Colin was born in the south of England in 1954, the youngest of four, they lived with his grandparents until he turned six when his mother remarried. The family migrated to Australia in 1967 and settled in Adelaide.

At the age of fifteen, he joined the Royal Australian Navy and served twenty years as a weapons technician before retiring to settle in Queensland.

Married in 1977 and with two children, seven grandchildren and three great-grandchildren, he lives with his wife, Lesley, just outside of Brisbane.

This is his first published work.

My wife, Lesley, for her support in allowing me to indulge my desire to write and publish this book.

My sister Lee for reading it and providing constructive criticism where needed.

Colin Plenty

BORDER WARS

AUSTIN MACAULEY PUBLISHERS™

LONDON * CAMBRIDGE * NEW YORK * SHARJAH

A CIP catalogue record for this title is available from the British Library.

ISBN 9781398462908 (Paperback)
ISBN 9781398462915 (ePub e-book)

www.austinmacauley.com

First Published 2023
Austin Macauley Publishers Ltd®
1 Canada Square
Canary Wharf
London
E14 5AA

Chapter 1
A Lesson in History

The middle of the 19th century was a period in history which could easily be given the name of "Globalism". The major powers had already discovered all of the territories and land masses of the world and the most powerful of them had laid claim to the ones they wanted.

The Portuguese and Spanish had almost completely divided South America. The Portuguese also had well-established bases of operations in India and the Dutch had the East Indies. The British had their immense Empire stretching across the entire planet. The Germans and Americans were trying to establish their international bona fides and the French had large swathes of Africa and Indo China.

Into this mix was the strategically placed Empire of Japan.

The isolationist nation had only permitted a couple of western nations the rights to trade with them and that trade was restricted to the port city of Nagasaki. The Dutch and the Portuguese had been granted a very privileged position.

The balance changed when the Americans and Russians basically forced Japan to open their borders to trade. The threat of invasion was all too real, and the Japanese decided to trade rather than fight.

Treaties

The Islands to the North of Hokkaido were known to the Japanese as the Kuril Islands; the Russians call them the Sakhalin Oblast. These islands have been in dispute for longer than anyone could be bothered to think about.

The first Russo-Japanese agreement to deal with the status of Sakhalin and the Kuril Islands was the 1855 Treaty of Shimoda; the treaty was the first that managed to establish official relations between Russia and Japan.

Article 2 of the Treaty of Shimoda, which provided for an agreement on borders, states "Henceforth the borders between Russia and Japan will pass between the islands Iturup (Etorofu) and Urup (Uruppu). The whole island of Iturup belongs to Japan and the whole island Urup and the other Kuril Islands to the north constitute possessions of Russia".

The islands of Kunashiri, Shikotan and the Habomai Islands, that all lie to the south of Iturup, are not explicitly mentioned in the treaty and were understood at the time to be a non-disputed part of Japan. The treaty also specified that the island of Sakhalin/Karafuto would remain un-partitioned between Russia and Japan, as in the past.

In the 1875 Treaty of Saint Petersburg; Russia and Japan agreed that Japan would give up all rights to Sakhalin in exchange for Russia giving up all rights to the Kuril Islands in favour of Japan. However, a controversy remains as to what constitutes the Kuril Islands, due to translation discrepancies of the official French language text of that treaty.

The Russo-Japanese War of 1904-1905

The Russo-Japanese War of 1904-1905 was a military disaster for Russia.

The "Treaty of Portsmouth", concluded at the end of this war, gave the southern half of Sakhalin Island to Japan.

This war was fought from early 1904 until late 1905 between Russia and the Empire of Japan over rival ambitions of both nations in Manchuria and Korea. The major theatres of operations were the Liaodong Peninsula and Mukden in Southern Manchuria and the seas around Korea, Japan and the Yellow Sea.

Russia was seeking a warm-water port on the Pacific Ocean Coast for its navy and for maritime trade. Vladivostok was operational only during the summer, the winters would often see it iced over and not navigable; whereas Port Arthur, a naval base in Liaodong Province leased to Russia by China, was operational all year. Since the end of the First Sino-Japanese War in 1895, Japan feared Russian encroachment on its plans to create a "sphere of influence" in Korea and Manchuria. Russia had demonstrated an expansionist policy in the Siberian Far East from the reign of Ivan the Terrible in the 16th century.

Seeing Russia as a rival, Japan offered to recognise Russian dominance in Manchuria in exchange for recognition of Korea as being within the Japanese sphere of influence. Russia refused and demanded Korea north of the 39th parallel to be a neutral buffer zone between Russia and Japan. This was to be the original division between North and South Korea. The Japanese government perceived a Russian threat to their plans for expansion into Asia and chose to go to war.

Russia suffered multiple defeats by Japan, but Tsar Nicholas II was convinced that Russia would win and chose to remain engaged in the war; at first, to await the outcomes of certain naval battles, and later to preserve the dignity of Russia by averting a "humiliating peace".

After negotiations between the antagonists broke down in 1904, the Japanese Navy opened hostilities by engaging the Russian Eastern Fleet, at Port Arthur in China, in a surprise attack. With the Eastern Fleet all but destroyed the Russians decided to send the Baltic Fleet to the Far East.

After leaving the Baltic and beginning to make their way across the North Sea, in a fit of panic, the Russians opened fire on fishing boats in the North Sea, the so called "Dogger Bank" attack, which resulted in the British closing access to the Suez Canal. As a result, the Russians had to sail around the Cape of Good Hope (southern tip of Africa) to get to the Far East.

The extended journey took its toll on the Russians and the fleet was ultimately destroyed by Admiral Togo's Japanese Fleet in the Battle of Tsushima. This would be the cause of the cessation of hostilities and the end of the Russian Navy's presence in the Japan Sea.

Russia ignored Japan's willingness, early on, to agree to an armistice and rejected the idea to bring the dispute to the Arbitration Court at The Hague. The war concluded with the Treaty of Portsmouth, mediated by US President Theodore Roosevelt. The complete victory of the Japanese military surprised world observers. The consequences transformed the balance of power in East Asia, resulting in a reassessment of Japan's recent entry onto the world stage. It was the first major military victory, in the modern era, of an Asian power over a European one.

World War Two
The Yalta Conference

The Yalta Conference, also known as the Crimea Conference and code named the Argonaut Conference, held from February 4 to the 11th 1945, was the World War II meeting of the heads of government of the United States, the United Kingdom and the Soviet Union for the purpose of discussing Germany and Europe's post-war reorganisation. The three states were represented by President Franklin D. Roosevelt, Prime Minister Winston Churchill and Premier Josef Stalin respectively. The conference convened near Yalta in Crimea, then a part of the Soviet Union; the conference took place within the Livadia, Yusupov and Vorontsov Palaces.

The aim of the conference was to shape a post-war peace that represented not just a collective security order but a plan to give self-determination to the liberated peoples of post-Nazi Europe.

The meeting was intended mainly to discuss the re-establishment of the nations of war-torn Europe. However, within a few short years, with the Cold War dividing the continent, Yalta became a subject of intense controversy.

Roosevelt wanted the USSR to enter the Pacific War with the Allies. One Soviet precondition for a declaration of war against Japan was an American official recognition of Mongolian independence from China (the Mongolian People's Republic had already been a Soviet satellite state from its own beginnings in 1924 and through World War II), and a recognition of Soviet interests in the Manchurian railways and Port Arthur (but not asking the Chinese to lease it), as well as these conditions they wanted to deprive the Japanese of much disputed territory (such as Sakhalin and Kuril Islands) to be returned to Russian custody having been lost in the Treaty of Portsmouth.

These were agreed upon without Chinese representation, consultation or consent; all stemming from the American desire to end the war early thereby reducing American casualties. Stalin agreed that the Soviet Union would enter the Pacific War three months after the defeat of Germany. Stalin also pledged to

Truman to keep the nationality of the Korean Peninsula intact as the Soviet Union entered the war against Japan.

The Kuril Islands dispute, also known in Japan as the Northern Territories dispute, is a disagreement between Japan and Russia and also some individuals and groups of Ainu people over sovereignty of the four southernmost Kuril Islands. The islands separate the Sea of Okhotsk from the Pacific Ocean.

The four disputed islands, like other islands in the Kuril chain that are not in dispute, were annexed by the Soviet Union following the Kuril Islands landing operation at the end of World War II. These disputed islands are under Russian administration as the South Kuril District of the Sakhalin Oblast. They are claimed by Japan, which refers to them as its Northern Territories or Southern Chishima, and considers them part of the Nemuro Subprefecture of Hokkaido Prefecture.

The Invasion of the Kuril Islands was the World War II Soviet military operation to capture the Kuril Islands from Japan in 1945. The invasion was part of the Soviet invasion of Manchuria, and was decided on when plans to land on Hokkaido were abandoned. The successful military operations of the Red Army at Mudanjiang and during the Invasion of South Sakhalin created the necessary prerequisites for invasion of the Kuril Islands.

The San Francisco Peace Treaty, signed between the Allies and Japan in 1951, states that Japan must give up "all right, title and claim to the Kuril Islands", but it also does not recognise the Soviet Union's sovereignty over them. Japan claims that at least some of the disputed islands are not a part of the Kuril Islands, and thus are not covered by the treaty.

Russia maintains that the Soviet Union's sovereignty over the islands was recognised in post-war agreements; including the Soviet-Japanese Joint Declaration of 1956, but did not resolve the territorial dispute. During talks leading to the joint declaration, the Soviet Union offered Japan the two smaller islands of Shikotan and the Habomai Islands in exchange for Japan renouncing all claims to the two bigger islands of Iturup and Kunashir, but Japan refused the offer after pressure from the US.

The dissolution of the USSR in the late 20th century came and went without changing anything as did the passing of the millennium. By the beginning of the 21st century many diplomatic efforts had been started and finished trying to resolve the possession of the islands; all had ended without actually managing to resolve anything at all. Several times one side or the other would restart efforts but an agreement on where to put the border eluded them all.

More Recent Efforts

In 2056, to commemorate the 100th anniversary of the last reasonably successful conference, the Russians finally gave way to some impressive diplomatic efforts from many nations in the Northern Pacific. The islands from Hokkaido up to the island of Raykoke would be returned to Japan. The islands to the North would be retained by Russia. The new border would be established between Shiashkokan and Raykoke and all the water between the islands was to be a "mutual access gateway", which would permit free use for all shipping.

The other significant point of this new treaty was that all the islands were to be free of military bases and equipment. The Ainu, the traditional occupiers of these lands, were instrumental in the negotiations and it was they who had forced the "no military" clause to ensure that they would be left to live and raise their families in peace.

And it was to prove to be a lucrative peace for them, the fishing rights and restrictions were observed by all and rigidly policed by both sides. The crops they grew on the larger islands and the ability to sell the excess and much of their fish catch, allowed them a significant level of prosperity and with it came a previously unknown level of autonomy. Life was good for them all.

Unfortunately, as is often the case, it was not to be the continual peace that they all desired.

Chapter 2
Prediction

Family and close friends had gathered for the birth of a new addition. The lives of the two principal families had been tightly interwoven since the late 20th century.

The family of the descendants of Tokugawa Musashi was large, as was that of the descendants of Ichiro Okubo, and the two families would have large gatherings several times a year.

This year, 2150, would prove to be no different. The occasion this time was the birth of yet another cousin, this one was a little removed from the direct line of descent but in this family, that did not make it any less important.

It was almost expected of the old woman that she would give both a blessing and a prediction, at the birth of a new member to her extended family. Her name, Kana, had the meaning of "the powerful one", and here, late in life, she was a famous Senkensha (seer) and a direct female descendant of the powerful Ai Okubo, who was herself the mother of the famous and formidable Hitomi Maki. Theirs was a powerful family and their predictions and foretelling's were always heeded; never were they wrong.

It was around an hour after the birth; the mid-wife was giving the baby back to her mother and the family were all chatting among themselves, when Kana stood up suddenly and looked at the heads of the family. Her voice deepened and her eyes glazed over. Those that already knew her were silent as they awaited the foretelling that was evidently coming.

'This child born here today will be happy and she will be successful in all that she undertakes.' Everyone was pleased at the positive message for the future; then, after a few minutes as all watched mother and baby, Kana continued, 'Wars will come, they will be brutal and it will take an exceptional warrior to overcome the opposition that are even now amassing.' At that point she collapsed on the floor alongside the body of the midwife, who had apparently fainted just before her.

Several of the gathered family moved forward and gently picked up the old woman. As they sat her in a lounge chair, she came back to consciousness.

'Oh my, was that as bad as it feels?' she asked no one in particular.

'It was obviously very important and it sounded like you were straining to give as much as you did,' replied her daughter, Reina.

'Is the midwife alright?' Kana asked.

Looking at the prostrate woman, Reina announced, 'She is coming around, father caught her before she hit the floor.'

'What happened?' asked the confused woman.

'You fainted. What was the last thing you remember?'

'I felt very warm and then had no energy, I could not stop myself from falling.'

'She is an empath,' Kana announced, with the authority of one who knows exactly what had happened. 'She will be fine.'

'What do you mean, mother? You have not spoken of an empath before?'

'That is because they are very rare, especially one that is as sensitive as this one.' Kana gestured towards the midwife. 'She is the first one I have seen. The only one I have heard of was a friend of Great-grandmother Ai, and she only appeared once when Ai foresaw the coming of the new Shogun towards the end of the 20th century. Empaths are only apparent when the message is very important. Get her some sweet tea to restore her energy.'

'Do we know if this message is for us or for those in the future?' It was Dai, Kana's husband, that was asking.

'Given that it took both a Senkensha and an empath to bring the message, I would say that the message is for the future, and as a family we will have to be ready when we are needed. Now, let us have a better greeting with the new addition to our ever-expanding family.'

The baby was presented ceremonially to the old woman, no more would be spoken of the prediction for many years, however the heads of the family groups would always keep the second part of the foretelling at the front of their minds, the prediction of war was always going to be worrisome; if it was dire enough for a long-range prediction then it would be important for all to remember.

Chapter 3
Planning

The public voice of Russia was rapidly becoming angry. The people were getting angry because the prestige of being one of the pre-eminent nations on the planet was being eroded.

Industry was no longer effective and imports of all materials and manufactured goods was costing jobs at home. Many were out of work; food was not as plentiful as it should have been; other countries were simply outproducing them and while that meant lower prices no one could afford to buy if they did not have an income.

As so often happens with such situations, a charismatic new leader eventually managed to "read" the mood of the people and with the promise of better times ahead he was elected to the position of President of Russia. Now all he had to do was deliver on his many promises.

After the first two years he was not hopeful of being re-elected, a major drought across the grain growing areas and an early and very severe winter had decimated the livestock industry. Threats against his life were being received daily in his office in the Kremlin and he was actively, but very privately, looking for a place he could escape to, if it all went wrong.

His lifeline came one day when the news feeds showed that the Ainu people of the Kuril Islands, north of Japan, had managed to find a new oil source, the first in almost a hundred years and the flow rate was so high that they had, almost overnight, become one of the highest income groups in the entire world. Instantly the prosperity made them more comfortable than they had ever been.

Descended from hunter gatherers theirs was an ethnic minority that had been variously governed by themselves, China, Japan, Russia, some of them Japan again and finally under their own control but a part of Japan. They did not see what their new found wealth would bring them along-side their new found prosperity.

They didn't see it, but the Russians did!

In the Kremlin

'How can we get some of that oil?' The Industry Minister, Karpov, demanded.

'We can't,' answered Resources Minister, Dmitri Saklin, with a tint of anger in his voice.

'Why not?'

'Because we agreed to let those god-forsaken islands go back to Japan,' replied the Foreign Minister.

'Is there any way we can get access to the edge of the oil field? From our Lands?'

'We have tried, but the bulk of the field is close to Iturup Island, the field plays out before Chirpoy Island. There is none near Kamchatka.' Resources Minister Saklin replied.

'What if we just go and take it?' None of the ministers were ready to voice that option, but the President was.

'President Tokmakov, do you realise what you are suggesting?' asked Rubashkin, the Foreign Minister, obviously in a panic at the thought.

'Settle down, Evgeny. We are all thinking it, I just said it that is all.'

'I understand that, Kolya. But we must be very careful in how we assess and plan our way forward. There are many hurdles to overcome if we go that way.'

'But you think we can do it?'

'The Chinese will be angry that we are able to get there, they cannot get access to that area. The Americans will jump and shout and rattle their swords but they will not commit soldiers to stop us. The United Nations will put sanctions on us but with access to the oil we will be in a better bargaining position.'

'The Japanese will be the most difficult. They have good soldiers, well trained and prepared, but we will be able to hold them off long enough.' The boast sounded believable, but the politicians were not seasoned soldiers, they did not understand what it would take to hold all those islands through the winters that were getting colder and more difficult to survive than ever before.

Summer was brief there, but also a hot affair; however, in complete contrast, the winters were windy, cold and wet and very long. Very short days and long cold nights. Only the hardiest of humans could thrive in such an area.

'We must be very careful; the Americans have just announced a new oil field they have discovered off the Aleutians they will be wary of any military action north of Hawaii,' warned Kozlov, the Defence Minister.

'Yes, Maxim, so true; but they will not be prepared to risk having us take their field as reparation for their interference in our affairs. I think the Japanese will be on their own in a military response to us.'

'I will establish a committee of the Army and Navy to assess the requirements for invading the islands, it will be at the highest level of security, any information that gets out will stop us before we get moving.'

'Very well, we are agreed.' The President announced, 'Now it is time for lunch.' The five men left for the restaurant and each was alone in their own thoughts, none of them thought that it was anything except right for them to take the islands from Japan; if anything, they thought it was overdue. The fact that an election was due in less than two years and a successful campaign would ensure the security of their tenure in the Parliament was also towards the front of their thinking; like all politicians, their minds did not go too far beyond the here and now, just as far as the next election. Done right they would be in power for many years to come.

Two weeks later

The very senior officers, chosen more for their connections than their abilities, were waiting patiently for President Tokmakov's arrival. Their discussion mostly centred around the fact that they had not received any pre-curser information about the meeting. All were nervous; an unannounced meeting was usually either a purge of the other senior officers, or even worse, a purge of them. None of them would be able to settle their nerves until it was done.

'Thank you for coming here at short notice,' the president announced as he entered the secure conference room attached to his personal suites.

'To set your minds to work, and at the same time, at ease; I would first like to say that this room has been screened every day for the last month to ensure that it is completely secure. Nothing that is discussed here is to be either removed or repeated outside these four walls.' As he waited for his words to sink in, he reached out and pressed a button to close the secure, bulletproof coverings for the windows.

'Forgive us, Mr President, what is it that requires so much secrecy?' Admiral of the Fleet Gennady Andreyushkin was not one to leave a problem to wait.

'In a moment, Gennady. Get a coffee, sit and relax for once. There are a couple of others we are waiting for.'

Minister Rubashkin and Minister Saklin were the last to arrive, so late that the morning meeting had now morphed into lunch and Admiral Andreyushkin was asking for preferences for when lunch was ordered.

'We are so very sorry for being so late,' puffed Dmitri Saklin, the Resources Minister. His smoking habit was very obviously impacting heavily on him, now he was advancing in age. 'The meeting with the Chinese Foreign Minister went so long; they would not stop asking questions on every little detail. I tell you, dealing with the Americans is far easier than dealing with them.'

'That is fine, Dmitri, we must be careful and considerate of the few allies we can count on, especially with our current project about to get underway. We will need all the good-will we can get in the coming months and years,' replied the President.

'Now we are all here we can begin. The first item is secrecy; It is imperative that what we discuss does not go further than these four walls, any and all discussions will be conducted in this room. That includes any information you gather from your staff. If you wish to have a meeting with some of your aides they must be vetted and approved. All work is to be conducted here, all research, all discussions. Am I clear?'

The overt warning, to so many of the highest members of the party as well as the Combined Chiefs of Staff, almost had the effect of stunning those present. Eventually, all murmured in agreement. This was obviously not a general planning meeting.

'The second item is that we will all have to sign a letter of consensus, that we all together undertake the project. This is to prevent any one of us deciding to leave and abandon the remainder. Are we all in agreement?'

'What if we get into the planning, for whatever this is, and it is not feasible?' asked General Fedin of the Airforce.

'Then we can destroy all references and the project will go no further, do not worry, Goran, we can all trust each other. All documentation will be held on computers that do not leave this office and when we are not here, they must be locked in the safe. It has been built so that each of us can access our work only when others are in the room.'

Goran Fedin just looked at the politicians assembled before them and thought to himself, *I cannot see any time where I will fully trust a politician.*

'Why so much secrecy?' demanded Andreyushkin.

'All in good time, Gennady. Please, be patient.'

The gentle knock at the outer door was almost unexpected and, with tensions so high within, it was also almost frightening.

'Victor, would you please?'

Victor Usenko, as Marshall of the Russian Federation he was the most senior officer in all of the armed forces, rose from his seat and went to the door. When he opened it an army Colonel was waiting with a trolley of food for the occupants. Once the door was opened the Colonel stood to attention and then turned and left. He had complied with his orders to deliver the trolley and leave when the door was opened. The Colonel had no clue as to who else was in the room as he could not see inside, he did leave wondering as to why the Marshall of the Army was taking delivery of a food trolley.

Once he had returned to his desk, he began to voice his opinions aloud and the next morning he was "attached" to the army outpost that overlooked the sea access to Murmansk harbour. Not quite the end of the world, but on a clear day you could see it from his office window, and many were privately wondering just who he had upset so badly that he was sent there in such a rush.

The meals were completed without any reference to the, as yet unstated nature of their meeting. Eventually, the empty plates were stacked on the trolley and the Foreign Minister left the trolley outside for collection.

'Now, gentlemen, it is time to get down to business.' The President began, 'The Ministers and I have been discussing the embarrassing losses to Japan of the Islands in the Sakhalin Oblast. There have been many outbursts of public opinion around the subject and the general feeling of the people is that we should never have conceded the islands in the first place. It is my intention that we shall retake the islands at the first opportunity.'

'Are you certain it is the "people" that are lobbying for the return of the islands? Or is it your politicians mind that wants the oil the Japanese have discovered further down the chain, and with it the political prestige and improved chances of re-election?' Gennady Andreyushkin had never been one to mince his words, and this time he had not wasted a single second before laying the politicians nerves bare.

'You are as perceptive as always, Gennady. If this discussion does not agree with your "moral obligations", you may leave now, before we have actually discussed any specific issues.'

'Thank you, Mr President. I shall return to the Baltic Fleet where we are preparing for war games.' Gennady Andreyushkin collected his uniform cap and made for the exit. As he opened the door, he turned and said, 'Good day to you all. Good luck in your endeavours.' With a nod he left the meeting, closing the inner door behind him.

Tokmakov followed him into the ante-room and closed the inner door. 'Let me call for your car.' The president picked up the phone and ensured that the car was waiting when he emerged from the building.

No one heard the president make another call.

Getting in his car, he told the driver, 'Back to the airfield, I will take my helicopter to the Baltic Fleet Headquarters.' As he sat in the quiet of the rear seat of the plush limousine he pondered if he had made the right choice to leave at that early stage of the discussions. Throwing pros and cons at his brain he came to the conclusion that he was right to leave at the first opportunity, before he was too deep in commitment and could not get out at all.

Arriving at the Airbase, he got into his helicopter and set off for the Fleet Base.

The president returned to the conference room and resumed his place at the head of the table.

'Now, let us get down to business. This will be very short and then I will leave you to your discussions. I want you to devise a plan that will enable us to get control of the islands from Raykoke in the north to the strait between Iturup and Urup in the southern end. Include, if you wish, a possible plan for taking Iturup as well. We need this to be a quick affair and ended swiftly. The faster it is done the less chance there will be for retaliatory strikes and repercussions from the UN and Japan's allies.'

'Discuss this here only and if you want a replacement for Gennady then we shall get one; perhaps someone from the Eastern Fleet, someone that knows the area of operations.'

'Mr President,' began Marshall Usenko, 'I feel it would be best if we all gave this our undivided attention and we should return here in two days for discussions on our first thoughts. However, I would ask you to be patient as you wait for us to formulate a plan as there may be some items that will require extra input before we can agree on the final operational directives.'

'Excellent idea, Victor. We will meet here tomorrow morning to discuss the first thoughts on the operation and then in two days' time for lunch? Yes, that will suffice for the initial briefings.'

With that last statement, the meeting dissolved with all the attendees going their separate ways.

Later that evening, Dmitri Saklin, the Resources Minister, was watching the evening news.

'This is the late news,' the television announcer stated in his usual monotone. 'In our earlier bulletin, there were reports of a helicopter crash North-West of Moscow late this afternoon. Reported by onlookers; there were reports that there were no survivors. Just thirty minutes ago, a spokesperson from the Kremlin has confirmed the death of Admiral of the Fleet Gennady Andreyushkin, and his pilots are also deceased. Mechanical failure is thought to be the cause of the crash. In other news, Brazil has moved through to the next round of the world cup…'

Also watching, in his Moscow apartment, Victor Usenko was suddenly distressed by the bulletin. The remainder of the bulletin faded into obscurity as the Marshall pondered the ramifications of what he had just heard.

The following morning at 8am President Tokmakov entered the secure conference room and was pleased to see that all the attendees were there.

'Good morning all, I trust you slept well?' he asked, and as he looked around the table, he could see that none of them had. 'I saw the news last night; so sad that Gennady did not wish to continue with us; if he had, he would not have been on that helicopter. Wretched bad luck.'

His statement was greeted with a mixture of grunts and mumbles from his associates; he noted that none could look him in the eyes at that point.

'Do you have any thoughts of a replacement for him?'

'Here or in his usual duties?' was the rather terse reply from The Defence Minister.

'Both if we need to.'

'In keeping with the secrecy requirements, I feel that we can complete the planning without input from his position,' replied General Fedin.

'Explain your reasoning, Goran,' the President insisted.

'It has always been well known that the Navy, and in particular the senior ranking officers, have always been,' he paused for effect, 'somewhat independent. They have always completed their duties as assigned but they prefer to be less encumbered in their thinking and their actions.'

'Why is that, do you think?'

Usenko interrupted, 'I have addressed this many years ago, they seem to feel that as they are usually operating more or less away from direct contact with their headquarters as they move across the globe and they have a large measure of independence in that respect, they need to be able to make decisions instantly, with regard to their particular position at that time. Not an unreasonable theory but it does have some limitations.'

'How do you think we should proceed then?' The President was no fool of a politician, he already had the Chief of Staff and the Commander of the Airforce creating his plan and apparently without his overt control. This is exactly as "the puppet master" had wanted it to go, if it failed, he could claim no responsibility for it. If it succeeded, he would be guaranteed an election win, probably two, if handled correctly.

'How do you plan to cover the involvement of the Navy, without a Senior Admiral assisting in your planning?'

'I would like to discuss all planning proposals first, and I ask that all keep in mind that we will most likely be controlling the maritime aspects ourselves. If it becomes apparent that we need to have an officer here to assist, then we can find one that is similar to us in our thoughts.'

'Excellent, we are beginning to make headway. I will leave you to your discussions; as I am not a military man, I may impede your processes by constantly asking for explanations. Shall we plan for a conference in one week to explain your progress?'

All present nodded and agreed, the die was now cast, whatever plan they could devise was now theirs and they would be fully responsible.

And so it began, every day for the next week the two military officers worked from 8am to 8pm, never wavering they would put together concepts and routines, they would explore strategies and form possibilities; then they would try to conceive ways that they could be thwarted or that the plan would fail.

The one part of the plan they could not cover was how they were going to get the Japanese and the UN to agree to permit some military access to the area without alarming the locals and their government representatives. The Russian islands were easily dealt with, they would be told they had to move and that was it; however, the occupants of the Japanese islands would need to be given a reason to move and that was going to take some innovation.

The planning schedule was endless, there were no pressing deadlines to meet and the two could break whenever they wished. The President was, however, becoming agitated. Seeing little or no apparent progress he began to make covert threats.

'Perhaps, Victor, you both should take a break. Perhaps you would consider using my dacha, it is empty at this time of year and it is also quiet, away from the distractions of everyday life. I can arrange for a helicopter to take you both there. It may provide you with the incentive to complete this task in a timelier manner.'

The threat was, while unstated, clear. Come-up with a plan soon or a disaster would befall them. As it happened, the planning took a sudden turn for the better when, late one evening when he could not sleep, Marshall Usenko saw a long-forgotten film on the video feeds.

The following morning, he was already in the planning room when General Fedin arrived.

'Goran, I have what may be the answer to our most distressing problem.'

'What is it? Can I get coffee before you explode with the news?'

'Yes, yes get a coffee and I will show you.'

The two sat before the 80-inch television and Usenko pressed play. The opening credits had already ended when Victor had pressed play on the remote. Goran watched for a moment and demanded, 'What does an old movie about submarines have to do with our problem?' He was clearly upset that his friend had been so easily diverted.

'Watch, you will see.'

Eventually, the movie had progressed to the point that the Submarine Captain needed to get the crew to evacuate without dissent.

'Do you not see, Goran; this is how we can get the locals on our side of the border and the Japanese on their side to leave the area immediately and not wish to return.'

'What is the name of this movie?'

'It is a piece of American drivel called *The Hunt for Red October*. The Captain wanted to steal the submarine and defect. But if, as you saw in the movie, we can create the thought of a nuclear radiation accident then the locals will all want to leave. Of course, we will have to apologise and agree to "clean-up" the radiation but once we begin, we will have total control over who enters and who does not.'

'And then we can do as we wish with the islands, and the resources, we gain access to. That is a brilliant concept. All we need to do is work out how to create the "accident".'

The two began to throw ideas at each other until they came up with a solution.

'It is disappointing that Gennady is not still around, we could use his expertise at this point,' remarked Victor.

'Yes, but he decided that he would not be working with us.' They both left their thoughts of the demise of Gennady Andreyushkin unsaid; neither of them trusted the "security" of the room they were working in. 'We will need to find someone to give the maritime perspective on the proposal, perhaps the President will have someone in mind?'

'Quite possible, we can ask him tomorrow when we give him a little good news.'

The following morning the President opened the door to the conference room and looked around, only to see two very tired and dishevelled senior officers.

'Good morning Victor, Goran; I hope your work is progressing significantly faster than when we last met.' It was not spoken in such a manner just to be rude, rather to place a sense of urgency on the part of the president to get his political plan in place.

'Indeed, it is, Sir,' replied Victor; as the senior of the two it befell him to be the one to make the reports. 'We have managed to come up with a plan that will ensure that we can get access to both the Northern and the Southern Islands for many years to come.'

'And without any real complaints from the Japanese until it is too late, then we may need to enlist some political assistance to ensure the completion of our works.' Added Goran.

'Very good, show me.'

'Perhaps some tea first?' offered Victor, after your long journey.

'Very well.'

The drinks and snacks had been placed on the table and the three men engaged in some small talk before the full presentation began. It was almost an hour before they finished talking and the President just sat and pondered for a long time as he ran through the proposal in his mind. Eventually, he spoke.

'Now that we do not have Gennady to assist, god rest his soul, you will need to have some help from the navy.' The president's words were as hollow as an empty barrel.

'That is correct, we are unsure as to who we can trust with what is probably the most important phase of the plan. Do you have anyone in mind that we can include in this group?'

'Actually, I do. The son of Dmitri Saklin, the Resources Minister, will be a suitable candidate. He is a senior submarine commander with extensive experience with both ballistic and attack submarines. He is waiting for promotion to Admiral and with his assistance you can put your plan in motion; and when it is fruitful, he will be rewarded for "An exceptional career and exemplary service to Mother Russia." And I think you will also be rewarded in a significant way.'

'Thank you, Sir, you are most generous.' Victor thanked the President.

'Let us not get too far ahead, you have to get the plan to work first.'

'As you say, we must be successful first.'

Marat, the son of the Resources Minister arrived in Moscow the following week and was spirited away to the president's dacha without any explanation.

On arrival he was escorted to a private suite where he was searched, and all his electronic devices were locked away. Next, he was taken to the conference room where his father was waiting.

'Papa? It is so good to see you again; it has been far too long.' The two embraced and had time for a little private chat. 'What are you doing here? What is going on?'

'You have not been briefed?'

'No, I was in the mid-Atlantic when I received a signal informing me that I was to rendezvous with a cruise ship off the coast of Cuba and then I was taken by helicopter to the airport and then Moscow. What is going on?'

Dmitri sat down and poured a drink for each of them. As he slowly explained the problem that was facing them, and the presidents wish to correct it, his son sat and listened earnestly to ensure he did not miss any detail.

'So, you are telling me that the plan is to take back all of the islands north of Hokkaido and keep them?' he asked incredulously.

'That is correct.'

'But why am I here? There are any number of senior officers, Fleet Admirals included, that could do this with ease. Why me?'

'The plan that has been put together, and agreed with in principle, has the need for the involvement of a ship or submarine or two. You are the most capable of the officers available.'

'I see, and when will I get to see this "plan"? I assume it is on a computer here?'

'No, actually it is not on any form of electronic device. There is only one copy.'

'How am I supposed to give my input if I cannot have a copy?' Marat demanded, 'I will need to study it first!'

'And so you will my son, all in good time. The only copy is held in a safe nearby, it is a paper copy and if needs be it can be destroyed completely. It cannot be scanned, there are no scanners here; and as such it cannot be sent to anyone via email, that keeps it secure.'

'You are certain about this Father? To take the lands of Japan?'

'It is only right that we do this Marat, those islands were ours and the feeble politicians of years past did not have the right to give them away. We are simply getting back what is ours.' The statement was simple enough, but it gave strength to the lie that the islands had always been Russian Territory, a lie that was now essential for them to verify.

'I see, when do I meet the others on the planning team?'

'When we have lunch; now tell me what is happening in your life, it has been far too long since we talked.'

Father and son talked for the next hour and a half slowly catching up on each other's lives. Their conversation was friendly and open, discussing family friends and other mundane subjects, however there was always an underlying tension which neither wished to address.

Eventually, the clock wound its way towards then past 1pm and around 1.30 there was a knock at the door, before either could speak the door opened and all of the "conspirators" entered. Marat rose from his seat and introduced himself to all of the arrivals, snapping to attention when General Fedin and Marshall Usenko finally entered the room, saluting each as they met.

'Please not so formal here, Marat. We will need to be working much closer together and as such we will need to be more familiar with each other.' Victor said as they began to get comfortable.

'Now, Victor, would you please give us your plan?' demanded the President.

Victor rose and moved to the front of the room, 'Please, understand the plan is still in its infancy. There is much detail to be added.'

'Just the outline will be sufficient, for now,' replied Kolya, we can ask for explanations as it is revealed.

'As you wish, Mr President.' Marshall Usenko was about as far out of his depth as it was possible for a the most senior officer of the military to get.

For the next half hour, he gave an outline of the plan as it stood, answering the few questions that arose as best he could.

'That is it?' asked Kolya. 'That is all you have?'

'Please, we have been trying to devise a way to get the population to leave the islands of their own free will; add to that the possibility that we can get the Japanese Government to ASK us to put our people onto their islands as well as have them leave voluntarily has been a difficult task. With Marat to assist us, we anticipate our efforts will accelerate from now.'

'Do you have a timeline?'

'We anticipate that we can be ready to move in just six months if we can iron out the fine detail.' Added Goran, as he tried to take some of the pressure from Victor. 'As I see it, if we can do it right, we will be inhabiting the islands for as long as we wish.'

'Very well, we will meet again in two weeks. Work as quickly as possible, the less time you spend the less people will ask about where you are.'

With that the meeting was understood to be over, and the political masters left the military men to continue their quest for a method to keep the politicians happy and keep their heads as well.

It was fortuitous that Marat had been seconded to the "team"; his perspective on the problem was a breath of fresh air and the speed of progress ramped up when he was given permission to engage a gifted nuclear expert who could also double up as a programmer for the computer systems that would be essential as a part of the final plan.

The next progress meeting came and went without fuss and the third meeting did the same. When the politicians arrived for the fourth meeting, they entered the room with a decided air of frustration, they had been more than patient and now they wanted to get the full plan and they wanted to set a date and they wanted it NOW!

'Yes, Mr President, we have all but completed the project.' Stammered Marshall Usenko.

'What do you mean "All but completed"? I thought you were finished as you promised?'

'Yes, we are; but we need to find the right date when it is not too cold and the tides are right. Everything else is ready.'

'Very well, describe the plan to us and what you think will be the start date.'

The Senior officer handed the video controls to the youngest, most junior, officer for him to give the presentation. It took almost an hour before he was finished. The plan was detailed and complete.

'I can see why it has taken so long for you to complete this task,' remarked Maxim Kozlov, the defence minister. 'Are you certain you can do this?'

'As certain as we can be. Nothing is perfect and there may be a number of circumstances that we cannot conceive; but we have been able to create a plan that will appear, at worst, as an unfortunate accident and at best as a disaster which we will "do our utmost" to reconcile for our "good neighbours" and trading partners, Japan.'

'We believe that it will insure us all against any form of complicity, as well as give us the expected benefits.'

'Very well, do not tell us the date you wish to move on this plan. We will need to be as surprised as everyone else in the world when the news breaks.'

'Understood Mr President, we will begin when we are ready. Perhaps we should announce the fleet movements around a month before we start, so that the movements are expected and not sudden?'

'Good Idea, Goran. Good luck gentlemen, the future is in your "invisible" hands.'

The politicians left and the military men had the final discussions on timing. A final, sumptuous, meal marked the end of the formal discussions and they all left for Moscow the following day. All except Marat, he would need to oversee the beginning of the plan.

Chapter 4
A Not Quite Unexpected Disaster

The calendar moved so slowly that some in the cabal thought it had almost stopped altogether. The team had been working hard at the planning meetings, or more correctly summit, had been finalising the fine details of how they wanted to proceed. Eventually, they believed they were ready and called the President to give him the final approval of the plan.

All the co-conspirators arrived during the morning and were all busy with their own conversations when Captain Marat Saklin made his grand entrance into the conference room. The silence was as deafening as it was instant, Marat moved to the front of the room and began by addressing and greeting each of the guests individually.

'Thank you all for coming here, so far away from your usual places of work. We, the planning committee, believe we have come up with a plan that will provide a solution for all of the questions and problems that arose from the proposal we were given.'

For the next two hours, he gave the full briefing for the project, code named Lenin for their political forbear. Every individual item, no matter how small, was covered and fully explained both individually and in context of the forward momentum of the plan itself.

'And that, gentlemen, is how we propose to proceed. I believe that we can cover ourselves with glory for the return of the islands as well as the "environmental concerns". If we adhere to the plan, we will be successful.' For the next few moments, no one spoke; eventually, Kolya Tokmakov stood and began applauding. Followed by all the others, they offered their congratulations for their work.

'You have all done wonderfully well, this will be a great leap forward for us all. Thank you,' he gushed, barely able to keep his enthusiasm in check; he could see his political star ascending to the point where he would be lauded for many centuries as a true political patriot.

His co-conspirators were no less enthusiastic in their praise; they all could see the future for themselves.

The auditorium of the General Assembly was, as it usually was, full; more of assistants and hangers on than Ambassadors but it was full none the less.

'Good evening,' began the Secretary General. 'The first item on the agenda is from the Ambassador from the United States of America; if you please?' He indicated to the American who pressed the button on the microphone stand before him and began to speak.

'Mr Secretary General, fellow ambassadors, we from the United States wish to request an affirmative and unambiguous agreement from the Russian delegation that they are going to finally come to agreement with the remainder of the Security Council, and the other members, and finally agree to retire the last of their extremely dangerous High Pressure Fission Reactor powered fleet and join us in using the safe, low pressure fusion reactors that we all have signed the treaty for?'

'For far too long they have been dragging their feet and they have been recalcitrant in refusing to agree to this move which will make the rest of the world a safer place in which to live. They only have one submarine left which uses this old, dangerous technology and it is high time they joined us all in making the world safe from nuclear meltdown accidents.'

Choruses of 'hear, hear' and 'Yes, when?' echoed around the chamber.

After a few minutes of raucous noise, the Secretary General called for silence and eventually everyone sat and waited for the response.

The Russian Ambassador was nothing if he was not considered to be straightforward. His decision making always came with the air of one who was always right in what he said and he was never in doubt or flustered in anyway. Today, however, he appeared to be considerably doubtful in his speech. It was not that he was in doubt as to his response, far from it he felt very comfortable, he did, however, want everyone to assume that he was unsure and not completely at ease with his reply.

'I thank the Secretary General and the Ambassador from the United States,' he fumbled his documents and gave the impression of a man under considerable pressure as his hands shook slightly while he found the correct page. 'I have here, in my hand, a directive from the President, Kolya Tokmakov himself. In it he has given the following directive, and I quote.'

"On this day, 5 October 2160, I order that the submarine known as "Boris Yeltsin" be taken to the Naval base at Murmansk for removal and decommissioning of her weapons, and the decommissioning and disassembly of her propulsion plant. This is the last of the "fission" nuclear-powered vessels in the entire world and it is right that now is the time for the decommissioning of this ship."

'As you can see, this is signed by the President just last week and he asked me to present it here for you all to witness our recognition of this major step forward in international relations.'

The entire auditorium erupted in applause; at last there would be no more threat of a nuclear accident and its associated meltdown. This was a great day for all the world.

After the good news had been given the Secretary General asked a very pertinent question.

'Thank you for this wonderful news,' he began. 'Do you have a time schedule for this decommissioning or is it just a proposal at this time?'

'Yes, we do have a schedule,' replied the ambassador. 'Marshall Usenko, General Fedin and Captain Saklin, a submarine specialist, have been planning this for some time and we expect the submarine to be moved around the beginning of November, give or take a week, certainly before the winter sea ice takes over the ports and we cannot transit the required route.'

'Very good, thank you.'

'If I may Mr Secretary General?' asked the American.

'Certainly.'

'While we are well aware of the dangers that may be posed taking this ship half-way around the world, we would like to permit the use of American controlled waters for this final transit. While restrictions are still in place for the Panama Canal and such, we would still like to offer the ability to use our waters.'

'Thank you, sir. We will be in contact if the route we need to use is going to be through your waters,' replied the Russian Ambassador. Smiling inwardly, he was very pleased that it had all gone so smoothly.

Any other business was delayed for a few days so that they could all confer about how good it all was. Even though the spectre of nuclear weapons still abounded, finally there was a great danger to be removed from the world, and all could relax, just a little.

As is usual with such things, there were a couple of "minor issues" to be resolved before the ship could sail. First there was the problem with the main engine lubricating oil system, the water separator had literally broken. The shaft driving the machine had snapped inside the oil separator and a replacement had to be installed. Not a real problem, but no one wanted the engines to seize during the long voyage.

Then there was a problem with some of the computer systems which was eventually ignored, no one was going to be firing intercontinental ballistic missiles anyway.

The last problem was the desalination plant. That was essential, and it was eventually repaired by a little dockyard ingenuity in the creation of some replacement pipe work, not neat or tidy in any way, and it wound its way through watertight hatches instead of through the bulkheads as would be usual, but it was good enough to ensure showers and drinking water for the men for the three months it was expected to take to get to Murmansk.

Eventually, the submarine was ready, and the crew were all on the casing waiting for the speeches and the official farewells.

At the top of the conning tower, Captain Saklin was preparing for the departure. Marshall Usenko, General Fedin and President Tokmakov had all left the ship and were now on the dock watching.

'Remove the gangway,' ordered Saklin.

'REMOVE THE GANGWAY!' shouted the office of the watch, repeating the order in the time-honoured way of navies the world over; repeating the order ensured that it was heard correctly and repeated without error. All watched as the crew removed the securing lines and the crane gently lifted the gangway away from the ship.

'Single up all lines.'

'SINGLE UP ALL LINES!' again the officer of the watch repeated the captain's orders.

'Tugs take the weight.'

Again, the order was repeated, but this time it was the Navigator that was repeating the order and he was speaking to the tug captains already alongside.

The ship lurched slightly as the tugs began to pull gently at the submarine.

'Let go forward, let go aft.'

'LET GO FORWARD, LET GO AFT!'

The submarine began to move away from the dock, with only the two mid-ship lines left there was little still holding them in port.

'Let go midships, tugs, take us away.'

'LET GO MIDSHIPS.'

'Tugs, take the weight, pull us off the dock.'

Just as the last line was released the band, waiting patiently on the wharf, struck up the Russian National Anthem. All the crew standing at attention began to sing as did the watchers ashore.

As moments go in the life of a warship, it was as poignant as it gets. Some of the older members watching remembered singing when she had first put to sea straight from the builder's yards, and tears were beginning to run down their cheeks. For them this was the end of a fond memory; for the "Boris", as they affectionately knew her, was the holder of the most coveted title a warship could have; she was always known as a "Happy ship" and all that had served on her were sad to see her go as they relived their memories in their minds.

Once they had been moved away, Captain Saklin saluted the watchers ashore and gave the order, 'Ahead slow. Release tug lines.'

Once again, the orders were repeated, and the giant propeller began to turn sending a wash behind them as the ship began to take control of its own motion.

'Navigator, take us down the channel and out to sea.'

'Yes sir.'

Once clear of the naval base the navigator set course, basically heading south west passing Russky Island they continued around Reyneke and then headed east in the general direction of Sapporo, then north east along the west coast of Hokkaido, they were to travel along the deep-water channel towards the Vries Strait between Iturup and Urup. From there they were to submerge and travel south in the Western Pacific towards the western tip of West Papua and an eventual a port visit in Surabaya, Indonesia.

At least that was the official plan. The official reason was to let the sailors and the shore population see the "Boris" for the last time. The actual route, however, took them a lot closer to Japan than anyone actually knew. The journey was scheduled to be between five and six days, at 20 knots, to get to the open ocean and from there it would be 25 knots all the way to Surabaya.

On the morning of the third day, Captain Saklin's electronics wizard knocked on his cabin door.

'Enter.' The door opened and then closed behind the visitor.

28

'Yevgenney, come, sit.'

Yevgenney sat and waited while Marat called for coffee and cake to be brought in.

'I trust that all is going well with your project?' He asked.

'Certainly, Captain.' The two paused their conversation while the steward served the foods. 'Better than good, actually. All the programming is complete and the other works are also done. All is ready.'

'Good, we should be close enough at midnight tonight, call me then to confirm.'

The two continued their conversation with private discussions about families and football and such, more to fill in the time than anything else. As with all such events time seemed to pass very slowly, their minds were constantly travelling the planned course of events and they were both distracted by the gravity of what they were doing.

Meals came and went as did everything else, still they waited for the right time. Their plan was almost undone when just after sundown the Navigator called on Marat.

'Excuse me Captain, but there seems to be something wrong with my navigational readings,' he said as he waited at the door to the Captain's cabin.

'Come in, tell me what is wrong?'

The Navigator entered the cabin and closed the door behind him.

'I have been updating my chart and it seems that we are very close to the Japanese Islands, well inside their national waters.'

'How did you come by this discrepancy?' asked Marat, trying to find a way to allay his Navigator's fears.

'I have been checking the inertial navigation system and the readings it has given put us a long way to the East of our expected track. I have rechecked and it appears to be correct.'

'What of the compass? You know the ring-laser device was never as accurate as we needed. Maybe it has malfunctioned in some way?'

'I will have it tested.'

'Ask Yevgenney to assist, he may spot something you do not.'

'Yes Sir.' The Navigator left and before he could find Yevgenney, Marat had already warned his friend that he was about to get a visitor.

'Can we check the operation of the compass, please?' The Navigator asked.

'Why, what is wrong?'

'By my calculations we are considerably off course, I was trying to find the cause and how far off we are.'

'I will check it now, come with me if you wish.'

The two men made their way into the compass room. Almost in the centre of the ship it was situated in the most stable position to try to keep errors away from the sensitive part of the device. As Yevgenney accessed the computer system the Navigator waited for a result. Eventually, the readouts were put on the screen and the two began to analyse the results.

'Sorry my friend, there are no errors in the Inertial Guidance system, perhaps the captain will allow you to surface to take "star shoots" the old-fashioned way, to assess our position.'

'I would rather not, if there is any way around it,' he joked, 'I have not done star shoots since I graduated from the Navigation School.'

The two laughed together at the thought of him trying to calculate their position using a sextant and star charts.

'Let us speak with the captain, it is best if we can do this straight away and again at mid-night.' Yevgenney was impressed by the Navigator's sudden switch to professional seaman, no joking this time.

'Very well,' replied Marat. 'Meet me in the control room.'

The three senior officers appeared almost together in the control room.

'Periscope depth!' Marat ordered the helmsman, and the ship began to rise noticeably by the bow.

'Ship is at periscope depth, Captain.' Reported the Officer of the watch.

'Very good,' he replied, 'Time check?'

'2215 local sir.'

'Up periscope!' The larger of the two periscopes slid noiselessly up its feed tube until the eyepiece was at the Captain's preferred height.

'We should have a good view, sir. The almanac shows a full moon in two days.'

Marat pressed his eye to the silicone rubber protective eyepiece and slowly spun around looking at the horizon in every direction. Then he raised the top mirror to check the overhead view and did the same again.

'You may be disappointed; the sky is in full cloud cover.' Marat said as he handed the periscope to the Navigator who immediately pressed his eye to see for himself.

'What are your recommendations, Captain.'

'We shall keep going as we are, there may be a cloud break in the morning, we can recheck then.'

'As you wish, Sir.' That was the end of the discussion as the three officers made their way to their rooms to sleep as they cruised through the night. As they left the control room Marat ordered 'Down periscope, depth 150 metres.'

'Yes Sir, Down periscope, depth 150 metres.' Repeated the Officer of the watch. And he was again repeated by the helmsman who made the adjustments; and they all settled down for an uneventful night.

'Less than two hours to go.' Commentated the helmsman to his understudy. 'Go fetch the coffee.'

'Why is it always me?' the seaman complained.

'Because you are the junior member on watch. Your time will come when you can order someone else to get your coffee; now go!'

The junior seaman almost leapt to his feet, after all it was his first sea duty and he was still learning what was happening. What he did know was that he would have to obey his orders, literally everyone on the ship outranked him.

He had just poured the coffee when the alarm bells rang. Rushing back to the control room he was greeted by the senior officers, emerging from various cabins and rooms, demanding answers to their constant stream of questions.

'What is going on?' demanded Marat. 'Shut that alarm off!'

Seconds later the silence felt almost as loud as the alarms had been.

'The alarm is automatic, Captain.' The officer of the watch explained. 'The indicators are that there has been a fire in the electrical switchboard. The automatic fire dousing systems have put it out. I have sent the electricians to check what damage has been sustained.'

'Reactor systems?' demanded Marat; no one wanted a reactor accident anywhere, let alone at sea where the skeleton crew would be hard pressed to cope with the damage.

'Reactor appears undamaged. No contrary indications.'

'Very good. Are we holding depth?'

'Depth steady at 150 metres, Sir.'

'Very good, be ready to surface at short notice. Seaman; get some coffee for all.'

'Yes Sir.' The seaman replied and left to complete his previous task. "How can they be so calm?" he pondered to himself "We had a fire, and no one seems worried?"

He returned with the coffee and handed everyone a cup. As he gave one to the helmsman, he asked just that question; in a very quiet voice, lest he be overheard.

'Remember they are vastly experienced; they understand what is happening.' The reply did little to calm the young man's nerves.

'I want damage reports from the technicians, NOW!' demanded Marat, he was not in the habit of waiting for anything.

A few short minutes later the Chief Electrician emerged from the after end of the ship.

'There has been a number of short-circuits within the main switchboard, the systems have been left without maintenance for so long they have deteriorated badly.'

'Can you fix it?'

'Sorry Sir, no. There is so much damage and we do not carry the materials to rebuild the switchboard. We have redirected the essential systems through the secondary switchboard and isolated the damaged sections on the main.'

'Very good. Can we complete our mission to get to Murmansk?'

'I have inspected the systems and there appears to be no collateral damage. As we are not operational, we should be able to complete our mission, after all we only need to keep life-support and navigational systems online through the switchboards. Reactor systems are run local for just this reason.'

'Very good, thank you Chief. Well done to you and your technicians.'

'Thank you, Sir.'

The Chief saluted and left the control room to try to get the main switchboard back in an operational condition.

The fire had most of the crew on edge. Fire on any ship is dangerous enough. Fire on a submarine, 150 metres below the surface, was unthinkable.

Marat was thinking the same.

'Come up to fifty metres.'

'Set Depth 50 metres.' Repeated the Officer of the Watch, the order was repeated, and they began to head towards the surface.

It was two hours later, almost, when the ship shuddered throughout and then listed slightly.

The shudder was severe enough to shake the Navigator out of his bunk and sent him racing to the control room. All the officers arrived at the same time; none knew what had happened.

'Damage report!' shouted Marat as he entered the room and several voices began to shout back at him.

'SILENCE!' he shouted, 'One at a time.'

'Electrical report no further damage.'

'Engineering, we are unable to move the control surfaces. We cannot manoeuvre.'

'Reactor closed off, in standby and stable.'

'Life support good.'

'No flooding at this time. That may change when we get off this rock, or whatever it is. Hull is intact at this time.'

'Good, full checks on all systems. Reports as you finish.'

The section heads and their Chiefs left for a much more in-depth analysis of their domains.

'Navigator, we need to know exactly where we are; and what we have hit. Once we have a clearer view of how we are we can make plans.'

'Should we inform the Kremlin, sir?'

'Not yet, we will let them know once we have answers for their questions.'

It was almost dawn when the final report came in.

'No extensive damage, Captain. We can attempt to float off when you are ready.'

'Good. Blow all ballast, periscope depth.'

Again, the orders were repeated, and the ship began to float off. All was well and everyone breathed a sigh of relief. Marat swung the periscope around to ensure he was not going to surface in front of a freighter or under an oil rig. Once he was satisfied, he gave the order.

'Surface!'

The ship again began to rise and once it had made it to the surface, they were all dismayed when they realised the swell was rising under them, not a force 9 gale; or worse a late season typhoon, but still very uncomfortable and even the seasoned sailors began to feel queasy.

As the officers emerged on the top of the conning tower Marat ordered the Navigator to determine their correct position.

Pulling the chart from under his jacket, he marked the few positional indicators that he could find and then double checked his calculations.

'It appears that we are considerably East of our predicted track, there must be an error in the predictor navigational control systems.'

'Very well. Get it fix—' Marat was interrupted by the firing klaxons blaring loudly and all were stunned when the missile tube covers opened all together. Before anyone could react, the missiles began to launch. "Terror" would be the feeling that they all would attest to feeling at the later enquiry. Which would be replaced by relief when the first stage engines all appeared to cut out prematurely, at least they had not started a nuclear war by mistake.

All wondered, as they looked on, "Where would the warheads land?"

They did not have a lot of time to wonder, however, the radiation alarm took over from the launch klaxon.

'CAPTAIN!' the power plant officer shouted into the intercom. 'We have a leakage of radiation into the ship.'

'The reactor?' Marat quizzed the reporting officer.

'Reactor is scrammed and secure; but there is an uncontrolled release of radioactive steam and water from the propulsion system. We MUST abandon ship.'

Marat Saklin thought for a few minutes and then ordered the abandonment of the submarine.

'We need to submerge the ship. Release the lifeboats, Radio make emergency transmission to Kremlin. Message reads "We have run aground following navigational systems failure. Reactor is secure, radiation leak internal and contained. Missiles have auto released without full boost engines. Landing position unknown. We are abandoning ship and scuttling onto rocks approximately 50 metres deep. Send retrieval teams." Make that in plain language, Russian and English. Send from main radio now and repeat every three minutes. Once off the ship continue to send using the emergency radio.'

'Yes Sir.' The message was sent but the radio room called back urgently. 'Captain, the radio is not transmitting.'

'Wait there, we need the power of the main radio to ensure Moscow receives it. Yevgenney, see what you can do.'

As Yevgenney began to work his magic there was an unearthly groan from the hull as the already damaged frames let go. The sea flooded in with enough force to knock over an elephant. Nothing could stand against the incoming tide.

'EVERYONE, OFF' the crew pushed the lifeboats off and jumped in as fast as they could. Paddling frantically, they gathered together and tied the rafts to each other to keep any from drifting away.

The submarine Boris Yeltsin sank quickly, so quickly that even the captain was washed off the conning tower into the sea and was rescued by frantically paddling sailors.

As first light began to filter through the leaden sky it saw six life rafts bobbing in the slowly rising sea. A head count revealed that there were two missing, the radio operator and Marat's friend Yevgenney. Sad, to be certain, but an acceptable loss given that an entire ballistic missile submarine had been sunk.

'DOES ANYONE HAVE THE EMERGENCY RADIO?' Marat shouted against the increasing wind.

'Here, sir!' came a voice struggling against the wind.

'Navigator, get to the radio and transmit our position, plain language.'

The navigator fought the rising seasickness and began to transmit their situation to the world.

'Put out your sea anchors, we need to remain close to where we went down.' Marat ordered, and the rafts stopped drifting quite so fast.

It took two days before anyone heard the helicopter, when they did, they all cheered loudly. They would be saved.

Chapter 5
Rescued

'There,' shouted the observer 'Turn right to 060 degrees, then straight ahead.' As the rescue helicopter turned the pilot announced 'I have them in sight. All units converge on my position. Rescue ship? there are six or more life rafts to be picked up as well as passengers.'

The Japanese Coast Guard had been incredibly efficient in finding the castaways so very quickly. They were not far off the coast of Iturup when they found them. The one topic of conversation, both offshore and on, was "Why are they so close to the island?"

The sea had abated a little from the previous two days and the wind had also died down. One by one the sailors were taken from the rafts onto the Coast Guard rescue ship where they were all given clean, dry clothes and warm drinks to bring their core temperature up towards normal. Foods were provided but they did not have much flavour, they had been chosen as bland foods specifically to enable the seasick sailors to digest them after two days without any sustenance.

The survivors began to recover rapidly and as they felt better, they were all beginning to wonder what had actually happened and what had become of their shipmates.

Captain Saklin was taken to the captain of the rescue ship and he was immediately questioned as to what ship they had been on and what had happened. It took around an hour before the full story had been told, and the signals were sent informing the Japanese Ministry of Defence of the disaster. From there it was directly to the Prime Minister and the Cabinet and they sent an envoy to the Russian Embassy to demand the Ambassador meet with the Foreign Minister to explain their shockingly bad navigation and to outline their plans to rectify the situation.

At the Office of the Japanese Foreign Minister

'Mr Ambassador, please come in and sit. Will you have tea or coffee?'

'Thank you, tea please, call me Anatoli. We can get by without such formality.'

The Foreign Minister called for tea and wondered why the ambassador was being so accommodating, most unlike the Russians to be so nice.

'As you wish, will you call me Genzo?'

'Certainly.'

At that point the refreshments were brought in and the attendant served the two men, even while he was serving them, he could feel the tension in the room. After being assured there were no more requests the attendant left the room, closing the door quietly behind him.

'Mr Ambassador, Anatoli, I understand there are many operational provisions that you need to observe. However, we demand answers. Why was your submarine so close to our shoreline? Why did your Captain not take action to move further out to sea? Why were missiles launched in our Territorial Waters? How many warheads were they carrying, and have they all been accounted for? Where were they programmed to land? What do you plan to do to rectify the situation? We have several hundred radiation readings that are well above the acceptable level, how do you plan to clear the sources away and restore the land and sea?'

'Firstly, I must apologise. And I do so on behalf of President Tokmakov and the Russian people unreservedly. I have spoken with Captain Saklin, and he has given me a briefing on the subject. Firstly, they had a problem with the navigational system, and they were trying to navigate the old-fashioned way, by the stars. This was not an issue, but a fire broke out in the main electrical switchboard. This fire caused many short-circuits and computer failures throughout the ship. Life support systems were placed in emergency mode and only critical systems were repaired at that time.'

He paused for a sip of his steaming hot tea, while he tried to gather his thoughts. "How much do they really know?" he wondered, before he continued.

'The most crucial error came late in the night when the ship ran aground. The electronics officer had just diagnosed the error in the inertial navigation system, which had placed them off course, when it was too late.'

'The submarine crashed into a reef at 20 knots and needed to surface to release itself. Once they were on the surface, they could determine their exact position, but before they could make plans to return to base the malfunction in the missile control computer began to launch the missiles.'

'I know it will be of cold comfort to you all, but the same malfunction that caused the launch error also caused the missile engines to malfunction and they all cut-out after a few seconds. Not having attained sufficient altitude the missiles did not have their targeting or directional control systems fully functional and they all returned to earth but not, in any way, in close proximity to each other. We will need to launch search teams to find the warheads.'

'Exactly how many warheads are you speaking of?' the Foreign Minister asked, barely disguising his anger that the Russians could be so blasé about something so important.

'Of the thirty missiles on board twenty-seven launched. With fifty warheads each we are looking for just over 1300 warheads.'

'YOU LOSE MORE THAN 1300 NUCLEAR WEAPONS OVER JAPANESE TERRITORY. AND YOU SOUND LIKE YOU CAN'T FIND A SOCK!' All sense of decorum had disappeared from the Foreign Minister. 'THERE WILL BE CONSEQUENCES, I CAN ASSURE YOU!'

'Again, I apologise. There is more, if you wish me to continue?'

'Go on, may as well get it all on the table now.'

'There was an uncontrolled release of radioactive steam and water inside the submarine. The reactor is safe and in itself it poses no danger. But it will need specialist work to raise the submarine again. Unfortunately, there was also a breach in the ship's hull, and it split in two. We do have the position of the wreck but as I say it will be difficult to retrieve the vessel.'

'Tell me, Just HOW do you plan to rectify this situation?' Minister Suzuki was getting angry now. How could they be so indifferent to anyone and everyone around them.

'I have received instructions that all works will be paid for by us and completed by Russian workers, many will be serving members of the Russian Navy, but they will do it all.'

'And what of the residents? What is to become of them?'

'The President and the Government have authorised that all will be compensated for any inconvenience. We will also pay for any that wish to relocate to the main islands of Japan; this includes their accommodation and relocation expenses as well as any other losses they suffer.'

'Very well,' replied Genzo, somewhat mollified by the repatriation offer. 'I will report to the Prime Minister and the Emperor and await their response. We will be keeping a very close watch on your progress. Do not be surprised if they demand compensation for this breach of internationally recognised safety protocols regarding nuclear ships and weapons.'

The Ambassador stood and bowed to the Minister, in a nod to Japanese tradition, 'I will make myself available at any time for you.'

'Domo arigatō.' Genzo returned the bow and the Russian was escorted to his car.

"Thank the gods that I survived that without being jailed. Now I have to inform the President."

'Back to the embassy, I need to speak with the President,' he ordered his driver as he closed the privacy screen between them.

Once he was in his private office he sent for a double vodka, he needed it after his meeting with the Minister. The drink was delivered, and he locked the door before he set the hologram system to place a call to the Kremlin.

'Anatoli, tell me you have good news?' The image of President Tokmakov smiled widely at him.

'Yes, Kolya, I believe I do. The Foreign Minister was very angry, and he has made demands for compensation. But I believe that when he has had his meetings with his Emperor and Prime Minister, they will give us the authorisation to begin to relocate the affected locals and start the collection of the "lost warheads" and the raising of the submarine.'

'Good, I have heard from Captain Saklin. He informed me that his radio operator and his electronics officer were both lost in the "accident". A great disappointment to all, no doubt. Once we have retrieved the bodies, we will have them repatriated to Moscow and they will be interred as "Heroes of the Nation" for their sacrifice in trying to avert a disaster.'

'That should be a suitable epitaph for them, and the pension will ensure that their families are cared for,' replied Anatoli, his words began to lose their veracity, he did not want to think that all this was deliberate, but the more he thought about it the more it appeared to be. *Best not to dwell on that possibility or I may end up like Andreyushkin,* he mused.

'You took the words from me, my friend. You only have a year left in your posting, do you not?' Kolya asked innocently. 'What do you think you will do after that?'

'Well, given I was extended here and have been Ambassador for seven years now, I think I will retire and spend my days fishing and golfing. Maybe even visit my family in Sochi, I have not seen them for some time.'

'That sounds like a great idea. I may join you after the next election, if they do not want me anymore,' Kolya joked. 'How would you like to come home early? You have done more than anyone else could, and I would like you to be one of my advisors for the election. What do you think?'

'Yes, it would be good to come home.'

'Then home it is. I will organise your replacement and you can begin working towards your retirement with a lowering of your workload. We will speak again soon.'

'Goodbye, Kolya. My regards to your family, see you soon.'

The call was terminated, and Anatoli relaxed somewhat. Deep in the back of his mind he knew that his reference to family would remind the President that he had married a first cousin of the soon to be "former Ambassador to Japan" and there were ties that had to be observed. Anatoli hoped that the ties would be strong enough to ensure he would survive. This was, in every description, a dangerous game and he would need to be careful if he were also to avoid becoming collateral damage.

The UN General Assembly

'The meeting will come to order!' commanded the General Secretary. 'The first to have the floor will be the Ambassador from Russia.'

Suddenly everyone became attentive, this would be either a poorly disguised attempt at a cover up, or it would be a reasonably believable report on the disaster they had caused in the Kuril Islands north of Hokkaido.

'Thank you, Secretary General and members of this auspicious chamber.'

"Pretty quick to be sucking up to us." The Australian Ambassador whispered to his New Zealand counterpart.

"Fifty bucks says it is a whitewash."

"You are on." The two close friends sat back to listen to the explanation.

'As you are all well aware by now, the Submarine "Boris Yeltsin" has run aground and sunk off the west coast of Iturup Island in the Japanese Kuril Islands. The preliminary investigation has revealed that a failure of the inertial navigation system placed the ship in an incorrect position, far off its expected track. Subsequent to this error there was an unrelated fire in the main switchboard; this fire and the resulting electrical short circuits damaged many of the onboard computer systems. The result of these system failures was the launching of most of the Intercontinental Ballistic Missiles she was carrying.' Uproar echoed around the Assembly.

'Are you saying there was an uncontrolled and unauthorised launch of nuclear weapons?' demanded the U.S. delegation. A sentiment that was repeated by almost every one of the assembled diplomats.

'Please, let me explain fully, then you may ask for details of the results,' begged the Russian.

The room eventually became quiet again. But it took quite some time for this to happen, many delegates were already making reports to their political overlords.

'There is a small light at the end of this incredibly difficult tunnel. The missiles were not programmed with targets and the rocket engines were shutoff automatically after sufficient flight to clear the ships' location.'

'What of the warheads?' demanded the Japanese Ambassador. 'Are we to assume they are just lying around on our territory?' He knew the answer, he had been well briefed before the meeting had even been scheduled, he just wanted the Russians to admit their grievous failure.

'The warheads? Yes, I was getting to that.' The Russian explained as he paused for a much-needed drink. This was going about as badly as he had foreseen. He didn't want to give out the next, secret, information but he would not be able to keep it secret any longer.

'Part of our safeguards,' he began nervously, 'is that if a launch is unauthorised the engines shut off prematurely and the warheads are deployed at the same time. As they were launched prematurely, they were not fused and ready for detonation. This means that we can collect them from wherever they landed.'

'So, there will not be any explosions?'

'No, all we need to do is find them and retrieve them.'

'Just how many are we talking about?' asked the American, not interested in the plight of Japan and her people, just sensing an opportunity to gather important information on the Russian Fleet's capabilities.

'We are looking for 1350 warheads in total, but that is not the most important task which faces us.'

'Really, you lose thousands of weapons, nuclear weapons, and it's not that important? Are you even listening to your response?' The UK Ambassador was almost white with rage, he saw not only the danger to their close ally but also the danger to humanity on a grander scale.

'You win, it is a whitewash. Here is your fifty.' The Australian whispered to the New Zealand Ambassador, as he handed over the winnings.

'I apologise. During the grounding there was a release of radioactive steam and water from the power plant. While the reactor is secure and safe there is a good deal of danger in and around the wreck. We will be working to raise and remove the ship and all its equipment.'

'Do you need assistance?' This was an unexpected question from the New Zealand Ambassador. Long known for their opposition to nuclear power and weapons it was not a field they were known as being experienced in.

'Thank you for the offer, but no we have all the people and equipment we will need.'

'Where are we to put our citizens while this "recovery" is underway? We cannot just move them to another island. There is insufficient infrastructure to do this.' The Japanese ambassador was now getting just a little worried about the direction the disclosure was taking.

'I have been authorised to provide all assistance for those that wish to be relocated to one of the main islands of Japan. We will build housing, schools and any other items which are needed.'

'That is a huge undertaking, there are many tens of thousands of people there. How will you build everything quickly enough?'

"This is good" the Russian thought, "they are already looking towards the people and helping them, not worrying about the weapons."

'The President and people of Russia are not capable of the physical construction required in the short time available. We would ask that the International Community assist us in this endeavour, we will cover the cost, of course, but assistance from you all will help in making this as smooth a transition as possible for those we have effectively displaced by our error.'

Everyone was silent. For the first time ever, the Russians had admitted fault. Not just among one or two nations but before the world.

'As Ambassador for Australia I would like to affirm the assistance from our construction industry. As a close ally of Japan, we are similar in our building codes and construction methods. We are well placed to assist.'

That was the beginning of a veritable tsunami of offers from around the world. Those that could not actually assist with the building were offering materials and others were offering catering for the huge numbers of workers and refugees.

The planning was to take another week or two but eventually the agreement was made that as soon as possible the local inhabitants were to be relocated to Hokkaido and Honshu until the clean-up had been completed. This was international cooperation at its best.

The construction began almost immediately. The road builders followed hard on the heels of the electrical and water supply companies; and new substations, water supply treatment plants and sewerage treatment plants were established at lightning speed. As the roads were being laid down the schools were being constructed and the first houses began to emerge almost like mushrooms growing overnight into new towns and suburbs.

But even with the vast quantity of materials and expertise it was still almost a year before any of the displaced people could be relocated to their new homes.

Eventually, the new inhabitants were settling into their new surroundings. For many it was almost as foreign a place they could find. If they had somehow been transported to the moon, they would not have been less familiar with their surroundings.

The predominant ethnic group were the Ainu. These were the descendants of the original inhabitants of the island chain; and whilst they were technically Japanese, the same as those further north in the island chain were technically Russian, they still held on to their own way of life. Traditional methods of farming, fishing and the growing of crops were still observed, and they were very comfortable with the creation and use of their traditional clothing and artefacts. Going to the supermarket was almost frightening to them; the sheer abundance of foods and the variety available was, to them, an alien way of life.

Time would prove to see some of them embracing their new life; however, many would forever decry the loss of so much they held dear, not the least was the slower pace of life they craved; just like it once was.

For President Tokmakov and his co-conspirators the relocations were taking far too long. They wanted to begin the retrieval of their weapons, and the wreck of the submarine, at the first opportunity. Reality would force them to keep up the appearance of apology and concern for the well-being of "those poor people, deprived of everything by an unpreventable incident".

The retrievals were still however second to the planned rapid deployment of the "Technical Retrieval Teams" that would be the forerunners of the final establishment of the permanent new inhabitants. In a secret stockpile just outside of Vladivostok, huge numbers of prefabricated buildings were arriving; waiting their turn to be placed on a ship to be transported into place. The Army engineers had been planning for this almost as long as the politicians had. The training had seen the construction and assembly brought down to just under four days to assemble a house or other small building. The larger buildings that would be needed would have to wait until the smaller requirements had been completed, for no other reason than to delay the suspicions of invasion and seizure of the lands. It would be a slowly completed mission that would give them the longest tenure in the Kuril Islands, and they all had to abide by the planned program sequence.

It was the northern most islands that were occupied first. Starting at Raykoke they established their "working" sites and appeared to be very industrious. At the same time there were a number of Russian Navy ships close to the site where the "Boris Yeltsin" had gone down. These were the only ones actually attempting to do some real work. They had surveyed and mapped the position of the submarine and a deep submergence vessel had recorded the exact layout and positioning of the wreck.

Their first assignment was to retrieve the bodies of the two sailors lost. And this alone took almost a month. Clearing away damaged parts of the ship first they eventually managed to make their way into the radio room, just off to one side of the Control Room, the two were jammed behind the door and the door was eventually removed with remote controlled underwater cutting equipment.

The bodies were retrieved by a remote submersible and, after the decontamination teams had finished their work, the two were repatriated to Moscow where, amid much pomp and ceremony, they were interred as Heroes of the Russian State.

The Russian elections came and went. As usual there were accusations of collusion and bias. More accusations of vote tampering and eventually, after the third recount, Tokmakov was announced as the re-elected President. No one actually believed the result, but no one could supply any evidence that there had been any fraudulent activities; at least no one that valued their lives were willing to speak up. It would be noted, eventually, that an unusually high numbers of important officials and opposition members had suffered motor accidents during the unusually harsh winter.

The last of the island locals had been relocated around eighteen months after the "disaster". At this point the invasion began in earnest.

Japanese Foreign Ministry

'Call the Russian Ambassador and ask him to come here for a meeting.' The Japanese Foreign Minister demanded; and his assistant immediately began making phone calls.

Eventually, the meeting was set and the two waited for the refreshments to be provided.

'I will come straight to the point,' the Foreign Minister said abruptly, 'It appears to us that you are moving far too much staff and equipment into the Kuril's. How do you justify so many military groups on the islands?'

'We have only placed those we need to complete the work,' replied the Ambassador testily.

'Again, I ask you, why so many military personnel?'

'The military, in particular the Navy, have the greatest number of experienced members that are available at short notice. Larger numbers permit us to rotate them quicker.'

'That sounds like an excuse. We demand you provide weekly updates on the progress you are making. You will set down the dates for the completion of the search and locating of the "lost" warheads and for the retrieval. You will also set down the expected dates for the raising of the submarine and its reactor system.'

'I apologise, these items are unable to be defined exactly. We must proceed slowly, especially with the retrieval of the submarine. The hull is far more damaged than we first believed, the latest sonar and video scans show that the supports under the reactor are in poor condition, and we must not move so quickly as to have them break.'

'Why are they so bad?'

'Please understand, the ship was very old, and much of the maintenance was not completed as she was not expected to go to sea again. The original plan was to decommission it at the Eastern Fleet Base. But budget cutbacks saw the decision to close one decommissioning port and only have the one at Murmansk as an operational area.'

'I understand, but I also understand that you are delaying as much work as you can. Many here believe that you are deliberately stalling in an attempt to establish a permanent presence in the Kuril's; this will not be tolerated. For centuries now we have had too many of your attempts to invade and steal our lands and we believe that is your ultimate goal.'

'I will convey your concerns to Moscow immediately.' The Russian stood up and turned to leave. 'Please, Mr Foreign Minister, do not threaten my political overlords, they will not be pleased with the stand you are taking.'

'Pleased or not, that is how your actions have been assessed. You must increase your efforts to complete the clean-up of your mess. Make no mistake, the nations of the world are assessing you the same as we do, and we will soon be making representation to the United Nations.'

'Again, I say, do not threaten us.'

The Russian left, he was angry, and his demeanour did not improve when his car was not waiting for him when he left the building and he made certain that his driver was very sorry for the entire journey back to the embassy.

The message was delivered to the President and he took the hologram call from the Ambassador just hours later.

'What do you mean? They suspect we have an ulterior motive. Are we not doing all we can to clean up the mess?'

'I apologise, Mr President. I am merely conveying the accusations that the Foreign Minister has levelled at us.'

'Unbelievable, I will raise the subject with their Prime minister at the G20 meeting next month.'

Kolya Tokmakov sat and pondered deeply. The reports from Japan were only the tip of this iceberg. Many of his political opponents were making the same accusations. And there were also rumblings of discontent from the streets as well. How had he misread the populace so badly? Why were they complaining about his actions? He had simply put into action the plans his political advisors had insisted were the best way ahead. "I must tread carefully for a while; we must be seen to be taking the right and honourable steps." But no matter how he tried to reorganise the thoughts inside his head the outcome was the same. "Either they give us the islands, or we just remain forever and fight them if they insist on going to war."

The high-level meetings came and went, G20, The Pacific Forum, the Northern Pacific Trade Alliance and even the General Assembly of the UN. Everyone thought the same and no one was willing to do anything about it. After ten years and two Russian Presidents, Japan was looking to be more isolated as the subject became less important each year.

Chapter 6
An Auspicious Birth

Hokkaido 2190

The two "Old" men sat looking at the images embedded in the apparent haze before them. Eventually, one of them spoke.

'Zaphiel, are you near?' He called out.

'I am here.'

'Do you see before us?'

'I do; I see a new child has been born. Am I to protect him?'

'Yes, Zaphiel, you will. But not as closely as the last we assigned to you. We need you to bring Tokugawa Ieyasu, Miyamoto Musashi and Jackson Teague to us. They will need to assist him.'

'Very well.' The Angel Zaphiel disappeared and returned very quickly closely followed by three men dressed in the style of the samurai of centuries past.

'You wish to see us?' asked Jackson.

'Yes, do you see the child before us?'

The three men looked into the haze and watched as the new-born babe slept peacefully in his mother's arms. 'Yes, we see him,' they agreed.

'Jackson, this is your seven times Great-grandson. His parents have named him Jackson in your honour.' The three all looked at the boy and waited for a few moments.

'He is a wonderful addition to my family line, but why are you showing us this?'

'His destiny, like all, has been set in motion. Zaphiel will care for him until he is ten. After that time, you will all need to mentor him. Ieyasu, you will need to teach him leadership and diplomacy. Musashi, you will need to teach him "The Way", as he will need to be a warrior, one of unrivalled skill. Jackson, you will need to teach him determination, how to solve problems by not looking as others do, and how to lead warriors in battle.'

'Why is this so important as to require all of us?' asked Musashi. 'What is it that he must achieve?'

'That we cannot say, but rest assured there is more at stake than ever before.' 'Very well.'

The three "men" and the angel left to discuss the methods they would need to use if they were to be of assistance to this new-born child.

Born into one of the few devout Christian families in Japan his christening was held not long after his birth. It was probably a misnomer to say they were devout Christians, because they did not actually go to church on a regular basis. Still, their beliefs were very strong; prayer and God were ever-present, and all of the family were believers. One thing they did believe was that they did not need a priest to lead them in prayer. They could do that for themselves. It was well established that private prayer was better, for them, than a tightly organised religion.

As babies went, he was a quiet child, rarely crying, always watching those around him. At his Christening, held at the family chapel on their estate in the far north of Hokkaido, his sister would remark that he was always watching those around him. And if you could observe him from afar, that is exactly what he appeared to be doing. Watching and assessing everyone he could see.

He went to the local primary school and while he did not excel in every subject, he did manage to be in the top few of the students. His innate intelligence and consistency of effort would show when he had the compulsory IQ tests at age nine. He was assessed as being over 130, and this score was to be held as the reason he took on so many formal subjects at school as well as extra-curricular activities. He was outstanding at Judo, Karate and Kendo. The discipline of the traditional martial arts was what had attracted him, and his dedication to these arts was rewarded by high rank black belts in all.

This was not enough for him. He also took on Kung Fu, and boxing. Achieving National Age Championship status in all disciplines. Despite them attending the same school, the Kung Fu dojo was where he met the man that would be his life-long friend, and sensei, Akio Takamatsu, and the two trained together so often and so well that the Sensei pushed them harder than all his other students. Jackson took up Mixed Martial Arts fighting and at eighteen he had won the National Open Championship. Many of the top promoters wanted him to tour the U.S. and Europe but he was not interested in a life of exhibition fighting. He had ambitions of his own; at least he thought they were his own.

As soon as he had graduated from high school he enlisted in the army. No one tried to prevent his enlistment, indeed his father thought that it would be the best place for his energies to be used. His original preference was to be a tank driver, but the psychological testing would put him so high that he was placed in the Officer Training School and his career as an Infantry officer began.

'Do you think we will ever need to go to war?' His Tactics Instructor asked the class, one day during the latter stages of his training.

Almost everyone spoke or shouted their enthusiastic agreement; the mass opinion was yes, we will.

'Nakagawa, you did not answer, why not?' demanded the officer.

'We are here to learn how to fight if we have to, we are not here to start a war but to prevent one. If we need to go to war it will be because the politicians have failed in their work. As it has always been, we will be left to fix the mess they make.'

'Very wise answer, but non-committal, do you think we will go to war?' The instructor was insistent in his demand for a definitive answer from Jackson.

'I feel we are already at war, the shooting has not yet begun, that is all.'

'Explain yourself?'

'It is many years, decades, since the Russians invaded the Kuril Islands under the thin veil of clearing up a nuclear mess that they engineered. In my opinion we will eventually go to a full war footing and try to take back the islands in the not-too-distant future.'

'And what is your timescale for this "War" you insist we are in?' The officer could barely contain his dismissive attitude.

'It will be in a few years, maybe a decade or two, before fighting breaks out. We will need to be ready when it does.'

'And tell us all, if you please Cadet Nakagawa, what do you think will be the outcome?'

'Many will die early in the fighting. It will take innovative thinking to defeat the Russians and take back the Islands.'

'We will see. I will make a note of your words and we will all see how close to correct you are. Class dismissed.'

The cadets left the building and were making their way to their rooms when one jumped in front of Jack.

'Why do you always make it difficult for everyone?'

'What do you mean, he asked for my thoughts and I gave them. That is all.'

'Really, that is all, you will get us all into trouble if you do not stop! Try giving a normal answer sometime.'

Jack walked off, wondering why no one else could see the inevitability of a war with Russia, when he could see it so clearly; when the other cadet again jumped in front of him.

'You think you know it all!' he shouted, just a few centimetres from Jack's face. He was well known for intimidating his fellow cadets before challenging them to a fight.

Jack tried to walk around him when the challenge came.

'You are always refusing to commit. I will fight you today, after class in the gym. OR ARE YOU AFRAID?'

Jack had never been afraid of anyone and this particular cadet was no exception. Again, he tried to leave, ignoring the challenge.

'What's wrong, Nakagawa, frightened?' he taunted.

Jack spun around with a speed that stunned everyone. 'Very well, 1700 in the gym, what do you prefer, boxing, karate or MMA?'

'Let's make it MMA.'

The decision had been made. All the cadets were waiting before the appointed time. The challenger was getting his hands bandaged in preparation for the fight but there was no sign of Jack. 1700 came and went, as did 1715. By 1730 his opponent was cursing and complaining about Jack not being man enough to turn up.

Eventually, to the sound of much shouting and taunting, Jack arrived.

46

As he was preparing in his corner of the ring his friend asked why he had taken so long before arriving.

'Read the deeds of Musashi.' Jack said 'One of his duelling tactics was to make his opponent wait. Look at him, he is so angry he will fight a steel post soon. He will not be concentrating, and his tactics will be controlled, not by his mind, but by his anger. It will be a short fight.'

Jack's second looked across the ring to see his opponent jumping and twitching while he yelled abuse at Jack.

'I see what you mean. Be careful, he will be dangerous in that mood.'

'I will not be here long enough for him to be a danger to me. If I do this right, he will not be a danger to anyone else either.'

At that point the senior officers and course instructors arrived and took their seats. It would be normal for them to stop the fight, but the Camp Commander decided that they would let this particular lesson in life play itself out.

The referee called them to the centre to give them the fight instructions, "Three five-minute rounds, no biting, no gouging no foul blows" etc.

Jack held his hands out for the usual "fist bump" which took the place of a handshake but all he got was a shove from his opponent.

The referee pointed at the timekeeper and he rang the bell to start the fight.

At the sound of the bell, his opponent charged across the ring intent on doing damage. Jack just jumped to one side and hit him in the side of the head as he ran past. This simple punch enraged his opponent far beyond the simple fact that he had been hit. Again, he charged at Jack, swinging wildly without any real chance of hitting him. This time jack drove his knee into his opponents' passing ribs, leaving him gasping for breath on the canvas.

The crowd was silent, no one had expected this to be the start of the fight. The senior officers were making comments among themselves.

Once he had regained his feet someone shouted, 'Stop running past him, hit something!' and that was probably the worst advice that anyone could have given at that point.

Instead of running at Jack, this time he walked up and tried to get a close in grapple; all he got was more knees to the ribs and a couple of hits to his head. Still, he did not realise he was outclassed.

Jack's second shouted out, enough Jack, finish this off. And he did. Jack moved in quickly when they broke apart and ended the fight with a flurry of fists, knees and elbows. The referee tried to stop the fight but by the time he had separated them it was over. Jack had almost raised a sweat and his opponent was being assessed by the doctors to see if there was any lasting damage, and at the same time Jack asked for his, now dislocated left little finger, to be reset. A quick manipulation and some strapping tape completed his medical needs.

The crowd dispersed and left Jack and his second almost alone in the ring. The Commandant went to Jack and said, 'That was fairly brutal Cadet Nakagawa.'

Jack stood up and bowed. 'In the words of my ancestor, there is no such thing as half a fight. He challenged me to a fight, and that is what I gave him.'

'May I ask, did you tell him of your experience in the ring?' The Commandant asked, clearly well acquainted with Jack's earlier career.

'No Sir, if he wanted to, he could have found out for himself. I was not about to let him goad me into a fight and then back out because I am experienced. He wanted to fight, and no one was going to change his mind.'

'Perhaps next time you may consider giving him time to back out.'

'I always gave my opponents the chance to "not fight". He chose to do it.'

'Very well.'

The Commandant left and as he made his way back to his office, he commented to the Course Instructor, 'He will make a very good fighting commander, I don't think he is one for an office.'

'I completely agree.' Was the reply.

Later that evening Jack went to his old dojo and sought out his friend.

'I don't get it Akio; I can see what is going to happen and they all act like I am the idiot in the room for saying what I know in my heart to be true.'

'If you believe it, then hold on to that belief. Just because they will not see, does not mean that you have to be blind as well.'

'Wise words, arigatō, that is exactly how it is. Let's train.'

'How about katana's today?' Akio asked his friend.

'Are we permitted?'

'I was awarded my Preliminary Sensei Accreditation today; I can now officially train you in the harder weapons.'

'SENSEI! Fantastic. Make it a shorter session and I will buy you dinner.'

'Better, loser buys. There is a small sushi shop just down the street we can go there.'

The "short" training session eventually ended two hours later. Showered and changed the two friends made their way to the restaurant just as they were about to close. The owner let them come into the shop and locked the front door. The two enjoyed a private dinner and a long overdue catchup over their lives and general discussion.

'Did you ever make a go of it with Mya?' Akio asked.

'Only for a few weeks, long enough to finish school and do the formal evening. After that she decided to leave me, and she took up with the baseball captain. The last I heard they had three children and then they had divorced. I did hear she was living on Okinawa with a man now, but nothing more than that. How about you?'

'No one serious, just a few "friends with benefits" as they used to call it.'

The two laughed at their complete lack of life companions.

"Never mind, Jack, when the time is right you will find someone." He said imitating his older sister almost perfectly. He never knew if she was mocking him or trying to give him real life advice, but he took it as well meant.

The two parted ways promising to continue their sessions as often as possible. Before Jack graduated, top of his class as usual, Akio had been given full accreditation as a Sensei and he took the position at his dojo alongside the

Master. And his training of Jack was to be a lifelong pursuit as well as some fun for the two friends.

Jack's graduation at the top of his class was a not unexpected result, and he would eventually be sent to an active combat battalion as his first posting as a commissioned officer.

Chapter 7
An Important Addition

Jack was almost twenty-two, a few weeks from his birthday, and just a month away from completing his training when he received a call from his father.

'Jack; I have been speaking with Reina Maki.'

'All is well, I hope?' Jack was well aware that Chie Maki had been close to the end of her pregnancy and he was concerned that she may have had problems.

'Yes, all is well. The doctors have just left after attending Chie; if she has not given birth before, they are going to induce her this Saturday. She has asked specifically for you to be present, at least at the hospital if not actually inside the birthing suite.'

'Where is she now? Why does she want me to be there?'

'She is at home, with us and her mother Reina, and grandmother Reina of course. She said she will explain later, you know how senkensha are, they will make odd demands when they need to but there is always a good reason. Will you be able to make it?'

'I will make certain to be there. I will speak with the Course Officer right away.'

Father and son made small talk for a few minutes more to be polite than out of any pressure to speak for a suitable length of time. Neither father nor son was known for their love of telephone conversations, they would rather be sitting with each other than talk endlessly on the phone.

Eventually, Jack bade his father farewell and left to speak with the Course Commander to ensure he got the time he needed.

'Cadet Nakagawa is here to see you, Sir,' announced the Course Commander's secretary.

"Now what does he want?" he wondered to himself, "Every time I speak with him something unexpected happens." He sat and grinned as he remembered the huge argument over tactics; with the General Commanding Southern Forces on one side and Jack on the other. Eventually, the General had to pull rank to win the debate. "Never seen a cadet with such a depth of knowledge of past commanders" He is going to make a lot of people rethink their ways one day.'

Shaking off his reverie he pressed the intercom button and announced 'Send him in.'

The door opened and Jack marched in stopping a polite three paces away from the desk. He saluted and then bowed to his superior officer.

'How many times do you need to be told! It is not necessary to salute and bow. One or the other will suffice, not both.'

'Again, I apologise Sir. I was always told that a salute is to honour the uniform and the rank; a bow is to honour the person. It seems right to me that you receive both.'

The man before him looked at Jack for a few moments and indicated for him to sit.

'How do you do it, Nakagawa, you always have the right answer?'

'I don't think it is a case of being right, I feel it is just polite. I will try not to bow next time, but then I will not be separating the ones I respect from the others.'

'You do realise that there are a number of other cadets that think you are just trying to ingratiate yourself to the higher-ranking officers here?'

'May I be blunt, Sir?' Jack asked.

'You usually are.'

'I do not care for the approval of others; their thinking and actions are not what I believe a commander should be doing. My ancestors have had a habit of doing what feels right not what is popular. I will keep doing things their way until a better method is presented to me. If that means saluting and bowing, then so be it.'

'You have a lot of your ancestors' ways in you. Be careful they are not your undoing.'

'Their ways have been proven to be worthy of replication, Sir, as such I will learn from them as well as you.'

'Well put, Nakagawa. Now I am guessing that you actually have a purpose to your visit here?'

'Arigatō, Sir. I have received a call from my father, he tells me that Chie Maki is expected to give birth this weekend and she has requested that I be present at the facility. She is currently at my family home waiting to go into hospital for the birth.'

'Why do I know the name "Chie Maki"?'

'Chie is a direct descendent of Shogun Akira Maki and Hitomi Okubo.'

'The formidable one?'

'Hai, she is sometimes referred to as such.'

'Your family does move in esteemed circles, doesn't it?'

'Our families have been intertwined for many years, centuries.'

'Is she likely to turn me into a frog or something if I do not give you the time off?' he began to laugh at his statement.

'Hardly, Sir. She is senkensha, not majo (witch). She cannot turn you into a frog; but she can tell me who will and when they will do it.'

The two laughed together for a moment; at the same time the Commander brought the class report onto the screen before him.

The Course Commander watched Jack, as he checked the course progress on the computer screen; and studied Jack's reactions for some time as he weighed his options. 'I assume you are up to date with all your studies and assignments?'

'I am, Sir, yes.'

'What of your class officer?'

'When I asked him, he seemed to be of a mind that a weekend or more without me would be a blessing in disguise. Do YOU know what he meant by that?'

Jack tried to keep the grin from his face and, more or less, achieved his aim.

The officer opposite him had considerably less luck at disguising his emotions.

'Let's not get into that right now. You can have a four-day pass. If that proves insufficient let me know.'

Jack stood up and saluted, then he bowed again, this time slightly deeper and then left the office closing the door behind him.

"It is impossible not to like him." The Course Commander thought, "He will go far on personality alone and with his brain, he will probably end up as Chief of Defence Forces."

'Papa?' Jack spoke quickly when the phone was finally answered, 'I have been given four days. I do not have to be back until Monday, later if I need it.'

'Wonderful news my son, we are all looking forward to seeing you.' The two hung up and Jack quickly packed a bag. He had already booked a cab to the airport and within the hour he was on his way North, to his ancestral home.

'Jack so good to see you, Army life is looking after you I see. You have put on so much muscle.' His mother was so proud of him; the military option in life was one all her boys would take, the other two would join the navy in due course and all would be successful in their chosen careers.

'Thank you, Mama. It comes from hard work, not the fine foods they serve us.'

'Now I know you are lying. Come inside. Tea, Coffee? After your long journey you must be hungry?'

'Mama, it is only an hour by plane; add a little for travel at the other end I only ate just two hours ago. You can't count airline food; it isn't really food after all.'

Mother and son laughed as they hugged, both thinking, "It is good to be home."

Jack greeted the rest of his family the same way. They didn't see a lot of each other, but when they did gather it was as though they had only been together the day before. They never had arguments or fought like some families, they genuinely enjoyed family company.

'Well where is Chie?' he eventually asked.

'She is sitting on the rear veranda, watching the afternoon go by. She has been waiting for you to get here.'

Jack went out to the rear of the huge, spacious home and sat beside Chie. She looked at her watch and said, 'You are three minutes and twenty seconds late.'

'Me? Late? Impossible,' he replied.

'I know what time you arrived, and you should have been here three minutes and twenty seconds ago.'

'Sometimes, Chie, you senkensha can be very hard to live with.'

'He hugged her as closely as he did his sisters.'

'I knew you would be here. Now I can have this baby.'

'Why? Why is it so important for me to be here?' Jack was perplexed at her words; even though he knew deep inside what the answer would be.

'This baby will be most important to you in the future; when you can, keep her near; this is important for all.'

Jack looked at Chie and thought deeply about her words. 'Very well, I will do this. But first we will need to have the baby in the outside world.'

'Tonight, just as the sun goes down.'

'Should I call the doctors?'

'No, they will only get in the way. Just the mid-wives will do.'

The statement was more than words, everyone knew exactly what she wanted, and they also knew how she knew. The "old ways" were very strong within the family groups and those ways had never failed them yet.

At that moment, as Jack sat and held Chie's hand, his mother came out and sat with them.

'Early dinner this evening, mama,' he announced.

'Really?' she looked at him quizzically.

'Chie has a need for an early dinner, while it is still light.'

'I must organise the staff.' His mother disappeared into the house and soon the beginnings of meal preparation could be heard.

This was how it had always been for them. With a senkensha near, all it would take was for a mention of something and that was enough for everyone to begin preparations. This time an early meal had been called for, and that is what would happen.

It was just after seven; as the last light of day morphed from oranges, pinks and purples into the blackness of night that they heard the gentle cries of a new-born. Not the raucous scream so often portrayed in the films and television, this was a gentle cry of love for all around her.

'What are you going to call her?' Jack asked after a few short minutes.

Chie lifted a small hand out of the blanket that surrounded the child and looked at her face.

'She has asked to be called "Fumiko" The approximate meaning is "Intellectual" or "Knowing".

Jack gently stroked her forehead and said 'Welcome to our world, Fumiko. May your life be as wonderful as ours is.'

The rest of the family would, one by one, greet the tiny baby. This was a momentous day for all. A new generation of senkensha, to continue the strong line of the Okubo/Maki women. A new generation of family to be welcomed and cared for by all. A new connection to the universe that would prove to be at least as formidable as her ancestors had been.

Chapter 8
Baptism of Fire

'The objective of this exercise is for Red team to infiltrate the lines of Blue team and take as much ground as possible in the allotted time...'

The Operational Briefing was for Jack's first exercise as an officer commanding soldiers in the field. The exercise itself was not that big, restricted to the Northern Command it was to be the first of the "Summer" season, as they called it. The program was for ten separate exercises across the Spring/Summer seasons culminating in a multi-national series in Hawaii late in October.

'Nakagawa you will take your platoon (30 soldiers) and you are to disrupt the enemy as you see fit.'

'Hell, Sir,' whispered his sergeant, 'they are going to hang you out to dry with that for a directive, ask for more information.'

Jack raised his hand when the Intelligence Officer asked for questions.

'Yes, Lieutenant Nakagawa?' He asked testily.

'Sir, you have given me only a brief outline of an objective, is that all there is or are there specific objectives for me to accomplish as well?'

'Your mission is to disrupt the enemy operations. We don't care what you do, just disrupt them while we attempt to take their command post. Is that enough or do you want me to hold your hand while you take a piss as well?'

Jack replied. 'No need for you to do that, Sir.'

"Unless you really want to," he thought.

'The exercise begins in four days-time, get your teams ready and be at your start line at zero hour.'

The briefing broke up and as they left Jack's sergeant was wondering what plan Jack would come up with.

'Sergeant, meet me in the mess tent with the other NCOs.'

They all assembled in the mess tent and waited for Jack.

As he walked in, he said, 'What no coffee? Some mess tent this is.'

A cup of coffee appeared out of nowhere and they all waited for Jack to begin the meeting.

'As we know our objective is to disrupt the enemy. Let's have a close look at the maps.'

The maps were laid out on the table and the relative positions of the objectives were laid out.

'I know this place,' Jack suddenly said. 'My father knows the owners. We would visit as children,' he said as his memory returned to sunny summer days visiting friends during the school holidays.

'What do you mean Sir?' asked a corporal.

'The enemy headquarters are in this house,' he replied indicating the blue flag marked on the map. 'They must have agreed to the use of it for the exercise.'

'Sergeant from this moment on we will make our plans here in the mess tent; we will make this our base of operations; we will be comfortable in here.' Jack indicated the small dwelling shown on the map. 'No radio contact with anyone. If they want disruption, that is what they will get.' Jack indicated a house on the very edge of the map.

'How do you know we will be able to use the house?'

'It is the gatekeepers house on my uncle's estate, he will give us access. Now no uniforms are to be worn. Take them with you we will need them later.'

The plan for "war" was beginning to take shape.

'Ieyasu, are you driving this or is he doing it?' asked Musashi.

'I have sparked the idea; he is driving it now.'

'Let us see if he has learned from our efforts. Jackson, come see, our protégé is about to begin his journey.'

The three watched the progress from their vantage point, this would prove to be enlightening.

'Uncle; Konichiwa.' Jack bowed deeply to show his respects to his uncle.

'Konichiwa, Jackson. What brings my nephew to my home?'

'I have been tasked with a project for the upcoming war games here, and I thought I would make use of it to see some of my beloved family.'

'Come in, do you have time for tea?'

The answer would always be "yes". Despite the passing centuries, there was still a large amount of protocol that would need to be observed, and the offering and receiving of tea was just the beginning.

'How is your career in the army progressing? I trust you are doing well?'

'How well I do will be judged in these games, I have been given the task of disrupting the enemy headquarters. A big part of the strategic scenario.'

'How much can you tell me?'

'I don't suppose it will be a problem. I would like to use the gate keepers house as a base of operations, if at all possible?'

'Certainly, why the gate keeper's house?'

'It is quite close to the home that the enemy are using as a headquarters and if we do not wear uniforms we can come and go as we please.'

'Which house are they using?'

'Apparently Sato san has let them use his home, he will be away for the next two months in Australia, on holiday.'

'Sato's place?' he replied quizzically. 'You do know you can get inside from here, don't you?'

'Tell me more, Uncle.' Jack replied; suddenly more than interested in the small revelation.

'During the time of the Boshin War; the Sato clan, in this area, were known to hide samurai that needed to escape the searches. There are a number of houses that are connected by tunnels and some tunnels emerge a long way from the homes of people like Sato.'

'Do you know where these tunnels are?'

'Only a couple of them. If I remember there is a hidden opening near the small waterway that runs alongside the gatekeeper's house. They believed that emerging in a relatively open place would not place friends and allies in danger.'

'If we can use it, where does it emerge in the house?'

'If it is still usable it has a hidden chamber that is accessed from the main room. I would assume that if your enemy is using the house, he will use that room as his base of operations, it has enough space for map tables and such. Come finish your tea and we can see if it is still where I remember it.'

'Uncle, even you are not so old you can remember the Boshin Wars!' Jack laughed as he spoke, and his uncle joined in.

'No, but I was good friends with the family as a child and we would play in there, running from my home to his and back. Now there are memories for me to relive one day.'

'After my "war" is over I will return, and we can do just that.'

The two men drove the one kilometre or so to the area where the tunnel emerged and after about twenty minutes of pulling at weeds, they had uncovered the opening.

'This is fantastic, we can set up in the gate house and access this when we wish.' Jack's mind was now beginning to work at a feverish pace, a trait that would stand him in good stead far into his future. 'Will we be able to use the house before the games begin? I would like to have a presence there early so that they do not become suspicious.'

'You are a very devious thinker; I would like to see how your plans come to fruition.'

The two turned on their torches and entered the tunnel. The first hundred metres or so was full of twists and turns, to keep light from escaping, his uncle told him. As they progressed further the tunnel straightened out and it was possible to almost run for the two kilometres to Sato's house.

'Don't run upright,' his uncle warned him. 'There are hanging rocks left to stop the unwary.' Jack looked up just in time to see a large jagged rock that would split open the head of anyone not aware.'

'Traps for the pursuers, I assume?'

'Yes, the lights they had were not as bright as our modern ones, the overhead rocks would often be missed in the shadows and many chasers were almost killed by running headfirst into them.'

Eventually, and without injury, the two arrived at the other end of the tunnel. As they looked at the rock wall that apparently blocked their way Jack was wondering how they could go further.

'Just around the corner there is a ladder, steel steps set into the rock. When you go up there is a landing at the top, big enough for four men, if they don't want to dance.' Jack stifled a laugh and began to climb. The ladder was a lot longer than he first thought, and halfway up he thought he could hear voices. Looking down at his uncle he could see that they could both hear them.

Continuing to climb they both, eventually, were standing on the small landing.

Whispering to Jack his uncle said, 'Turn off your light and let your eyes become accustomed to the darkness.'

Jack did as he was told and soon enough, he could make out a small opening at eye level and he put his eye to the opening and saw the advance troops putting the operations room together. Some were putting maps on the panels they had erected around the walls; some were assembling radio equipment and others were assembling the planning desk.

The two moved back from the wall, and Jack was whispering as he asked, 'How do we get in?'

'We can wait an hour and they will be gone, then we can get in and see what is going on.'

As they waited, they spoke almost nothing for fear that the soldiers on the other side of the wall would hear. Jack was churning scenarios over in his mind as his uncle watched in the dim light. "He is very preoccupied with this access I have shown him. I wonder what he is thinking of?" he thought. Almost as if Jack could read his mind, he replied in a voice that was almost inaudible.

'I think I can make their lives miserable; I can disrupt so much from here that they will not understand why their careful plans are going so wrong.'

A sudden shout from inside and the soldiers all left. The two watching from the peep hole waited, and hearing the trucks drive off, they waited for an extra ten minutes before Jack's uncle showed him the intricate latching mechanism that kept the access panel hidden from those that did not know of its existence. Gently pulling on one lever while turning another the panel clicked, not loudly but enough to know it had released and the panel opened slowly and silently until they were able to enter the room. Jack was surprised that the entire panel had opened, not just a small opening halfway up a wall; this was an entire wall panel that had been covered with a painting of one of the Sato ancestors. An ally of Oda Nobunaga his place in history was almost as important as any of the early Shoguns.

The two looked around and Jack quickly took some photos of the early defensive plans that had been left behind.

'It is getting late, Jack. If you want, you can come back whenever you wish.' The two left the room, carefully closing and locking the panel behind them.

The return along the tunnel seemed to be a lot quicker than the outward journey and soon they were sitting and enjoying a small whiskey as they discussed the days revelations.

'Would I be able to begin tomorrow?' Jack asked.

'Certainly, how many would you be bringing with you?'

'I have thirty men to consider, but I would like to start with only four. Two to keep watch and record the goings on and two to relieve them around lunch. The games begin in earnest in a little over a week so that will give us enough of a noticeable presence here and we can gather intelligence at the same time.'

'You should be far enough away to have all of them on hand, the old stable is clean and dry, and you can set a fire there to keep warm at night, they will not notice you being so far away.'

'Then we shall move in tomorrow. I hope I can do this right; my career has a lot riding on it.'

Jack returned to the barracks and gave the order to be ready to move out the following morning at 7. There was a bit of grumbling from some of the younger ones, No one likes early starts and to be ready to leave at seven meant a lot of preparation first. Most of the older, more experienced soldiers were just waiting to see what this new officer could do. Was he going to be creating a workable plan or was he full of tactical theory and a stickler for the manual?

The trucks arrived and the drivers assigned were told they would not be required; Jack's platoon would transport themselves. This alone was enough to raise some eyebrows in headquarters but one of the aims was to see how effective the new officers were. It was almost that they were "given enough rope to see how many could hang themselves" as the old saying went. So, his superiors were happy to let Jack try his plans. They had tried to get him to explain his plans, but he had refused to give anything away saying "You have given me the task of disrupting the enemy headquarters. If I tell you how I intend to do this, and you don't like it you will stop me. I am trying an innovative approach and I would like you to judge it by its results not its apparent intentions."

The Senior Colonels and Generals that were judging the exercise were not very pleased, but they decided that they would let him try. Given his name and his heritage they would like to know if his abilities were learned, or were they innate and inherited. Only time would tell.

Jack and his platoon left the barracks and soon they were far enough away for them to relax. No one had followed them, and they stopped for a break just off the main road heading north.

'Lieutenant, I have disabled the tracking devices as you ordered.' Reported one of his communications experts.

'Good, let them wonder what we are up to.'

That simple exchange gave him more credibility than a dozen other orders or requests could have. Instantly he was a man that planned his actions and was not above ignoring the rules when it suited him, he was not one that simply followed the doctrine.

Another hour down some smaller roads and they found themselves at a gate into a private estate.

'Are we allowed in here, Sir?' queried one soldier.

'Yes, I have permission from the owner, this will be our base of operations until the end of the exercise.'

'Sir that is almost three weeks away. What about food?'

'One of the trucks has sufficient food for us for over a month. We will make ourselves comfortable here tonight and then tomorrow I will lead the first four out for their surveillance shift.'

The trucks moved off with Jack giving the instructions as to where to turn and which track to take. Suddenly, just as they thought they were getting lost, they rounded a bend in the track and the stable appeared, at the top of the adjacent rise they could just see the roof of the house.

They all unpacked and set up camp. A good fire was made, and two sentries took a walk around after dark to ensure the light could not be seen from outside. Satisfied they all bedded down and Jack promised a full briefing the following morning.

The sun rose to reveal a clear day and following on from a good breakfast they all sat and waited for Jack. The door opened and Jack strode in followed by his uncle.

'Konichiwa.' They all replied the same and waited.

'This is my uncle he owns this estate. If you have any issues, please do not hesitate to call him or me.'

Jack's uncle left his number on the wall of the stable and made his excuses, demanding that Jack have dinner with his family that evening.

Jack then started by giving them a little of the history of the area and how he was planning his assignments. As each part was explained he gave the names of those that would be responsible.

The detailed briefing was long, and no stone was left unturned. When he was done, he asked for questions and any recommendations or corrections, if he had missed something. So detailed was his briefing that there were no questions, or corrections at all.

'Right, as you heard my presence has been demanded elsewhere for the evening. Tomorrow I will take the first surveillance teams to their position. Settle in and enjoy, tomorrow it becomes real.' Jack left and went to visit his family.

'Sarge?' asked one soldier. 'I have not been in the army for long, but is that what it is like? Do all officers give such information?'

'To be honest, this is the first time I have ever had such a detailed briefing by any officer, let alone a Lieutenant straight out of Officers School. His plan seems good and workable we will need to see if he is right. Gut feeling? He has this bull by the horns and if he is as good as his plan appears, we will be eating steak.' The inference was that Jack had the right plan and, more importantly, the support of his senior NCO.

The next morning back in camp, Jack was first up, and he was stoking the fire for breakfast when the others began to rise.

'Sir, that is not an officers' job.' One of the corporals told him, 'Let one of the others do it.'

'Corporal, I am an officer simply because I have the rank on my uniform. This exercise has us as an infiltrating team and we all need to be doing whatever needs to be done. If that means stoking the fire, then whoever is there will do it.

We will be better if we all work together and I am not so precious that I will not get dirty if needs be.'

The corporal was taken back by Jack's words and later he spoke with the sergeant.

'Corporal, from the little I have seen of this one, and I have seen a lot of new officers in the field, he is going to shake up a lot of people. If he does right by us, and he seems to be doing so, then he will get our backing. If he wants to stoke the fire let him, he does not appear to be doing it to gain favour among us, he is doing it because it needs to be done.'

One of the men had twisted his ankle, severely enough to be a real problem if left untreated. Jack immediately organised an ambulance and had him transported to the local private hospital.

'Why not return him to base and let the medics take care of him?' was the first question that arose.

'Because he will get better treatment here and the officers will not know where we are and what we are doing.'

This simple act of caring for the men under his command was enough to raise him in the estimation of the others, he actually did care.

As a new officer, on his first exercise, every move from Jack was always going to be analysed. By those above him to see if he would be an effective officer and by those below him to see if he was going to be worthy of respect and support. Jack did not care for either side of the argument; he felt that if he did the job well, he would benefit, and that was all the incentive he needed. Just do the job well.

The surveillance team left just after dawn that morning. They were surprised when Jack led them into a tunnel and, if it were possible, they were more surprised when they found they were, effectively, inside the enemy headquarters. The first two began the listening and recording of plans from inside and the others returned to the base of the ladder.

'Sir, can I make a suggestion?' one of the privates asked.

'Certainly, always open to a good idea.'

'If we get a chance we can "kill" their radio operator and put one of ours in. As a private he will not be noticed.'

'And we will get a chance to send out incorrect orders.' Jack agreed immediately 'Or give their General some false information. This could be interesting. Let's try, see if we get a chance.'

The chance came early that night, a single radio operator had been left on watch to wait for some extra signals that were due in. The soldier was very pleased to be left alone, he would have a nice warm bed to sleep in, lots of food and no one to order him about.

Just on sundown Jack and his sergeant, along with two others entered the tunnels. Making short work of the run to the house they almost surprised the "spies" that they had left in place. Waiting for the right moment, which just happened to come along shortly after they arrived when the soldier left for a "comfort break".

As he returned to the room he was quickly silenced by a knife to his throat.

'Sorry, you are now dead and out of the war.' The sergeant said firmly.

The radio operator was stunned and lead away down the ladder and back to Jack's base.

One of Jack's communicators was left to do the work and when the officers arrived the next morning he was quizzed as to the whereabouts of the original radio operator.

'I am sorry Sir; I do not know. All I know is that I was brought here as he was sick. No one told me any more than that.'

'Very well. Just do your job and keep out of the way.'

'Hai, Colonel,' he replied and already his impression of Jack had risen, again. The Colonel was abrupt and dismissive, "his" Lieutenant was inclusive and caring about his men.

The exercise began and instantly there were problems for the Blue team.

'Sir, Message from surveillance.'

'Read it out,' the General ordered.

"Two squadrons of light tanks proceeding towards the western perimeter. Suggest intercept at point AA23."

'Very well, send a squadron of Main Battle Tanks. Dragon 3 can deal with them.'

'Hai, Dragon 3 to point AA23.' The operator repeated as he sent half of the blue divisions armour to a point almost twenty-five kilometres away from the real position of the fake attack.

Four hours later the report was received, 'No enemy armour at AA23, Sir.'

'Tell them to keep searching, they must be hiding somewhere.'

'Hai.'

And so it went on for the first two days of the operation. Report of movement, dispatch teams to deal with it and find no one. The General was getting very frustrated.

On the third day the General decided that he needed time to think and left the Tactical Colonel alone with the radio operator.

The Colonel did not hear the latches, but with the radio desk alongside the moving wall panel, the radio operator did.

'Colonel Sir.' The operator called.

'WHAT' he shouted angrily.

'I think you are dead, sir.'

'What do you mean?' he responded as he turned to confront the private.

His face could not have conveyed the concept of surprise any better than at that moment. In front of him stood Jack, with a wakizashi pointed directly at his throat.

'Sorry sir, you are dead, and you didn't have time to call out before I slit your throat.'

The Colonel almost exploded with rage and he would have shouted except a burly sergeant had already stuffed a gag down his throat and a corporal had his hands bound. Before the reality had fully set in, they had him in the tunnel and were taking him away.

When the General returned, he wanted to know where the colonel was.

'I believe he went to the toilet, sir,' the radio man answered without even looking up from his work, and a grunt was all he got from his superior officer.

Back at the stable the Colonel was making all sorts of demands, but no one bothered to answer him.

'Who is in charge here?' He insistently asked, despite not getting an answer the first ten times he asked he still asked again.

Eventually, Jack appeared and the Colonel became even more aggressive.

'You can't do this; it is against the rules of engagement.'

'I am sorry sir, all my rules said were "disrupt the enemy as I see fit", that is what I am doing.'

It took almost three hours before the Colonel settled down and he began to discuss the events rationally. It was late into the evening before Jack managed to get his agreement to watch the operation unfold without interfering, after all he was "dead" at that time.

The next morning Jack called his uncle, explained how the exercise was progressing and asked for another favour.

'You really know how to upset people, don't you?'

'My apologies, uncle, I am merely operating within the very few boundaries I was set when this "war" erupted.'

The two laughed and even the enemy officer joined in.

'I would love to see the Generals face when he sees what you are going to do.'

'I will try to get a video recording of it for you Colonel.' Jack replied as he put the next phase of his plan into place.

'OK. Time to go, into the old truck for the first ten, don't forget you are grumpy men doing dirty work. Its ok to be angry.'

'You can rely on us Sir, replied the veteran Sergeant.'

The truck bounced and lurched its way up to the gate of the Sato residence. The sentry held up his hand up to get them to stop and the driver was good enough to make it appear as if the truck had no brakes as he almost ran over the sentry.

'Sorry, the brakes need work. We are here to fix the leaking sewerage pipes.'

None of the men had showered for three days and they all smelled as if they were worse than the sewerage they were supposed to fix.

'Wait here, I will get approval.' The truck sat there, so much smoke pouring from its exhaust it was almost a bigger environmental threat than the sewage leak could ever be.

The sentry returned, 'You can't come in. The General has ordered you are to be refused access.'

'Don't care about your general, we have got a pipe to fix and the owner has sent us. If you don't want the toilets to back up again you had better let us get to work.'

Not quite an ultimatum, but a big enough threat to give them a fair chance of gaining entry.

A few minutes later the sentry returned again. 'OK, the General says you can work, just keep out of the way.'

'Yes Sir, thank you Sir.' The driver said, almost grovelling, as he moved away from the sentry, "drove off" would be a misnomer as the truck could barely move of its own accord. Eventually, they were around the corner of the house and headed to the delivery doors. As they stopped Jack opened the door and most of them entered, leaving the "smokers" outside for a "cigarette" break before starting work (and as sentries to stop their work being discovered).

'Listen up,' Jack whispered, 'This oven is not an oven at all.' With a push on the handle the door swung inwards to reveal another entrance to the tunnel complex. As we "kill" them take them back to our base; if we do this right, we can leave them with a general only. Remember only take the ones alone, they will simply go missing without anyone to report how or why.'

It was only ten minutes before one of the staff officers arrived. The sword against the neck was sufficient to tell him he was "dead" as Jack led him down the tunnel, he asked 'Why are you carrying a sword?'

'Does not everyone go into battle carrying one?' Jack asked innocently.

The officer could not give an answer and the remainder of the trip back to base was quiet.

When they emerged, the officer was taken away and made comfortable for the remainder of the exercise.

One by one the staff were taken and delivered to Jack. No one could understand where everyone was. The tanks and Infantry Fighting Vehicles were being sent here and there, never seeing the enemy. Companies of infantry were being marched all over the area and they were becoming tired and distrustful of every order that came from headquarters.

Eventually, it got to the point that the General was not game to go outside. But that did not help him, late one-night Jack and his sergeants opened the access into the planning room. Emerging silently, Jack crept up behind the General and gently placed his sword against his neck. The General stiffened but did not move.

'General, officially you are now listed as dead. My apologies, for your sudden demise.'

Slowly the General turned and looked at Jack. 'How did you get in…' He stopped speaking as he saw the open panel and the sergeants in camouflaged combat uniforms holding their assault rifles ready.

'Is this a real sword? Am I in danger?'

'No sir, it is a training weapon from my dojo, but it serves the purpose.'

'You do realise there is still three days to go in this exercise?'

'Yes sir, and I intend to put the tank divisions and the infantry far enough out of the way to allow us to take victory.'

'You do not have the capacity to do this! You cannot command them.'

'Really Sir!' Jack responded with a good deal of disbelief. 'Send Dragon to AA23 the Red Tanks are amassing near there for a final push.'

'Hai, AA23 it is.'

'YOU! You are a part of this?'

'Hai, I am, Sir. I apologise for the deception,' replied Jack's radio operator.

'Send the IFV's to AA25 to support them.'

'Hai IFV's to AA25.'

'How long has this been going on?'

'Since your operator was taken "sick" sir.'

'That was right at the beginning.'

'Hai, it was.'

'And how did you get to know of this access?'

'My uncle lives near here, he played in the tunnels as a child.'

'That is unethical, and it is against the Rules of Engagement.' Trumpeted the General.

'Hardly, sir. My brief was to disrupt your operation anyway I could. So, I did.'

'There can be no precedent for this behaviour, you are as far out of your operational parameters as could be.'

'Actually, Sir, there are many instances of this happening.' Responded Jack as the argument began to escalate.

'Name one instance, any one,' demanded the General.

'During the Falkland War, in 1982 between Argentina and England; the English Marines needed deployment information on the Argentines, so their officer picked up the phone and called the Post Office, I think it was, and got the information he needed. So, there is a precedent to getting "local knowledge" as it were. All I did was to push the use a little further along.'

'How are the tanks and IFV's going?' Jack asked, more to drive home the loss of control rather his actually needing information.

'Have them deploy on the far side of the reference point, tell them the enemy are expected to arrive in the early hours of tomorrow.'

'Hai.'

The instructions were passed and eventually a report was received that they were ready.

'Good, send to Red command "Enemy searching in force AA23 AND AA25. Approach through FS12 via ring road. Approaches clear for at least 12 hours. Sign that Taipan 1".'

'Who is "Taipan 1"? That is not an authorised call sign?'

'That is me. My personal call sign for this exercise. I told my command team that any signal that was signed with that call sign was guaranteed to be authentic, and this is the only time I have used it.'

The General and Jack sat and talked for several hours. Now that he was no longer a part of the fighting force, he could get a little better acquainted with what appeared to be a great field commander in the making.

The two spoke of Jack's family and his esteemed ancestors.

'Why have you not married? I thought that there would be any number of eligible women lining the streets to be married into your family?'

'To be candid, I never found anyone that made me want to be married. I have had some close personal connections if you wish to call them that, but most of them seemed to be more interested in the family name and fortunes than they were interested in me.'

'So, you were never tempted?'

'No, sir. I do not have a need to carry on the family name, I have brothers and sisters that are doing that quite well without me. When I meet the right one, I will make the commitment, not before.'

The dawn eventually began to break, and off in the distance the heavy rumble of main battle tanks could be heard. Soon they were close enough to be visible as they charged up the access to the estate at close on seventy kilometres per hour. No matter what happened now, the exercise was effectively over.

With the tanks forming a defensive ring around the main property and the infantry deployed on the flanks it was now time to bring out his captives.

One by one they emerged from the tunnels into the compound. All were blinking in the harsh light as they emerged into the bright sun.

As they were all assembled now "guarded" by just one man, with a dressing on his foot they watched as a small sedan made its way up the drive to the main house.

'Uncle, come in, I owe you tea at least.'

Jack introduced his uncle to all the senior officers and as the groups split into several discussion groups one of the senior officers asked his uncle how he managed to do it.

'Never underestimate him. Give him a task and let him go, he will make it work. Somehow his mind will not go straight at a problem, he will mostly go around it. Unpredictable is the best description. And he thinks quickly, very quickly.'

'That was masterful to watch.' Musashi observed.

'I think that is an understatement,' replied Ieyasu, 'I could have used a tactician like him many times, he will be very difficult to defeat.'

'I think we have done all we can to help him, his mind is working faster than we can help him now. I feel we can watch and wonder from here on.' Added Jackson Teague, 'He is what they used to call a "game changer" his methods will change the way many things are done on the battlefield.'

The three left the view before them, all were pleased and impressed with their "Protégé."

Chapter 9
Debriefing

"Sergeant Higashi is here Sir." The statement issued from the intercom on the desk of Colonel Fujita, Commander of the Northern Infantry Group.

'Send him in.'

The door opened and the veteran Infantry Sergeant entered and stood at attention before the colonel's desk.

'You wanted to see me Sir?'

'Hai, sit down.'

Sergeant Higashi sat and waited for his commanding officer to begin.

'Sergeant, as I see from the action reports that you were assigned to the platoon commanded by this new Lieutenant,' he paused as he referred to his notes, 'Nakagawa; is that right?'

'Hai.'

'I will be blunt; I am copping a lot of trouble from above for the way he conducted his platoon during the exercise. What is your assessment of him? Is he worth defending?'

'May I speak my mind Sir?'

'Sergeant we have known each other for many years. Speak up.'

'When we were at the exercise briefing, General Onishi's second-in-command gave us only the barest of information. We were told to "disrupt the enemy as we see fit." That is exactly what we did. The Lieutenant asked for more specific instructions and he was basically told to shut up and do as he was told.'

'If General Onishi did not like what we did, he should have given a more detailed and inclusive briefing. Lieutenant Nakagawa came up with an outstanding plan and it worked perfectly; without him the General would not have been able to claim a victory. Add to that the fact that General Nomura almost burst a blood vessel when he was "killed" shows what a completely unexpected method he had used. No one had even properly assessed the building.'

'Good, that will look right in my report. Now, tell me what you really think?'

'Lieutenant Nakagawa is one of the few officers that seem to instantly have the support of his troops. He has no need to demand respect, it is already there. He asked for our input and he actually demanded we tell him if he was wrong or there was a flaw he had not seen. He is a very different officer to all the others I have seen emerge from the College.'

'OK. Short answer. If you had to go to war, would you rather have him in charge or someone else?'

'Tough question, I think I would go with him; he inspires the men, I have not seen so many **want** to be included in his projects.'

'Thank you, Sergeant. I am thinking I may have you assigned as his permanent 2I/C would you be agreeable with that?'

'Certainly, Sir. It would be a real eye-opener to see if he is a "one shot" officer or if his methods are adaptable to the tasks assigned.'

'That is what I want to know. If he is as adaptable and innovative as he first appears then we may be able to make use of his particular talents.'

The Senior Officers of the Northern Command were all waiting for the General Commanding and the Chief of Army Staff to enter. The conversations were all being carried out in whispers, no one was speaking out loud. Suddenly the door at the end of the room opened and the two Generals entered and took their seats at the head of the table.

'This debriefing is to assess the Exercise completed two weeks ago in the North of Hokkaido.' The Chief of Staff began, 'We will be analysing the deployment of the resources and the adherence to the Rules of Engagement as laid out in the exercise briefing.'

'First General Nomura.'

'The First task of the Blue Army was to protect the Headquarters and to engage and destroy the Red Army as opportunities became available. The units assigned were 3 Companies from Dragon group; sections 1, 2 and 3 main battle tanks and two sections of Infantry Fighting Vehicles.'

'The exercise results show you were defeated, why is that?'

'Do you want fact or opinion in this?'

'Both I think,' replied the Chief of Staff, wondering how the General was going to justify his loss.'

'The loss was due to the failure of the Red army to remain within the boundaries of the Rules of Engagement. The methods used were so far away from the accepted methodology that there was actually no means of combating them. In short, we believe that the Red Army cheated in their pursuit of their objectives.'

'General Onishi, what were your objectives?'

'The original objective was to control the access routes and to attempt to take the enemy headquarters by force if possible.'

'And do you believe that you have been successful in your assigned tasks?'

'The record shows that we have won the exercise, but I believe the methods employed by Lieutenant Nakagawa were not permitted under the instructions handed down.'

'So, in short, you say that you won but only because one of your most junior officers cheated, Is that it?'

'As much as it pains me to say it, yes.'

The Chief of Staff whispered to the General beside him and their little private conversation was observed but not heard by the others in the room.

'Colonel Fujita, do you have anything to add?'

'Arigatō, Sir. I have conducted an inquiry into the actions of the platoon commanded by Lieutenant Nakagawa. I have found an officer, even at this early stage of his career, that is at once at ease with the burdens of his command and also, he is a clear and innovative thinker. He learned his lessons from history, and he displayed a clear and innovative thought process that has stopped the methodology of our exercise regime in its track. The method he used in this exercise was to fully investigate his field of combat and analyse the benefits and pitfalls of the area. He used local and personal knowledge to his best advantage, and he was not above a fair amount of deception to force his enemy into a bad position.'

'How does this condone his forcing our troops into unknown positions without consideration for their safety, this is a peacetime exercise!' demanded General Nomura.

'I have asked him this question, Sir, his answer was simply "Go Rin No Sho" and even I had to ask what the writings of Musashi had to do with his actions.'

'And, how did he justify his actions?'

'One of Musashi's thoughts on opponents was "put your enemy where you want him" and that is what Nakagawa did, he put your tanks and IFV's where he wanted them, out of the way. His tactical thinking is as different as beer and sake; I feel if we can understand what he is doing and how he is thinking he will change many ways that we conduct manoeuvres and ultimately, he may change the way we conduct war itself,' he paused for a sip of water.

'I implore you all, do not dismiss this as a single event, his mindset appears to be of the same type as his ancestor. He thinks very fast and very differently, so everyone else will not know what he is doing, and he cannot be second guessed. Even though he is still a very junior officer we need to learn from him.'

'Very good, thank you Colonel, do you have a soldier assigned to him, for intelligence purposes?' Asked the Chief of Staff.

'I have permanently assigned the Senior Sergeant that was with him. He will be reporting to me directly if there are any important issues to be investigated.'

'Very good. I feel we can rely on the Colonels recommendations. He is in the best possible position to advise on anything important. It is very important that we gain as much insight into this subject as we possibly can. If he is a once only genius, so be it. But I feel that we will be gaining if we can take advantage of what seems to be a different way of working.' The Chief of Staff finished the meeting and all left wondering if it was as good as it seemed.

Time would tell.

Jack's combat methods were to prove a continuing success. So much so that for the next few years the Army High Command would give him more difficult tasks with each exercise that arose.

Promoted to Captain in minimum time he was give tasks far beyond the usual purview of a junior officer. In the final exercise of the year he was tasked with defending the headquarters of the "Blue" army. This was to be the first time he had not been the aggressor but had to conform to the demands of securing the garrison and preventing the "red" army from attacking the headquarters.

'Captain Nakagawa, you will be responsible for keeping the enemy away from the direct access road from the East.' General Onishi announced during his operational briefing for the final exercise of the season. 'Here are the start points for the exercise. The enemy are holding around fifty kilometres away somewhere to the east of our headquarters.'

'Any questions?' General Onishi braced himself for the usual awkward question that Jack Nakagawa would come up with; however, this time all he got was silence. 'No questions Captain?'

'Not at this time, Sir. Defence of the Eastern perimeter seems to be reasonably straightforward, perhaps I could ask for the second platoon to be assigned for this exercise as well as the fourth?'

'Why do you want two extra platoons? is the third insufficient?'

'The Eastern perimeter road is a winding and steep road. I cannot get surveillance and coverage for the entire track with just one platoon.'

The General paused in his thoughts, "Why does Nakagawa's every statement appear to have two meanings?" He thought to himself. "Why can he not be a normal junior officer?"

'Very well, the second and fourth platoons are assigned to Captain Nakagawa. If there are no other questions this briefing is complete; return to your positions. You have tonight to get your plans implemented. The exercise begins at 0500.'

Jack and Sergeant Higashi left and neither spoke until they were out of hearing.

'Sir?' Higashi asked.

'How many times do I have to tell you, call me Jack when we are alone, it makes it so much easier to work. We can keep the official stuff for mixed company.'

'Sorry, old habits. Jack?'

'That's better; Yes?'

'This project seems more difficult than the others. We cannot attack and there is very little we can conjure up as subterfuge.'

'Maybe, maybe not. Let's wait until we are with the troops and I will explain my plan; and don't forget, I will be most displeased with anyone that can spot a hole and does not tell me.'

Jack and Okimoto waited for the last of the soldiers to enter their briefing tent before he began.

'Right let's get the map up.'

The two platoon sergeants pinned up the map and waited for the, now familiar, stream of information to emerge. For the next hour Jack explained, in depth, the concept and methodology he would be using to "Defend" the eastern Perimeter.

'...And don't forget to take working style clothes with you. If we are to make this work, we will need to appear to be workers not soldiers.'

'Okimoto, get the NCOs and come back for coffee. I have questions.'

Just five minutes later the two platoon sergeants and their corporals as well as the second and fourth platoon officers were all sipping coffee when Jack reappeared.

'Thanks for waiting. Now you have had a few minutes to discuss the plan, what are your thoughts?'

'I am glad it is your plan,' replied one officer, I think you will be answering to the General when he finds out about it.'

'That is one way of looking at it, I guess.' Jack answered, 'but I want to know if you think it can be done, will it work?'

The other NCOs were not so used to speaking out in the presence of officers but Okimoto opened up.

'To be blunt, it is probably the most outrageous battle plan I have ever heard.'

The other almost held their breath as they waited for Jack to absorb the Sergeants words.

'Don't hold back, tell me what you really think.'

'The entire concept relies on the enemy commanders doing what you want. Do you really think you can get them to do that?'

'Good point, that is exactly what I want them to do. Think of it this way; if the police tell you to take a detour, you do. If the Roads Maintenance controllers tell you not to drive a certain direction or on a certain road you do, you don't argue with them you just do it. I believe they will do the same.'

'If that is the point of your plan then I will ensure that my dress uniform is ready for my next appointment with the Chief of Staff to explain what happened this time.'

Jack spluttered into his cup as he began to laugh. 'And so will I!' he snorted, still laughing. But I will have to front Colonel Fujita and General Onishi beforehand.'

At that point a new voice was heard, and all looked in the direction of the sound.

'Colonel Fujita, an unexpected honour. Please, sit. Would you like coffee?'

'Thank you, Captain, or should I call you Jack, like the others?'

'I would be pleased should you consider using my given name.' Jack bowed in the Colonels direction just as a cup appeared, seemingly from nowhere.

I will be the Command Observer for your group, for this exercise. So, I will be assessing your capabilities directly, this time.'

'And most welcome you are, Sir.'

'Now, give me a briefing on your plan, so I know what you are up to.'

'Very well, Sergeant Higashi stay, the rest of you begin the preparations for your assignments. We will leave at 2300 tonight and be in position ready for the start at 0500. I will be at map reference Alpha 21 for the commencement. Get ready and be believable.'

A chorus of "Hai, Sir" emerged from every member of the group as they left. Colonel Fujita just watched as Jack gave his commands and the soldiers all left to complete their duties. "Jack has this lot right behind him." He mused, "I wonder what he is up to this time."

'You have them, Jack. They believe what you have planned. I can see it in the way they react when you speak. How do you do it?'

'To perfectly honest, I don't know. I think that they may believe in the plan I have put forward and as it is a viable alternative to the "march here and die" type of command they have usually been given; they are willing to push it forward with all their energies.'

'Is that how you see it Sergeant?'

'If I may be completely open, sir?'

'Please do. It seems to be a normal event around here.' The three of them had a small laugh as Okimoto answered the Colonel.

'Jack has the ability to put forward an unusual battle plan when he needs it most. He can create, out of nothing, a method that will either put the enemy at a complete disadvantage or send them somewhere they should not be; and they are quite happy to go there. I believe, and I have not told him this, if we have to go to war then it will be his type of thinking that will be the difference between winning and losing. I can assure you Sir; I would want to be standing beside him if he does go to combat.'

'A powerful recommendation Sergeant, Let's see how it unfolds.'

The platoons were ready to move out around 2230, As was normal, for Jack's teams, they drove themselves to their assigned starting points. At just five minutes after the official start Jack put a call through to the headquarters.

'General, sir?' the signalman called.

'Hai, what is it?'

Call from Taipan 1, he wants a squadron of main battle tanks in hiding at grid reference BZ35 and a squadron of IFV's at BZ33.'

'Get him on the radio!' the general was not impressed by a mere captain demanding heavy armour to be left at his disposal.

'Why do you want them there? BZ35 and BZ33 are out of the boundary of the exercise area.'

'Actually sir, if you get the cartographer to reassess the boundaries, using the exact co-ordinates as given in the briefing, you will find that they are within the area by around fifty metres. As such we can use the position to our advantage.' Jack continued to explain his proposal, 'If I can get this right, I will drive the enemy armour directly into your guns with almost no chance of return fire.'

'Put the Colonel on.'

'Hai, General?'

'Is he right, Colonel?'

'He has explained his theory and shown how the boundaries should be calculated. He is right, everyone assumed that the land, south of the road, was out of the exercise area; all he has done is checked the actual boundary. This will be impressive if it works.'

'Very well, let's see if he can pull it off.'

'Hai, Sir.' Colonel Fujita put down the radio, 'OK, Jack, you are on. The General will put the armour where you want them.'

'Good. Once we have the plan under way, I will move ahead of the enemy to keep a close watch on the progress.'

'All units standby,' Jack spoke into the radio with a voice that conveyed not only his position as commander of the Eastern Defensive group, but also his innate command of their portion of the exercise. From that point on, his word was an order.

'Platoon three to BG12 and four to position CX30, platoon two to BZ35 to greet the heavy armour. When you get there, wait for me.'

The platoon officers departed, and they began to take up their assigned positions.

'Are you coming with me, Sir?' Jack asked innocently.

'Try and stop me, this I have to see.'

Jack, the Colonel and his Sergeant jumped into the truck and were soon bouncing over the rugged terrain to the start position. Stopping in a covered area they made their way to the first of Jack's checkpoints on foot.

'Who is setting up the roadblock?' Colonel Fujita asked.

'Platoon 3 have the first task. We are going to get the enemy to take a different route, this is how we will do it.'

Just thirty-five minutes later the rumble of heavy armour could be heard as the Main Battle tanks wound their way up the relatively steep and narrow roadway. As they rounded the corner they suddenly came to a halt as a "Road Traffic Warden" held up his sign and ordered them to stop.

'Get out of the way!' demanded the commander of the lead tank, Major Hyashida.

'So sorry, sir,' replied the "civilian" before him, 'there is a landslide almost eight kilometres up the road. You must go back; this road is closed.'

'This is an Army training area; you cannot close the road.'

'Again, sir, sorry. The road is a public thoroughfare through the training area, there has been much rain recently and there is around two hundred metres of road that cannot be used, there are many large rocks we cannot move until special equipment arrives tomorrow. I apologise.' The man bowed very deeply; which was just as well as he could barely keep the grin from his face.

'Very well.' Major Hyashida was less than pleased at this unexpected problem. Calling into his microphone he ordered the column to turn around and return in the direction they had come.

'Sir if I may?' shouted a man with "surveyor" written on his overalls.

'WHAT!' shouted the Major.

'If you go back around ten kilometres there is an unpaved road to the west. That will take you to the ring road around the town. Three kilometres along you will find a track which will lead you to the north again.'

The Major consulted his navigation system and grunted. 'Yes, there is, thank you,' he still could not disguise the anger in his voice, but eventually the column began to turn around; a very difficult process on the narrow sloping road. An hour later they began their journey away from the roadblock.

'Part one complete. Lieutenant, pack up and take half of the platoon to BZ35, go over the hill, that will be shorter, the rest can remain here and we will collect them on our way back. Come on Colonel we are going to part two.' Jack, Colonel Fujita and Sergeant Higashi left in a fast-all-terrain vehicle; making their way to the second check-point. It was almost an hour after they arrived that they heard the sounds of heavy armour approaching for the second time that day.

The column was travelling fast as they rounded the bend, trying to make-up lost time.

'ALL STOP!' Major Hyashida screamed so loudly that the men on the small bridge all looked up to see what was going on. As they watched they saw a tank, around five back from the lead slam into the rear of the unit in front.

Almost at the same time two IFV's collided in much the same way and there was instant chaos.

'What are you doing on this road?' the Major demanded, getting angrier by the minute.

'So sorry, sir. The rains have damaged this bridge, the underpinnings have been eroded and it cannot take the weight of your tanks until it has been surveyed for damage and passed as safe.'

'Dammit, how can we get through? I must get over the ridge this morning.'

'If you try going back there is a small track leading over the ridge, just a few kilometres away. That is how we got in this morning.'

Again, the major screamed into the microphone. The two damaged tanks and the two IFV's were "abandoned" on the side of the road for the recovery vehicles to attend later. The slightly injured soldiers would have to wait for the recovery teams to take them to the base hospital.

Once the armour had moved off, Jack and the Colonel emerged from hiding with the entire platoon behind them.

'Excellent work; pack up and make for BZ35. Sergeant Higashi leave five men to "guard the prisoners". Let's go Sir I don't want to miss the finale.'

'Neither do I, Jack.'

The three jumped again into their vehicle and headed off. Arriving at Map Reference BZ35 well before the tanks of the opposing army. When they arrived the Major in charge walked up to Colonel Fujita, saluted and asked, 'How do you want us deployed, sir?'

'Don't ask me, he is in charge.' Fujita replied indicating Jack who was standing to one side.

The Major looked confused, he could not reconcile the fact that the officer in command of the exercise was only a Captain. Jack walked up and saluted.

'If you please sir, I would like the tanks on either side of the small cutting, pointing downhill and camouflaged. The Light tanks and IFV's should be around three hundred metres down the track ready to "attack" from the rear of the enemy column.'

'Lieutenant put the platoons behind the IFV's ready to attack with support if required, no point in exposing them unless absolutely necessary.'

'Hai.' The Lieutenant replied and dashed off to ensure the infantry were placed exactly where Jack wanted them.

'And now, Sir's; we shall wait. I estimate we have around three quarters of an hour so let's get some coffee and let the troops prepare.'

The more senior officers almost had their mouths open in a perpetual stare. The junior officers and NCOs were busy double checking the camouflage and ensuring that they were all well-hidden.

'Can we push that big rock into the road? Just far enough to make them stop. We should be able to clear it away easily enough after we are done.'

A quick shove with a reserve tank blocked the road and all waited to see how it would work out. As fate would have it, they would have more than sufficient time to drink their coffee and relax for a short while.

While they were waiting for their enemy to appear; Jack moved through every defensive unit under his command. Speaking with all he came across and ensuring they all understood what was going to happen. It was almost ten minutes after he had returned to the observation position that they finally heard the roar of straining engines as the tanks tried to make their way up the steep incline.

'Standby, all units!' Jack called into his microphone, and they all waited for the "enemy" to appear.

Chapter 10
"Slaughter" and Debrief

The tanks finally emerged around a bend and into the view of the concealed observers.

'STOP! STOP! STOP!' Screamed the Major. Everyone in the column stopped; this time without hitting each other.

'ENGAGE!' Jack ordered the "attack" to begin. Just as the Major jumped down to survey the boulder he was confronted with a cacophony of noise as the trap was sprung.

The enemy column was completely "destroyed", for the most part without returning a single shot. The tanks in Jack's squadron accounting for their direct opposition; a combination of IFV's and infantry attacking the enemy's smaller units saw them, also, out of action.

The cacophony of noise was overpowering in its intensity and one by one the "Umpires" declared the vehicles out of action. The Major stood powerless in front of his column and watched as Jack's troops fired an almost endless supply of blank rounds at them.

Eventually, Jack approached the Major and, holding his pistol directly at his head, asked 'Do you surrender?'

For a long while the Major tried to reconcile the action, but he could not conceive that he had been defeated. He had held a numerical advantage of almost two to one in all respects and yet here he was alone and confronted by a junior Captain demanding his surrender. The only response he could muster was "NEVER" at which point Jack "shot" him. The umpires ruled him dead before he could protest.

'CEASE FIRE!' Jack shouted and his defensive teams stopped shooting.

'Colonel Fujita, your assessment please?'

'Well, Captain. You have won this engagement. But you still have to defend the approaches.'

'As you say, Sir.'

'All units make for the headquarters. Infantry hitch a ride on something. All possible speed. Wait for me at the bridge.'

Suddenly the vehicles turned and began to make their way down the incline in the direction that the enemy had come. Soldiers jumped into the IFV's and on top of the tanks as they passed by.

'Colonel, I protest!' shouted the opposing commander.

'On what grounds?'

'He has operated out of the boundaries of the exercise area.'

'We have had this discussion and the consensus is that he has operated in accordance with his operational directives. You lost Major; if you wish to make further representation then do it at the debrief.' The umpires all nodded their agreement and that was the end of the argument; at that time.

'How is he going to get to his headquarters? The roads are out.'

'Jump in Major, Colonel. We should be able to get to the head of the column before we get back.'

'But the roads are out!' insisted the Major.

'With all due respect, Sir, wait and see.'

The command vehicle bounced and leapt over the track as Jack's driver made up time; meeting the column just before they arrived at the bridge roadblock. As Jack's car passed the column, they could clearly see the smiling faces of his infantry as they made their way to the front. As they entered the bridge the Major was astounded to see the, so called, engineers waiting patiently for the truck to take them and their roadblock back to base.

Jack's car stopped and he jumped out to personally thank each one of his men for the successful completion of the pivotal part of his battle plan. As they got underway again the Major asked.

'I suppose there was no landslide either?'

'That depends on your definition.' Jack replied, 'There were two rocks that landed beside the road, they had slid down the embankment, so I guess that does constitute a landslide, just not as big as we made out.'

Colonel Fujita stifled a laugh and covered his mouth, to disguise his amusement at Jack's concept of what actually constituted "a landslide". As they approached the headquarters Jack again began to deploy his forces to best provide a defensive perimeter on the eastern flank.

'Put the tanks behind the wall, ensure they have sufficient height to be able to fire over the top, IFV's towards the left flank of the tanks. Infantry platoons take your positions; Second platoon between tanks and IFV's; Fourth between the IFV's. Third set-up a defensive perimeter closer to the headquarters itself. Get something to eat and drink, you have all been very busy this morning. Same for tanks and IFV crews.'

The column dispersed and everyone began to make tea and something to eat. The Colonel and the Major left to speak with the General and as they walked away, they could see Jack moving amongst his troops stopping to speak with them all.

'How does he keep going?' General Onishi asked no one in particular as he watched the officers approaching him.

'Actually, Sir, he has not slept since the day before yesterday. He was busy planning for his assignment.'

'General I must protest!' demanded Major Hyashida.

'Good morning to you too Major,' replied the General with a hint of sarcasm in his voice, he was more than just slightly irritated that the tank commander did not even attempt to observe the simple courtesy of "Konichiwa" or a "good morning". 'Come inside and you can tell us exactly what it is you wish to protest about?'

The three officers made their way into the small anteroom off to one side of the operations room. And once inside the three sat and waited for the steward to serve them and close the door behind him.

'Now Major, your complaint?'

'The area that Captain Nakagawa used to transit and assemble his forces is out of the boundaries of the exercise area. His use of subterfuge and misdirection are not included in the Operational Directives. His disobedience of these directives has resulted in damage to two Main Battle Tanks and two Infantry Fighting Vehicles. His operational control is not permitted, and it is outside the permitted variances of the directives.'

'And what do you propose we do if your assessment is proven correct?'

'He must be censured and placed on the "not for promotion" list.'

'A harsh punishment. But what if he is found to be correct? Then what do you propose?'

'I do not propose anything, he is WRONG.'

'Settle down Major. Colonel Fujita, what is your assessment?' General Onishi calmly shut the Majors complaints down and deflected any further complaint away.

'At first explanation, I too, felt the same. I asked; no, I demanded, a full explanation from Captain Nakagawa. He laid out the maps, the operational parameters and the operational directives. When he was finished, I was convinced that he was correct in his assessment that the boundaries of the exercise area were incorrectly transcribed many years ago and the area he used for his assembly and for his ambush of the attacking column were indeed within the correct boundary.'

'He can't be within the boundary!' the Major shouted. 'I have used these grounds for many years; the road is within the boundary and the outer edge of the road is outside. HE CHEATED!'

'Settle down Major, Colonel Fujita ask the Captain to come in here and give the full explanation.'

Fujita opened the door and ordered the nearest private to find Captain Nakagawa and bring him to the anteroom.

A short while later there was a knock at the door and when Major Hyashida opened it he saw Jack standing there with Sergeant Higashi who was, in turn, carrying a tray of tea, coffee and biscuits.

'We thought you may like some refreshments,' announced Jack as he entered the room.

A chorus of "Hai, arigatō." met his entrance and he poured for them all.

'Higashi, I want you to stay as well.' General Onishi ordered.

'Hai,' replied Higashi and waited off to one side.

'You may as well join us in the drink, Sergeant. I shall want your assessment as well.'

'Hai, General.'

'Captain, explain your reassessment of the area boundaries.'

Jack asked Higashi to put the map on the table, and following that Jack pulled out his copy of the operational directives and found the page noting the delineation of the exercise area.

'General these are the co-ordinates of the boundaries, is that right, Sir?'

He offered the page to the general who looked at it and replied 'Hai.'

'Good, Colonel do you agree?'

'Hai.'

'If we transpose the boundary corner points onto the map it shows that this line,' Jack drew the line on the map, 'is the correct boundary according to the operational directives. As you can clearly see it gives us an area of around fifty hectares in which we can operate; that is the area that was usually considered out of bounds.'

The three senior officers looked, checked and rechecked his lines and none could come up with an explanation for the error.

'Jack, how do you explain this difference between the assumed line and the correct line?' Colonel Fujita had slipped into the familiarity that Jack used with all of those he worked with; and he was surprised as to how easy it was for him to do so.

'When the pre-exercise plans were released, I studied them closely. It did not seem right that the boundary was outside an easily identifiable landmark, the road would normally be such a boundary line. A quick phone call and the reason was explained. The boundary was supposedly changed when the road was realigned following a real landslide around ten years ago. No one has changed the alignment of the actual boundary; it was always assumed to be the road. I merely ensured that I had as much legal room as possible to work my battle plan. Think of it as an International Border, I kept within the real border lines not the assumed ones.'

'And your deceptions? Are they also permitted?' Major Hyashida was clearly not liking the prospect of being denied what he believed was natural justice.

'If we were actually at war, I would do this and much more to ensure victory. The deceptions were not listed among the illegal manoeuvres for the exercise, that is why I used them. The so-called "workers" were members of the 3rd platoon creating a diversion for my enemy, nothing more.'

'Sergeant? Your thoughts?'

'General, I have worked with Captain Nakagawa since he first graduated from the academy; almost every time we go on exercise, he has been able to create an effective battle plan and emerge without significant casualties. I am constantly amazed at how hard he works to create his masterpieces; he will spend hours finding little escapes that provide us with an advantage. This time he forced the enemy column to take a road they did not want to, and they ended up being confronted by a numerically inferior force that had a superior position and he won the encounter.'

'Thank you, Sergeant.'

'General, if I may, I have one more observation.'

'Go, on.'

'Arigatō, Sir. The operational directives given to the Captain have all had very little in the way of direct and specific instructions. It is almost as if the planners want to see if they can force him to make errors in both judgement and planning. From my position as his 2I/C I have seen him work almost miracles in getting his soldiers back intact as well as completing his assigned tasks. We may never be allowed to look inside his brain to find out how he does it, but I would rather go to war with him than any other field infantry commander I know, present company excepted.'

'Thank you, Sergeant, for the unsolicited comments. Dismissed.' Jack's sergeant left the room and as he moved to the door, he received a small bow from Jack in appreciation of the support.

'Anything else Major?' Colonel Fujita asked.

The Major began to rant about how a junior field commander was undermining the command structure by deliberately diverting away from the assigned instructions and a dozen other minor complaints. Eventually, the General became wearisome of the tirade and stopped his complaining.

'Major Hyashida, I feel your primary concern is that he handed you your "arse on a plate" as the Americans would say. Think for a moment; are you more concerned that you were beaten? Or is your problem that you were beaten by unconventional means? Many of us have suffered this ignominy over the last few years, Nakagawa is a brilliant Infantry Officer, his methods are unpredictable, and he will be very hard to defeat at war. Do not hate him for his ability, learn from his dedication and we will all benefit.'

'As you wish General.' The Major bowed but before he could leave, he was cautioned.

'Major, there are more exercises coming up soon. Command has decided to give Nakagawa an entire battle group to determine if his methods are suitable for a larger sphere of operations. You will be a part of that group; learn to work with him.'

'Hai, General.' Hyashida left the office to spend the next hour thinking about his day and what the future would hold. He was met outside by Jack.

'Sorry you were on the receiving end of the fight today. They seem to keep giving me more difficult tasks without any specific orders. Come have coffee with me, after all you are dead, and the rest of your army are not expected here for a few hours.'

'I guess it's not actually your fault; all you are doing is trying to complete your missions.' The two sat and discussed the events so far for two hours or more. Eventually, the "enemy" were sighted making an attempt to out flank the defenders.

'Tank squadrons proceed to Jump point Bravo. IFV's and Light tanks in support.' Jack's orders were simple and in plain language.

'How do they know where the jump off point is?'

'I gave it to them this morning when we were waiting for you to arrive at the ambush. I planned for any incursion that may come late in the exercise time scale and this was one of them. Come on, watch if you wish. Okimoto, ask Colonel Fujita if he wishes to observe.'

'Right Jack. Honda, pass the message to the Colonel.' The sergeant ordered a private and he dashed away only to return a few minutes later followed by the Colonel.

'More action, Jack?'

'Hai, they are trying to outflank us.'

'Your plan?'

The tank squadron is already deployed with IFV's in support. The light tanks have formed a visible line to tempt them into the firing trap.'

Once again, Jack's plan worked. The attacking tank battalion chased the retreating light tanks and as the ground began to deteriorate Jack sprung the trap. Occupying the enemy main battle tanks with his own; the light tanks and the IFV's attacked almost with immunity. Two platoons of ground infantry were so well camouflaged that no one actually saw them until it was too late; by then they were busy throwing "grenades" and "explosive packs". Either the tanks were "destroyed" or damaged so badly they could not continue.

'You planned this this morning?' He asked incredulously.

'Yes Major, I did.'

'Remind me never to get into a bar fight with you. I can think ahead but not that far.'

The two officers would eventually be close friends, until a disaster one day far into the future.

Chapter 11
Into the future

The remaining exercises of the season were conducted and completed without anyone actually accusing Jack of cheating. The Head of Northern Command, The Chief of Army Staff and the Chief of the Defence Force had all become supporters of his unconventional ways. And even though some were still complaining about his methods, none were willing to voice their concerns out loud.

The final exercise, before the winter break, was to be held in the late autumn. The weather had been unseasonably dry and many of the small creeks and rivers in the exercise area had dried up.

It was so dry that the planners had to make arrangements for extra drinking water to be trucked in. So much was required that there was a constant stream of trucks going both in and out of the training area supplying both the defenders and the aggressors.

'The final order of the briefing is for the attack group,' announced General Onishi. 'Captain Nakagawa will lead the assault group. Captain your objective is to gain access to the enemy camp and disrupt their defence lines. When you have infiltrated them, report to headquarters and we will begin the final assault.'

'Any questions?' The General waited for the usual request for something out of the ordinary from Jack and he was slightly surprised when there were no requests.

'Very well. The exercise begins tomorrow at 0500 and the scheduled finish at 1800 in three days' time. Good luck.'

The meeting broke up and Jack called for all his subordinates to meet in the mess tent and go over his battle plan.

'Any questions?'

'Just explain the "road" we will be using again please.' Asked one new lieutenant.

'Map please Sergeant.' Jack asked Okimoto, 'This line is the access route we will be using.' Jack drew a line along the twisting route and the officers all marked it on their maps.'

'Captain, if I may make a suggestion?'

'Certainly, Hiro.'

'Sir, if we divert here,' he pointed to a spot on the proposed track. 'We can circle around the rear of their camp, enter through here,' he pointed to another part of the track. 'This part of the track is well below the ground level on the camp side and just a little further away, as such it will reflect our sound away from the camp and muffle the remainder.'

Jack studied the map closely. 'It is not too steep for your tanks?'

'No Sir, we can make it easily. And the weather forecast is for a half moon and clear skies. Wind will be from the south-east and it will assist in blowing our noise away as well.'

'Very good. We shall do that. Everyone onboard with that?' No one dissented. 'Now, timing. We will need to be flexible in our timing, we need to be able to disguise as much of our noise as possible. No over driving the engines, no excess noise from exhausts, no talking. Finally, use these for communications.' Okimoto opened a box of civilian two-way radios and began handing them out.

'Why these? We have perfectly good radios to use.' One tank commander asked, slightly confused.

'If we use these then they will not be able to listen in to our chatter. Keep your language ordinary, not military. We can use an obscure channel that they will not be monitoring. It will double the confusion if they cannot hear us.'

'OK. Let's go I want to be well away from this position when the exercise begins, move out at 2200. Good luck.'

The meeting broke up and Major Hyashida stayed to ask a question.

'How did you come up with the radios?'

'They were used by the engineers to control their vehicles during major earthworks, I just asked the engineers if I could borrow some.'

'Isn't that outside the parameters?'

'Not at all, we were told to use radio communication. They did not specify which radios, or which channels. So, I just improvised. They didn't say I could not do it.'

'And this is the point that we tell the Captain that we all need to get our dress uniforms ready for the enquiry.' Added Okimoto.

The group burst into laughter and all left to begin their preparations.

'Major, a word if I may.' Colonel Fujita had been waiting at the rear of the tent, sipping coffee and listening to every word.

'Hai, Colonel.'

'Your thoughts?'

'Never had a mission briefing like it. He gets information from everyone. It gives me a good feeling; like we can accomplish anything.'

'I notice you called him "Sir", a reflex reaction?'

'Actually, I think it is more personal than that; he is in command and it becomes automatic to refer to him that way, and it feels right. I don't think his rank really has much to do with it at all, where he is concerned. As you well know he works best when he is on a first name basis with his team. This is one time it is the man that gets the respect not the badge.'

'Well put. Time to go or we will miss the start time.'

Jack's assault team were at their jump-off point well before the start time of 0500. In the hour or so before they were due to begin, he made his way through the entire group, ensuring that each was comfortable with their particular place in the jig-saw puzzle that was an army exercise.

He accepted tea from most and ensured that they had all been able to get breakfast before they started.

'You don't know when you will get a chance to eat again, so get some now,' he was heard to say many times.

As the start time approached, he made his way to Major Hyashida at the head of the tank column.

'All ready, Hiro?' he asked. It was not a real question, just a way to begin their day.

'Ready as I will ever be, Jack.' Hiro replied, still surprised how easily the use of first names had become; but more surprised as to the results he achieved with his persistent ignoring of the protocol of army hierarchy.

'I have been thinking about the push into the enemy camp.' Jack continued, 'I think we should find an area where we can stop for a couple of hours and make our approach at night. The water and supply trucks will be most active in the evening, they may give us some extra sound cover.'

Good idea,' replied Hiro 'We can hold up here,' he said pointing at a clearing well away from the expected infiltration route.

'How long to get there?'

Hiro made the calculations. If we can move at a leisurely pace, to keep the noise down, we will be there just on sundown, around two hours before full dark.'

'Good, let's do that. Let everyone know, get the surveillance drones up from around midday to give us enemy deployment information.'

'Hai,' replied Hiro and then he proceeded to give the instructions to the remaining field commanders.

The drones went up at midday and soon came up with some very interesting video feeds.

'Have a look, Jack,' announced Hiro when they had stopped for their planned break. 'Grass fires all over the north-west of the assigned combat zone.'

'Grass fires! Great, there will be a lot of fire trucks in the area soon and they will help disguise us as well. Let's see if we can adjust the approach line closer to the south-west.'

Jack, Hiro, Okimoto and the junior officers all began to pore over the maps looking for an extra advantage. Eventually, they found one.

'Sir,' shouted a new Lieutenant.

'Let's be a little quiet, shall we.' Jack chided him gently, never being one to put someone down unless it was inevitable, and more importantly, warranted. 'What do you have?'

'If we can split the team, one half can approach using the original track. The other can move through here,' indicating a barely visible track on the video from the drones.

'And then we can meet up at the enemy headquarters.' Jack finished the sentence for him. 'Good idea. Okimoto, send the drones to get a better idea of the condition of the track. Hiro, will you do the calculations, please.' Jack looked up at the new officer, 'That is a good idea, well done.'

'Thank you, Sir,' he looked a little embarrassed to be singled out for praise, but he had earned it.

Just twenty minutes later the drone footage came back and Hiro emerged with the transit details. Jack simply waited for them to finish their summary and then he spoke.

'Good work. Comms! Make to General Onishi; Taipan 1 requests plan Bravo 43 implemented at 0530 tomorrow. The Infantry Fighting Vehicles will use this track, leaving at 0500 and the tanks will use this track leaving at 0430,' he ordered indicating the tanks would use the new route and the IFV's and foot soldiers the original choice. 'Any questions?'

'No? Good. Okimoto, unfortunately the men will have to use the "ready to eat" meals tonight and tomorrow morning, we cannot risk alerting the enemy.'

Hai.' Okimoto left to pass the message.

'Lieutenant Ushida, call support and get the fuel and water tankers up here under cover of darkness, quiet as possible if you please.

'Hai.'

'Hiro let's get as much done tonight as possible. Fuel all vehicles. Everyone is to be well rested before we set off. I will call the officers for a confirmation briefing at 2100 tonight.'

'Hai.'

The officers left to get their extra work completed. When they all gathered that night, Jack was off to one side listening to the conversations from a corner where he was not visible.

'Why don't we just attack tonight?' asked one new officer.

'We should have attacked as soon as possible.' Agreed another. The conversations were all roughly the same, the instructors at the Officers School had done well in schooling them as attack troops, but Jack was more of a "let's surprise them." Type of leader, he had some extra parts planned that he had not let out, yet.'

Eventually, Jack "entered" the tent and as they became aware of his presence, the group became quiet.

'Everyone got a coffee?' a murmur of agreement rolled through the small group present. 'Everyone ready?' he asked, it was a rhetorical question, but he asked it just the same.

'This is the plan…' Jack began the official, modified briefing and the officers were all taking notes of their expected parts in the morning's events.

'Any questions?' he eventually asked. As was normal no one had any requests for information or other items.

'No questions? Good everyone is to be ready by 0400. Get your troops ready and rested; tomorrow will be a lot of fun, for us. Not so much for the "enemy" I hope.'

The tent emptied quickly and soon Jack was left with just Colonel Fujita and Sergeant Higashi.

'Dare I say you are right on the edge of both the boundary and the rules of engagement?' he asked.

'That may be so, we can explain the change in our positioning by the fires, the trucks bringing water into the camp and to the firefighters, and we can use the drought as well. Maybe they will all simply say, "Damn Nakagawa" again, and not make a big deal of it.'

'That is probably closer to the truth than we would like to give it credit for.' Fujita responded, 'When did you give General Onishi the new plan?'

'I didn't. I just gave him a possible requirement, gave it an important sounding code name and that was that. Now anyone that hears of plan "Bravo 43" will wonder what is in plan "Bravo 42". It just gives a little more confusion to everything we do.'

'As usual I will be waiting to see what your plan works like.'

Colonel Seijin Fujita enjoyed Jack's little deceptions much more than he admitted.

If you had bothered to ask, Jack did not sleep that night. It wasn't as though he didn't want to; but there was something about the plan that he was not happy with. To begin with he was unsure that he had the best plan; not a conscious decision, just a gut feeling. Then there was the nagging fear of amassing too many casualties, something he had always worked hard to minimise.

The last of his concerns was how to find the best access into the enemy camp. Finally, at 0230 he felt he was ready to proceed.

Walking to the darkened corner of his briefing tent he nudged the foot of his messenger.

'Sorry to wake you so early, wake the officers and the senior NCOs, briefing here in ten minutes.'

The sleepy private staggered out of the tent and made his way to the Officers' quarters first and then he began to rouse the NCOs. Eventually, they had all gathered and each was presented with a coffee from Jack as they entered for the briefing.

'Don't you ever sleep?' asked Major Hyashida as he took the offered cup.

'Not dead yet, leave coming up in two weeks, I will sleep then.' Jack laughed as he spoke, and Hiro joined with him.

'What's up Jack?' asked Hiro as he sipped from his steaming cup.

'Changes in the battle plan. Have a look.'

The two moved to the map table and studied the plan.

'I was having trouble reconciling the easiest access route with the easiest method of infiltrating their H.Q.'

'What changes have you got, Jack?' Okimoto Higashi, Jack's long term second in command asked.

As Jack explained to the Major and the Sergeant a voice from behind was heard to grumble "What could possibly need changes now. I thought it was ready to go."

'Sergeant Higashi, what is the first rule of combat?' Jack asked without looking up.

'No battle plan will survive first contact with the enemy.'

'And why is that?'

Okimoto looked at the young lieutenant, 'Because the enemy does not have a copy of the battle plan, he will not be where you expect him to be; unless of course you have put him there.'

'Second Lieutenant Yoshida,' Jack announced, still looking down at the maps, 'If you want a life of routine and certainty, I would suggest you apply for a transfer to the Airforce. They never do anything without it being authorised and promulgated on the squadron bulletin board. If you wish to be a part of what I am doing, then you will learn to be flexible.'

'Hai, Rikugun-Tai-I (Captain), I apologise for my outburst.'

'Very well.'

Suitably chastened, he remained silent; as did all the junior officers.

'I have decided that the two columns will meet here,' Jack indicated a position that would prove to be Just out of sight from the enemy headquarters. 'We can enter the area here,' he pointed again. First squadron tanks are to wait outside to guard approaches. Infantry Fighting Vehicles will follow the light tanks into the compound. The third and fourth platoons will infiltrate the building as quietly as possible, I want to try to take them out before they realise it is not their armour.'

'Lieutenant Yoshida, you will be beside me for the duration,' ordered Jack. 'Any further questions?'

All the officers were busy making notes and preparing to brief their troops.

'Major? Is the communications disrupter working yet?'

'The technicians got it going at 0100. The problem was an antenna connector that was incorrectly installed. They have rewired the aerials and tested it. They are happy.'

'Good, can we ensure they are active before we can be discovered? I would like to be able to ambush their armour when it returns.'

'Hai, leave it with me.'

'OK,' Jack addressed all present, 'Let's get ready; get them up, fed and briefed.'

At that order, they all left. All except Major Hyashida.

'Be with you in a minute Jack,' he called as Jack left the tent.

'Lieutenant Yoshida, a moment.'

'Hai Major.'

Hiro ensured they were alone and then he turned towards the Lieutenant.

'If you have questions or comments make them at the appropriate time. Smart comments and complaints are not welcome or needed. If the Captain has called for an extra briefing it is because he feels that there is an unacceptable risk to those he commands.'

'Just so you know; he has only had four hours sleep in three days, you managed that last night. If you are unhappy with this level of attention to detail, then we will make arrangement for your transfer. Do you understand me?'

'Hai. Rikugun-Shōsa (Major). I apologise.'

'Good now get out there and do your job.'

The Lieutenant left and Jack came back in.

'Tough words, Hiro.'

'I know, but he will be a better officer for it.'

'How about you? Do you agree with the changes?'

'It is somewhat outrageous, but then again most of your plans are. As for my feelings, it will be a huge slap in the face for General Nomura. He may well be asked to resign if he loses another exercise to you.'

'Well, let's see how I do then.'

'Put up the surveillance drones!' Jack ordered at 0430, let me know when there is movement.

The small drones flew off towards the enemy headquarters and Jack waited patiently for the reports.

Blue Army HQ

'General, I apologise for intruding,' the Adjutant announced as he woke General Nomura. 'There are reports of heavy armour moving towards us from the North.'

'Very well, confirm as soon as you can.'

The adjutant left and the General began to dress. As he arrived in the command room his steward handed him a steaming mug of tea and several planning officers began to give him briefings. 'Are the reports confirmed?' he asked.

Again, several officers began talking.

'One at a time!' Nomura shouted.

'Infra-red surveillance reports heat blooms in as many as ten heavy vehicles.'

'Scouts report tanks pushing up the main access road.'

'Intelligence reports IFV's in support.'

"So, he has finally tried to bluff his way with a frontal charge." The General thought. 'Send three squadrons of main battle tanks down the road to meet them head-on; send the remaining tanks and the IFVs down the forest track to cut them off from behind, at the bottom of the road, spread them out to ambush the enemy as they emerge.'

'Hai.'

The orders went out and almost the entire armoured group moved out to "ambush" the incoming enemy. Just after the enemy tanks rounded the downhill bend in the road, Major Hyashida and his armoured column made their way out of hiding and began the run up the hill towards the enemy headquarters. The perimeter guards watched as the column appeared before them through the early morning mist.

For the next three hours it was a game of cat and mouse. As the blue tanks began to hunt down their enemy, the red tanks would melt away into the trees, only to emerge nearby forcing the blue column to change course, time and again.

Throughout the early morning no one received a message. This was considered normal as they were always under radio silence. This time it would prove to be an error of judgement; the lack of signals was due to the enemy disrupting their communications, not an adherence to protocols.

The guards reported the column and were told that it was their own armour returning after chasing down the enemy, they promptly ignored the column entering the compound.

Meanwhile, the ground infantry had infiltrated the Blue headquarters from the rear corner and had "silenced" all the guards they encountered. The IFVs and light tanks took up positions around the headquarters itself and the main battle tanks formed a defensive line facing the road, waiting patiently for the return of the enemy column.

Jack signalled silently to his ground troops, the senior NCOs and Officers gathered for their final instructions.

'First platoon, cover all access at the rear; second right side, fourth left. The IFV's will cover the front with the fifth and ninth. Sixth, seventh and eighth setup cover fire for the tanks. Third platoon, we will wait for ten minutes to let the others get into position then we can go capture as many as we can. All the commanders left and deployed their teams as Jack had ordered.

Exactly ten minutes later Jack signalled for his team to breach the first door. Breach was probably a strong term; the door was actually the entrance to the kitchens and it was unlocked. Quietly opening it Sergeant Higashi directed his men to cover all possible directions. The kitchen staff were quickly and quietly rounded up and held in the office.

Emerging from the kitchen, they made their way through the lower rooms, Jack always at the front and Lieutenant Yoshida was right beside him. It only took ten minutes to clear the lower levels and the then made their way slowly up the stairs to find the planning room.

Silently calling his most experienced soldiers closer he indicated which ones were to go which way. As he stood upright his team raised their weapons ready to "fire". If this had been a real war with live ammunition this would have been the moment that was most dangerous.

Jack gently leaned forward and slowly turned the door handle. The door opened silently and the foremost soldiers looked left and right through the crack to determine the position of the occupants.

The door was actually a pair of doors, which was just what Jack needed at that moment. Testing the second door he found it was not secured either and this would allow them to get almost the entire platoon inside within only three seconds.

Jack held up his hand with three fingers extended. Slowly, counting down he lowered one finger, then the next. When the third finger dropped the doors burst open and thirty men rushed into the room.

The occupants inside were so surprised that they did not react immediately, and before they had time to do more than look, each one was effectively "captured".

General Nomura was almost at the point of having a heart attack. He was threatening anyone and everyone with Court Martial for allowing the enemy to get inside his headquarters.

'General, please!' Colonel Fujita pleaded with him, 'You are defeated, shouting and threatening will not change that fact.'

Nomura was not yet ready to admit defeat. 'He has cheated again! How can you let him continually flout the rules of engagement?'

'I have stood beside him for the entire process of his planning. It is my assessment that Captain Nakagawa has once again been able to circumvent the defences of your army.'

'My tank division will soon return and then he will be done.'

'Excuse me Sir?' asked Sergeant Higashi.

'Hai?' replied the Colonel.

'Message from Red Tank Command, Major Hyashida reports the enemy Main Battle Tanks have been successfully ambushed. Their infantry and IFV's have also been defeated.'

'Arigatō, Sergeant.'

'Sorry General, it appears that you have been completely defeated in this battle. Congratulations Captain.'

'Arigatō, Colonel. Sergeant, estimates of casualties?'

'The umpires are finalising the totals; it seems we sustained around ten "dead" and thirty-five "wounded". Enemy reports only one hundred survivors, not including the command group and kitchen staff. one tank is left damaged all other vehicles are destroyed.'

'A decisive victory, Captain. You have performed well above what your experience and training would predict.'

Jack bowed in the direction of General Nomura, 'Domo arigatō, General. I have tried to keep my casualties as low as possible.' Jack replied. This was high praise from a newly defeated General of Nomura's standing.

Chapter 12
The Aftermath of Exercise Season

The knock at the door was unexpected, the reason Colonel Fujita had arrived was not.

Jack rose to his feet from behind his desk and bowed to his visitor.

'Please come in Sir. Would you like coffee or tea?'

'Tea, arigatō.'

Fujita did not wait to be asked, he took a seat in the lounge chair under the window of Jack's office. Jack poured the tea and served it to his visitor.

'Let me guess why you have visited today; You got bored with the lack of entertainment in your office?'

'No.'

'You wished for some intellectual company and in-depth conversation?'

'No.'

'You wish to raise your spirits with witty chat?'

Colonel Fujita laughed, 'No, but that is always available when you are around.'

Jack put his hand to his chin as if he was pondering some weighty problem.

'I am at a loss for further suggestions, I give up. What can I do for you Sir?'

'I think you already know; the Chiefs of Staff have been investigating the summer exercise season and they have a few questions for you and Major Hyashida as well as Sergeant Higashi.'

'All of us? Well I can't say I am surprised. Any clues as to the nature of the questioning?'

'Let's just say there are a number of "senior" officers that are not best pleased at the methods you have used.'

'Still? I thought we had already thrashed this out.'

'Put it this way, you have managed to master ground infantry, mechanised infantry, tank, support armour, and combined ground operations in less time than most take to become comfortable with just one discipline, let alone master it. They are going to probe your brain; they want to know how you managed to do it.'

'Should I be worried?'

'I don't think so, I get the feeling that they are accepting of your successes, they just want to know how much they can push your capabilities.'

'The Major and Sergeant?'

'They want to know their opinions of your work methods, are you relying on too much local knowledge or are you taking the lead and your reputation from the input of others.'

'Hmmm. How much time do I have?'

The conference is scheduled to begin after lunch, about 1330. Get your documentation ready, you will need it.'

Jack prepared as best he could. His "documentation" consisted mainly of his maps and mission briefing statements. For the detail of each mission, he would rely on his incredible memory.

The first called in was Colonel Fujita.

Fujita entered the conference room and saw a long table placed across the room. Seated at the Centre was the Grand Marshall of the army with the Marshalls of the Northern and Central commands alongside him. Several other senior Generals, including Nomura and Onishi, were arranged around the table, leaving the side closest to the door empty.

'Be seated, please Colonel.'

'Colonel Fujita,' the General Commanding the Northern Forces began. 'You first raised the issue of the methodology used by Captain Nakagawa, why?'

'His first combat exercise, as a Lieutenant, was relatively straight forward. His Battle Orders were to "disrupt" the enemy headquarters for as long as possible. He overstepped the mark and, in the end, he had completely overshadowed the entire exercise.'

'For the record, how did he do this?'

'He managed to attack and takeover the enemy headquarters, effectively ending the exercise early. He had disobeyed the orders, in that he captured the enemy command, he did not disrupt them.'

'I see. How did he justify his actions? Why was he not disciplined for disobedience?'

'The problem was that no one had given him the correct boundaries for his command. He had family living close to the exercise area and he enlisted them in providing extra information on the enemy base. This information allowed him to penetrate into the building and capture the command group.'

'What exactly were his orders?' Asked the Marshall of the Army.

'Specifically, he was ordered to "Disrupt the Enemy". No more, no less. That was all that he was given by way of battle instructions.'

'That was it! It appears that his orders were at the very least light on detail for a junior officer in his first exercise.' The Marshall was incredulous at the revelation. 'On a professional note, he should have requested more detail; on a personal note he embarrassed us all.'

'Tell us about his subsequent actions?'

'Every time he was deployed, he would come up with a new method of circumventing the envisioned system. An exercise would be planned and he would find a way around the restrictions. I do not understand how he did it, his mind can find the smallest details that are lost to others.'

'His last foray, how did he get around the enemy defences?'

'He used dry riverbeds as roads, and when he was ready, he asked General Onishi to draw the enemy armour away from their headquarters. He then deployed his forces and his ground troops entered and again captured the headquarters of General Nomura.'

'Very well. Send in the Sergeant.'

Sergeant Higashi entered the room and saluted the officers. If he was impressed with their high positions, he did not show it, his was the casual air of a man that had seen it all before.

'Sergeant Higashi, tell us about Captain Nakagawa,' demanded the Chief of Staff for the Army.

'I have never seen an officer like him. He has the uncanny ability to get so many people do what he wants; and they seem happy to do it for him. His command of the soldiers below him is automatic, they appear to have an immediate "bond" if I can put it that way. He inspires confidence in those around him. His control seems to be innate and natural.'

'Would you say he is an effective officer?'

'His record speaks for itself.'

'I understand he had some dissent from a junior officer at the last exercise, what was that about?'

'One thing that Ja…Captain Nakagawa does is give highly detailed briefings, not just what he wants but also why he wants it. The officer you refer to was questioning the need for so many changes in the plan, especially at the last minute.'

'And what did he do?'

'It is one of the most difficult things to do, reprimand someone when they are in a room full of lower ranks. All he said was that if the officer, a new Second Lieutenant, was unhappy with the possibility of change then perhaps infantry was not the place for him and he should possibly think about a more defined and rigidly controlled branch of the defence force, like maybe the Airforce, where they don't even go to the men's room without it being planned and authorised.'

'The response from the officer?'

'Major Hyashida took him to one side and ensured that the officer would not interrupt and he would be more accepting of the planning process.'

'Hmmm. Your personal thoughts? You have been in the Army for a long time?'

'I have seen most things that the Army can throw at us. Nothing seems to upset him. I have seen officers reduced almost to tears with the complexity and the harsh reality that is a difficult battle problem. Captain Nakagawa just studies the plans and the deployments and every little detail. His final plan will all but guarantee success with the minimum number of casualties. Cannot ask for more than that from a field officer.'

'Would you serve alongside him? In an active arena?'

'Without even a hint of hesitation, sir. If he goes to war, he is the one that will have the best chance of not only success but also bringing us back.'

'Arigatō, Sergeant. Send in Major Hyashida.'

Okimoto stood and saluted, leaving the room he closed the door before sending in the Major.

'How was it?' asked Jack.

'Funny; I don't think they are out for blood, but they do want to know how you do it.'

'That will be hard to explain; half the time even I don't know how!' the friends all laughed together.

'Major, they want to see you now.'

'Must be leaving the condemned man until last!' Jack joked and they all laughed again.

Hiro entered the room and saluted.'

'Sit, please Major.'

'So far we have heard from his Colonel and his Sergeant. I believe you had some harsh criticism of Captain Nakagawa following on from your encounter?'

'That is correct, sir. It was harsh, at the time I thought that he had been operating out of the boundaries of the exercise area.'

'Well, was he?'

'When the boundaries had been first drawn the outer edge of the existing road was the edge of the usable area, effectively the road was the end of the battleground, whilst actually still being within the boundary. Captain Nakagawa studied the maps; and I have to say that he studied them more closely than even the Command Cartography Group, the ones that actually supplied the maps.'

'And what did he find?'

'The actual boundary had not been properly mapped following the realignment of the access road; the original boundary was almost fifty metres outside the road area. We have all been accustomed to using the road as the boundary, I have done so for my entire time as a tank commander. Captain Nakagawa simply ensured he had the correct working area.'

'And how did he explain his actions?'

'He likened the boundary to an international border; assuming that a border is in one place will prevent the use of nearby lands, however if the border is actually elsewhere, he was able to use more room. In this case he was able to camouflage his ambush more effectively and his action was successful, specifically due to his attention to detail.'

'I believe that he had you running around all over the area, is that right?'

'Much to my embarrassment sir, yes. He had managed to conjure up the "fact" that there had been a landslide on the first road we used and then he had a bridge "under repair" on the second road. This pushed us directly into his ambush.'

The Grand Marshall and the Chief of staff were trying to stifle their amusement.

'Your record, Major, shows you as the top tank commander we have.'

'Arigatō, sir. It is most kind of you to say so.'

'And yet you were convincingly out manoeuvred by a relatively inexperienced infantry officer. How does that sit with you?'

'At first, I was angry that he had used so much subterfuge. But following on from an in depth debrief from Colonel Fujita and then from General Onishi; I could see the methods he was using. As the Australians say "The devil is in the detail." And he finds the detail so easily. Give him a paper map and he will almost see it as a hologram. Show him the limitations of the area and he will find the gaps he can exploit. Give him the weapons and he will find new uses for them.'

This last revelation caused the Marshalls to sit up and listen more closely.

'How so?'

'During the last exercise he was using the small quad-copter drones as surveillance units, quiet and small they are very difficult to find. He found one of his privates was the current world champion at drone racing and used those skills to get highly detailed information of almost everything that was happening. The pilot was able to fly so much faster than any other and he got his drone in and out of the enemy area before anyone could stop him. Add to that he is now asking if the delivery drones that the online food companies use, can be modified to take a couple of grenades and drop them amongst the enemy.'

'And? Can they?'

'He is getting the engineers to try to get the release mechanism to work reliably, as I understand it, it is just a case of being able to "pull the pin" at the right time.'

Thank you Major. We asked the Sergeant and we ask you the same; would you go to war with him in charge?'

'In a heartbeat. We all have faith in his ability.'

The Major left and closed the door behind him.

Looking at Jack he said, 'I think you are in luck; it seems they want to exploit you, not crucify you. Sorry, forgot you are Christian.'

'No problems, no one has actually been crucified for over a thousand years anyway,' he laughed at his own joke, 'Stick around, we are all going for a beer after, no matter what the outcome.'

Jack was finally called into the conference room at almost 1500. As he entered, he made note that almost every senior General as well as the Field Marshalls from Northern Command and Central Command and the Grand Marshal of the Army were all present. These men were as high as "High Command" got, and as experienced as officers were in the Army; this was not going to be an easy group to win over. At this point Jack decided that he would have to be, not only full in disclosure, but also careful with the phrasing of his answers, he could not afford to anger any of them, despite the good feelings he was getting from his friends.

Jack stopped and stood at attention, saluting and then waiting, for further instruction.

'Sit please, Captain.' The Field Marshall ordered; and Jack sat in the chair directly opposite the Marshall.

'Do you understand why this hearing has been assembled?'

'I believe it is because I do not automatically follow orders as blindly as some others.'

Every eye in the room suddenly looked at him, as though they had been compelled by some unseen force.

'THAT! Is a big understatement.' Nomura almost shouted.

'And why is that, Captain?'

'Battle orders usually come in one or two different forms. The first is a direct, concise and explicit order. Such as "Stand there and stop anyone that approaches." The second type is less rigid and allows the receiver a greater degree of latitude in their understanding and compliance with the order.'

'Can you give us example of this second type?'

'Certainly Sir. If the order "Disrupt the enemy in any way you see fit", is given; then the receiver is then able to use their own discretion as to what is the best way to comply with the order.' Jack had deliberately used the language from his first briefing as an example, more to bring the concept forward than to embarrass the General.

'Can you give us an example of how the second order can be used?' The Marshall was hoping to bring Jack's first exercise into the discussion.'

'Certainly, Sir. History is the greatest teacher we have, if we do not learn the lessons of history then we are doomed to repeat the mistakes; if I may loosely paraphrase George Santayana. In June 1944 the allied forces were launching the D-day landings on the coast of France. One of the little-known groups operating behind German lines was a team of saboteurs from what Churchill dubbed "The Ministry of Ungentlemanly Warfare". These operatives were given the task of disrupting the enemy ability to bring reserves into the battle.'

'Can you be a little more specific?'

'The group were far behind the German lines and their task was to try to slow the advancement of a battalion of tanks, and if possible, prevent them from reinforcing the defensive line. This one small group, given a monumental task and only their own methods and plans to complete it. They were not given the possibility of support, nor were they given any method of escape should they be captured. The history of the encounter shows that this small group slowed the tanks so much that instead of taking just three days to get to the new front line they were still not close enough to be effective nineteen days later, long after the allies had established their beachhead and had begun to deliver supplies and reinforcements.'

'And how did they achieve this feat?'

'They took the approach that if they blocked two kilometres of road through a forest, the enemy would simply go around the blockage. But if they dropped one tree in the wrong place then their opposition would try to clear the one tree away, quicker than trying to clear a new road, after all it is only one tree. But then they would drop another tree, again in a place where they would hold them up, much longer than normal.'

'Why did they not attack the column while it was stopped?'

'They only numbered less than twenty, they did not have the weapons to stop a Tiger or King Tiger tank. So, they decided to slow them. History shows us that after almost three weeks of disruption the enemy column was forced to turn around as they were then needed elsewhere. This small band had achieved more than their objectives with clever thinking and good strategy.'

'So, you tried the same?'

'Not exactly the same Sir. My first orders were to disrupt the enemy, so I found a way no one had thought of. I took them away, one by one and "killed" them. Until only General Nomura was left. My apologies for the deceptions, Sir.'

'And all your other victories? They were brought about the same way?'

'Not exactly the same, Sir. In one I simply mislead the enemy into thinking there was a numerically inferior force trying to infiltrate. When they arrived, there were none to be found. In another I let them enter the area I wanted them in and then destroyed them in an ambush.'

'What about Major Hyashida? What did you do to him?'

'I used subterfuge, I lied to him a little and forced him to enter the ambush area where he was overwhelmed by a vastly inferior, but better placed force.'

'General Onishi, it appears you were a party to this deception?'

'When the Captain shared his rather audacious plan, I was completely intrigued by it. I have never seen a plan like it. He proposed to give me the enemy armour "on a plate" as he put it. The plan allowed for me to escape if it did not go as he saw. His vision was perfect, the enemy armour came right up to my tanks and just stopped waiting. A perfect target, but he did not fire immediately, he waited for the Major to begin to remove the rock blocking the road and then he attacked. They could not fire back as they had all shutdown their systems to help get the rock off the road. A most impressive command of operations.'

'Arigatō, General. Captain will you wait outside please.'

Jack stood and placed his cap on his head, saluted and left the room.

'How was it, Jack?' asked Hiro Hyashida as soon as he saw Jack emerge.

'Good, I don't think they will shoot me just yet.' They all grinned and sat to await the verdict.

It was almost twenty minutes before the usher called them all back inside. The three men, four if you include Colonel Fujita, saluted and waited at attention. Eventually, the Grand Marshall addressed them all.

'This hearing was convened to investigate an apparently unique methodology for the formulation and implication of battle plans. Whilst we find that Captain Nakagawa is a very junior officer and his experience is restricted to only a relatively few exercises, he has shown the ability to out-think the most experienced officers in the army.'

'As he has shown such a command of ground forces operations, it is our decision that he be promoted to Major immediately and then to Colonel at first opportunity. Congratulations Major, you are to report to the Directorate of Army Planning at 0800 next Monday; have a few days off, go and see your family. Your thinking will transform the way we plan and execute exercises.'

'Domo Arigatō, Sir I will try to live up to your expectations.'

'Dismissed.'

'You are buying!' Jack's friends said together as they left the hearing.

'ME, why me?' he asked with a good amount of mock indignation.

'Because you have just been promoted, well ahead of more senior people and far quicker than is normal. Add to that a pay rise with the promotion and that is why you are buying!' replied Okimoto.

'I guess that is a fair reason.' Jack conceded as they entered the small bar.

The four sat and talked far into the evening. Food came and went as well as more than a few drinks. As their evening slowly began to wind down Jack looked at his friends and spoke.

'I have to thank you all for your help and your friendship. Without you all it would have been very different and much more difficult for me to progress so far, so fast.'

A chorus of slight denial was all the reply he got.

'It is now the end of October; I want you all to come and visit with me for Christmas at my family home. You do not have to bring anything with you. Rest assured that the holiday is not a strictly religious observance; more of a family gathering to enjoy each other's company. Feel free to bring your own families, there is more than enough room for everyone.'

'I think,' Slurred Hiro, having had a little too much to drink 'you will have to email us to confirm this offer of hospitality once we have all sobered up. Otherwise we will not be able to remember it.'

Jack laughed and was quickly joined by the others. 'Consider it done.'

At that moment there was more than a bond of fellow soldiers between them, now they had become personal friends, a friendship that would last until it either "died of natural causes" as many friendships do; or it was torn asunder by outside forces, forces they had no control over.

After they had bid goodnight to each other, Jack made his way back to the barracks and began to pack his kit. The following morning, he called his parents with the good news that he would be home for almost a week before beginning his new role at Army Headquarters.

Chapter 13
A New Job

Jack arrived at Army Headquarters at 0730 on the following Monday.

'You are early, Major?' the duty guard queried him on arrival.

'Only a little, I don't want to upset the General on my first day by being late.

Jack was ushered into the gate office where an access pass was waiting for him along with his inbound information pack. Once he had checked all the items and had gotten directions to his new office he left and ensured he was fully settled in before the day was scheduled to begin.

No sooner had he familiarised himself with his office and staff he found a private and said, 'Go to the gate and inform the guard that there is a button on his jacket that is almost falling off. Tell him that we don't want the General to see it.'

The private disappeared quickly and returned around ten minutes later. He knocked on the door frame and waited for permission to enter. There was no immediate response from within, so he knocked again.

'Private if you keep knocking on the frame so much you will end up with sore knuckles, and I will end up needing a new door frame. Just knock once and enter. If the door is closed then wait for me to respond. Either way, one knock is all that is required.'

'Hai, my apologies Major.'

'The guard asked me to convey his thanks for you noticing the button, he has replaced his jacket and will correct it during his break.'

'Very good.'

The private left and began wondering about this new Major. Was he as good as he first appeared? Or was there a different face underneath. He decided to make a couple of calls during the morning break and he was both surprised and pleased with the replies he got. It seemed that this new officer would be a breath of fresh air in the planning headquarters.

By the close of day, the word had spread throughout the Planning Group; the general feeling was that the Major was really worth the effort to be on his right side. The responses garnered from the field units was that Jack Nakagawa was an officer worthy of respect and as such he quickly managed to get the staff running around to get what he wanted from them all.

His quickly established rapport with the lower ranks was noticed almost immediately by his superiors, and more than one had called the office of General Onishi to get more information on this new planning officer.

'Give him what he wants.' Onishi replied to one inquiry 'Watch what happens when he is done and presents his work for evaluation.'

And that was how he worked; the exercise plans were concise, but they also left a lot of room for an officer to manipulate the situation to his liking.

Up to this point his career had been described by some as "stellar" in its rise. After around eighteen months he was promoted to Lieutenant-Colonel and just two years later he was a full Colonel. It seemed as though someone had lit a fuse under the rocket ship that was his destiny, and all were waiting to see if he was to continue as he had started.

'What do you think, Musashi?' asked Jackson 'Is he good enough?'

'I think he is far above good. He is forcing all around him to lift and become better. He has much to do and some to learn, the time is coming for him to put all he knows into battle. His decisions will decide who will be alive at the end.'

It was not all plain sailing for Jack; but on the whole, he managed to get the junior officers to begin to think for themselves and the senior officers simply had to let them get on with the job.

One thing that everyone was slow to realise was that Jack almost always left an unstated shortcut in the Battle Instructions. Those that were clever enough to find it would be able to complete their mission in short time with spectacular results. Those that didn't? well it is enough to say that they were often called in to the debrief to explain the high number of "casualties" that their units had sustained.

One officer, a newly promoted Lieutenant, complained loudly that the mission he had been given was impossible. When asked to explain he stated that there was no physical way for the mission to be completed and he would lose all he commanded if he were to follow the directives.

'Ask Colonel Nakagawa to come in,' the General Commanding the Planning Group was almost comfortable with the number of complaints he received from the junior officers that could not come to grips with yet another of Jack's battle plans.

A short while later a knock at the door was met with a gruff "Enter!"

'You wish to see me General?' Jack announced immediately following his salute.

'Yes, read this!' The General handed a report to Jack and he quickly completed reading it.'

'I am sorry Sir; I do not see the problem.'

'This Lieutenant has made an official complaint that the battle problems are far too difficult to complete without excessive casualty lists.'

'Well, Sir. That is a big call from an officer that has yet to be fully successful in completing the "Battle Readiness" evaluation.'

'Yes, I was thinking that. What can you do? This is an official problem now; I have to act on it.'

Jack sat back and thought for a few moments. 'There is still a month left in the summer exercise season, is it possible to set up the same exercise that was my first defensive challenge. We can enlist the assistance of General Onishi, and General Fujita can be the overseer and umpire. and we can see if this officer can find a method of completing the task.'

'The basics of your method is taught as a lesson in the Academy now; I think he will be aware of it.'

'I know, but if he is as unthinking as he appears, he will not remember it. After all we do not teach the entire event, just the points that made it such a good lesson.'

The General looked at Jack with suspicion evident in his gaze. 'If I didn't know better, I would say you have a surprise in mind?'

'I would like to keep that private for now, If I may?'

'Certainly. I may just tag along and watch for myself.'

'I think that would be a good idea, after all you do have to act on the report. Perhaps we could have you take the place of the "blue" commander in the house?'

'Done. I will make the arrangements, Colonel Hyashida should be able to provide the armour, some of his teams need an extra workup as well.'

The planning was completed within the week. The units assigned were informed that they were to be the subject of an extra exercise, following on from the raising of an official complaint. That alone made the soldiers less than enthusiastic; no soldier ever "wants" to do extra work "in the field" as it was known.

The phone rang on the Generals desk. As he answered he heard Jack giving extra orders to someone nearby.

'General, we are ready. I have taken the liberty of asking for Warrant Officer Higashi and the third platoon as my defensive forces, Colonel Hyashida has put a Main Battle Tank Company on the list as well, apparently they failed their last inspection, so he gave them this as extra duty.'

'What about the house? Is it available?'

'Hai, I have spoken with the owner and he is happy to take a week to visit his family on Okinawa.

'Good. Have the team pick me up from the Officers' Quarters on the way.'

'Very well, I have taken the liberty of getting your staff to pack for your week in the field.'

'Arigatō.'

The five officers were all waiting for the lieutenant to arrive at what would be called the "planning and control" room in the house they had borrowed for the exercise. While it was not usual for the Army to use a private estate for any exercise, let alone one involving an armoured group; the owner was a former Colonel from the Tank Regiments and he enjoyed the fact that he could give something back to his colleagues.

Eventually, the Lieutenant arrived and he was taken inside for the briefing.

'It's all yours Colonel Nakagawa.'

'Arigatō, General. First thing; jackets off, no rank in here.'

The Lieutenant looked around with a good deal of apprehension, only to see the two Generals handed their uniform jackets to the Warrant Officer who hung them up. The two Colonels were already waiting as they had draped their jackets over the backs of a chair.

Jack looked at the General and announced, 'Motoyuki, would you like tea or coffee?'

'Tea, arigatō Jack.'

Jack looked at the others, 'Okimoto? Hiro? Seijin?' They all requested coffee. 'Hurry up Ginjiro, tea or coffee?'

'C…c…coffee please,' he stammered in reply, totally overwhelmed at the concept of so many high-ranking officers on a first name basis with both him and the Warrant Officer.

'Hiro, would you give the staff a hurry-up? don't want to die of thirst while we wait.'

The Colonel left the room and returned a few moments later. 'On its way.'

They sat and made small talk until the refreshments were served, the steward almost spilled the tray when he heard them all discussing the latest news and weather reports, and giving their opinions on the upcoming Rugby World Cup which was being held in Australia just a few weeks later.

'I still think the New Zealanders will be top, again.' Stated General Onishi, with an air of certainty that should have been a finality.

'As the Americans say "Bullshit",' replied Okimoto, 'Uruguay will back up their last effort and take it again.'

'Care to wager on that?' asked Jack.

'Sure, Jack. Put up or shut up.'

'How about $500 US?'

'A gentleman's bet? OK.' Jack and the General shook hands, and the bet was set.

'Is this a private wager or can anyone get in?'

'Get in if you want Hiro,' replied Okimoto. 'How about we make it a pool. We each nominate our preferred team and as they get beaten the money goes into a pool. Whoever gets the furthest gets the money.'

'Great idea, are we all in?'

The question was answered by a chorus of "Hai" from all present, and the matter was settled.

Just then an aide entered the room.

'General, please forgive the intrusion.'

'What is it?'

We have received advice that the typhoon has changed track and is expected to begin landfall in just twelve hours, only thirty kilometres from here.'

'Very well. Tell me, Jack, if you were in charge what would be your recommendations?'

'Send the armour and ground troops back to barracks immediately.'

'Why so?' asked Hiro 'Explanation of your thinking please?' Not because he needed an explanation, he had known Jack long enough to be able to understand some of his thought processes.

'A typhoon will cause a lot of damage; the troops and their equipment will be better protected if they have returned to barracks. As well they are then available for relief works should they be needed.'

'And our involvement? What do you propose we do?' Enquired Motoyuki seeking full information from Jack.

'We can continue the exercise almost as a "virtual" one. The hologram projectors are ready and we will have the advantage of abandoning the exercise if we need to.'

'Very good, make it happen. Lieutenant, sit here and watch.' General Onishi ordered the almost bewildered junior officer.

For the next fifteen minutes they watched as Jack dispatched the armoured companies and the infantry to return to barracks, each group was given a different route for their return, to keep the disruption to a minimum, not block a highway with almost a hundred vehicles. Tank transports, IFV's (Infantry Fighting Vehicles, ARV's (Armoured Reconnaissance Vehicles), and supply trucks all take up a lot of space. This was Jack's way of trying to reduce the congestion on the roads.

'If you listen carefully Lieutenant, you will notice that Jack has made all his deployments without using any reference documentation. He knows who is deployed, where they are holding, where they are going and the simplest route for each to take to return. They will all be gone in around thirty minutes. Learn from his methods, he is rewriting the Operations Manual, he is changing the way we work.

The lieutenant took closer notice of the way Jack manipulated the giant chess set that was the operation in hand. He watched as Jack sent the columns where he wanted them, never looking for the unit name or even the unit's commander's names; everything was in his memory.

As he watched and listened, a call came in from a tank transporter that had broken an axle and sustained a crack in the trailer frame while onloading.

'We cannot on load, the trailer is not usable.' The driver reported.

'Leave it there, use the tank to drag the truck and trailer to a safe position. I am sending a truck to take the crews to barracks. We can retrieve it later.' Was the simple order from Jack.

The entire operation was complete within thirty minutes, every single unit on exercise had been dispatched to return to barracks, leaving just the senior officers at the "headquarters" of the exercise.

'What do we do now Jack?' asked Seijin Fujita.

'We can still complete the exercise we came here for.'

'How? You have just sent all the units back to their barracks.' The young Lieutenant was clearly confused as to how they would be able to continue their work.

'Hiro, Seijin will you please program the exercise into the computer system. Okimoto, give them the details of the units that we had planned on using. Don't forget to use the strengths and weaknesses that were the result of their last Battle Readiness Evaluation; nothing earlier, we need to get this as close as to how they would react if they were still here, and put the system controls to "actual time elapsed" please, not accelerated transit. This needs to be as close as we can get to actual warfare. Can we get this mess cleared away please? then we can begin.'

'Ginjiro, you will use the hologram projector in this room to plan for the first phase of the exercise. I will use the one in there.' Jack announced as he indicated the second planning room. The empty refreshment trays were removed. 'You be the defensive controller for the first phase of the exercise. You have twenty minutes for analysis and a further fifteen for deployment.'

'Computers will be ready in fifteen minutes Jack!' announced Okimoto.

'Very good,' Jack acknowledged the report.

'Lieutenant,' General Onishi almost whispered to the junior officer, 'What you are seeing is a fully confident officer at ease with his work and his handling of the soldiers appointed to his command. No shouting, no indecision. Just calm control. Learn from his example.'

'Hai.' Was all the young officer could say, as he watched the continuous stream of commands send people and machines to do as he had ordered.

'Now!' Jack suddenly spoke. 'We have time for tea before the computers are ready.' And just as suddenly the steward arrived with more refreshments for them all.

The two made their preparations for the upcoming battle problem. Ginjiro worked hard deploying his defensive systems to the area's most likely to be the routes used for the attacking forces, and placing his defensive positions for the expected assault.

Jack, meanwhile, had already completed his battle plan in the first ten minutes and had the orders ready for his deployments in the following five. As he waited for the official start time, he spoke with the others present.

'How do you plan to attack?' asked the general

'Broadly speaking,' he said quietly, 'I expect he will try to use some of the tactics I used. He may think to be a little more realistic and actually have a landslide and a broken bridge, we can do this on the computer. I will approach from a different line, here.' Jack pointed to a position on the hologram map. 'This was not previously used, that will give me the ability to outflank him. He will not be expecting me to arrive so easily or quickly, I should be around a day earlier than he expects me.'

'You are so good at circumventing the "normal" ways things are done. Sneaky is a good description,' replied General Onishi.

'Thank you, Sir, so kind of you to say so. I believe "sneaky" will keep real soldiers alive more than "bravely predictable" will.'

They all laughed at Jack's acceptance of the somewhat brutal assessment of his methods.

The lieutenant was finished just five minutes overtime, an acceptable overshoot given the circumstances.

'Well Lieutenant. Give me your plan for the defence of my position.' Onishi demanded.

Suddenly in the spotlight, the Lieutenant instantly became very nervous. He had clearly forgotten that he was defending the Generals Headquarters.

'I will put diversionary units here, here and here, Sir,' he indicated positions on the map. He will be forced to enter from this position and there will be an ambush force waiting here,' he indicated again. 'That should either see his destruction or at least force him back.'

'Very well. Begin in ten minutes!' Ordered Onishi. "This will be a bloodbath." He thought to himself. 'Don't forget to give your orders aloud so I can hear what is happening.'

At the appointed time the exercise began.

'First platoon to grid A9B, second to B9H, third to C13A. Armour to junction position C13E.'

The teams he had ordered left the prime defensive position and made their way to their designated points to await the attackers.

Jack, meanwhile did nothing.

'Not moving out Jack.' Asked Hiro.

'Not yet. I will wait until the enemy has begun his deployments then I will put up drones. Get a good look at the battleground.' Hiro smiled and waited until almost an hour had passed.

'First teams deployed, Sir.' The lieutenant reported.

'Arigatō.' Was all the reply he got.

'Drones up, check approaches along vectors 183, 197 and 215.'

Everyone waited for information to be returned.

'All teams at assigned positions Sir.'

'Arigatō.'

'Drone reports in, Jack. These are the defensive positions occupied.'

Hiro illuminated the "enemy" positions on the hologram. Jack simply looked for a few moments.

'Good. Put your armoured division here, with the light tanks at the fore, the IFV's and ARV's next. Main Battle Tanks next.'

'Can I ask why the MBT's are last? Or is that classified?' Hiro asked with a mix of a real need for information and a joke at the expense of his friend.

'Look, what do you see?' Jack posed the question to get Hiro to say how he saw the battle ground, this would most likely be what his opponent saw as well.

'The proposed track is narrow but not too steep. A small stream running through the centre is the only natural barrier.'

'Right. The stream is almost a metre deep at the fording place. Tanks will have no problem but the IFV's will be at their fording limit as will be the ARV's. If they get stuck the MBT's will be able to push them through. Once they make the other side, they will all be able to climb the hill. They will turn left at the track a kilometre on and that will bring them around the rear of the outer defences. We can the shift the MBT's to the front and with a little luck we will all be eating dinner at the "enemy" headquarters.'

'NO one has used that approach for a very long time, certainly not with heavy armour.' Stated general Onishi.

'I understand General, but isn't that the purpose? To find a way around the enemy and strike where they do not expect it?'

'Once again, you are right. Let us see how the Lieutenant is going to handle this.'

'You go, Jack. I will drive them from here.'

'Arigatō, Okimoto.'

Once out of the room they closed the door. 'You give your Warrant Officer command? Am I allowed to ask why?'

'Certainly, Sir. He has been working with me on this type of plan for many years now, he understands the principles and the reasoning behind what I do and how I do it. HE can complete this exercise without me, if necessary.'

'You really think so?'

'I do.' Was Jack's simple reply.

'We shall see.'

They entered the "headquarters" planning room where the Lieutenant was busily trying to find Jack's mobile division.

'Where the hell **are** they?' He spoke softly but not quietly enough, General Onishi was closely watching his new officer, he watched as the officer slowly became more and more out of touch with reality as he lost control of the battle. Onishi was not pleased with what he saw.

The battle was over just ten hours after it had begun. The defences were completely overrun and the headquarters were captured with only three casualties on the attacking side.

'Come in here Lieutenant,' ordered General Fujita. He closed the door behind him and gave the officer the debrief on his performance. The others could not hear the details of the conversation, but the looks when they emerged were enough to tell them that the assessment was less than flattering.

'We shall reconvene at 0800 tomorrow. Ordered General Onishi. Lieutenant, tomorrow you will be in command of the attacking force. You will need to bring your best effort.'

'Hai, General.' Was all he replied. But everyone could hear the significant doubt in his voice.

'This morning the roles are reversed, Lieutenant you have thirty minutes to plan your assault. You have the same teams as were available to attack yesterday. The defending teams will be the same,' announced General Fujita. 'Report when you have completed your preparations.'

Just fifteen minutes the defensive team reported as ready. The lieutenant was not quite as quick, taking a little over ten minutes extra to report as ready.

The exercise began at 0900 and it was slow going from the first.

The defensive team let the attackers get further up the first track before they encountered the "landslide" they turned around and tried the bridge road and were only three kilometres from their target when they came under fire from the defensive battery. 127mm rounds smashed into their position forcing them back down the road. One in six vehicles had been assessed as "lost with crews".

They tried to use the previous ambush road and they attempted to go around the ambush site, running into another ambush losing almost half of their remaining number. Getting more frustrated the remaining attackers tried an ill-fated frontal assault; getting wiped out in the process.

'Call a halt please Seijin. Get the Lieutenant in here,' ordered Onishi.

The lieutenant emerged, clearly distraught at his inability to give even a good account of himself. As he waited for his opposition to emerge, he was stunned to see Jack sitting and waiting for the assault team to come into the room.

As he waited, he took note that the two Generals and the two Colonels were deep in conversation, on the other side of the room. Something was not right, but his brain simply refused to process the information.

'Seijin, where is the defensive commander?'

'Believe it or not, he is ensuring his "men" are "fed and rested" after the battle problem.'

'How is he doing that?'

'He has ordered the return to headquarters and stand down.'

'Very good. I assume this is another of your ways, Jack?'

'It is, Sir,' Jack replied, a huge grin crossed his face. 'One of the parameters of the battle problem is the well-being of the assigned units, are they rested, fed etc. Do they have a dry sleeping area? This is not known by most that use the program as they use it for one battle program at a time. If it is in campaign mode it will use a lot more parameters to gauge the efficiency of a unit. If you take the units further into the campaign, they will lose efficiency if they are not looked after.'

'Well bring him out when he is done. He must be getting hungry by now.'

Just at that moment Warrant Officer Higashi opened the door and bowed to the array of senior officers before him.

'Mission accomplished,' he announced. 'The defensive headquarters is safe for all.'

'Well done Okimoto. Come sit and eat. We will debrief you shortly.'

'He wasn't in command? Was he?' demanded the lieutenant.

'I am afraid so. Colonel Nakagawa wanted him assessed and we felt that this was as good a time as any.'

Turning to Higashi he continued, 'Congratulations, Warrant Officer Higashi or should that be Captain Higashi.'

Okimoto stood silently in disbelief, eventually he replied.

'Captain? Domo arigatō Sir.' And he bowed deeply. When he stood upright, he was greeted with pats on the back and handshakes all round.

'I must say I did not expect this.'

'You have passed all of the requirements for promotion to Officer Level. Well done.' General Onishi announced.

Okimoto looked straight at Jack. 'Did you have anything to do with this?'

'Me? You suspect ME?' Jack could not disguise the false indignity he tried to portray. 'Of course, I did. No one else would do it. You have always had a better grasp of infantry operations than anyone I know, of course I wanted you promoted.'

'I don't understand?' The lieutenant said surprised at the events before him. 'I thought I was against Colonel Nakagawa?'

'And so you were.'

'But why was I not put against him today?'

'Your assessment was yesterday, which you passed by the way. Today was for the Warrant Officer.'

'I, I passed? I thought I had lost the engagement?'

'You did. But then again so has everyone else that has taken on Jack. You had three attacks at him. Most only got one, I only managed two.' Fujita tried to give the young officer some sense of the fact he had done well enough to pass his final assessment. 'Now you have had a chance to take on Colonel Nakagawa in the field, do you really think he is unrealistic in his demands when he plans an exercise?'

The lieutenant thought for a minute or so; eventually he broke the almost uncomfortable silence.

'No Sir, I don't. Now I have been able to see both sides of the argument I can understand why he creates such demanding tasks.'

'Good. Now let us eat and relax for the rest of the day. The helicopter will collect us in the morning.' Onishi insisted that they stop the exercise regime for the remainder of the day.

During the afternoon Okimoto cornered General Fujita.

'Why did Jack go to such lengths to get me promoted? Do you know?'

'Ask him.' Was all Seijin would say.

That evening, during dinner he did just that.

'Jack? Why do you want me promoted to Officer ranks? Don't get me wrong, I am more than pleased you did, I just want to know why?'

'Well, when I was a young cadet I was asked if I thought we would ever go to war. I said I thought we were already at war with Russia; the shooting had not begun but I thought that it was just a matter of time before it did. I feel the same now; and we will need commanders like you if we are going to win.'

'You think we can win a war against Russia?'

'That depends on when and why the shooting starts. There can be a chance for the diplomats to get them off Japanese soil but do not be surprised if that does not work. I feel we will have to be ready to fight when the time comes.'

'You really think there will be fighting?'

'Hai. I do, and just to make you all a little more worried I have been told to expect it.'

'Who could possibly tell you that? No one can possibly know!' the Lieutenant almost shouted his thoughts.

A short silence waited while Jack appeared to give his next words a deep consideration.

'During my last leave break, I received a visit from a very close family friend. Chie Maki and her daughter Fumiko came to my ancestral home for a visit. As I sat with Chie, she said that Fumiko had something very important for me. I called Fumiko to come to sit with us and when she had gotten comfortable, she looked at me.'

Jack paused for a sip of his tea, no one spoke, they simply waited for him to continue.

'Fumiko did not speak for a few minutes and then, after Chie had prompted her a couple of times, she looked at me, straight into my eyes. Her voice lowered as she spoke.'

'What did she say?' Almost everyone jumped at the Lieutenants words.

'Her exact words? "War is coming, many will die. There will be no peace until you force them to surrender." A simple enough statement but one that is full of danger and concern.'

'How old is this Fumiko?' demanded General Onishi.

'She is just turned eight.' Jack answered, slightly perplexed at the thought that her age was somehow a factor. 'Why?' 'How can one so young know such things?'

'Good question, how?' echoed Hiro.

'Her original family name is Okubo. She is known as Fumiko Maki.'

'Do; do you mean she is related to Hitomi Okubo?' The lieutenant joined the conversation suddenly.

'Direct family line.'

'That explains it all.'

'What do you mean Lieutenant?'

'When I was young my grandmother would tell me tales of the old ways. She told stories of the Majo (witches), Majutsu-shi (sorceress) and the Senkensha (seers). She told stories of Ai Okubo and her daughter Hitomi, the formidable one, that is how I know the name; through her stories.'

'Yes, Fumiko is still learning but she shows signs of being just as powerful as her ancestor.'

'Then we should be ready. If grandmother is right, those senkensha are not often wrong.'

'That is one reason I wanted Okimoto to be promoted, we will need officers of his calibre. Unfortunately, we cannot be seen to move onto a "war footing" until it is completely necessary, there can be no other way.'

'So true Jack. We must be seen to be the aggrieved in this. Right now, we have no proof and no reason. We must wait.' Seijin was, for once, philosophical in his reply.

Chapter 14
Other Pastures

'Jack, General Onishi wants you in his office at 1100, Sir.' Jack's assistant announced on the intercom.

'Formal or informal?'

'Informal, his staff say he has a proposal for you.'

'OK. Clear my morning meetings.'

'Hai, sir.' A few minutes later, 'Sir? Your meeting with Colonel Hyashida for tea is cancelled. But he wants you to have lunch with him and General Fujita. Captain Higashi of the Fifth Infantry will also be there.'

'Very well, arigatō.'

The remainder of the morning disappeared as Jack wrestled a deployment problem into submission. At precisely 1100 he knocked on the Generals door.

'Enter!' came the reply from within. 'Jack, sit please.'

Jack sat and waited while Onishi completed the reading and signing of the documents in front of him. Once he was done, he placed them in the tray for his staff to take away.

'How is the Planning Group going?'

'Fine, Sir. I have got them confirming the existing maps and holoprojections of the regularly used training grounds.'

'Anything interesting come up?'

'Actually, yes. We have been using around thirty acres of prime rice growing land that belongs to a "small holdings" farmer. We have not even been paying him for the use.'

'How long have we been doing that?'

'It looks like around twelve years. It was taken as a buffer zone for some exercises, big multi-nationals, and it was never given back.'

'Didn't he complain?'

'Apparently, his letters went unanswered.'

'Do we need to do anything?'

'I feel we should pay him arrears for the time we have occupied it; but I also think the engineers should spend some time to re-establish the rice fields he had there before we took it. I also feel that he should be compensated for the lost productivity.'

'That is going to be expensive? Who is going to be covering the cost?'

'I think that the office of the Defence Minister should cover it, after all it was the minister that ignored the letters in the first place.'

'OK, I will back your judgement in this. Get him paid, quietly, we don't want to be inundated with demands for payment.'

'I will get onto it this afternoon.' A short lull in the conversation led to Jack asking, 'I don't think you asked me here to discuss rice paddies?'

'No, actually I didn't. I have been ordered to send a Combat Group to the new exercises in Hawaii, Trans-Pac they are calling it. I was going to have General Fujita to be in nominal command with yourself as 2 I/C. However, things have changed and you will now be in command; Colonel Hyashida as Armour Commander. Captain Higashi is to be your Infantry Commander and Second Lieutenant Hasegawa is to be his assistant.'

'Hasegawa? Why do I know that name?' Jack pondered aloud.

'He is the one that took command of the landing exercise in Okinawa when the hovercraft exploded. Saved a lot of men that would have otherwise died. Like you, he is a fast thinker.'

'Yes, I remember now; he organised the rescue and triage of the injured. Good man to have.'

'Indeed, his commendation was approved last month, should be awarded soon.'

'Nice to have a good man rewarded. Now, how many will I be taking to Hawaii?'

'The Fifth infantry will supply IFV's and ARV's, a dozen of each and two companies of ground troops. Hyashida will take two companies of Main Battle Tanks. The first will be needed for the defensive part and the second company will arrive for the beginning of the second week. The first week will consist of "semi-virtual" exercises, both defensive and offensive.' Onishi paused while he spread the map on the table. 'For the defensive you will be commanding the garrison here,' he pointed at the defensive H.Q.

'You will have your infantry and armour as well as a Colonel Garcia from Mexico.'

'Garcia? That is another name I know!' Jack stopped and thought for a moment, suddenly he smiled widely, 'He won the Pacific Rim Gunnery Competition last year accuracy of 99.5% if I remember. Spectacular display of Gun Battery control.'

'That's him, get his number from my assistant and get in touch; you will need to be familiar with each other's methods before you go.'

'Now, the second week. You will be commanding the landing into heavily defended positions, same people but you get an American in control of the ships and LCH's (Landing Craft Heavy); same thing goes, get in touch. Any questions?'

'Just one sir, why me?'

'Fujita has had his appointment changed and he is going as a referee; I was asked to send someone that has the ability to give the opposition a difficult time. Yours was the only name to come up.'

'I don't know if I am offended or flattered by that, Sir.'

'Let me guess; offended and flattered in equal measure?'

'I have become transparent,' Jack answered, with a wry smile. 'You know me far too well.'

'There is three months before the exercises begin, you have a lot of work to prepare for this series, it is important that we show the rest what we are capable of. I am relying on you for a good outcome.'

'You can depend on me, Sir.'

Jack stood and saluted; turning as he left, he asked one final question.

'If I can find some gaps, can I create as much havoc as I wish?'

'We are all confident in you finding gaps that no one else has, and we want you to show them all what happens when they are unprepared.'

'Arigatō, Sir.' Jack bowed. 'They will be wondering what has gone wrong when I am done.'

He turned and left, his mind already spinning lists of requirements; and at the very top of the list was maps. Paper, holographic, drone views, even GOOGLE would be useful, especially for the older views that would show changes and improvements in the layout of the training areas. Jack had worked out long ago that maps, and the information buried in them, were the vital lifeblood of a successful campaign.

The restaurant, situated just down the road from the rear access gate to the Planning Centre, was a well-known haunt of Jack and his friends. With good food and equally good Sake it was always going to be well patronised by the higher-ranking officers from nearby.

Jack and his friends sat waiting for their meals in the, unusually quiet, corner of the dining area.

'No one in today, Jack.' Offered Okimoto

'No, very quiet. The owners say that it is getting to be this way most days; it gets better late in the evening. It is good for us; we can talk without having to make ourselves heard over the crowd.'

The meals were delivered, and the owner tried to say he was "Very privileged to have such an esteemed group dine in his humble rooms". He also tried to refuse payment, as a "thank you" for their service. Jack would not hear of it.

'Are we going to have this argument every time we eat here?' he demanded 'We are not here because the food is free, we are here because the food is very good and we prefer to be able sit and talk without being moved on. Your hospitality is worth every Yen we pay. So please do not try to give us the meals; we are grateful that you offer but if we all ate for free you would be out of business very quickly. We will pay and we will be happy to pay full price and we will come back next week as well.'

'Arigatō, Jackson san. As always you are more than welcome to dine here.'

'Arigatō. I hope the unagi (eel) is as good as usual.'

The owner left them to talk; he would put a bottle of sake on the table and not charge them but Jack would note the cost of meals and put the price of the bottle back on the bill when it was paid. It was almost a game between them, the owner would offer and Jack would refuse. The bill would be paid in full with a healthy tip for the staff and it would all start again when they returned.

Much later Jack would give them a plaque of the Army and much later the Imperial Guard and they would be recognised as having provided exemplary service for them. To the casual observer there was a wall which was adorned with the insignia of the many army units in the area, but pride of place would always be the letter of appreciation from Jack.

'Come on Jack, confess. What did General Onishi want?'

'I have no idea what you mean!' He filled his statement with innocence, but no one bought his deception.

'Really?' asked Seijin Fujita. 'Do I have to remind you that I am a General and I actually had breakfast with Motoyuki Onishi this morning?'

'NO, no, no. No need to remind me; even though you just did. If I have to tell you…'

'And you do!'

'We are all going to Hawaii, but we are not going to be surfing at Waimea Bay or Pipeline or Sunset. We are taking part in the Trans-Pac exercises. First as a semi-virtual exercise which will be for us only. And then as a part of a real landing assault with fleet units from several nations.'

'Dare I assume that Seijin is going to be in command?' asked Hiro.

'No, Seijin is getting on a little, he is going to be one of the referees.'

'Getting on! That's harsh, Jack.'

'I know, I actually thought you had gone to sleep while we were talking.'

Seijin spluttered a short laugh into his drink and the others joined in.

'Just remember Jack, I may be older than you but you are yet to make it to my age. Have respect for your elders.'

Another round of laughter was followed by another round of drinks.

'You win, General san.' Jack announced as he raised his glass in a salute to his friend. It was good to be among friends.

'So, who is going, exactly?' was the next question.

'All of us, plus a new officer as my assistant, a Second-Lieutenant Hasegawa. Very promising as an administrator and as a field officer. Hiro, you will be bringing two companies of Main Battle Tanks; The Fifth Infantry will be supplying IFV's and ARV's; pick your very best teams we are going up against the best that the Americans can give us.'

'Okimoto you have been nominated as commander of the infantry companies, three in total, again pick the best we can get, and be ready to join us.'

'What about support? Jack. Are we taking our own?'

'No Hiro, we are getting support from others. The Americans will give a Naval Landing Force, Commanded by a Captain Tyrell Backhouse, top man, one of the best in terms of Fleet Operations. Changed a number of the way's fleets operate, especially in combined force operations. The Land Gun Battery will be from Mexico, commanded by a Colonel Roman Garcia.'

'I have heard of him,' interjected Seijin.

'Yes, won the Pacific Rim International Gun Contest. Really good at his craft. I will be speaking with him tomorrow morning as well as Backhouse. Tell you what, meet at my office and I will get them both on the holo at the same time. It will be good to put faces to names for all of us, we can get an idea of how we can pursue this problem; and when we finish, we can lunch here and discuss the information we have got.'

'We could make this our daily briefing session. Out of the office for an open and private discussion, no interruptions.' Offered Okimoto.

'Good idea; everything is to be put on hold until after this is completed. The confidential work is to be done in my map rooms.' Jack ordered, 'Other discussions as we need them. If you have someone you wish to be included, ensure they can be spared from their usual duties. Remember, gentlemen, we carry the reputation of our ancestors with us, we must not fail them. I will clear everyone to be assigned to my staff until it is done. General Onishi will second the supply division for our support.'

They all raised their glasses and invoked their gods for a favourable outcome. The meeting broke up and they all returned to their respective offices.

'Hiro?' Okimoto called out to Colonel Hyashida.

'Hai.'

'Is it me or did we all just accept that Jack is in overall command? Without even questioning the more senior ranks involved?'

Hiro thought for a moment, 'I think we did; He just seems to know when he is in command, I know he does not care much for rank anyway, and when he makes a decision it seems to be accepted, no one seems to be concerned and they all accept his being in charge, it all works out in the end and I am yet to see him make a major unrecoverable error. Happy to follow him into battle.' 'Me too.' Agreed Okimoto, nodding as he spoke, 'Me too.'

'Colonel Garcia, there is a Colonel Nakagawa from Japan calling?'

'Thank you, please put him on.'

Jack's image suddenly appeared as though he was sitting in the chair opposite Garcia.

Colonel Roman Garcia was a veteran of the Mexican Army. A career man he had already served well over twenty years and was destined to be promoted to General within a year. Not overly tall, he came in around 177cm or 5'9" in the old measurements. Weighing around 95kg he was a solid man with little or no spread around the midriff.

Married for almost twenty years, with two grown children, his perspective was considerably different to Jack, who was still yet to find a suitable life partner.

Jack had already read the appraisal that Intelligence had provided; and from what he read Garcia seemed to be a professional man who would demand the best his men could give. As well as being the ultimate professional soldier he was also a likeable man who enjoyed the company of all that he came into contact with.

As it is with many such men, ones that set a high standard for both their men and themselves, he could be a strict disciplinarian when it was needed.

Destiny had thrown the two together and they would form a strong and lasting relationship from this very first meeting.

'Colonel Nakagawa? Nice to meet you, put a face to the name, so to speak. I have heard many stories about you.'

'Please, call me Jack. I hope the good stories were true and the bad ones were all false.' Jack joked and he hoped the slight levity would be an enhancement to their first meeting.

'If I am to be brutally honest, you are reported as being one of, if not **the** most fearsome field commander seen for many, many years.'

'Let's hope the lower ranks believe that before they meet me, I don't want them to be disappointed by the real me.'

The two laughed together and their bond was sealed. This would be a good friendship.

'Enough of the admiration society, how can I help you?'

'As you know I have been tasked as Ground Forces Commander for the upcoming Trans-Pac exercises.'

'Yes, I was hoping to meet before we go.'

'That is why I am calling. I can get a hyper-jet to your nearest airbase to bring you here for a face-to-face planning meeting. Can you get a weekend off?'

'I would love to; my wife may not be so happy though.'

'So, bring her with you.'

'She may be a little lost in Tokyo on her own.'

'Sorry, I am not explaining myself. I want to hold the meeting in a more relaxed atmosphere than my planning rooms; I was going to suggest having it at my family's home in the far north of Hokkaido, right at the foot of the mountains.'

'That sounds like a "planning meeting" we could both enjoy.'

'So, you're in?' Jack asked hopefully.

'Absolutely, I shall let Grace know.'

'Unfortunately, I will have to leave you now, I need to get Tyrell Backhouse for the same meeting.'

'Backhouse? Can't say I can give you any leverage there. I have heard of him, but I have never met him.'

'That's ok, I will win him over with my sparkling wit and engaging personality.'

'Well, aren't we confident.' Garcia laughed.

'Well, if that doesn't work, I will simply order him to attend, as Commander Red Forces he will have to be there.'

The two shared a laugh and the conversation ended with 'I will call later today to confirm date, flights and scheduling.'

The hologram closed off and Roman Garcia called his assistant to place a call to his wife.

'Hi darling,' she greeted him. 'Is everything ok?'

Roman looked at Grace with the same love that he always had for her. 'I thought you may like to go away for a weekend, before the next round of exercises gets too busy.'

'That would be wonderful, where to?'

'How does a heritage home in the foothills of Hokkaido sound?'

'Don't you mock me Roman Garcia. Are you serious? You know I have always wanted to see Japan.'

'I have just spoken with Jack Nakagawa, the Commander for the next exercise. He has invited us to his home for a "meet and greet" with the other senior officers, he will send a jet for us and Tyrell Backhouse, the American. We will do some planning but I get the idea he has a more relaxing weekend planned.'

'I will get packing straight away, the kids can look after the house for a few days.'

'OK. I will be home in a few hours to help. Love you.'

'Love you too.'

They closed the communications links and Roman began to make his arrangements.

'Captain, there is a Colonel Nakagawa waiting on the hologram for you.'

'I was wondering when he was going to call. Put him on and cancel my other calls until we are done.'

'Aye, aye Sir.'

The hologram burst into life and Tyrell Backhouse got his first view of the man that was going to be commanding the upcoming exercise. He was slightly surprised at how young Jack was for a full Colonel and even though he was surprised he didn't show it.'

'Tyrell Backhouse, here.'

'Jack Nakagawa.'

Jack now had at least met both of the senior ranking men he was going to command in "battle".

Tyrell Backhouse was a surprise, to say the least. He would be a little over six feet tall (184cm to be precise) broad shoulders and no visible fat. The briefing Jack had been given showed him to have been drafted as a professional football player but had forgone that career as he felt he would be better off as a serving member of the military.

Despite his slowly advancing age, the tall African-American was still a competitive basketball player and could be seen playing for the Navy against the other services, not only in basketball but also baseball and ice hockey.

'It is good to meet you face to face, or as close as we can get from opposite sides of the pacific.'

'Same here,' Tyrell answered. 'I have heard a lot of good things about you. They say you like to stir things up, is that right?'

A direct question needed a direct answer.

'I certainly do. I don't see the reasoning behind knowing both sides of a battle problem when exercising, we only get one side if it is real. Everything after that is a reaction, best to get used to being controlled by reactions. Or better still make the enemy react to us.'

'That is the best reasoning I have heard; I will have to push Washington to accept your thinking. What can I do for you?' Tyrell Backhouse was already liking the man opposite him, this man could prove to be a game changer.

'I have a proposal for you,'

'I am listening.'

"Likes to get down to business quickly," Tyrell thought.

'I am hosting a "meet and greet" at my ancestral home; for all the senior people going to Trans-Pac. I would like you to come as well.'

'Sure, where and when?'

'I will send a hyper-jet for you and Roman Garcia.'

'Garcia! He is one great asset, best gunner in the world.'

'Yes, that is why he was assigned. Roman, and Grace his wife, are coming. Bring Daisy too please. It may be just a weekend or it may be a little longer. We will get some planning done but I want the time to be spent getting to know each other more than just planning.'

'Why don't we fly in Thursday and see where it goes? That will mean a Tuesday take-off though.' The American suggested.

'Thursday it is. I will get the Flight Planners to co-ordinate with you and Roman for departure times. I will send them to Mexico first and have them stop off at Hawaii on return.'

'Great, see you Thursday.'

The two closed the call and Jack sent his staff to finalise the arrangements.

'Call Daisy, please.' Tyrell spoke into the intercom and moments later the image of his wife appeared. Holding her beloved Baumblatt violin, he had caught her as she practised. Almost two hundred years old, the violin had been a wedding gift from Tyrell and she played it at almost every recital and concert she had performed in since then.

'Honey, we have been invited for a weekend in Japan, all expenses paid.'

'Who on earth would do that?'

'Fella by the name of Jackson Nakagawa. Red Forces Commander for the Trans-Pac exercises. He wants a meet and greet before we actually get into it. Going to his house in the far north.'

'When are we going?'

'The flight will be Tuesday over the dateline it will land Thursday their time.'

'I had better get moving, need to pack.'

'Don't panic, I will send my staff steward to help. She can prepare for both of us.'

'OK. Bye hon.'

'Bye.'

The hologram call closed and Tyrell called his personal assistant from the outer office.

'Yes Sir?' She queried, wondering what had suddenly happened, did she hear right? Were they really going to Japan?

'Cancel all my calls for the next week. Send my steward to my house to assist

Mrs Backhouse to pack, then go and pack for yourself for a week or so away; Red Forces Commander has ordered us to Japan for a planning meeting.'

'YES, SIR,' she said with a lot of enthusiasm. 'Never been to Tokyo.' She continued as she left the office.

'Petty Officer,' he shouted as she left. Returning to the office she asked 'Sir?'

'No one said we were going to Tokyo; we are in fact going to the far north of Hokkaido. So maybe pack some warm clothes as well.'

'Aye, aye, Sir.' The Petty Officer left, wondering who was so senior that he had a Captain, who was already so senior he was listed for promotion to Admiral before year's end, rushing around and leaving at short notice.

The hyper-jet left Mexico City bound for Hawaii, the improvements in the aviation industry had made a mockery of the 12 hours in the air of the early 2000s, by completing the journey in just 4 hours and fifteen minutes. A thirty-minute turnaround had them bound for Japan in almost record time.

Once in the air, the cabin attendants served drinks and food to the passengers and the crew and the aircraft almost fell silent.

Tyrell moved seats to the spacious "conference" area at the rear and began going through the information bulletin his staff had given him. At this time Roman came and sat with him. With their primary introductions completed as they left Hawaii; the two began to share what they knew about their host.

'I have not met him and the dossier that H.Q. sent me yesterday does not give me much information. What have you got?' Roman was eager to get some information, any information.

'From what my lot gave me, he is a bit of a prodigy. The little they managed to get shows a first-rate ground commander that has been able to turn his mind and skills to any field of warfare.'

'Yes, my bulletin said the same. But no one seems to be willing to tell us what he is like, what sort of commander **is** he?'

'It seems that no one wants us to know. I suppose we will have to wait and see?'

The two settled in and made small talk. Families, children, likes and dislikes; discussions found them as very close in their lives and outlooks. Joined by Grace and Daisy the four sat and chatted until it was time to retake their seats for the landing.

A total flight time of just seven hours showed that the pilots had been careful in the timing of their arrival at the airbase east of Sapporo, landing at the right time for the passengers to fly to Jack's home and arrive just before lunch.

'Please retake your seats for landing,' announced the pilot.

All the passengers and cabin crew sat down and the automatic restraints slid silently across each of them.

It was testament to the skill of the pilots that no one felt the aircraft actually touch down. Quickly hustled into the helicopter they were told their baggage would be delivered a little later in the afternoon.

As they approached their destination, they all looked at the lush green pastures below and as the house came in to view, they were all stunned into silence.

The house they were nearing looked more like a centuries old Japanese castle. Which was just as well, as that is exactly what it was. Originally built in the seventeenth century it was the home of the local Daimyo (roughly the equivalent of a Duke or Earl) it had served as the local seat of power up until the Boshin Wars and the Meiji restoration (1860s).

Immaculately restored, it was so impressive that the visitors were almost certain that they had been brought there in an attempt to impress them. And impressed they were.

They expected to be greeted by a soldier, dressed in at least a day uniform, if not dress uniform. What they got looked like he had stepped out of a movie. Dressed in a pale grey silk kimono their host was almost out of place in the early 2200s.

As the guests emerged from the helicopter, they all waited, almost stunned in awe they were unsure as to what or who was waiting for them.

Jack moved forward and bowed respectfully.

'Welcome to my home, I am Jackson Nakagawa, please call me Jack. Come inside and make yourselves comfortable.'

Jack led them into the house and through the hallways into the "Sun Room".

'Would you all like coffee or tea?'

His guests mumbled a reply which he took as a "yes" and he brought the tray from the small preparation room off to one side.

'I must apologise,' Jack said as soon as he had placed the tray on the table. My family are not here, just me and a couple of staff. My parents are in Tokyo visiting my brothers and my sisters are working in Sapporo.'

'This is your home?' The question came from Grace Garcia, as she looked around the artworks and artefacts around the room.

'It is, it has been in the family for centuries and we try to keep it as authentic as possible.'

'Who is this?' Asked Daisy Backhouse, pointing to a painting of a smiling European man. 'And what is the uniform he is wearing?'

'I assume you are Daisy?'

'Sorry, I should have introduced us. It's just that you have caught us by surprise with the magnificence of your house.'

'Domo arigatō; it is nice of you to say so.'

'I am Tyrell Backhouse; this is my wife Daisy. Roman and Grace Garcia.' Tyrell indicated each one of them in turn.

'Very pleased to meet you all,' replied Jack as he shook hands with them all.

'Did you say Daisy Backhouse?'

'Yes, Sir. I did.'

'THE Daisy Backhouse?' Jack asked as his mind made the final connections.

'You have heard of me?' Daisy asked, somewhat incredulously.

'Heard of you? I have recordings of you performing at The Royal Albert Hall and Madison Square Garden. It is a real privilege to meet you in person.'

'That is so kind of you to say.' Daisy blushed a little as she spoke, it was always a little embarrassing for her when she met a fan.

'You enjoy the classics?' Asked Tyrell.

'Most certainly, I have season tickets for the Tokyo Symphony. Although I have not attended very often this year, for some reason the General seems to think I should be doing Army work for him.'

They all laughed and that little exchange seemed to relax everyone.

'We must have an evening of "culture" while you are all here.'

'I have brought my violin with me. If you wish…?'

'I was hoping you would agree. I have heard you play several times, but a private concert? Now THAT would be wonderful.'

Jack poured drinks and served everyone as they found comfortable seats with a view of the fields, all the way to the foot of the mountains off in the distance.

'I am sorry,' announced Grace, with a huge smile. 'I do not play any instruments.'

'Nor do I,' replied Jack 'but I do appreciate the skill and dedication it takes to rise to the top of such a profession. I would be surprised if anyone in the world plays like Daisy.'

Daisy blushed again.

'Don't blush honey. There are maybe two in the world that are as good as you, and they have both retired.' Tyrell was clearly proud of his wife's achievements.

'Daisy, you asked about the painting, over there?' Jack broke the silence with a direct question.

'I didn't mean to pry.'

'No, no it's not prying. That is the man known as Tokugawa Musashi, the first Shogun of the new era. He was my seven times Great-grandfather.'

'That is Jackson Teague?' Tyrell asked 'He was one impressive man. I was unaware that you were related?'

'His adopted daughter, Sara, married my six times Great-grandfather Isoroku Nakagawa.'

'Can I ask, who owned the house? Jackson or Isoroku?'

'The house was always a part of the Nakagawa clan. It has been our family home for many centuries. My parents do not like living here it is a little large for their tastes, so they allowed me to have it and they live in one of the smaller homes in the grounds. My brothers are in either Yokosuka or Tokyo and my sisters are in Sapporo so when I get the chance I come here. It lets me rest and think.'

'I can understand that.'

At that point there was a polite knock on the door frame.

'Please excuse the intrusion.'

'Emika, come in. What is it?'

'I have heard from Chie Maki. She says that little Fumiko is insistent that she see you as soon as possible.'

'Have them come as soon as possible. Send them tickets and have the car waiting at the airport for them.'

'Hai.' Was all that Emika said before she left.

Jack stood silently looking out of the huge French doors at the mountains in the distance.

Eventually, Tyrell asked, 'Who is Fumiko?'

Without turning around Jack replied, 'In our culture, we have people known as "Senkensha" or in your language "Seers". Fumiko is the latest in a long line of very powerful Senkensha. If she insists on speaking with me it is because she has a message for me. We will not know until she has arrived.'

Jack turned, the look on his face suddenly turned from concern to a smiling host. 'Now, let's find you some rooms. There must be some somewhere in this place.'

No one knew what to make of the statement, was he serious or forcing the humour. Grace broke the moment when she giggled 'I hope so, you don't have enough couches for everyone.'

Jack joined in with the humour and everyone relaxed, just a little more.

The afternoon was spent with everyone getting to know each other, dinner passed with more chat and the evening was submerged in sake and smiles.

Jack didn't let them go too late announcing that he was ready for bed and leaving his guests to speak without him.

'I thought we would be preparing for the exercise, checking maps and engagement rules?' Roman was at least a little confused as to the beginning of their first meeting.

'Same here,' replied Tyrell. 'But then again he did say it was a meet and greet and that is exactly what we have been given.'

The following morning found Jack kneeling on the decking facing east. He was so completely silent and still that neither Roman or Tyrell dared disturb him. He remained that way for a few minutes, eventually the sounds of Grace and Daisy could be heard at the other end of the house.

'Are you two going to stand and watch me all day? Or will one of you make the coffee?'

His two guests jumped at the sound of his words.

'Sorry, we did not want to disturb you.'

'Arigatō for your kindness, I was just finishing my morning prayers and my meditation.' He stood up and turned around. 'How did you sleep? Were the beds good enough? Are there any amenities you require?'

The two simply stood and watched him. Eventually, Tyrell answered his questions.

'Well, thank you; very comfortable and no, we have everything; in that order.'

'Good. Roman?'

'Same here, Jack.'

'I was worried that the beds would not be very good, they do not get used much and I was unsure of the condition of the mattresses.'

At that point Emika entered the room closely followed by Grace and Daisy.

'Coffee and tea for all.' Emika announced as she placed the tray on the table. 'I will prepare breakfast when Chie and Fumiko arrive, they should be here within the next thirty minutes.' Emika turned and left, not waiting for a reply as she had announced her intentions and there was no more to say.

Jack poured the tea and coffee for his guests and they all sat in the comfortable chairs as they waited. More small talk was beginning to surface when Jack asked, 'So, did I make your approval?'

No one spoke immediately. Eventually, after a short awkward silence, Tyrell asked 'What do you mean?'

'I deliberately left you two to talk last night. I just wanted to know if I have "passed muster" as it were?' Jack smiled as he asked.

'You would be the most enigmatic person either of us have ever met.' Tyrell continued, hoping not to offend too deeply. 'Roman and I have both seen a lot of service and neither of us have ever met a commander like you. You have requested our presence here for a meeting before the Trans-Pac exercises and we have been treated as though we are friends here to pass the time of day.

In the past, if I have been asked to attend a meeting for planning, then that is what we do. If I am to be honest, we are just a little confused.'

'I am sorry, if I confused you. I wanted to have a meet and greet to get to know you. We are going to be living in each other's pockets for the next three months, I thought it would be best if we actually liked each other.' Jack continued smiling. 'Of course, if you want a planning meeting, only, we can get to it.'

'Don't listen to him, Jack. Despite his own words he was restless last night, always is if he is unsure of what is happening. More so if he is suffering from jet-lag.'

'Thank you, Daisy. I apologise, I didn't think of jet-lag. I don't suffer from it myself and as such I do not think about it. As today is Friday I propose we have a full day of simply resting and chatting. If any of you have a question ask. I am never offended by an honest question.'

At that point Emika entered the room. 'The driver has called; Chie and Fumiko are only ten minutes away, breakfast in fifteen minutes. Dare I assume you are all happy with eggs, sausage and bacon?'

A chorus of "yes, thank you" was the reply and Emika left to complete the preparations. Just a few minutes later a rush of black pony tail flew past everyone closely followed by 'WALK Fumiko.' Which the owner of the pony tail promptly ignored.

'JAAACK.' The young girl screamed as she landed in his lap. Arms wrapped around his neck as though she was frightened to let him go.

'And Konichiwa to you too, my personal typhoon.'

His guests were stunned into silence at the close personal greetings.

'Fumiko, get down and behave, Jack has guests.'

'Mama, I already knew that.'

'You know way too much.' Jack had managed to get untangled form the girl and greeted his long-time friend.

'Chie, we do not get to see enough of you.'

'Try coming home a little more often and maybe you would.'

'Ouch, I will try.'

'No, you won't,' answered Fumiko.

'And why is that?' he asked.

'Well…'

'After breakfast, Fumiko. You agreed.'

'Hai, I apologise Mama.'

They all moved into the dining room where a group of steaming platters were waiting for them.

'Please help yourselves, eat what you wish.'

They all filled their plates and sat for a hearty breakfast.

As they chatted Grace asked, 'Jack, I don't want to appear to be nosy, but is there a Mrs Nakagawa?'

'No, never found one that I wanted to be with.'

'I thought you would have a line-up of eligible women wanting to be your wife?'

'There is, every time I go into town or to an evening event there are any number that want to be with me. The problem is that most of them either want the name, the prestige that goes with the name or the position that my family occupies in our society or, sadly, the family fortune. It is difficult to find one that wants me for who I am, not for what I have.'

'I see.' Was all Grace replied.

Suddenly from the far end of the table came a small voice, quite deep in tone and sounding insistent 'There will be one for you. She will emerge at the most unusual time. You will not be looking for her, but she will be there. You will bond almost instantly and the two of you will be inseparable. You will conquer all that stands against you, side by side; the world will never be the same again for any of us.'

Grace stared at little Fumiko, the hair on the back of her neck beginning to bristle. Automatically she crossed herself and silently she prayed to the saints.

'What do you mean?' Roman eventually asked. 'How can you possibly know this?'

Fumiko turned and looked at the guests, one by one she looked; and one by one they all became slightly unnerved by the darkened eyes and deeper voice than the little girl had when she had entered the room.

'Please, do not fear. Fumiko is simply telling what she knows.' Chie announced; and just as she did the girl appeared to emerge from her "trance".

'I am sorry, Mama. I could not stop myself.' She announced with a tear in her eye. 'I am sorry, Jack. I was supposed to wait.'

'No need to apologise, Fumiko. You did what you had to.'

With that, she again climbed onto Jack's lap and snuggled into his arms.

'Was it a good one?' she asked in a very small voice, still unsure of what she had done, what she still needed to do.

'It was very good. Apparently, I am going to get married.'

'Good, but that was only part of what you need to know,' her reply was as enigmatic as it could get.

'Can the rest wait while we finish breakfast? Or do you have to say it now?'

'It can wait, I think.'

Breakfast was finished almost in complete silence and they all moved out to the rear deck to enjoy some conversation.

'Tell me, Daisy, do you ride?'

'Horses or motorbikes?' Daisy replied.

'Either.' Jack answered with a laugh, it was the reply they needed to break the ice that had formed around their conversation.

'I grew up on a farm so horses are a yes. Never cared much for motorbikes though.'

'Grace?'

'I have ridden one or twice, not very well though.'

'Roman, Tyrell and I will be doing some planning this afternoon. Would you like to ride while we are busy?'

'Sure, sounds like a great idea.' Daisy agreed.

'Fumiko would you go and ask Gin to come in, arigatō.'

Fumiko left and disappeared to find the senior groom.

When they returned Jack asked 'Gin, this afternoon please saddle Mai for Grace and Takarra for Daisy. Take Danuja and show our friends around the estate, just after lunch will be fine.'

'Hai,' replied the groom and he disappeared around the side of the house.

'They are two of the quietest horses we have, excellent for those who are inexperienced or out of touch.'

'Thank you, Jack, it will be good to get back in the saddle.' Daisy thanked him. 'Now stop evading the issue, tell us all about Fumiko!'

'As I said yesterday. Fumiko comes from a long line of senkensha. Sometimes the line will give us one of exceptional capabilities. Fumiko is one of those.'

'No one knows how she does it, but if she says something will happen then it will. No question, it will happen.' Chie added.

'She said there is more?' asked Grace. 'Do we have to wait? Or can she give a reading at will?'

'I don't know, ask her.'

'Fumiko,' began Grace, 'you said you had more for Jack, are you ready now? Or do you have to wait?'

Fumiko moved in front of Jack and put her hand out to gently touch his forehead. No one moved or spoke, they all stared intently at the girl waiting for something to happen.

Suddenly she withdrew her hand and she looked straight into Jack's eyes, her voice deepened, and her eyes appeared to glaze over; 'Before you meet her, she will go through a great ordeal. You will be there but unable to assist,' her voice got a little deeper as she continued. 'There are wars coming, some will be near, the others will be far. No one else can win these wars but you. You will be victorious in the first one; but you will need HIM,' she pointed at Tyrell. 'And HIM.' She pointed at Roman, 'and many others to gain victory in the wars that will follow.' At that point she sat down and slept at her mother's knee.

Again, Grace crossed herself and prayed, this time Roman joined her.

'Is she ok?' asked Daisy.

'Yes, she will be fine, the fore-telling's take a lot of energy and she needs to rest now.'

'Jack,' Tyrell asked, with a tinge of both hope and fear in his voice, 'I don't suppose she is referring to the exercise, is she?'

'No, her fore telling's are for the real world. Jack, you will need to be wary when the time comes,' replied Chie.

'How accurate is she?' asked Daisy.

'Accurate enough for no one to argue with her,' replied Jack. 'Her family are renowned and now I will have to work extra hard to be ready for whatever the world has to throw at us.'

No one had heard the door open and, to the surprise of all, Reina Maki, Fumiko's Great grandmother walked into the room. Every head turned to look at the sudden arrival. Jack immediately stood up and bowed.

'Reina, Konichiwa. What brings you so far from Kyoto?'

'Konichiwa, Jack; some time ago I had a warning that little Fumiko would be giving you a fore telling. I needed to be here for her.'

Reina turned and looked at Chie. 'You need sugar, your energy level is very low, and so is hers. Sweet tea for both, now!'

No one moved at first and before Emika could enter the room, Jack had already prepared the very sweet green tea that Reina has prescribed. Fumiko woke and, with tears in her eyes, she said 'I am sorry, I know it was not good, please do not be angry.'

'I am not angry; how could I be? You have given me a great deal to think about. I now know that I will have to be at my very best in the events that are coming, second best will not be good enough. Domo Arigatō, Fumiko, you have done me a great service.' Jack bowed deeply to the little girl and she giggled a little before returning the bow.

Mother and daughter sipped their tea, at first and then they simply drained the cup before asking for another, quickly supplied by Jack, they finished that in quick time as well.

'Jack, I don't want to appear to be a complete luddite in this,' it was Tyrell that broke the silence, 'Does Fumiko mean that we are going to war? As in bullets and such?'

'She does,' replied Reina, her own eyes darkening as she spoke. 'You will all be safe, but you will need to be open to new innovations to succeed.'

'OK, this here is a gittin' spooky. I'fn I says so myself.' Daisy had suddenly reverted to her former "farm girl" self, for just a few moments. 'Tyrell, you needs to do a pile a work to git through this, by the sounds of it.'

'Well said, Daisy.' Chie butted in, 'Be assured, they will all be safe.'

'Actually, may I ask another question? A personal one?' It was Daisy, but her voice and mannerisms had completely reverted to the urbane and refined lady that she was.

'Fire away, that is why we are here; to find out about each other.'

'I noticed that there is a Christian cross in your entrance; Are you Christian or do you follow another religion? Please feel free to ignore the question if it is too personal.'

'Congratulations, you are the first with the courage to actually ask. Yes, we are Christian in our beliefs; We are not church goers though, we prefer to keep our beliefs private. We have a private chapel here in the grounds if any of you wish to use it for prayer or just as a small sanctuary.'

'This is embarrassing; how do you reconcile the predictions with your beliefs?'

'I prefer to think of it this way. If God has a message for me, then I do not care how he gets it across. If that means using Fumiko or any others to do the hard work, then so be it. It is the message that is important, not the messenger. No, that did not come out right; The message is more important than how it is delivered.'

'Jack, you don't seem surprised by all this?' Roman eventually asked after, what was almost, an uncomfortable silence.

'Actually, I am as surprised as all of you. The content of Fumiko's message is deeply troubling for me. However, my family and hers have been intertwined for centuries; we are accustomed to hearing their words and we are ready when the time comes for action. This will allow me to assemble plans long before there is a need for them.'

'Jack, I believe that Chie and Fumiko should be close to you for the future, they may need to say more as events unravel.'

'Thank you, Reina. I will make the arrangements.'

Chapter 15
Planning

The remainder of the morning was spent with everyone getting to know each other. Following a light lunch, Daisy and Grace left for their ride and Jack's groom took them all around the vast estate.

'Daisy, I have to say it makes me uncomfortable listening to all this talk of predictions and such. It goes against everything I was taught as a child.'

'I fully understand how you feel.' The two were silent for a couple of minutes, 'Grace can I speak freely, without upsetting you, I mean?'

'Sure, go ahead.'

'If you are uneasy with the way Jack lives, just let it pass. We will not be here forever.'

'Does it not bother you, using the supernatural to achieve his ends?'

'I don't think he is using anything; he has not asked for anything at all. He has been given a message freely and he is using that as a basis for preparation. Did you notice that there is a shortage of detail? The message seems to be more of a warning that things are not going to be perfect in the future.'

'I suppose you are right; It just seems to be a little difficult for me to understand. I have always placed my faith in the Lord and he has not given me any direct contact; and here is Jack who seems to have him on speed dial.' Daisy laughed and a short while later Grace joined in as she became aware of just how funny her words were.

'Roman, Tyrell come in here please.' Jack ushered his new friends into his study. 'We can plot and plan our lives away in here without any interruption.'

Jack pressed a button on the desk and the curtains closed. Another button and the planning holoprojector burst into life with a 3D rendering of the island that was to be used for the exercise.

A third button and the planning desk lit up with a translucent map of the island for them to work on.

'Funny enough I still prefer to use "real" maps for my planning. The 3D is useful for getting defensive positions and transit routes right though.'

'3D is best for me; I can plot trajectory arc's and fall of shot easier if I can see where the high points are,' replied Roman.

'Good point, I am not a gunner so I need you to bring that to my attention. Tyrell?'

'Maps and charts are all we require for war at sea, but if you want to include anti-submarine and air war then we need 3D rendering as well, not for planning but for combat.'

'Again, I didn't think of those scenarios. I think we have everything we need for the project ahead, if you think of something we don't have call out, I will get it delivered.'

'Now, the first part of the exercise for us is a defensive scenario. It will be a semi-virtual assault and we will be defending.'

'What do you mean "semi-virtual"?'

'We will have a "live fire" exercise. Even the Americans object if we actually kill people, so we will be firing live and the opposition will be virtual. They have already planned their half and they completed it last week. It will be projected onto our screens and we will have to "fight" them in real time. The odd part is that we will need to get our fire-control data; course, speed, range and so on, in real time.'

'The second part is to be more traditional, except we will be the assault team, and both us and the defenders will be firing blanks. The First half will be for Roman and me to work out; for the second half, I have come up with a battle plan that will require all of us.'

'Roman, who are your best gunners?'

'For the 127mm (5 inch) field guns the 123rd, 165th and 187th are the best. For the 155s (6 inch) the 86th Heavy Bombardment along with the 93rd Battery Support group are best.'

'What were their accuracy scores last time out?'

'All were 99.5%.'

'I still think that is incredible, out of 200 shells only one was not perfectly placed. That is a level of accuracy and reliability we can exploit.'

'Now this is what I have so far…'

Jack began to lay out his battle plan for the first part of the exercise; a little over thirty minutes later he was finished.

'Well, what do you think?'

A slightly awkward silence fell on the room; eventually Tyrell spoke out.

'Just how long have you had the "Rules for Engagement"?'

'Well, you arrived Thursday so they would have been delivered on Wednesday afternoon.'

'You put this all together in just a day?' Roman was stunned.

'Well, actually it was about four hours before I went to bed Wednesday night. Is it OK?'

His two guests simply stood looking at each other, neither willing to be the first to speak. Eventually, Tyrell broke the silence.

'I have seen worse plans emerge from a month of deliberations from a room full of highly placed and very senior officers and they were all pleased with what they had made.'

Roman continued, 'Can I get you to show my planners how you did that? It is so simple and yet, if we look deeper, it will make the entire exercise proposal redundant. The enemy will simply not know how to defeat us.'

'I will take that as approval then?' Jack's face creased with a broad smile, he knew what he had was good but, to have two highly credentialled warriors give it the "rubber stamp" of approval was a sign that he was on the right track with them, they would be able to work together, each with trust in the others.

'Time for coffee; then we can set to work with the second phase plan.' Jack turned and left the room to get the refreshments.

'How the hell did he do that? Complete a battle plan so easily?'

'I don't know, but I get the feeling that if we let him work, he will have the second phase done before dinner.'

The two smiled at the thought that they could relax and concentrate on getting the assigned troops ready for the exercise and not concern themselves with the planning.

Jack returned with the tray and put it down on the coffee table. The three sat around the table and Roman asked, 'Is the second phase ready? Or will we have to wait for tomorrow for that?'

Jack spluttered into his coffee, spilling a little as he did so. 'Am I really that transparent?'

'Not sure, I feel that if you have this done,' he waved his arm at the planning table, 'it makes sense that you will have at least the genesis of a plan ready for phase 2.'

Jack looked out of the window and mused to himself "I really must work harder at disguising my works." And that made both the others laugh into their drinks as well.

'If you really must know, I think that this is how we can do it…'

For the next hour Jack outlined the plan he had, eventually he asked for any input and his visitors could not provide any changes.

'You know you are very close to being "out of bounds" for the approaches, don't you?'

'Close, yes; but not actually out. It will depend on the tide and a couple of other variables, that is where you come in, Tyrell. I will need your people to be absolutely spot on for that part.'

'What will happen if you are out?'

'Nothing that has not happened before. People will yell and shout, complain loudly and bemoan their losses. But the fact is that if this was a war then the boundaries they set would not exist, and that is how I justify the small errors; we are training for war, errors happen and if they are going to cry "foul" if it does not go their way then there is no real point in holding the exercise at all. Is there?'

'Now you have put it that way, no. I will be beside you when the enquiry begins.' Again, Jack spluttered into his coffee. Wiping his chin, he said 'A good friend of mine puts it this way. After I hold the final planning meeting, he will tell his fellow officers "And this is where we get our dress uniforms ready for the inquest." And every time there has been an inquest, I have been exonerated.'

'Then we shall be certain to have our dress uniforms ready.' Added Roman.

The three moved out to the rear deck and watched as Grace and Daisy rode into view. Dismounting at the stables, off to one side of the house and giving the horses to the grooms, the two eventually made their way to the deck and sat with the others. Seemingly from nowhere, Emika appeared with drinks for them.

'How was your ride?' Jack asked no one in particular.

'It was great, you have a beautiful piece of land here.' Daisy seemed to stop short in her answer.

Jack waited for a few seconds and said 'You have a question don't you.'

'Well, it is a bit personal.'

'Ask away I don't mind answering.'

'This place must cost a small fortune to run, how can you afford it?'

Jack gave a smile and replied, 'My family has been very wise in its investments for many generations. In general terms, I am considered to be very wealthy. I enjoy a number of pursuits, which include the horses and fast cars, and I can afford to indulge myself; so, I do. Sadly, it is that wealth that I must protect when the "prospective ladies" call. Which is one reason I am fussy as to who I keep contact with.'

His guests kept silent as his words sank in.

'What sort of cars?' Tyrell eventually asked.

'My favourite, for daily use, is a current model Bentley Continental, with the hydrogen fuel cell engine. For exhibitions I have a two-hundred-year-old Aston Martin Vanquish, heavily modified to run on a biofuel of course, but boy does it move. I am lucky that one of my grooms is an ex racing driver and he keeps the cars in top condition.'

'Wow, impressive,' replied Roman. 'I am still driving my old Chevy.'

'If I can ask another question?' continued Tyrell.

'Sure.'

'In your study, the armour. One set is severely damaged, why?'

'That was the dress armour that Jackson Teague was wearing when he fought off the rioters in London way, way back. His daughter Sara inherited it, eventually, and it has been here ever since.'

'You have a lot of weapons too?'

'Mostly my family, they are heirlooms now. The museum in Tokyo has requested some for display; and if they have a special exhibition, I will send a couple. But there are some that just do not leave here. The ones beside the battered armour are Jacksons, Emperor, Queen, Vengeance and Vendetta are all on one side. Repulse and Vindictive are on the other.'

'The medals in his picture, I see there are many for bravery, what is the story there?'

Jack stood up and moved to one of his bookshelves. Reaching into one of the drawers at the bottom he retrieved four books. He opened each one, dedicated and signed them with a personal message and then presented them to his friends.

'This book, "By Emperors Choice" was written by Takusan no Korin. It is almost a documentary of his life, enjoy reading it, it explains everything that happened to him.'

'Are these re-prints?'

'No, original editions from the first run.'

'Jack, we can't accept these, they must be worth a fortune?' Daisy chided him.

'Actually, they only cost around two thousand Yen or twenty dollars. So, they are quite cheap.'

'But they are almost two hundred years old!' Daisy continued her protest 'They must be worth thousands now.'

'Maybe, but I still have quite a few of them and I would rather have you read them than leave them in the drawer. Besides, they have your names in them now so I can't take them back.'

'Thank you so much, you are very generous.' They chorused.

'And you are all welcome.'

Chapter 16
An Enjoyable Weekend

Sunrise Saturday morning found Jack in his usual place, on the deck facing east and meditating. Lost in his peace he thought he heard a noise, but in the silence that followed he dismissed it as one of the dogs moving around as it woke in the early morning.

'Get to your feet!' the voice suddenly shouted from behind him. Jack didn't move, even though he was now fully aware of his surroundings and every sound in the house.

'I said; "Get to your feet!" Or have you gone deaf as you get older?'

'No, I have not gone deaf, I just didn't realise that my sensei was so rude as to not say, at the very least, "Konichiwa" when he arrives in my home. I suppose you also want breakfast, Akio?'

Jack stood slowly and turned around, the smile was spreading across his face as he saw his long-time friend and his house guests waiting for him.

'How did you sneak in here? The dogs are obviously not doing their duty.'

'Do not blame the dogs, they greeted me as the friend I am. As for your house guests, I begged them to wait until I had surprised you.'

'I see,' Jack mused, 'betrayed by everyone in the house.'

'Actually, Jack, Fumiko told us you were getting a visitor so we made certain to be awake when he arrived,' Tyrell interjected.

'Betrayed by a young girl in my own home? What is the world coming to?'

The two finally greeted each other with the bow and handshake that was normal for them; neither being totally comfortable with the "man hug" that had become so prevalent as a greeting.

'To what do I owe the visit?'

'When Emika told me that you had friends coming I booked a flight. It has been far too long since we had time to just sit and pass the time of day.'

'You think that after disturbing my meditation, you were just going to sit!' Jack feigned indignation. 'Get your armour, SENSEI! We will train first; then if you have earned your meal, we will eat.'

'AS YOU WISH!' Akio replied, just the greeting he wanted, the two had not trained together for over a year and he relished the opportunity to engage in full battle training. 'I assume you wish for "full battle" today?'

'Certainly. Tyrell, will you get Emika to provide some tea or coffee while we let off some steam?'

Tyrell disappeared into the house while the others made themselves comfortable. Emika emerged with a tray of streaming drinks and was closely followed by Jack and Akio who were both dressed in full training armour; two weapons in one hand and kabuto (Helmet) and mempo (face mask) in the other.

The two moved across the deck and out onto the grassy area at the rear of the house, in full view of the visitors. Almost from nowhere Chie and Fumiko emerged from the house and approached them. Jack and Akio had both finished dressing as the two approached, Jack held out his weapons to Fumiko, she grasped the sayas (scabbards) and Jack withdrew the weapons, Chie doing the same for his opponent, then the two retreated to the relative safety of the deck.

'Are they real swords?' asked Grace, almost fearful that one or both would end up severely wounded.

'No, my lady they are just practice weapons, they do not have the sharp edge of a combat katana.'

The two looked at each other and, as tradition dictates, bowed and then took a fighting stance. Slowly, they circled and suddenly Akio struck first, or more correctly he tried to strike first. Jack simply leaned to one side and the downward blow missed his arm, but he was off balance and the return stroke slammed into his side accompanied by a grunt as the blow struck home.

From that moment the two were trading blows, until Akio slipped just slightly and as his body leaned forward Jack drove his knee deep into his friend's ribs closely followed by a blow to each side of the kabuto from his weapons. Akio staggered backwards but the hits kept raining down on him. Eventually, he dropped his weapons and sank to his knees.

'Enough, you win!' he shouted at Jack. Jack took three paces backwards and bowed; kneeling he placed both his weapons on his left side with the tsuka pointing towards his opponent.

This is the traditional method of saying "I am not a threat to you", the placement put the weapons in the least favourable position to be retrieved and used in a hurry. Placing them on the right and with the tsuka towards his own hand indicates he is ready pick up and continue fighting.

Jack stood up and helped his friend to his feet, both removed the kabuto and mempo and they bowed again to acknowledge their opponent's skills.

As they walked back to the deck Akio said 'You still lift your rear leg as you strike, you must anchor your feet a little better.'

'So says the defeated one!' Jack began laughing and Akio joined in.

'Just a moment. Tyrell would you lend a hand here?' As Tyrell approached Jack removed his kote (arm protection) and as his hand came into view, they could all see the distorted shape of his left fingers.

'Hold the arm still against my side.' Tyrell held Jack in a "bear hug" and Akio grasped the offending finger; with a pull and twist it popped back into place and Chie appeared at his side with the medical kit to strap the wayward finger and give him a small dose of pain relief.

They slowly divested themselves of the rest of their armour, with a little assistance from Chie and Fumiko. Finally, they settled into a chair each and they began to field the questions.

'How did you evade my first strike, Jack?' Akio asked before anyone else could jump in.

'I saw you shift your feet, as you leaned forward to strike you were slightly off balance, it would not matter if the blow had struck but as it missed your following hit was weak and without good placement.'

'Wait a minute!' Akio began. 'I am the Sensei, not you.'

'And so, you are.' Jack grinned widely, knowing he had, for the first time ever bested his good friend. Next time, it was certain to be a different outcome.

Fumiko came out of the house with cold drinks and coffee for the two, almost slipping on the polished floor she was having a little difficulty with the large tray.

'Fumiko, I said I would take it out.' Emika gently scolded the little girl.

'If I am to fulfil my future duties I will need to practice now.' Fumiko said with a determination that no one argued with.

'How often do you two do this? Fight each other?' Asked Roman

'Around once a month, if we get time. Unfortunately, there are many that want to take some of my time every day so I do not get to practice as much as I would like.'

'Is it always this hard?' was Daisy's first question.

'No, sometimes we actually make each other work for a win,' replied Akio.

The questions came and went while the two recovered. Eventually, they went to shower and they all sat down for breakfast.

Once they had all eaten and the table had been cleared Jack asked 'Fumiko, what did you mean when you said you would need to practice to be able to fulfil your future duties?'

She looked firstly at Jack, then her mother and then back to Jack.

Looking down at the table, unable to hold the stares of all present, she said, 'When I have finished with school I will be working as your personal assistant. I need to begin to learn how to do this now, as there is much to know and only a little time to learn how to do it.'

'Did you not think to ask if I wanted you to perform such a role?'

'No, it is going to happen and that is all I know.'

Grace silently and surreptitiously crossed herself, still unable to come to grips with the predictions.

'I hope you are not upset with me.'

Jack looked at her for an uncomfortable minute or so. Eventually, he nodded and said 'Well, if you are going to work for me then we will need to get this properly setup,' Fumiko's face broke into a very wide smile, 'but not until after you have finished school with good enough results.'

'That's the easy part, I am always passing with good grades.'

Jack looked at Chie. 'She does, always in the top three of her classes.' Chie replied to the unasked question.

Again, Jack looked at Fumiko, and again he waited for an uncomfortable time to pass. 'It is settled then, I suppose no amount of argument will change this. On completion of your schooling you can work for me.'

'Arigatō JACK!' she squealed, and jumped up to hug him.

'Congratulations, Jack. You have just gained a personal assistant.' Tyrell announced, 'it is funny though, I don't remember anyone abolishing the child labour laws?'

'We tend to do things our own way, here in the far north,' before Jack could continue his phone began to ring. 'Excuse me, I need to take this,' he said as he made his way inside the door. The one side of the conversation seemed to be a quiet, respectful conversation; spoken entirely in Japanese. 'Arigatō, ashita o ai shimashou.' (Thank you, I will see you tomorrow) Even though they felt that Jack had completed his discussion; Jack returned to the deck and handing the phone to Daisy said, 'It's for you.'

For just a few moments she sat almost unable to move; finally, she held out her hand and took the phone from Jack. Tyrell and the others looked at him as though they had a hundred questions waiting to be asked. Jack just held his forefinger to his lips indicating them to be silent; the huge grin on his face showed that some fun was about to be had.

For the beginning of the conversation Daisy said nothing and no more than a few words could be heard from the, as yet, unidentified caller.

Eventually, the voice fell silent and Daisy replied. 'I am sorry, I will not take the place of "Concertmaster" your first violin has worked far too hard for me to walk in and take their place. I will either be a guest soloist or I will play as a part of the string section.'

Apparently, the voice tried, again, to convince her.

'No, you have my terms. You may take them or leave them; it is your choice!'

A few short words and the argument had been decided. 'I think Mendelssohn's Violin Concerto in E minor op64 would be suitable. Can you have your orchestra ready for that?'

A few more words were heard, but not understood. 'Thank you, we will meet tomorrow morning and have a final rehearsal tomorrow afternoon. Sayonara.' Daisy ended the call and handed the phone back to Jack.

'That was not very fair,' she protested, 'putting me on the spot like that. Can you believe he wanted me to push his Concertmaster out of place? Does he not know what it takes to get to that position?'

'I understand you put him back on the right path?' replied Jack.

'That is a polite way of saying it.'

Daisy was grinning widely as Tyrell asked. 'Just what is going on?'

'I am playing as a guest soloist tomorrow night at the Concert Hall in Sapporo; dare I assume you have transport organised, Jack?'

'Helicopter will pick us all up at 9:30.'

'Will someone please explain to the rest of us?'

'I have arranged for the family private box at the Sapporo Concert Centre to be prepared for us for tomorrows concert by the Tokyo Philharmonic Orchestra. Daisy will be performing as a guest soloist. So, we will all need to have our best outfits on.'

'Just as well I had my staff pack my dress uniform and an evening dress for Grace, isn't it?'

'Yes. Tyrell you have everything?' asked Jack.

'Always packed for emergencies,' he replied.

'Good.'

'Since I now have to entertain several thousand strangers, I suppose I should practice, at least a little.'

Daisy left the group and soon the sounds of a beautifully played violin could be heard throughout the house.

'I think I will make a start on your gift,' announced Grace.

'Use the sun room, Fumiko show Grace where the reading room is, please.'

'Hai.' Jack's newest "employee" led Grace to a brightly lit room, decorated with a number of antique paintings on the walls and furnished with very comfortable chairs. Perfect for a reading room.

As Grace settled in and opened her book Fumiko asked 'Would you like tea or coffee or perhaps a cold drink, my lady?'

'Thank you, Fumiko, coffee would be nice.' Fumiko left for the kitchen and Grace began reading. Just a few minutes later Fumiko delivered the coffee and left her to read in peace.

The men sat on the deck swapping stories, as soldiers do and they were enjoying an afternoon of good camaraderie, and equally good Japanese whisky.

After around half-an-hour Fumiko returned to the sunroom and retrieved the empty cup. Once she had returned it to the kitchen, she went back to the sunroom, almost shaking with nerves as she approached the doorway.

Somehow, she managed to knock, all but silently, on the door frame. Grace looked up from the book and invited Fumiko in.

'What is wrong, Fumiko?' Grace had noticed the small girl would not lift her head and look at her.

'May I speak, privately with you?'

Grace was now fearful that the girl had done something wrong or some unseen cultural barrier had been breached. 'Of course.' She closed her book and placed it on the table beside her chair. 'What is it?' she asked.

Fumiko could not bring herself to raise her head and look Grace in the eyes. She approached the chair and stopped around two metres from it. Kneeling down she sat back on her heels, holding her hands in front of her.

'My lady, I must apologise. I have not been respectful of your beliefs. I have been showing my capabilities without thought for those who do not believe as we do. I shall try to be less obvious in my ways. Again, I apologise.'

'You do not need to apologise to me. I have not had much to do with those that hold your capabilities. I am unsure how to respond. In history, your ways would have been punished, simply because you were not understood. I will try to be more understanding, even though it goes against everything I have ever been taught.'

Fumiko bowed lowly from her kneeling position. 'Arigatō, thank you, my lady.' She regained her feet and as she left the room she turned. 'Congratulations, my lady.'

'What do you mean "congratulations"? Why should I be congratulated?'

'You will have a grandson. He will be very strong and a source of much pride and pleasure to your family.'

'WHAT? HOW?'

'Perhaps you should call your son.'

Grace dug frantically through her bag and found her phone. Shaking with both anticipation and fear she dialled her son.

'Sergio, do you have news for me?'

'I am not sure of what you mean?' he replied.

'It is simple, do you have news that we should know?'

After a few moments of uncomfortable silence, he responded, 'Si, mother. Angelina is expecting, she is just ten weeks along; but how do you know?'

'I pray, I listen to God's word. He listens to the faithful, you know.' Then Grace moved the phone from her mouth. 'ROMAN!' she shouted, and all three rushed into the room.

'What is wrong?' Roman asked, clearly thinking there was bad news on the other end of the phone.

'Here, speak with your son. He has something to say.'

Roman took the phone with an overpowering sense of apprehension. Grace looked at Fumiko and smiled widely, holding her finger across her lips. The two sharing a common secret.

'Sergio? What have you done?'

Sergio and Roman spoke with the rapidity that only the Latin languages can convey. Eventually, Roman ended the call and handed the phone back to Grace who said goodbye.

The room had fallen silent as Grace moved across to Fumiko, grabbing her in a huge embrace she kissed the now embarrassed girl on each cheek.

'Now I believe you have a miracle for a mind. Can you believe it; I am going to be a grand-mother. We had given up hope, Angelina had a lot of trouble and the doctors said she would never carry a child.'

Fumiko smiled, slightly embarrassed. As she began to reply her eyes darkened and her voice lowered, 'The pregnancy will be trouble free and he will be a strong baby.'

Again, Grace hugged her, this time joined by Roman. She had gained a convert in the belief of her uncanny abilities.

Chie hugged her daughter and whispered into her ear, 'Well done, you have made a believer of a doubter. She will be your friend for all time.'

Just then Daisy entered the room.

'What is all the noise about? I am trying to master Mendelssohn in a day.'

'Daisy, I am sorry to have interrupted you.' Grace began, 'but this little angel has given us the most wonderful news.' Again, she put her arms around Fumiko, holding her close. 'God's angel told me that we will be grandparents and our son has just confirmed it.'

The entire group descended into hugs and kisses. The difficulties were explained and, her practice forgotten, Daisy joined them for the small celebration.

Jack left the room and beckoned Fumiko to go with him. He led her into the kitchen where the two prepared some snacks. As they worked Jack began to speak.

'I do not know how you did that, but I must tell you; getting a devout Catholic like Grace to believe and accept you is a huge step forward. If you keep going like this you will be a very important part of my household. I am very proud of you.'

She bowed her head and smiled widely. 'Domo arigatō, Jack san.'

At that point Chie joined them. 'I am very proud of you, to be able to stand and not only prove your capabilities but also to explain them is a huge step; the family will be impressed with your sudden improvement.'

'Come let us get the foods into the reading room.' The three left the kitchen, Fumiko holding a tray of confectionery, Chie with savoury items and Jack with the drinks, he didn't get to leave the kitchen before Emika took the tray from him saying, 'you are the head of the house, you should not be doing the staff works.'

Jack took the pots of coffee and tea from the tray. 'But as the head of the house it is up to me to host the guests and as such it is my duty to serve the drinks; just because we are not in the chashitsu outside,' he said referring to the traditional "chashitsu" or tea house in the ornate gardens which lead away from one side of the house, 'does not mean that I am permitted to forego my duty.'

'As usual, you are right. I will carry and you can pour.'

'Agreed, now let's get in there before they eat all the foods.'

As they sat and shared the news, the conversation swung back and forth and slowly the subjects changed. Eventually, Daisy got up and began to make her way back to the room she had been using to rehearse.

'Jack,' she called. 'Can I ask you to call your friend, the conductor, and let him know I will be performing "Allegro Molto Appassionato" "Andante" and "Allegro non-Troppo Molto Vivace". Each one takes around ten to fifteen minutes, depending on how he wants me to play, tell him he can place them wherever he wants in the schedule.'

'Certainly. Is there anything else you require?'

'No, I just need to re-familiarise myself with the pieces.'

'Consider it done.'

Daisy left, and Roman asked 'I thought it was the Conductor that set the program for a concert?'

'Daisy is the guest artiste, given her standing in the professional rankings she gets to decide,' replied Tyrell.

The following morning a helicopter arrived and the entourage left for the concert centre in Sapporo.

The only ones not overwhelmed by the greeting were Tyrell, who had seen it all before, and Jack, a seasoned concert goer. The rest were almost agog at the considerable bowing and grovelling that were on display.

Finally, once they were inside and out of public view, Grace said 'WOW. I had no idea just how much of a reception you would get?'

'Daisy is right at the top of her profession; it is a big plus for the orchestra to have her play as a guest soloist.'

'Thank you, darling. Now I must practice or it is not going to be very good.'

Daisy left with the conductor and the other dignitaries. Jack led the way back outside to a waiting bus which gave them the VIP tour of the city. Returning to the concert centre they collected Daisy and left for an early, light, meal before dressing for the evening. A limousine arrived at six thirty to take Daisy back to the venue for final tuning and preparations. At seven thirty a second limousine arrived and took the rest.

The concert itself was, in Jack's words, "A wonderful experience, marvellous to behold the skills of the very best violinist in the world."

The rest could only agree, even though it was their first experience of a classical concert. They were still talking excitedly when they arrived at the private dinner Jack had arranged for after the concert.

'How do you feel, Daisy? First concert in a year or so?' Asked Jack.

'I didn't know you were such a fan. Or have you been secretly stalking me?'

'Call me an enthusiast; I made certain you were in practice before I asked.'

'Thank you for that, it could have been embarrassing if I wasn't. Did any of you pick the missed note in "Andante"?'

No one admitted to hearing the error, although both Tyrell and Jack would privately say they did, much later.

'I noted that the conductor did not pick it either, perhaps he will need to brush up on the piece at a later date.' Daisy mused to no one in particular.

The following morning, they all made their way back to Jack's home where they relaxed, they were due to leave for home on the Monday and they all wanted to simply sit and chat, just be friends before leaving.

'Jack, the big mare in the stable. What is her name?'

'The Friesian?'

'Yes, her.'

'That is "Maiko" she is one of my favourites. We are preparing her to return to being a part of the Imperial Breeding Program. A stallion called "Osaka" will arrive in time for her to come into "season" this year and we will try to get a foal next year.'

'You mean we have been here and this is the first we hear of you being a horse breeder?'

'Well, to be fair, I am not in charge of the breeding program. I am simply providing the location and staff to look after her.'

'So, you are providing horses for the Emperor?' Tyrell joined in the conversation.

'In a manner of speaking. The Imperial Palace needs a number of horses for the carriages and the Imperial Guard. I was approached by the Breeding Captain to see if I could provide a place for the mare to birth and raise a new foal. Couldn't say no, and this year will be the third.'

'All of them are in the guard?'

'No, the second born, "Ame" which means rain, was not quite tall enough. He didn't reach the height that would look right in either a team on a carriage or in the line of the guard. So, he was sold to an enthusiast and he made his name in equestrian circles.'

'I hope you got your money back for him?' asked Roman.

'Well, not so much.'

'You sold him at a loss?' Roman was astounded. 'I don't know much about horses but I do know that Friesians are expensive.'

'Yes, they are. But if he is no use to us, either as a breeder or as a worker, he will just eat his weight in feed every few months. So, we, as in the other breeders and carers, sell the not so perfect units to someone that will be able to give them a good, useful, life.'

The last few hours were given over to cementing the friendships that they had formed during the previous days. Chie and Fumiko left to return to their home, in Tokyo, with the command that Fumiko was to ensure that she completed her schooling at the top of her classes. Jack didn't tell them that they would be moving into his private quarters as house guests, he felt that it should be a surprise for the two.

As the other guests climbed into the helicopter to take them back to Tokyo, Jack said, 'We will arrange for a further planning session in two weeks, sorry ladies, this one will be for our planning groups and we will be head down for a full four days. However, I would be privileged if you and your families will come back here for Christmas, if possible. Don't say yes or no yet, make certain they are available first. If not then, maybe next year.'

'Thanks, Jack. That is very kind of you. See you in two weeks,' replied Roman as he shook Jack by the hand and Grace gave him a hug and kiss on the cheek.

'I am certain we can make Christmas; the kids are off doing their thing but if we say that they can have the holiday here they will be packing their bags early. Thank you so much Jack, playing in that concert was a wonderful experience. I had no idea that I would get such a huge ovation, I did not know that the classics were so popular in Japan.'

Tyrell and Daisy both said their goodbyes and suddenly Jack was left alone watching the helicopter disappear into the sky.

'They are all lovely people, Jack.' Observed Emika 'I will have to make sure I have all that I need for a Christmas feast, especially when I tell your family it is going to be so big.'

'Yes, they are all in for a free feed when it is on offer.'

Chapter 17
More Planning

The next two weeks saw Chie and Fumiko settle in as Jack's houseguests, Fumiko was enrolled in her new school, luckily it was not too far away, and Jack began to push his battle plans together.

'Do not wait up for me, I will be working late again tonight.'

'Again, when do you sleep?' Chie demanded. 'You did not stop all weekend and you were at it again this morning, I heard you.'

'I apologise, I will try to make less noise.'

'Less noise, nothing. You need to sleep and eat properly. You do not set a good example for Fumiko. She is already imitating your work habits; I do not want her doing the same with her eating.'

Jack was almost dumbfounded; was he really such a strong influence on young Fumiko?

'I am very sorry; I will try to be a better example to her. I didn't understand the power of my example to her.'

'I do not ask you to change everything you do, just the things that impact on a young girl as she looks up to the one that she idolises.'

'Really?' Jack asked in genuine surprise. 'She idolises me?'

'Not only that but she knows more about you than she will say openly. She knows much more about what is coming for you. Be wary, she spoke in her sleep the other night; she is worried that your wounds will be too severe.'

'Wounds?'

'Yes, wounds. She says you will be shot in the war that is coming soon. And you will receive other wounds in the wars that are yet to be revealed.'

'I see,' Jack looked out of the window, Chie's words had a much more profound effect than she had wanted. Now he had another reason to be careful in the future. 'Can you ask her, please, to see me when she gets in?'

'Hai.'

When she came in from school Fumiko knocked on Jack's door. 'You wanted to see me?'

'Hai, come in and close the door.' She closed the door gently and sat waiting as Jack poured tea for them and placed a plate of biscuits in front of her.

'You know that mother disapproves of me eating chocolate biscuits before dinner.'

'Don't worry, I won't tell her.'

"You don't have to!" shouted a disembodied voice from outside the room.

'Dammit, sometimes I forget how difficult it is to keep secrets around you two.' Jack and Fumiko both laughed and the voice outside joined them. 'So, come in and join us then!' Jack called out, and Chie entered the room carrying her cup with her.

'I have heard you are worried about me? In the future, I mean?'

Fumiko bowed her head as a small tear made its way down her cheek.

'I am frightened sometimes; the visions are so real. I worry for you.' The tear was joined by another.

'Can I ask what you see deep into the future, if anything?'

'The best I can manage is that you and your family will have a long life together, that is all.'

'Then there is nothing to worry about, is there? If I am to have a wife and family, and live to an old age, then whatever injuries or wounds I get will not kill me, will they?'

'I suppose not.' She sniffed.

'I will make a pact with you. I will not worry about my injuries and you will do the same. Is that a deal?'

She looked into his eyes, not blinking or moving for a few moments 'Deal, just remember that you will be hurt and you will survive, just don't blame me for not telling you again.'

'Good. We are agreed. Now tell me how you went with your examinations.'

'I passed.'

'That's it?'

'She was top of her class in all subjects. She had been nominated for High Achiever classes but the school counsellor felt she would be better served by jumping a year and moving on from there.'

'Well done. You don't think that the others will give you a hard time?'

Her voice lowered as she replied, 'Once they know who I am and what I can find out about them, they will all want to be my friend. The bullies will stay away because I can see what will be. Most will be happy to be friends, the others will not want to anger me.' She shook her head as she "came back" as she called her recovery. 'That was a surprise, I didn't expect that.'

The three spent the next half hour or so chatting. Suddenly Jack stood up.

'Let's go out for dinner, there is a ryokan (guest house) near here that has just opened a new dining room, we can eat there.'

The three dressed and left for their dinner.

'That was marvellous.' Chie said as they left the room. 'I have not had such a good curry for a long time.'

The others agreed and they all walked the two kilometres or so back home. Tired and ready for bed Chie and Fumiko said their goodnights and left Jack siting in the lounge.

Not yet ready for sleep, Jack began to push his battle plans around his mind. For the next two hours he simply sat and played the "chess game" that was military exercises, inside his head.

'What am I missing?' he asked himself, "why can I not let this be? It is a good plan, so what is wrong."

Finally, as he slept in his chair, his dreams led him to the words of the Chinese General Sun Tzu *"When you surround an army, leave an outlet free. Do not press a desperate foe too hard."* Suddenly awake he rechecked the combat hologram and within ten minutes had the answer to his problem.

Stretching he made his way to bed and fell into a deep, dreamless sleep. When he finally woke it was to the sound of Chie telling the caller that he was not ready for work as he had been planning all night. 'I will ask him to call you when he wakes, not before.' Were her last words, before ending the call.

'Konichiwa, Chie.'

'Konichiwa, Jack.' She replied.

'Who was calling?'

'Someone by the name of "Onishi" I think he said.'

'You told off General Onishi? I suppose I had better find an excuse.'

'Do not bother, he will be fine with or without explanation.'

'Never the less, he is still my Superior Officer, I must show him respect.'

'It does not matter. Sit, eat your breakfast, or should that be lunch?' Chie smiled at her little joke and Jack sat as he had been told.

Eventually, he made his way to the Planning Directorate, forgoing his usual path he went directly to General Onishi's office, where he spoke with the Generals secretary.

'The General called for me earlier.'

'I will see if he is free.' A quick check, and Jack was permitted to enter the room. A gentle knock on the door was answered by "enter" from within.

'You called for me sir?'

'Yes, come, in sit.' Pressing the intercom button, he continued, 'Coffee for the Colonel and tea for me!'

'Hai,' replied the disembodied voice from outside and just seconds later an administrative aide entered with the drinks. Serving the General first the aide left and closed the door behind him.

Jack simply sat and waited for Motoyuki to begin.

'Ugh, I don't know what they think is used to make tea, but I can tell you that is not it.'

'I am afraid I must agree, sir, the coffee is no better. May I?' Jack gestured to the intercom and Motoyuki nodded.

Pressing the "talk" button he said, 'Will you get my Admin Officer to have refreshments delivered from my office, please?'

Again, the voice replied 'Hai.'

Jack and Motoyuki made small talk until just five minutes later the door opened; the intense aroma of freshly ground and brewed coffee instantly filled the room.

'Dammit, Jack. Now I want coffee as well.'

'It is just as well that he brought a jug then.' Jack smiled and made a mental note to thank his staff for their forethought.

Once the door was, again, closed Jack asked.

'Now, Sir, you wanted to see me?'

'Cut the Sir; the door is closed.' Motoyuki replied, smiling widely as he thought "Jack's method of using given names certainly makes the simple tasks easier."

'As you wish, Motoyuki.' Jack replied and the two visibly relaxed.

'How is it that you were late today?'

'I was up most of the night putting the finishing touches to my first battle plan for the Trans-Pac exercises. It will do no good asking my house guest to wake me, she will do it but only when she is ready.'

'Who is she?'

'Chie Maki.'

'Not another one of the "Maki Senkensha", surely?'

'She is that.'

'Just as well I did not upset her then.'

'To be honest, I have never seen her upset at anyone; and even if she were upset, she would not let it show.'

'Not surprising, Tell me more about your battle plan.'

For the next thirty minutes Jack gave a detailed rundown on the plan he had devised and included the sticking point that had kept him up most of the night.

'You put it all together, without assistance?'

'Not quite, I had help from the Cartography Group and from Tyrell Backhouse and Roman Garcia. There were a few details I had to "mine deep" to get right.'

'Have they all been told?'

'I sent word and a precis of the plan this morning, actually I have a hologram meeting in an hour to get their responses. I will be hosting them next week for the detailed workings.'

'Very good. Would I be able to attend the briefings?'

'Certainly, sir; sorry Motoyuki.'

'On a separate subject I have some good news.'

Jack looked up, directly into his friend's eyes. Quickly he thought "Chie did not mention good news?"

'As you know,' Motoyuki continued, 'I have been appointed to the position of Chief of the Northern Army. It is expected to be a short-term promotion as I have been notified that I will be the Chief of the Army by the middle of next year.'

'That is wonderful news, congratulations.' Jack stood up, bowed and shook hands, then he sat down again.

'Thank you, but that is not all. The Chief of Defence Forces has asked me to nominate my successor as Head of Planning and I have nominated you.'

Jack spluttered into his coffee cup; 'Me! But I am only a Colonel, that position is for a General!'

'Yes. I know that.' Motoyuki replied.

'How will that work? I will not have the rank to order the Army commanders to comply.'

'You know, for one so smart you can be quite slow off the mark sometimes,' he sat back and let his words sink in for a few moments. Suddenly Jack's eyes lit up.

'You mean?'

'Yes, Congratulations General Nakagawa.' Motoyuki Onishi stood and saluted him, 'I must say this is the fastest promotion anyone has ever seen. Officially it will be promulgated on June 1, that is the minimum time for you to be in rank before promotion.'

'That is next Monday!'

'Yes, just in time for you to give your briefing to the other commanders. This will ruffle a few feathers, the ones that complain will be asked to provide a plan for Trans-Pac, any that are better than yours will be pushed up the promotion ladder. Between you and me, I do not expect any will be able to complete the planning in less than two months. Do not let this be known before the CDF (Chief of Defence Forces) has had time to get it out.'

'Wow, promoted so soon. It will be hard not to say something, especially with Chie and Fumiko living with me.'

'Just think about what you just said, Jack.'

Jack repeated his words in his head and began laughing.

'Yes, I see what you mean. They will already know, won't they.'

'I believe so. Just don't let it out around here.'

'No, I won't.'

'Hologram connected, Sir.' Jack's admin assistant was nothing if not efficient.

'Colonel Garcia and Captain Backhouse are waiting.'

'Arigatō, please ensure we are not disturbed.'

'Hai.' The door closed gently behind him as the assistant left the room.

'Tyrell, Roman, I want you to meet General Motoyuki Onishi, Commander Planning and Logistics Group.'

'Afternoon Sir,'

'Buenos tardes, Sir.'

'Konichiwa, to you both. Jack has shown me his plan and I asked to be here, firstly for your initial thoughts and again next week for your detailed briefings.'

'Welcome to the world of chaos that Jack's mind lives in.' Answered Tyrell.

'Yes, it is a little like that, isn't it?'

Both Roman and Tyrell laughed and, almost unexpectedly, so did Motoyuki and Jack.

'You think this is bad? You should try living in this mind, it is really crowded and busy in here.' Jack's response had them all laughing and agreeing with the concept. The small jokes had cemented the close friendships for all.

For the next hour Jack explained each and every detail he had managed to cover. The deployment and firing positions of the Main Battle Tanks, as well as the IFV's and Light Armour, positioning of the Infantry Companies, rules of engagement, even the use of deception. It was all covered.

'That's it for now,' he finally stopped the briefing. 'Next week I will send a flight to collect you and your senior commanders as well as the core of your planning groups. Roman, I would like you to leave on Sunday, early; you will collect Tyrell on the way and arrive here what should be late Monday or early Tuesday, I have not worked out the time differences yet. I will meet you and get you settled then we will begin the last planning objectives on Tuesday. I have allowed four days to complete the final planning. That will bring us up to Friday and, if all goes well, we can spend the weekend at my home. Any questions?'

'Are we permitted to bring the wives?' Tyrell was under strict instructions to see if they could all get together again.

'I actually do not see you surviving too well if you don't. Motoyuki, you and Yumi are also welcome.'

'Arigatō, Jack. We will be pleased to come. If you have enough room.'

'ROOM!' Roman had almost shouted, have you seen his place?'

'No, I have not. Is it large enough?'

'OH, have you got a surprise coming.'

The three began to laugh and that simply left the General wondering what was so amusing.

Chapter 18
Even More Planning

The hyper-jet left Pearl Harbour/Hickham Air Base and was quickly at its 80,000 feet cruising altitude. Drinks and food were served and the conversations, generally speaking, circled around who was Jack and what was he like; unlike Roman and Tyrell, most of the staff had not heard of Jack and they had no concept of how he worked.

The aircraft landed at Tokyo and a fleet of cars took the planning teams to the Directorate to leave their briefing notes in a secure office, before going to the Officers Accommodation to rest and eat before beginning the planning briefings the next morning.

Come in, everyone. Please remove your jackets and hand them to the stewards, they will hang them up along with your caps.

Jackets were duly removed and handed over. Each officer found their assigned seats and waited for the briefing to begin.

'Everyone settled?' Jack asked, no one dissented. 'First let's get the important stuff out of the way. Coffee or tea?' Most of those present simply sat and stared in disbelief. The usual beginning for a briefing was, get your own drinks and take a seat; the most senior officer would give the briefing after being announced by his 2I/C.

'Coffee for me,' called Tyrell.

'And me.' Added Roman 'And don't be afraid to hand out some of those biscuits you keep hidden.'

Jack smiled and nodded to the staff who scurried away returning soon after with trays of biscuits and cups and saucers for the drinks.

'Tea for me.' Motoyuki called out and one by one the others gave their preferences.

Once all were served and a few hushed conversations had begun, Jack let them speak for a few minutes.

'You must give my staff the supplier of these biscuits.' Tyrell demanded, 'They are too good, far better than our cookies.'

'Sure, I may get a "fee" for introducing new customers,' replied Jack, much to the surprise and amusement of all present. Jack watched to see how many were relaxing and he was pleased to see that the initial tension had dissipated. Calling for silence Jack began.

'I am Jackson Nakagawa; I have been nominated as the Red Forces Commander for Trans-Pac. I am also the Senior Planning Officer for our part in the exercise. Would you please give your names and position as it pertains to this exercise. Please stick with first names, I do not permit rank in my planning meetings, it stifles energy and free speaking, and things get missed if we do not speak freely.'

Again, most of those present were almost confused. This was not how planning briefings were conducted. For a few moments no one spoke.

'I am Motoyuki, Commander of the Northern Army.'

'Tyrell, Commanding Fleet Operations.'

'Roman, Artillery.'

'Greg, air defence.' And so on, each spoke in turn, introducing themselves and their position.

The last was a small, Japanese woman.

'I am Mai, I am secretary to Gener—sorry, Motoyuki. I am to take the minutes of the meetings.'

'Ah,' said Jack. 'The most important of us all.' She blushed and looked down somewhat embarrassed. 'Without you, none of us will remember what we have said.'

Again, she blushed and began to take notes and operate the recording equipment.

'We are one missing, who is to operate the holo-projector?' No immediate response came from the group.

'Sorry, Jack.' Motoyuki eventually replied. I believe he was taken ill this morning.

'I can do that.' Mai announced, 'I will set the audio recorder to auto and the other secretaries can print it later.'

'Good, arigatō. Let's begin.'

'The exercise is set in two phases. The first is a semi-virtual live fire exercise. I will be commanding the defence of the subject base firstly utilising Romans Heavy Bombardment group and the field artillery. Later the Main Battle Tanks, IFV's and the ground troops will be used. Roman, your deployments and requirements?'

'Thank you, Jack.' Roman began to detail his layout and demands and he was quickly followed by the other commanders. This, initial briefing, was to give all present the overall plan and the expected outcomes.

It went for almost two hours before there were no more details to be revealed. 'Any questions so far.' No one spoke immediately. 'Good, take a break, rest rooms down the hall. Resume in 30.'

Most of the planners stood and left, more to stretch their legs than anything else, leaving only Roman and Motoyuki with Jack.

'How did that go? Seemed ok.'

'To be honest, I think they are somewhat overwhelmed with the detail that has already been completed.'

'I got that feeling too, Jack. Several times someone was about to ask a question and you answered it in the next sentence.' Roman added.

At that moment Tyrell re-entered the room. 'You have them in your palm, Jack. They are all enthusiastic about what has already been done and they can't wait to get to the exercise itself.'

'Good. I was hoping they would be pleased.'

The groups slowly returned and almost all of them poured an extra coffee or tea before sitting down and continuing their conversations.

'OK! are we all ready?' Jack asked; not waiting for an answer he continued. 'Next subject; are there any special requirements not yet covered?'

Roman raised his hand. 'Do we have accurate ranging data for the firing area?'

'It is available, but in the spirit of the exercise, we will need to provide our own ranging data, just as we would if we were at war. How accurate do you need to be?'

'That depends, how accurate do you want my gunners to be? We can guess the range and adjust for fall-of-shot, that may result in us following the enemy as they approach. Or, if we are accurate, we will put the barrage down on their heads.'

'Right where it should be.' Jack interjected.

'Exactly.'

'How accurate do you want it?'

'Within a metre, if possible. Remember the Heavy Bombardment Group will be firing blind, we will not see our splashes.'

Jack sat for a moment, seeming to stare into his cup. No one spoke.

Pushing the intercom button Jack spoke 'Get Captain Higashi on the line.'

Moments later a voice asked 'Konichiwa, Jack. How can I help?'

'Konichiwa Okimoto, I need to speak with our "drone racer" and the head of cartography, can you get them to the planning division after lunch?'

'Certainly; you do realise the head of cartography does not like your briefings, he always seems to end up trying to redraw all the survey maps.' Okimoto was almost laughing as he spoke.

'That's ok, bring him in chains if you wish.'

The room was almost silent; the notable exceptions were Roman, Tyrell and Motoyuki who were joining in with the amusement.

'Tell him I will send him to map Antarctica if he does not want to come!' Motoyuki added, and the rest of the room were unsure if he was joking or not.

'Bring yourself here as well, Okimoto, as you are the Infantry Commander; I need your input as well.'

'Are you sure? There are several here almost fighting to get that position.'

'That's good, I like it when they are eager. I will include your company in the order of battle.' Jack pointed at Mai and she made special note of the requirement. 'See you after lunch.'

'Hai.'

The call was terminated, and a small voice asked, 'Jack, what company is that?'

'Fifth Infantry, Fast Response Company 3.'

'Hai, they are added as the lead infantry group.'

'Very good. Keep that up and I will steal you from Northern Headquarters for my planning group.'

'I think that would be a good thing.' Mai replied, almost oblivious to the double meaning of her words, or the looks of the rest of those present.

As Motoyuki looked, almost sideways, at Jack; he wondered "How does he get people on side so easily? I think it must be his personality, everyone just wants to be a part of what he is doing. I wish I could bottle it, whatever it is."

The remainder of the morning was a simple question and answer for the items that had been outlined. Breaking for lunch they all left for the Officers Mess for lunch. All except Jack, as usual he would spend the time going through his notes looking for "the deliberate mistake" as he called it.

Finding none, so far, he sat in the easy chair in his office and began to relax.

'Not coming for lunch?' Roman asked.

'No, I will let them talk amongst themselves for now. If I am there, they will simply wait for me to control the conversation.'

'True. I will eat and speak with the Battery Commanders and the Gun Fire Controllers and get their thoughts.'

'Good idea, I am trying to get the best method of ranging into my mind. We will have a chat after lunch.'

Roman left Jack to his deliberations and sat with his people.

Lunch was over soon enough, and the planners began to drift back to the conference room. Just as the last made their way to their seats there was a knock at the door. Before anyone else could speak Motoyuki said 'Enter! Sorry Jack, your conference.'

'Not a problem, arigatō. Okimoto! Konichiwa. Jack stood and bowed to his friend and the gesture was immediately returned. Come in, sit. Gentlemen this is Captain Okimoto Higashi, He is the C.O. of 3 Company 5th Infantry, and this is "Drones", that is all anyone calls him.'

'Why "Drones"?' asked Tyrell.

'He is the World Champion in Quad Copter Speed Racing,' replied Okimoto, 'He can fly into spaces so small that no one can follow his craft; as such he can gather visual information faster than anyone else, as long as the target is less than two hundred kilometres away.'

Drones looked down as he felt a little embarrassed by the accolade.

'Really, how do you do it?'

'Arigatō, Okimoto, but now I am the Former World Champion. Now I have access to military grade equipment the sports controlling body feel I have an unfair advantage over the other competitors.'

Everyone in the room was suddenly attentive, this was a field that they were not familiar with.

'What information can you gather with your drone?'

Drones looked at Jack and Motoyuki, for approval. Jack held up his hand, thumb and forefinger a small distance apart, Motoyuki nodded his assent.

'Depending on the hardware package I can photograph documents through a window; if the building is vacant and a window large enough is open, I can enter and retrieve items as well. I can gauge distance down to 1 metre or less, and the improvements in the release mechanisms has now made a reality of the dropping of three or four grenades or an IED from around 3 metres to fifty metres in altitude at around 100 kilometres an hour.'

'How many drones can you put up? I mean one drone is not going to make much difference?'

'No, one won't. The exact numbers are classified but let's say I can provide an attack force or a defensive shield.'

'OK, enough of the secrets for now.' Jack continued. 'We need to be able to range the enemy position in real time, at sea. What can you do?'

'I can either use GPS systems to give the distance from the controller, that is a satellite, or I can send a drone carrying a reflective unit that can give laser sights a more accurate figure; that has the difficulty of being a "line of sight" measurement, far more accurate but you need a clear view.'

'Won't the enemy "kill" the drone first?' asked Tyrell.

'No, we will usually be moving too fast.'

'What of the EM guns used to defend against these?'

'I am not at liberty to say, Sir.'

Tyrell looked at Jack and Motoyuki in turn and both shook their heads in a gesture for him not to ask any more questions. This just left Tyrell in a quandary; should he report this to his superiors or respect the confidence he had been privy to.

'I am putting on my "Generals Hat" for a moment. Announced Motoyuki. 'The information you have just heard is highly secret, your development and procurement people have been made aware of the advances we have achieved, in general terms, but we are still the owners of the information and the hardware details. As such any disclosure of this information will be against the agreements that have been put in place by your respective governments.'

'This exercise will be the first that has used this system and the proof or otherwise will be the deciding factor as to whether it will become a regular tool in the military hardware inventory. AM I CLEAR?'

Everyone present nodded and all recalled the disclaimer and disclosure document they had signed when they had first arrived for the briefings.

'Good, I apologise for the overt threat, but this is important.'

'If I may?' asked Roman, Jack nodded. 'We would like to test both methods. It may be that one is more suitable for certain conditions than the other.'

'Good idea, we will talk when we close for the day.' Jack replied, he could already see that Roman was thinking along the same lines; whatever is best for the situation and that would take some testing.

The afternoon slowly wound to a close, the various planning teams leaving for their accommodations and some private discussions.

Jack and his team sat with "Drones" and Roman after all had left.

'Mai, when you get the notes drawn up, please delete any discussions on the drone capability.

'Already done, Jack.'

'Arigatō; Motoyuki I was serious when I said I wanted her to be a part of my team.'

'And I was equally serious when I said you were going to be the Head of Planning. You get to choose your staff.'

'Again, arigatō. Drones I will get you attached as remote systems advisor; your assistant will be Mai.' Jack had a cunning smile on his face when he said it. Mai and Drones instantly blushed, CAUGHT!

'Yes, I thought so.'

'How did you know?'

'You should never play poker, Drones. The moment you walked into the room your eyes went directly to Mai and hers to you. It was obvious then and there.'

'And I thought I was covering up so well.'

'You were,' replied Tyrell. 'I had no idea.'

'How will you get my ranging right?' Asked Roman, getting the subject back on track.

'The drone system can use several methods, the least efficient is using the GPS system, only good down to a metre or so. As it is prone to external information it is also at risk of being "hacked" so data may be corrupt or at least inaccurate. I can attach a laser system but the range of such a small unit is low, not much use for Heavy Bombardment. I can use a reflector and the laser can be a part of the Aiming Company, this is the most accurate at less than ten centimetres.'

Mai stepped forward and handed Motoyuki a note, after he read it, he announced. 'We can be a little more open with Roman, the government has signed a contract for the sharing of sighting and associated technologies with Mexico,' he held up the note, 'here it is.'

'Can you now disclose a little more about the defences your drones have?'

'The safest system we have is a pre-programmed unit that does not require me to fly it. The course, speed and altitude requirements are set before launch and the drone is sent away. It will be automatic from that point, it is capable of maintaining its position from any designated item such as a building or even a moving ship if necessary. The drone guns will not interfere with the control system as it is independent and there is no external control, no signals to be interfered with.'

'That is great, when can we test?' Roman was clearly enthusiastic.

'I think we can test at a private facility that I know about,' announced Jack.

'This wouldn't be your place would it?' Roman was ahead of Jack for once.

'Now that you mention it, yes. We can test this Friday. I think the briefings will be over by Thursday afternoon. Is that sufficient time to get a ranging unit here?'

'Just a moment.' Roman called his Battery Commander.

"I don't care what time it is there. Get the range controllers and their equipment for the 127s and 165s onto a plane and have them land at Sapporo Airbase on Friday at 8am." The reply was not heard by the others.

'They will be at Sapporo early Friday.'

'Good, this will be interesting.' Said Jack; Motoyuki and Drones both nodded in agreement.

The rest of the week was head down in planning and by Thursday afternoon everyone was getting tired and tense. Everyone except Jack and his team, they all knew the demands, and were accustomed to how Jack pushed for a result, it wasn't that they didn't get tired or testy, they did; it was just that with Jack doing more than any of them they got no sympathy when it came to complaints about being worked too hard.

Friday came around and all were farewelled at the airbase just outside Tokyo. The staffers slept the entire trip home.

'Now, let's collect the ladies and go for a break.' Tyrell was looking forward to spending time at Jack's home again.

The ladies were all waiting at Motoyuki's home. As Tyrell and the others walked in, they were met with a chorus of "let's go, we are tired of playing the tourist without you." They all climbed into the staff cars that were waiting and headed off to the helicopter landing pads.

Daisy and Grace spent most of the trip back to the base chatting like the old friends they had quickly become. They all had a short wait before boarding the waiting helicopter and they eventually made their way towards Jack's home.

Looking out of the window Motoyuki was watching the scenery pass and suddenly he nudged Yumi.

'Look, Yumi, it is one of the Meiji castles,' he announced as they watched. Grace and Daisy just smiled, Roman and Tyrell simply kept quiet.

The helicopter slowly circled and began to hover as it began to lose altitude prior to landing.

'Is that a "re-enactment actor", look, in the kimono.' She pointed at the figure emerging from the building, as she indicated the man to her husband.

By now everyone was staring, fascinated, at the man. Suddenly the helicopter jolted as they landed, and the engines began to shut down. Once the rotors had stopped the boarding stairs were lowered and, being the most senior officer on board, General Onishi and Yumi were first to leave.

'Konichiwa, welcome.' Jack bowed before his guests; he had managed to arrive almost twenty minutes before them and had changed into his preferred clothing.

Both were stunned; 'Jack is this your home?'

'Hai.'

'I said you were in for a surprise.' Added Roman.

'That you did, and I must admit, I am surprised,' replied Motoyuki. 'I had no idea it would be so grand.'

'How did you manage to get a castle, Jack.' Yumi asked directly; she never was one to skirt around the subject.

'The fortunes of the family have managed to ride out the financial woes of the last three hundred or so years. The investments that were made have performed well enough to make us sufficiently wealthy, all of us, to be able to live how we wish. This has been the family home for a few centuries, I am the current occupier. My parents are the official owners, but they prefer to live in a smaller home, here in the grounds.'

Jack and his guests all made their way inside where Chie and Fumiko were waiting to serve them drinks and confections, all created under the watchful eye of Emika.

'Come to the rear, it is warm enough to be able to sit and watch the view. We can do the tour later; it is time to relax.'

'I still don't understand, Jack,' Motoyuki began, 'surely this is a National Heritage Home, how do you get to live in it?'

'Because it has been in the family for so long, and we have had a continual presence here, they assist with the upkeep as it is a part of the National Heritage; and we do our part to keep it in its original conditional. I can assure you, the craftsmen that work here have great difficulty in repairing when a timber is in need of replacement, don't forget they did not use nails or screws when it was built, and they still do not use them now; "a dying art" is how my lead tradesman puts it.'

'It is testament to his skill that the house is in such good condition.'

'Yes, and he trains apprentices in the historic skills to ensure they are going to be capable in the future.'

The conversations continued to circle around the home and the artefacts they had witnessed already. Around two hours after they had arrived, just after lunch, the Range Controllers and their equipment arrived.

'Jack, where can they leave their equipment?' Roman asked.

'Put it in the old hay shed, just to the east of the stables. It will be dry there. We will begin the tests tomorrow. Drones, sit with the Range Controllers and get an idea what you can do together, Mai, keep notes on the discussions and working plans, we will need to be able to replicate the results in the future, no doubt.'

'Hai,' Drones and Mai left to check the equipment and become familiar with it and its users.

'Drones, do you think Jack sent us so we could be together?'

'Certainly, he knows we will not do a lot of work today and when we finish, we can be alone for a while.'

'Is Drones as good as you say, Jack?' Asked Yumi.

'I have watched him pilot recon drones of all sizes; from those a little smaller than a strike drone, right down to the little toy ones. He is fast and accurate. Have a look at this, his winning flight at his last championship.'

The holoprojector came to life and they were treated to the view from the drone as it hurtled through the complex maze of buildings, stairwells, vehicle parking lots, outdoor manoeuvring and technical courses. Each of the watchers would jump and duck as the view came perilously close to the obstacles of the course. Once the tiny craft flew through the final gate everyone visibly relaxed. 'WOW! That was amazing.' Daisy finally gave voice to the feelings that everyone had. 'That is incredible.'

'I have to agree, I have never seen anything move so fast and so close to an object, without hitting it,' admitted Tyrell. 'He has a real skill.'

'Not only that, you will see he is already a Sergeant Major, despite only being in the army for a short time. He is the original member and the official Training Officer of the Group; he has recruited a number of the best and the most promising racers in the country, their training has improved their skills and Drones has been designing modifications and new craft as well as coming up with improved methods of using it as an offensive weapon.'

'Jack has created a new branch of the Army by his innovative thinking but there are some that think it is a personal pet project and will not amount to anything important.' Motoyuki continued, 'but let me tell you this, from the very first reconnaissance flight it showed promise. Jack has been continually improving the usage and Trans-Pac will make everyone sit up and take notice. We believe it has the ability to change the outcome of some battles.'

The following morning, they began the testing program.

'You can tell us all about it later,' announced Yumi. 'We will stay here and be civilised while you go outside to "Play War".' Effectively she dismissed them all and they did as they had been ordered.

All the men left and began to make their way to the old hayshed. Most were wearing jeans and a "T" shirt. Jack, ever the individual, was wearing a kimono.

Most were also carrying binoculars to give them a better view of the entire testing area.

'What is in the briefcase, Jack" asked Tyrell, noting the small aluminium case in Jack's hand.

'The last survey maps of this area. We will need to have benchmark measurements if we are to be certain this is going to work. The surveyors needed to map the area accurately for the last of the Heritage Surveys.

The group arrived at the shed and Drones was in a deep conversation with the head of the Range Controllers.

'We can attach the reflectors with some form of adhesive for the test. I will need you to help me in the engineering workshops, if this works as well as we hope we will need to have a better system for mounting though.'

'You are going to glue the reflector on your drone? How will you get it off when we are done?'

'Actually, I was thinking more of duct tape for this trial. We can prove the operation here, then, once we are ready, we can do a full trial with a properly engineered solution.'

'That will take months!'

'Not really, if it works, and I have no reason to think it won't, we can print a carbon fibre mounting and attach the reflector material, the only parameter that will be doubtful is the size of the reflector itself.'

'How much weight can the drone lift?' The two spun instantly and saw Jack and his "entourage" entering the shed.

'The smallest drone can lift half a kilo without affecting its operational range. The next one can hold two kilos but it is a bit bigger, easier to spot in flight.'

'What is the reflector made of?' Roman already knew the answers to his questions but asked anyway to ensure the Range Controller was on top of the requirements.

'A standard reflector is made of concave titanium which has a gold-plated surface. The reflective curve is calculated to be the premium for the frequency of the laser in use. That way we get the best reflection and the strongest return signal.'

'What are these reflectors normally used for?' Asked Tyrell.

'The Airforce use them for landing approach when they are flying "covert", no lights or radars. We adapted them for use in gunnery ranging, but we usually have them on a truck or other heavy vehicle.'

'Can we do that, Drones? Can we build these?' asked Motoyuki.

'Unfortunately, no. It is extremely difficult to electroplate onto carbon.'

Jack thought for a moment, as did everyone else. Turning to the Range Controller he asked, 'What if we got the space labs to spray coat the reflector base with gold and then polish it? That way all we need to do is make the base.'

'That will work, Sir, sorry Jack,' replied the Mexican, warming to the obvious capabilities of the people he was now working closely with.

'Drones, your thoughts?'

'As soon as we can get the specifications, I can get the workshops to begin a full-size test unit.'

'Get them on standby, please.'

'Hai. What error in the surface is acceptable?' Drones had asked a question that is difficult to answer.

Stunned into silence the Range Controller suddenly had to try to recall the parameters of the reflectors. 'I, I think it is around 3 to 5 microns.'

'Don't think, we need to find out,' Roman insisted. 'We can go with what we have for now, but we will need the information by the end of today. You, Lieutenant Sanchez,' Roman pointed to a nearby officer, 'get onto your technical people and find out, now!'

'The stunned officer rushed away and began to call everyone he could think of. Roman indicated to Jack and the others to come outside.

'The maximum acceptable surface error is 10 microns. A space engineering company should be able to cope with that with ease.'

'How do you know that?' Tyrell asked.

Roman grinned widely. 'There is a reason that Jack is one of the premier infantry commanders, it is because he KNOWS what is important. That is the same reason why my gunners are the best in the world. That junior lieutenant was simply standing there idly waiting to be given a job, now he has one. And next week he will be transferred to a store's facility in Merida. He is not good enough to be attached to the Premier Gunnery Battery in the world.'

Drones looked at each of the officers in turn. Eventually, he said, 'Thank the gods I am good at flying these things, at least I know my job is safe.' No one spoke for a moment until, all at once, they began laughing.

'You are absolutely right. Now let's see if we can get this to work.'

It took an extra hour before Drones was happy with the stability of his craft and its flight characteristics with the extra load underneath. They began the test by measuring the range from the shed to the stable.

'Range 26.3 metres!' The Range Officer called out.

Jack checked the survey maps and simply nodded.

'Next target!' Motoyuki called out and the drone shot away to the next agreed test point.

'1654.5 metres.'

'Good. Next!'

And so, it went for almost two hours; the drone was brought back twice for replacement batteries. And each time it went out was the same. Drones would announce he was on target and the Range Controller would say how far away it was.

Eventually, they had sufficient data for the first day and as they were packing up the bedraggled Lieutenant returned.

'Well Lieutenant, what is the answer?' Roman demanded.

'The best information I have is "around twenty microns" sir.'

'Jack, can we get a flight back to Mexico for him tomorrow?'

'Hai.' Was all Jack replied.

'Lieutenant, you will return home and ask the manufacturers of the reflectors for the technical specifications. Dismissed.'

'Sir,' the officer saluted and began to make preparations to return home. As he walked away, he had the feeling he would not be returning.

As the group approached the house, they could see the ladies waiting for them. They had been watching on the huge monitor screen that had been setup for just that purpose.

'How did it go?' asked Fumiko.

Jack smiled widely. 'You tell me,' he challenged.

Fumiko thought for a moment as she stared intensely at him.

'You are well pleased with today's outcomes, but tomorrow will prove your work. Roman, sending the lieutenant home will be the making of him, he will be well suited to logistics.'

Those that knew Fumiko simply smiled, the others were left stunned. How did that little girl know so much?

As they sat and discussed the days works, they began to relax.

'Jack, would you like Daisy to play this evening?'

'No, Tyrell, she is on holiday, it is us that are working.'

Dinner came and went with a lot of conversation and love for friends. The newcomers were scrutinised and questioned, they all "passed muster" as Jack would put it, and yet more had joined the select group of friends.

The next morning, Saturday, the soldiers were up and about early. Drones was testing the unit he was going to use that day and he ensured the extra-large battery was securely attached.

'First flight, take it over to the top of that ridge, alongside the communications tower.' Jack ordered.

All watched as the small drone slowly lifted from the lawn just behind the house and suddenly it simply disappeared into the distance. They watched as Drones let his fingers skim across the control unit, his vision obscured by the 3D video headset he wore while "flying". It was only a minute or so until it was completely out of sight.

'How fast is it going?' Roman asked no one in particular, not expecting an answer, he was surprised when Drones replied 'around 120kmh, at the moment.

'Is that it? As fast as it goes?'

'No, I will show you when it gets back.'

It took over thirty minutes of intense concentration before Drones finally announced, 'Look at the screens, here is the comms tower,' he slowly rotated the hovering craft. 'Your controllers should have it about now,' he finally announced as he manipulated the position.

Roman looked at his gunners and he was well pleased when they gave him a "thumbs-up"

'Range?' he demanded.

'67 decimal 656 kilometres.'

'Jack?' Roman enquired, waiting for approval.

'Excellent! Well done everyone, this is fantastic. The principle is proven. Now bring it back and get a new power pack, there is one more test I wish to see.'

Jack watched as Drones manipulated the control unit and then simply placed it on the table and removed the headset. As he tried to walk, he could not manage a straight line.

'Are you alright, Drones?' Asked Tyrell as he watched the "pilot" hold onto Mai's shoulder for stability.

'Yes, just give me minute, the difference in sensation of watching a 3D rendering inside the headset and then coming back to reality can be unsettling sometimes. I will be fine in a minute or so.'

Jack leapt to his side and assisted Mai in getting him settled in an easy chair. Jack then disappeared inside the house and seconds later he returned with Chie following.

'Here,' she said, 'drink this ginger tea, it helps with dizziness and motion sickness.

'How did she know what to bring him?' asked Grace, then just as suddenly she continued, 'never mind, we know the answer to that question.'

Jack smiled and everyone else followed suit, they were all becoming accustomed to the extraordinary goings on at Jack's house.

As Emika served them all Roman asked 'How long until it returns?'

'About another twenty minutes,' replied Drones. You will not hear it approach; it will simply settle out there,' he pointed to the grass clearing about twenty metres from the house.

As it turned out he was slightly out in his calculations, just eighteen minutes later they finally saw it approach and set itself down on the ground.

'Sorry everyone, I miscalculated the tail wind.'

'Don't apologise, that was fantastic to watch, and extremely accurate.' Roman was excited to see what else they could achieve.

Drones picked up the unit and tested the replacement battery. Once he was satisfied, he gave Jack a nod and then set it down on the grass again.

'This time, I want you to range across to the rail yard in town.' Jack demanded.

'Hai.' Drones replied as he checked the computer mapping. Eventually, he said, 'Ready.'

'Launch.' Roman ordered, 'Get to it start tracking and calculating!' he ordered his team and they began to follow the tiny drone as it hurtled across the town. Just minutes later Drones consulted the control unit and announced '27.486.4kilometres.'

'Confirm range, 27decimal486decimal4. Repeated the range officer. Drones pressed a button and the drone came back to him. As it approached, he again put the headset on and said watch this.

They all heard the drone before they could pick it out in the sky. Suddenly it shot past the rear of the house, so fast that three of the watchers didn't even see it. Flying in a huge circle Drones took it to the front of the house and, as everyone watched on the monitor he flew through the house and landed on the coffee table beside Daisy.

'And that is why he is a champion racer,' announced Jack as the others sat, almost dumbfounded.

'I assume that you pre-programmed that flight?' Roman asked.

'Hai.'

'Range, is that good enough?'

'Yes Sir, the signal was a little weak though, but that will improve with a better reflector.'

'Good. Now we can all relax. Let's enjoy the remainder of the weekend.' Motoyuki ordered, then he noticed Jack was not even listening, his mind was off solving yet another unasked question as he looked out from the deck towards the mountains.

Finally getting everyone's attention he indicated that they should leave Jack to his thoughts and they should relax in the sunroom, well away from Jack and his deliberations.

'What do you think he is concentrating on this time?' Tyrell asked no one in particular.

'You may as well ask the gods; his brain goes off and looks for things we don't even think exist,' replied Chie.

'Fumiko? Any ideas?'

'Sorry, at this time Jack's mind is as difficult to work with as a snow monkey. It is random thoughts that Jack pushes around until he has something that he can exploit.'

The conversations swayed through any number of topics from how hot it was in Hawaii when the exercises would be held, would Grace be able to visit while the men went to "war", how was the pregnancy progressing? And a number of other topics, just to fill in the time.

Suddenly Fumiko got up and made a cup of coffee, just in time for Jack to enter the room; Fumiko handed him the cup and announced 'You need to eat, your body needs fuel if you are to push it this hard.' With that simple announcement the other conversations halted and everyone waited for Jack to speak. 'Arigatō, Fumiko.' As he took the cup, 'Food it is.' Just then Emika and Chie entered the room with platters of food for each to help themselves. Still the conversations were stilted, as though they were waiting for a phone call or something else to happen.

'Tyrell?' Jack began, suddenly breaking the slight tension. 'Can we get a small ship to do some recon before the exercise?'

'Sure, I can get a patrol boat or something a little bigger, if that's what you want?'

'Drones? Can you get good surveillance footage from your small units or do you prefer to use a larger one?'

'Larger is better, if we are not at war; if we are fighting then the smaller the better.'

'Very good. Get five of your best pilots to come here tomorrow bring six identical video recon units, no side numbers or anything else.'

'Hai.' Drones jumped up and called his unit, one word from Jack and they were all on a plane within just two hours.

'What **are** you doing, Jack.'

'I feel we are ready for the first part of the exercise; I would like some extra knowledge of the conditions in the assigned area and that is why I asked Drones to get some surveillance units here. We can go to Hawaii and get the information I need and then we can plan the second half.'

'You do understand that no one conducts surveillance of the exercise areas prior to commencement, don't you?'

'Actually, if you read the Combat Instructions there is no order preventing it.'

'You are wrong, Jack.' Tyrell picked up his tablet and thumbed through the long document. Eventually, he stopped scrolling and said, 'Here it is, Section 19, paragraph 9. "No person is permitted to tour or inspect the exercise area prior to commencement. No person is to permit another to gain access prior to commencement." The rules are simple, and in black and white.'

'Actually, they are various shades of grey. We will not be "accessing" the area; no one will be landing or walking on the battleground. If you read the full instruction on Mapping and Planning it does allow us to use overhead and satellite information.'

Quickly Tyrell and Roman searched the Combat Instructions.

'Be damned, he's right.' Roman said after a fruitless search. 'So, you are planning to send your genius pilots out to get video of the entire area without anyone knowing?'

'That about sums it up.'

'And you will use that information to plan for both halves of the exercise?'

'Yes, I believe the saying is "Forewarned is Forearmed" or that is what an Australian told me once. The more we know about the area the better we can exploit it.'

'And this is where we get our dress uniforms ready!' Okimoto picked the exact time to join the argument.

They all burst out laughing. 'Now I understand the words.' Roman added.

Once they had settled down Tyrell spoke up. 'You really do like to push things, don't you? The hierarchy will blow a fuse if this gets out.'

'They usually do,' Okimoto replied for his friend, 'but they have never won an argument against him. He is able to confuse so many by the use of language and logic. That is one reason why he is now a General, he has defeated everyone that is senior to him, and when they complain, they lose that fight as well. It is no secret that many do not like him because he is so good; but ask Hiro Hyashida, Commander Ninth Tank Brigade, he lost many engagements because Jack out-thought him.'

'You can ask him when we go "flying" next week. I want his input for the final deployment of heavy armour and that is dependent on the surveillance we get.'

'So how do we get the drones over the island, without anyone knowing what we are doing?' Roman asked, his interest in the proceedings were becoming more professional with each section of the plan and now he wanted to more about the capabilities of the "flyers" as Jack called them. Deep inside, both he and Tyrell liked the sneaky side of Jack's approach to battle plans, and both could see the benefits of correctly used drones as a war asset.

'That is where Tyrell and his fleet come in. If we can go out on a patrol boat or a destroyer, and launch six drones for let's say two hours of "attack and interception" training; we can manage two hours of flight can't we Drones?'

'Hai, three if we use the high-performance battery packs, but they do take longer to recharge.'

'Good bring eighteen of them as well as some smaller ones for flight testing and a few extra pilots.'

'Hai.' and Drones disappeared to call his team again.

'Where was I? Oh yes, we can launch six or twelve drones to make a series of aerial attacks to "test" the air defences of the fleet units. While they are keeping the sensor systems busy, we can send an extra six to video and map the exercise area.'

Drones returned and gave his commander the "thumbs up" indicating the request had been passed.

'What about returning all to the ship? Wont someone be suspicious of twelve drones attacking and eighteen returning?'

'I think that we can get away with that, if they know we have launched eighteen, just because they do not all attack at once does not mean they are not there.'

'May I ask? Please.' Mai interjected.

'Of course, what is it?'

'What if someone notices the video equipment on the drones?'

'Good question.' Jack thought for a moment. 'Tyrell, would your commander like some video footage of his ship at sea and defending himself against a threat?'

'That is a story they will accept, just have to edit out the best bits for ourselves.'

'DRONES!' Jack shouted. 'Get a video editing unit as well.'

'HAI!' came back from the next room.

'You certainly don't let the grass grow under your feet Jack,' commented Motoyuki. 'This is the first I have watched him plan a full exercise; he is really impressive. It is no wonder so many have difficulty keeping up,' he added.

'Now that that is done, can we relax a little?' It was Grace that asked after watching them for so long without comment.

'Of course, that is all for the weekend,' announced Jack. 'Now who wants to dine out tonight?'

The decision was unanimous, and all made their way to the dining room at the ryokan that Jack, Chie and Fumiko enjoyed on a semi-regular basis.

'Why is it empty?' asked Daisy. 'Where I come from a good measure of a restaurant is how many people are there.'

'I booked it out for us for the evening,' replied Jack. 'I didn't want Emika to have to cater for us all. And it is my privilege to be your host for the evening.' Jack bowed to all and they all replied in unison, "arigatō".

Chapter 19
Covert Surveillance

It was eventually two weeks later that they all met again, this time in Hawaii. Jack's plane landed at Hickham and he was met by the Base Commander's Adjutant.

'Good morning Sir,' he spoke as he saluted. 'I trust you had a good flight?'

Jack returned the salute. 'Konichiwa, yes thank you it was good, nice and smooth.'

'I have a car to take you to Pearl (Harbour Naval Base.) Is there anything you need?'

'No, thank you for asking. Has Colonel Garcia arrived?'

'General Garcia arrived just ten minutes ago, if that is who you mean?'

'General! I knew it was close, just didn't know it was that close.'

Then a voice from behind, with a strong Spanish accent, 'Admiral Backhouse is here too.'

Jack spun around and immediately spotted the "Generals" insignia on his friend's shoulder.

'Congratulations Roman. This is a surprise?' Jack pointed to Roman's shoulder badges. 'It was a little early; when the Chiefs of staff heard that both you and Tyrell had been promoted, they thought I should at least be the same rank as the other commanders.'

'What time is it here?' Jack had not yet corrected his watch for the change in time zones or the International Date Line.

'Just after 0900, Monday, Sir.'

'Arigatō. Call Admiral Backhouse and inform him we will pay our respects to the Base Commander before we sail.'

'Aye, aye Sir.' The adjutant saluted and phoned for a driver to collect Tyrell from the officers' mess and to meet them at the Commanders office.

The drive to the office was short and soon they were sitting in the Commanders office with the obligatory coffee, making small talk.

'I don't suppose you are willing to divulge the nature of the tests you are going to conduct from one of my ships?'

'Suffice to say the tests are an integral part of the battle plan for "Red" forces for Trans-Pac. The results will determine how we conduct the exercise.'

'Is he always this evasive, Tyrell?'

'Only on days ending in "Y" I believe.'

The four had a small laugh at the quip.

'Seriously, Sir,' continued Jack, 'the trials I have requested are new and they have not yet been divulged to more than five people, three of them are here and the other two are already onboard the ship designated for us to use.'

The Base Commander looked at Jack with suspicion. 'And if I decided to forgo your request for a ship?'

'Then I would simply have a destroyer and support ship sent from Japan and bypass your involvement. After all you are the Head of the "Blue" forces, so I could not permit the information falling into your hands.'

Again, he looked at Jack, as a Fleet Admiral he was not familiar with, relatively junior officers, denying him information. 'What about after the exercise?'

'After, well we are all friends and as such we will share all the intelligence we gather beforehand.'

'Tyrell, are you ok with this?'

'It may appear to be unusual and somewhat surprising, but Jack does not conform to traditional methodologies. He will never rely on given information nor will he use the full "enemy" deployment information. He believes he would not have the information if the "war" was real and so he depends on gathering his own intelligence and he plans from there. As he said one day, following the initial contact, everything is a reaction; so he plans and deploys his resources that way.'

The Base Commander thought for a moment; 'There are many conventions and even directives that prevent us from simply giving over control of a ship, we want to know where it is going and when it is due to return. There is nothing more embarrassing to explain than why we lost a ship. To circumvent these requirements, I will give control of the ship to Admiral Backhouse. I understand your requirements and I will not have you tracked or under surveillance. As soon as you are done you are to make contact with Pearl and give your position, course and speed. Understood?'

'Yes, sir. Thank you.' Jack replied. 'Now, we are to sail in just twenty minutes, and we are yet to meet the C.O. of the ship.'

'Good luck, I expect full disclosure after the event.'

'Hai.' Jack replied

The three saluted and left the office. None of them spoke, they would wait until they were alone to express their feelings.

The short trip to the wharf was quiet and, as per Jack's instructions, there was no official welcome when they finally boarded. As they stepped onto the deck each asked, "Permission to come aboard?" which was answered with "Granted" and they moved aside.

While they waited to be shown to the C.O.'s cabin, Drones approached them.

'Konichiwa, Drones. What is happening? All settled?'

'Konichiwa,' Drones replied as he saluted. 'I feel we have created a great deal of interest, so many boxes and no indication of what is inside.'

'Did they give you a hard time?' Tyrell asked.

'No Sir, once I told them they would need permission from you and Jack to see inside they left us alone. It is handy to have a little rank to beat them up with.' Tyrell stifled a laugh as the ships C.O. arrived at the gangway.

'Drones, get the men settled, once we have sailed and we are out of sight of land test your equipment.' Jack ordered.

'Hai.' Drones left with his guide leading the way.

'Admiral Backhouse, Welcome aboard, Sir. Commander Alan Dalton Captain of the Sainsbury.' The ship's captain saluted and held out his hand.

Tyrell took his hand. 'Captain, I would like to introduce General Nakagawa, commander Red forces for Trans-Pac and General Garcia Artillery Commander.'

With Tyrells introduction the Commander became instantly aware that he should have addressed Jack first, as overall commander. Salutes were exchanged, as were handshakes.

Looking at the gangway staff he pointed at one and ordered 'Show our guests to my cabin.' and the three were led away, with Jack first.

The route to the captain's cabin seemed torturous, twisting this way and that, up ladders and along passageways. Finally, the sailor opened a door and the captains steward waited to take their hats. The door had barely been closed behind the escort and it opened again; this time the captain entered.

'Can I offer you drinks? Sorry only soda or tea and coffee.'

'Coffee, Alan,' replied Jack, the request was repeated by Roman and Tyrell.

The drinks were delivered, and they all sat, waiting for one to break the ice as it were.

'Dismiss your steward, please. We can get by without him for now.'

The captain was stunned. Never in his long career had he been ordered to send his staff away from the cabin; let alone by a foreign officer. The captain looked at Tyrell and all he got in return was a nod.

The steward was told to wait in the wardroom (officers mess) for further instructions. He had no sooner entered the wardroom before he began to ask his fellow stewards what was going on as he had been ordered away from the captain's cabin.

No one could give an explanation and it was the Electrical Officer that took him aside.

'If you wish to continue in your chosen career, you will not ask questions that do not concern you. The three officers are the Command Group for Red Forces; they have discussions that do not need to be repeated in whole or in part. Do you understand me?'

'Aye, aye Sir.' The steward replied. The conversation simply led to more, this time unstated, questions.

Captain's Cabin

'Can someone tell me what is going on? I got a message on Friday to single up for sea Monday morning, important passengers embarking for two possibly three days' work-up. I am the captain; I do have a right to know.'

'Settle down Alan. Jack is going to explain it all.'

'I must apologise, Alan, for the secrecy. I do not enjoy doing it this way; but I will be discussing some aspects of Trans-Pac and I do not want them to get out. I could read you the Official Secrets Act but that is not how I work.' Jack had a sip of his coffee and took a deep breath before he continued.

'You understand that there is a fine line between what we can do in preparation for a major exercise and what we can get away with?'

'Yes, but what does that have to do with me?'

'Roman needs the most accurate possible information data for his battery if we are to complete the battle plan we have devised. I understand that the battle plans are usually given to us and all we do is comply. This time I managed to get General Onishi, Chief of the Northern Army, to demand that we are given maximum freedom to prosecute the "war". This was given reluctantly but we got it anyway.'

Jack paused to pick up his telephone, pressing a couple of times on the screen he spoke rapidly in Japanese, and less than five minutes later there was a knock at the door.

'Enter!'

The door opened and Drones stood there holding a single black protective case.

The captain looked at him and was about to speak when Jack started. 'Come in Drones. Put the case on the floor and open it.

Drones looked at Jack, silently questioning the order.

'It's ok, show Commander Dalton what we have.'

Drones opened the case and gently pulled the small craft from its protective padding and placed it on the table. At only fifteen centimetres across the tips of the propellers it was no giant of a machine. The colour of matt black all over was enough to draw interest.

'This is the latest in surveillance drones. It has three camera systems, one visible light, one infra-red and one high resolution still camera. It also has an operator's visual system to allow the operator to drive it. It can fly faster than any other drone in its size range and most of the larger ones as well. It can be fully controlled or programmed. It can also deliver a payload if we wish.'

'But why do we need it for the exercise?'

'Roman needs the most accurate range data of a moving target if he is to shoot it. We need to know how well we can use these, and other similar units, to give him the accuracy he wants. We need the shortcomings to be understood before we go to "War" that is why we are here.'

'I see.'

'Arigatō, Drones. Get the units ready and then stand down until we are ready tonight. Get your escorts to show you around the ship. Enjoy it for a while.'

'That's all you tell him? Get ready and stand down?'

'Strange isn't it?' Tyrell commented. 'But wait until you see what they do when they are ready.'

'So how are we going to do this? What exactly will you be doing tonight?'

'We will launch a number of drones after dark, the ship will be darkened. Once launched the drones will be sent to a start point, not defined, and they will conduct approach and attack runs against your systems.'

'I still don't get it? Why? We have anti-drone tech, we can "shoot" them down. What do you expect to achieve?'

'Let's just say that we have a few systems we need to test. For Trans-Pac we need to be certain of the possibility of detection. That is where you come in, we will make our attack runs and you have to find us. It is that simple.'

The meeting was interrupted by a knock at the door.

'Enter!'

The door opened and one of Romans gunners stepped inside.

'Guzman, all ready?' Roman asked.

'Si, General, all tested and ready.' 'Good, wait for us with the ranging unit.' Guzman left and left them alone again.

'What equipment does he have?' Asked the Captain, slightly in awe of the three guests and their easy, relaxed method of command.

'The other task we have set our teams; is to test the capabilities of the ranging systems we have created. It is a combination of both the drones and the gunners.'

'I have to say, this is a little overwhelming. You seem to have a lot to do and all of it new.'

'That is true, Alan,' replied Tyrell. 'But here is the secret part. Firstly, it is not written down anywhere so it cannot be proven to be more than speculation. We will be conducting surveillance overflights of the exercise island while we are out. Now while the covert operation and the ranging are extremely important it is the surveillance that is most important. You are the only person, officer or enlisted, outside of those onboard today that knows our full scope. This is top secret, if we can get the information we are after then in time of a real war we would be saving lives.'

'I don't understand. The Operational Directives do not permit an inspection of the exercise area prior to commencement of the exercise. That is specific.' Jack gave Roman and Tyrell a wry smile.

'And that is why we are conducting a "drone based, high speed, camera survey" not surveillance.'

'And as Okimoto says, "This is where we get our dress uniforms ready for the inquest".' Roman added, and the three again began laughing at the inside joke.

'I am not so certain I agree or approve of this, I need authority to even get within fifty miles of the island.'

'We will be conducting our "equipment assessments" fifty-five miles from the subject area. So, no, you don't need authority.'

'Can I speak off the record?' He directed the question directly at Tyrell.'

'Sure, go ahead.'

Alan Dalton, thirty-year veteran and at least ten of those as a ship's captain took a deep breath.

'I have never heard of senior officers plotting and planning an exercise this way. You seem to be ignoring all conventions and almost all of the Operational Directives. Are you not afraid of repercussions?'

'Actually, I have been doing this for all my career,' replied Jack. 'People jump up and down and threaten me with everything from a dishonourable discharge to jail time for direct disobedience. The fact is, if we were at war, I would do this and a lot more to ensure victory at minimal cost. The first part of this exercise is to defend against a hostile seaborne assault. To do that I need the data to be accurate and a part of that data is the placement of the Heavy Bombardment Group and the 127 Medium Battery. This is how we make certain we get the data and we have faith in our ability to repeat our efforts in a combat situation.'

'Do not panic, Alan.' Roman continued, 'If it all goes wrong, you are not in the firing line. I have seen the reports of Jack's work so far, and even the ones that he has defeated are grudgingly appreciative of his unique approach to solving the problems. All we ask is for your teams to do what is needed to enable us to win. And remember, you are part of the Red Teams, if we do well it will be a feather in your cap as a significant part of the planning, testing and command group.'

'OK, you win. Let's do what we can. Now it is time to leave.'

'Good. Guns, get your ranging team to target several buildings and landmarks on the way out, get some idea of how ready we are.'

'On it Jack,' replied Roman. 'Let's have some fun.'

'The run out of Pearl Harbour saw the Range Teams identifying and ranging buildings all the way out, and once at sea they all stood down and relaxed for a while.

During the afternoon many of the crew could be found watching the Japanese soldiers assembling and testing their machines. Comments ranging from "look how small that is" to "Just how much more can they give that as payload and still have it fly?"

Late in the day Jack was watching the preparations and he called down to the soldiers below as they completed their preparations.

'Drones? Have you given them a test flight yet?'

'Just waiting for clearance, Jack.' The sailors were astounded at the use of first names, and that started comments amongst themselves.

Jack asked his escort to call the bridge and get clearance for test flights.

'All clear, Drones. Launch when you are ready.'

The first off were the small units completing two laps around the ship then landing again.

'Force launch, standby!' Drones ordered his team to prepare for a full group launch.

'All units ready.' Drones assistant reported. As he looked for Jack, Drones could see there were many waiting to see some of their capabilities.

In Japanese Drones told his flyers "Give them a show."

'LAUNCH!' he shouted; and eighteen drones lifted vertically from the deck in unison. 'CATCH ME IF YOU CAN!' and the chase was on.

Drones' unit shot off vertically closely chased by the rest. Showing off, just a little, Drones made his team chase him all around the ship, diving beneath the bow and hurtling down the side of the ship at close to 130kmh only to suddenly rise vertically again spinning all the way until it was out of sight and then dropping just as suddenly to hover just above the deck. All the time closely followed by the chasing units, never close enough to catch him but not far behind either.

Following a ten-minute display of top class flying they all landed exactly where they had launched from.

As the motors stopped spinning the crew began to applaud loudly. Jack smiled at Roman, Tyrell and Alan. 'Well done. Get recharged and attach payloads for tonight's flights. Check operations and stand down. Flying begins at 2200.'

Jack turned to his command team and announced, 'They are ready.'

'You know the crew are going to talking about this for days, right?'

'Maybe, maybe not. Tonight, we intend to evade all your sensors so they may not be quite so happy when we are done, such a defeat can be dispiriting to say the least.'

As the clock slowly made its way towards 2200 the drone teams, assisted by a number of sailors, erected a small marquee. Inside they setup their Combat Control System. Far from the usual radio control units, this drone control equipment was a sophisticated computer system which recorded the video feeds as well as giving the flyers a covered control room. Open on one side they could launch and retrieve the units away from prying eyes. It was now time to prove they could get the data required and their drones would now be carrying the secret laser reflectors for the ranging group to test their skills.

Jack and the others were settled into the Command Information Centre. The operational centre of the ship was where all the information from the radar, sonar and other sensors was collated and sent to the gun and missile control systems.

'Are your teams ready?' Jack asked.

'Ready as we can ever be,' replied Alan as he looked around the room which was almost full with operators, technicians and onlookers.

'I don't think anyone is sleeping tonight, everyone onboard is interested in this.' Commented Tyrell.

'It is novel for them; they don't usually get to see this up close.'

Jack pressed his communicator, "Drones, launch at 2200. You have control of formations and attack sequences."

'Hai.' Was the only reply.

All eyes in the CIC, on the bridge and around the deck were watching the clock as it appeared to take forever to get to 2200. At just 2 seconds past, the distinctive sound of high-speed motors could be heard as the flying units prepared to leave.

'Departure formation Delta 3.' Drones ordered. Then, just a few seconds later, 'LAUNCH!' and eighteen drones hurtled out of the marquee and within ten seconds they were lost to sight.

'Ops, Surface Control.' The tracking system operator called out. 'New contact on the plot. Designated Skunk One Four.'

'Very good, track contact.'

The system had detected the drones and was now actively tracking them. Held in a tight formation by their pilots they appeared as a single contact on the screens.

'Ops? Are we tracking them?' Alan asked his Operation Officer.

'Affirmative, Sir. Holding contact at 30,000 yards.'

'Very good.'

Sitting in his own control centre Drones was listening to the feeds from the CIC. Very quietly he said, deliberately using Japanese language to disguise his tactical orders, 'Units 12, 15 and 16 break formation and proceed to primary target.'

No one replied; the three units simply dropped at ten second intervals from the main group and left at full speed for the exercise area. The rest continued at a leisurely pace for a few more minutes, still in a close formation.

'Still tracking, Sir.' Was the report from the Combat Control system, a message that was repeated every few minutes during the opening hour of the trial.

Still the drones moved away from the ship in a very tight formation. At forty-five miles out, Drones gave the order, 'Hold formation, turn 180 degrees, approach target (the ship) for first run.

'Target has reversed course, inbound at 50knots (approx. 100kmh).'

'Very good, still got full track?'

'Yes Sir, tracking systems holding target.'

"We will see." Drones thought to himself. 'Standby formation Bravo 1, standby, standby, GO!'

Every one of the drones broke formation at the same time. All dropping to just a few feet above the sea they increased speed to maximum and were now closing at almost 150kmh.

Then just a few seconds later, 'Lost Track. Last known position Green 135 at 23,000yards.

'GET THEM BACK!' Alan ordered. Jack looked at Roman and Tyrell; all three gave a slight nod to each other; they were inwardly very pleased at this sudden turn of events.

The next few minutes were very tense in the CIC. No one spoke fearful that they might break the operator's concentration.

For all concerned this was the point that would either make or break Jack's battle plan. Alan was trying to get his teams to find the incoming aircraft; Jack, Roman and Tyrell were willing Drones to evade the technological wizardry of one of the newest units in the Navy's inventory.

The tension was suddenly broken by a call from the bridge.

"CIC-Bridge."

"CIC" came the reply.

"We have located Skunk One Four."

Alan looked at Jack with a smile on his face. "Where is it?"

"About ten feet in front of the bridge windows, Sir."

Alan's face said it all, crestfallen he began demanding how the target managed to get through their defences so easily. This was a question that almost no one could answer; or perhaps that should be no one was willing to answer.

Before a coherent reply could be uttered, the drones all formed up again and began to fly away, this time away from the port side of the ship. Again, the reports began.

'Ops, Surface Control. New contact on the plot Designated Skunk One Five. Course 335, speed two zero knots.'

'Very good track contact.'

'Aye. Sir.'

The Surface Controller issued the orders and three separate systems began to track the drones as they slowly flew away from the ship.

After around twenty minutes, Drones ordered his pilots to swing around the bow of the ship and drop to sea level.

'LOST CONTACT, SKUNK ONE FIVE has disappeared from the plot.'

'Pick it up again!' Alan again demanded, even though he knew it may be a fruitless attempt.

Just ten minutes later, "OPS SURFACE."

'Yes, Surface, tell me some good news.' Alan asked hopefully.

'Sir, I believe we have regained contact. Skunk One Five has emerged twenty miles off the starboard bow.'

'Can you confirm?'

'System shows the same identifiers as Skunks One Four and One Five before it dropped off the screens, Sir.'

Very good, Keep tracking it.'

Just as the report was being made, Drones ordered his pilots 'Formation Bravo six, approach now!'

Before the CIC could confirm the report from Surface Control another message was passed.

'Sorry Sir, Skunk One Five had disappeared again.'

'Very good. See what you can do.' Alan was becoming somewhat dispirited; Jack's small aircraft were proving to be a lot more difficult to catch than anyone had thought.

Still sitting at the rear of the CIC Jack and the others were in a deep and private conversation.

'Looking good at the moment.' Jack whispered, 'The next twenty minutes will tell us if we are going to be successful.'

Roman and Tyrell simply nodded, and they all waited for the next significant moment.

'CIC Surface; New contact on the plot. Surface vessel. Dead astern range 20 miles. Designated Skunk One Six.'

'Very good, report.'

'Commander,' Tyrell called out. 'That will be the "Hendrix" she is joining us for the exercise.'

'Thank you, Admiral. Surface, rename Skunk One Six as USS Hendrix.'

'Aye, Sir. Hendrix is holding at 20 miles dead astern.'

'Very good.'

All was silent for a few minutes, then 'Commander, ask Hendrix to report all air contacts.'

'Yes Admiral. Surface?'

'The Surface plotters were busy relaying the order and, once it had been passed, it again fell silent. Ten minutes or more passed by, then suddenly a report was received.

'Command this is Hendrix, we have an unidentified air contact on your port side. It has left your position and now appears to be stationary.' As the ships continued to move across the ocean the reports continued to come in.

'Hendrix, your stationary contact is our Skunk One Five. It has been shadowing us for a while.'

'Roger that. Skunk One Five has disappeared from the plot.'

Now with two ships searching for the drones it was assumed that they would eventually find them. But the assumptions were mostly incorrect.

'Roman, get your Ranging Group to give us the distance to Hendrix.'

'We have the distance sir, twenty miles, 40,000 yards.' The report came from the surface plot and was as close to accurate as they could get.

Roman was speaking in Spanish with his ranging group which had setup at the stern of the ship.

'Jack, Alan, Ranging Group put drones at 36,787.2 metres or roughly 40,230 yards.'

'Arigatō, Roman. Well done to your Range Group.'

Everyone in the CIC looked at the visitors; from the lowest seaman to Commander Dalton, they all had one question, "How could they be so accurate?"

Alan Dalton was the only one that asked, and he was, at first, met with a strange order. In Japanese Jack ordered Drones to return his units to the ship; the message was relayed and soon a group of drones was seen to be circling the ships bridge before landing back inside the take-off marquee.

Jack looked up at Alan and said, 'We will discuss this in your cabin.' Not a request, or an order as such, but it was an order, nevertheless. As Jack left the CIC Tyrell spoke to those present.

'This exercise has been a great success. However, as with so many such things, there is a warning. The capabilities we have all been witness to this evening are in all respects "Top Secret" and the results are the property of the Japanese government. Any disclosure will start with ten years in Leavenworth and then the sentence will be enforced after that beginning. Do you understand me?'

A chorus of 'Sir, YES SIR.' Rang out behind him as he left for the captain's cabin and a debrief with the others.

Chapter 20
Final Preparations

'Roman, that was the single most impressive action I have ever seen.'

'Thanks Jack, it was good wasn't it.'

'Can you tell me now what the hell was happening?' Alan demanded answers, he felt he had been used as a plaything.

'Just a moment,' Tyrell answered. 'Steward, coffee and food for all; this has been a very stressful evening.'

The food was brought up from the galley and the four officers waited for the steward to leave. As he opened the door to leave the steward was confronted by Drones waiting to enter.

'Come in Drones, we will need you for the debrief as well.' Tyrell invited him inside and they all sat around the table. Before anyone could speak, Drones handed Jack a tablet and said 'Have a look.'

Jack had a quick check and handed it to Roman and again it was approved with a simple nod. 'Got it all, Jack.' Was his only comment.

'Full story, we have been trying to get the 3D maps of the exercise area, we needed them to get the deployment of the guns right. At the same time, we needed to ensure we can get accurate ranging information for the battery. While Drones here was testing your defences; by the way that was an impressive display of flying out there.'

'Domo arigatō, Jack.'

'Three of his pilots mapped the entire defensive and offensive areas of operation.'

'That is against the Operational Instructions. I said it before, and I say it again now.' Alan was becoming concerned about his future in the service.

'Yes, so you have said. But the directives forbade us visiting the area, it did not say we could not conduct photo reconnaissance. That is all we did, don't worry, I will be the one that has to explain the actions of those I command,' replied Jack; he was becoming a little annoyed that he was constantly defending his actions in minute detail, not in the overall picture of the entire exercise.

'The intelligence we have gathered has given us the most advantageous positioning for both the Heavy Bombardment Group and the Supports. It has also given us the landing and infiltration routes we will need for the second half.'

'And what was with the "attacks" on us and the Hendrix?'

The attacks were to determine the effectiveness of the fleet's defences against us, while we cannot carry a payload large enough to do any more than burn some paint, we can fly alongside the ships and landing hovercraft giving Guns here almost perfect range information; the point of today was to determine if we can go undetected, and I think we can. Flying just in front and below the bow will give us the hidden aspect we need to succeed.'

Roman smiled, he liked the nickname Jack had given him; everyone else had only ever used his rank or his name.

'The ultimate fact is that we are now closing in on the final planning details. Tyrell, your thoughts?'

'I think the first phase is ready, the second needs a little creative equipment procurement but that is a simple enough thing to achieve. The third phase simply requires us to have our retirement plans ready and our dress uniforms cleaned for the inquest.' The last of his statement was spoken with a huge grin on his face and the others joined in.

Drones stood up from his seat. 'Jack san, I should be honoured to be your second for your "seppuku" (ritual suicide), if you consider me to be reliable enough,' he bowed deeply in mock deference to his commander.

'Domo arigatō, Drones san. I would be most pleased if you would do so.' Jack joined in the joke, 'However, I would prefer it if you waited until after the inquest to perform your solemn duty.' And again, they all burst into laughter. Once again, Jack had forged a cohesive fighting group from nothing.

Chapter 21
Trans-Pac

"This is the evening news." The hologram of the news report began, and even though there was always something important at the beginning of the report, further along the mundane assignments were eventually being read.

"A special Shipping Information bulletin has just been released by Pearl Harbour Authorities. A work barge has broken free of its berth during last night's storm. The barge is almost 160 feet long and has two large shipping containers on deck. No one was aboard when it broke free. In a "Notice to Mariners" All shipping is to be aware that it may be freely floating or half submerged. Its current whereabouts are unknown. If the barge is sighted, reports to the Shipping Control office on area code 808-555…"

No one had paid any attention to the report. All floating objects were routinely reported so no one had to do anything out of the ordinary.

'Hiro? Have you had the opportunity to fully appraise the new "paintball" ammunition yet?'

'Yes, it looks good. Range and accuracy have been "faithfully recreated" as the engineers would say.'

'Good we will use it on Trans-Pac instead of blanks. Make sure your crews are fully familiar with it. When we are on exercise, we will only be carrying that for your tanks for the duration.'

'Consider it done. What about the IFV's and the others?'

'Okimoto reports the 6mm ammunition for the assault rifles as well as the 50 calibre and 30mm are also ready. Yours will be black paint, 30mm will be yellow, 50 cal. green and assault rifles will be red. Makes it easy to determine the effectiveness of the teams.'

'And no one can complain that their Main Battle Tank was taken out by a rifleman with a bayonet.' The two grinned at the thought.

'I will speak with Roman and Tyrell tonight. We will set out at 0830 for our insertion into the exercise area. Remind your teams that we will only have 24 hours to get fully prepared before the games begin.'

'No problem, they are really looking forward to it.'

General Fujita suddenly appeared at Jack's breakfast table. 'Jack! We have a problem.'

'Really? Sit, tell me.'

'We need to be alone; I can't risk this getting out.'

'We can find a quiet place while we are in transit to the exercise area.'

'We have extra time to get there, the exercise has been delayed for two days.'

At that moment Jack's phone rang. 'Just a moment, it is Chie.'

'Yes Chie, what is it?'

Seijin could not hear the whole conversation, but the few words he did make out only led his mind to the same conclusion that he had already arrived at.

'Many thanks to Fumiko and you. I will be home in a couple of weeks. Sayonara.'

Jack closed the call. 'I am going to say two words,' he whispered to Seijin. 'Hai.'

'Sainsbury, Dalton?'

'How? Never mind. Yes, that is why I need to talk to you in private.'

Jack beckoned a steward to come to his table. 'I need a conference room, in thirty minutes. Coffee and tea, please. And call my aide; Lieutenant Hasegawa, please.'

'Yes Sir.'

The steward left to attend to the urgent request immediately. Before Jack could finish his breakfast, his aide entered the dining room and sat beside him. 'You wanted me, Jack?'

'Yes. Something important has come up, I want the entire command group and NCOs in the conference room in thirty minutes. The steward will tell you which one.'

'Hai.'

Twenty-five minutes later the conference room was packed. Everyone waiting for Jack. He arrived exactly at the thirty-minute mark.

'Jack, Admiral Backhouse is on the Sainsbury and will join with Commander Dalton shortly. Hasegawa was, as usual up to the minute with his Commanders requirements.

'No. Not Dalton.' Jack pulled his phone from his pocket and called Tyrell directly.

'Yes Jack?' Tyrell asked, his curiosity peaking at that moment.

'I need you on the hologram, alone!'

'Sure. Be there in a minute.'

The hologram projector beeped once and the image of Tyrell appeared beside Jack.

'First!' Began Jack. 'This is Top Secret! Understood!' Everyone murmured their agreement. 'General Fujita, you have the floor.'

'Arigatō, Jack. We have been ordered to change the exercise,' he paused for a moment. 'The Americans have been informed as to a part of our battle plans and they have removed the "Virtual" portion to a full opposed landing. As such we will NOT be carrying out a "Live fire" exercise. Instead, we will have to use the paintball ammunition.'

'How did they get this information?' Roman was the one that asked the question first, it was on the lips of each of those present, but he was the first to ask.

'I was unsure at first,' Fujita continued 'But as each new condition was placed on the conduct it became clearer.'

'Dalton?' Tyrell asked quizzically. 'Surely not?'

'At the risk of placing some unrelated persons in some danger,' Jack butted in. 'I received a call this morning and the caller simply said two words; Sainsbury and Dalton. This caller has no previous contact with the exercise regime and as such does not know those participating. Tyrell, I need you to confront Dalton.'

'Be right back!' Tyrell's image disappeared from the conference room.

'Roman, what would you need to increase the firing rate of your Heavy Bombardment unit?'

'The main restriction is the loaders get tired. 155 shells are heavy. Around a hundred extra gunners should do the job, and a second support group should be sufficient.'

'Get them on a plane to Honolulu. We can get them into the country without suspicion there. Get helicopters to ferry them to our position. Also get as much paintball ammunition as possible, bring that into Hickham at the same time, that should keep their spies busy enough.'

'Hiro, Will this affect your tanks?'

'No, we are ready for anything they throw at us.'

'Good. Okimoto?'

'No problems, we are ready in all respects, but if they are going to land in force then we could do with a couple of extra companies of infantry.'

'Do it, get a company of jungle trained and a company of armour support on a plane into Honolulu. I want all the reinforcements here within twelve hours, we are going to need a couple of days to get them integrated to the battle plan.'

'Drones?'

'Hai?'

'Can you get twelve extra pilots and a dozen or more long-range UV and IR surveillance units as well as some of the miniature units we discussed last week onto the same plane as the infantry?'

'Hai, consider it done.'

Captain's Cabin USS Sainsbury

'Enter.' Alan Dalton called out in answer to the knock at the door. The door instantly opened.

'Admiral Backhouse. How can I help?'

'You can begin with the sudden changes to the Battle Planning for Trans-Pac?'

Alan Dalton suddenly felt as though his stomach had fallen through the deck under his feet.

'I, I, I am unsure of your meaning Sir?' he stammered.

'Red forces have been forced to change the entire battle plan; someone has divulged secret information to the Blue forces command. You are the only one that has had contact with the plan and Blue Command. Explain yourself.'

Alan Dalton had been caught out. Thirty years and ready for promotion to a position that may have given him command of a Cruiser force, if not a Fleet Carrier; and now he could see it all disappearing.

'The battle instructions were outside the parameters of the briefing; I am not going to jeopardise my command and my position as Captain by complying with, what I consider to be, illegal orders.'

'Hmmm. You do realise that your orders were to place your ships as directed by Red Forces Command? The decision as to whether the orders were compliant or not was not yours to make.'

'Never the less; I will not be a party to such flagrant flouting of the Rules of Engagement.'

'Did you read the entire Rules? Or just that part that applies to "Seaborne" engagement?'

'I was only given the Seaborne Engagement Rules.'

Tyrell was silent for a very uncomfortable few minutes; the longer he was silent the worse Dalton felt.

Eventually, Tyrell continued, 'Did you read the "Combat Warnings" at the end of your document?'

'No, they are just the usual items like don't run the ship aground, don't run out of fuel and such.'

'You will need your lawyer to explain them to you.' Tyrell got up and went to the door. Alan Dalton was confused as to the last statement, until the door was opened and two Marine Sergeants waited outside.

Tyrell turned around and faced the ship's captain. 'Commander Alan Dalton you are hereby relieved of command and placed under arrest.' Tyrell nodded to the two marines and they entered the room to handcuff the now bewildered Dalton.

'You can't do this?'

'As Naval Forces Commander, I can.'

'What are the charges?'

'Wilful disobedience of the "Rules of Engagement" for the Trans-Pac Exercise. Divulging "Secret" information to the enemy in contravention of the Rules of Engagement section 107, para 9, sub para 12. Headed "Confidential Information". Take him away, deliver him to the Brig at Pearl they will be waiting for him.'

The two Marines escorted the ex-captain ashore.

Tyrell closed the door behind them and called out to the steward. 'Come in here, please.'

The steward entered and was visibly nervous.

'You obviously heard all of that?'

'I am sorry Sir; I could not help but hear.'

'Give me your thoughts.'

'May I speak freely, Sir?'

Tyrell suppressed a small smile as he thought of how Jack's ways were beginning to rub off onto him and the other commanders.

'Please do, everything you say will remain in this room, as will everything you heard, understood?'

'Yes Sir. Commander Dalton was a very strict disciplinarian, the smallest infraction of the regulations would be punished severely. No one on the ship was well disposed to him. We all wanted him promoted so he would leave the ship.' The steward took a deep breath. 'I saw and heard a very little piece of how you and the Japanese General treated the ones he commands; that drone pilot was so eager to help that I wondered how we could get to be that good. I told some of the guys a little, only a little, and they did not believe me until the Operations guys confirmed that it was all good humour and first names during the short time you were at sea with us.'

'The sad part is that once you left us, Commander Dalton became even worse, as if he thought it was all going to end badly; I suppose it has, hasn't it?'

Tyrell smiled. 'Yes, it has. You can reveal the fact that he had given our battle plan to the opposition and had been removed from command for that failing, no more. Understood?'

The steward smiled; thankful he was not in trouble. 'Yes, Sir.'

'Now, before you go and spread the good news; let's get some coffee and get me back on the holo-conference.'

The coffee appeared at the same time the holoprojector beeped reconnecting Tyrell to the others.

'Welcome back Tyrell. All sorted I trust?'

'Sadly, yes. I have relieved Dalton from Command of the Sainsbury; he was the one that ran to Blue command with the details. He has been arrested and landed to the Brig at Pearl.'

'Good, at least he is out of the way. Now here is how we can still win.'

Jack spent the next thirty minutes giving Tyrell the updated information and new deployments.

'What do you think?'

'At first it was disappointing to have a relatively senior officer go down this track. But now, I think we have a better chance at winning. I have an idea that may cause some more headaches for Dalton, during the second half we can still use the initial part of the plan but can we try this.'

For twenty minutes Jack and Tyrell pushed a plan around. 'Just a minute.' Jack called out 'Hasegawa, get Drones, Okimoto and Hiro in here please.'

Moments later the three entered 'Tyrell, give them a briefing.' Tyrell repeated his hastily formed plan which was met with smiles and enthusiasm.

'If Dalton thought the first plan was a worry it is just as well that he isn't here now; this would give him a heart attack.' Drones was, as usual, speaking the thoughts of all around him.

'Good, now we have a landing to oppose, we have two extra days to prepare so let's get to it. Time to make the Blue command sorry they trusted the former command of the Sainsbury.'

'Speaking of the Sainsbury, I will be commanding the Naval Forces from here until Washington can appoint a new captain.' Tyrell announced.

'OK, 0830 tomorrow we can land on the island and set our defences.'

At precisely 0830 the following morning Colonel Fujita and his tanks rolled off the transport ship and onto the wharf of the island designated for the exercise. Closely followed by the remainder of his tank force and the IFV hot on their tails. At the same time, Romans guns were lifted by helicopter and placed on the ridge overlooking the approaches.

For the next four hours the only sound was the roar of hard-working engines pushing the heavy machinery and guns into place.

'ROMAN!' Jack shouted as he approached the firing position of the Heavy Bombardment Group.

'Yes, Jack?' he replied.

'Soon as you are ready, get your ranging tested with Drones. Get your gunners fully familiar with the paintball ammunition. What colour did you have delivered?'

'I asked for pink; that should be annoying and embarrassing for them, returning to base with pink machinery.'

The two shared the humour despite the nerves that were now beginning to surface.

The remainder of the force were busy setting up their defensive positions while Jack and his command team established the Command Post in one of the concrete blockhouses that had been established for the purpose.

'Jack? Can I have a minute?' Drones appeared at the door.

'Sure, come in. How can I help?'

'I think it is me that can help, or perhaps that should be give you an extra problem to cope with.'

'OK, now you have my undivided attention.'

Drones helped himself to a coffee and sat down with his commander. 'We were testing the IR Drones this morning and one of the guys decided to go for a joy flight. Not normal procedure, I know, but this one was flying in circles at around two thousand feet when he picked up a heat bloom.'

'Around here? What was it?'

'A US Navy surveillance drone. We are tracking it at the moment and it appears to be circling in a slowly shrinking spiral which should end up overhead in a couple of hours.'

Jack waited for some time as he thought about the possibilities; eventually he said 'Keep tracking him, get the new pilots ready with the interception units. We will have to be quick.' Jack picked up the radio 'Hiro, shut down all units; no heat signature,' he turned to his aide, 'Hasegawa, set up the mess arrangements in here cooking etc. We will move the command post in the mess tent, this drone may have already plotted our deployment. Drones, if he gets closer than three miles let me know.'

The two replied "Hai." in unison and just thirty minutes later the exchange of places had been completed.

Reports came in one by one confirming the deployment and preparedness of each unit.

'Jack,' Roman called out as he entered the command tent. 'I would like to try a few ranging salvo's, to ensure the coverage is correct, not the 155s just the 127s.'

'Fine, just give us an hour or so to deal with this illegal surveillance drone and we can start.'

Just at that time the position report for the enemy drone confirmed he was within the "controlled airspace" over Jack's position.

'OK Drones, get them up.'

The commands were issued and thirty tiny drones shot vertically into the sky, directed by the pilot flying the defensive unit they eventually began to hover waiting for the enemy plane to arrive.

'Target has broken three miles.' The report came from the flight zone controller.

'Very good, Drones let's see if our plan works.'

'Hai. Place the intercept group in his flight path and just a little higher.'

The tiny drones flew across the flight path and waited, their pilots watching the target as it approached.

'Ready, Jack.'

'Very good, take it out.'

The pilots played kamikaze with the little drones, with frames made of titanium and metal battery shields the pilots flew directly into the engine cowling of the rapidly approaching surveillance unit.

The explosion was spectacular. The titanium of the frames and the high-capacity batteries tore the engine to pieces and then set the ruptured fuel lines on fire. The resulting fireball was as brief as it was violent. The shards of the remains dropped into the ocean and the surviving interceptors returned to base.

'Well done Drones. Red 1 Blue nil. I wonder what that will do to their plans?'

'I feel it may well make them rethink; they would not be expecting to lose an expensive piece of inventory so soon.'

It was three hours later that the holoprojector beeped into life.

'Tyrell. All set?'

'Certainly; but I do have a small problem.'

'Let me guess, a surveillance drone has gone missing.'

'How do you know?'

Jack smiled at his command group. 'We saw the fireball in the sky, since all our units are accounted for, we assumed it must be someone else's.'

'CINCPAC (Commander in Chief Pacific) is absolutely spitting. He wants to know how they lost their aircraft.'

'Would you like to "stir the pot", as the Australians like to say?'

'Sure.'

'Ask why their surveillance unit was overflying our position before the official beginning of the exercise. The Rules of Engagement strictly forbid surveillance after deployment has begun.'

'Get back to you.'

Just an hour later Tyrell called again. 'Jack, you did it again.'

'What did I do?'

'Two Intelligence officers have been reassigned and the Surveillance Commander has been ordered to explain himself to CINCPAC himself.'

'I think they should have been a little more careful.'

'Maybe so, Jack. But you have made some powerful enemies. Blue Commander General Crasten has vowed he will "bury" your lot.'

'Good.'

'What do you mean by that?'

'Crasten and his team will be so bent on revenge they will not be concentrating on the problems at hand. They will be so angry they will miss some of the evidence of our deployments.'

'You are one devious pirate. Have no fear, my dress uniform is ready.'

The two smiled at the thought. 'How did you do it? How did you take it out?'

'We flew some little drones into the engine, blew it to pieces.'

'That is major combat thinking. Remind me to stay on your good side.'

'Certainly, but only if you keep your spies active, we need as much information as we can get.'

'Sorry, but I think I will only be able to give you the departure date, which is tonight at 1900, that will put them off your position before dawn.'

'Will they chance a night landing?'

'No, they will at least want the sun in your eyes as they approach.'

'Good to know. Rest assured, when it is our turn, we will be doing it differently.'

'Now how did I know you would say that.'

Tyrell signed off and the final planning was put in place.

Out of nowhere Drones appeared carrying coffee.

'Arigatō, Drones.'

'When will we start?'

'Keep some of your IR drones up all night; from 0430 tomorrow we will need all the UV and Infra-red sensor units up and watching east. Get your pilots as much rest as possible. We will need a full complement ready and that includes the ranging units.'

'Hai.'

'Drones, give your pilots a pat on the back from me; not only did they destroy an enemy unit, but they have annoyed Blue Command far beyond the loss of one aircraft. They have given me a bonus in the prosecution of this exercise.'

'How?'

'Tyrell reports they are angry with me. An angry man does not focus on all the problem, just on the cause of his anger.'

'In that case we should make sure they get angry more often.' Drones grinned and left the tent.

The day began to dawn and was forecast to be a warm and sunny day.

'A good day to fight.' Hiro volunteered.

'It certainly is. The spotters are up already, and they say there are signs of the approaching landing fleet.' Answered Drones as he entered the tent.

'How far away are they?' Jack asked.

'Still twenty miles, the hovercraft are having to travel slowly to keep the LCH's (landing Craft Heavy) near.'

'Good, the intelligence we have says that Crasten will want to land his heavy armour first. Roman? Your boys ready for some fun?'

'Definitely. They think it is time to show what real gunners can do.'

'Good. Okimoto? Your lot ready?'

'Certainly, just waiting for someone to shoot.'

'OK, if we are already fed and ready let's get back to our positions. Hiro? Start all units and make certain you are ready, then shut down and relax for a few hours. If it blows up early, I will call you. Now, let's show them all what we can do.'

The section commanders returned to their assigned positions and Jack simply sat with his coffee.

'Nervous?' asked Hasegawa.

'Not really. The plan is good, the enemy is uncertain, and the troops are confident. From now on it is all down to timing.

An hour later Drones called in. 'I am bringing the Ranging drones in for battery replacements, enemy is still ten miles away.'

'Agreed. Quick as possible.'

'Hai.'

Within ten minutes the drones were again airborne and waiting just seven miles away.

'Enemy landing fleet has crossed the seven-mile line!'

'Roger. Drones report when ranging drones ready.'

'Ready now.'

'Roman, ENGAGE!'

The next sound was seven 155mm guns letting loose the first rounds of the "Game". As if to increase the confusion, just six seconds later the same happened and then again after a further six seconds.

None of the enemy had considered the high rate of fire that Jack's gunners could attain, just as they could not conceive the accuracy, either.

From the very first salvo, the enemy ships were taking hits. By the time they were just five miles from the landing zone they had lost almost a third of their number either "sunk or disabled".

Just as their commanders were beginning to bemoan their high losses, the resounding bark of the big guns was joined by the crack of the 127s, firing faster and with the same accuracy as their big brothers the landing force was now in real trouble with more than half their number out of action.

Suddenly, at range of just one mile, the guns fell silent. The attacking fleet had been decimated, just seven in total managed to get through; three hovercraft and four LCH's. The landing force was reduced to just eight main battle tanks ten Infantry Fighting Vehicles, three ARV's and a single company of soldiers.

The landing "force", or more correctly, what was left of the landing force finally made it to the beach and began to try to move inland. As they moved up the beach, the small road off the beach led them towards the Red Command post.

As they approached the road they expected to come under fire, but nothing happened. With the foot soldiers riding on the IFV's the column made their way inland.

Suddenly, as if to guide the Blue team, the 127s again began to fire, but this time the shells were landing in front of and to their right of the column. This tactic had the effect of guiding them towards an escape road away from the deadly accurate fire of the Mexican Gunners.

'This will lead us, in a roundabout route, to the Red HQ. Keep moving.' The most senior officer that remained had taken charge, but as a newly promoted Major he was well out of his depth.

With the Tanks leading, he slowly worked his way along the twisting tortuous route, sometimes steep and sometimes very narrow as they headed to their enemy headquarters.

After two hours or more he called a halt.

'Check all directions, IR and UV. I can't believe they have not followed us.'

'All clear all round.' Was the eventual report.

'OK, Senior officers to me, we need to come up with a plan.'

The tank commanders and the infantry officers gathered around and they all checked their maps. Finally agreeing on their position, they made a plan for the approach to the enemy command post.

'At least they don't know where we are,' he exclaimed, not realising there were five surveillance drones watching their every move. 'First IFV see how far along there we can go, be careful.'

The Infantry Fighting Vehicle set off up the little used track.

Red Headquarters

'They have stopped for a conference, Jack.'

'Coordinates?'

'Road Junction, grid GK73.'

'Good, they will probably turn right, that is impassable so they will have to turn back. We have around three hours.' Jack replied.

'Drones, put up two extra units to check their progress along that track, replace the pilots on the chasers, send new units. New batteries when they get back and some down time for the pilots.'

'Hai.'

'Okimoto, you have time on your hands, get your men food and drink; and let them rest a little. Hiro, same for you. When the time comes you will bear the brunt of the first assault.'

A chorus of 'Hai.' Followed and the radios went dead.

Blue Column

'What do you mean we can't get through?'

'Sorry Major, the track simply peters out, just ends up as jungle.'

'OK, take ten and then we move out up the other track.' The Major had the uncanny feeling that he was being manipulated, but by who or why he did not know. What he did know was that he did not like the feeling, but at least he had not led his entire column up the wrong trail.

'Right, everyone on a truck, move out! Armoured recon to the front; keep a close watch and report everything.'

One ARV (Armoured Reconnaissance Vehicle) slowly manoeuvred its way past the remainder of the column and, by default, the entire Blue assault army. They could almost sense they were closing in on the Red headquarters. The remaining foot soldiers took a hold on a vehicle somehow and the column slowly began its ascent towards the final goal.'

'Are you comfortable with your choices Major?' General Fujita asked, trying to get a feel for the situation.

'Not at all, General. But this is what I have been handed and I will try to make it work. Any way you look at it, we are in real trouble.'

Red HQ

'They are on the move, Jack.' Called Drones from his control position in the darkened corner where he could keep control of his assets and also watch the video feeds directly.

'Good, let Hiro know when they are approaching his position.' 'Hai.'

The trap was now set, and it was just time before it was sprung.

The video feeds from the surveillance drones showed the enemy were making slow progress, their selection of tracks showed exactly where they were expected to emerge from the jungle.

Blue

"Blue 1, this is recon."

The sudden sound from the loud speaker made all inside the tank jump for a moment.

'Blue 1.' The Major answered.

'Sir, we are at the edge of the jungle, the track continues on for some way. There is no sign of the enemy here and there is no evidence that they have been here recently.'

'What about tyre tracks?'

'None Sir, except the wide imprints of agricultural machinery, tractors and harvesters I expect, there seems to be some sort of plantation off to the far south; probably pineapples or sugar cane given we are in Hawaii.'

'Roger that. Move into the clearing and wait for us, the tanks can take the front from here. I think we are around ten miles from the enemy.'

'All units, when we leave the clearing it will be fast as possible to get to the enemy before we are discovered. Be ready, ground troops get a good grip, it may get bumpy.'

Red HQ

'Jack! IR three and six report the first ARV has emerged from the jungle. He has stopped and appears to be waiting.'

'Arigatō, probably reassembling before they charge in here. Hiro?' 'Hai.'

'What are you seeing?'

'Exactly what you want, a small group of tanks trying to get up the slippery sloping ground closely followed by IFV's and a couple of ARV's, all covered with infantry.'

'I expect the first to stop at the edge of the jungle and wait for the rest to close up on his position. When they are bunched up, take them out.'

'As you wish.'

The ARV had pulled off to one side, at the edge of the jungle, and was waiting for the others to emerge. Far off in the distance he could hear the hardworking engines trying to drag a 70-tonne tank up a wet slippery slope. Eventually, the lead tank pushed its gun out into clear air where it stopped and waited for the others to get closer behind him for the "sudden" push against the enemy.

The first indication that it was not going to end well came when the 30mm guns of the Red Team ARV's opened fire. The sharp sound of the ammunition hitting the enemy vehicles was accompanied by the splatter of paintballs; hundreds of them. The Major and his team had only seconds, five of them in fact, to work out what had happened before the sound of tank engines starting began to confuse them again. Closely followed by the crash of 101mm (4 inch) guns firing at point-blank range into his column; all the major could do was watch as his tanks were all "disabled" or "destroyed".

'Hiro and his Armoured Column continued to pour fire into the "enemy" and one by one the vehicles were put out of action. With the crews trying to get out of their vehicles it was Okimoto and his ground forces that completed the massacre.

The final assessment was not only that none had survived; but they had not even returned fire. The first time ever that an entire assault army had been, not only defeated, but wiped out without firing a shot.

'All Umpires and Referees report to me at the leading Blue tank.' General Fujita had called a quick conference for the preliminary findings of the conduct of the exercise. Once they had arrived, they began to compare notes.

'Never seen anything like it.' Was the first comment from the English Umpire, also travelling with the Blue team. 'Where did he get those gunners?'

'It can only be a Red victory,' the New Zealander said 'There are no Blue left.'

The comments continued for the next twenty minutes. Eventually, Hiro approached them.

'My apologies for intruding, but General Nakagawa has invited you all to use his Headquarters for your deliberations.'

'Arigatō, Hiro. I think it would be advantageous to be comfortable as we gather the requisite information.'

The "Independent Assessment Team" as their official title described them, all found a ride on the first of Hiro's IFV's and set off to the Red HQ. The rest squeezed in somewhere and followed soon after.

'Colonel Hyashida? Where should we go?' The young Major was unsure as to what he should be doing with the remains of the Blue Army.

'Follow us. I am sure Jack will give you a coffee and somewhere to rest.'

'Jack? Who is Jack?'

'Sorry, to you he is General Nakagawa; to us he is simply Jack.' With that Hiro gave the order to move out. Eventually, the defeated group joined on at the rear of the column and followed them towards the compound.

'They are all on their way, Jack.'

'Arigatō, get some refreshments for our visitors.' Drones whispered into Jack's ear causing his face to split into a wide grin. 'Sure, why not.'

As the long column approached the HQ, Drones and his pilots began to give a small demonstration of their capabilities. Flying around and in-between the vehicles at ever increasing speeds those that had not witnessed the skills were all wondering as to just how good they were; a question that was answered when Drones led his top pilots in a "slalom" race at full speed along the column.

As they finally drove into the compound, they were witness to over a hundred drones of many different sizes simply hovering and waiting for them to pass under.

'Impressive work Hiro!' Jack shouted to his Tank Commander as he bowed in respect as the column passed him. The drivers parked their vehicles and began to discharge the passengers. First out was General Fujita.

'Seijin, you would like a coffee, yes?'

'Arigatō, it is time to partake in your legendary hospitality Jack.'

'Hasegawa, take them inside and get them comfortable, please. Refreshments as they wish.'

Hasegawa bowed and gestured towards the "mess tent" as they referred to the HQ building.

'Not using the HQ building for command Jack?'

'No, Seijin. We were not confident that it was free from interference, following on from the leaked information before the start. So, we changed things around a little.'

'Probably a wise move.'

Chapter 22
Trans-Pac Part 2

One by one the Umpires and Referees made their way into the HQ building and once they had commandeered a table the refreshments were served.

'General Fujita?' asked Alex Johnson, the New Zealand General in overall command of the adjudicators, 'Where did he get all this food and drink from?'

'I will ask him. Jack!' Seijin beckoned Jack over. 'How did you get so much "luxury" food items here?'

Jack smiled widely. 'Just because we are at "war" does not mean we have to be uncivilised. I had Tyrell fly it in from the "Red Fleet" at sea.'

'It is really appreciated.'

'Arigatō, Seijin. Have the Blue team been attended to?'

A chorus of "Hai" met Jack's query and again he smiled at the forethought his team had given.

Just as he was about to speak with the Blue Tank Commander as loud commotion could be heard approaching from the outside.

'I thought we would at least have time for coffee before the angry ones arrived.' Hasegawa gave voice to the same thoughts that everyone was entertaining.

'Get some extra cups and plates for them.' Jack ordered; and from somewhere an extra tray of foods appeared.

The first through the door was a U.S. Army Colonel; and he was so fired up Jack expected him to have a heart attack. His main complaint seemed to be that, once again, Jack had somehow cheated.

General Johnson had his hands full trying to placate the irate American. Eventually, it was the Englishman that stopped him.

'If you have a complaint it must wait until the debrief, not before,' he told the Colonel. With his strong, almost indecipherable, Yorkshire accent leading the argument, the American had to stop and listen carefully just to understand the simple statement and this seemed to take the steam out of his words.

'Gentlemen, we must leave you. Our transports are arriving to take us out to sea to begin the preparations for the second phase of the exercise. Please, continue to use the provisions, may as well eat them all, I don't want to have to take this food back to the fleet; if I do it will destroy our reputation as "The Dirt People" living off scraps.'

Most of those present laughed; the exception was always going to be the Americans. Once out of sight Jack spoke to Hiro, 'Angry little man, isn't he?'

'I bet he complains about everything we did, starting with the artillery and ending with the colour of the milk for the tea.'

'Yes, but we can handle him when the time comes.'

Back at the Umpires conference the arguments were again becoming heated, the American Colonel was going to be heard and no one was going to stop him.

Several times each of the Umpires in turn tried to calm him but he was not going to be easily put off.

Eventually, General Fujita spoke up.

'Colonel! That is enough! If you feel so deeply about this, then put in an official complaint.'

'Complaint! I will challenge him to a fight, one on one. In the ring if necessary.'

Fujita stared intensely at the American, eventually all became quiet as they waited for the next outburst.

'Be very careful what you say, Colonel, and before you say any more watch this.'

Seijin pushed a few controls on the holo-projector and the image of an MMA fighting ring appeared. The two fighters inside the ring were waiting for the bell, to begin their fight.'

'Who is this? Why are we watching it?' the American demanded.

Seijin turned up the volume as the announcer introduced the event.

This event is for the Japanese National Open Title. It will be fought over five, five-minute rounds. In the blue corner, straight out of high school Jackson Nakagawa. In the red corner, The current National Champion and number one contender for the World Championship Daichi Hosho. The cheering for the champion was as loud as it was almost completely absent for the unknown Jack.

The two met in the centre of the ring and received their instructions, then they returned to their corner to await the bell to begin the fight.

The history books called it a fight. The spectators all wanted their money back. The promoters began to rub their hands together in anticipation of the vast amounts of money they would make, starting with the rematch. The bookmakers all made a fortune, no one had backed the winner.

The only one not interested was Hosho, he was unconscious and being attended to by the doctors. Jack was waiting patiently, unsure what all the fuss was about.

The eventual injuries were described as "Broken Jaw, fractured eye socket, concussion, broken nose, broken ribs, ruptured eardrum and missing teeth (presumed swallowed)."

The news feeds described it as the most unlikely victory ever.

So, what had happened?

When the bell rang to begin the fight Hosho charged across the ring to attack in his usual style. Jack took three steps forward and one to the side. A knee to the centre of the rib cage saw his, unprepared, opponent stop and gasp for air. The subsequent deluge of blows would see the man regarded as the toughest fighter in his weight class, smashed into oblivion.

So quick and clinical was his onslaught, Jack had barely raised a sweat and the fight was over almost before it began.

Seijin turned off the holo-projector and looked around the, now silent, room.

'If you are certain you wish to step into the ring with Jack, I will arrange it. But be warned he still trains for this and several other martial arts; he has lost nothing over the years.'

'Were that 'im?' asked the English General.

'It was,' Seijin replied.

'Colonel, you have bitten off a lot more than you can chew. Be careful who you challenge,' warned General Johnson.

The American looked around and waited for someone, anyone, to speak; something to break the extremely uncomfortable silence. With nothing being spoken, eventually he turned and stormed out of the room; still angry but having no one or nothing to blame it on or to rant at.

'You know he is going to push this as far as he can don't you Seijin?' General Johnson finally broke the silence, a good while after the American had left.

'I have no doubt he will try. But let me tell you this; starting as a new Lieutenant out of the College Jack has stood against generals, The Chief of Staff, The Chief of the Army The commander of the Northern Army and several others. All of them came out of it defeated, Jack can handle him both on and off the field of battle. Now I could use a fresh coffee.'

A steaming cup suddenly appeared before him, being carried by one of Jack's staff.

'arigatō, shouldn't you be on your way back to your unit?' Seijin asked the steward.

'Once you have finished Jack will ask Tyrell to send a helicopter for me, to bring back his family dinnerware.' The steward gestured to the table covered with expensive looking cutlery and crockery.

'Very good.'

The umpires collated their documentation and had an in-depth conference while the combatants prepared for phase two.

'Seijin? Can I ask why you let the steward call his Commanding Officer by his first name?'

'That is Jack's preference, he feels he gets a closer-knit group and better results if everyone is comfortable with the situation. To be honest, I didn't like it at first, but let me tell you, he gets results from his teams that no one can predict; and that is the one difference we can point to. His teams are comfortable with him at the top. That is how he made General so quickly; yes, he embarrassed many of us, me included, but he is good. If he is going to get such results simply by the way he speaks with people then I am all for it. Watch his performance in the second phase, then think if you could pull it off. I know it will be nothing short of spectacular.'

Red Fleet, Captain's Cabin, U.S.S. Sainsbury

'Are we all ready?' It was a rhetorical question but one that had to be asked, even if it was just to ensure that no last-minute issues that had arisen.

'Nothing? Good. Tyrell the barge is ready?'

'Yes, Jack. The internal layout should convince anyone.'

'Drones, your heavy drop units are ready?'

'Hai, the payload has been tested and the drones themselves have been load and range tested. All exactly as we wanted them.'

'Have the batteries been capacity drain tested?'

'Hai, the batteries are able to complete two runs minimum.'

'Arigatō. Okimoto? Are the lead troops ready?'

'Hai, soft shoes for quiet; and night vision gear for safety.'

'Good. Hiro? The plan does not call for your insertion at first, but when the time comes you will need to be fast.'

'All ready, we are planning on landing a tank, two ARV's (Armoured Reconnaissance Vehicles) and two IFV's (Infantry Fighting Vehicles) from each LCH (Landing Craft Heavy) in that order. The smaller units can deal with foot soldiers and small vehicles while the tank can protect them should they encounter the enemy armour.'

'Roman, I know this is out of your field of expertise, but can you drop some rounds onto the enemy position from the Heavy Bombardment Group?'

'From out at sea you mean?'

'Hai, is it possible?'

Roman thought for a few moments. 'Of course it is possible, just don't expect any accuracy.'

Jack began to laugh as he thought of Romans hyper-accurate gunners getting frustrated with the constant motion of being at sea and trying to hit a target.

'No, I don't need accuracy, just an annoyance factor that is off the scale. Same with your gunners, Tyrell. I expect that they will try something similar to our tactics, except they will not have the 155s or our gunners. If they are lucky, they will have the 105s on their tanks, and the 127s from their artillery, nowhere near the range. We should be able to annoy them without being effectively shot at. Roman, where did they come at the Gunnery Competition?'

'Oh, they did really well; by their standards. They came in twelfth, accuracy score of 85%.'

'Not in the same game, sounds good. Now what does the latest intelligence give us?'

'Just a moment, Jack. I will call the intelligence officer.' Tyrell moved to his phone and made a call. Just two minutes later a junior officer knocked on the door. The look on his face was one of surprise when the door opened with a Japanese General doing the honours, the young officer clearly expected a steward to open the door.

As he looked around, he saw the assembled Command Team, however his mind could not calculate the hierarchy of those he saw; none of them was wearing a jacket the only rank insignia was worn on the collar or the shirt. A young Japanese Sergeant-Major was arguing a point with Admiral Backhouse; A Mexican General asking for information from a Chief Petty Officer, the point seemed to be something to do with lashing down guns.

'Jack,' called out the, apparently older Japanese Captain. 'If we can attach some steps or footholds on the side and some ropes on top of the IFV's we can double the travelling capacity of the units, get more men ashore earlier.'

'Good idea, Okimoto.' The man holding the door called out to the steward 'Set a place for two extras and then find the Engineering Chief, please. Come in, take a seat. What is your name?'

'Thank you, sir. Cruz, James Lieutenant JG.' (junior grade, as low as qualified officers get).

'Come in James or do you prefer Jim?'

'Er, um, Jim is fine Sir.'

'Call me Jack. Everyone this is Jim, introduce yourselves.' Around the table each in turn held up their hand.

'Roman Artillery,'

'Okimoto, Infantry.'

'Drones, drones.'

'Mai, conference notes and audio/video equipment.' And so on around the table.

The lieutenant was completely dumfounded when the Admiral introduced himself by his first name.

'Tyrell, fleet operations.' Just at that point there was yet another knock on the door, and again Jack opened it.

'Master Chief Harold Masters, I was told to report.' Jack held out his hand and the Chief took it. He was not quite overawed, as Drones had already told him of the informal ways of the command group.

'Harold; come in sit. Introductions again if you please.' And the names went around the table again.

'Shuffle around a bit, I need the Chief next to me.' Okimoto announced, and the senior officers all moved chairs so that the Chief took the required position.

'Jim, get a coffee and then give us a rundown of the latest intelligence.' The lieutenant did as he was told and sat at the only seat left at the table, between the Admiral and the Mexican General. He felt very much out of place and the look on his face showed it.

'Don't panic, Jim, we don't bite.' Tyrell attempted to ease the young officer's mind.

'Unless you are a smart-arsed Blue Army Colonel that deserves a flogging.' The room burst into laughter and the lieutenant simply looked confused at the inside joke.

The room slowly became a mass of individual conversations and Jack let them go for a few minutes; eventually he asked 'Jim, what are the latest deployments of the enemy? Start with the heavy armour and the artillery.'

The intelligence officer was, if not shocked then at least self-conscious, to be the centre of attention and he began to speak, describing the current known positions and spread of the enemy equipment.

After around five minutes Okimoto interrupted him. 'Hold on Jim, how old is this information?'

'Twelve hours, or there about.'

Okimoto looked at Jack, no one saw the imperceptible nod.

'Drones,' continued Okimoto. 'Do you think you can get something a little more up to date?'

'Hai.' Drones picked up his communicator and spoke rapidly in Japanese. 'Six IR and UV drones on their way.' Jack nodded and the conversation continued for the next fifteen minutes.

Suddenly the holo-projector beeped and the live feed appeared before them. The steward dimmed the lights and the group watched as Drones described the findings before them. When he was finished Jack spoke. 'Hai, arigatō Drones. Can we get a flight up one hour before the sun starts to make the sky light as well as one an hour after nightfall?'

'Hai,'

Tyrell called the Navigator and asked for the appropriate times to allow Drones to fly in and out undetected.

It seemed that, to the young intelligence officer, any of the people present could ask for something and the ship would move heaven and earth to give it. It didn't matter if it was an enlisted man or the Commanding General.

When he returned to the wardroom, he made the comment to another junior officer and it was overheard by the ship's operations officer.

'You seem confused by the goings on in the captain's cabin?'

'I didn't mean it to sound like criticism, but I have never seen the way they work. It seems that it is all against the way we were taught at Annapolis.' (The US naval academy).

'Did you see the preliminary results of the first half of the operation?'

'No Sir, I have not.'

'The Red Army, the ones they are running from the captain's cabin, won the first part. The Blue army were wiped out, only two survivors and they were privates that fell off an ARV. Red army casualties, one private twisted his ankle and one cook cut a finger. More than impressive by any standards. The way this General Nakagawa works is different and very effective, we will all benefit from watching his ways. We may never be able to replicate them, but he is showing the world a new way of commanding an army in the field.'

The wardroom phone rang and was answered by a steward.

'Lieutenant Cruz, Sir. Admiral Backhouse wants you back in the Captain's Cabin.'

'Very good, tell him I am on the way,' he stood up and took a look at the wardroom clock. 'Three am, looks like no sleep tonight,' he commented to himself.

'Look on it as a learning experience, Lieutenant.' Was the comment from the Operations Officer.

Moments later his knock on the door was met with "Enter" from within. He opened the door and was surprised to see everyone still there. The Chief Engineer and the Infantry Captain were busy with the creation of a modification for the IFV's. The General and the Artillery officer were trying to resolve the problem of firing guns without any stabilisation. Several other parts of conversations were being heard and not quite understood.

Suddenly a cup of coffee was thrust into his hand. 'Come and sit, we are about to get the first of the mornings intelligence from the drones,' he took the coffee without even realising he had done it, and found a seat.

'Don't they know we have been checking their positions?'

'They probably suspect but the units we use are so small they will never see them anyway.'

'Just how small?'

Drones looked at Jack and got a small nod in return. He called his pilots and then opened the door. He asked the steward to open a door to the open deck. Just as he did so a small drone entered the ship from outside and flew directly into the captain's cabin, landing on the table. Barely 100mm across it was so small that the Intelligence Officer could not believe it would be useful, until the holo-projector showed the people in the room from its position on the table.

'That is impressive. Now I see how it can help.'

'Jim,' called Jack, 'I want you to work closely with Drones, your analysis will be helpful. Get the navigator to plot the enemy positions on a map of the area that will give us a two-dimensional view of the battlefield.'

'I will speak with him at breakfast.'

'Just a minute.' Tyrell interrupted, and just five minutes later the navigator appeared at the cabin door. 'Nav, work with these two,' Tyrell indicated Drones and Cruz. 'Plot the positions as they are revealed two and three dimensional.'

The navigator seemed somewhat disoriented at the strange demand.

'Yes Sir, I will get my assistant on it this morning.'

'That will be too late, NOW, if you please, Commander.'

The navigator spun around to see who was speaking, and locked eyes on a tall Japanese man. He was about to speak when his brain eventually made the connections. 'Yes, Sir. Right now.'

'Get my assistant and have him bring charts and maps of the area.'

It seemed amusing to Jack that everyone that entered the captain's cabin was stunned; the navigators assistant was no exception. Eventually, the maps began to come together. The positions of the enemy guns and tanks were being plotted and updated and the battlefield began to take shape.

Breakfast came and went; taken at their makeshift work station the steward was kept very busy bringing and removing plates of food as well as what was almost a never-ending supply of coffee and tea.

Eventually, the first of the projections was ready and they all relaxed.

'OK, time to stop. Everyone; take a shower and rest. We start again at 1600.

The entire command team stopped working and rested, as ordered.

That afternoon the system was again updated and the possible assault plan was refined.

'They don't have too much imagination, Jack.' Tyrell announced, they have put their artillery in the same place as you did and I would bet they have laid out an ambush on the side access tracks as well.'

'That is a shame, we won't be going that way. They will have to change their plans.'

'I think we should wait an extra day before we attack, the command group can do the brunt of the work at this time. DRONES!'

'Yes Jack?'

'Have you had your guys test the special weapons we devised?'

'Yes, we had to change the underside pads but the new ones are perfect.'

'Good. Get your team to charge the battery packs and then stand down until the sun goes down.'

'Hai.'

Drones left Jack to his deliberations. Just after Drones left the room Jack went for a walk around the deck and was far away with his thoughts when Tyrell came up behind him.

'Special project is ready and tested Jack. Electric motors are well hidden and silent when running. I think we are ready to go.'

'Yes, new moon in three days they will expect us to use the dark night, we will start tonight, put the barge in place for them to find in the morning. We will attack tomorrow.'

'Consider it done. Now you need to sleep the same as the rest of us.' Tyrell announced. The two made their way to their cabins and slept instantly. Like all good military people, they could sleep anywhere and survive and function on almost no sleep at all.'

With no pressing business to keep him awake, Jack managed some sleep and, as his mind actually did not have a problem to solve while he did so, his rest was deep and uninterrupted.

He woke with a start; he was rested and ready. Looking at the clock he knew it was after dark and following a shower he returned to the captain's cabin.

'Evening all. How goes the war?'

'Ready and raring to go. We have already sent the special unit an hour ago, it will make landfall in about seven hours.'

'Good, the game has begun. Latest intel?'

'On the holo,' announced Drones. The entire command group had gathered by this time and were all watching as the relative positions of the enemy forces were placed on the image. Separate colours for artillery, armour, ground troops. The experienced eyes of the commanders began to analyse the deployments and the positioning. The strong points and weak points becoming clear with each new piece of information.

The latest positioning was plotted as soon as it was received.

'This is good Tyrell. They are well clear of the initial landing site, the intended approaches are well defended, as we expected and our preferred landing site is off their radar. We will win this as well.'

High confidence, was how their mood would be described later at the debriefing.

Blue Headquarters

The captain in charge of an observation platoon was significantly agitated to burst into the Operations Centre. 'Colonel, Colonel, there has been a barge washed up in the storm channel to the west of here.'

'Why are you making a fuss over a barge? One was washed away from its moorings a while back. No one cares about an old barge.'

'But this one shows signs of having been occupied in the last day or so.'

The Colonels head spun so quickly he almost gave himself a sore neck.

'Occupied! So that is how he intends to fight. He has already landed, get search teams out, I want them found.' The captain left to organise the demanded search teams.

'General?'

'What is it Colonel?'

'A barge, showing signs of being occupied, has been found to the west.' 'And?'

'I believe the Red Army have begun their infiltration; I have dispatched search teams.'

'Very well, keep me informed.'

'Yes, Sir.' The colonel saluted and left, "I will find him and beat him this time." He thought to himself.

U.S.S. Sainsbury

'Heat blooms in IFV's and ARV's Jack.' Drones put the new data on the projector.

'Good they are out looking for us. I think we shall take an extra day before we land, they will be getting tired and irritable. Tired men make mistakes.'

The game of cat and mouse would normally be one of hide and chase. This time it was chase, chase and more chase; but there was no one to chase, it was all shadows and the soldiers quickly became distrustful of their superiors. Rest was in short supply as was food; and fatigue would prove to be a huge factor in the Blue Army's ability to withstand any attack, let alone a full invasion force.

The appointed day arrived and Jack spent most of it ensuring his teams were ready, fed, rested and motivated.

The sun went down and Jack waited for any last-minute intelligence that would change his plan. Nothing changed.

Just after mid-night Jack gave the order 'Drones, special deliveries if you would be so kind.'

'Hai.'

Almost fifty heavy delivery drones, at just over 400mm in diameter they could easily lift and deliver the 5kg payload required, lifted off and headed for the enemy positions. With his team working as fast as possible Drones had them flying at about half a metre above the sea surface, so low that they would be all but invisible.

They approached the island from the inhospitable north and as soon as they arrived, they began to place their packages on each of the tanks and the artillery Just at the base of the barrel. Being so late at night the gunners and tank crews were resting, the attacking fleet of drones had not been seen or detected, so they took the opportunity to rest. It was a decision that their command group would regret.

As quickly as they arrived the, now empty drones, left and flew away from the island the same way they had arrived. Undetected and safe they returned to the ship without incident.

'Prepare them for tomorrow and get some rest.' Drones ordered his team.

He entered the "Planning Room", as they had taken to calling the captain's cabin and gave Jack the good news.

'OK, Roman, Tyrell at dawn tomorrow you can begin to fire on the enemy position. Drones you may have the pleasure of completing your work at the same time.'

'About that Jack.' Roman had been quietly analysing the demands of the battle plan.

'You have something?'

'Well, we know my gunners have no chance of actually hitting something, anything; having the guns move up and down ruins any chance of accuracy. So, why don't we use my lot to fire "star shell", that will keep them awake and Tyrells lot can fire for effect. Their stabilisation will give them the extra range to keep the ships out of range of the Blue's. We can fire from mid-night and the placed charges can be detonated at our pleasure.'

'Great idea. Let's go with that. The final phase can be implemented at any time during the week following.'

Roman's gunners went to work; with two guns mounted on the bow of each ship they began bombarding the shore installations with monotonous regularity. Every four seconds a star shell would illuminate the sky above the Blue defensive positions. This would be followed by three or four paint shells from the Red Fleet.

The ships were getting some hits from the shelling, but not enough. The Blue team had not returned fire as they knew the Red units were out of range, all they could do was wait. An unnerving experience to be certain, but there was nothing else to be done.

Just an hour before the beginning of sunrise Jack gave the order and dozens of remotely detonated charges were set off. The umpire's adjudication was that the defenders had no heavy guns left; all had been destroyed from a long way away. And the Blue team could only try to recover.

A good commander would have been able to still defend the position, if he were up against a normal aggressor; but this was not any other officer and Jack was far from finished with his plan.

'What do you mean our armour is destroyed? The enemy didn't even score a hit; how did they defeat us?'

'Colonel, your teams failed to notice the explosive packages attached to your tanks and artillery. He has effectively blown them all to pieces. Now you get to devise a new plan.' General Johnson was less than gentle with his assessment; and he made certain the Colonel understood that it was not looking very well for him. For his part, the Colonel could see his promotion was slowly disappearing and he had the odd feeling there was little he could do to stop it.

He stormed out of the building and began to demand reports as to the search for the teams that had obviously already landed and were, to his slightly confused mind, responsible for the loss of all of his heavy units.

Completely obsessed, he sent virtually all of his ground troops to search for the "elusive saboteurs" and, predictably, they reported nothing. It could have been called a "cat and mouse" strategy, except there was no mouse and the cat would continue to chase it for days if necessary.

'Colonel, we have searched the eastern extremities and the north as well; nothing to report.'

'Then search the central area and the west, they must be there.'

'Sir, the men need to rest.'

'Rest! No, you must find the infiltrators, dismissed Major. Shut down the radar search units and take them as well for your search parties.'

'Yes Sir.' The Major left the building to return to the ground troops; all the time thinking he would have to go and tell them to continue working without rest. Well to hell with him. 'Go get a feed and rest some. Then we go out again,' he told his troops. They were grateful but suspicious.

'What about the colonel?' one asked.

'Let me worry about him, just take your break where he cannot see you. If we are out of sight, he will assume we are doing his bidding.'

Referee's Control Room

'That Colonel is out of control,' General Johnson commented.

'I would not worry too much; Jack will sort him out. And if I am not mistaken it will be sooner rather than later,' Seijin replied.

U.S.S. Sainsbury

'Do not let up on the bombardment Roman. We are going in tonight.' Jack had committed his forces to the final assault.

The high-speed boats would make the trip into the "unusable landing area" that Jack had chosen for his infiltration, in around three hours. The only factor that was uncertain was would they be tracked by radar or some other means.

'Surveillance reports?' Jack queried the team that was sitting in the captain's cabin.

'Last intel shows the heavy armour, most of the ARV's and IFV's are out of commission,' replied James Cruz, now more familiar with his role in the team he was more confident in his dealings with the hierarchy of the team. 'Latest reports show they have shut down their radar and fire control systems, no need for gun control when there are no guns to control.'

'Anything else?' Jack asked, hopeful there was nothing to jeopardise his plans.

'There is one thing, Sir,' he began, almost frightened to continue he looked around for consent.

'Spill it.' Tyrell demanded.

'Well, Sir. We hacked the Referees communications; the Colonel is becoming more "unhinged" as they say. He now has no effective battle plan and his commanding general is no better.'

'YOU HACKED THE REFEREES!' Jack shouted with glee. Turning to Tyrell he said 'This one is really one of us.'

Tyrell smiled widely. 'He certainly is; Lieutenant you will need to get your dress uniform ready for the inquisition.'

The Lieutenant was confused, and his face looked like it.

'I don't understand?'

'Sorry, Jim. It is a standing joke that we will be asked to explain ourselves to a board of enquiry. It seems to be that everyone takes offence to being beaten; and around Jack that happens with monotonous regularity.'

'So, you are only joking?'

'No, there will be a board of enquiry and Jack will stand before it, wearing his dress uniform and we will all be there in support. But he will be the only one he will permit to answer questions. Don't worry, Jack will protect you.' Okimoto was speaking with the certainty that experience brings. 'The way the Blue Command team has performed, it is more likely that the enquiry will be "How did they get beaten so badly" rather than investigating Jack's methods. We have one thing in our favour, General Fujita is the number two referee for this exercise and he will be able to deflect a lot of the criticism.'

'Arigatō, Okimoto, your words are good to hear. Unfortunately, we must now prepare to end this "war".'

And end the "war" was exactly what he did. The boats landed the infantry in the secluded bay Jack had found hidden amongst the mangroves. Three hundred ground troops were put ashore unopposed and they made their way quickly around the rear of the HQ building, "killing" or wounding all they encountered on the way. Seijin was expecting them but no one else even suspected.

Jack waited until the reports of the rapidly advancing landing craft were becoming more prevalent, then he gave the order for the massed infiltration of the building. One by one the ground troops, aides, and assistants were removed from the defensive rings and that gave space for them to penetrate further.

Eventually, they were in position and ready.

'Hiro, land en masse, fast as possible. Proceed towards the HQ building, Tanks at the front.' Jack whispered into his comms unit. There was no reply, there was no need for one, Jack and Hiro both knew the end was close and Hiro understood the need for a distraction to let Jack get inside to complete the exercise.

Blue HQ

'General, there are massed landings.'

'Where?'

'Right along the beaches, where we tried to come ashore.'

'Who is opposing in that sector?'

'Colonel Hicks has gone in search of the "infiltration" teams he thinks were landed the night before last.'

'Dammit. He was supposed to be guarding the beaches.'

The noise of hard-working engines was becoming louder as the assault teams sped towards their final objective. The defending General was trying to assemble as many of his teams as were available, but every time he assigned a position to a team they stopped transmitting and were assumed lost.

'General Johnson; I can no longer offer resistance to the assault teams. As head referee I would appreciate it if you would contact Red Army Command and offer our unconditional surrender.' Just at that moment the door crashed open and thirty Red Army infantry entered the room. Followed by a tall Japanese General.

'Your offer of surrender is accepted.' Jack announced as he entered the room.

Seijin could only just hold in his amusement and he caught the eye of General Johnson who was almost as stunned as everyone else in the room.

One private off to one side decided he would try to "kill" the enemy general and he tried to shoot. Before he could get his weapon level, he was hit by over thirty paintball rounds.

'That was foolish, he should have understood that the time for heroics had passed.' Jack was philosophical at that moment, a mood that dissipated completely when the Colonel entered with his weapon in hand. Okimoto and his group "shot" the colonel so many times there was little of his combat fatigues that was the original colour.

Once the noise died down, it was Jack that spoke.

'That was just stupid. What do you think your General meant when he offered his unconditional surrender?'

'YOU F****N CHEATED!'

'Oh shut up, you are DEAD. Your army has been defeated, you are dead and your general is in custody. Will somebody give him a glass of champagne.'

The room was silent. No one understood the last statement. Eventually, Seijin asked the question.

'Jack, why would you give him champagne?'

'Winston Churchill once said, "You should drink champagne for defeat as well as victory. It tastes the same and you need it more." Give him a drink.'

'F*** YOU!' the Colonel screamed.

'Sergeant-Major, remove the Colonel.' It was General Crasten of the newly defeated Blue Army that gave the order and his NCO grabbed the officer and literally dragged him out of the room.'

'My apologies, General Nakagawa. That was his last chance at field command. He will be in charge of "parks and gardens" at a remote base in northern Oregon from now on.'

'No need for an apology, Sir. Many have taken offence at being defeated. He is just the latest in a long line of angry opposing commanders that are waiting for me to make a mistake.'

'Now we are done, would you be able to give me a debrief on your tactics? I for one would like to find out how you did it?'

'Certainly, I will make an appointment after the official debrief.'

'Congratulations Jack. You and your team have just been declared the official winners of the exercise.' It was General Johnson that offered his hand. As Jack took it, he was asked, 'If I asked you what would you say was your main advantage?'

Jack thought for a moment and then said 'I think it would be the teamwork as a whole. Every time I needed to assign a new person to a position, the others would help to bring them into the team. The trust engendered would be spread and all felt included and valuable. Everyone helped in their own way.'

'Hmm; and equipment wise?'

'Oh, that is simple. Drones. The variety and purpose of our drone equipment as well as the superior pilots gave us a distinct advantage.'

'Hmm. Speaking of drones; a long-range battlefield interdiction drone was lost right at the beginning of the exercise. Know anything about that?'

'That's illegal, Sir. The Rules of Engagement do not allow for the use of those units.' Jack's words were tinged with his trademark sarcasm.

'We will discuss that at the debrief, any idea how it was lost?'

'None whatsoever,' Jack answered innocently, 'but we also lost five or six of our IR detector units early. Maybe a coincidence?'

Seijin could not hold the laugh inside. 'Jack you should not play poker. That is the worst bluff I have ever seen.'

'I do not know what you mean.' Was Jack's response, but all could see the smile creeping across his face.

'Sure, we all believe you. Don't we?' Even Seijin and Hiro could not disguise the sarcasm in their voices.

'Gentlemen, there is a meal and hot showers for anyone that wishes to join us on the Sainsbury.' Tyrell's offer was accepted by all and soon the fleet was onloading the ground units for their return to Pearl Harbour.

Once settled onboard, Jack called a holo conference of all the senior commanders for the Red Army.

'Congratulations gentlemen, we are victorious. As such I believe we should be rewarded. Once the equipment has been cleaned and prepared for transport, all, and I do mean all, personnel will take a week's leave and enjoy the tourist traps of Hawaii.'

Jack's offer was met with enthusiasm by all and they began to make plans for their week off.

'DO NOT,' Jack continued, 'get too drunk. Remember there is still the debrief to be concluded so...'

'Get your dress uniforms ready!' they all chorused together.

Chapter 23
Trans-Pac Debrief

The room was full of high-ranking officers. Army and Navy alike, the place was packed with the commanders and their advisors as well as the referees and umpires.

Eventually, General Johnson entered the room and all became quiet. With the Blue Army Staff on one side and the Red Army on the other.

The "Blue" table was covered in documents, several copies of the Rules of Engagement, Combat Reports, Engagement Results. Ammunition reports; everything that could possibly be needed. General Crasten was seated with six of his deputy commanders at the table and almost a dozen others behind him. A very powerful group.

The "Red" table was, by comparison, empty. A single copy of the Rules of Engagement had been placed at the centre of the table with a holo-projector beside it. Jack sat behind the table with Mai beside him to control the projector and supply reference material if needed.

'This meeting will come to order.' General Johnsons assistant ordered and the room fell silent.

'Thank you. The purpose of this meeting is to analyse the results from the completion of the Trans-Pac exercise. The final conclusion was a resounding victory, in both sections, to the "Red" army, commanded by General Nakagawa. The result is not in dispute, what we do want to know is how it was achieved?'

'General Crasten?'

'Thank you, Sir. I have been completing army exercises for the last forty years. Some I have won some I have lost. In this instance I was completely out manoeuvred and out fought by the opposition. Their tactics, right from the beginning, had us on the run. We could not land a blow on their defences and we could not defend against their attacking methodology.'

'How did you do it, Jack?'

'Thank you, Sir. To begin with, I was given team members that wanted to achieve high results. The artillery I was told to use were Mexican. The language barrier was difficult enough, but we managed to adapt.'

'You cheated!' came a cry from the rear. 'You used 155mm guns and the rest of us only had 127s.'

Jack didn't even turn to see who had spoken. 'These were the regiments that were given to us, and as such, were approved during the original planning stage. The advantage we conceived was to improve accuracy. This was a major issue for us, how do you tell the World Champions that their gunnery was not good enough? We improved the ranging by using laser drones, this improved the accuracy from 99.5% to 99.99%. Instead of having one shell in 200 miss we had lifted their work to one shell in a thousand. General Garcia tells me that his gunners are more than pleased with the benefit they have gained from the exercise, and we have given them some of the ranging drones so they can continue their record-breaking work.'

'The Rules (of Engagement) do state that 127mm guns are to be used.' General Crasten posed the question.

'It does. However; Section 5, para 7.3 states that "In the event that artillery regiments are a part of a greater unit then the weapons of that unit may be used." The 86th Heavy Bombardment Regiment are a part of the 9th Field Support Group. There are, I believe, five Regiments to each Field Support Group. Three regiments of 127s, one of 155s and the artillery support group, technicians, range officers and such.' Jack looked at Roman for confirmation and simply got a nod in reply.

'Did the 155s give an advantage?'

'Certainly, we could shell the opposition as they approached the landing area. The longer range meant that we could destroy more of them before they could land. They simply continued to charge straight at us, despite the heavy fire.'

'What would you do if you were on the receiving of this type of bombardment?' General Crasten wanted to know how Jack would protect his own should the places be reversed.

'I would have kept out of range, to start with, then I would have sent the majority of my units to a secondary landing site.'

The Colonel could not stay quiet any longer. 'We only had the beach landing grounds!'

'Colonel, you may have only had one landing ground; but we had a landing ground in the north, rocky but usable. There was one along the storm drainage channel. Another hidden in the mangrove swamps. You could do a lot of damage with a little foresight.' The Colonel had no answer.

'You destroyed most of the attacking forces before they landed, why did you not finish them off on the beach?'

'The short ranging limitation of the 155s did not allow us to drop shells into their lines once they got ashore, this is one of the reasons we needed to stop most of them before landing. The plan was always that some would get through and we needed to control that event. So, to paraphrase Sun Tzu and Miyamoto Musashi I placed my enemy where I wanted them. By forcing them to use the escape road to get away from the bombardment I put them on the road to my ambush, and that is where I completed the defensive phase of the exercise, with an ambush.'

'You destroyed a surveillance drone, WHY!'

'Ah, you are referring to the lost Battlefield Interdiction Drone are you not?'

'Section 19 para 12 Prohibited Units states "This exercise is for ground units, as such Large Assault drones are prohibited." The definition of large units is contained in annex 3 part 2 and it specifically states that Battlefield Interdiction Drones must not be used. Just for information section 19 para 19 also states that surveillance of the combat arena is not to be conducted after the units have been deployed. Why was it flying over the exercise area?'

No one could give a reason.

'Call the pilot Commander at the Pentagon see what he has to say. Or should I save you the bother. The flight was authorised by the Blue Unit Commander, wasn't it Colonel?'

The Colonel could not return Jack's stare.

'As a part of this question I would like to ask if you also had a part in the loss of six of our IR detection quad-copters?' Still the Colonel could not look up. Jack did not care about the lost units they were cheap and easily replaced, he just wanted them all to know that the cheat was seated at the other table.

The questioning continued for the next two hours. Each time they tried to trap Jack, he answered their questions and quoted the section and paragraph number to prove he was right, without ever opening the "Rules". Eventually, they gave up.

'I think that is enough for the first part of the exercise, we will reconvene for the second part after lunch.' General Johnson was becoming just a little weary of the constant claims of cheating against Jack's team; an allegation which always turned out to be the result of nothing more than an intense attention to detail by Jack's Red Army Command Team and a level of innovative thinking previously not applied.

'That went well.' Jack said as he sat down at the table set aside for them at the Pearl Harbour Investigations centre.

'Went well!' exclaimed Jim Cruz. 'I was terrified the whole time.'

'Nothing to worry about, it is all in hand,' replied Okimoto, his words were accompanied by agreement from Hiro, both of whom had seen it all before.

The meal was completed without fuss, everyone relaxing and comfortable with the proceedings.

The second half went as well as the first; for Jack and the Red team. Not so much for the Blue team. The Conduct of the Commanding General was not in question, he had done all he could. The conduct of several of his support commanders was, however, not so easily dismissed.

'Welcome back. How did you achieve such spectacular results firing the 155s from sea?'

Jack turned and smiled at Roman. Turning back, he began. 'We didn't. The results were the worst ever for the 86th.'

'You used them for shore bombardment, didn't you?'

'That would be a kindness to say it. The fact was the gunners could not be accurate in any measure, the motion on the sea prevents anything other than stabilised mountings from being accurate.'

'So, what did you use them for?'

'One of the oldest uses of guns is what we call "star-shell" a brightly burning flare that illuminates the enemy positions. We knew the enemy would be worried if we could use star-shells at that range, they would instantly think they were in range of the guns but they could not fire back at that range. The use of stars let us covertly detonate the explosive charges we had placed on their tanks and artillery and left them with the certainty we could bombard them at will. A deception I was happy to encourage.'

'Once they had no heavy units left, we could land with almost immunity from return fire. That was when I sent my Assault groups ashore. Each section comprised a Main Battle Tank accompanied by ARV's and IFV's. The light units carried extra infantry, they kept the remnants of the enemy defences occupied while I accompanied my Infantry Captain and one of his company's as they captured the enemy headquarters.'

Over the next three hours every move made by the Red Army was dissected. The feint with the barge which sent a disproportionate number of troops away from their required positions. The supposed landing in the north, also diverting soldiers. And several other tactics.

The time eventually came for summing up.

'We are unable to come to a certain conclusion as to the failure of the Blue Army. While the top of the command structure appeared to be able to accommodate the changes to the flow of battle, it appears that some of the lower commanders became distracted and confused by the tactics of the Red Army. The Blue assault phase was plagued by unit commanders not completing the tasks assigned; this was not due to any negligence on their part, the opposition forced their responses. This is not a failure of the Blue Army; it is a victory of the Red Command and the tactics used.'

'During the Red Army assault phase, their tactics and the fluidity of motion allowed them to completely out manoeuvre the Blue Defences. Congratulations General Nakagawa, A resounding success for you and your team.'

'This hearing is complete.'

The Referees and Umpires stood and left the room. Suddenly Jack was being slapped on the back by everyone, all congratulating him on his successes. 'Sir, If I may?'

'Yes, Jim. What is it?'

'I know I am the most junior officer on your team and I know I was the last to join you. But if you want an Intelligence Officer in the future, I would like to volunteer.'

'Actually, I would like to thank you personally for your work. Even though you were late to the party, your input was crucial to our success.' Jack shook his hand, 'and you are welcome any time.'

'So, what is next Jack?' asked Okimoto.

'I am having a week in the office to put the paperwork and reports away then I am going to take a week off.'

Chapter 24
Posted, Overseas and Back

Jack answered the call at his desk.

'Hai, Motoyuki. How is life at Headquarters?'

'Boring without my "laugh a minute" General to amuse me.'

'I apologise for my absence; how can I help?'

'This time it is I that can help you. I have been asked if I can send you to Sandhurst, in England for a period of eighteen months or so to teach planning and tactics.'

'Why me?'

'I will treat that as the worst question I have heard in a long time. They have been given a copy of the combat reports from Trans-Pac and they want to hear from you.'

'Do I get a choice?'

'No.'

'Well then I will be happy to go. Can I have a few days at home first? I would like to catch up with my family as well as Chie and Fumiko.'

'Of course, I am still wary of upsetting the senkensha you seem to have on hand.'

Jack smiled and the two spent a little time catching up before he was due to leave for the other side of the world.

Eventually, leave over and farewells bidden, Jack was taken to the airport where he began the next chapter of his life.

Landing at Heathrow he was collected by a staff car and driven to the Academy, south-west of London.

His accommodation was a very generous suite of rooms in the Officers Mess and he quickly settled into the routine of the daily life of lectures, parades and exercise.

For the first time in several years he had sufficient time to concentrate on his martial arts expertise and as soon as he found a dojo nearby, he quickly returned to his peak fitness and began honing his skills, which he had ignored for far too long.

It was at the dojo that he quickly made friends with a Marine Major, Mark Gibbs, and the two could often be heard debating historical battles, an offshoot of their shared love of military history.

One evening after a particularly hard training session Jack made comment that he would often go for dinner with his sensei.

'Why don't we go? There is a nice Japanese restaurant just opened on "The Kingsway" just over the Blackwater River. You can teach me the finer points of Japanese cuisine and how to use chopsticks.'

'That sounds like a great idea. We can go once we have cleaned up.'

'The meal was to become a Friday evening ritual for the two. Once they had completed their work for the week, usually on a Friday, they would train for two hours and that would see them seated and ready for dinner at around eight.

It was almost six months later, long after they had become regular diners, that one day Jack noticed the owner was particularly concerned with something.

Jack caught the owner's eye and beckoned him over.

'Kobayashi-san, come sit with us for a moment.' The owner sat and was unusually quiet. 'Katsuo, you seem distracted, what is concerning you?'

Katsuo could not look either of the men in the eye, he simply stared at the table.

'Tell me, my friend, what is so wrong?'

Very slowly he lifted his head and Jack could see the tears beginning to form. Very quietly he began.

'Nakagawa-san, for some months we have been "visited" by men who demand money from me to keep my little restaurant "safe". Last month I was short and they demanded they get extra this month. They are due here tonight and business has still been slow. I fear for my staff.'

'A stand-over man?' Jack looked at his companion and received a nod in return. 'Do not concern yourself, we will take care of this business for you.'

'But I cannot afford to repay you either.' His first thought was that Jack and Mark were going to pay the debt for him.

Mark smiled at Jack and said, 'No one said we were going to pay him, we are just going to take care of this business.'

'I cannot let you do that; they will be armed. I do not want you to get hurt.'

'Let us do this for you. You are a friend and we will help.'

Katsuo stood and bowed. 'Arigatō, but please be careful.'

'It was almost an hour later that three men charged through the doors. Customers tried to become invisible, fearful of the men and their machete's.

'We warned you, old man. Now everyone, put your valuables on the tables, do it now and no one gets hurt.' The youngest of the three moved to the rear of the room and began to force the customers to put everything in the small bag he was carrying.

Jack stood up and threw his wallet on the floor.

'There it is, come and get it if you are brave enough.'

'Oh, smartarse is it,' he raised the machete and started towards Jack. No one could say for certain if he was actually going to swing his weapon or was it just posturing, it was of no consequence in the end. As he lifted his arm Jack sprang at him and kicked him in the knee. A throat punch before he hit the ground and the man was never getting up to repeat his challenge.

His companion started towards Jack but found the arm holding his weapon was unable to move. He turned his head and looked directly at the big Marine

Major that held him. His mind was confused, right up to the point that he was hit with the most powerful head-butt and he too collapsed, unconscious, on the floor.

Turning to Jack he asked, 'Where is the third one?' The youngest had witnessed the "fight", if that was the right word, and was trying to hide.

'COME OUT HERE BOY!' Jack shouted and the third assailant slowly appeared from behind a curtain, bag in one hand and a small billy-club in the other.

Wielding the weapons taken from the others Mark and Jack stood over the fallen bodies like a pair of colossal statues.

'GET ON YOUR KNEES, BOY.' Jack ordered. The boy did just that, fearful of the fate that had already befallen their venture.

'ARMS OUT TO THE SIDE.' Again, he obeyed.

'Now, get over here.' The boy again obeyed and shuffled over on his knees. When he was around three metres away Jack ordered him to stop.

'Put the bag and weapon on the floor!' He was shaking in fear as he complied with the order. 'Now put your hands on your head and lock your fingers together.' As he once more complied Jack could hear some fearful tears being shed from the rear of the room. Gesturing towards the rear of the room Jack silently asked Mark to see to the patrons and ensure they understood there was no more danger.

'How old are you?'

'Th, thirteen Sir.' The fearful boy stammered, 'What happened? he was still unsure as to what had gone wrong. 'Dad told me there was no danger, he just wanted me to hold the bag.'

Jack was not listening to questions; his eyes were moving frantically around the room. Finally deciding that there were no extra assailants, he turned to the owner.

'Katsuo, call the police please.'

Just five minutes later a group of six officers entered the room. Expecting to walk into an armed robbery they were met by cheers and good wishes. The two principal assailants were still unable to move, although this was now more from fear than from injury.

The Sergeant in charge began by asking the owner for a rundown on what had happened. With his constables taking statements he finally came to speak with Jack and Mark.

'Can I begin with your name sir.'

Jack replied.

'Can you spell that for me? Thank you, sir. Now in your words what happened?'

Jack told the Sergeant what had happened, and then he said, 'Do not blame the boy, his father forced him to be here.'

'Are you certain?'

'I am. He is not a thief; he was here because he was forced.'

'Are you willing to testify to that Sir?'

'I am, he told me and his father admitted to it.'

'Thank you, you gentlemen have been most helpful.'

The paramedics had administered sufficient pain relief for the boy's father to begin to rant and threaten Jack. Despite several attempts to keep him quiet he eventually got to the point where he began to threaten to bring his mates back next time.

At that time Jack had heard enough, he stormed over to the man, now strapped onto the gurney ready for the ambulance, and grabbed him by the throat. You still want a fight? DO YOU! Major Gibbs, how many marines can you get here by Monday?'

'Mark had to stifle a laugh, Three companies from 2 Marine (Second Marine Regiment) and one from 3 Para (Third Parachute Regiment). Roughly four hundred.'

'Arigatō, I can call General Onishi and have a division from the Northern Army here by Sunday, that makes over ten thousand soldiers, how many are you going to bring? We need to know how many body bags we will need.'

No one spoke for a full minute. Finally, it was the Police Sergeant that broke the uncomfortable silence.

'Can I ask, Sir. Exactly who are you?'

'General Jackson Nakagawa, Deputy Commander of the Northern Army, Japanese Land Defence Force.' A small untruth, but it served the moment better than "Director of Planning". Then Jack turned to the prostrate man and again grabbed him. 'If I hear of you or any of your friends threatening Katsuo or any other hard-working people anywhere near here I will come for you first, do you understand me? These businesses are now effectively under the protection of the Royal Marines and the Japanese Army. Tread VERY carefully.'

Eventually, the police, ambulance and other onlookers left and Jack turned to Katsuo.

'I think we have that little problem sorted out.' Then turning to the room, filled with, now, less fearful patrons, 'Ladies and Gentlemen, I must apologise for this evening's event. Please enjoy your meals. Katsuo, charge it all to this card.' Jack pulled his holographic credit card from his pocket and handed it to the owner.'

'No, Jack. I cannot let you pay for it all.'

'I insist; business has been quiet for some time, you said so yourself. Why should you lose even more because those fools thought they should take it? Go on, every meal and drink are to be on here.' Again, Jack offered the card and Katsuo returned with the receipt. Jack glanced at it and returned it to his friend, 'You forgot the tip for your staff, they too have had it bad tonight; let's say 25%'

'You are too kind.' Again, he returned with the corrected receipt and bowed to Jack and Mark. 'Arigatō again my friends.'

'Now I feel like sake to celebrate. Hand them around.' Katsuo left to assemble the drinks for the room.

'Jack,' began Mark, 'That must have cost a fortune?'

'I can afford it. It is good to know that the evening will be the start of better times for Katsuo and his family. These diners, the police and the press will improve the reputation of this place and the business will pick up quickly.'

'Just from this? You paying the bill?'

'Not just that, but the restaurant will get a reputation of being a safe place for families to eat. That will bring patrons.'

And bring them it did. The news was all over the area the following morning, hologram news feeds, all the social media and word of mouth spread it very quickly and it was not long before there was a long wait for bookings. But every night there was a small table waiting in the corner, just in case Jack or Mark happened to come in, which they did a lot.

Chapter 25
The Diplomatic Waltz

UN General Assembly

'This meeting is now in session.' The Senior Administrative officer banged her gavel and the auditorium slowly became silent.

'For the first item of business I call upon the Ambassador for Japan to begin her address.'

The Ambassador pulled her microphone closer. 'Domo arigatō Madam Secretary General.' She looked around the room to ensure she had the attention of all present. 'It has been several decades, YES DECADES since the Russian Army established a military presence on the Kuril Islands.' At that point she was, predictably, interrupted.

'I protest, we did not establish a "Military Presence", we are simply trying to rectify a situation that was the result of a mishap.'

'It does not matter how it happened; The Russian Armed Forces have established a presence in the Kuril Islands. These islands were ceded to us in an act of good will and now they have, following what could only be described as a deliberate occurrence, they have now occupied Japanese lands and it is now time for them to be returned to us.'

'We have not completed our clean-up mission. We must be permitted to stay until the job is done.'

'NO. You have had more than enough time to complete the works, our satellite images show you have been creating a military base, this so-called clean-up was completed a long time ago. You must leave, and leave NOW!'

At that point the meeting descended into what could be arguably described as chaos and it took a long time for the Secretary General, amidst much shouting and banging of the gavel, to re-establish order. Eventually, everyone became silent.

'We shall vote, given that there has certainly been sufficient time to complete a clean-up mission the motion is "That the Russians shall leave the Kuril Islands and return them to Japan." Vote now please.'

The vote was all but unanimous, China and North Korea abstained and the rest voted in favour of Japan.

'As the Ambassador for Russia, I have been instructed to use our Power of Veto. This matter is now closed.'

'The Ambassador forgets, the power of veto was amended thirty years ago to being only for matters of international aggression. As they have indicated that this is not an aggressive stand the power of veto does not apply.'

'I thank the Ambassador for Germany. You are quite correct,' replied the Secretary General. 'It is the ruling of the UN General assembly that Russia will remove its presence within six calendar weeks from this date.' The gavel banged three times to signal the end of the debate.

It was only three weeks after the attempted robbery at the restaurant that Jack was called to the Commandants Office.

'You wish to see me General?'

'Yes, Jack. Please sit.'

Jack made himself comfortable and waited for the Commandant to begin. Eventually, he put the signal he had been reading in front of Jack and said, 'This arrived just twenty minutes ago. It seems that you are needed back home a little earlier than we anticipated.'

Jack read and then re-read the signal. 'It seems so,' he replied. 'I wonder if this has anything to do with the goings on in the UN?'

'I think it may have. The signal is unequivocal, you need to be back at the 'Planning Directorate" in Tokyo by the day after tomorrow. I can tell you; we will be sorry to lose you. Your unique insight and methodology have really set many of our officers thinking very hard about the existing work methods. You will be missed, and not just by Katsuo Kobayashi. You have made a huge impact there as well. Come back and see us sometime.'

'Thank you, Sir. I will return as soon as possible. But there may be a few things that need sorting out first.' With that Jack left the office.

That evening it was farewell drinks at the Officers Mess and the following morning Jack was on his way to Tokyo.

The Kremlin

'What do you mean, we have to leave?' The president had been completely blindsided by the UN decision.

'I am sorry sir; the General Assembly has ruled in Japan's favour.'

'Then we shall take it to the International Court of Arbitration.'

'Again, sorry sir; the word from the Justices is that we should have been finished twenty years ago. We cannot expect a favourable decision from them.'

'Then we shall ignore the decision. We will not leave.'

'I wish it were so easy, Mr President. But the mood of the populace has shifted significantly from the time of your predecessors.'

The Prime Minister had been quiet so far but now it was his turn. 'The general populace is tired of being a life support system for an overweight and self-indulgent military. They want to be included in world affairs, not left as international pariahs on the side-line. It is a small thing, internationally speaking, to give these insignificant islands back, to enable us to gain so much in international affairs and respect.'

'It does not matter what the "populace" wants; we have control of the islands and we will keep it. We will tell the populace what it wants, they have no say in the matter.' With that definitive statement the meeting was deemed to be over. The high-ranking politicians left to return to their offices and to ponder what the hard line would produce for them.

They did not have long to wait. The sitting of the Court of Arbitration was over almost as soon as it had begun. The Justices ruling seven to zero in favour of the Japanese.

The Americans, always ready to "sink the boot in", almost immediately turned the screws with financial sanctions. Germany, The United Kingdom, Australia, India, all of the Nordic Nations as well as all the Eastern European Nations followed suit. The sanctions bit hard but the Russian President would not concede.

Oddly enough, even the Chinese and North Koreans joined in the wholesale slap-down of the Russians. Investigations, many years into the future would reveal their motivation was they may have been able to retrieve one or two nuclear weapons and avail themselves of some Russian technology.

Still, the Russian President stuck to his guns and refused to bow to international pressure.

After a long series of negotiations, the Diet (Japanese Parliament) made the decision that more diplomatic sanctions should be put in place.

The Prime Minister's Office, Tokyo.

The communications unit on the desk buzzed, The Prime Minister pressed the answer button. 'Hai?'

'The Russian Ambassador is here for your 1.30 meeting.'

'Arigatō,' he released the button and went back to the documents he was signing. Following a long five-minute wait, the P.M. eventually pressed again and asked 'Send him in.'

The door opened and the Russian Ambassador entered the room; pausing to bow to the top politician in the country he was astounded to be ordered, 'Sit, please.'

The Russian sat in the indicated chair and waited for a moment. He was considerably confused at this point. Normal diplomacy would have a staff member arrive with refreshments, but this time there was nothing. Normally he would be greeted with a handshake and some small talk, but this time there was nothing.

'You have been summoned to explain your country's unwillingness to abide with international legal rulings.'

Normally the subject would be approached gently in a civilised manner, this time there was nothing. So completely stunned at the ignoring of traditional Japanese hospitality, the Russian was almost unable to speak.

'Well? What have you to say?'

Eventually, he managed to frame a response, 'The fact of the matter is that we now control the islands, and the President has informed me that the originally proposed return will not happen at any time in the near future.

The Prime Minister did not respond in any way for at least five minutes, possibly more. Eventually, he spoke; not with the gentle, fatherly tone he was famous for, this time it was an order, spoken in direct unequivocal terms.

'Your diplomatic mission has to close. Diplomatic immunity for your buildings, people and everything within will expire at midnight tomorrow. You are to be at the airport ready to leave the country by 11pm.'

'But we will not have sufficient time to pack all our items.' The Ambassador was now clearly worried that a lot of Russian secrets will fall into Japanese hands.

'As they say in American movies "That is not my problem." You have your deadline, meet it!'

'I will inform the President; he will demand the same from you.'

'He may demand whatever he wants. Our diplomatic presence left Moscow two hours ago. You may leave.'

The Russian stood up and only now did his diplomatic bluster begin to surface.

'You will regret this stance you take.' It was bluster by name and nature, they both knew there was no conviction in the words and neither was offended by the "protestations" or the responses. This was the usual way of diplomatic negotiations; demand, argue, concede.

'Perhaps we will regret it,' replied the Prime Minister as he made a conscious effort to continue reading the documents before him, ignoring the Ambassador would allow him to reinforce his position. 'All further diplomatic contact will be made through the offices of International Relations in The Hague. I am sure you know it; their building is just around the corner from the International Court of Arbitration.'

With no further course of action open; the, now former, Ambassador to Japan turned and left the room. All the way back to the Embassy he could only think that the world was now bent on bringing the regime down. "I will resign in "shame" and retire. Maybe I can live out my life in Cuba, the weather is nice there." he thought, as the car wound its way through the busy streets of Tokyo. A small tear left his eye, he had always thought of Japan as a second home and now that idiot of a President had taken it away from him. "Maybe I can negotiate a place with the Japanese government as a special advisor, that would suit me very much."

His musings were suddenly shattered as the driver announced that they were back in the Russian compound. For now, he would have to oversee the disassembly of the Russian Diplomatic Mission. But his mind was firmly set on securing his future; and with each passing minute his future did not appear to be within Mother Russia. "Never mind, it is nicer living here as an old man than it would ever be in Russia, and if I help them, they may even like me." were his last thoughts on the subject, for that day.

Russian Embassy, the next evening.

'Ambassador Gripkin, there are a large number of Military and civilian police at the gates.' The third undersecretary was clearly disturbed and confused by the events. This was his first position following his training and he had only been in the country for three weeks, and now he was furiously packing his few personal office items before being unceremoniously thrown out.

'Settle down, they had to arrive sometime, and that time is quite obviously now. Leave my office, there are no important documents left here, just my private items and I will pack them.'

'Yes, Sir.'

'And close the door behind you.'

The undersecretary left the former ambassador to his private items and set off to assist with the transporting of the secured items.

A knock at his door brought the Ambassador back to reality; he had been trying to formulate the speech he would need in the very near future.

'Enter!' he called and the door opened, this time it was the Military Attaché that was waiting.

'Your family has just arrived; shall I show them up?'

'Yes, please.' A few moments later Ambassador Gripkin's second wife entered the room with their three years old daughter in tow.

Alex gathered his wife and daughter in his arms. 'Sakura, my love, my darling Yui. Why so many tears. We will be fine. I have almost finished my preparations. The Prime Minister has agreed to meet me for an official farewell at midnight in his office, he knows you will be with me and as such I feel that this meeting will be far more cordial than the last.'

A brief tap on the door frame interrupted their private moment.

'WHAT?' shouted Alex, more to give the impression of his disapproval at the interruption than out of real annoyance.

'The last of the trucks has left for the airport; it is now 10.50 and the last car is leaving soon.'

'Go, I will be paying my respects to the Prime Minister and he has allowed me two days to complete the diplomatic rounds before I must also leave. I have been allocated a driver from the Japanese government. Good luck to you all.'

'And to you, Sir.' The Military Attaché left the room and was soon in the car on his way to the airport. Alex and Sakura both watching from the third-floor window. Suddenly the embassy was a very quiet and lonely place. Just twenty-four hours ago there had been almost three hundred people working there, now there were just three.

Alex made tea and sat with his family, no one speaking. Eventually, Yui fell asleep on the floor. It was just one minute after midnight when they heard the sound of the gates opening and a car entering the compound.

'This is it, my love. Pray for a good outcome.'

'That is all I have been doing for the last day.' Sakura replied as she gathered the sleeping little girl in her arms; she watched as Alex opened the door behind his desk and retrieve two massive brief cases. Clearly very heavy they contained, what he hoped would be, his retirement "fund". Soon enough the driver arrived at the office door and carried one of the cases as they made their way down to the entrance. As they approached the doorway for the last time Alex pushed his hand deep into his pocket and withdrew a single key. Handing it to the Officer in Charge he said. 'This opens the keyboard in my office, in there you will find the remaining keys to the building.'

The Officer gave a brief bow and escorted the three to the waiting limousine.

Prime Minister's Office. 12:30 am

'The former Russian Ambassador, sir.' The assistant bowed and placed the heavy brief case he had been given just inside the door, then he stood aside to allow the late-night guests to enter. 'Would you like refreshments, Sir.'

'No, I already have them. That will be all.'

'Hai.' The door was closed silently and the three watched each other carefully.

Eventually, it was the Prime Minister that broke the silence. 'Will tea be acceptable, Alex?'

'Yes, thank you, very nice.'

'Please sit,' he said as he poured for the guests. Serving them he also placed a small plate of confections for them.

'Would Yui be more comfortable in a bed? I can get one made up for her?'

'Actually, just a pillow and a blanket on the couch will be fine. I do not wish her to waken in a strange place without me beside her,' replied Sakura.

'Yes, of course.' Pushing a button on his desk he spoke quickly and just a minute later an aide appeared with the requisites, Sakura laid Yui on the couch and covered her.

'Now, Alex, you said you have a proposal for us.'

'I do. In these two cases are many official documents, they are copies of course I could not risk the political masters in Moscow becoming suspicious when they found original documents missing. They are important enough for me to now be a fugitive from my own government. Therefore, I now formally request Political Asylum for myself and my family.'

'Asylum! that is unexpected. Why should we give it to you?'

'First, I have betrayed my country. I am now in great peril and I fear I will be killed if I should return. Second, I am married to a Japanese citizen, whom I dearly love, and she would also be in fear for her life if we go to Russia. Third, our daughter is a Japanese citizen and as she is a minor she would need to be protected by your government. And lastly, the documentation I have provided, as a show of good faith, will be important enough for you to be able to justify my remaining here.'

The Prime Minister simply thought for a while, pondering the implications of the request. 'Very compelling reasons, all of them. But, why have you decided that you would not return? It was all but confirmed that you would return with the rest of your mission, why stay? Political asylum is one reason only, a good reason yes, but only one. Why decide to betray your country?'

'I have been at a personal mental impasse for some time, I have passed your demands for the return of the Kuril Islands many times, marrying Sakura was always regarded as a political ploy by your government, a method of ingratiating myself to the Japanese people. There were even some that openly accused Sakura of being a spy. I wish to live in relative peace, that is not now possible in Russia. I could go to Cuba, but their government is far too closely aligned with Moscow. This is the place we feel most at home.'

'And where would you live?'

'Eventually, we would like to go to Kuzumaki, in the north, and be close to Sakura's family. I realise we would need to be hidden for a while, but Kuzumaki will be our preferred final destination.'

'Let me make a couple of calls. If you are granted asylum you do realise it will be on the basis of the documentation being useful?'

'Of course, that is why I ensured I got the most important of all the information available.'

The Prime Minister left the room and, through the closed door they could not hear anything clearly.

Prime Ministers Call

'Home Affairs Office, how may I help you?' The dis-embodied voice on the other end of the line sounded tired, which was to be expected at almost 1.30 in the morning.

'This is the Prime Minister; I need to speak with the Minister right away.'

'Hai, I will have him call you directly.'

The line went dead and within two minutes it rang again.

'You wish to speak with me, Prime Minister?'

For the next five minutes the two most senior politicians in Japan discussed the proposal. The call ended with the Home Affairs Minister promising to call, back as soon as possible.

The phone beside Jack's bed rang incessantly. As he woke, he groggily told himself to get a more civilised ring tone.

'Jack here,' he announced, his cheery demeanour belying the fact he had only just woken.

'How do you do it Jack? It is three in the morning and you sound as though it is nine?'

'Would you believe it is a lie? I am as tired as you are. What can I do for you Motoyuki, must be important?'

'It is…' Motoyuki Onishi outlined the request he had received from the Chief of Staff and gave Jack the rundown on why it had made its way to him.

'So, you want me to put the former Russian Ambassador and his family into one of my guest houses until their claims can be verified and their final settlement arranged?'

'In a word, yes.'

'OK. I will inform my house keeper to be ready. They can live in the main house as the only usable guest house is where my parents live. I do not have any pressing projects at this time, so I will get a helicopter to transport all of you from Tokyo Airport and I will meet you there.'

'Thanks, Jack. We can use private hangar 23, the Emperor's hangar. The palace has given permission.'

'Right. Be there at 8. Have the car drive into the hangar and the passengers can transfer in private before the helo is pushed out for take-off.'

'Thanks Jack, can you get one with two extra seats?'

'I see, this is just a ploy to get a weekend at my place!'

'Not JUST a ploy, but I thought Yumi and I would take advantage of the opportunity.'

'Fair call. I will see you in a few hours.'

The call was terminated and just as Jack was getting ready there was a very small knock at his door. 'Yes, Fumiko?'

'Are we all going home?'

'Why not. It will be good to have a weekend at home for once. Let your mother sleep for a while then we can get ready.'

'Far too late for that, Jack.' Chie appeared at the door. 'You make far too much noise inside my head when something like this happens.'

Jack and Fumiko both burst into fits of laughter.

'My apologies, Chie, I did not mean to wake you.'

The three had a quick bite to eat and Jack arranged for an early helicopter to take them to his home before the others arrived.

They arrived just before seven and Emika was already preparing a full breakfast for them. As they ate there was a tension in the air that eventually none could ignore any longer.

'Do not worry Jack.' It was always going to be Fumiko that would break the silence. 'All will be well.'

'She is right,' Chie added. 'The one who you wait for has his home in his head, but it is his heart that holds Japan dearest.' Fumiko nodded her agreement, only because she had a mouthful of food; otherwise she would have beaten her mother to the words.

Jack simply looked at his two close friends and agreed. 'I knew I could count on you two for the important information.'

They finished breakfast and then showered and changed. The ladies decided to wear kimonos and Jack chose the traditional Hakama pants, Montsuki and Haori kimono jackets but with western style shoes. Once they were all dressed, they looked like they were a part of a re-enactment group; an impression that would be reinforced when they emerged from the castle gates.

Motoyuki and Yumi were watching the faces of their guests as the helicopter began to make its descent approaching the grounds.

'Is that where we will be staying?' Sakura asked, pointing to the small guest house just visible near the tree line off to one side of the sprawling estate that was emerging before them.

'In a manner of speaking.' Motoyuki replied, carefully disguising his smile.

'Alex, it looks so peaceful. We should be comfortable here.'

'I hope you are; it is a private residence and the owner has made all the arrangements for you. The housekeeper will meet us on the ground.'

The helicopter landed and the five got out once the rotors had stopped.

'You say this is a private home, who is the owner?'

'A family friend, Jackson Nakagawa.'

'I have heard of him; so that is his house.' Alex pointed to the guest house away to one side.

'No, that is where his parents live. This is his home.' Motoyuki pointed towards the castle and at that moment Jack, Chie and Fumiko emerged.

'Konichiwa, Yumi, Motoyuki; welcome back. You must be Alex Gripkin, welcome to my home. And this must be Sakura and Yui.' Jack bowed and was copied by the ladies. 'Come inside, you must be hungry or at least thirsty. I hear you have had a difficult couple of days, do not worry you are safe here.'

'How much does he know?' Alex whispered to Motoyuki.

'Everything.'

'Everything? You have spies watching us?'

'No, he doesn't,' Jack butted in. 'But I do.'

Alex and Sakura both looked alarmed, they had not considered that their intentions and whereabouts had been divulged so quickly.

'Do not worry, my spies are here and they tell me that you have Japan's interests at heart.'

'Dare I ask who they are?' Yumi asked, even though she already was certain of the answer.

Jack simply looked at her and smiled.

'I thought so.' Yumi grinned widely as she walked to the house. 'Emika, so good to see you again.' Emika had emerged from the house to lead them all inside and through to the rear deck where there was a breakfast waiting.

Once they had all had their fill, Sakura asked 'Yumi, you know who his spies are? Are they here?'

Yumi looked at Jack and he simply shrugged his shoulders and gave a brief nod. 'This is Chie and her daughter Fumiko. If you wish to know anything these are the two to ask.'

Sakura and Alex both looked from Chie to Fumiko and back several times, clearly unable to grasp the revelation.

'Keep going Yumi, they do not yet understand.' Jack prompted.

Yumi spent the next half hour explaining the unique abilities of Fumiko and her family.

'I am sorry, but that is all too fanciful to be real.' Alex announced, he had not been able to come to terms with their capabilities.

'Mama, may I?' asked Fumiko

'Of course.' Chie replied.

Fumiko moved slowly to Sakura and placed her hand on the almost frightened woman's head. As her eyes glazed over, she spoke, 'You doubt what we know, yet you wish to believe. There are more coming.' Then she moved to Alex and placed her hand over his heart. 'You are safe here, your motives are pure, you wish to remain in Japan for the rest of your life. This will happen. Go with your first instinct, resign in "shame" and "live as an outcast" your former political masters will believe you.'

'How can she know? What does she mean "There are more coming" more what?'

'I am sorry, I do not explain myself very well. You will have twins.'

'How do you know THAT?'

'Am I wrong?'

'No, you are right; but how do you know?'

'It is who I am, and the matriarchal line I come from.'

At that point, Jack spoke up, 'If you are going to stay with us, you will need to become comfortable with Fumiko and Chie. Sometimes Tomoko, Fumiko's Grandmother, and Reina, her Great-grandmother, will visit. It is no place to hide a secret when they are all here. Now, Fumiko, what is it with you and the babies?'

'Just because they are not yet born does not mean they do not have something for us. Babies are particularly easy for me to find; it is just one of my talents.'

'Twins? Are you certain?' Alex was beside himself with amazement and curiosity. 'How far along is she?'

'I am certain, you will have a boy and a girl, you are almost twenty weeks, half way through.'

Alex got to his feet and embraced Sakura. He kept repeating, "Twins? we are having twins".

The friends sat watching and smiling as tears of joy slowly wound their way down the cheeks of Sakura and Alex. Yui took that moment to jump up and hug her parents as well.

It was Jack that broke the moment, 'Chie, gather the family midwives and doctors. This will have to be kept as close to a secret as we can.' At that moment Chie's phone rang, once she had spoken for a few minutes she turned and announced 'Mother, Tomoko, has already asked two midwives to come here.'

'Your family seems to react quicker than anyone I have ever met.' Alex was astounded when just six hours later two midwives entered the house and demanded to see the expectant mother. Half an hour later they all emerged announcing, 'All is well, mother and babies are fine. One of us will stay here until they are born.' With that one left immediately and the other organised her place in the house with Emika.

'Is that how it is? Jack, they turn up and make themselves at home? Do you not even have a say?'

Jack smiled, just a little enigmatically, 'I have found it is best to not argue with the Senkensha, they will always know what is best and what is right and most importantly what is going to happen. Agreeing is just a simple way to make life easier.'

'I see,' Alex pondered, he was about to ask a question when Chie spoke.

'You want to know if you will all be safe here? The simple answer is yes, as long as you fully disclose everything you know. And just to be clear, we do not do "foretelling's" on demand, so you cannot just ask a question and get an answer. If we did that, we would all be fabulously wealthy from winning at the casinos.'

Everyone laughed, the mood was broken from a serious dive into the unknown into a morning with friends. Later in the afternoon, Alex, Sakura and Yui all took time for a little rest, it had been a very eventful three days for them.

Fumiko found Jack sitting in his favourite "thinking" chair on the rear deck, as the sun began to set. Sitting with him she was quiet for some time, then finally she said, 'It is getting close. The die has been cast. War is closer now than ever before. You will need to be careful.'

'I knew you were going to say that,' he smiled.

Grinning at him she asked, 'Are my ways becoming a part of you?'

'No, not at all. I can see that the movement of the political boundaries and the posturing of the high-profile players is changing. Their standings show us that they are going to war and as usual it is others that will do the fighting; after the politicians have done everything to ensure it happens, and nothing to prevent it.'

Fumiko put her arms around his neck, 'Be careful,' she whispered. 'You are needed for a much larger concern than a few islands.'

Jack held her close and said, 'I will be more than careful, after all I cannot afford to let your family loose on an unsuspecting world, can I?'

She giggled, 'No, they won't understand like you do.' The two sat close together for almost half an hour when a small cough came from behind.

'Am I interrupting?'

'Not at all, Motoyuki. Come sit.'

'I will get tea.' Fumiko announced and she left the two generals to talk.

'She is worried, Motoyuki. War is close.'

'Yes, we can all feel it. That is why I recalled you from England. I need you to begin planning so we are ready when the politicians run out of words.'

'I need to know everything that Alex brought with him. Not just the big bits, everything. I will set up a planning cell here, in the library. I will get one of our linguists to transcribe all the documents for ourselves, I don't want to rely on the Secret Services for their transcriptions, they will only give us what they want to. Who is commanding when we put men on the ground?'

'That will be General Tanaka, a capable officer. He will be going first as he currently commands the Northern Army.'

'Can you get him to give me his requirements, what he wants to take into the area as assault troops, then I can begin to plan the attacks for him?'

'Sure, if you can foresee a need then tell him he should take whatever **you** think is going to be useful for the battle plan.'

'OK, I will. Let's begin with the documents. Suddenly Jack reached forward and pushed a button on the hologram, his private secretary in Tokyo appeared before him. 'Get satellite control on the line please.'

Just a moment later the hologram beeped, Jack pushed the receive button and a Major appeared before him.

'Major, I need up to date photographs and assessments of all of the Russian positions on the Kuril Islands.' The Major looked as though he could possibly care less, but it would take a lot of work.

'That will take two weeks to get, sir.' Was the curt reply.

'I didn't ask for it in two weeks, get it done now, photos by am tomorrow and assessments the day after.'

'The task will take two weeks; we need to wait for the next satellite pass.'

'Major, this is General Onishi. General Nakagawa has asked you to get him information and you will.'

'I am sorry sir, but to redirect the satellite will cost millions of Yen.'

'Listen Major, I didn't ask for a financial report on satellite operations, get the information!'

Motoyuki ended the call and sat back in his chair with an exasperated look on his face. 'How did we get to the point where a Major can argue with a General?'

'Not certain; but when we do go, officially, he will not last long with his attitude.' Jack was incensed at the way Major had responded to the order; it was simply not good enough with war on the horizon.

For the next five days trucks and helicopters arrived and left again with monotonous regularity. Equipment was off loaded, the important and expensive art works and artefacts in the library were packed and placed in storage in the underground vaults as the library was transformed into a planning centre for Jack and his team.

Crates were unpacked and the equipment assembled and tested. Communications were setup in a separate room high in the castle and a veritable forest of aerials and antennae erupted on the roof.

As the equipment began receiving data Jack and his team began to plan the invasion of Iturup, the island that held the bulk of the Russian forces. Sensing the need for more information Jack had a "hotline" installed direct to Satellite Control.

As he began to look at the transcription of the Russian documents Jack was finding a few discrepancies.

'Hasegawa, get a translator in here please,' he asked his personal assistant; Hasegawa was probably the only member of his close-knit staff that he addressed by simply using the family name. No one could say why, it was just the way it happened. Jack had tried several times to use his given name but when he didn't get a reply he simply gave up.

The door opened and a rather nervous young private stood waiting.

'Don't just stand there, come in.' Jack tried to calm the young man, his words only managing the smallest effect of reducing the worry.

'Have a look at the map, just here.' Jack pointed to a small area. 'The satellite images do not show anything in this area yet Mr Gripkin has it referenced as a vital position, is that right?'

'Y-Yes sir.'

'Find the reference in the documentation and re-translate it please. Sit over there.' Jack pointed to a chair in the corner with a small table beside it. The translator sat and began to sort through the document until he found the page he needed. Working slowly, he eventually completed the retranslation first directly from Russian to Japanese and then again converting from Russian into English first and then Japanese to see if there was a missed element.

'It appears that there was a couple of items missed in the original translation, sir.'

'Keep going.'

'The document actually says that there is a type of storage underground in the area. The original translation simply notes it as "supply point", I don't think that their first translation is accurate.'

'Certainly not accurate enough for us.' Jack reached out and pressed a button. 'Motoyuki, have you got a minute to spare before you leave?'

In just seconds Motoyuki appeared in the doorway. 'What's up Jack?'

'This young man,' Jack pointed at the very self-conscious private, 'has found an important error in the original translations.' Jack explained the error to his friend.

'Leave it with me, I will have words at the highest level about this.'

'Stay for a couple of days extra and see if we can get a bigger noose for their necks.'

OK, Yumi will love it any way. Can we make this my command post for a while?'

'Certainly, I can charge the Army for the electricity if you do.' The room burst into laughter at the comment. 'What! Are you all listening into our conversation?'

'Of course, we are listening, wouldn't be the Planning Group if we weren't learning from you,' replied a sergeant from the other side of the room.

'Good answer, Noro.'

Jack pushed the connection to Satellite Control.

'SatCon?' came the reply.

'General Nakagawa here, I need a fresh set of surveillance photos for Iturup North East quadrant sectors J23 to J60. Give me UV, IR, Radiation Spread, Gamma Radiation, Alpha and Beta radiation levels and any other scan data you can manage.'

Jack could hear a few grumbled words and the planning room went eerily silent as his teams waited for what would surely be a problem for someone.

'Can't do it today, three days at the earliest.'

'Major are you refusing an order?'

'Err, no sir. I will get it done at first opportunity.'

'I will get back to you.' Jack shut down the call and he was furious. He walked to the open doors that faced across the estate towards the stables. As he tried to find a way around this particular road block no one spoke or even moved. The experienced members of the planning group knew that a flurry of orders would soon be coming.

Suddenly Jack turned and went back to his desk, as he walked, he called out 'Hasegawa, get Drones for me please.' By the time he had sat, the smiling face of Drones was waiting for him on the holoprojector.

'Drones, good to see you again, it's been a while.'

'It certainly has, Jack. What can I do for you?'

'How is Mai?'

'She is fine, sends her regards and wants to know when we can visit your home again.'

'Pack up now, get a helicopter up here. Charge it to Project Tosa. While Mai is packing, do you still have your contact in SatCon?'

'Sure do.'

'Can you trust him? You know how we work; will he be a good fit for us?'

'He will, he is the guy I beat in the National Championships; he has moved on to satellite work. He is a Captain now, he enlisted before me.'

'How senior?'

'I think he has just passed three years in rank.' Jack looked at Motoyuki and got a nod in return. 'Bring him with you.'

'OK, see you soon.' The call was terminated and Motoyuki asked, 'Are you going to do what I think you are?'

'If he is as good as Drones says, then yes, I am.'

'Let me know when they arrive.' Motoyuki left the room and Jack returned to the problem at hand. Just what was the puzzle behind the differing descriptions of the sectors Jack was looking into. The private sat and waited, unsure what to do next.

'We have a little time; would you ask Mr and Mrs Gripkin to come in here please.' The private disappeared quickly and returned with the guests.

'Coffee please.' Jack ordered and the private quickly returned with a steaming carafe and cups on a tray. Serving the drinks, he waited for a moment and he was almost shocked when the Sergeant said 'Keep translating, Jack will need information quickly and very soon.'

'May I ask a private question?' Jack began, looking directly at Sakura.

'Of course.'

'Where in the Kurils does your family come from?'

'What, how do you know?'

'Your tattoos on your upper arms, they are from the Ainu of the Southern Kurils. I was wondering if you were from the northern part of Iturup?'

'You are without a doubt the most incredible and knowledgeable man I have ever met. You are the only person that has ever asked me that question, many have wondered and I have had to explain to them, but you are the first to know.'

'I try to keep up with the history of our part of the world.'

'My family were the village elders of our area.'

'Show me where you are from?'

Sakura moved to the map and pointed to a small clearing in the centre of where Jack was wanting information.

'Here, this is where we lived.'

'Your parents, are they still with us? Would they be able to help?'

'Yes, they are, and they would be delighted to assist you.'

'Just a moment.' Jack again contacted his friend. 'Drones, this is Sakura Gripkin. She will tell you where to find her family, collect them on your way.'

'Hai.'

Sakura gave her family address and within an hour they were on their way to Jack's home.

While they were waiting for the new arrivals Jack began his assessment of the island, trying to determine the best landing place for the assault force that was slowly being put together by General Tanaka.

Turning to, his now "personal translator", 'What is your name?'

'P...p...p...Private Takashi sir.' The stammer was more from being suddenly addressed than anything else.

'No, your first name.'

'Eiji, sir.'

'OK, Eiji, take off your jacket.' The now confused private obeyed the strange order.

'While you are in here it is first names only, understood?'

'Hai, sir.' Jack looked him in the eyes.

'That includes me and Motoyuki,' he indicated General Onishi who turned and nodded. 'The reason I had you remove your jacket is that there is no rank in my planning rooms. We need to be comfortable and at ease with each other; there is a lot of important information that is going to be flying across this room, we need to be more concerned with the information itself than the personal niceties. Outside Rank is fine, in here not so much use.'

The private seemed slow to realise what was happening, this was new territory for him. He was about to respond when a Sergeant on the other side of the room called out.

'Jack, inbound helo reports arrival in ten minutes.'

'Good. Drones?'

'Hai.'

'Arigatō. Land them in front of the garage and have them escorted to the rear deck.' Jack pressed his communicator. 'Emika, refreshments for eight on the rear deck, when you can.'

The flurry of exchanges served to embed the command from Jack in the mind of Eiji.

'Eiji, find Mr and Mrs Gripkin and little Yui. Bring them to the rear deck and bring your notebook. We will be discussing a few items and we may need translation and interpretation.'

'Hai.'

Jack and his guests were waiting on the rear deck when the doors opened.

Sakura jumped up and ran to her parents. Grabbing them both at once, she was a mess of happy tears; it had been a very long time since they had even been in the same city, let alone the same room.

Drones walked up to Jack and extended his hand. 'Konichiwa, Jack. This is Haruto Saito.'

'Welcome Haruto. Alex, I will need to leave you for a while. There are things I must attend to.' At that moment Emika appeared with the refreshments and the Gripkins settled in for their own private family reunion.

'Come into my office, we need to discuss this in private.'

Haruto looked puzzled. 'What are we discussing?'

Jack didn't reply and when they were away from the others, he closed the door and indicated to the seats.

'What is going on, Jack?' asked Drones. 'This is not like you, meetings in private.'

Jack just held up his hand as he pressed the communicator. 'Motoyuki, can you come to my private office please?'

Moments later Motoyuki arrived and took the last empty chair.

'Haruto, this is Motoyuki Onishi, Chief of the Army.' The two nodded in acknowledgement.

'I have closed the door because this discussion is important to the near future, and it is private. Haruto, what is with the Major in charge at SatCon?'

Haruto looked as though he was a deer caught in the headlights of an oncoming truck.

'I am sorry, Sir. I do not understand?'

'Please, call me Jack. We have been trying to get information from SatCon and all we get is grief from the Major in charge. Why?'

'May I speak freely?'

If you don't, Haruto, we will be here all day. Say what you know,' replied Motoyuki.

'The Major is a strict disciplinarian. Any and all infractions of his rules are punished quickly.'

'Punished? How?'

'Usually loss of leave.'

Motoyuki looked at Jack. 'That explains the high attrition rate in SatCon.'

Jack looked at Haruto. 'Why does it take so long to get information from the surveillance satellites?'

'It doesn't. He just won't send the information off until he is ready. If he says it will take three days and he sends it after two, he looks good for completing the demand ahead of schedule.'

'Does he do the work or does he simply take the credit?'

'He rarely leaves his office. We do all the work; he gets the praise.'

'Can you do the work?'

'I do now.'

Jack looked at Drones and got an imperceptible nod. He then looked at Motoyuki and gave a nod.

Motoyuki looked at Haruto. 'Major Saito, you are hereby appointed Commander SatCon. We assume you can do your job from here at the Northern Area Planning Office?'

'That's Captain, sir.'

'MAJOR Saito, can you work from here?'

A huge grin spread across his face. 'Hai, anywhere there is a secure computer terminal.'

'Good get one setup in the next twenty-four hours.'

Haruto smiled at Drones. 'I told you it would be a good thing, didn't I?' Drones assured his friend.

'You did, but I didn't think it would be this good. What will happen to my predecessor?'

'There is a job at Northern Command, I think we will assign him to Colonel Higashi's Rapid Response Teams. That will make him understand what rapid means.'

'Now, we shall get back to our guests, we need information.'

As they left the private office all of them smiled at the thought of the Major being commanded in an infantry role, instead of a warm quiet office.

The Major lasted almost three months before resigning, the real army was far too tough for him.

'I apologise for leaving you, there was a pressing matter to be addressed.' Jack bowed before his guests. 'I assume you are Harucor Anchicar and you are Chikap Anchicar?'

Sakura's parents stood and bowed in return. 'That is us. May we ask why you have demanded to speak with us?'

'I hope I can trust you; I am currently investigating the Russian troop deployments in the Kurils, Sakura tells me that you once lived in this area?' Jack pushed the button and the holo-projector displayed a three-dimensional map of their former homeland. 'Can you indicate where you previously lived?'

'Before I do, or say, or commit to anything, what is your intention?'

'If needs be, I will fight and destroy the Russian hold over your lands.'

Harucor thought for a moment and then he looked first at Chikap then Sakura. 'And what will you do should you win such a fight?'

'I will return your lands to you and let you live in peace. We have the Emperor's assurances on this.'

He thought for a moment and the reached out to indicate the area of what was once his village.

'Just a moment, Drones, get Mai in here, please.' Moments later Mai arrived.

'Yes Jack, how can I help?'

'Take note of the co-ordinates please. Sorry, again the position of your village.' Again, Harucor reached out.

'Arigatō, what are the roads made of?'

'Originally there were dirt tracks but I believe the Russians have put hard roads in.'

'Drones, coordinate with Haruto. I want satellite images of the roads in this area as well as the Russian camp, buildings etc. Familiarise yourself; as soon as we are "on the ground", I will need drone images of all of it.'

'Harucor, Chikap; do you understand how the Russians forced you to leave?'

'We do.'

'Is there somewhere they could hide the weapons? Caves or underground areas?'

'Just here,' again he put his hand over the image, 'there is a system of caves. If you approach from the north there is a large, open entrance and it appears to go back around two hundred metres and then stops. But if you approach from the south-west, here, you will find a much smaller entrance hidden amongst the rocks. Once inside there is room for four men to stand together, upright and it will lead into the larger area. It is twisty and not easy to walk on the broken ground but it is easy enough.'

Jack sat back, deep in thought. He appeared to be far away in his musings and none dared to interrupt. Suddenly he began.

'Haruto, first task; I.R., U.V., and radiation images of the entire area focus on the cave areas. Mai give him the exact coordinates. Drones, can you get a spy drone close enough from here for a detailed examination of the remote entrance?'

'Hai, it can be done.'

'Once Haruto has the satellite images get to it.'

'Jack, what are you thinking?' asked Motoyuki.

'We know that there have been no reports of the warheads being relocated back to Russia. I believe they have found them all and they have been stored in these caves. It makes sense, the Russians would have found them all by now. They may have left a couple lying around on the ground to try to fool surveillance into thinking that there are a couple of hot-spots still to be cleaned up, but I would be willing to wager that over thirteen hundred warheads are in these caves.'

'Don't tell me what you think you can do? Are you really going to try to steal them?'

'Of course. We know the Russians are lazy in these matters. If we can get to them from the south-west entrance and get them out. we can send them back to Japan. If we can't get them out, we may be able to move them deeper into the cave system and then close the caves off with a fake wall or rock-fall or something. Either way we can steal them.'

Not a single word was said, no sound was made. They were all still trying to comprehend the possibility of stealing over thirteen hundred nuclear weapons.

'And what would you do with them?' asked Motoyuki, despite being very familiar with Jack's outlandish schemes he was still incredulous at the thought of such audacious action.

'If we can get them, and that is a big IF, we will then have a very good bargaining place at the negotiation table. I know we have been opposed, as a nation, for over two hundred years, but if we get these weapons then the Russians will have to engage in dialogue and they will have to concede some positions to us.'

'You astound us all.' It was Chikap that spoke. 'We have been trying to find some way of negotiating our claims for years and you have just put it down on the table. How long have you been planning this?'

'Actually; about five minutes. The concept of stealing weapons is always a possibility in war. This proposal is just an extension of that possibility. What to do with them just popped into my head as we were discussing it.'

'For some strange reason I believe you can do this.' She replied.

'Haruto, now we have a reason for the surveillance we can get moving when you are ready.'

'Let me call MY office and get the "bird" into position.'

'Good idea.'

The plan had been set in motion; this was the opening gambit in this huge chess game. The revelations of the satellite would be crucial in the continuation of the prosecution of the first stage of the war.

As they all set off to begin their tasks the young translator, Eiji, caught up with Drones.

'Is that all it takes; he comes up with a fanciful idea and everyone agrees and does it?'

'Not so much a fanciful idea; He has already worked out that there must be somewhere for the Russians to have put the weapons. The cave system is the easiest solution for them. It is close to their camp, easy to put guards if they need to. Difficult to detect, unable to be seen. Where else would YOU put them?'

'He has already taken that into account?'

'Certainly; and a lot of other information as well. By tomorrow morning we will know if they are where he says. The satellite images will either confirm or deny their storage.'

'WOW. I have a lot to learn about this work. I thought planning was how many rolls of toilet paper do we need, and how many bullets for an exercise. This is way more exciting.'

Drones laughed. 'Welcome to the ride of your life. Jack has chosen you to be a critical part of this, do your job well and we will all, benefit.'

Chapter 26
The Game Begins

The Kremlin

'What the hell do you mean? Gripkin resigned?'

'My apologies, Mr President. We received notification two days after the Tokyo embassy had been abandoned.' The Foreign Minister was clearly concerned, whether it was for his own position or the life of his comrade no one could say.

'Exactly what did he say?'

'His letter said he was overcome with shame and remorse that he was unable to negotiate a better outcome for Russia. He has decided that he would rather live in exile and disgrace than continue to work and take the Ambassadors pay in what he called "false circumstances". He felt he did not deserve to continue as a representative of the government.'

'Does he not realise we do not blame him?'

'He does, but there are many that blame his wife for his inability to perform correctly.'

'Ahhh. She is Japanese born is she not?'

'Yes, sir. Born in Sapporo, I believe.'

'Very well. We have no option but to accept. Get the Head of the Security Services to check the documentation brought back, see if anything is missing.'

'Yes, Sir.'

It was almost a week before the report was handed over. All documentation was accounted for, the secure documents were all intact and none were compromised.

'Alexy, see if we can get a message to Alex Gripkin somehow. Tell him we accept his resignation with great reluctance and hope he can see his way to return home soon.'

'Yes sir.' The private secretary began to pass the message through a convoluted sequence of friends, helpers and former associates until it arrived at the headquarters of Amnesty who took on the task of actually delivering it.

'Eiji, get Alex and Sakura please.'

'Sure Jack.' It had taken a while, but Jack's private translator had finally become almost comfortable with the use of first names. A short while later the Gripkin's sat in Jack's office.

'Good news for you both.' Jack smiled widely as he handed over the letter. Alex was hesitant when he saw the official stamp of The Kremlin in the corner of the envelope and he was almost shaking as he opened it.

'I apologise for reading it first, it was delivered to me open, I simply put it back in its envelope.' Jack explained.

Alex read the letter, then read it again and then a third time before he handed it to Sakura. Unexpectedly she performed the exact same ritual, with the small exception that she burst into tears of happiness when she had read it for the final time.

'Alex? Does this mean we are safe?'

'It does my love. But let's not forget that we need to still keep a low profile. As long as we are helping Jack and his people we are, technically, aiding an "enemy" so until the conflict is resolved we need to be unobtrusive.'

'But where will we live?'

'For the foreseeable future, here. Unless my home is a little crowded for you?' Jack's open invitation, delivered with abroad smile, was eagerly accepted.

'Jack, the latest analysis shows the cave system has the warheads stored inside, gamma radiation levels are higher than surrounding areas. There are three guards permanently at the access. Our analysis of the surveillance images shows it has not been accessed for over a week now.'

'Arigatō, Haruto. Keep the analysis going, I need to know how often they access the warheads. If they continue this way it will be as I expected, they believe they are secure.'

'Drones, have you got close to the south-west entrance yet?'

'Close? We have its position mapped and I am getting a set of close-up video and still pictures tonight. If we can get an operator closer, we may be able to fly inside and confirm your suspicions.'

'Leave it with me.'

Just three days later a submarine was waiting to take Drones close to the north-east coast of Iturup. The next night saw the real time images transmitted directly to Jack's planning rooms.

'There they are.' Jack announced as he watched the stockpile appear on the holo-projection. For the next five minutes Drones flew the tiny video drone around the cave system.

'Drones, get some vision of the access route from our end right up to the weapons. When you are done come back and we can analyse what we have.'

'Hai.'

Two days later Jack was studying the satellite and drone footage. As he looked, he was becoming more pleased with what he saw. Not only were the images clear and concise but they also gave him the perspective of what the teams would find when they finally infiltrated the area.

'Hasegawa? Get General Onishi on the line please.'

Moments later Jack was met with 'Konichiwa, Jack. What do you have for me?'

'Konichiwa. I have just sent the latest Field Analysis to you.'

'Just a moment while I get it on the hologram.' A minute later, 'Very interesting, Jack. What are you proposing?'

'I think we should keep this between us, we don't want anyone getting suspicious over any sudden moves. It seems the Russians are willing to let the weapons just sit in storage. My satellite analysts have been going back over what data we have and it seems that the Russians have had them stored for some time. They do not enter the cave system at all and if we just leave them be, we will have a better chance of getting them later.'

'What about Tanaka?'

'We can let him know what is going on, but I feel the less that it gets out the better.'

'Agreed. If and when the final decision is made, I will decide whether or not to let him in on the positioning. Until then we will keep the location and the access routes secret.'

'My thoughts exactly.'

The Office of the Prime Minister of Japan

'Please come in, sit. Will you take tea or coffee?'

'Coffee, please,' replied the Ambassador for Mexico.

The drinks were served and some small talk was completed before the main topic could be addressed.

'I understand you are canvassing for support and allies?' asked the Ambassador.

The Prime Minister looked directly into the eyes of his guest, silent for a moment he eventually said, 'We are. Are you here to offer assistance in this matter?'

'More than assistance, we are willing to be a proper ally, we are willing to provide physical support as well as Diplomatic.'

'Arigatō, it is gratifying to receive your offer. While we believe that ours should be the sole combat divisions engaged, we may need support for those actually on the front line.'

'We are ready to assist however you need it.'

The Prime Minister sat for a moment and then spoke, 'May I make a call, I would like to define what assistance we may need.'

'Certainly.'

The image of Motoyuki Onishi appeared on the hologram.

'General, this is Ambassador Sanchez from Mexico. His government has agreed to kindly give us support both in the UN and in the field, should we need it.'

'Arigatō Ambassador Sanchez.'

'General can you give some idea as to what we will need?'

'Just a moment Sir. I will bring our Head of Planning into this conversation; he will be the best placed to answer you.' Just moments later Jack appeared.

'Konichiwa. How can I help?'

The introductions were made and the P.M. asked the direct question.

'How can we use the offer of help, General Nakagawa?'

Without hesitating Jack replied, 'Send the 93rd Heavy Bombardment Support Group to the Artillery School, along with a detachment of the 86th Heavy Bombardment Group with the 155mm Field Guns.'

'That is very specific, why those units?'

'Mr Ambassador, I worked with them during exercise Trans-Pac. Best gunners I have seen. I would like them to teach our Heavy Gun Groups the finer points of accurate gun-fire support.'

'Just a moment, are you saying that our gunners are not good enough?'

'Actually, Mr Prime Minister, yes. The terrain we will be crossing and the enemy positions will require us to be bringing fire support almost onto our own positions. I know I would want the very best there is to be dropping shells less than fifty metres from my position.'

'Just a moment, I will need to speak with the Officer Commanding Artillery,' replied the Ambassador.

'Say Konichiwa to Roman for me.'

'You know General Garcia?'

'Certainly do. It has been a while since we have had a drink together, though.'

A few minutes later Roman joined in the conversation.

'Jack, good to see you again.'

'And you Roman, how is Grace?'

'Clucking like a mother hen now our grandson has arrived. Thank Fumiko when you see her, we still thank God for her counsel; wise far beyond her years.'

'I will do that. Don't forget, visit when you wish, there is always room in my house.'

'Thanks, Jack. We will do just that.'

'Ahm.' The Ambassador cleared his throat before continuing. 'General Garcia, the offer has been made for us to assist Japan in their dispute with Russia. General Nakagawa has requested the use of the 86th and 93rd for training. How long will it take for them to be ready?'

'I can have them on the ground in three days, and one of those days is lost in the flight across the pacific.'

'Fantastic Roman, bring Grace for a few days as well.'

'I will; but you will have to get Drones and his team to teach them how to get the range correct.'

'Drones is busy, I will fill you in when you arrive. But he will give you his best pilots.'

'Deal. We will see you soon, there will be many that will want to be included, now I have to thin out the list somewhat. Mr Ambassador, if it comes to actual fighting will we be included or is it just training?'

'That has not been decided, yet. Would your men be willing to go?'

'If it means supporting Jack, they will be fighting amongst themselves to get there.'

'Very well; dispatch your teams and we will meet in Tokyo on your arrival.'

'Yes Sir.'

Roman disappeared from the hologram and the Ambassador turned to the P.M.

'I do not understand? They will drop everything to come here? And what did he mean when he said "Supporting Jack"?'

'If I may, Sir?' Motoyuki interrupted, 'Jack is the one officer that the men respect, without exception and usually on first meeting. They first met him during Trans-Pac and they liked the way he worked with them. They want to be a part of his teams, they know they will be welcomed and respected, not just for what they do but also for what they know.'

'Arigatō, Motoyuki, but I am now blushing.' Jack told his friend.

'Good, about time I won for once.' The two smiled at the personal reference.

'Unfortunately, I must leave; there is new satellite data that has just come in and I need to analyse it.'

'Before you go, the Americans are rattling their sabres at the moment, but they do not appear willing to draw their swords.'

'OK, I will see if I can find some leverage for you. Sayonara.' Jack's image also faded from view.

'That was simple enough, how did he know what units he wanted? And how did he know he does not need assistance elsewhere?'

'The man does not have a memory as we know it. His mind is full and at the same time he knows exactly what he needs. The frustrating thing is he will ask for assistance and everyone will be falling over trying to get it for him,' replied Motoyuki.

'General, what did he mean when he said he would try to get some leverage over the Americans?'

'I am unsure, knowing Jack he will find a small gap in their arguments and tear it open. That usually has one of two outcomes. Either they will be embarrassed about what he can reveal, and they will give him what he wants. Or he will threaten to expose their lack of willingness to assist an ally and they will give him what he wants; if only to shut him up. Either way, he wins. If I know Jack, he already has some concept of how to get assistance and he is just waiting for the right moment.'

'Well, we shall see. The American ambassador is due in two days.'

'May I suggest putting Jack on the Hologram call, he is not bound by political niceties; he will call a spade a f***ing shovel and then hit them with it, if it means he will get what he wants.'

'Very well, let him know the time of the visit, my secretary will let you know.'

With that the Ambassador left and the P.M. continued to gather support from the nations of the world.

Two Days Later

'Mr Ambassador, please come in, drinks?'

'Thank you, yes, coffee please.' The American sat down and seemed to have the air of being in charge; after all he was there because the Japanese wanted U.S. support so he had all the bargaining chips, or so he thought.

The refreshments came and went as did the small talk. Eventually, the American demanded. 'Why have you asked me here? What are you after?'

"Rude to a point." Thought the P.M. "Just as his reputation had described him." 'As you know the Russians are refusing to return the Kuril Islands to us. We are gathering the support of our allies before going to the UN to make a formal demand for their return. I asked you here for your official response.'

'Hmmph.' The American was almost openly contemptuous of the request.

'What makes you think we will go to war with Russia?'

'We did not ask you to go to war, just to support our claims and possibly supply a couple of warships to help enforce an embargo of the Russian ports, should it come to that.'

'Let me tell you,' the American was now getting forceful and aggressive, for absolutely no reason at all. 'We will NOT be getting involved militarily or otherwise, beyond financial sanctions. Not for these "Small Insignificant Islands".'

Just at that moment the hologram beeped and Jack's image appeared before them.

'A fine sentiment, Mr Ambassador. But as usual one that only has the effect of supporting the American Banking Industry.'

'Who the hell are you?'

'General Jackson Nakagawa, Sir.'

'Why are you here? This is meant to be a private conversation.'

'I understand that, the Prime Minister thought that I may be able to provide a slightly different aspect on the conversation.'

'Such as? We will not be talked around this.'

'All we are asking for is a few ships to, as the P.M. explained, enforce a trade embargo if that happens. And I would like two or three Marine Reconnaissance platoons to assist in the analysis of the battlefield. Is that so much to ask?'

The P.M. was sitting back, allowing Jack to run full speed into this fight. Up to this point he was pleased with what he was watching.

'NO WAY!' the American almost shouted. 'There is nothing you could say to get that from us. WE WILL NOT COMMIT COMBAT TROOPS.'

'Your choice. Mr Prime Minister, I feel we should negotiate a position along the lines of 'If the Russians return the Southern Kurils to us, as agreed in 2056, then we will not oppose their annexation of the Aleutians.'

'You would not dare!' The American Ambassador was almost exploding with indignity. 'What possible reason do you think the Russians would use to annex the Aleutians?'

'Maybe it would be because they were not specifically named in the original "Bill of Sale". As I understand it the description was for the "Territory of Alaska" no more no less. I would say that is very ambiguous and open for interpretation.'

'They would not even worry about those worthless islands.'

Jack could see the Ambassador was backpedalling furiously and he was now over the argument, "All in now, Jack," he thought. "Time to attack."

'OH, please. Do you think you are the only ones that know about the new oil field off the coast of Dutch Harbour? Or the off shore underwater drilling rigs off the coast of Attu? Or even the giant storage facility on Umnak Island? It is common knowledge. And if the Russians decide to give us the Southern Kurils back; we may, in the "Spirit of Co-operation between new administrations", decide to ignore their claims on these "Small Insignificant Islands".'

'You are bluffing!'

'I am a combat general. I do not bluff, I fight. And may I add, when I fight, I fight to win.'

The American was suddenly silent. He was obviously thinking deeply about the consequences of the threats and discussion that had suddenly turned very one sided.

'A moment please,' he asked and just two minutes later he returned. 'The President has agreed to the request. We will provide three Marine Recon Platoons and five fleet units should you require assistance with a trade embargo.'

'Arigatō, Mr Ambassador. In return for your generous gesture I would like to place an American Admiral in command of the embargo. Tyrell Backhouse will be an acceptable choice.'

'Again, a moment,' he returned quicker this time. 'Can we get Admiral Backhouse on the line?'

Jack could be seen leaning forward and a moment later the image of Tyrell joined the conversation.

'Jack, good to see you.'

'And you Tyrell.'

'Admiral Backhouse, General Nakagawa has requested you command any combined fleet that is put together for any trade embargo that occurs against the Russians. Are you available?'

'Certainly, Sir. Jack where are you running the planning from?'

'My house, Hokkaido.'

'Be there as soon as I can.'

'Bring Daisy she can keep Grace company for a while.'

'Roman too? Great. Looking forward to catching up. See you soon.'

The hologram beeped and Tyrell disappeared from view.

'You two know each other?'

'Yes, Sir we do. He commanded my fleet units at Trans-Pac a while back.'

'Humph. If there is nothing else, Mr Prime Minister?'

'No. Thank you for your time and your generous offer, Mr Ambassador.' The American turned and left, he had the distinct feeling he had been herded into a corner and left with no way out.

'Jack, you really stamped on him, hard.'

'No more than he deserved, as usual they are only fair-weather allies, and as long as it suits their agenda.'

'Remind me not to argue with you.'

'No need for us to argue, we understand what is needed. He thought we were coming begging and he could run the show and he got surprised, that's all.'

'Arigatō, Jack. Sayonara.'

'Sayonara, Sir.'

The diplomatic meetings were to go back and forward for some months. One by one the various diplomats made their way to either the P.M.'s office or the Foreign Ministers. One by one they all agreed to support Japan in, mostly, the UN vote. Some were able to push a more vigorous line and applied financial or diplomatic sanctions. Even the ones that did not apply sanctions spoke against the Russians throughout the seemingly endless rounds of speeches and votes on the floor of the General Assembly.

At the end of almost six months of political jockeying in the halls of power and considerable late nights at the planning cells in both Hokkaido and Tokyo; the matter was scheduled for a formal hearing at the General Assembly and that was to be followed by the Security Council vote.

This was to be the crucial time, one wrong move by either side and the Kurils would be lost, this time probably forever.

Northern Army Headquarters

'General Tanaka. You are ready, yes?' asked General Onishi.

'Hai.'

'General Nakagawa, a brief rundown of the combat plan if you please.'

'First objective is for the fleet to establish a "no go" zone on the south-eastern side of the island.'

'Second; extend this zone around the southern half. This is expected to be a straight-forward matter as all enemy supply routes are via the north-western approaches, these approaches are open during the summer however considerable sea-ice is forecast for the winter and they may try to resupply using the southern routes. Have the supporting governments been appraised of the necessity of the zone?'

'They have, they are understanding of our needs and are willing to send shipping around the southern islands.'

'Third; once the army divisions have been landed and they have established a camp; we will be ready for the initial assaults, beginning with the destruction of the deactivated airfield on the western side. If we can destroy the fuel dumps and buildings there, they will be forced to fly from Urup. This is no great inconvenience to them however it will clear more of the island for our benefit.'

'Fourth; once we are established, a push into the enemy lines with armour and artillery support; this will see the enemy pushed back towards the shore.'

'Under no circumstances attack the eastern defences and we must steer clear of this area. We cannot risk the Russians knowing we understand what is there; nor can we risk damaging the equipment.'

'Very good. General Tanaka, your preferences?' Motoyuki asked.

Tanaka stood up. A senior career officer, who was overlooked for the position of Chief of Planning when Jack was catapulted into the job. His anger and embarrassment were only somewhat assuaged when he was announced as "Commander Invasion Forces".

'General Nakagawa,' began Tanaka. He had always been at loggerheads with Jack, at various times he was angry at being pushed aside and at other times he was amazed at the simplicity and detail of the battle plans that emerged from the Planning Group. Either way, neither was going to be best friends of the other and so they referred to each other by rank and family name, none of the easy familiarity Jack had with the others he works with. 'Has estimated that there are twenty thousand Russians in the two encampments in the north; eighteen thousand in the western camp and two thousand in the east. I have requested five divisions of ground troops. This includes two Tank companies and their support groups. I have asked for two anti-aircraft batteries totalling ten launch vehicles and support teams as well as battlefield surveillance systems. I assume the agreed Naval blockade will be sufficient.'

'What about support for the troops? Food, shelter etc?' Motoyuki was disappointed that he had to ask for specific information.

'We will create a ground camp, tents and such. Two field kitchens for each division. Total food supplies will need to be around three thousand calories per man per day. There is sufficient fresh water in the rivers and streams, we will not need to have treatment systems in place. Latrines will be placed well away from water supplies to prevent contamination.'

'Very good. Any other matters?' Motoyuki asked, half wanting more information and half wishing that the plan was sufficient.

'Just one,' Jack replied 'I have placed a company of Drone Pilots on standby should we need extra surveillance. I believe that the ground surveillance teams provided by the Americans will get sufficient information, but just in case.' 'Arigatō, Jack. I am certain they will call you if they are needed. For now, we must hope that the diplomats can find a way forward for us that does not require fighting.'

The General Assembly

'This meeting will come to order,' announced the Secretary General, the gathered diplomats and their entourages became quiet. Everyone knew why they were there and everyone was almost certain of the outcome.

'The motion has been debated and the votes have been cast. Is there any question on the validity of the process?'

'My government and the delegation here do not recognise the authority of the UN to hear these claims. We demand that the International Court of Appeals hear the claims against us.'

'You demand!' The Japanese Ambassador jumped to his feet and shouted at the Russian. 'You have done nothing except deny the rights of those that the islands belong to, the Ainu people, and you still demand what is not yours,' he sat down and waited for the inevitable counterclaims.

'These islands were seized following World War 2, they are Russian!'

'You really need to read your history books, comrade.' The Australian Ambassador had picked the perfect point to join the argument. 'Japan was ordered to relinquish all claims to the islands, according to the San Francisco Treaty of 1956,'

'Exactly!' shouted the Russian.

'If I may continue. The fact that Japan was forced to relinquish their claims did not mean that Russia was automatically given title, in fact the title was specifically NOT given and the Russians were NOT given sovereignty over the Kuril Islands. Mr Secretary General, the Ainu people were given the choice as to whether they would prefer to be Russian, Japanese or independent. They chose to be an independent prefecture of Japan. THEY CHOSE. Not the Japanese or the Russians. We should abide by the agreement that the Russians themselves put forward over a hundred years ago. The Russians must leave and leave NOW.'

The General Assembly erupted in vigorous applause, leaving no doubt as to who supported which side of the argument.

The Russian Ambassador could be seen frantically trying to save face; his assistants and researchers were poring over the copies of the relevant treaties, trying to find a possible loophole. One minute, two, five minutes passed.

'Got a problem?' asked the New Zealand Ambassador. 'Let me help. There is no loophole for your claims. Fact 1, you invaded under a manufactured excuse simply to get the oil that had been discovered. Fact 2, you have not done your research, if you had you would have left by now. Fact 3, Not only were you wrong to invade but you were equally wrong to steal, yes, steal the oil that belongs to the Ainu. Fact 4, you have been ordered by the highest law courts and the United Nations to leave the islands and you have ignored the orders. I propose that Russia is to be removed from the Security Council and stripped of the voting rights associated with the position.'

'The Chair recognises the proposal from the Ambassador of New Zealand. Please vote now.'

It was almost four minutes before the initial vote had been completed. China and North Korea were always going to abstain, and it came as no surprise that the final votes were one "no", two abstentions and the rest were "yes".

'Vote as much as you want, we will not kneel to your demands.' The entire Russian delegation left the Assembly.

The fallout from the vote would see immense financial sanctions. The resulting credit squeeze would see an almost immediate cessation of the importation of foods and other goods into Russia and there were shortages of everyday goods across the country.

The one result that the Russians did not bother to try to negotiate was the stopping of fuel imports, by this time there was no point in trying to negotiate anything; and soon their heating, electricity, and transportation systems were almost frozen; immobilised by the lack of fuel; unable to move the necessities of life around the country the Russian people quickly became restless. Still their government would not relent.

It was almost inevitable that the next move would be political. The political powers that, up until that time, could not even entertain the hope of being elected were now circling in the water like sharks. They could sense that political blood was ready to be spilt and they slowly began to manoeuvre their positions so that when the time came, they would be well placed and ready to strike.

Despite the diplomatic wrangling being performed behind closed doors the Russians were not getting any support from anyone, even those that were staunch allies before the invasion, and the ones that were friendly after, were now trying to ingratiate their administrations with the rest of the world; after all, now there were many goods and produce in excess, the prices would be more easily negotiable and goods would be cheaper as the excess would now need to be reduced.

The opposition politicians were pushing hard for new elections to be held and it was only the fear of being arrested that kept the general populace in check and even that fear was now being eroded.

General Headquarters, Tokyo

'Get General Tanaka on the line please.' Motoyuki asked his personal secretary. 'Hai.'

The hologram beeped once, and General Yoshiro Tanaka appeared.

'Konichiwa Motoyuki, you wish to speak with me?'

'Hai, Yoshiro. Please come and visit me this afternoon, any time will be suitable.'

'Hai, just after lunch.'

'Arigatō, sayonara.'

'Sayonara.' Tanaka shut off the hologram. "I wonder what he wants?" he mused to himself.

Just after 1.30 Motoyuki's secretary announced 'General Tanaka, Sir.' And ushered him into the office.

Siting on the side table were the usual refreshments; tea, coffee and sweet delicacies.

'Tea, I believe.' Jack was busy pouring tea for Yoshiro and Motoyuki and coffee for himself.

'Nothing better to do with your time than pour the tea?' Tanaka could not disguise the animosity he felt towards Jack. A comment well noted by Motoyuki.

'Right here and now? Actually, I have nothing I would rather be doing than pour the tea for you.'

Yoshiro had great difficulty in deciding whether it was a compliment or an insult; while he understood sarcasm, he could never quite come to grips with the precise wording that it required to be effective. A trait that Jack, most decidedly, did not share. In fact, having spent so much time with foreign armies, and picking up on the nuances of the English language, Jack was quite adept with the wording.

On this occasion, however, there was no hidden meaning; Jack was simply stating a fact.

Sitting on the desk was the thick document that was the detailed battle-plan for the invasion of Iturup Island. In large letters at the top right corner was printed the legend "COPY Number 1", and on the top and bottom of the cover, in red to emphasise the statement, "TOP SECRET" was printed and it was repeated on every page.

'Still sticking with paper? I thought you would have joined us in the twenty-third century by now.' Yoshiro tried to get one up on Jack.

'I thought about it, but by using paper it is easier to skip sections to find a specific part. It is also easier to control a secret document if it is printed. Electronic copies can be generated by anyone with a computer or tablet and an email address and they can be distributed without restriction.'

Motoyuki simply waited for the sniping banter to finish before he began.

'Gentlemen, we have now arrived at the place none of us wish to be. The diplomats and politicians have failed in their pitiful attempts at resolution. The UN is unable to pressure the Russians into leaving and it will soon be time for us to force them out.'

He paused to take a sip of his tea.

'This is really good; I don't often drink black tea, but I like this. Where is it from?'

Tanaka also took a sip and he was, almost, forced to agree.

'I have a friend in the Royal Marines, he is currently on exchange with the Australian S.A.S. He sent it to me; apparently it is grown in the far north of Australia and it is a blend of raw organic teas. It is not cheap, but the extra cost is worth it.'

'Australian tea.' Mused Yoshiro 'Who would have thought that a country that is mostly desert could create this? Can you get some extra?'

'Certainly, I will get Mark to arrange for a delivery, should be able to get it by the end of the week.'

'And some for me as well,' added Motoyuki. 'Yumi will like this.'

'Now, time for business.' Motoyuki rose from his chair and went to the safe behind him. Looking into the biometric decoder the safe determined that the man waiting was permitted to access the information contained within.

"Passphrase, please."

"Spring is the time for Hanami" A loud click of the locks and the door swung open silently, reaching in he retrieved two more copies of the battle plan.

"Close" the safe door swung closed and waited for the order to lock.

Motoyuki turned and handed copies to Yoshiro and to Jack.

'These are the only complete copies of the Battle Plan. I understand you have had the opportunity to read the important parts?'

'I have,' replied Yoshiro.

'Do you have any questions?'

'Yes, one immediately.' Yoshiro began to thumb his way through the document, mumbling "where is it" as he went.

'Where is what?' Jack asked.

'We are not to attack from the East.'

'Section 9, NO GO ZONES. Para 3.2' Jack replied.

Yoshiro looked at Jack, he had not even opened the document before him. Quickly he found section 9 and flipped pages to the quoted paragraph.

'Yes, this is it. Why are we not permitted to attack from the east?'

Jack looked at Motoyuki and got a nod in return.

'This is so secret that we did not dare to include its reference at the battle plan briefing.'

Yoshiro was stunned; what could be so secret that it could not be included in a strictly controlled, three copy, "Top Secret" document. He waited for Jack to continue.

'There is a system of caves at the eastern edge of the Russian camp. It is fully sealed, or so they think, and that is where they have stored the nuclear warheads, the ones they claim to have been searching for all this time. The eventual plan is to steal them, and that can only be done after we have defeated them.'

'Who else knows of this?' Yoshiro was incredulous at the revelation, no one had mentioned the warheads until now.

'Five in total; the three of us and my Drone Commander, as well as the Ainu Chieftain that gave us the information on how to infiltrate the system.'

'How did your drone commander become included?'

'He is the one that flew into the cave system and gave us the video confirmation of the placement as well as the access routes that may be used.'

'Can I ask why the drone commander flew and not one of the pilots?'

'I had him do the recon as he is the very best. A former world champion speed and agility racer, he is the one that found the entrance and accessed everything inside. We are better informed because of his talents.'

As so often happened around Jack, the fates decided to intervene at just that moment.

'General Onishi, there is a Warrant Officer here that insists on speaking with you and General Nakagawa.'

'What is his name?'

'He just says, tell them it is "Drones"?'

'Send him in.'

'I wonder what has brought Drones in from the Northern Planning Cell?' mused Jack.

The door opened and Drones entered, ensuring the door was securely closed behind him. Then he turned and saluted the three generals, who were all looking at him.

'Konichiwa, Drones. What brings you so far from home?' Jack asked informally, 'Coffee?'

'Konichiwa, Jack, General Onishi, General Tanaka. arigatō, coffee would be nice.' Jack got up and poured the coffee; Tanaka sat dumfounded as he watched a General serve a Warrant Officer.

'How is Mai?' asked Motoyuki.

'She is well Sir, thank you for asking.' Drones sat down before continuing.

'OK, now we are comfortable, why did you come? Surely you could have used a hologram to convey your information?'

'I could have, Moto—General.' Drones suddenly realised that maybe Tanaka did not approve of the informality that the others were comfortable with. 'However, the information I have is best delivered by spoken word and not written down, ANYWHERE,' he placed emphasis on the last word and that managed to get the attention of all three senior officers.

'OK, you now have our undivided attention. Out with it,' demanded Motoyuki.

'I assume you are all aware of the location of the Russian warheads?'

'We were just discussing that very point.'

'I gave it a lot of thought and spoke with the engineers and a cousin of mine. Between the three of us we created a remote-control lead lined box. Inside we placed a source of radioactive material; Alpha, Beta and Gamma radiation. Last night I placed it inside the cave system, hidden out of view. In a day or so we can open the cover a little and give the Russians a collective heart attack with the rising radiation levels.'

'YOU DID WHAT?' Tanaka was incredulous.

'We have artificially increased the radiation levels in the cave system. If the Russians react in their usual fashion, they will monitor it for twenty-four hours. Any increase in the levels will be reported and they will then place a six-hour check on the area. They won't enter the caves; they are far too frightened for that. If we then open the box a little more, showing a further increase they will seal the caves and leave everything exactly where it is. When the time is right, we can remove whatever we want.'

'Unbelievable, how did you come up with this idea?' Tanaka was now becoming curious.

'Mai and I were talking late one evening and she said she thought it may be a viable method of forcing the Russians to leave everything where it is. The rest was simply creating the hardware.'

'And where did you get radioactive material?' Motoyuki was concerned about the possibility of the material being available.

'I have a cousin that is stripping the last of the nuclear power stations and he got a low-level spent fuel rod. The management did not even notice that the end had been severed.'

'And how did you convince him that it would be a viable concept to just give it to you?'

'I told him that we could use it as a radiation source for training if we actually go to war. He was more than happy to assist.'

Tanaka could not hold his tongue any longer. 'I do not want any part of this, it is illegal and immoral.'

'Settle down Yoshiro,' Motoyuki was disappointed that such a simple and effective plan was beyond the thinking of such a senior general. 'You will not have to deal with it. When the time comes, Jack and his people will deal with the source as well as the warheads. Just keep to the plan and do NOT attack the eastern end of the Russian camp.'

Jack had been quiet while the explanations were made and to see his friend dismayed at the rejection of the tactic was almost too much for him.

'You may not like it, Yoshiro, but I can see the value in it. We will be able to control the destination as well as the destiny of these weapons. Well done Drones, give my thanks to Mai. Motoyuki, a commendation for both of them I think.'

'I agree, this is the kind of innovative thinking we need.'

The plan worked so well that all were in awe of the simple effectiveness of it. Within two days the Russians were busy building lead lined, reinforced concrete doors for the cave front. The satellite images showed them sealing the cave entrance and then moving the sentry positions away from the area. In one move the most dangerous items in the entire island chain had been isolated and removed from the tactical thinking. The only reason behind it all was the rise in radiation levels.

'Arigatō, Drones. Will you wait for us and we can dine this evening?' Jack asked his friend.

'Certainly, will you bring Chie and Fumiko?'

'That is a good idea, I think I will.'

At that point Drones stood and saluted before leaving the room, closing the door behind him.

'I must protest, Motoyuki. Jack is far too familiar with the lower ranks; it undermines the chain of command.'

'I used to think that as well; then I saw the amount of work and innovation he was able to extract from those under his command, and their willingness to go that little bit further for him. It will not work for most of us, I know I could not do it, but it works for him.'

'Now, any more questions?'

'I need to know why a priority has been placed on the destruction of the old airfield?'

Motoyuki looked at Jack.

'Section three, para 3.2, initial phases.' Jack responded, still not having opened his copy of the battle plan.

'How do you do that? Is it all memorised?'

'Actually, it is. The destruction is a priority as the old base is still usable even though it has been deactivated, there have been a few landings and deliveries made there in the last few months; almost everything is being shipped in, and to be honest I would like to keep it that way.'

'Would it not be an advantage for us to be able to use it?'

'Certainly, and we will; but we will land most of our items by helicopter or from landing barges. It is too vulnerable in such a small island to have aircraft sitting unloading and tanks and supply trucks waiting when it is a very short flight from even Urup to the north.'

And so went the rest of the afternoon; question, answer, move on. Eventually, they were happy with the plan and its expectations.

'Domo arigatō (thank you very much) Jack, let us hope we will not need most of the plan.'

'You are most welcome, Yoshiro. Unfortunately, the politicians and diplomats will not be able to negotiate their way forward. We will need to be ready when the time comes and come it will.'

Tanaka bowed to both and left the room. His car was waiting for him and as he was driven to the airfield to return to the Northern Army Headquarters he sat and thought over the afternoons work. "I may well have underestimated him. The plan is very good, every possible contingency has been catered for. Let us hope it all works." He watched the countryside for a few minutes and then suddenly a thought burst into his head "How does he know that we will go to war; he is so certain of the failure of the negotiations."

Inevitably the weeks dragged into months and then the seasons began to change.

'General Onishi, you have been summoned to the Imperial Palace.' His personal secretary passed the "Immediate" signal that had been rushed to his office and waited for a reply.

'Eleven tomorrow morning. Very well, have my full dress uniform ready.'

'Hai.' The secretary left to make arrangements with his staff for the requisite uniform to be made ready.

The ringing of his personal phone brought Motoyuki from his musings back into the real world.

'Yes, Jack?' he answered.

'This is it. We are going to war.'

'How do you know? Never mind. How will it go?'

'My sources say we will win a great victory, but it will be difficult and costly. Not so much in money but a lot of good troops will not make it home.'

'I feel I must tell you it is very difficult to send so many to fight and know that many will not come back.'

'And that is why you had me prepare the battle plan, it will increase the chance of survival for many.'

'True. Have you been summoned as well?'

'I have, I will collect you at ten thirty, if you wish?'

'That is ok, I have a staff car.'

'Far too important for a staff car, I have just collected my new Bentley we can arrive in that, I have a driver as well. May as well look the part of important visitors at the palace.'

'Agreed, it may be some time before we can partake in such a luxury again.'

'See you at ten thirty. Sayonara.'

'Sayonara, Jack.'

Right on ten thirty the next morning the gleaming burgundy coloured Bentley rolled to a gentle stop in front of the headquarters building where the Chiefs of

Staff had their offices. General Onishi emerged from the building and as he got in there were heads watching from every window in the building.

The Chief of Staff along with the Chiefs of the individual services and General Tanaka, had left only minutes before with a police escort along the freeway to the Imperial Palace. Travelling at a respectable 100kmh they were making good time.

'Inspector, can we push the limit upwards a little?' Jack asked the Police inspector in charge of the official escort.

'How far up, sir?'

Jack thought for a moment and then replied. The Inspector looked stunned.

'You really want to go that fast?'

'Why not. You have closed the freeway for us, let's make use of it.'

'Very well, I will give the order.'

Only a minute later Jack's Bentley left Defence Headquarters and rolled gently onto the freeway. The lead riders of his escort had shot off into the distance at almost 200kmh and it was only a couple of minutes before the gap had closed and his driver was flashing the headlights in a signal to go even faster.

The single car shot past the Chiefs of Staff convoy at well over twice their speed and arrived at the Imperial Palace almost five minutes before them.

The gates were opened, and they rolled slowly through and pulled up at the official entrance. Once the car stopped, palace staff opened the doors for the passengers; and as they waited at the entrance for their compatriots to arrive the Shogun, commander of the Emperors Personal Guard, emerged to greet them.

'Konichiwa, good to see you all again. I just wish it were under better circumstances. Jack, good to see you it has been far too long between drinks. We must get together soon.'

'Hiroshi, you are right, as usual. For the foreseeable future I will be working from the "Northern Planning Cell", come any time you wish. There is always a room for you, you know that. I know we all hope this will be over quickly, but my sources tell me different. Come for Christmas, bring your family as well.'

'Sources? You still have Chie Maki with you?'

'I do. But it is not only Chie, her daughter Fumiko lives with me as well.'

'Is she as powerful as her ancestors?'

'It is early yet to say; but she appears to be at least the equal of Hitomi Maki if not more powerful.'

'Her omens?'

'She foretells of victory, that is all.'

'That alone is a good thing.'

'Hai.'

'Just how fast were we going, Jack? Down the freeway.' Motoyuki asked as he puffed slightly from the sheer exhilaration of the drive. 'That was amazing, your driver was very confident at that speed.'

'A little under 240kmh. He was a racing driver before he came to me, so he would have to be good, won at Le Mans, Bathurst and several other endurance events.'

'Wow, I have never travelled that fast on land before. It is no wonder you like that car; it was so smooth, even at that speed.'

'I will take you out in the Aston one day; the ride is a little stiffer, but it goes a lot quicker.'

'How quick?'

'Top speed is around 385kmh.'

'I don't think so, I will leave those speeds to aircraft.'

Inside the Imperial Palace

The two continued to exchange banter until the remainder of the entourage arrived and they were then ushered into the Emperor's private chambers.

'Please wait here.' The Emperor's Private Secretary ushered the six senior members of the Defence Forces and the Shogun into the Emperors private meeting room. 'His Majesty will be with you soon.'

They made their way into the room and all began to take in the artefacts spread around the walls and the pictures that adorned almost every horizontal surface. The display of swords and armour, the portraits of the Emperors and Empresses, and the images of the Shoguns for the last two hundred plus years. Each looked in awe at the display, so many items from so long ago.

'There he is Jack, your namesake.' Commentated the Shogun. They all looked at the portrait of Tokugawa Musashi. 'Let us all hope he is looking down on us with positive support.'

They all agreed, but before anyone could speak again the Emperor entered with the Empress beside him and the Crown Prince and Princess following closely. The other members of the Imperial Family all filed in and waited, they were followed by the Prime Minister and the Foreign Minister, each with their wives beside them.

As the Emperor stopped, the heads of the Defence Forces and General Tanaka, stood to attention and saluted; all except Jack. He immediately unclipped his dress katana, knelt and offered it to the Emperor with both hands. The tsuka to his left (to prevent him from grasping it as a weapon) and the Mune (the back of the blade) directed towards the Emperor (a sign there is no aggression intended).

'Arigatō General, keep your weapon.' The Emperor told him, as he gently touched the offered weapon.

Jack bowed his head and then stood up and reattached the weapon to his belt.

A brief nod was all it took for the staff to enter with the obligatory refreshments. Even though the greeting was formal, and the small talk was friendly, there was a decided tension in the air. Everyone could feel it and yet no one addressed it.

'General Nakagawa, may I ask a question?' Prince Hitachi of Mikasa spoke in hushed tones, almost fearful he would be rebuffed for being so forward. As the sixth in line, his was very much a junior role in the Imperial Family.

'Of course, Your Highness.'

'Why did you kneel? The others did not?'

Jack looked the boy in the eye and said 'I am descended from a long line of Samurai. Even though there is now, in modern times, no longer a need or even a requirement to kneel, I feel it is right for me to show my allegiance, and I do this by acknowledging his position as my Emperor. Simply kneeling and offering my weapon shows that I am a loyal officer.'

'Why do the others not kneel?' the prince asked in a whisper.

Jack leaned down and whispered back, 'Because they prefer to use the modern ways; a salute and bow of the head is sufficient.'

'I am not certain I understand.'

'Ask your uncle, the Crown Prince, he will be able to answer you better, later on.'

At that point the Emperor called for quiet; instantly those present stopped speaking and waited for the Emperor.

'It is with great regret that I must inform you all that the diplomatic measures undertaken in an attempt to have the Russians remove themselves from our lands, land that they themselves ceded to us, have failed.' A murmur of discontent rolled around the room.

'The time is now near when we will have to retake what is ours, I understand that there will be much discussion both in the corridors of power and in the streets, but we are resolved; we will force the Russians from the Islands and restore the Ainu people to their ancestral lands. General Onishi?'

The open-ended question was the signal for Motoyuki to give the formal orders.

'The time is now right; General Tanaka prepare your forces for landing.' General Motoyuki Onishi had given his first order as Chief of Defence Forces.

'General Nakagawa signal the Combined Fleet that they may now enforce the Naval Blockade of the Islands of Iturup and Urup. It is understood that summer is now ended, and winter will soon be upon us. May your Gods go with you General Nakagawa?'

'Arigatō General Onishi,' Jack replied.

'I am not fully conversant with the methodologies of modern warfare, as you all well know.' Began the Emperor, 'However; I think we are all wondering why you would choose a winter beginning for the campaign?'

'Your Majesty,' Jack replied, 'We have chosen this time to begin the blockade as the winter sea-ice will soon be on us, and the weather forecasts are for early and severe winter weather and the ice packs will be forming soon; the far northern Russian Ports will soon be iced in. This will aid us in preventing the enemy from resupplying their bases. This will place the enemy at a distinct disadvantage by the end of winter. They will be short of all supplies; food, heating oils, generator and aircraft fuel, everything. That will be favourable to us. We will increase the surveillance efforts and get some covert units on the ground around the end of January, this will give us the best and newest information possible. Once the ground troops are ready, we will land and prepare our attacking forces. That should allow us sufficient time to complete the construction and testing of some new weapons hardware I have asked for as well as the training of several hundred "drone" pilots.'

'Arigatō, General Nakagawa; if I understand your thinking, we can use the weather as an ally. General Onishi, why do you have a smile on your face.'

'I do most humbly beg your pardon Majesty.' Onishi bowed deeply. 'It is well understood by his compatriots and those he commands that no one actually "understands" how Jack's mind works. It is one of the great mysteries of the world.' The entire room began laughing.

The Crown Prince had the next question. 'Why do you need so many pilots?'

'We have been trialling a number of new tactics utilising resupply drones as well as attack and "suicide" drones. I have asked for some specialist versions that are still in the testing phase. The number of these units we will require, demands that we have many pilots trained and proficient in their use. That will take some time, we expect them to be ready before the end of winter.'

'That is only five months away, how do you plan to complete this task?' The entire room was suddenly attentive, Jack was now firmly in the spotlight.

'I have given the recruitment and training process to my Drone Commander; he has been recruiting from the ranks of the best recreational and professional agility pilots in the country and we have had a lot of interest from around the world as well.'

'Foreign civilians wish to fight for us?' It was the Emperor that asked; every new revelation was opening questions about weapons and tactics that were, up to that time, secret.

'They do, Majesty.'

'Have you found out why?'

'Word spreads quickly in the online world. Drones, the Commander, is highly respected and his friends and colleagues wish to do something more than just dodge trees and walls. This is an, almost, natural progression for them.'

'Does your commander have a name?'

'He does, but it is all but unpronounceable.'

'Well, what is it?'

'Khemkhaeng Thamrongnawasawat. His family are Thai by ancestry, they have lived in Japan for almost two hundred years. Their family dynasty was founded by his namesake; when he was given permission to stay after his tenure as a Professor of International Relations at the University of Nagasaki was complete. They have lived in the area ever since.'

'With a name like that it is no wonder you call him Drones!' Onishi had perfectly framed the sentiments of all present.

'What rank does he hold?' Again, it was the Crown Prince asking.

'He was promoted to Warrant Officer not too long ago.'

The Crown Prince offered his opinion. 'Father, if this man is commanding so many as we go to war, would it not be better for him to be a Major or even a Lieutenant Colonel?'

'I think so, General Onishi, have him promoted to Major at the first opportunity. If he completes his work, then we can promote him again in the future.'

'As you wish, Majesty. Jack, see to it when you return to your base.'

'Hai.'

There was a fair amount of small talk that followed. Many times, Jack was asked by almost everyone if he would reveal the tactics and disposition that he had planned; and every time he would either deflect the question or simply not answer.

One by one the Chiefs of Staff left to attend to other matters and the various members of the Imperial Family departed to other pursuits. Eventually, the only ones left were, The Emperor, Onishi, Tanaka and Jack. During a slight lull in the conversation there was a knock at the door.

'Enter.' The Emperor ordered, and an orderly entered the room.

'Majesty, I apologise for the intrusion but there is a Major Saito insisting on speaking with the Generals.'

The Emperor looked at the three officers before him and saw a slight nod from Jack and Motoyuki, 'Send him in.'

Haruto Saito entered the room, saluted and then removed his cap before bowing to the Emperor.

'An unexpected visit Major, something very important I assume.' Tanaka was still unused to the easy access that Jack's teams had to him.

'It is General, I apologise for the intrusion, Your Majesty.'

'That is fine, what is your message?'

'I have been completing a surveillance assessment of the satellites and space areas above Iturup. The Russians no longer have a surveillance satellite in place; the last one, um, "failed" when its power spans unexpectedly "twisted away from the sun".'

'That is an advantage,' replied Tanaka. Onishi smiled and Jack simply looked directly at the SatCon Commander.

'What did you do?' Jack asked, almost accusingly.

'Nothing, Sir. "Someone" hacked into their control systems and the satellite stopped functioning. The Russians have spent a week trying to regain control, but they have not been able to command the computers to restart.'

'Dare I assume that "Someone" means someone you know?'

Haruto simply smiled gently. 'I don't know what you are inferring.'

'I think you do know.'

The Emperor and the others listened carefully at the exchange between the two.

'Well, if I had to guess, I would say it was an error filled triple translation from Russian to Swahili to Pidgin English and then to an obscure Aztec dialect.'

'And how did you manage that?'

'I have met many people during my travels, friends like to help.'

'Very good work, Haruto. Keep it up. See if you can work such magic again, should the Russians divert another satellite.'

'Arigatō, I will do what I can.' Haruto saluted, bowed to the Emperor and left the room.

'General Nakagawa,' the Emperor began. 'If I understood that exchange correctly, your Satellite Controller has put the Russians out of the surveillance picture?'

'Absolutely correct, Your Majesty. He is very good at his job. The Russians will be flying blind now and will still be so when we begin to land our forces, and that will make our job a lot safer if they do not know where we are or what we are doing.'

'Where did you find him?'

'He is a friend of Drones, and a very good drone pilot as well. He was in SatCon and I promoted him when the C.O. was transferred.'

'Do you have to teach them to be so sneaky?'

'No, Sir. I do let them know that if it improves our chances then I don't particularly care what they do; especially if we are at war.'

'Dare I assume you take good care of your "assets"?'

'He certainly does,' Motoyuki answered for Jack. 'In fact, he takes such good care of them that they are willing to try almost anything for him. That trait is something that Jack brings with him to the job; he trusts them, and they give everything to make the plans work. They get a lot of; how do the British say it? "Leeway" I think is the word; and they bring him working solutions. A most satisfying method of working. If only it could be taught, but I believe it is a character trait, not a learned method of operating.'

'Whatever it is General, it appears to work well.'

'Let us hope, Majesty, it will continue to do so into the future.'

'You sound dubious?'

'I have spent a long time working with many people that have provided different insights into the solutions for different battle problems, mostly on the training grounds however. The difference with the battle plans Jack arrives at is that they are not remotely similar to other solutions; as such they are much more difficult to counter. It is no secret that Jack will find innovative ways to defeat his enemies. I do not doubt that this will be any different.'

'Very good. Good luck to you all.'

The three Generals stood and bowed to the Emperor; then they turned and departed.

'Yoshiro, will you come with us?' Motoyuki asked inviting him to travel in Jack's car.

As they slowly drove to the palace gate Jack rolled down the window, 'Do we still have use of the freeway, Inspector?'

'We do, same for the return; I assume?'

'If we can, arigatō.' They worked their way onto the freeway and Jack spoke out. 'Right, Gin, let's see what she can do.' His driver grinned widely.

'OK, I hope the escort can keep up.'

The car surged impressively and soon they had not only caught the escort but had easily passed them.

'They will catch up when we leave the road.' Gin announced, and minutes later they had almost reached the gates of the Army Headquarters when the police escort finally caught them. Leaving the car at the Planning Group building the Traffic Inspector asked 'OK, how fast this time?'

Standing, holding the door open, Gin smiled broadly. 'Just a shade under 320kmh, but don't tell Bentley; we are not supposed to go over 260 for the first 1500km.'

'Well that explains it,' replied the Inspector. 'Our traffic bikes only go 275 at the most, those riders will get some embarrassing questions when they return to the station.'

Jack smiled as he answered, 'Go easy on them, some of the best racing drivers in the world had trouble keeping up with Gin when he was racing for Bentley. Good car with a very good driver, difficult combination to beat.'

'May I ask would it be possible for some of us to ride one day? We can get access to a testing track and it would be good for some of them to see what it takes to drive like that?'

'Sure, keep in contact with Gin and organise it for the near future. I will not be able to attend; the Russians need my focus for a while.

'Domo arigatō, Nakagawa san. You do us a great honour.'

'You are most welcome; just remember they will not be permitted to drive it, only passengers.'

'Understood. Good luck to you all.' The inspector saluted and left.

Jack and the others moved inside to complete the formal works and get the latest intelligence from the surveillance teams. One of the orderlies handed him a small sheaf of papers which Jack read through immediately.

'Well, all looks good, or as good as war gets.' Jack offered. 'I think we can begin the initial deployments tonight.'

'The troops will not be in position until the day after tomorrow?' Tanaka instantly countered Jack.

'Not the troops, Yoshiro, the Fleet. I have decided to begin by closing the Etorofu Strait. And placing fleet units to prevent access by sea to the port area. This will force them to land supplies further down the West coast of Iturup. The Navy will be waiting to intercept and seize them as they come further south, and they will escort them to the next deeper water harbour.'

'That is not in the battle plan!' Tanaka almost shouted his disapproval at the change to planning.

'No, it isn't, but it makes sense. The old airstrip is not long enough for the big transports so they will have to use the smaller slower ones. If they land safely; they will the need to truck their supplies along the small roads and tracks, that will make them vulnerable to attack.'

'Jack,' interrupted Motoyuki, 'won't the fleet be vulnerable to attack in that area?'

'They will, but the water there is shallow, no self-respecting submarine commander will risk running aground on the rocks and most of the Interdiction

Fleet will be from the Foreign Navies that are supporting us. The Russians will not want to risk beginning an all-out war with ten or more nations.'

'Really that many? We know about the Americans, who else?'

'As is usual in these cases the Australians were one of the first to promise support; they were closely followed by Canada, New Zealand, Germany, Brazil, Mexico and South Korea. Several Pacific Island Nations have also offered support for inshore patrols and the Chinese and North Koreans have closed their ports to Russian shipping.'

'Why did you not tell us this before?' Tanaka demanded, feeling as though Jack had deliberately left the information out of the official briefing, to make himself look good.

'The orderly just handed it to me, you were watching when he did it.'

'You read all that in a few seconds?'

'Yes, here see for yourself.' Jack handed the papers to Tanaka who then spent a full five minutes reading them. While he waited Jack made the tea and ordered a hologram conference with the Fleet commander and the ships Captains.

Eventually, Tanaka handed the papers back to Jack, with only a grunt as either acknowledgement or thanks. Motoyuki smiled to himself, "They will never be best friends, Tanaka's ego will see to that; he will be in command of the land forces but Jack is certainly running this show."

'Very good Jack; I would like to sit in, is that possible?'

'Of course, happy to have you; I want you too Yoshiro, you need to be aware of the operations supporting your ground troops.'

'I need to be at the departure.'

'We will share a helicopter; you can drop me off at the Planning Cell and then go on to the landing fleet. Tyrell Backhouse will be commanding from the USS Blue Ridge, the Marine carrier, keep in contact with him, he will be closest to provide fire support as well as logistics; just in case you need a rapid insertion or extraction.'

'Hmph' was his only reply.

Central Planning Room

'Mai, let me know when all are connected, please.'

'Hai.' Came the familiar voice from the Northern Planning Cell as Jack returned to studying the 3D hologram maps of the approaches to the strait.

'Hmm, ah, oh. Good.' A series of semi grunts emerged as Jack looked and probed for weaknesses.

'All ok, Jack?'

'Yes, Motoyuki, yes. I have plotted the positions for a possible minefield in the approaches to the seaport. We may need to use them as a last-ditch offensive ploy if things don't go to plan, time will tell.'

'I thought that your plans were supposed to be perfect and they would ensure the destruction of all enemy forces. All we are supposed to do is turn up.' Yoshiro was scathing in his attempt at a sarcastic response.

'And so they are, perfect and fool proof. There are, however, two issues that we need to address; first the enemy is not governed or controlled by my plan, so they will not play nice. Second no battle plan will survive first contact. What I am doing is trying to have contingencies in place should things go wrong in a big way. If we can force the Russians to react to us then we will win decisively, if they force us to react to them, then we may find ourselves in trouble.'

'And you think a minefield in the strait will stop them?'

'Think big, Yoshiro. We need to have whole of theatre plan; the island is just a small part of it. I am not going to divulge all aspects as that will take a month, a month we do not have to spare. If we all stick to our part of the plan then we will be in a good position come the end of winter.'

Just at that moment the hologram began beeping incessantly. After almost five minutes of beeping and introductions Mai's voice could be heard.

'Good afternoon all. Your host for this afternoon's meeting is General Nakagawa. Present in the Planning Cell are General Onishi, Chief of Defence Forces, and General Tanaka, Commander Northern Army.' A series of greetings resounded around the room.

'Jack, you have the meeting.' Mai moved into the rear of the room and began to control the communications and imaging systems.

'Arigatō, Mai. Konichiwa all; this is the final briefing before deployment. I assume you have all read and understand your position and your duties in regard to the plan?' Everyone present nodded in agreement.

'Good. Initial deployments are as follows. Tyrell, I want your Interdiction Fleet placed to cover the Western Approaches to the Etorofu Strait. Force all incoming ships to divert to the south-west where the Navy will board and take them to ports well away from the islands. This is critical, we need to begin to starve them of supplies before winter sets in.'

'Roger that, Jack. How much time do we have?'

'A review of the Russians previous supply schedule, addendum 9.3.3 in your plan, shows that the important food and fuel deliveries, supplies for winter, are due in three to four days. We need to stop them from being landed.'

Everyone was impressed as along with Tyrell's aide they began to shuffle through the copy of their part of the battle plan. Tyrell's aide eventually found the correct page and handed it to the Admiral; Jack had not even opened his copy of the plan.

'Very good; if we are expecting three ships, we can deal with them easily enough.'

'Be careful. Tyrell. The first intervention will be easy enough, the following ones are likely to be heavily escorted. Admiral Kobo; once intercepted, the ships should only require one escort to the nearest suitable port, Yokosuka or Sasebo where their cargo will be confiscated and the ships interned.'

'Submarines?' Kobo asked.

'Not expected, the waters are shallow and dangerous for a submarine to operate in. but keep your under-water defence systems ready just in case.

'Air strikes?'

'Again, not expected in the early phases, keep your systems ready anyway. The first moves will annoy the Russians and I expect they will retaliate heavily when they send the replacement ships.'

'Jack, if I may?'

'Certainly, Motoyuki.'

'We have just received notice from a number of extra Allied Nations that they are willing to send some ships to assist. These will eventually be used in the escort duties, this role will release ships from our Navy to take on the positions of radar and anti-aircraft picket as well as anti-submarine defence. For these early phases there will simply not be enough ships to go around.'

'Domo arigatō, Motoyuki. A good note, our forces will become more powerful as the weeks go by. Tyrell will you liaise with Yoshiro to get your Marine recon patrols into place in the next twenty-four hours. I would like to speak with their commander after we wrap up here.'

'Sure Jack.'

For the next two hours Jack spoke with every commander in turn, each given a briefing on their part in the overall plan. Eventually, the meeting began to wind down; the questions became less often and less demanding. Finally, the meeting was closed with Jack thanking them all and wishing them good luck for the future.

Once the majority had left it was just Jack, Motoyuki and Tyrell in the meeting.

'Jack, this is Gunnery Sergeant Rodrigues, he will be commanding the recon patrols.'

'Good afternoon Gunny.'

'Afternoon sir.'

'Please call me Jack.' Rodrigues looked at Tyrell, silently asking for permission to use the most unusual method of speaking with a very senior officer. Tyrell simply nodded.

'As you wish, si…Jack.'

'Good, your name?'

'Mike.'

'Good, welcome to the command group, Mike.'

'Thank you.'

'Tyrell, why is there a Sergeant in command of the Recon group?'

'The Commandant decided that there would not be any other officer as they are under command of a foreign national and they are not front-line combat troops.'

'I guess that is going to be their loss. Mike, do you have any questions?'

'Only one, I am concerned that we have been ordered not to be a part of the offensive army, just recon?'

'Don't worry, yours will be the first boots on the ground and the work you will be undertaking will be some of the most important of all. Tyrell, as they are not to be considered as a part of the Offensive Army that infers that they not permitted to fight?'

'That is right Jack. The Pentagon has decreed that we are only supplying some ships as combat units. Mike and his teams are not to be included as an integral part of the offensive groups.'

'I pray the good lord will save us from people that cannot see the wood for the trees.'

'Dare I say "amen" to that.' Mike replied and Jack began laughing.

'You are going to fit right in here.' Tyrell observed. 'Jack, I think it is important for us to define the policy for the recon group.'

'What have you in mind?'

'While the Pentagon has demanded they do not form a part of the offensive army, they should be given the capacity to defend themselves, should the situation demand.' Jack thought for a minute.

'Mike, your thoughts?'

Jack could see Mike turning the possibilities over in his mind. 'Such a ruling appears to be open to interpretation; we can fight to defend ourselves, sure. But what about defending those near us?'

'I am of the opinion that such action is within the broad operational parameters handed to us by your Pentagon. There is no definition for the possibility you propose. Therefore, I would say if your actions, in defending yourselves, also defend those nearby then you are in the clear.'

'Even if we do not come under direct fire?' Mike clearly wanted defined orders.

'If you feel you are under attack then defend yourselves.'

'I think Jack wants to say; if you have to shoot then shoot everything that is not us.'

'Thank you, Tyrell. Well put. Mike, we do not hold onto rigid lines or orders, around here, General Tanaka will probably argue that point so keep out of his way as much as possible, he thinks that his divisions should be the only offensive people in the area.'

Mike grinned widely. 'Thank you Jack, I think I will enjoy working for you.'

'I hope you do. Get your teams familiar with the comms equipment and weapons we are using, you may need to get replacements at some time and we won't have time to train you in the field.'

'Certainly will.'

'Motoyuki, can you get someone to assist?'

'Hai. I will assign a platoon from the fifth division to assist. Tanaka will not like it, but then again I am still the Chief of Staff.'

That was the end of the pre-action briefings, everyone bid farewell and returned to their duties.

'Are you confident Jack?' Motoyuki asked, out of the blue.

'Short answer, yes. The biggest issue we will have in the initial phases is Tanaka, I get the feeling he will do as he pleases and ignore the bulk of the plan.'

'Let's hope he does not stuff it up too badly.'

USS Blue Ridge

'Sir, is he always that easy to work with?'

'He is. You will be at the front, keep to his plan and he will get you home, be flexible and stay safe.'

'Aye-aye sir.'

Marine Deployment Area

'What's happening Gunny?' It was one of Mikes privates that asked what everyone was wondering.

Mike gave them all a detailed account of his part of the briefing and the exchange following on from it.

'So, we don't have to run away if it turns hot?'

'No, he has given us orders to "defend ourselves" and his definition is very broad.'

'You don't think he will use us as an excuse if it goes wrong?' The PFC (Private First Class) was concerned that they could be used as some sort of scape goat if there was a problem.

'I asked Admiral Backhouse and he told me as long as we don't attack the Russian lines ahead of schedule and stuff up the entire battle plan, he will cover our butts, come hell or high water.'

'Never heard of a general stick his neck out so far.'

'According to the Admiral, he has never seen an officer look after his men as well as this Nakagawa. Make it work, men. Our lives depend on it and so do many others.'

At that point a platoon from the Fifth Division arrived and with one Japanese soldier to three Americans they began to instruct them in the differences in the equipment that would be used.

In just two days' time Gunnery Sergeant Mike Rodrigues and the American Marines would be the first troops on the ground in what was to become known as "The Border Wars".

Chapter 27
Insertion

The term insertion, for the military, broadly covers the act of placing troops into an area that is under enemy control, and that is exactly what happened.

The helicopters hugged the terrain as they flew from the "Blue Ridge" towards the enemy airfield. Keeping as low as possible the three helicopters managed to evade the Russian Radar and other detection systems to discharge their cargo just two kilometres from the, supposedly, unused airport. Their first priority was to get information on what was housed in the revetments. (Armoured coverage for the parked aircraft, arranged to prevent damage from bomb blasts. One aircraft damaged does not cause damage to any other aircraft in the immediate area.)

To their utter surprise, they found that the airfield was far from unused, in fact it was very much in full working order, it just looked abandoned. As the marines looked through their binoculars Mike commented "Well, I guess this is why we are here, to find things like this." 'Get video of as much as possible. Comms, get in touch with "Tornado" (Blue Ridge) and ask for this to be patched through to "Taipan 1".' The radio operator began to make the satellite connections and the video images were being viewed in real time in the Northern Planning Cell.

'Mai, can you get me a line to the Emperor, please?'

'Hai.'

'Here it is, Jack.'

'Arigatō.'

Jack took his seat at his desk. 'Your Majesty, I understand the Prime Minister is with you?'

'He is.'

'I would like to inform you that the first teams are on the ground and they are already bringing us important information. Mr Prime Minister, if you would convey the fact that the Marines are already providing vital information, to the American Ambassador. I am certain he will puff up and take the credit anyway he can; it will make him feel good and it will cement our demands should we need extra assistance.'

'Arigatō Jack. Reports as you have useful information.'

'Hai, Sayonara, Majesty, Mr Prime Minister.'

Jack closed the hologram connection and began to make adjustments for the near future.

For the next ten days the nightly flights brought thousands of troops into the area. The first to be landed were the ARV's with their infantry support teams, their job was to establish the controlled area for the assault base. Setting the boundaries and the sensor systems they rapidly set up the beginnings of their operational base.

Once the base perimeters had been set, the support teams arrived. Field kitchens were quickly set up and a medical area, complete with operating rooms were prepared; no matter how good the planning or the execution of the individual assault phases were, there were always going to be casualties. Latrines and ablution buildings were also high on the list of early requirements.

Next were the Armoured Companies, Main Battle Tanks and their associated workshop support would be vital. The improvements the Russians had made to the road infrastructure would permit the easy movement of the tanks along the established transit routes. Add to this the relatively hard ground and the low number of large trees; the long cold winters made the growth of big trees a difficult and slow process even for mother nature, the ground was favourable for the use of heavy armour.

And so it continued, the landings became a constant stream of events, for the next three months the helicopters and landing craft, working at the opposite end of the island brought in the light and not so light equipment.

A clearing was established for the guns of the Heavy Bombardment Group to fire without interference from overhanging foliage. The Ranging Group, with the assistance of Drones and his pilots, as well as the vastly improved Gen 3 Ranging Drones, were sending so much information that the battlefield had already been rendered into a three-dimensional model.

'General Garcia?'

'Si, Sanchez, what is it?'

'We have been analysing the firing trajectories and it appears that we are too close to the airport.'

'Too close? Explain.'

Sanchez displayed the trajectory map on the targeting hologram.

'These buildings are the ones that we will need to destroy,' he said indicating several brick block buildings scattered around the field. 'Unfortunately, they are too close to the surrounding hills. To shoot directly at them we would need to be on top of these rises.' Sanchez indicated the small hills between them and the airfield. 'That position is too exposed for the 86th and we cannot drop shells from here as that requires gun elevation that is beyond the capabilities of the 155s and the 127s.'

Garcia sat and waited for a moment; a trait he had adopted from Jack, as he let the information settle in his brain. 'Solution?'

'If we can move the battery back around four or five hundred metres, we will lower the barrel angle for loading, the extra range will allow us to drop at a more useful angle directly into the enemy base.'

'Show me.'

Sanchez adjusted the hologram to display the expected trajectory of the shells from their current position and then the same from the proposed position. The indicated positions of the bombardment from each position showed that the advised change in position would indeed provide a better result.

'Good work, you and your ranging teams. Please have the engineers identify and prepare a location for us to move to. Get General Nakagawa and General Tanaka and ask them to join a conference call; get all Battery Commanders to call in on hologram immediately.'

'Si, General.'

Sanchez left and passed the message. "That was a lot easier than I thought it would be, he is a lot easier to work with than anyone else I have had."

The Battery Commanders joined the conference one by one, and waited patiently for the General to begin the call.

'All present? Good. Jack, Yoshiro; Battery Sergeant Sanchez, from the ranging group has identified a problem with the current position of the battery. As such we will be moving the battery around four hundred metres further away from the enemy. This predictive indicator explains why.' Roman began the video prediction for all to see. 'As you can see the move is essential. My apologies for the oversight; the engineers are preparing our new position and we will move at the first available opportunity.'

'Arigatō, good work Roman. Give our thanks to the Battery Sergeant, a commendation is in order. We have sufficient time to cover this event. Report when you are ready.'

'Thank you, Jack. We will keep in touch.' The hologram was shut down and the teams left to begin the relocation.

With the reconnaissance teams sending a constant stream of information and the establishment of the Assault Headquarters the time was rapidly approaching when the bullets would start to fly.

'Konichiwa, Yoshiro. Good news I hope?'

'Konichiwa, Jack,' Tanaka still did not actually like Jack, call it a clash-of personalities, and he could not even be bothered to try to disguise his feelings, 'We are now established and we will be ready to launch the first attacks in the next seventy-two hours.'

'Good to hear. The gun battery should be ready by then. Send one of the Marine Recon platoons back to the airfield to check on their readiness. I would also advise that the other two platoons be dispatched, one to the central camp to report on the enemy preparations and dispositions and one to the East to report on the possible reinforcement from that end.'

'Very good, I will hold for the expected reports.'

'Excellent, I will inform Admiral Backhouse to intercept all shipping and aircraft in the area, that will leave their ground forces as the only defence they have.' 'Hai.'

The call was terminated and Jack reported to the Joint Chiefs of Staff and then the Emperor. The die was now cast, the assault was ready to begin.

Russian H.Q. Iturup Island

'I don't like it. Something does not feel right.' General Ilya Plishkin said to no one in particular; he could do nothing more than convey his discomfort, he had no evidence that there was anything wrong. True the satellite data was old but that was nothing more than an inconvenience and not that unusual. No, there was a large amount of gut feeling in this. It could have been a combination of the lack of satellite data, the non-arrival of the expected supply ships, the increase in the radiation level inside the cave, the early cold burst of winter weather. There were a lot of indications that alone were not unusual, and even together were not a problem. He just felt uneasy, and unlike Jack, he had not yet learned to trust his gut instinct.

'Have the routine patrols returned yet?' Plishkin demanded.

'They have, General; but they have nothing to report replied his adjutant.

If the truth be known, the patrols had not completed the coverage of their entire patrol area, it was far too cold and wet for them, and so they had done just enough to keep the General from becoming suspicious and, more importantly, keep him from deciding that a stint in the Military Prison in Northern Siberia would be a suitable incentive for them to improve their enthusiasm.

'Good, maybe I am just getting paranoid since the Japanese closed our Embassy in Tokyo.'

No one replied, to say "yes" would be to all but accuse the General of being paranoid; saying no would be a direct disagreement, neither response could possibly end well. That left everyone, from experience, simply keeping silent.

'Move to the jump off point!' General Tanaka ordered the advance into the enemy territory. Tanks and Armoured Reconnaissance Vehicles followed by Infantry Fighting Vehicles all moved into position. The ground infantry had moved into position ahead of the vehicles during the night and were now almost within sight of the enemy camp.

Everyone was nervous, this was the first attack and it was essential that it succeed.

'Pass the word, we will be moving out at sunrise.'

'Hai, General.'

The word was passed and the commanders all checked their watches, two hours to go.

Russian H.Q.

'General, wake up please, General.'

A grunt was the only reply the aide got. He grasped the Generals foot and called again as he shook it, none too gently.

'WHAT!' General Plishkin was not an easy man to wake.

'My apologies, sir. One of the forward lookouts has reported that he can hear heavy engines off in the distance.'

'Where?'

'Due south of us.'

'Intelligence?'

'We have nothing in the area.'

'Alert the airstrip. Bring the base to full alert status. Place extra lookouts.'

'I took the liberty to increase the lookouts and begin to wake the remainder of the force, Sir.'

'Good, well done. I want coffee in the briefing rooms.'

'Waiting for you right now, Sir.'

Good, send in my steward.'

'Sir.' The aide saluted and left the General as the steward began to dress him in his combat uniform and body armour.

Plishkin arrived in the rooms as the picture of the incoming data began to emerge onto the hologram.

'REPORT!' Plishkin demanded and almost instantly everyone began to speak.

'One at a time!'

'The forward scouts report columns of heavy and light armour moving towards our position, ground troops are moving with them.'

'Air cover?'

'Fixed wing and rotary wing strike aircraft are preparing to take off.'

'NOT OURS, THEIRS!'

'Sorry, sir. None observed.'

'NUMBERS?'

'Two Companies each of heavy armour, armoured troop carriers and recon vehicles. Total estimated at three to four thousand.'

Plishkin thought for a moment, "This is unusual, no air cover, ground forces only. No precursor bombardment. They must be trying to take us by surprise."

'Estimated attack position?'

'Best estimate at this time is centre south of our encampment.'

'Very good, strike forces in the air as soon as possible, ground battery concentrate fire on centre approaches. DO NOT OPEN FIRE. We will wait until their choice is known.'

'Yes, sir.' The divisional commanders immediately turned to direct their units towards the expected attack.'

'Where is my coffee?'

'Right here, Sir,' replied Plishkin's steward as he handed the General a steaming mug of black liquid.

Plishkin took a sip and almost vomited.

'Since when has engine oil been a suitable substitute for coffee?'

'My apologies General. This is the best we can get since the trade embargos were enforced.'

'Typical, I am willing to wager the politicians have a better coffee than this.'

'I have a comrade who works in the Kremlin, he may be able to send some of the preferred beans.'

'That would be nice, make certain he does not get in trouble, I may want more at a later date.'

'As you wish, General.' The steward left to try to make the arrangements, thanking the gods that he was serving a realistic officer and not a rigid disciplinarian.

Northern Planning Cell

'What do you mean when you say you have a bad feeling, Fumiko?'

'Sorry, Jack. Something is going wrong, NOW, but I can't say what.'

'Relax, child. Finish your breakfast. Exams tomorrow, you must study today.'

'Hai, Mama.'

Just as Fumiko and Chie were finishing their meals Emika arrived to retrieve the plates. Suddenly Eiji, the translator, burst into the room.

'I am so sorry for bursting in like this, there are reports that Tanaka has begun the assault.'

'Already, his heavy battery is not yet ready to support him?' Jack was thinking out loud, 'and Tyrell is out of position.'

'Get it on the hologram, I am on my way.' Jack left the sun room and moved onto the rear deck. Turning to face the dawning sun he suddenly knelt down and bowed his head.

'What is he doing, Mama?' Fumiko whispered, lest she disturb him by speaking out loud. Chie waited for a moment and the replied.

'He is praying, he knows they are not ready and he is asking his god for help.' Fumiko moved to him and knelt just a little behind him, bowing her head she copied the man that held the lives of so many in his hands. No one moved for about three minutes, a short time, but in the complete silence it seemed as though it was a lifetime.

Just as suddenly as he had begun his prayers, he stopped. Lifting his head, he turned to Fumiko. 'Domo arigatō, your prayers will be heard as were mine,' he made the sign of the cross on his left breast and stood up. He bowed to the others and left for the planning room.

As he entered the room all were busy trying to get as much information as possible.

'Haruto! What is going on?' He demanded of the Satellite Controller.

'This is what we have, Jack.' The hologram came to life showing the multiple heat blooms from the ground troops as they moved along the route designated as "C1".

'What the hell are they doing on C1?' It was a rhetorical question; he knew that no one there had the answer. 'Zoom out.'

The image zoomed out to give a view across the wider area.

'Why are there heat signatures on that airfield? It was to be the first target. There should be nothing moving. Get Rodrigues and Garcia on line.'

'Gunnery Sergeant Rodrigues.' Came the reply, almost instantly. Before Jack replied he ordered, 'Get this image to General Onishi.'

'Mike? Why am I seeing heat blooms at that airfield?'

'I am in the dark on the why. I can only assume they have not been neutralised. Sorry Sir, we have been out of touch with H.Q. we only get what they send us and at the moment that is only instructions on gathering the information that General Tanaka wants.'

'OK, not your fault. Gather every scrap of info you can, send Tanaka what he asks for and send me everything. Roman, what have you got?'

'We were ordered to target the main compound first. We had to move the battery to clear the trajectory and then re-range everything. Still not yet done.'

'OK, keep your heads down, Tanaka has taken the assault into his own hands. Tyrell, you there?'

'Here Jack.'

'Get your fastest ships to the strait and be prepared to take down any aircraft that get close enough.'

'Roger that; I will launch the air wing as soon as possible. We should be able to take out any support from Urup.'

'Thanks, Tyrell. OK, listen in, everyone. The attack plan has altered, probably permanently, be on the lookout for enemy forces approaching your areas. Be careful of friendly fire; and above all else PRAY, we are in deep and we may struggle to get out of this. Mike, can you get close enough to take their aircraft out as the launch?'

'Sorry Jack, no. If we get that close, we will not have cover.'

'OK, stay down and report.'

'Roger that.'

The teams began to try to make the required changes; information arrived at breakneck speed and Jack was the one trying to assemble a workable battle plan from the mess that Tanaka had created.

'Jack, what the hell is going on?'

'My apologies, Motoyuki. Tanaka has ignored the battle plan and appears to be launching a direct assault on the centre of the Russian camp.'

'OK, have you contacted him?'

'I have been trying but he is keeping radio silence.'

'So, that part of the plan he obeys; I will brief the Prime Minister and the Chiefs of Staff. Keep me informed.'

'Hai.'

Jack sat and watched as the Hologram updated with the positions of the units as they moved into position. Suddenly the heat signatures of the armoured companies brightened, "At least I have satellite information" Jack thought to himself. As he watched he found that he actually wished he didn't.

'Multiple launches from the airfield!' reported Mike Rodrigues. "This is not going to end well." Jack thought, and for the first time ever, he wished he was wrong.

To say the battle was brutal would be an understatement. Of the five thousand soldiers that Tanaka had sent forward, two in five died in the one-sided firefight. And another two in five were wounded.

The entire armoured column had been wiped out; Main Battle Tanks, Armoured Reconnaissance Vehicles, Infantry Fighting Vehicles and Troop Carriers. Over a hundred in all, lost in the first fifteen minutes. Caught in the open, travelling down the road C1, they had no chance. The air strike came at them from the rear and combinations of missiles, bombs and ground strafing saw the column destroyed.

Tyrell and his air teams had managed to stop the secondary air strike from the north; virtually none of the aircraft or missiles got through, but there was simply no defence for them from the south.

Most of the survivors came from the ground troops who simply ran into the low-lying bushes and returned as much fire as possible; too little too late. The fight went on in savage spurts for most of the day. Thankfully it was a winters day and the day-light was relatively short. As night fell the ground troops emerged and began to rescue as many of the wounded as they could as well as bringing back the bodies of many of the fallen.

The mood in the camp that night was sombre and silent. The mood at the Planning Cell and in Headquarters in Tokyo was angry. Why had Tanaka not adhered to the battle plan? Why did he attack before they were deployed and ready? These and another dozen questions would remain unanswered for a long time.

'Now is not the time for an inquest.' Jack told the Chiefs of Staff.'

'That is not your decision.' The Head of the Airforce promptly told him.

'Then hold your inquest, it will only slow down the assault and give the Russians time to reinforce their garrison.'

'I remind you that you are addressing a senior officer.' The Airforce General was a stickler for the rules.

'Then hold your inquest, I have a war to win!' Jack left the conference; he was angrier than he had ever thought he could be. 'Why are they so blind!' he almost shouted.

'It is because they do not see what you see, they do not understand what you do and they only understand the brutality of war not the subtleties of combat, as you do.'

Jack spun around to see who had spoken; the entire planning cell were looking at him, waiting for his reply. Would it be angry? Would it be violent? No one knew, and they all waited.

Jack focussed on Fumiko, she tried to smile but a small tear slowly wound its way down her cheek. 'I am sorry Jack, but I had to say it.'

'Never be sorry for speaking out, your words hold more truth than Tokyo is capable of understanding.' Looking at the remainder of the planners he said, 'You all heard her words, now we must begin to correct this problem,' he took Fumiko and held her close. 'You are too young to see and hear what is happening, I am sorry you are caught up in this.'

'Jackson Nakagawa, you say that as though I have a choice; I will know what is happening, whether you like it or not. I also know that this will be one of several setbacks and I know you will be victorious.' She pulled him down to her level and whispered, 'And I know the Emperor will want to sack the Airforce General for lack of fighting spirit. But don't tell them that, let them work it out for themselves.' She released Jack and smiled at him. 'Now; you plan, and I will supply the coffee.'

'No, Emika will supply coffee, you will study. Final exams, remember?'

'Oh, Jack. Please try to keep up. That was yesterday and even though the grades have not yet been finalised, I am still top of the graduating class. That fact is going to upset a couple of the others, but that is their problem. Now GO.'

Again, Jack smiled at Fumiko, and he turned and began to call for information. Soon the general hum of a large group of people all conducting separate conversations at the same time had returned and with it the business of war, once again, became the focus.

'Get Drones in here!' Jack shouted across the room, and a short while later Drones appeared.

'Get the analysis from Mike Rodrigues, I want to know what aircraft are flying out of the old airfield on Iturup. Get a hold of someone smart from the Air Force and find out the best way we can cripple them on the ground. Also, find out how long we will need to wait before the "Amazon" and "Kamikaze" drones are going to be available in numbers.'

'Hai.' Drones turned and began to leave.

'And get onto the manufacturers, find out how long I will have to wait for the "Kraken" as well.' Drones kept walking and waved his hand in the air to signal that he had heard the final request.

A dozen more orders were being thrown around, and information was coming to hand. Jack had not noticed that Motoyuki was waiting patiently on his hologram.

Although he had no reason to say it, he asked 'What can I do for you, Sir?' an uncharacteristically formal greeting between the two.

'You can begin by explaining why you stamped on the General so hard.'

'I planned a very good campaign. Everything from tank parts to toilet paper was ready. The scheduling and progress were set. Almost everyone was in place. Then Tanaka turned it all upside down with an early, unauthorised assault; and someone that has not been seen since we began this, demands we stop and chat about a setback? Why do you think I jumped on him? If I don't get this back on track we will lose, and I am a very sore loser.'

'Domo arigatō, thank you, Jack,' the unmistakable voice of the Emperor came just before his image appeared. 'It is good to hear you speak with such candour and passion.'

'Your Majesty, I did not know you were there.'

'I was an unseen visitor to the previous conference. General Onishi assures me that you can retrieve the situation?'

'It will be difficult, but yes we will turn this around.'

'Is there anything you will need, extra?'

'I will need to be able to call for supply support from the air force, though I doubt I will get much assistance now; the Generals toes will be sore for a while.'

The Emperor laughed. 'You have a way with words. If he does not assist you then I am certain that we will find a Chief of Air Staff that will.'

'Domo arigatō, Majesty.

'Jack, there is one more important item,' Motoyuki sounded almost mournful as he spoke. 'There is no easy way to say this. The casualty lists have been received from Iturup. Hiro Hyashida and Okimoto Higashi were both killed in the attack. I am sorry.'

The room fell silent, all Jack's staff knew and liked the two commanders, Jack's close, personal friends; suddenly the war had taken on a personal feeling.

The Emperor and Motoyuki sat and watched Jack. His face did not change, almost as if he had not heard the horrible news.

'Jack, do not seek revenge at this time.' It was the Emperor that broke the awkward silence. 'There will be time later for that. Know this, all at the palace and the entire population support you. Do what it is you do best, that will ensure defeat for the Russians.'

At that moment the door opened and Harucor Anchicar entered the room. 'Jack! Is it true? Your friends have died on the battlefield?'

'It is true Harucor.'

'Is it worth it? What if you lose more of your friends and comrades?'

'Worth it?' Jack asked wistfully. 'That is probably a question best left for the Gods of War to answer. For me; there is only one way forward now, I will remove the enemy from your lands. It will not be simple, and there will be hardships to come, Fumiko tells me that. But; I will remove them!'

Harucor bowed to Jack and then to the Emperor. 'I can only speak as I see it. We will be forever in your debt if you can do this.' Then he turned and left.

'And now Jack, General Onishi and I need to do some of the work needed to support you. Report as you can.'

'Arigatō Majesty.' Jack replied as he bowed, his mind already churning over changes to the battle plan. As the hologram closed off Jack began to issue orders.

'Signal to General Tanaka, "Secure your current position; do NOT, repeat NOT recommence offensive operations at this time."; Get Tyrell on the line, and Roman.'

Once again; the hologram beeped, and two images appeared before him.

'Jack, condolences. Hiro and Okimoto will be sorely missed.'

'Thank you Roman. Now we need to prove their loss was not a waste. Tyrell, can you redirect your fleet to ensure we intercept any aircraft and missiles coming from both the mainland and from Urup?'

'Sure, we just had another of our allies provide a couple of Air Warfare Cruisers, they and a few destroyers should be able to hold the strait and I can take the rest to the west coast of Iturup and deploy there.'

'Good. Roman, set your Ranging Group to target every building at the airfield, leave the revetments, just the other buildings. As soon as Drones is ready, we will take them out. Also redirect a couple of your 127s to drop some shells into the main camp, four or five a night, after midnight tomorrow will do for a start.'

'No problem, I will contact Drones and get a targeting unit out tonight to get the ranges exact.'

'Good, arigatō. Tanaka has pushed the "button" early; I wanted a couple more weeks before we got to this stage. Now we go with what we can get.' At that moment Drones walked back into the room.

'Good news Jack. The "Amazons" are ready and being shipped today, they will be here before sundown. The manufacturers have had a little delay in building the numbers of "Kamikaze" units you require, but the first two hundred will be in the same shipment, a thousand by next week; and the "Kraken" is in the final phase of testing the new control software, they are confident that they will be in production in the next two or three weeks, first deliveries in a month.'

'That is great news, coordinate with Roman and prepare for some night work, get your pilots rested; take the IT people and double check the flying room.'

'Hai.'

The hologram closed and a small smile crossed Jack's face. "If Tanaka cannot do it from there, then I will cover the long-range issues from here." His thoughts remained private although many were feeling the same way.

Northern Army Forward Command Centre

'General, signal from Chief of Planning.'

Tanaka read the offered signal and slowly turned a vivid shade of red.

'Who the hell does Nakagawa think he is? I am in command here and I will decide when to attack.' Just as he finished reading the signal from Jack a second signalman entered the room.

'General, signal from Central Command.'

Tanaka held his hand out and the signal was passed. He read and then re-read the second signal.

'Call group commanders, meeting here in thirty minutes.' The two signalmen left in a hurry to begin to summons the commanders.

Once they were out of hearing range, 'Not certain, but I think he just got his butt kicked.' The second signaller remarked.

'How do you mean?'

'From what I over-heard, General Nakagawa has ordered him to hold position and General Onishi all but confirmed it in the signal I brought in.'

'Oh GOD. He will be unbearable to be around. I may just report sick for a day or two,' he grinned at his friend as he remarked.

'Me too.' The other agreed; 'General Tanaka is not a good person to be near when he gets angry.'

The unit commanders arrived in time for the Generals briefing.

'We have been ordered to hold in our current position and wait for the order to attack.' Tanaka began with a snarl, or it could have been a sneer; no one could tell the difference. 'The Planning Group are organising reinforcements and replacement vehicles; these will take time to be landed and deployed. I have been informed that there will be some strikes during this time, forward units will provide analysis to me for collation and transmission to Central Command. I know we have almost finished with the winter clothing for now, but the meteorologists have predicted a short and mild summer. Winter will be back before we know it. Keep your equipment prepared as for winter conditions. That is all.'

The unit commanders left the briefing and began making their way back to their units.

'Let's hope they are a little more careful when we attack next time.' Hyashida's replacement was speaking with the new commander of the infantry units. 'That last attempt was simply suicide.'

'Or murder; depends on your point of view really.'

The two looked at each other and then around to see if they had been overheard. A voice suddenly whispered, 'I think that we all need to keep those sentiments inside our heads. We don't want to be facing a Court Martial, do we?'

The two finally spotted one of the Artillery Commanders who was behind a bush having a cigarette.

'You feel the same?' The tank commander asked, quietly.

'Everyone feels the same. Let's hope that Nakagawa can retrieve the situation before we all die.'

The three looked around again to ensure they were still alone.

'I feel we should keep a private diary each, I can get it into a cloud account that can be sent to Command if we need to do so.' The Artillery Colonel was far ahead in his thinking and his preparations.

'Good idea, we can keep it to ourselves and have a "Weekly Commanders Meeting" to resolve any Issues we face. If it turns sour then we can send it to General Nakagawa.'

'Agreed?'

The three agreed to what would normally be regarded as mutiny; but in this case they would prefer to be a live mutineer than a dead soldier, especially if their deaths were to be caused by poor judgement from above.

Jack's Private Quarters Two days later

'Chie! We are having special guests for dinner tonight, will you ask Fumiko to help, please?' Emika called out.

'Certainly, it will keep her busy for a while.'

The three set to work preparing the meals for them all. After some time, Fumiko put down her apron and walked out of the kitchen.

'Fumiko? Where are you going?'

'To the cottage to assist in preparing for the evening.'

'Arigatō. She is such a god-send, Chie.' Emika was rare in praising someone and her words carried a lot of weight.

'I know she is; I just pray she is not badly affected by the war and all she knows.' Chie replied to the unexpected praise.

Eventually, the evening sky began to give way to the full darkness of night; and the guests gathered at the cottage in the grounds.

Following on from greeting long-time friends, the chatter was lively and full of laughter. The time for dinner was drawing close and eventually they all began to wonder where Jack had disappeared to.

Chie and Emika searched the main house and some of Jack's staff were looking around the grounds. But no one could find him.

'He will have to be here soon, or he will not get fed.' Jack's mother insisted. But no sign of his appearance was to be found.

Eventually, just as everyone was sitting down, Fumiko said, 'I will get him.' And she left the house. Taking the short walk along the dirt track she entered the estate chapel and there kneeling before the altar was Jack, not moving in the least, she was at first worried. When she calmed her mind she simply said, 'Jack, you have special guests for dinner, it is time now.'

As she watched he drew a deep breath; bowing forward while still kneeling he placed his hands on the floor and his head on his hands. Again, he didn't move for a few moments. As he slowly raised his head and began to prepare to rise, he made a sign of the cross on his left breast, rocked backwards and stood upright in one motion. Turning in the direction of the voice he finally replied, 'Arigatō Fumiko. Let us eat.'

The two entered the cottage with Fumiko almost shouting as they entered the room "Found him!".

For once Jack was completely unable to speak. Standing before him were not only Emika and Chie and his parents but also all his brothers and sisters as well.

'To what do we owe this family gathering?' He asked, slightly bewildered as to the reasoning.

'Chie told me that you were struggling, no that is not the right word, you were having difficulties in changing your battle plan to accommodate some setbacks. We discussed it and decided that a family meal would distract you enough to let you find a different way around your problem.'

'As usual, I can rely on Chie and my family to rescue me. Arigatō Papa.'

'Now let us eat, it was a long journey from Yokosuka.' Reo, Jack's brother, demanded.

'How did you two get leave?' Jack asked both his brothers. 'I had all leave stopped pending future activities and deployments?'

'You will need to ask General Onishi; but I believe his words were "Detached to the Northern Planning Cell for special instruction." We will need to be back by tomorrow night and we will need to be able to give our commanders some sort of special information to justify it.' Sora was laying down an order for his younger brother, not to demand anything but to cover the story.

'That I can do. After we have eaten then we can go to the planning room and see how the latest phase is working.'

'Is that possible? Are we allowed to see?'

'Of course, Mama. Not much use being in charge if I cannot make such decisions. You have been kind enough to permit the use of the family home, you should get to see what we can achieve.'

The meal was large and sumptuous. More of a banquet than dinner with the family. Eventually, they were all sated and the children were in bed and fast asleep.

'Go, all of you. We will keep watch over the little ones.' Fumiko told the family.

'We will, it is well for you to not see what is going on; you are too young for such things.' Reo made the observation in an attempt to protect the younger of those present from the horrors of war.

'Too late,' Fumiko replied. 'I already know what will happen. Congratulations, Jack, this will put the Russians "on the back foot" as the Australians say.'

'Arigatō.' The family walked slowly to the main house and eventually emerged in the planning room.

'Just a moment. Hasegawa, General Onishi on hologram please.' The hologram came to life with the image of Motoyuki smiling at him.

'I gather you like my surprise?'

'Arigatō, Motoyuki, they have cleared my thoughts. We are about to begin the next phase; are you willing to permit them to observe the strike?'

'If they wish to observe, I can't see a problem.'

'Arigatō. Drones, are the pilots ready?'

'Hai.'

'Roman, Guns?'

'Ready Jack.'

'Tyrell, bring the fleet to full ready state. When I am done with them, I expect a strike from Urup.'

'Very good. Sound action alarms.' Over the hologram they could hear the alarms bells ringing as the fleet prepared for battle.

'General Tanaka, pass word to your divisions, a major strike is about to take place. Be ready for counter-attack.'

'Very well.' The terse reply was noted by everyone that heard it.

'Drones, are the kamikaze units ready?'

'Hai, and a special delivery from Amazon has been prepared as well.'

'Arigatō, please ensure we get as much on the holograms as possible.'

'Surveillance units are ready. Holding at 1000 feet.'

Turning to his family, now seated around his planning table and all watching the projections.

'Here we go.' Jack announced. 'All units, all units. Begin Phase 1.'

The simple command saw several dozen "Amazon" delivery drones drop from their holding pattern. The majority made their way towards the airfield and a number split off to place charges on the communications mast and the generators and fuel storage. No one spoke as they watched the first move, almost fearful that their words would somehow distract the pilots.

The vision of the drones flying through seemingly impossible spaces was as spectacular as it was mesmerising. More than once a spectator could be seen ducking as a particular drone skipped perilously close to a wall or some other object.

Even though the time seemed to go so slowly, it was just five minutes later that Drones reported.

'All pilots report deliveries are complete and ready, Jack.'

'Arigatō. Roman, time of flight?'

'32 seconds.'

'Arigatō, standby for volley fire.'

'All guns ready.'

'SHOOT!' Jack's command was unusually loud, but not as loud as the crash of twenty 155mm guns firing simultaneously. Just ten seconds later they fired again, then again. Just before the third salvo Drones was heard.'

'Special delivery units drop your presents now.' The special Amazon drones, now just 500 feet above the main Russian camp began dropping fragmentation grenades, right amongst the Russian infantry as they emerged from their accommodation expecting an attempted attack. What they got was several dozen grenades exploding as they reached the ground. The devastation was not widespread but it was debilitating, as dozens of troops simply fell, some already dying, to the ground.

Again, Drones gave the order. 'Return Amazons, pilots take up Kamikaze's.' The delivery drones were switched to their auto-return control to allow the pilots to begin other duties.

'Drones, well done to your team.' Jack's praise was always well given and received.

All this occurred just as the first shells smashed into the buildings at the airfield. Just as the survivors emerged from the wreckage of their base the carefully placed packages detonated inside the aircraft revetments. The combined explosions saw every single aircraft destroyed where they sat. The communications mast crashed to the ground. As luck would have it, the collapsing tower shorted out the electricity supplies just before the fuel supplies and generators were blown to pieces.

'A few more salvo's please Roman, just to piss them off. Drones, return Amazons, prepare Kamikaze's.'

No response could be heard, it was not necessary. The orders had been passed and were complied with, it was such simplicity that ensured that Jack's missions were successful, no unnecessary radio traffic.

General Plishkin was fast asleep when the strike began, he charged into the command room in his pyjama's demanding information. The single item he would not get. No one could get in contact with anyone else, they were blind and deaf to what was happening. Eventually, he got word to the airbase on Urup and they were scrambled into the fight, not knowing where or how it would play out only increased the wariness and indecision that would plague them.

Forty-five aircraft took off and Tyrell's fleet had disposed of ten before they were within sight of Iturup. The big shock was yet to come.

'Target now ten miles out.' Came the report from the tracking ships. 'Kamikaze's up. IR cameras only, don't warn them.' The small, less than 150mm across, drones rose all but silently into the air. 'Targets are at 300 feet.'

'Incoming!' Reported one drone pilot and he was instantly followed by the remainder of the pilots giving the same report.

The hologram lit up with the approaching enemy.

'Show drones, please.' Asked Jack and the hologram instantly glowed with the positional indicators of almost three hundred drones.'

The general opinion was stated by Motoyuki Onishi, as he watched form Tokyo. 'My god, how did you do that?'

'Questions later, please.' Jack answered the rhetorical question just as the two groups of indicators began to merge.

Many of the small green Kamikaze lights blinked out; no one spoke, unwilling to break the fascination of the event as it unfolded before them. As more of the green lights faded the red "enemy" indicators began to also disappear from the view.

It actually only took five minutes. In the end there were around two hundred green lights and no red ones on the screen.

'Tyrell, any further take-offs?'

'No Jack. I think drones got them all.'

'Very good, keep watch. Put your pickets on long range duty, we don't want to be surprised with a strike from the mainland.'

'Already done, but the weather people say the mainland airfields are all but getting drowned in that almost typhoon that passed us to the north last week.'

'Good. All units return to local command. Well done everyone. Domo arigatō.'

Jack turned to his family they were all stunned.

Eventually, his father asked, 'How did you do that? So much devastation in such a short time?'

'I have been having great deal of difficulty, getting the timings right. The combination of the different units with the very different capabilities was simple enough; but getting them to strike at the exact right time had eluded me. This is the result of being able to stand back and rethink my strategy.'

'Son, it is no wonder you were in the chapel trying to clear your mind. Which Saint were you praying to?'

'It was St Jude, the patron saint of lost causes.'

'But the cause was not lost? Was it?'

'No, and that was how I wanted it to remain.' Smiling widely, Jack continued, 'I think my prayers were answered.'

The hologram again came to life. 'I am impressed General Nakagawa. I am unsure if it was the power of prayer or of your incredibly detailed, and followed, battle plan. Either way congratulations to you and your teams.' Once again, a member of the Imperial Family, this time the Crown Prince, had been observing, unseen, from the sides.

'Domo arigatō, Your Highness, I will pass on your message.' Jack bowed his head as he spoke.

'Now, Jack, explain how you destroyed almost three dozen strike aircraft please.'

'It is simple, Your Highness. The drones are very small and agile. Each carries a steel bar almost 300mm x 35mm x 10mm. The pilots, our very best, fly the Kamikaze drone into the intakes of the engines, the steel bar literally tears the engine to pieces and the engine will explode bringing down the aircraft.'

'I see, hence the name "Kamikaze". Clever thinking.'

'Arigatō, Your Highness. We use whatever methods we find that will work. We could not do it without the expertise of our pilots, and we must thank Drones for finding them for us.'

'I feel Drones is far more valuable than just a pilot. We need as many like him as we can get.'

'I agree, and he is finding them all the time. Before this war is over, we will have all but created a new branch of the army.'

At that moment, over the hologram audio, was heard a mighty crash.

'General? What was that?'

'Unless I miss my guess, Your Highness, that will be Roman Garcia and his 127s giving the Russians a reminder that we are still here.'

'Sorry, Jack. Forgot to mute.'

'That's fine Roman. Good work.'

'I think I will let you get back to work. I will inform His Majesty of your work this evening, I feel he will be pleased.'

'Domo arigatō, your highness.'

The image of the Crown Prince disappeared from the hologram.

'Jack, what is the next step?' General Onishi was being the formal head of the defence forces and Jack understood he was asking for the benefit of other service chiefs that were with him.

'I will put Mike Rodrigues and his recon teams back on surveillance. One team to gather information on the airfield and one for the main camp. I will keep one in reserve and rotate as necessary.'

'You are not seizing the airfield? Why not?' It was the Chief of the Airforce that was asking.

'At this time, the airfield is a very difficult area to defend. Open from the enemy side it will be a simple thing for them to continuously drop shells on us, or have infantry and armour assaults. The hills and heavy forested areas on our side, make it hard for us to move and resupply. I am going to leave it for them to use. As they bring in transports and fighters, we will destroy them. This is now a war of attrition, if I can make their lives miserable, I will.'

'You should be attacking NOW!' The Airforce commander was showing he was not completely familiar with the difficulties of ground warfare and a verbal attack on Jack and casting suspicion on his methods was never going to end well.

'General, if you want to lead such an attack, please feel free to come to the Northern Planning Cell and I will arrange transport to the front. I will call for volunteers to FOLLOW YOU into battle, but I fear you will be running a lonely race.'

'You overstep your position, Nakagawa.'

"All in Jack, all in." he thought.

'No General, I am stating the facts as they stand at this time. We lost almost half a division because we were not ready and the enemy were. If you want to take over, feel free. General Onishi, keep me informed please. If required I will submit my resignation before dawn. Please be mindful of the consequences.'

'And what consequences would they be?' sneered the Airforce officer.

'One, you have not read the battle plan. You do not know the attack sequences. Two, air defence support is not viable, the enemy strike planes are too close to our lines, if we detect an incoming raid they will be gone before you get here. Three, the Northern Planning Cell is currently on private property. You will have only twenty-four hours to relocate. And four, there are new, Top Secret, weapons being prepared for delivery. Their use will not be laid down until they are deployed.'

'And most of us pilots won't fly your drones for you.' Came voice from the far side of Jack's rooms.

'Who was that, I want him Court Martialled!'

'That was one of our civilian drone pilots, he and 90% of the pilots are doing this out of a desire to assist us. They are under no obligation to continue to fly.'

'If they won't fly, then don't pay them.'

'Listen, PAL. We all fly professionally; we all took a pay cut to work with Major Drones because he is a friend and we respect him and Jack. We are quite happy to return to our day jobs; the pay is better and the hours are as well. So, DON'T tempt us.'

'ENOUGH. General Nakagawa, you are hereby ordered to continue to prosecute this war as you see fit. And you General will report to the Imperial Palace tomorrow at 11am. My father will have something to say about this.'

Everyone had thought the Crown Prince had left, but now he had stamped his authority on the whole situation.

'A-as you wish; Your Highness.' The general stammered as he began to understand just how much he had erred in his assessment of the situation, and how much support Jack had.

'Get some rest, all of you. You especially, Jack. We need you at peak performance.' Motoyuki closed the hologram and it was only then that Jack realised that the entire planning cell had been witness to a verbal fight between two very high-ranking officers.

'If you want my opinion,' began the errant pilot, 'he needs a kick in the arse.'

That statement appeared to relax the team and all drew breath.

'Were you serious? You would have left?' Jack asked.

'It is a possibility. We are here because Drones asked us to help. We do not respond well to threats.'

Jack bowed. 'Arigatō, I thank you for your loyalty.'

'Loyalty, nothing. I enjoy blowing up Russians, my family are from here, for me it is a religion to hate Russians,' he smiled as he spoke.

'The we shall pray to our gods together. We will win this, with a team like all of you,' Jack swept his arm around the room to include the entire team. 'And with some surprises I have in store; the Russians will be very sorry to have begun this.'

Spontaneous applause erupted from his team. Jack stood and bowed to them all.

'Now, clean up and get rested, I feel the Russians will want some form of retribution tomorrow and we will need to be ready.

Central Command (0730 the next morning)
'General Onishi, you have received a request from the Imperial Palace. You are to attend at 1030 and they wish to have General Nakagawa on standby on hologram as well.'

'Very well. Get Jack on line.'

'Morning, how did you sleep?'

'How do you do it, Jack. Sound so cheerful first thing?'

'First thing? I have been up since 3, it is almost lunch time.'

'Do you never sleep?'

'Time for sleep when the war is won.'

'OK. The Emperor wants you on line at 1030. I will be in the palace. I think last night is going to blow-up in someone's face.'

'I thought it might. I will call my driver; you can arrive in style.'

'Careful Jack, I may get accustomed to that car of yours.'

'Use it, it needs to be driven. With me here and Chie and Fumiko here as well it is not getting used at all. Just let the Airforce General use his normal staff car, don't want his boots dirtying my carpet.'

The two began to laugh. 'OK, Jack. See you in a while. Sayonara.'

'Sayonara.'

The communications link was terminated. Jack looked at Mai, I will take this call on the rear deck. I do not want others hearing all the dirty laundry being aired.

'OK. I will get it setup.'

'Mai? What rank are you?'

'You know very well I am a Corporal.'

'Not any more, Sergeant. Send a signal to Central Command to that effect and get new badges for your uniform. Congratulations.'

'Arigatō, Jack.' Mai turned to leave the office, as she reached the door she turned back and asked 'Don't tell Drones, I want to surprise him with my new uniform.'

'OK.'

Jack smiled inwardly, it made him feel good to promote someone for good work, and he knew his planning team would not function nearly as well if she were not there.

Imperial Palace (1030)

'General Onishi.' The Emperors Personal Assistant announced Motoyuki's arrival as he entered the receiving rooms.

'Your Majesty,' he bowed deeply and waited the requisite time to honour the Emperor before standing upright.

'Come, sit Motoyuki.'

Moving to the proffered chair; he waited for the Emperor to sit first.

The two sat in silence waiting for the refreshments to be served and the staff to leave the room.

'I see you are using Nakagawa's car; does he know?'

'He offered me the use of his car and driver while he is deployed in the north. Unfortunately, it is far too comfortable, I may never use a staff car again.'

'Yes, he does use his place in the world to make sure he is well catered for. Enough small talk, The Crown Prince has given me a detailed report on the argument between Jack and that Airforce General, Ito. What is your take?'

'We all know Jack's mind works battle plans differently to everyone else. Ito does not seem to either appreciate, or want to accept, his thinking. He only sees the opportunity to attack and take enemy positions, his concept of attack does not appear to include the welfare of the lower ranks.'

'Is he right? Is that airfield too difficult to defend?'

'Most certainly. May I?' Motoyuki indicated the hologram projector on the table.' The Emperor nodded and a connection was made to Jack.

'Konichiwa, Your Majesty, General Onishi; how may I assist?'

'Can you describe the issues with us seizing the airfield?'

'Certainly, the approaches from our side are difficult terrain, steep hills and thick forest; minimal tracks to follow all of which are certain to be already targeted by the enemy. There are several choke points along these tracks which will concentrate our convoys and that will result in many avoidable casualties. The airfield is open on the enemy side, that means they can counterattack from around a dozen different directions, that alone makes it impossible to defend unless you wish to place the entire Northern and Central Armies there. The enemy aircraft are too close, they can strike at will and we would be hard pressed to stop them.'

'How do you plan to proceed?'

'Well, your Majesty, the broad plan is to leave it to the enemy. They will expend a huge amount of resources trying to reinforce it. For them it is a position that they can use to launch surprise raids on us.'

'Then how will you defend against such attacks?'

'They cannot launch ground raids for the same reason as we can't, the terrain is all but impassable; air assaults will require them to re-establish it as a forward airbase. New generator and communications equipment will be just the first. They will need to bring more aircraft in, and we have proven we can destroy them either on the ground or as they land or take-off.'

'How long can you continue to do this?'

'As long as the Russians wish to try to bring aircraft in. If we make them crash on the strip then they will have to repair the strip before they can land. Helicopters cannot move sufficient heavy equipment and if they try then we can shell the strip until they only have holes to land in. We have been there almost a year, and winter will be evident in the northern latitudes sooner rather than later, if we can restrict or close their resupply lines then we will have the upper hand come spring.'

'And why would the Russians keep trying this resupply?'

Jack thought for a minute. 'In a word, pride. They will not admit defeat, they are prideful enough to believe they can do as they wish. Their General, we think it is Plishkin, will not admit defeat to the Kremlin. He may as well shoot himself if he does.'

'Very well, keep this link open, we may need extra information.'

'Hai, Majesty.' The hologram imaging system closed down, but the audio kept running. Jack muted his end as he was only to speak if the Emperor wanted him to.

'I am satisfied that Nakagawa has the situation in hand. Now let us hear from General Ito.'

The Emperor's aide announced General Ito and he repeated the actions of Motoyuki when he entered the room, bowing in respect and sitting where he was shown.

'General Ito, The Crown Prince tells me there was a significant argument over tactics last night?'

'Majesty, General Nakagawa is showing a distinct lack of aggression in his dealings with the enemy. He has let the opportunity to seize a significant enemy ground asset slip from his grasp. If we are to win this war, I believe we must take everything we can when we can.'

'I have spoken with him. Broadly speaking, his plan is to let the enemy commit as many resources as they wish and to destroy them as they arrive in the area. In short, he has planned a war of attrition.'

'He lacks the courage to take the fight to the enemy. He should be dismissed.'

'General Onishi? Your thoughts.'

'I have had detailed briefings on the battle plan and I have questioned the thought and planning processes behind it. This is not a war we can win in a short time frame. General Nakagawa's plan is to cause as much death and disruption to the enemy as they can stand and then take back the islands; when the enemy cannot justify the seizure any longer.'

'That is rubbish. He lacks the will to engage the enemy.'

'Then tell us, General Ito, what is the political situation in Russia? How is it being perceived there?'

'What do you mean?'

Motoyuki continued, 'The news reports from the Kremlin are all full of victory and success; we have been, covertly, issuing the real reports, numbers of casualties, the losses of ships and aircraft. Even the possibility of the loss of control of the nuclear weapons they were supposedly retrieving. The political mood is swinging and swinging fast against the government. Our plan will ensure that when the war is won, we will not need to worry ourselves with this again.'

'General Ito, I feel you are as out of touch with this war as could be. Perhaps you should consider your future a little closer than you have so far.' The Emperor's words could have been interpreted several ways; the only way that was suitable was that he should retire, he was far beyond the notional retirement age anyway.

The silence was almost deafening as they waited for his response. Eventually, he spoke.

'I understand, Majesty. Perhaps I have no longer the spread of thought to fight such a conflict as this; a broad international conflict fought on a microscopic scale. In retrospect I believe that a mind such as Nakagawa's has the capacity to succeed, in the longer term.'

'If it pleases you, I should prefer to submit my resignation next week, after I have had time to clear my schedule.'

'Your Majesty, forgive my interruption. Perhaps a closer briefing on the battle plan would give the General a better understanding of the next phases and the role of the Airforce in them. A better understanding will be beneficial to all.'

'Arigatō General Nakagawa, General Onishi and General Ito will be there this afternoon.'

'Arigatō, Your Majesty.'

With that last exchange, the meetings were seen to be over. The future was yet to be fully decided.

Chapter 28
A New Perspective

The helicopter landed in the grounds of the castle and, as with all visitors, General Ito was impressed with the grandeur of it all.

'Nakagawa said the planning cell was on private property, who owns this?'

Motoyuki smiled as he replied, 'We all feel the same when we first arrive. This is Jack's ancestral home. Technically his parents own it; but he lives here and as the current occupant he is regarded as the owner.'

Ito simply stared at the impressive building, trying to take in every aspect.

'Come, we shall most likely find Jack either in the planning room or on the rear deck.'

The two approached the front of the castle and the helicopter crew shouted out asking where to take the luggage.

'Just leave it for now and come with us.' Motoyuki replied. 'We will sort out accommodation later.'

Just as he approached the door it was opened by a young girl. 'Motoyuki, welcome back. And you must be General Ito. Jack is waiting on the rear deck for you.'

'Arigatō, Fumiko.'

'Is Yumi with you?

'No, strictly work this time.'

'That is never going to work around here. Send your helicopter to get her, Grace and Daisy will want to see her.'

'Do you think I should?'

'I know you will. Knew it before you arrived.'

'Of course, you knew.' Motoyuki turned to the pilot 'Return to my house and collect my wife. Bring her here when she is ready.'

'Hai General.'

'And stop at General Ito's house as well. Kei, call your wife and have her come here it will be a good holiday for both of you, even though you are working.'

The helicopter lifted off and as they flew south again the pilot was left wondering "are we a private shuttle now".

'Come let's find Jack.' Motoyuki lead the way and Kei followed, the same as everyone. His eyes jumping from one priceless artefact to another and from one portrait to another.

'There is so much here, it must be worth a fortune.'

'It is; even the Emperor is impressed with the displays. See these,' he indicated a display of swords, 'Belonged to Tokugawa Musashi.'

'Surely they should be in a museum somewhere?'

'Not really, Jack owns them and he will loan them for special displays only.'

They finally arrived at the rear deck to find Jack in deep discussion with Drones. Fumiko followed them out with a tray of drinks and confections.

'Arigatō, Fumiko. I will serve, can you…'

'Get the rooms ready for Yumi and Himari, of course.'

Fumiko disappeared and Jack simply said 'Don't know why I bother to give her instructions; she already knows everything.'

'How?' Kei asked no one in particular.

'It is a long story, time for that over dinner,' replied Jack.

At that a voice called out, 'Early dinner for you and your guests. You will be working late tonight.'

'And thank you, Chie.' Jack called back. 'Same story,' he said to Kei.

'Drones, tonight After midnight I want a close detailed survey of the enemy main camp. I need to be able to pinpoint any and all individual buildings.'

'IR or UV as well?'

'Both, and if possible, raw video footage.'

'I will pilot a drone out just before sunset, I can fly fast enough to get the general layout in video. We can take two extras and analyse from 1000 feet, cross reference with a satellite mapping and that will give us most of what you need. I have modified a Kamikaze to take a camera and we can send two out, one IR and one UV, at the same time, they can fly lower and get a more detailed view at a slightly higher speed.'

'Good. Are your pilots rested? I expect the Russians will try some form of resupply tonight.'

'They are all rested and ready to fly. I have to say they are all really enjoying their time, the Kamikaze pilots are relishing the opportunity to fly into a really small space, more than one has said it has already enhanced their chances at the next world championships.'

'Then we must hope it is all done by then. Are the Amazons holding up to the work?'

'I have some new propellers coming in soon. The old ones flex a lot during high-speed manoeuvring, the new Kevlar composite should prove better, and give a higher top speed as well.'

'Good, test them and we will try them tomorrow.'

'Do we have enough explosives?'

'Fixed pack, yes, several hundred units. We will probably need more units late in winter. Anti-personnel units, we have thousands, more than enough. 'Order around five hundred blast packs, we will test a plan tonight.'

'Hai.'

Drones left to begin his latest concept testing and to prepare his pilots for a long night of flying.

'That is how it is done here; Jack lets them have a long-rein as it were and they produce the goods.' Motoyuki was open in his praise.

'You are going to make me blush if you keep that up.'

'I doubt that very much, Jack. You keep your mind on the war, that is where it needs to be.'

'Kei, this is the plan for tonight.' With only a hologram image of the battle zone for support, Jack gave a detailed briefing of what he wanted to achieve and how he was going to do it.

'You make it sound so simple.'

'That is because I don't concern myself with how Drones and his team fly their units, I just give my concept of the next move and they prepare for it. Not much goes seriously wrong and I feel that tonight we will annoy the Russians into doing something really rash. Just a moment.'

'Jack opened a channel to the fleet. 'Tyrell?'

'Here I am Jack. What can I do to help?'

'Just a heads up, I have guests here and we will be having a late-night snack. Sorry I can't get you here, Daisy sends her love.'

'That would be right, have fun without me! Enjoy, and you owe me.'

'Yes, I know I do; put it on my tab.' Jack closed the line.

'Please tell me you are not planning a hologram dinner party.' Kei asked incredulously.

'No, but that is a great idea. We will try one day. Once this mess is over and done. Thank you, that will be a great way to catch up.'

'So, what is this late-night meal you spoke of?'

'That is just a way to tell Tyrell that I intend to "poke-the-bear", so to speak and I will be poking him with a very sharp stick. He has to be on the lookout for a response. We don't want to be caught by surprise. Anyone listening will think we are having guests for dinner so we let them think that.'

'You are deliberately trying to confuse me.'

'Not at all. We work somewhat differently to other units; we work very closely together and we all have a lot of room to change what is not working. This series of attacks were not due until the middle of this winter, Tanaka changed the timing with his assault. Now we are trying to get the basic plan back on its schedule. We have actually lost very little of the plan. Losing so many men, so early was not calculated, we now have to work smarter. To do this I need more information, and I need to advance a certain secret mission.'

'Am I permitted to know what this secret mission is? Or is it a puzzle like everything else you do?'

Jack looked at Motoyuki and got a small nod in return.

'In just one month, plus or minus a week or so depending on the weather, we will begin to remove the Russian nuclear warheads from the cave system they are stored in. This will need to be done over many nights and it will be very dangerous work. To achieve this end, I will need to keep the Russians guessing our intentions. That begins tonight with the surveillance and some attacking of their main camp.'

'That is the "late night snack" that Jack was referring to. Tyrell and the fleet will need to be vigilant and the drone pilots will need to be alert and ready to do their part.' Motoyuki added.

'What about the Airforce? We can bomb the camp as much as you want.'

'That would be nice, except the Russians will have interceptors waiting for you. They are so much closer to the action than you are, and the fleet will not be able to protect you, it is possible that one of our missiles could get side-tracked. That risk is unacceptable. So, we will be a lot more covert in the operation.'

'And I thought you were ignoring our capabilities. What do you need from us?'

'Firstly, logistic support. Soon enough the 155s and the 127s will need more ammunition. We will also need food and other supplies. Second, when the time comes, we will need to move the warheads away from the combat zone. This too must be done without alerting the enemy. Third, should it prove necessary we will need you to deliver the new weapons, that will be a very dangerous, long-range business.'

'So, you are not out of the picture,' Motoyuki concluded. 'It is just not quite your time to shine.'

'And now "Yuki" it is time to stop speaking and time to say hello.' Yumi had arrived just at the right time and had used her pet name for her husband. 'Konichiwa, Jack.'

'Konichiwa, Yumi. Have you come to take him away?'

'No, I have come for dinner and a visit with my friends. You boys can continue to do your war thing.'

'Arigatō, my lady, you are most kind.' Jack bowed and just as quickly as she had arrived, she left.

'You have people just coming and going as they please? I think I am still confused.'

'Not at all, Yumi is a close friend with Grace Garcia, Roman Garcia's wife; and Daisy Backhouse, Tyrell's wife. They meet here as often as they can and enjoy each other's company, sometimes they even speak with us.'

'Be careful, Kei,' Motoyuki warned him with a smile. 'If Himari joins forces with them, then we will be outnumbered for ever.' At that point Mai knocked gently on the door frame.

'Hai, Mai. What can I do for you?' Jack enquired.

'A moment of your time in private, please?'

'Excuse me for a moment.' Jack rose from his chair and he and Mai walked a short way out into the lush grass away from the house. As they walked Mai could be seen to be talking animatedly, determinedly making several points.

They turned and began to make their way back to the house, and as they walked it was easy to see that Jack was deep in thought. The two climbed the few steps to the deck and as he sat down Jack finally spoke.

Looking out at the green lawns he gave a simple order. 'Mai, send them to me and return with Drones.'

'Hai.' Mai left the three Generals alone for a minute.

'Trouble Jack?' Motoyuki asked tentatively.

'Nothing I can't handle.'

'Do you want us to leave?'

'Actually no, it is a problem with two junior ranks, I want these two idiots to feel the weight of their errors. A little rank will help.'

'OK.' Then in a whispered aside to Kei 'This will be interesting; I have never seen Jack have problems with his lower ranks. Let's see how he handles this.' A short time later two very sheepish looking corporals appeared at the door with Mai and Drones behind them.

'Over here!' Jack ordered the two men, and they quickly moved before the three Senior Officers. It was easy to see that whatever it was, the issue had gotten out of hand far too quickly.

'I have had a report that you wish to fight each other? Is this true?'

Both began to plead their case at the same time.

'One only, you,' he pointed at one of the two. 'Speak.'

'It was his fault. I told him in private that I was going to ask Mai for a date and he asked before I could. He took the opportunity I wanted and he is a poor companion, he should have waited until after I had asked.'

Jack shook his head slowly. 'You,' he indicated the other man. 'Speak.'

'He does not have the right to demand I stand aside; I have the same right as he does. If I want to date Mai I will, I don't need his approval or permission.'

'And you want to fight over this?'

'He has challenged me and I accepted, we agreed that the winner gets to ask her.'

'You two are idiots. Did it not occur to you that she may already be in a committed relationship?'

The two looked confused; looking at each other and then Jack and back again, they had no answer.

'Do you really think that she would even consider either of you as an option? This is what will happen; Since Mai is the subject of this conflict, she may decide how it is to be resolved.'

Mai smiled gently and began, 'I will not have two potential suitors fight each other over my affections, and,' smiling at Drones, 'I will not have my fiancé fight anyone. Therefore, I request Jack to be my defender and he will fight you both at the same time. If one of you survives the fight then I will consider his proposal if neither of you win then there shall be no more spoken of this.'

'Arigatō, my lady. I accept the appointment as your defender.'

'Arigatō, Jackson-san.' Mai replied formally.

Turning to the two she continued, 'You have five minutes to prepare.'

Just five minutes later the two, now very apprehensive, soldiers were on the lawn as ready as they would ever be.

It was a fight by name only. Jack had not even raised a sweat when the two were lying on the grass nursing some massive bruises and black eyes.

'Have you had enough? My sensei would be incensed if you were his pupils.'

'Incensed is not the word I would use. Perhaps the two should try to learn some of the more basic levels of junior fighting before such a challenge is issued again.'

Jack spun around and his eyes immediately found his closest friend and sensei.

'AKIO!' Jack shouted, so good to see you. 'What bring you to this far-flung outpost of the Empire?' Jack bowed formally and the gesture was returned.

'It's not so far, and I felt it was time for you to hone your skills, you still hold your elbows too low you know.'

'That depends entirely on my opponent.'

'True, and if these two are indicative of the calibre of your opposition, then it says volumes as to why you have become lazy and do not attend the dojo.'

'Ah, yes, there is a reason.'

'A reason, or an excuse?'

'You know how to hurt a man. You do know that we are planning a war here?'

'Always the excuse; you are planning a war against one of the largest armies on the planet and you use that to prevent you from training.' Akio was as adept with sarcasm as Jack was.

'Well, that hurt.' Jack said smiling, 'Let me introduce my co-conspirators.' Jack re-introduced Motoyuki and introduced Kei.

'Are you always so hard on him?' Kei asked, with a fair amount of incredulity in his voice.

'No, Only, when he deserves it.' Akio continued in a staged whisper, 'Don't tell him, but his performance showed he has lost nothing of his skills, he is still a difficult opponent to fight.'

'Speaking of fighting, You two are hereby removed from tonight's operations. Report to the recharging group, and ensure the drones are all prepared for the strike.'

The two corporals slowly and stiffly bowed to Jack and the others and before they left, they spoke to Mai.

'I apologise, I was far too involved in my own desires.' Bowing again they left to start the important work of preparing the strike drones.

'Jack, can I ask if it decreases your standing to stoop to fighting junior soldiers?'

'Actually, Kei,' Motoyuki jumped in, 'I will be willing to bet that defeating those two will have generated a lot of good will and respect for Jack. He has shown that he is willing to resolve a problem and not have it appear on a soldier's service record. The others will recognise that and they will understand the effect. Jack protects them from official problems, they will respond favourably.'

'Unbelievable, now I know why so many are requesting positions in his world.'

'It does not work for everyone; I know I could not do it myself. But it works for him.'

'Arigatō Motoyuki, your words, as always are most gratifying to hear,'

'All true. Now, we will need to finish preparations before dinner.'

'Fumiko?' Jack called out, and a small voice replied from the distance.

'I know an extra for dinner. Welcome Akio!'

'Arigatō, Fumiko,' he called in return. 'Has she settled down any?'

'No, getting more sensitive if anything.'

'How do you mean, Jack.'

Jack explained the rather unique capabilities of Fumiko and her family history.

'Why is it that every time I ask a question, your answer is so much more than straight-forward?'

'I think it may be because sometimes there is so much more to tell.'

Over dinner the blushing Fumiko and, to a slightly lesser extent Chie had their family capabilities explained. One question that always surfaced was can she give fore-tellings when asked?

'Only under exceptional circumstances, most of the time it is an unexpected revelation.'

'Are you ever wrong?' asked Himari.

'No, my lady, I have never been wrong. But I have wanted to be, sometimes people do not wish to hear what I have; like the time I predicted health issues and the lady did not want to hear about it. I think she already knew and did not want to deal with it. She did survive, but it would have been easier if she had listened to me.'

'I think I may come to you instead of my doctor.'

Fumiko looked up and her eyes began to darken. 'You have no need of doctors in your near future.' She intoned and then shook her head. 'Oops, that just slipped out.'

'Jack, your life must be crammed full right now. With everything else that is going on you still have a private senkensha or two here. Do they keep you busy or are they just on the sides?'

'We have given Jack the reasons that he needs to achieve his aims. How he does it is all his. But I will warn you all, though this conflict is large enough and important enough to be given every ounce of energy, there is another coming, it will be bigger and more difficult to overcome than any before. Jack, you will need to keep your allies very close when the future becomes today.' Chie breathed deeply, and appeared to be almost asleep as she rested on Fumiko's shoulder.

'I apologise; mother does not often give such deep thoughts. This was a rare insight for her. By the way, Grace, another grandchild is coming, congratulations.'

'Really, gracias, little one. I will speak with my son and let him know that we knew first, again.'

The small talk moved from one subject to another and then another. The sun had long since set and the clocks were slowly moving to the late evening, closer to the time for the strike to be launched.

'Jack?' Drones moved close to Jack's side as the two of them studied the hologram before them. 'Thank you for looking after Mai, for me.'

'No problem, those two have been sniping at each other for a long time. Now they can do some good and put their minds to the task at hand. Are you ready?'

'Hai, all units are prepared, we lift off at 2330, the strike units will follow at 2345. All being good we will return before 0215 and the strike drones will follow us onto the ground.'

'Good.' Jack turned to his guests. 'We will begin soon.' Then he returned his gaze to the hologram which at that time actually showed the inside of the launch area.

'Jack, important signal.' Mai handed the paper to him and then disappeared again as Jack read the signal. He had barely finished reading when the image of Haruto Saito appeared before him.

'Haruto, what have you got?'

'Konichiwa, the latest surveillance shows the Russians have moved a second surveillance satellite into position.'

'Arigatō, that will upset our plans a little.'

'Not really, the idiots put it in the same position as the last one.'

Sensing there was more to hear Jack replied 'And?'

'It seems that someone with a working knowledge of ancient Aztec languages has hacked the damaged satellite, the two crashed this evening. The "shooting stars" you will be seeing around two tomorrow morning are the resulting debris of their new unit. Breaks my heart to see such incompetence. You should hear the screaming and accusations being hurtled around at the Cosmodrome. Most ungentlemanly language, thankfully the ladies will not have to hear them.'

'Good work, well done to you and your team.'

'We didn't do anything, just playing around with the control units we adapted and suddenly the two came together.'

'OK, we believe you. Thousands may not, but we do. Keep it up, keep watching the hologram; first strike soon.'

'Jack, did he say what I think he said?' Kei was totally astounded.

'Yes, some time ago he hacked their surveillance satellite and now he has used it to destroy the replacement. Brilliant work, keeps our movements more secret.'

'That is amazing,' Kei whispered to Motoyuki. 'I wonder what he will do next?'

'Watch and see.'

Chapter 29
On the Offensive

'Standby all units. Drones, you have control.'

'Hai. All units; game play "Misery" is now in play. First unit in five, four, three…' When the count reached zero Drones could be seen concentrating on the screen before him. His unit lifted and shot off into the inky darkness and the hologram switched from the flying room to the drone camera.

Trees and shrubs flew by as he reached ridiculous speeds zipping over the tree tops. Finally, it slowed a little and the eastern end of the enemy camp came into view.

'Good to see they are still keeping away from the cave system.' Drones commented as he flew only half a metre above the buildings along the main street. The low-light cameras recording every aspect of the enemy camp.

Twice he covered the enemy buildings and then he hovered over a generator shed and pointed his camera at a specific building.

'As far as we can tell, this building is the headquarters for the Russian General.'

Jack pointed at Mai and she "tagged" the building for special attention later.

'Noted and tagged on the hologram.' Jack replied.

'OK. Let's have some fun. IR and UV units, have you completed your tasks?'

'Hai,' replied the pilots in sequence.

'All good, Jack this is the moment. Permission to set "Misery" in motion?'

'Approved.'

'Big Eyes (surveillance drones) return. "Amazons" commence your run.'

The strike units began to fly down the length of the enemy camp. At 500 feet altitude they were silent to those below. As they approached the centre of the enemy camp the watchers at the Northern Planning Cell, Central Command and the Imperial Palace almost held their collective breath.

Suddenly, without any extra commands, the drones began to drop the first portion of their payload. Just five seconds later the fragmentation grenades, designed to maximise the injuries to those on the ground, began to explode.

Only three were dropped at first, a long distance between them saw the damage restricted to the walls and doors spread along the road.

The reaction was for hundreds, possibly thousands, of soldiers to emerge from their confines and begin to fire wildly into the air. Once they were busy shooting at an almost non-existent foe the other hundred drones dropped their deliveries.

The carnage was all but complete. Hundreds of soldiers wounded and dead laying in the street. As more soldiers emerged to try to get the wounded to safety a second round of grenades were dropped with the same effect as the first.

No one had even thought of drones; the Russians were seen to be rushing into the nearby forest trying to find the assaulting troops with no chance of even seeing them.

As the Russians tried desperately to save so many of their comrades none of them heard the third wave.

This time, instead of dropping grenades they carefully placed explosive charges on the roofs of the buildings one on those targeted and two on the suspected Headquarters building. In just three minutes the only drone left was the first one in; holding at the eastern end of the Russian camp, Drones camera unit was filming the proof of the strike capability.

The detonations were carefully timed, every package exploded at the exact same time. Some buildings simply had a hole blown in the roof; some had the roof blown off. The generator shed was one that had its roof collapse inside, covering the generator with debris. The headquarters building was a complete wreck. The roof collapsed inside and the fire, left burning to keep the occupants warm, ended up burning down the building.

Drones waited for the right moment, with chaos erupting all around he began to fly through the camp. This time at around four metres above the ground. Most of the Russians were far too busy with the wounded, the fires and the collapsed buildings to even notice the drone flying so close to their heads and at over a 140 km/h he was gone before he was seen.

'Well done Drones, you and your team.' Jack congratulated his pilot. 'All units. Be ready, surveillance keep us informed.'

'Hai.' No reports were forthcoming for a short while; then a call from SatCon.

'Jack, Heat blooms from Urup Airfield. Multiple, two dozen or more.'

'Roger, Tyrell you get that?'

'Ready and waiting.'

'Tanaka, Tyrell they are heading straight for you.'

The watchers heard the reports, and all were listening to the communications from the fleet.

Suddenly through the noise they heard, "Multiple bogies, inbound!"

The retaliation was underway, the question was, did the Russians know where the strike had originated.

'Assign and engage as you can.' Tyrell had handed the prioritisation to the Weapons Offensive Systems.

"Splash, one," a short while later "Splash two" and so it went. Still a dozen got through.

'Drones, You ready?'

'Hai.'

'Send up the kamikaze.'

'A hundred kamikaze drones lifted into the air as the aircraft passed over the Russian camp. Standing between the Russians and the Japanese encampments the drones waited at 1500 feet looking for prey.

As the fighters emerged on the I.R. screens the pilots could easily see the open intakes of the engines. They had worked out that two into one engine would be the easiest way to destroy them. Blowing one wing off unexpectedly, sent the aircraft spiralling down every time.

Before the retaliatory strike got anywhere even close to the Japanese lines there were simply none of them left.

And just to rub salt into the wounds, the gods that be decided that it would now be a good time to snow.

'Good work everyone. Mai send to Tanaka, "All strikes successful, be prepared for counterstrike's" and send to Tokyo "First strike successful."

'Hai.' Mai left to send the reports. Jack turned to look at his friends, the first time that he had let his gaze deflect from the hologram.

'That was a very good outcome. Now we must be ready for the next phase.'

'I had no idea, no concept of not only the methodology but the firepower you could bring to bear; and yes, you were right, we could not have reacted quickly enough in that scenario. Congratulations, Jack.'

'Arigatō, Kei. Now you know what we are trying to achieve and some of how we will accomplish it.'

Imperial Palace

'It is most distressing to watch such carnage.'

'I agree, Father. Judging by the comments from the North and from the Commander on Iturup, the raid has been a total success. It seems that General Nakagawa has been able to begin this part with success, now we must wait to see if that translates to victory.'

The Emperor waited for a moment and then summoned his Army Communications aide, 'Send word to General Nakagawa; Having watched your efforts, we congratulate you on your first strike. Well done.'

'Hai.' The aide left to send the signal and just as quick a reply was received.

"Arigatō, Your Majesty. We are continuing to plan and execute operations as the opportunities arise."

Russian H.Q. Iturup

'What the hell happened? We just got flogged and NO ONE knows HOW?' the commanding general was almost incandescent with rage. His personal staff were smart enough to be well away from the outburst; but the H.Q. planners were directly in the firing line.

'Get the gunners on the line. Where is the Commander of the Airforce? I WANT ANSWERS!'

He had almost begun to calm down when the Gunnery Commander finally called in.

'What took you so long?'

'My apologies General, the lines are down. The primary communications tower was taken out in the attack. And the lines to your H.Q. are not answering.'

'That is because they blew up the building, dammit. How did they manage such long range and accuracy?' The Russian Command had no real information on the conduct of the attack, they could only barely conceive the level of devastation was due to either an air strike or gunnery; and given he had not had reports of aircraft overhead he assumed gunnery. 'Well, answers or excuses? Which will it be?'

'We do know the Japanese have the support of the Mexican Artillery, they are the very best, that will explain the accuracy; as for the range I can only assume they are using a new type of rocket assisted shell, but that counters the accuracy. The rocket shells are less accurate than the 127s alone. There is some information that indicates the presence of the long-range 155s, but we have not been able to confirm that.'

'Find out how they did that to us.' The general pointed to the devastation all around them.'

'Yes, General.' The Artillery Colonel left, his 2I/C with him and neither spoke.

Russian Battery Control

'Christ we were lucky to get away with that.' The Major said, 'I don't think the Airforce will get away as easily, though.'

'We didn't get away with it, I managed to spread enough bullshit to cover our backs. We need to show we can strike back at the enemy, get the battery ready to return fire.'

'Yes, Sir.' The Major left to prepare for, what promised to be, a long exchange of fire.

Russian H.Q. Iturup

'Where were your aircraft? You do realise they were supposed to support us?'

The Airforce Commander was now in line for the renowned abuse of the Theatre Commander.

'As soon as the attack was confirmed we launched a counter-offensive. We lost almost two thirds of our planes before they had crossed the straight, the others were taken out before they could reach a launch point for their weapons.'

'HOW IS THAT EVEN POSSIBLE!' The general was now in serious danger of giving himself either a heart attack or a stroke; either would be welcomed by all those around him, the Airforce Commander especially so.

'We do not know, Sir. It is possible they have a new long range I.R. laser. The planes that were destroyed over land appeared to disintegrate in flight.'

At that moment a series of bright 'meteorites' shot across the sky, part omen and part man made demonstration, everyone stopped speaking and watched as they transited and fell somewhere in the Pacific Ocean.

'Get on to Satellite Command, I want to know why our surveillance has not pinpointed the enemy launch areas.'

An hour and a half later, just before the first vestiges of dawn would show more clearly the devastation wreaked by their enemy, the Generals personal assistant knocked on the door frame.

'General, please excuse the intrusion but I have information from Satellite Command.'

'Come in. What is it?'

The assistant was more than pleased to notice that the Generals demeanour had abated to almost civilised levels.

'Satellite Command has confirmed that the surveillance satellite initially tasked with our support went "rogue" almost eight months ago.' Before the general could respond his assistant continued, in an attempt to get all the bad news out before he could be blamed. 'The replacement satellite crashed into the wreckage of the first two days ago, the meteor shower earlier was the remnants of them.'

'How is this even possible?' The, now somewhat confused, general was asking himself the rhetorical question, he knew that Moscow was incompetent in many areas, but to leave an army in a hostile arena without surveillance was almost criminal.

'Very well, get me a conference with the Kremlin when they have had time for their breakfast, no point in making them angry earlier than that.'

Just as they began the conference, the distant boom of heavy artillery could be heard, just before the crash of explosions amongst their own battery. For once Tanaka had timed the retaliatory strike to perfection.

'General, what is going on there?' No reply. 'General Plishkin answer me!' demanded the President. Still no response.

'If Plishkin wanted a conference he should at least have the decency to be present.' The Presidents words were completely overshadowed by the constant explosions emanating from the other end of the hologram. Eventually, the General appeared. 'My apologies, our main battery is being shelled.' Another crash.

'Do your duty, General, go. We will call back in an hour.' The hologram closed off without Plishkin acknowledging the order.

An hour later there was no response from the hologram in the temporary command bunker. An hour after that a signal message reported the hologram would be back on line that night.

'Somehow I think the old adage "No news is good news" will not apply here.' The defence minister gave his opinion more to break the sullen silence than as an actual observation.

Eventually, the hologram clicked into life, and the dirt encrusted form of General Plishkin appeared before them.

'What has happened?'

For the next forty minutes Plishkin gave a detailed report on the strike, the counter strike and the horrendous bombardment they had endured with no method of striking back.

'What do you mean, you can't strike back?'

'We have no air forces left in the area; their guns are too far away for us to shell them, as is their headquarters. They out number us over two to one and we have no surveillance of the battlefield. We are almost defenceless and blind at the same time.'

'What about the satellites? Surely they are giving you information?'

'Apparently, the overhead satellite went rogue last year and the replacement crashed yesterday.'

'General why has it taken so long to get this information to us?'

'The information from Satellite Command was that all interested parties were informed and we would get a replacement at first opportunity. We literally have no idea what will happen next.'

'Minister for Defence? What have you to say for yourself? Why is this the first I am hearing of this?' The President was clearly angry about the short comings of the support. 'The political mood is turning, if we lose this war, a war you said we would have no problem winning, we will be international pariahs for a century. How do you plan to resolve this?'

'I...I...I will dispatch strike aircraft from the Vladivostok base this evening. We will hit them back.'

'And how do you plan on targeting their positions? Ask them for a map and to leave the light on?' General Plishkin was clearly under no misunderstanding as to the difficulties facing strike aircraft that do not have satellite targeting information. He knew they would be flying blind and attacking an enemy that had already proven to be difficult to stop.

'Have no fear, General Plishkin,' the Minister for Defence was bluffing and yet no one called his bluff. 'We can give the information from Moscow or Vladivostok.' His tone, all at once both dismissive and condescending, would be his eventual downfall. But here and now it had sealed the fate of many Russian soldiers and pilots as well as the loss of many aircraft.

'We will see, Minister.'

'We understand the difficulties you face, but try to keep us informed General.' The President was far more worried than his tone indicated, he was beginning to think they may have to sue for peace. The plan, laid down so long before, had started to unravel and there did not appear to be a way to stop it.

Northern Planning Cell

'Well done all. However; at this time, we have only given him a bloody nose.'

'And broken ribs, and lost teeth.' Came responses from the rear.

'Yes, as you say, we have hurt our enemy. He will undoubtably strike back at us.' Jack smiled at the enthusiasm his team were displaying. 'So, we now need to be doubly vigilant, keep a close watch on all sensor systems, get as many drones back on line as possible. The Kamikaze units will be the front line of defence for us; pilots rest as much as possible. Above all, remember the front line is not here, there are friends in the direct line of fire. It is up to us to protect them as much as possible. Good work and good luck.'

Jack left with the entire team understanding the work was nowhere near complete. His part was to keep their enthusiasm levels high. Motivation was the most important tool he had.

'Hasegawa, do we know the enemy commander?'

'We are almost certain he is General Plishkin, a career officer but he is an Armour specialist, infantry, artillery and aviation tactics do not figure high on his list of achievements.'

'See if we can confirm it, and get a dossier on him, we may need to exploit his weaknesses in the future.'

Just three hours later Hasegawa returned. 'It is Plishkin,' he announced as he placed a folder on Jack's desk. More information is coming, but it appears he is prone to rash decisions and then shifting the blame if it does not work out.'

Suddenly the hologram came to life, blaring with the notification of an important message. Jack pressed the control and Haruto appeared before him. 'What's up Haruto?'

'Multiple heat blooms, over one hundred at Vladivostok Combined Military base.'

'Analysis?'

'Best we can guess is a retaliatory strike on Iturup.'

'Very good, keep the information coming.'

'Hai.' The hologram link closed and as Jack pressed the alarm he said 'Well that took a little longer than I thought.'

Calling Drones, as he spoke with Hasegawa, he said 'Get as many kamikaze units airborne as possible. All pilots report for duty, include the pair on battery duty.' Pressing the control again he called out 'Tyrell, you on?'

'Here I am, Illustrious Leader.'

Jack gave a laugh. 'Reports of multiple heat blooms over Vladivostok; looks like a strike heading our way. Are you in position to render first line of defence?'

'Sure are, after the strikes last night, and their success, I sent reinforcements to cover the flight path inbound from there. I have two dozen air warfare cruisers and destroyers waiting. BUT; I don't think we will stop them all.'

'Thank you, faithful servant. We will have the Kamikaze's airborne once they have passed over your boys.'

'Touché.' Tyrell replied and the two smiled together.

'Be careful out there, Tyrell. This is going to get hot, very hot.'

'No problem Jack, I have got my fighters standing by for any that get past your boys, I will keep them in reserve, waiting for the enemy to return to base. Should be a bit of a turkey shoot, if there are any left. And I can assure you my pilots are ready to have go at them.'

'Good. Just be careful. I will get Haruto to keep you up to date with satellite information as it comes to hand.'

'Good luck.'

'And you.'

Jack pressed the hologram control again, this time both Yoshiro and Roman appeared.

'Yoshiro, we are expecting air attacks in the next hour, they have just left Vladivostok, get your teams into position. Roman get as many of your guys into as safe a place as possible.'

'OK Jack, Listen, I know it is almost impossible to do but if we can get the enemy into the shell path of the 127s we may be able to at least confuse their attacking systems, face it several hundred extra targets suddenly appearing is going to upset any pilot.'

Jack thought for a minute and then 'That sounds like my type of plan; if you think you can, go for it. You may just get the distinction of being the first artillery commander to shoot down a strike aircraft.'

'OK, Good luck Yoshiro, hide well and shoot when you can. Let them know we are not giving up.'

'Arigatō, Roman. You too Jack. Are we expecting a host of our small friends?'

'Yes, sorry, forgot to say. Drones and his team are preparing now for another day at the races.'

'Great, good news. Let's hope for the best.'

'Just remember, you are the front line; let me know if there is any way I can assist.'

Jack closed the hologram and sat back. "Let's hope the plan holds up when the enemy is aware of us."

'Admiral Sir, Force 2 (Air warfare ships.) Report multiple bogies; in bound.'

'Very good, Jack? You hear that?'

'Hai. Here we go.'

The force of one hundred and sixteen strike aircraft were still eighty nautical miles from the fleet when the first three fell from the sky. The rest tried to either evade (primary mission was the ground forces on Iturup) or engage. By the time they had passed the fleet there were only fifty or so remaining.

They made the biggest mistake just as they approached Iturup; they dropped from cruising altitude to just two hundred metres and flew directly into a swarm of Kamikaze drones. One after another they either blew up, or their engines disintegrated. Around twenty managed to escape the drone net. 'Red 5 to Red Leader.' The radio call sounded desperate. 'Go ahead.'

'My targeting radar is picking up dozens of contacts but I cannot see them.'

'Keep a watch, something is out there.'

No sooner had he said it than a 127mm shell smashed through the scout, red 5. Before he could send a message or call for assistance his plane was engulfed in flame and his bombs exploded.

'What the hell is doing this?' A rhetorical question, asked by the now, via the selection process of attrition alone, attack leader. 24-year-old Lieutenant Kavlov was now the most senior combat pilot on the east coast.

'GET DOWN! As low as you can and get out to sea at top speed.' The first order he gave was to be the saviour of the remaining pilots. Almost reaching Mach 6 the now much smaller strike force was escaping at breakneck speed. Just three minutes later he ordered, 'Climb to 5000 metres, speed 300. The planes immediately rose to 15000 feet and slowed dramatically, Kavlov was not the only one breathing very rapidly, almost hyperventilating he finally managed to call.

'Who is left?' One by one the pilots replied with their call signs. "Twenty, that's all I have left?" he wondered; then, with his training finally kicking back in, he asked, 'Who has weapons?'

Again, one by one they answered. Doing the mental calculations, he managed to work out that he must still complete the mission, the Kremlin would not be pleased with any pilot returning with either fuel or weapons to spare.

'Heading 140, altitude 100 metres, Mach 3 to the coast. Then we climb to 800 metres for the run in.'

By the time the last of his force had released their weapons there were only six still flying. Badly mauled, the remains of the strike force would need a great deal of luck to get back to their base, and still they had not managed any real damage to Tanaka's ground forces.

'Yoshiro, Tyrell, Drones, Roman, let them go, they can cry their misfortunes to their Generals. I guess it will be some time before they can launch again, that was a huge number to lose.'

Flying erratically, to throw off missile and gun threats, they slowly returned home. One by one the remaining aircraft touched down. Just before Kavlov began his approaches he was called by Air Traffic Control.

'Sea Lion,' (his personal call sign). 'Do you have sufficient fuel to wait? We have a large hailstorm here.'

'How long?'

'Half hour maybe a little more.'

'I will hold out to sea at 3000 metres.'

'Very good, we will call when it has passed.'

Kavlov turned away and slowed to conserve fuel. He was pleased that he had taken the option to be the last to land, "A good commander looks after his team." He thought to himself. "Anyway, it gives me time to analyse what happened and try to form a report for the Commanders."

Flying in a huge circle he could see the towering clouds that were at that very minute dumping vast quantities of large hailstones on the base.

Eventually, he heard his callsign in his ears. 'Sea Lion, you are cleared for approach.'

'Very good,' he replied as he turned to the correct heading for the main strip at the Air Base.

As he approached the base, he slowly ran through the landing sequence check list. The second last item was "landing gear down", followed by "full flaps" and a final approach speed check.

'Control, this is Sea Lion. I do not have a secure light for my landing gear. Requesting a fly-by of the tower to confirm gear is down?'

'Approved, Sea Lion.'

He flew as close to the tower as he could, angling the aircraft to allow for a good view of the undercarriage, and his worst fears were realised.

'Sea Lion, this is Control. You DO NOT have landing gear down.'

'Roger control, please arrange emergency services. I am coming in without landing gear.'

Taking a long loop from the tower he aligned the aircraft with the landing approach signals and began the slow descent to what he hoped would not be a severe crash.

He was wrong.

The plane put down on the strip without problem. However; he soon found that the strip was covered in black ice, courtesy of the freezing hailstorm. With no effective control of his plane, he was about to eject when the plane slewed sideways and one wing dug in; the plane flipped twice before landing on its now mangled fuselage with a sickening bang.

However the wild ride was not over yet, sliding down the air strip at what seemed to be an ever-increasing speed he eventually ran out of tarmac and speared nose first into the drainage ditch at the end of the runway.

With the slippery runway and the taxiways alongside it, the emergency services took an inordinate amount of time to arrive. The few blessings of the day included the fact that the fuel cells had been torn off when the wings parted company with the fuselage. The already primed ejector seat, for some reason, didn't fire. The flight deck remained intact and the canopy had detached itself when the plane began to roll over.

The fire crews were first and doused the wreckage with retardant foam; close behind them were the rescue crew and they were followed by the ambulance.

No one was expecting to see a survivor but when he was extracted and gave a feeble "thumbs up" to the onlookers.

Base Hospital, Vladivostok 3 days later

'He does not look good, doctor. What is the prognosis? '

'He is strong and his improvements are being measured by the hour. We expect almost a full recovery.'

'Almost?'

'No matter how good the engineers are, a lost arm and leg may be replaced with prosthetics but they never function as good as the original items.'

'I understand. When do you expect him to regain consciousness?'

'He is showing good signs; in a day or so we will lighten his pain relief and bring him back to reality.'

'Very good. Reports by the hour.'

'As you wish General.'

The General Commanding the Eastern Seaboard left the Intensive Care rooms and made his way back to his office in the Administration Building. His mood was already sombre and losing so many pilots and aircraft was yet another problem he now had to deal with. The first in an ever-growing list of problems was how to explain the losses to the Kremlin. And that was occupying his mind almost completely for the flight to Moscow for a face-to-face report with his political masters.

War Room, The Kremlin, Moscow

'General, we are most concerned at the inability of the Eastern command to support the front-line troops on Iturup. Just how do you explain this?'

'There seems to have been a massive underestimation of not only the numbers of enemy ground troops but also the weapons they have at their disposal and the tactics they are employing. The support of so many other nations is also worrying. Food is getting short in the frontline areas and it is becoming more difficult to resupply.'

'They have the same weapons as everyone else, why are they so superior?'

'Their command team is not on the island, sir. They control almost everything from the Central Command Planning Group.'

'How can their tactics be so superior? Why are they out thinking and out performing us?'

'I am not certain as to who is planning for them; but he is good, very good. His methods are not usual, his actions and reactions are very difficult to counter. If we had better surveillance, we may be able to gain a better understanding of his methods; and his intentions.'

'You were given two full capability surveillance satellites! Why are they not sufficient?'

The general took a deep breath, he expected a grilling, but he didn't expect that the Chiefs of Staff and their political masters would be so misinformed.

'I apologise Sir, I assumed you knew. The first unit went rogue some time ago; we were unable to regain control.' The General had at least deflected a lot of suspicion away from his command.

'And the second?'

'Once the second had been tasked, Satellite Command began manoeuvring it into place. It was almost ready; they were orienting it and it collided with some debris. Best they could tell me was that they thought it may have struck the first one. It fell from orbit and burned up on re-entry.'

'So, you have been blind from the start?'

'As far as satellite surveillance goes, yes. Radar and I.R. have been working but we simply do not have the accuracy.'

At that moment there was a knock at the door.

'ENTER!' the Chief of Staff shouted, clearly irritated at the interruption. The door opened and a very senior communications officer entered.

Stopping once he had closed the door he saluted and addressed the senior officer present. 'My sincere apologies for interrupting. We have just had a signal from Iturup Command,' he continued without waiting for approval. 'General Plishkin reports a strike has damaged a number of units in his artillery battery, and the continual raids are taking a great toll on both his infrastructure and the morale of his troops.'

'How is it making such problems for his command?'

'I thought you may want further information so I asked him to elaborate. It seems they are under constant fire, Rocket Propelled Grenades. Small Tactical Missiles; 155mm gunfire and snipers. To add to the misery the enemy seem to be operating some new type of particle beam weapon that brings down aircraft and cruise missiles. Helicopters and transports all simply explode and fall from the sky.'

'Thank you, Colonel. You may go.' The Colonel saluted and left the room, stopping outside to draw a deep breath he looked at his assistant and said 'Thank god that is over, they must have a lot to get through, they didn't even challenge the information.'

'Let's go, before they think of something to abuse us for.'

The two left quickly; leaving those inside to try to find a way around the losses.

'How can we move forward, General?'

'Firstly, we need to get some form of retaliatory strike, something to make them think twice about attacking us. To make that happen we need to understand more about the command teams of the enemy. Secondly, we will need to increase the number of troops on the ground as well as feed them better.'

'What do you mean by that?'

'1700 calories per man per day may well be fine here in command central where the average soldier is pushing the keys on his keyboard, but over there they need three thousand just to function, extra work, deep deployment towards the enemy will require much more; four or five thousand per day.'

'That is not possible. The entire nation is suffering under the blockading of imported goods, not just your army. Deal with it!'

'Yes sir.'

'Anything else?'

'It would be helpful if we could get some information on the commanders we are facing. That may enable a change of strategy.'

The Army Chief simply pointed at one of the staffers taking notes and nodded.

'Return after lunch, General and we may have something.'

'As you wish.'

At that point the meeting adjourned for a meal break, the staff officers going their way and the Field Commander going his.'

It was just over two hours later that they were ready to resume.

'We have the information you wanted. The Ground Commander is a General

Tanaka. A capable officer, uses the units available to him well. Sometimes prone to rash decisions and rushing to complete a mission to the point of creating mistakes.'

'Tanaka, I thought he was not the preferred commander. Still, he is a difficult customer to deal with. What about the Head of the Army, he must be pulling the strings from their headquarters?'

'Chief of Staff is a General Motoyuki Onishi. More of an armour specialist than an infantry man. Tends to give his line officers a great deal of room; lets them make the decisions.'

'Onishi? I have not heard of him. If he is in central command then who is pulling the strings?'

'The only other name we came up with is a General Jackson……'

'Jackson Nakagawa! Oh god help us.'

'You have heard of him?'

'Ask any infantry officer that has been around for more than ten years. He is the pinnacle, the very best there is, he is the one that destroyed the American General Crasten in their Trans-Pac exercise. Not only is he a top line infantry commander, he also has mastered armour, artillery and a dozen other disciplines.'

'You sound as though we will not be able to beat him? Is he really that good?'

'Let me put it this way; if you rolled Eisenhower, Montgomery and Bradley into one and then sprinkled it with liberal amounts of Wellington and Nelson; add a touch of Patton for aggression and Rommel for his command skills then you have almost made him.'

'Really, that good?'

'That good? It is a good thing for us he is in planning and not on the ground. Any news on the coalition commanders?'

'Admiral Tyrell Backhouse, commands their fleet.'

'Good officer, masterful in his field.'

'They also have a General Roman Garcia. A Mexican gunner.'

'Not THE Roman Garcia.'

'You know him as well?'

'Reputation only. He is the current World Gunnery Champion. Accuracy rates of 99.5% or better. They have a formidable team against us. We may not be able to beat them.'

'Careful General, what you speak is treason.'

'Treason? No, I don't think so. What I am being is realistic; what I am saying is that they have the very best that are available from anywhere in the world, we are against a formidable team and with Nakagawa steering them it may well be that we should sue for peace now, before we lose all face and a lot of soldiers.'

'You may be right, but such comments do not belong outside these walls.'

'Understood.'

'How is the pilot that crashed?'

'Lieutenant Kavlov is in an induced coma. He is expected to survive his injuries but I doubt he will ever fly again. As good as they are, a pilot that has lost a leg from the hip and an arm from the shoulder is unlikely to regain the fine touch needed to fly a strike fighter.'

'Understood. Once he is well enough, we will visit. He is to be awarded the Order of Lenin.'

'A suitable award for one so young that took command and pressed home the attack despite catastrophic losses.'

The meeting went on for another half hour with the subjects becoming more and more banal now that the primary business had been dealt with. Eventually, the General managed to leave the Chiefs to their work, or as he put it "They can stuff their faces with caviar now they know they are off the hook for the total failure of the strike. Now I have to find a way to deal with their incompetence, and fight the dammed Japanese as well." A view he would hold more closely after being handed a signal when he arrived back at the Vladivostok base. He was now beginning to wonder exactly who the enemy were.

Chapter 30
Repatriation

Admirals Cabin USS Blue Ridge (Two Days Earlier)

'Enter.' Tyrell called out in response to a knock on the door.

'Signal from Picket Command, Sir.' (Lead ship designated for Long Range Radar Air Defence) Tyrell took the paper and looked at the address details.

From: HMAS Adelaide

To: Admiral Backhouse, USS Blue Ridge

Subject: Prisoners

HMAS Adelaide today retrieved the bodies of six Russian pilots, they are being held for handover at a date in the future.

Ten Russian pilots have been rescued and have undergone surgery to relieve them of the duress arising from their significant injuries.

Please advise course of action for return of both living and deceased.

Signed: C.O. HMAS Adelaide.

'Reply, "Make best speed to Yokosuka Naval Base. Transfer living to Naval Hospital for best result surgery/prosthetics. Deceased to be transferred to Funeral Directors for preparation for return to their home country." Sign in my name and Cc that to Yokosuka Command and Base Hospital, Central Command Tokyo and Northern Planning. Also get expected arrival date and time from Adelaide and include it.'

'Aye, aye, Sir.' The signal Petty Officer left to complete the assignment. 'I wonder how they are going to repatriate them? We don't even speak to them at all.'

The Command at Yokosuka received the signal within five minutes of it being sent.

'Call the Prime Minister's Office.' The Admiral Commanding Yokosuka Naval Base called to his secretary.

'Prime Minister's Office, how may I help you?' The receptionist sounded almost bored, it was late in her shift and she was looking forward to going home.

'This is Admiral Ashikaga; I need to speak with the Prime Minister.'

'Just one moment Sir, putting you through.'

The receptionist settled back and looked at the clock, only ten minutes to go. The P.M.'s call indicator lit up and she connected her headset to the line.

'Hai? The Swiss Ambassador, Hai.' Suddenly the boredom that had plagued her for the last two hours had left her, something was up and she wanted to know what it was.

She placed the call to the Swiss Embassy and then, listening covertly, she heard the discussion. So, the rumours were true, there were some prisoners. News from the Islands was in short supply, just the little that the Service Chiefs would release, no more no less, this was "real" news.

'I need your assistance, Mr Ambassador.'

'Certainly, how may we help?'

'I now find we are in need of a neutral conduit to contact the Russian Government.'

Instantly the Swiss Ambassador was intrigued. 'May I enquire as to the nature of the contact you wish to make?'

'We have rescued a number of Russian Pilots that were shot down earlier this month, they are being transported to a Naval Hospital for surgery and such. We also have a number of their dead that will need to be repatriated at the first opportunity.'

'And you want us to be the go-between?'

'If you are willing.'

'I will contact my government and get the requisite authority.'

'I, we, thank you for your consideration.'

The call was terminated, the wheels had been set in motion. "Now all we need to see is just how badly these pilots have been injured." The P.M. thought to himself.

The reports were requested and received by the P.M.'s office and the following Monday morning they were waiting in the P.M.'s computer inbox. As he read through them, he became just a little depressed. The description of the injuries was by no means graphic; however, it was the simple statements of injuries like "Three broken vertebrae with severed spine. Unlikely to walk again." And "Traumatic amputation of both legs. May walk with prosthetics." That had suddenly brought the reality of war into a sharp focus for him. This was what had actually happened and he was very upset at the consequences of their decisions, decisions that even now were far too advanced to retrieve.

'Get General Onishi!' he almost barked at his secretary, so fresh were his emotions. "Why am I suddenly so angry?" he questioned himself; but he did not have time to ponder further as the hologram beeped and the image of General Onishi appeared before him.

'Mr Prime Minister, how can I be of assistance?'

'I take it you have seen the reports from The Fleet?'

Onishi knew what was coming, but decided to play dumb, for now.

'Which reports would that be, Sir?'

'Don't play shy with me; the reports on the Russian prisoners that are being brought back here.'

Motoyuki waited for a few moments before he replied, 'Ah, yes. The wounded Russian pilots. Shame we could not find more of them.'

'Is that all you have to say about it? It's a shame?'

'I do not understand what else you wish me to say. They attacked us and we defended our positions.'

'But over a hundred died!' The P.M. was becoming emotional. 'Is this what Nakagawa wanted?'

'You are so right.' Motoyuki's words were painted bright with sarcasm. 'Over a hundred died, over a hundred Russians. Have you forgotten that thousands died during the first engagements? Thousands of Japanese? AND this is not Jack's doing. This is war, sir, and casualties are going to happen. NOT pretty is it? You send our young men to fight their young men and then complain that some of them die! What did you expect? A quick game of chess to decide the winner? And do not blame Jack for the deaths, he is trying to fight YOUR war and do so while protecting as many as possible.'

Motoyuki was now beginning to fire up. 'We try to tell you, time and time again, war is the failure of politicians to negotiate the way forward that does not include killing vast numbers of people. And what do you do? You send us to fight anyway. The answer is very simple, if you do not want men to die, then don't start a war! Be very thankful that we have such dedicated women and men that are willing to do your dirty work for you, and not complain when it becomes difficult.'

No one actually knew what the response from Motoyuki was expected to be but the Prime Minister was not expecting a tongue lashing and he was certainly not expecting one delivered with such venom.

'You are not being helpful, General. We need to restrict the numbers of wounded and dead we see.'

'Then don't look.' Was the terse reply.

'You forget, your position is a political appointment, it can be rescinded.'

'Are you threatening me? It may come as a surprise but not only do I have the full support of the Chiefs of Staff, I also have the full support of the Field Commanders. We are committed to completing this mission but we can only do so with the support of the government and the leaders of the country. The Emperor and the Imperial Family all support us, as do almost all of the politicians and yet you sit there threatening to dismiss us? Jack, I know you are listening, join the conversation, please.'

Jack suddenly appeared on the hologram. 'Mr Prime Minister, General Onishi.' For once Jack was not his usual quiet, reserved, unflappable self. This was him being an Army General and the change in his demeanour was unmistakable.

'Your thoughts, if you please.'

'We are at the crossroads. You can walk away and tell the world that the cost of retaking the islands is too high and concede defeat. OR, we can continue to take the fight to the Russians and show them that they should never have come to Japan in the first place. Which way will we go? It all depends on the political will.'

'So you place the onus on us then?'

'Why would we not make you responsible, we are simply soldiers doing our duty. Either stand behind us, in support; or beside us, as brothers. Do not stand in front of us, I will simply run you over, with enthusiasm, in my effort to complete my mission. And do not even think of dismissing General Onishi or any of the Chiefs of Staff. The Services will not put up with that level of political interference.'

'Are you threatening me? I remind you; I am the Prime Minister.'

'Yes, you are. So, act like one. And yes, I am threatening you. If necessary, I will run against you, next year. Let's see who will win an election after I have won the war.'

The politician rose within the PM's mind, no longer did he have the support of the military; that much was obvious. If that fact got out, he would be an ex-Prime Minister before dinner. Now he needed to worm his way out of the mess he had created.

'So, what do YOU think we should do, Nakagawa?'

Jack was angry at the way he was referring to him, Family name only and that was spat out as though it was distasteful.

'First, go to the Russians, and offer to repatriate their fallen. Not behind closed doors, as you usually do. Do it out in the open, force them to take the hand of truce; that will place them on the back foot. The political backlash for them will be they will look weaker, and while they cannot really afford that, they cannot refuse the offer either. Second, the injured should be classified as "Prisoners of war, too injured to travel at this time." Get the bio-medical companies to assist in treating them with prosthetics and whatever operations they need. If we send them back in the best possible condition then we get the "brownie points" again for being the good guys. Third, show full and unconditional support for the ones actually doing your dirty work, the front line. And fourth, show full and unconditional support for the Allies that have stood up to support us. I know some of them are ideologically your political opponents but now is not the time to put the Chinese or the North Koreans, for example, off side.'

'Jack's words had stung, at first. But after he had finished, the Prime Minister had a few moments before replying.

'You do not choose to clothe your words in niceties, do you? I can see you have a great deal of understanding of the entire situation that we face. I will take your advice; I do not have a choice at this time. Just promise me one thing.'

'And what would that be?'

'Don't become a politician, you will be unstoppable. None of us will have a chance against you.'

'You have my word, I prefer my enemies where I can see them and where I can kill them, not hiding behind a door waiting to stab me in the back.'

'I think it is time to get back to work for all of us.' Motoyuki was for once glad that he could call an end to what had been a fierce argument; and he was glad that Jack was his friend.

Chapter 31
A Resupply Mission

Eastern Command, Vladivostok

'Welcome back, General. I trust the trip to Moscow was fruitful?'

'If you call trying to get blood from a stone, and failing completely, fruitful; then yes it was. Maybe they will see some sense but I doubt it.'

'At the risk of giving you more bad news,' his personal aide paused, not quite fearful, but concerned at the reaction he would get.

'Get it out, may as well get it over. Then get some coffee.'

'The coffee is waiting for you, the news is that Moscow has managed to stuff it up, again. They have posted the news that a convoy has departed to deliver more troops and equipment to The Kuril's.'

The General could feel the bile rise in his stomach, he suddenly felt physically ill at the press release and the betrayal that it conveyed.

'Those bastards must be trying to crucify me. Show me the signal.'

The press release was offered and the General had trouble reaching out to take it, almost as if he would be tainted by the contents. He read slowly as he threw his cap onto the desk and sat, sipping at the now tepid coffee that had been poured for him.

If he was upset with the cooling drink, he didn't show it. A Tank Commander for many decades he was accustomed to poor coffee, drunk at very odd temperatures. Like most cavalry men he had long since become accustomed to what he sometimes referred to as "raw" coffee; he took it without sugar or milk; such luxuries were simply not available in a front-line tank squadron, and it was easier to brew without the extras.

'Have you read this?' he asked with a growing feeling of doom within his mind. 'I have, General.'

'How the hell do they expect us to protect a convoy, without air or proper sea cover? And why are they sending them such a long way around?' Why send them all the way north and then squeeze them through that narrow waterway?' The line of rhetorical questions was beginning to become endless.

'Get the Fleet Commander in here.'

'I will send the car for him,' replied the aide, he may well be asleep.

A disapproving grunt was all the reply he managed to give. It appeared to him that almost everyone was putting obstacles in his way, in one form or another.

Thirty minutes later the phone rang.

'What are you after Grigori? It is 2 in the morning.'

'What I am after is a conference with the Fleet Commander in my office.'

'Why so eager? Get some sleep and we can discuss the problem, or whatever, over breakfast.' It was obvious that Admiral Anatoli Litvak was not going to get out of bed without what he considered was a good reason.

'You may want some sleep, but I don't think that Jackson Nakagawa and Tyrell Backhouse are tucked away in bed.'

'What did you say?'

'I said.'

'No, don't repeat yourself, is that really who we are up against?'

'It is, and for good measure they have Roman Garcia running their Heavy Battery.'

'I will be there in half an hour. I will get my staff to supply the coffee, that tanker stuff is rubbish.'

'See you soon, Anatoli.'

Just under thirty minutes later Anatoli Litvak walked into Grigori's office, closely followed by a steward with coffee and some food.

'I thought you may want something to eat, having just arrived from Moscow.'

'Thank you. Now we need to discuss some very important information.' With a flick of his finger he dismissed the staff and the two sat looking at each other. 'Did you mean what you said? Or was that just a ruse to get me here?'

'Oh, I meant it alright, just to make it worse they have Tanaka commanding the ground forces.'

The Admiral sat and thought for a long while. 'Tell me about Tanaka, I have nothing on him?'

'Very experienced Ground Forces Commander, makes some rash decisions but he commands well. Works fast, like all their Generals, and he is unpredictable, makes him difficult to deal with.'

'We are really up against it; this is going to take some serious work if we are going to simply survive.'

'My thoughts, precisely. However, that is not why I got you in here. Read this.'

Grigori handed the press release to Anatoli and sipped his coffee as he waited for a response.

'Why are they saying they left Magadan? We have nothing there?'

'Perhaps it is to try to throw them off the scent.' Grigori replied. 'And why would they tell the world they are travelling down the west coast of the island chain? That much should be obvious.'

'Anatoli, you are the fleet commander; how would you do it, given we cannot guarantee air superiority and protection.'

After a few minutes thought, 'I would either surround them with every ship and submarine available and dash across the Sea of Okhotsk or hug the coastline all the way around the Kamchatka peninsula and then into open ocean eventually approaching from the east.' Anatoli was at least thinking tactically.

'Good, I thought the same. And it appears that that is what they are doing.'

'Well let us hope we can support them. It is most unusual for Moscow to do this without our involvement, though.'

'I think they are trying to get themselves the glory. Make it a politician's victory.'

'May the gods protect us from politicians. Can we contact them?'

'No, complete radio silence, for purposes they are civilian freighters going about their proper business.'

'We need to establish a command room. Probably best in the Fleet Headquarters, we are geared up for shipping movements.'

'Good idea, let me know when you are ready and I will move there, temporarily of course.'

Northern Planning Cell

'Jack, there is some weird radio traffic going around, all about a few freighters leaving Magadan and heading into the Sea of Okhotsk.' Hasegawa announced as he entered the planning room.

'Interesting, get Tyrell on line, and the Navy Chief of Staff.' Moments later the three sat looking at each other.

'What's happening Jack?' asked Tyrell.

'Listen to Hasegawa's report.'

The three waited is silence as Hasegawa finished the contents of the shipping movement report.

'Jack,' began Admiral Mana Yamaguchi, 'that sounds like bullshit to me. We have been keeping a close watch on the ports and there have not been any ships into Magadan, let alone leave the place. And for the last three weeks there has been too much sea ice for shipping to traverse the area.'

'Hmm; Tyrell?'

'Looking at the place and knowing how desperate they are at the moment; I would be more inclined to think they have left Vladivostok and have been hugging the coast all the way around. Probably going to exit to the Pacific at the end of the Kamchatka Peninsula. My guess? Get into the central Pacific and approach Urup under cover of night from the east.' At that moment Haruto interrupted.

'A little busy right now Haruto.' Jack responded.

'Not for this you aren't.'

Jack was a little annoyed, but he knew better than to ignore the head of SatCon. 'OK, what is it?'

'Satellite picked up several ships coming down the east coast of Kamchatka. The first has not made any move towards open ocean.'

'You win, I am interested. Arigatō.'

'Tyrell can you dispatch some American ships, try to heard them into U.S. waters.'

'Done, I will dispatch two U.S. cruisers and five coalition destroyers from the northern Task Force. Warn the Coast Guard at Dutch Harbour of our intentions. We should be able to force them into port somewhere in the Aleutians, hopefully Dutch Harbour itself. Intern them for the duration.'

'Consider it done.' Hasegawa confirmed as he left the group.

'Mai, get Yoshiro and Roman on the line, please; and Mike Rodrigues.'

'What's up, Jack?' The two asked the same question almost at the same time.

'We are being given a big advantage; Tyrell has just dispatched a task force to intercept what could be the last resupply mission for the enemy. If he is successful, we can go on the offensive during the winter when they are short of food, ammunition and warmth.'

'That is good news indeed,' Yoshiro could see the importance of the information. 'What do you want us to do.'

'First, Roman, keep their sleep to a minimum, mid-night bombardments. Not really interested in doing damage to their camp, or even killing them. Just want to keep them awake. Yoshiro, keep your snipers working and get some raids happening to keep them occupied. Mike, send one of your teams to the eastern end of the camp, I need detailed estimates of their disposition. Any questions?'

All was silent. 'Good. With a little luck and some hard work, we should be able to end this in the near future. Good luck, keep me informed. Mike stay on line for a moment, please.'

The calls were ended and preparations began.

'Mike, I want you to keep your other teams on the western flank, around 2 kilometres behind the 61st division, at the top of the long gully. There is accommodation there and you should be out of the way, if it goes hot.'

'Sir, I know I speak for the men when I say we would rather be in the front line, or a little ahead of it if possible.'

'Yes, I understand. But; your involvement is predicated by the agreement that ground troops would not be used as combat units. I have cleared it with Admiral Backhouse; you can defend yourselves, but you cannot be a part of the assault teams. I am sorry, but that is a political reality.'

'Understood. Not happy with it, but understood.'

'Arigatō. It is a necessary move; unfortunately, I need to keep the allied commands on side.'

Jack closed off the hologram and sat in silence as he mentally twisted the information and the deployments until he was reasonably satisfied with the way it was progressing.

Eventually, there was nothing else for him but to spend some time with his family; so he left the planning room and went to sit with them all before dinner.

'This is USS Independence; you have entered United States Territorial Waters. STOP YOUR ENGINES. Prepare to be boarded!'

The message was delivered in English and Russian, three times each. Eventually, the ship began to slow, its wake dissipating as the propeller stopped. The boarding party was already on the helicopter gunship and every offensive weapon on the cruisers, and their attendant destroyers, were trained on the freighter in the unlikely circumstance that the crew did not comply; the American Captain was quite willing to sink the ship with little notice and no empathy.

The boarding teams secured the bridge and a team of marines began to search the ship. With a crew of only ten it was a short search.

'Do you understand why you have been boarded?' The Marine Lieutenant asked the ship's captain.

'You say we are within the US waters; we dispute this.

The Lieutenant asked for a Navigator to board and a short while later, the Navigator with a Russian Interpreter plotted the position using the Russian equipment. Once it was proven that the Russians were indeed in American waters. The ship was boarded by the Coast Guard and taken to Seattle for "inspection and seizure of its contraband cargo". Broadly speaking that meant everything on the ship.

This scenario was repeated another five times and each ship was seized and taken away. Yet another winter would be spent cold and hungry on the ground of Iturup.

The Kremlin

'What do you mean, seized?' The Russian Chief of Staff was enraged and his voice showed it.

'It is not a double meaning. The Americans followed the freighters as they crossed in to US Territorial waters, seized the ships and the cargo.'

'How could you let this happen General Chernov?'

'Perhaps if you had kept me informed as to the dispatch of the ships and their expected route, I may have been able to give some advice as to the best method of protecting them. The first we heard of it, here in Eastern Command, was when we received the signal saying they had been boarded.'

A reluctant apology and a very reluctant "very well" were as close to admitting fault as anyone would get from the Kremlin. It was notable that two middle ranking officers were found dead in their crashed car the next morning.

Japanese Ground Command, Iturup

'Hear that? Yoshiro Tanaka asked his support team.

'Sounds like thunder; the Meteorological Officers did not forecast storms.'

A few seconds passed and suddenly Yoshiro shouted, "TAKE COVER!"

For most of them it was just in time, the first salvo from the Russian 130mm guns smashed into the camp. Unfortunately for Yoshiro Tanaka it would be the last ever order he would give.

'BROADSIDES, SHOOT!' Roman shouted and in the best tradition of Nelsons Navy every gun from both the Mexican and the Japanese battery's, 155's and 127's, fired together. Just ten seconds later they fired again and they continued firing every ten seconds until the gunners were about to drop from sheer exhaustion from feeding the heavy shells into the 155mm Heavy Artillery.

'Cease fire!' the order eventually was made and the silence was almost oppressive. Later observations would show that beyond the first salvo from Romans guns the enemy did not return fire. They couldn't return fire; the Mexicans were so accurate that the Russian Battery had been put out of action almost immediately.

The infantry emerged with a rush from the bunkers and began to search for survivors. It was to be to everyone's dismay that the command bunker had been hit hardest and the only survivor was General Tanaka.

Survival was only by name however; both legs were so severely damaged that no amount of surgery could hope to restore even some function. His left arm was dangling by a small scrap of skin. Add to that, broken ribs and internal injuries it was always going to be a lottery to see if he could be saved.

The medical teams worked like men possessed. Stopping the major bleeds and stemming the severed arteries were the first priority. The arm was so badly damaged that they amputated it in the field. It took almost four hours before he could be listed as "Stable for travel" to allow them to get him to the "Blue Ridge" so the hospital could try to keep him alive.

'How is he, Doctor?' Tyrell asked his chief surgeon, his concern for the General was personal as well as professional.

'I think he will live, not so sure how he will be once his injuries are explained to him.'

'We cannot dwell on that. Thank you, and your team for saving him. At least he will see his family again.'

'Yes, and with time he should be able to walk with prosthetics; his arm will be a difficult prospect, nothing left to work with.'

'OK. Put a priority on the surgical report, I need to get it to Tokyo ASAP.'

'Right on it.'

'Get a meal before you start. You need it.'

The Chief Surgeon smiled as he left Tyrell's cabin. He had served with a lot of commanders and Tyrell Backhouse was one of the best.

Northern Planning Cell

The hologram on Jack's desk beeped incessantly.

'Tyrell, must be important to make so much noise?'

'It is. No easy way to say this, Yoshiro has been severely wounded in a Russian attack. He is out of surgery but his injuries are significant. Surgeons report is on its way. Is his wife there or still in Tokyo?'

Jack didn't respond immediately; this was very difficult to come to grips with. Eventually, he replied, 'No she is in Tokyo, I will get Onishi to break the news.'

'We will need to relay him through your place, I need to keep my medevac choppers on hand.'

'Sure, no problem. I will get one sent from Central Command.'

The chopper from the Blue Ridge arrived almost two hours before the one from Tokyo. During the wait, Jack never left his side.

312

'Be honest, Jack. How bad is it?' Yoshiro asked.

'Honest! Are you certain you want that?'

'No one on that ship would tell me anything, not that it would matter, they had me so full of drugs I couldn't have understood it anyway.'

'You know you have lost your left arm?'

'Hai, that much I do know.'

Jack took a deep breath. 'You also lost both legs, a significant portion of your liver, a couple of ribs and a couple of feet of intestines.'

Neither spoke for a considerable time.

Eventually, Yoshiro replied, 'So not only will I not play the violin, I will not play rugby either?'

Jack could not stifle the laugh, even if he wanted to. 'You never played the violin and you hated sports.'

Yoshiro tried to laugh as well but simply ended up coughing. Once the fit subsided, he looked at Jack and asked 'Jack, finish this, finish them. Don't let the losses of our friends be for nothing.'

'I will do that.'

'You know Onishi and the Chiefs of Staff have been itching to get you the command, do it. Finish them off.'

'I will, and god willing I will buy you as much sake as you want.'

Smiling, Yoshiro said, 'I will take a rain check, have to wait for the liver to catch up.'

The two smiled and waited for the medevac. No more words needed to be said. Jack would now start to plot the final demise of the enemy.

Central Command, Tokyo

'Get General Nakagawa on the line.'

The hologram sat quietly until eventually Jack appeared.

'My apologies, I was in a planning meeting.'

'No need to apologise, we understand you are very busy. We will be brief,' Motoyuki continued, 'Is it possible for you to continue your planning function from Iturup?'

'Almost all of it is done by satellite and remote functions, it can be done from anywhere.'

'Very well.' Onishi looked around at his fellow Generals and Admirals; each in turn nodded. 'Jack, His Imperial Majesty would like to speak.'

Jack simply waited and eventually the image of the Emperor appeared.

'General Nakagawa, you are hereby appointed to the position of Commander of the Northern Army. With this position comes a promotion to Full General and command of all Japanese Forces Northern Pacific. You are to prosecute the war on Iturup to its conclusion. Any and all support is to be given in your prosecution of this war.' Good luck General.'

'Domo arigatō, Your Majesty. I will do my very best.'

The Emperor's hologram closed and the Chiefs of Staff watched as Jack sat deep in thought.

'What is it Jack? What is going on inside your head?'

'The ground teams we have at the moment need to be rested. I want ten divisions to replace them. We can take four from each of the Southern and Central Armies and two of the remaining divisions from the Northern. Ask our allies if we can rest the ships? Or, if not, we need to get them some time out of the patrol area to rest, maybe a rotation system over the winter. I need a minimum of one thousand Kamikaze drones and an extra two hundred Amazons. I also need someone to put a fire under the backsides of the manufacturers of the new "Kraken" units. We will need a minimum of four thousand calories per man per day. And don't try to short change me on that. It is COLD, they need two thousand just to keep warm.'

'If we can, I would like to get a second surveillance satellite over Vladivostok, and one over the Sea of Okhotsk.'

'Jack we cannot do the satellites. We simply do not have them.'

'OK, just a moment.' Off to one side Jack could be seen speaking with someone. After a few minutes he returned.

'What is happening, Jack?'

'I have sent my SatCon Commander to work, he assures me he can steal a couple of satellites from the Russians; if not he will be able to steal their data.'

'Are you serious?' General Ito was astounded. 'I have seen a lot of what you can do but steal satellites?'

Smiling widely Jack replied, 'Why not he has done it twice already, if he says he can, I will be surprised if he can't.'

'With the general noise from the staff in the room, and the discussion from the chiefs, the one word that was clearly heard was "Unbelievable".

Eventually, General Onishi regained control of the room. 'We will begin with your requirements immediately. Good luck.'

The hologram closed off and Jack simply sat and thought. "Well, now it is up to me." And he began to bring together the requirements that needed attention before he left for Iturup. The first item on the agenda was always going to be dinner with the family.

Chapter 32
Murder!

'Thank you all for coming tonight.' Jack was almost holding court as he sat at the table for dinner. 'As you all know, I have been appointed as Commander Kuril Forces. Tonight, will be the last chance I have for some time to sit with you all. While I have no fears that we will not be successful, I do have a lot of work that must be done before we are victorious. I thank you all for your love and best wishes.' Jack lifted his glass and saluted his family.

While there were many at the table the two that were most conspicuous by their absence were Chie and Fumiko. The official reason being that they had returned to Tokyo to be with Reina, Chie's Grandmother during a period of ill health. Jack, however, could see it in Fumiko's eyes; there was something that was bothering her greatly. The only explanation was that she had "seen" something distressing and she did not wish to confront it, at that time.

The evening stretched on for longer than anyone thought possible, they just didn't want Jack to leave. Eventually, they all made their way to their rooms knowing that Jack would be leaving in the early morning. When they eventually, rose it was to the sound of goodbye tears from everyone, as Jack boarded the chopper and left for war.

He had not been on the ground more than thirty minutes when it became obvious to everyone there that a Combat General had arrived to take his place as Theatre Commander.

'Hasegawa, Commander's meeting in twenty minutes. No excuses, on hologram if necessary.'

'Hai.'

Right on schedule the meeting began.

'First item, unit strength and current casualty status. Tyrell?'

'All Fleet units at full strength, nil casualties; unless you want to count a marine that managed to twist his ankle while trying to complete a marathon on the flight deck.'

'Nil casualties. We will be rotating the fleet for rest periods at Yokosuka during the winter. Roman?'

'All batteries at full strength, we have the upgrade ammunition for the 127s and the 155s; 20% increase in range and no reduction in accuracy. All ready to take it too them.'

'We will also be rotating your teams for rest during the winter.'

'You may have a problem there, none of them are willing to leave. They are all committed to you and the final task, winning the war.'

'Arigatō, can you bring in reserves? If we go to extended or 24-hour barrage, they will get tired and we will need to keep the firing rate up.'

'I will get back to you on that.'

'Mike Rodrigues?'

'Full strength, ready and raring to go.'

'Arigatō, Infantry?'

'All injured headquarters staff have been medically treated; all that are capable have returned to duty. 193rd Division at 75%, losses during the first assault. 161st Cavalry Division at full strength but no spare ARV's or IFV's. 122nd Cavalry 50% no vehicles. All others at full strength.'

'Arigatō, we will be getting replacement units in the near future; everyone gets rotated out.'

'You may have a mutiny there; they all want to stay. Various reasons but mostly they want revenge for the casualties inflicted already.'

'Arigatō, Drones?'

'All flying units fully stocked. Weapons and ammunition in excessive supply. Spare power packs for all units. All pilots ready with the exception of one that has been playing too many games during stand down, he has "Nintendo thumb".'

'Give him some pain relief and put him back to work, and he does not get a medal for combat injuries. That is just lazy.'

Everyone laughed at the thought that a video game could put a pilot out of action.

'SatCon?'

'We are at full strength; all programmers and hackers are working. Our Satellite is fully functional and the Russian captive is fulfilling its new mission as a "Space Junk Creator" with renewed vigour. The other captive satellites are functioning correctly, and the Russians are still wondering how to get their units back. By the way Roman, thank you for your programmer; Aztec is a really useful security language.'

'You are welcome, I hear he is enjoying his time.'

'Arigatō Haruto.'

'Now, this is the plan, going forward.' Jack began to layout the general plan for the future, and the immediate plan for striking at the enemy.

For the next month, between Roman and Drones the Russians did not get too much respite. The guns were working perfectly and every time the Russians tried bring their guns forward to a position where they could be effective, Roman's gunners almost literally blew them back behind the lines. The Russian artillery had one major flaw, their propellant was not as effective as the Mexican product and as a result their range was deficient; bring them close enough to attack the front line and the 155s of the 86th Heavy Bombardment Group would quickly have their position and the resultant heavy fire would push them back again before any real damage could be done.

If the Russians brought them far enough forward to attack the main camp, then the 127s and the 155s smashed them into oblivion.

It was just as big a problem if they left them far enough back to protect them from the guns, Drones and his pilots would simply drop fragmentation grenades and incendiary explosives on them at night. It was a real "lose-lose" situation for them and they were having difficulty finding a solution to the problem.

For the next three months, as Jack rotated his teams out for rest and then brought them back in, he had the drones and the guns dropping death into the Russian camp at will, and at the same time they would retrieve around a hundred and ten warheads per week and ship them off to a secret facility.

It was to be many years into the future before it would be revealed that the storage facility was actually a part of a disused nuclear power station. No one would go there and the radiation level would never be questioned. Yet another product of Jack's fully functional tactical mind.

When he put it to the Emperor as a viable solution, he was asked, 'Who will be willing to work there? Staff will be required.'

'We can ask for volunteers, as they did when the Fukushima power plant exploded. If we choose the elderly, they will have a very important position and that will be good for their sense of self-worth and any illness that may arise will not be evident until they are well into their old age, not so big a problem for the mature citizen as it is for young people.'

And so, it was agreed, the numbers of volunteers far exceeded the number of positions available and the facility was both manned and secure.

Finally, the schedule was set for the Russian weapons to be stolen and spirited away, and that would leave Jack to concentrate fully on the downfall of the Russian Expedition.

The barrage concentration on the Russian positions was definitely taking its toll. Many Russians were looking haggard, underfed and sleep deprived.

In contrast, the Allied positions saw well fed and rested troops, feeding off the constant damage they were doing to the enemy their morale was high, very high and the general feeling was that they could achieve anything.

The Russian Command, both in the Kremlin and on Iturup were both feeling the political heat.

The Kremlin

'How can we get better results?' asked General Chernov.

'Try delivering some relief troops and supplies.' The reply, from an almost completely ineffective Airforce General, was less than helpful.

'That is good coming from you, your planes cannot even stay in the sky long enough to deliver something, anything.'

'What about ships?'

'The last convoy was interned for straying into U.S. waters. We disputed it but the fact is that we tried and got caught. We are getting some through, but for every one that makes it three get caught.'

All the service chiefs sat in silence as they tried to find a solution.

'We have had some success with air-drops, we have kept up the deliveries of food and some reinforcements, but I fear it will be insufficient come spring.' Mused Admiral Litvak. 'What if we assemble a convoy with a large naval escort, if we can make it fast enough, we may just get through.'

'That appears to be our only way forward. Begin to plan for it, as soon as the sea ice has dissipated, we will move. I will signal Plishkin to begin work on providing sufficient landing areas to off load the ships. When we go, we will need to have full air cover for the entire trip.'

The Kremlin had finally arrived at a reasonable solution; unfortunately, it would all be unravelled by a rash decision, a decision that would be the result of not keeping everyone informed.

Russian H.Q. Iturup Island

'General Plishkin, the gunners report another three units out of action. That last barrage was particularly savage.'

'That's makes almost half our artillery and most of our armour. Who the hell is commanding them? I thought we had gotten rid of their General.'

'Not certain, sir. I will ask Moscow.' The Communication Officer was eager to get away from the General before his legendary temper surfaced.

Just four hours later the young officer returned. 'General, I have the dossier from Moscow. It appears that the Japanese have just promoted a General and put him in command.'

'WHO?' shouted Plishkin.

Opening the dossier, the officer began to read, 'General Jackson Nakagawa, 43, single. Home is in the Northern reaches of Hokkaido. Parents still alive and live in the family home. Two sisters, two brothers, numerous nieces and nephews.'

'Who the hell cares about kids? What about him?'

'Career officer, infantry, but has been known to dabble in other disciplines. Adept at Martial arts. Oh, he is a planner, has run the Central Command Planning Group for a few years.'

'So, he has no personal ties, promoted to take command, and he is a planner with no field experience. I want to rattle his little Japanese cage. Call Eastern Fleet Command.'

The comms officer called the Fleet Command and passed the call through to General Plishkin.

'Admiral, I want to deliver a blow to their new commander. I have been given the position of his home; it is somewhat remote in the north of Hokkaido; I do not have satellite vision but Google Earth has mapped it for me. It seems his home is in the grounds of a castle and consists of two smaller buildings and an outer area. I want you to put a cruise missile into each of these buildings. I want him to know that he is playing in the big league now.'

The Admiral took a long look at the images from the hologram and finally he asked, 'Are you certain? Blowing up a castle is a little extreme; and it is not going to get us any friends, destroying heritage buildings.'

'NO, dammit. NOT the CASTLE. The three small buildings!'

Again, the Admiral looked at the image and eventually he said, 'Yes, we can do that. I can get them to program the strike to approach from the west and fly over the mountains.'

'Good, when?'

'Three days? Is that good enough?'

'Yes, that is fine.'

'Do you want a day or night strike?'

'Night, I think. Reduce the chance of discovery.'

'Very good, I will let you know when it is underway.'

Three days later, at midnight, the grounds of Jack's family home exploded with the delivery of three cruise missiles. The first hit the small cottage, the second hit the family chapel and the last blew the stables to pieces.

'JACK! Call from your sister Hana.' Hasegawa called out from the communications room in the command post.

'WHAT? Why is she calling, must be important? Put her on.'

'Hana, is everything OK?' He could clearly see her tears. She was so upset that she could barely speak.'

'It's, its Mama and Papa, they have been killed.'

'What happened?'

'The investigators say it was a cruise missile. Hit the cottage.'

'I am on my way.'

'HASEGAWA!' Jack shouted.

'What's wrong?'

'There appears to have been a missile strike on my home. All Commanders on line in five.'

'Hai. '

Five minutes later, 'Thank you all, there is no easy way to say this, my family home was attacked this evening by a cruise missile strike. There can only be one reason for this, we are hurting them badly and they needed a distraction so they try to take me out of the picture.'

A chorus of sympathy erupted from the entire group.

'I will be leaving in ten minutes; you all have your assignments. All I can say is hit them hard, and I will return as soon as possible. Tyrell, the ships returning from rest can you redirect them to cover the western and northern approaches of Hokkaido? Just in case they try a second strike.'

'Consider it done. They will pay for this, mark my words.'

'Arigatō. Call if you need me.'

Jack walked away from the hologram and his IFV took him directly to the landing pad for the helicopter to take him away.

Jack, unusually, didn't say a word for the entire journey. He simply sat and waited. As they finally made the final approach, he ordered the pilot to fly around the area as he checked through the night vision goggles looking for the damage.

The chopper landed near the main house and the family ran out to grab him. Tears all round, it took a long time before they moved back into the castle.

As they moved inside, he pressed his communicator. 'Drones?' He enquired and he was pleased with an instant response.

'Hai?'

'I want full surveillance coverage of the entire estate and approaches.'

'Consider it done. Already got ten up. And Mai and I both offer our deepest condolences.'

'Arigatō, my friend.'

As they moved through the house, they were followed by Emika, who, despite her tears, had managed to put together some foods and drinks for everyone.

Just half an hour later Jack's Uncle arrived, his old truck wheezing its way along the driveway until it came to a stop beside the wreckage of the stables.

'Why has Uncle arrived at the stables?' Jack asked, it was a rhetorical question and he was surprised when Asa replied.

'The attack killed Maiko; the colt survived but he will need a brood mare to care for him.'

'Maiko too.' Jack was wistful in his acknowledgement of the information. 'They will pay dearly for this.'

Pressing his communicator again he ordered

'Roman, Drones. Continual bombardment; if it moves, kill it. If it doesn't, blow it to pieces.'

'More than pleased to assist.'

'Arigatō. Drones, send Mai down here, please.'

'Hai.'

Just moments later Mai appeared. It was evident that she too had been crying but she was ready to do what was necessary.

'Get Motoyuki on the line, please.'

'Jack, we are so sorry. This is terrible news.' Motoyuki gave condolences from himself and Yumi.

'Arigatō, my friend. I want ten anti-missile defence units here tomorrow with sufficient operators to adequately defend, not only my home but also the Northern Planning Cell.'

'Consider it done. Anything else?'

'Not at the moment.'

'We will visit tomorrow; let you have a day with your family before we fill your house.'

'Arigatō. You are always welcome.'

The family sat and shared their grief for almost three hours, one by one they wandered off and managed some sleep; all except Jack. He simply stood and watched the mountains. His body was not active, but his mind was churning through dozens of scenarios and tactical decisions that would inflict the maximum amount of pain on the Russians for their cowardly attack on defenceless civilians.

Emika, long accustomed to Jack's sometimes odd actions kept him supplied with coffee and confections to supply enough energy to keep his mind working and his energy up.

He still hadn't moved when Chie and Fumiko arrived.

Fumiko, now blossoming into a beautiful young lady, threw her arms around him and wept openly on his shoulder.

'I knew, I knew.' She kept repeating, almost as some form of mantra.

'I should have warned them, I knew something was going to happen.' She burst into a fresh wave of tears.

'You could do that no more than I could,' Jack tried to explain, 'and even if you had warned them, they would have still lived in the cottage. This is not your fault. I know who is responsible and I will make them pay for their actions.'

It took a long time, but eventually the tears began to dry. Jack and his closest friends sat and watched as the sun got up, no one spoke but Jack had most of a fully formed battle plan, waiting for him to say the word to begin the retribution that was heading for the Russians.

The local Police Chief, a self-important man, tried to take control of the investigation. He failed, miserably. With a host of family and many very senior Generals and Admirals flooding the house he was outranked by almost everyone. He gave up completely when the Emperor and Crown Prince arrived; it was finally clear that there was far more happening than he could hope to cope with.

The funeral, two days later, was no great lavish affair; but even with it being restricted to just family and close friends there were well over a hundred attending.

Two days after the funeral Jack began his retaliation.

'Drones, get the heads of manufacturing for the Kraken here in the morning, they can explain why they are so far behind in their production.'

'Hai, 10 early enough?'

'Hai, we can all have breakfast first.'

It was as well that Daisy and Grace had arrived for the funeral, they were sorely needed to help Emika get breakfast for so many. Eventually, the food was done and the adults sat on the deck chatting while the children played on the grass. Suddenly Fumiko said 'They are here.' And got up to bring them to the rear of the house.

They introduced themselves and settled down while a fresh round of coffee was brought out.

'We will leave you to your discussions.; Said Grace as she herded everyone out of earshot, leaving Jack and the other officers to conduct business.

The tension was obvious, the Heads of manufacturing were well aware of the circumstances for the visit and they were wary of how to begin. Jack saved them the worry.

'Why have you not completed the units I asked for?'

'We had some problems with the software, to begin with.'

'That was resolved last November. Next excuse.'

'The range was lower than specified, so we needed to redesign the battery system.'

'My Drone pilot gave you the information at the beginning of December. Next excuse.'

'There were some difficulties with the seals, they could not cope with the depth required.'

'What depth were you working with?'

'300 metres.'

'In what world did you think 300 metres was the desired depth? You were told 150 metres and that was achieved in the middle of last year! Next excuse.'

'We have now completed the testing, it is ready. We thought you may require the deep-water version.'

'Begin production on the Kraken 150. Continue the research on the Kraken 300. When will you have 1000 ready?'

'We can begin production immediately, we should have 500 units ready by the end of the month, that is three weeks. The remainder will be ready by the middle of next month.'

'Very well.'

'Sir, is it possible to know what the device will be doing?'

Jack looked a Motoyuki and got a nod in return; he then gave a short presentation on the proposed use of the device, and the results they wanted to achieve.

The two engineers had definitely turned slightly pale when Jack had finished.

'Well? Does this satisfy your curiosity?'

'Most certainly, I think we are both pleased that you are our General. Domo Arigatō, and good luck with your plans.'

'Arigatō.'

The two left and began to get the production lines moving, Jack would be ready to go on the full offensive in the near future.

'You were a bit hard on them, Jack. They have worked some minor miracles getting the units ready.'

'They have, but I would have had them deployed long ago if they had stuck with the original plan and designs. Honestly, who wants a unit that can submerge to a depth of 1000 feet?'

'Good point, Jack.'

'Arigatō; Drones!'

'Hai?'

'Are your special pilots ready?'

'As ready as they can be without real units to work with.'

'Good, delivery is planned for next month. Get them ready. General Ito, we will need your transports to deliver them at very low speed and low altitude. Can you get them ready?'

'Certainly, I must say this is innovative work, they will be curious as to the payload they are delivering.'

'Then let them watch when Drones deploys the units in an action situation, I must admit I am waiting to see the result myself.'

They all smiled and the conversation slowly turned to "non-military" subjects.

'I told you they were finished.' Fumiko announced as she led the ladies back outside. Sitting beside Jack she announced, 'Your devices will have the desired result. You will make them pay, Jack.'

'Arigatō, Fumiko.'

Chapter 33
It's Personal

'Get me General Nakagawa on line.'

'Aye, aye Sir.' Tyrell's secretary replied.

'Konichiwa Tyrell. To what do I owe the pleasure?'

'You may not be so happy when I tell you.'

'OK, you have my undivided attention.'

'The Pentagon have assigned a "Psychological Combat Command Analyst" to me.'

'I give in, what is it?'

'The purpose is to carry out an analysis of the stresses and the effects of that stress on those in command positions. Assignments for each of the ships Captains in the fleet have already been given and the Pentagon has demanded access to the ground forces as well.'

'And by what right has the pentagon "demanded" this access?'

'The Pentagon wants to get some real time information on the loads undertaken by field commanders. Before you ask, your Chiefs of Staff have agreed, as long as there is no interference with your operations.'

'Just a minute. Hasegawa, get Motoyuki and Roman on this line.'

A few minutes later they joined them. 'Something coming up Jack?' they both enquired, almost together.'

'Apparently the Americans, I apologise Tyrell, the pentagon wants to analyse us in the field. According to Tyrell it has been approved. Know anything about this?'

'Apologies, Jack. Just found out about it this morning. It was presented as a fact-finding mission for American commanders and somehow, we all got put in the basket. I have been trying to sort it out but apparently it was first agreed to by the Prime Minister.'

Jack sat motionless as he thought through the implications; finally, he looked up, 'I will allow this, observations only, no questions to anyone but me. He will not be permitted on the front line. That will at least let Roman and the Divisional Commanders off the hook.'

'Yes, well,' Tyrell continued, somewhat nervously, 'he is a she and she is a full Colonel.'

'To put it bluntly, Tyrell, I could not care if he/she was a flying fish. NO ACCESS TO THE FRONT LINE.'

'Yeah, I already told them that. They think they can change your mind.'

Everyone laughed and the recurring response was "Yeah, right. Like that's ever going to happen."

'Arigatō, thank you all for your support. Tyrell, I will wait here for the arrival she can follow me as much as she wants.'

'Thanks Jack. That has let me off the hook.'

'Has it now, you owe me then.'

'OK, dinner on me.'

'No, no. no that will not be enough. I want tickets to see Daisy perform.'

'That's unfair, put me in the bad books with Daisy. You play dirty.'

'Your call!' Jack smiled widely at his friend. They both understood that it was a "Gentleman's Wager." The penalty was one that was acceptable to all.

'What about Grace and me?' asked Roman; closely followed By Motoyuki asking for Yumi as well.

'OK, ok you all drive a hard bargain.' Then he added, under his breath, 'The things I do for friends.' And they were all smiling as they left the call.

Jack simply sat in his office and pondered the demand. It was completely unheard-of, to have a psychological evaluation during the prosecution of a war. Eventually, he was brought out of his musings when Chie demanded he sit with the family for dinner. Looking around the planning room he saw that all was well and progressing as he wanted; so, he did as Chie asked.

'He finally deigns to grace us with his presence.' Sora was joking as he "abused" his brother. They all sat down and enjoyed the family get together, even though they all knew it was only too close to the time he must return to face the enemy.

The next morning Jack had managed a sleep in, he did not rise until nearly six o'clock. He was shocked and he rushed to the planning room to ensure that he had not missed any important events or calls. Once satisfied that all was progressing as he wished he went to the small graveyard which was beside the wreckage of the chapel.

Kneeling before the fresh graves he was silent as he prayed and spoke to his parents. It was almost half an hour later that a female voice behind him pulled his conscience back to the present.

'Are you General Nakagawa?'

Jack stiffened at the voice; who is so unfeeling as to confront someone as the knelt before their parent's graves.

As the warrior inside him began to rise he decided to ignore the demand.

'I SAID, are you General Nakagawa?' The voice was more insistent. Jack knew exactly who it was and again, Jack decided to ignore it.

'I have been sent…' Suddenly Jack stood and turned towards the voice.

'HOW DARE YOU INTERRUPT MY PRAYERS. GO AWAY!'

She did not move, she began again, 'I have been sent to—' She stopped midsentence as he moved past her, speaking rapidly in Japanese into his communicator. As he climbed the steps to the deck, three of the drone pilots blocked her way.

'Let me through!' She demanded.

'You are not permitted in here. This is private.' She was told, and she was forced to stand and wait until Jack had finished his breakfast and then, only then, was she permitted to speak with him.

She was escorted to Jack's office where he had to force himself not to offer refreshments.

'Now, WHAT do you want?' Jack was, uncharacteristically forceful; and it had the right effect, she was now on the backfoot.

Just as she began to speak the hologram on his desk came to life.

'Jack! Surveillance reports the enemy 130s have been moved a little closer to the front.'

'Your thoughts, Haruto?'

'I think they are getting into position to launch a bombardment at the H.Q. Estimated start time of sunrise tomorrow, if they stick to their usual operational directives.'

'Wait, get Roman please.' Roman joined the conversation.

'Yes, Jack?'

'Haruto reports movement of the enemy 130's. Assessment?'

'The idiots are now too close; we can get them.'

'Start at sundown with the 155s and then hit them about 3am with everything. That should force them back.'

Roman agreed and left the conversation. 'Good work Haruto, keep it up.'

'Arigatō Jack, I do have some thoughts about the sat…'

'Say no more, we will do this in one hour.'

Haruto responded with a stunned silence, eventually he said 'Hai.' And closed the hologram call.

Jack turned to the visitor. 'Now you were saying?'

'Why did you stop your Major reporting? He obviously had something to say?'

'His report was secret; you are not permitted to know.'

'I will have you know I am cleared for secret information.'

'And I could not care less, you are not cleared for my information, ANY OF IT.'

'General, if this is going to work you need to trust me.' She was trying a little reverse psychology.

'Then I guess it is not going to work, pack your bags and report that to the Pentagon.'

She was nothing if not persistent. For the next three days she tried to get admitted into his inner sanctum, and she was rejected at every turn. Each time there was something important, a meeting or a call, she was taken away. Finally, Jack called a meeting of all his commanders and she was permitted to remain.

One by one the commanders joined the meeting and when all were ready Jack began.

'Right, the time has come. I will be returning to Iturup tomorrow first thing.

The first item on this phase is Operation Ocean. Kei, I want the Airforce to deliver the new units to the "jump off point" tomorrow night, drop time is around 0230.'

'Hai.' Came the reply.

'Drones, work with Haruto and ensure the enemy air assets are compromised. Send your ranging units to get information for Roman, and prep your special pilots.'

'Hai.'

'Roman, keep their heads down and knock out as many as possible.'

'Mike, are your teams watching targets assigned?'

'Yes, group one reports eastern end still clear, they are obviously still scared. Three, reports some activity at the western airbase but nothing serious, they may be trying to resupply.'

'OK, Keep in touch with Drones. Targets as they become available.'

'Roger that.'

'Forward divisions rest as much as possible; we will be annoying the life out of them soon enough and that is going to spur them into some sort of action. It is time to make Plishkin pay for his murderous raid on my home.'

'Tyrell, you can have your Colonel back. Chopper up in two hours.'

'Roger that.'

'Any questions?' Jack had given his quickest briefing ever; he simply didn't want information going where it could do damage. He knew his team would ask later, that was the purpose of giving a timeframe to the helo departure, now they knew when it would be clear to call back and ask the more revealing questions.

Admirals Stateroom, U.S.S. Blue Ridge

'When that chopper arrives bring the Colonel to me on the Admirals Bridge.' Tyrell pressed the stop button on the communicator. Just ten minutes later there was a knock on the door.

'Enter!'

The Colonel closed the door behind her and sat in the chair indicated, opposite Tyrell.

'Admiral, I do not know how to begin.'

'Try the start.'

'He is rude and misogynistic; he does not even acknowledge the existence of the females he commands. He has trust issues; he does not let others into the secret world he believes is his own to control. He is a control freak; nothing happens without his approval. He shows strong narcissistic tendencies and he all but refuses to sleep; that alone clouds his judgement. He is never open, and he always refused to permit me to meet his family.'

'Go, on.'

'Psychologically, he is not capable of commanding an army. He does not look at the larger picture, only what is before him here and now. My report will show that he needs to be removed from command at first opportunity. Or placed in command of infantry only.'

'You finished?'

The colonel looked slightly embarrassed at the sudden stop to her report.

'For now.' She replied.

'OK. Now let me show you what he is actually doing.' Tyrell called for his tactical commander to operate the hologram. The image appeared over the table.

'Now, you say he should be restricted to the infantry. Commander, infantry positions on Iturup, please.' The hologram showed the entrenched positions of the ten divisions on the front line. 'A hundred thousand men there.'

'Now zoom out for the Armour and Recon patrols.' The picture zoomed out a little. The coloured dots indicating each unit becoming a little smaller.

'Add Romans Heavy and light Battery's and the Northern Army Artillery.'

The positions of the dozens of guns were instantly marked.

'Out to include the enemy airfield. Out to include Mikes Recon teams, the headquarters positions, medical etc. As the image became larger the depictions of the islands became smaller.

'Add transit routes for enemy vehicles. Add resupply routes, enemy and us. Add sea transit routes.' The map became a little smaller as it showed more detail.

'Add fleet positions. Add expected enemy sea transit routes.'

'Is this enough for him? Is that enough for him to take care of?' Tyrell was now beginning to see why Jack had not wanted to speak with the interloper, there was far too much at stake.

'More than enough for any Commanding Officer.'

'Watch.' Tyrell replied.

'Show enemy Airfield and defences on Urup. Show enemy Fleet Base East and Vladivostok Combined Military Base.'

'Now this is what he needed to keep secret. He agreed to let me tell you now because we are under a communications blackout. You will have to remain with the fleet until this is over.'

'Show the intended deployment of Kraken, include transit routes and waiting positions.' A plethora of small spots appeared all over the sea transit routes into and out of the Vladivostok base.

'Is that enough?'

The colonel simply stared at the mind-boggling array of information.

'Show satellite surveillance positions.'

The hologram expanded to show the position of not only the Japanese satellite but also the captured Russian ones and the ones that had their data hijacked.

'Is that enough? Show known and suspected submarine transit routes.'

The now very complex hologram showed the three-dimensional battlefield. From under the sea into space, the psychologist was now stunned.

'He did all this?'

'This is not all of it. Show secure storage "November" and the deployment of four of the captured weapons.'

At that point the psychologist was stumped. How did one man put all that together? How does he keep track of what is going on?'

'It is all in his brain, he does not miss a thing.'

'Unbelievable. What is his next move?'

'Ask him. Jack, join us.'

'Konichiwa.'

'How do you keep all this up in the air? How do you keep control?'

'Fact is, I don't need to. I tell the commanders and they do it. I just coordinate and let them have the fun.'

'By the way, Tyrell, The Kraken will be in position by tomorrow night. I believe they will try to resupply, by sea, leaving in the next two days or so.'

'Where do you want us?'

'Keep the fleet well away from the central western approaches. Keep some close to the west coast of Iturup and protect the North of Hokkaido; there is still a chance of missile strike there.'

'Concur. How are the family holding up, Jack?'

'Hana and Asa are still shaken; they have decided to return to Sapporo for the duration. Reo and Sora have been recalled for the fleet rotation.'

'And Emika, Chie and Fumiko?'

'All good. Fumiko sends her regards and says stay away from Russians; they attract explosions at funny times.'

'HA, ha; trust Fumiko. Send our love to all, and Daisy has agreed to the concert.'

'Thanks Tyrell and tell your Colonel that if she wants to understand command she needs to stay up with the planners.'

'You mean you?' she asked, a little nervously.

'Yes, you need to stay up when I am up in the planning rooms.'

'Roger that.' Tyrell closed off the hologram and thanked the commander; he called the steward and refreshments were served.

'Can I ask, Sir. How does he do it? How does he know everything?'

'His mind is a military trap. If he needs something, he will ask for it; if he thinks he can use something he will ask how, if he needs a new weapon, he will get it made.'

'But how does that work?' The Colonel's mind was now trying to understand the thought processes behind the enigma that Jack appeared to be. 'What about the satellites?'

'We only had one, to begin with; then the new Commander of SatCon literally stole one from the Russians; no one asked him to, he just hijacked it. From there he smashed one of theirs and then hacked deeply enough into others to steal data.'

'It is a shame that you could not spend a lot of time speaking with the army he controls; we all trust him, and we all believe that he will win this war.'

'But the way he speaks, he seems to be a control freak, he does everything. It is almost a personal vendetta.'

'When you arrived at his house,' Tyrell began.

'No, I went to the Northern Planning Cell.' She interrupted.

Tyrell smiled. 'That is his house. He was praying, was he not?'

'Yes, he was. And he was quite angry that I had interrupted him.'

'That is because he was praying for the ability to protect the ones he commands; and he was probably speaking with his parents.'

'How does that change things?'

'General Plishkin attacked his home to try to put him out of the war, that is how much the enemy want him gone. When they attacked, they killed his parents. I would say that permits him to be angry.'

'Yes, I suppose that would do it. I really need more time, don't I?'

'I think it may be a little late for that. He will give the orders when he is ready.'

Imperial Palace

'Get Jackson Nakagawa on-line please.' The Emperor asked his personal assistant, moments later Jack's image appeared.

'Your Majesty,' Jack bowed in respect. 'How may I be of assistance?'

'I understand you are beginning a new phase of the war?'

'I am, Majesty.'

'Can I ask, how confident are you?'

'They will be defeated in months.'

'That is a very bold statement.'

'The loss of my parents was a very bitter pill to swallow, there was no reason for it, and I have promised to bring the criminal to justice.'

'Criminal is a very strong word.'

'It is mild as can be, every other description means I resort to profanity. Plishkin killed non-combatant civilians who were not in a war zone. The building was a private residence and the Russians targeted it regardless of who was there. That is a War Crime.'

'You are very passionate about this.'

'I make no apology, Your Majesty, up until now this war was a matter of principle. Now it is personal, and they will pay.'

'Very well, I would say good luck, but I do not think luck is going to play a big part in this.'

'Arigatō, Your Majesty. We will win.'

The hologram closed and the Emperor looked at the crown prince.

'I fear the Russians will regret their ill-advised attack on the homelands.'

'I agree father, I fear it is a huge cost, but it will end the war.'

Chapter 34
Operation Kraken

'Conference with Tyrell, please.' Jack requested, almost instantly the hologram came to life.

'Konichiwa, Tyrell.'

'Jack, how are things there.'

'Ramping up. We are nearing the end.'

'That close? What is next?'

For the next ten minutes Jack outlined his vision of how the war would progress.

'Does this meet with the Colonels approval?'

'It does seem to cover everything.' She replied.

'Everything with one exception. The enemy does not have a copy of the battle plan, it is up to me to force them into the position I want them. Drones is ready and I will be contacting General Ito shortly.'

'Good luck Jack.'

'Arigatō. Stay safe.'

Tyrell closed the hologram and turned to the Colonel. 'Now you get to see what he can do. I will have my steward ensure you are here every time I am. That will be as close as I can get to Jack's working hours. For now, get some sleep.'

'Thank you, Admiral.' She left with her mind in a whirl, how had she misunderstood the workings of the Generals mind? She decided that she would be able to write her master's thesis on this project alone.

Central Command

'General Nakagawa is on the line, Sir.' The hologram came alive and showed Jack smiling as he sipped his ever-present coffee.

'Konichiwa, Kei. I trust you and your teams are ready?'

'Konichiwa Jack. Ready as they will ever be. As you requested we have been flying through the area on a semi regular basis, the Russians do not seem to be interested in us.'

'Good, that is what I hoped would happen. I would like to get the others online too, is that ok?'

'Sure, go ahead.' The Hologram beeped with regularity as the other commanders and deputies joined the conversation.

'OK, this is the time. We will now begin the final phases of the war. Tonight, General Ito will deploy a new weapon, right under the enemy noses. The use will be brutal, but as the Russians will discover, we are in the business of brutal. I will give them a chance to reduce loss of life, but they will probably ignore it.'

'Tyrell, you and the fleet will be exposed as I expect this to play out at sea, have the special units been prepared?'

'All ready, Jack.'

'I will be running from the front lines. I will be with the 61st close to the left flank. The 59th will be on the extreme left. Towards the right flank, in order, 67th, 91st, 93rd, 97th, 99th, 131st, 132nd and the 150th on the extreme right. Armour and Cavalry with their respective infantry divisions.' Jack paused for a sip of coffee and to let his commanders catch up with their notes.

'Fleet. Be ready to dash into the Sea of Okhotsk. The enemy will be stalled when you are needed. Current estimates are less than 10 aircraft left serviceable, as for cruise and anti-ship missiles we must assume they are all available. Mike, your recon teams need to continue the assessment of the old airstrip, they may try to land troops there. Drones have some kamikaze and amazon units waiting to assist Mike. And send a couple of long range "big-eyes" (surveillance drones) to assist Tyrell.'

'Roman, can we move the 127s to keep the Russians occupied? If we can bring the 155s up a little closer, we can bombard their supply lines as well.'

'Consider it done.'

'Any questions?'

'We will need some extra ammunition for the guns,' Roman stated, the next delivery is expected tonight, can we get them pushed forward at the same time as the guns?'

'Certainly, get the supply teams to cover that.'

'What about our supplies? Ammunition and food?'

'General Ito will keep up the current rate of supply, we have sufficient ammunition and spare weapons at the stores depot in the rear. IF YOU NEED IT. GET IT! No excuses will be accepted.'

Another slight pause and then suddenly a different voice called out. 'Jack, we have been monitoring a number of Russian communications channels. SatCon analysis now shows multiple truck convoys approaching the Russian Fleet Base East.'

'Arigatō, Haruto. This is it people, they are beginning to fill their supply ships. Remember, your enemy is hungry, cold and dispirited. When they attack they will do so as desperate men. To paraphrase Sun Tzu "Do not press a desperate foe, always leave them a way out." We have given them a way out, but I doubt they will surrender, it is not in their nature. Good luck to you all.'

Tyrell watched as the hologram closed and he began to prepare his fleet. 'Well, Colonel, not quite how you first saw him, is he?'

'He certainly is not. He did not even refer to notes, you say it is all in his memory?'

'Everything is in there. Now get a little rest, we will be up late tonight.'

'Good evening Admiral, or should that be morning?'

'Morning, Colonel. You are just in time.' Tyrell pressed a button and the image of the cargo space on a huge air force transport appeared before them. Arranged in rows were what appeared to be gigantic brown spiders. Around half a metre across they sat, legs neatly folded into their sides and with some type of pack mounted on top of their backs.'

She could not stop herself, 'What the hell are they?'

Tyrell smiled. 'They, Colonel, are Jack's latest invention. He named them after the legendary sea monster that would drag ships to their doom, The Kraken.'

'How do they work?' Suddenly her curiosity was pulled away from the analysis of Jack's mind towards the serious business of war and the items being used to fight.

'They are an autonomous sea mine.' Jack suddenly appeared on the conference hologram. 'They will be dropped in the approaches to the Russian Fleet Base in Vladivostok where they will make their way close to the choke point of the deep shipping channel. When the time is right, they will be attached to the ships leaving the harbour, until that time they will lie on the sea-bed waiting.'

'Wont they be damaged by dropping into the water?'

'The pack on their backs is a parachute, they come down gently, and then swim away.'

'I am amazed, what happens to the parachutes?'

Jack grinned widely. 'That is the most amazing thing. They are made of a fabric that comes from corn starch, sugar and bamboo. They are coated with a substance that, on contact with sea water, causes them to dissolve completely. Twenty minutes after deployment there is no evidence of their existence. Tyrell, we have around two days before we expect them to put to sea, and around four to five days for them to be over the deepest portion of the sea. That is where we will stop them.'

'Very good, once we have the coordinates, we can keep just out of radar range.'

The three sat and waited for a few moments. Without warning the rear cargo door slowly opened and the surface of the sea could be clearly seen in the bright moonlight. As they watched the aircraft descended to the release height and the Krakens, were pushed out of the aircraft. The stream was almost never ending as they dropped row by row off the end of the ramp.

'How many are there?' The Colonel asked.

'Each aircraft carries two hundred and fifty. Tonight, we will be dropping five hundred.'

'That seems a lot?'

'Not really, five or six per ship; to ensure they sink quickly. I expect between twenty and thirty ships in this first convoy. They may have more to come. If all goes well, we will not need them. If it goes badly and the Russians try again, we will already have sufficient on site.'

Jack turned his head and called out, 'DRONES!' off in the distance the reply "Hai" could be heard. Then his image suddenly joined the conversation.

'How can I help?'

'Have the manufacturers given an expected underwater life for the Kraken?'

'Their data sheet shows a submerged serviceable life design of between two and four years.'

'Good. We can retrieve the unused units when a pickup system can be designed.'

'Actually, I have a prototype. It is only small, holds ten or so. But there is no reason it cannot be made bigger.'

'Well done. Put it either on the workload of the builders or on a back burner for after the war.'

'Arigatō, I will give it to the builders, they are so slow it may be needed to retrieve the "out of life" units after we are finished. Now I must go if I am to oversee the pilots as they put these into position.'

'Good work Drones. By the way, I expect the Russians will have minesweepers lead them out of the harbour, maybe even as far as Russky Island. I want to leave them alone; they are the one weak point of the Kraken.'

Before they could cancel the call, Mai emerged. 'Sorry to butt in, one of the pilots is a bit of a wizard with editing software. She created this map of the Sea of Okhotsk, with a slight modification.'

On the hologram an image of their operational area appeared. With Japan and the Kurils on the right side and the Asian mainland on the left, Russian Territory at the top it was a precision rendition of the entire Sea. Directly over the deepest portion of the water was a picture, originally taken from an ancient pirate chart, it depicted a sailing ship with the tentacles of a gigantic squid wrapped around it as it dragged the ship to the depths. Underneath the picture was the warning "Here there be monsters".

'That is awesome, get Haruto to hack it into the Russian Chart Database.'

'We thought you would like it, Haruto is already uploading it to their satellites, they download the latest charts as they need them, saves carrying copies that may be old and outdated.'

'Brilliant work, all of you. Arigatō.'

'You are welcome.'

'Did she just say you have modified the Russian Navigational Charts?' She asked.

'Well, not exactly changed, more of an included warning. It is not a good idea to make huge changes, their navigators are very good, if you change the depth readings, or channel markings they will pick it up really quickly, something like this is a minor change that they will have to be looking at to see and it does not alter the functionality of the chart.'

The Colonel fell silent and no one spoke for a few moments.

'General, Admiral. I have made a number of grave errors in my original assessment. If possible, I would like to begin again, in the near future.'

'I am ok with that, Jack?'

'Start now if you can keep up.'

'I will pack my bags and get a helo out to the island, if that is ok?'

'Certainly, Tyrell get a pilot that is familiar with the approaches, don't want an overly enthusiastic missile man shooting down the chopper.'

'What about me?' She asked, shocked that a passenger was dispensable item.

'Because you, like Tyrell, and me, we are all dispensable, in this environment the machine is very important. The passengers, not so much.'

'You tell Daisy that and see how far you get.' Tyrell almost shouted at Jack.

'Keep your hair on, I haven't been to the concert yet. Until that has happened YOU are the most important one here.' The two started to laugh and, eventually, the Colonel joined in; slightly unsure just how much was joke and how much was fact.

Chapter 35
War at Sea

'Welcome back to the real world, Jack.'

'Thank you, Roman. Are you where you want to be?'

'Given the constraints; the terrain, the hills and range we need to cover I would prefer to be around two hundred metres back. That way we can effectively drop shot over the hills on a short range. But if we stay here the enemy cannot get to us for the same reason and we can drop onto their supply routes as well, so this is a good compromise.'

'Good, gunners well rested?'

'I wanted to speak to you about that. We can sustain a huge rate of fire but only for a short time, the shell handlers get tired. 155s are heavy. We could do with some reserve muscle.'

'How many?'

'Therein lies the problem. With the numbers we have we could easily use three or four hundred.'

'Wow, that many?'

'Well, if you consider that each gun has a handling crew of eight or ten, we already have almost a thousand. If we can get extras, we can sustain fire for a very long time.'

'OK. Do you need to get them from Mexico, or can you go with untrained soldiers?'

'We can do untrained; they are only lifting the shells and cartridges.'

'If I give you the numbers, can you get them up to scratch in two days?'

'Sure, that is the easy part.'

Jack spoke into his communicator, 'Hasegawa, we need the biggest one hundred men from each division to be attached to the gunners for the duration. Speak with the Commanders and get them on duty at the heavy battery this afternoon.'

'Hai.' Was the only reply, and three hours later a thousand "trainees" arrived at the gun battery.

'You have just reinforced an entire battery from your existing troops, are your infantry not understaffed now?' The Colonel was frantically trying to juggle the numbers, but she was so far behind Jack that in the end she simply gave up and kept to making her notes and observations.

'The change is 1%, an acceptable variation. Illness due to lack of food can take 10% without fuss, so a 1% reduction is acceptable.'

The rest of the day was spent with Jack touring all the divisions under his control. Every infantry and cavalry division was visited and he made certain that they were all ready.

The medical staff were also on the list for a visit and Jack finished his meetings with "I hope you don't have anything to do."

When they arrived at the field kitchens there was a great deal of work going on.

'What are they preparing?' The Colonel asked.

'For the next three or four meals they will be on a high calorie high protein diet. Once we get fighting their meals will not be so luxurious, so we feed them the good stuff now.' Looking at the Catering Officer Jack asked, 'What have you planned for the next week?'

'Given the Russians are going to get a flogging, I suppose we will need to feed a lot of prisoners. They have been on starvation rations for a long time so we will have clear soups and bread ready for the first couple of days and then we can get them back on solids, once their digestive systems can handle it.'

'Good. What about delivering to the enemy lines?'

'We have a truck that can take several large kettles of food to the lines and we can move an entire field kitchen in a few hours.'

Jack sampled the food and his only comment was "That is good. You should open a restaurant when you leave the service. People will pay for that."

The Colonel tried it and she too was very pleased. Every time Jack spoke with someone, she could see the real concern for their welfare and their safety.

They finally made their way back to his field command position with the 61st division. Just as they sat down, she felt as though she could sleep for ever. All she heard was "Hasegawa, call to Northern Planning please."

All she could think was "Does he never stop!"

'Konichiwa, Jack. How can we help?'

'Any movement from the Eastern Fleet Base?'

'Not really. The usual harbour movements, water and fuel lighters and such. Ammunitioning was completed a couple of days ago. There is still a steady stream of trucks filling the freighters.'

'Numbers?'

'Freighters, eighteen, warships, of varying sizes, twelve. Three minesweepers, ten large harbour tugs.'

'Your thoughts?

'Spoke with Naval Command last night and they are thinking around 24 to 36 hours.'

'What time are the tides?'

'They will come out on high tide around midnight, the out flow for the next few hours will keep the sea ice out of the way and let them get to sea easily enough.'

'Get Drones, please.' Drones appeared before them.

'Hai?'

'I want to get the Kraken attached once the minesweepers have left the fleet, is that possible?'

'Sure, there is a bit of ice. NavCom (Naval Command) assures us that their minesweepers do not like the ice, hulls are not strong enough.'

'Good. Get them attached before Russky Island. I expect they will make it a high-speed run across the sea towards Urup. We will attack with plan "P".'

'Good idea. That will get us brownie points, maybe even their sailors will like us.'

'That is also a part of the plan. Arigatō, can you transfer me to Chie or Fumiko please.'

'Hai, Sayonara.'

The hologram was quiet for a few minutes and then 'Jack! So good to see you are safe.'

'Arigatō for your concern, Fumiko. Are you all well?'

'We are fine. Emika still has her moments but we are doing ok.'

'How about Hana and Asa?'

'They called earlier, they are doing ok, but it is still early days for them. They got calls from Sora and Reo they are doing well also.'

'Did you actually speak with them?'

'For a moment, then once I knew it was all ok, I let Mama do the talking.'

'Good, I will not be able to call for some time, so don't panic if you do not hear from me.'

'It doesn't matter if you call or not, I will still know if you are well or not. So, don't try to hide it.'

Jack smiled. 'Is it ever possible to beat a senkensha?'

'Some are not as forward as I am. So, you may be able to keep things from them, but not me.'

'You win. Hopefully it will not last much longer.'

Her voice lowered, 'Be careful, there is pain and suffering around you, not you but those near to you.'

'Thank you for the warning.' Jack turned off the hologram and the Colonel caught his eye.

'What did she mean by that?'

Jack then spent the next thirty minutes explaining the extraordinary skills of Fumiko and her family line.

'Can I ask, how is it that you can accept such "otherworldly" skills, surely as a Christian it goes against the church theology?'

'The traditions and capabilities of senkensha are well entrenched in Japanese life. It is as easy as accepting that Muslims do not eat pork. We accept the capabilities; her family and mine have centuries of history intertwined between us. We are accustomed to having her around, along with her capabilities. And we do not work within the usual theology of the church, we prefer to do it without the dogma or the priests.'

'Every time I learn something about you, it surprises me. Why do you think that is?'

'Most probably because I do not fit any of the usual boxes that we like to use to categorise what we know and what we understand about people. And that is just how I like it. I am not an open book, because I prefer to be a closed one. You are in a very privileged position, very few will ever get this close to being inside my brain. And I will say this only once, do not abuse the privilege.'

'Now it is time to rest, war will soon be upon us.' Jack leaned back in his chair and in seconds he slept.

The Colonel, however, did not. Sleep ran away from her as she tried to reconcile what she knew of human psychology, what so many years of university had taught her; what so many years of clinical practice had brought to her. None of it helped her to understand the enigma before her. Finally, she slept. And it was a deep dreamless sleep until she had a feeling there was an earthquake shaking her bed.

'UP!' Jack shouted as he vigorously shook her. 'Time to go to war.'

'Huh? What?' was all she managed to say.

'Haruto, assessment?'

'Heat blooms from machinery of at least thirty ships. Tide is starting its run out.

Minesweepers have left their berths.'

'Arigatō, Drones. Ready?'

'Hai!'

'All units on line.' All the commanders responded. 'We are live now. The enemy has begun to leave their Fleet Base. I want to know when we have all assets correctly deployed. I estimate we have three days at most.'

'Roman, wake them up.'

'With pleasure.' Just half a minute later the heavy crash of Romans 155s could easily be heard.'

'Big eyes enroute to enemy lines for assessment.'

'Inbound at airfield.'

'What have we got?'

'Looks like heavy helo transports.' Ten heavy transports were in the middle of landing on the damaged airstrip, and that was as close as they got.

'Was that you, Drones?' Mike Rodrigues already knew the answer; but asked anyway.

'Hai, Mike. How did we do?'

'Let's just say Kamov will be getting an order for replacements sooner rather than later. Sorry to say, no survivors.'

Sitting behind Jack as he orchestrated the weapons he had deployed, the Colonel thought there would be some cheering or at least a little jubilation. All she heard was silence as each of the commanders gave thanks it was not them. As each hour passed, she became more amazed as to how Jack and his team tried to minimise the casualties.

The shelling of the enemy base continued until the morning sun had well and truly risen. Following the last shell, in the eerie silence, Jack walked outside his room and faced the sun.

As he knelt, the Colonel noticed that he was wearing a katana. She only noticed it as he released it from its clasp and placed it before him. Tsuka to the right and edge pointing away from him; the samurai position for a warrior to collect his weapon and be ready to fight.

She was about to speak when Hasegawa grabbed her arm and put his finger to his lips, telling her to be silent. She understood and waited for him to finish.

Eventually, he bowed forward, his forehead on the ground. Then gathering his weapon in his hands, he stood up and clipped it to his belt. As he turned, he looked at Hasegawa and asked 'Reports?'

'Drones confirms correct attachment of Kraken units. NavCom confirms expected arrival in zone is 9am, day after tomorrow.'

'Local bombardment has taken down their generators again. Reports they have now completed an undersea link to the grid on Urup.'

'Good. Get Drones to put a couple of Kraken on the cable and blow it up six hours after we have dealt with their fleet. Speaking of the fleet, dare I assume that ours is still in one piece?'

'Admiral Backhouse reports all units in position and ready. "*Waiting for the Lord and Master to give instructions*"—his words.'

'Send a signal. "*I hope he was genuflecting when he said that*".'

Just moments later a reply arrived. "I am American, I bow to no one. But I will make an exception for him." Everyone laughed; just what Jack needed to lighten the mood.

'Haruto, anything from you?'

'Just that the Russians have accessed our new charts.'

Russian Flagship

"Navigator to the Admirals Bridge; Navigator to the Admirals Bridge." the main broadcast address system was insistent in its demands and the Navigator rushed to satisfy that demand.

'Admiral Litvak Sir, you wish to see me? What can I do?'

'Explain this on the chart, that will be a good beginning.'

The navigator looked and then looked again. 'I don't understand. I will check the database.'

He left for the Navigators chart room where he downloaded a new chart, it was the same. Then he tried a slightly different chart of the same area, then another and another, he quickly ran out of options.

No matter what he did, every chart of the Sea of Okhotsk had the legend in the middle, right across their expected track, "Here there be Monsters."

The navigator was not a religious man; he was a scientist, a mathematician and he was well versed in the ways of, and what was in, the oceans; he definitely did not believe in monsters. And yet, as he stood there alone in the charthouse, studying the charts, he prayed for salvation; from what he was unsure, but still he prayed to a god he did not believe in.

Returning to the Admirals Bridge he tried to formulate some response that would not see him getting deeper in trouble; a man like Anatoli Litvak was not to be trifled with.

'Admiral Sir, I have checked all the available charts. All the online two dimensional, and the three-dimensional hologram adapted, charts show the same image. I do not have any real reason for its existence. I have a very old paper chart that does not show it, I feel the archive copies may have been hacked by someone unknown.'

'I have checked with the individual ship Navigators and they all report the same image. Unfortunately, it is too late to get the charts changed. I have initiated a forensic examination of the database but I am unsure as to what they will find.'

'Very well, keep me informed. Meanwhile, can we use the charts?'

'Certainly, Sir. There appears to be no interference with the functionality.'

'Very good. Put the track data up for the fleet and don't forget to include the Kremlin and Central Command; the last thing we need is for them to be asking for information. Unfortunately, the trip across the sea is not a short one. I wish to change the track from the previously designated run across the North of Hokkaido, the enemy has a strong fleet there and we do not want to run into them. We will transit the west coast of Sakhalin and then hug the coast down to the eastern tip of the Poronayaskiy State Nature Reserve. From there it is just over two days to reach Urup.'

'A long time in open sea?'

'Yes, but we can assume the enemy cannot cover it all. They are, at last report, still covering the north of Hokkaido. Even they cannot be in two places at once.'

'I will prepare the charts and transmit them to the fleet.' As he left the Admirals Bridge, he could only think he was lucky to escape without censure.

Now he had to plot the fleet course through the narrow channel at the northwest of Sakhalin and the coast hugging transit down the east coast. "Thank god for computer navigation systems." He thought as he worked. "I do not know how people like James Cook and Ferdinand Magellan did it with only a sextant, stars and hope to guide their way."

Just two hours later the course was plotted and approved by Admiral Litvak and the fleet was directed to change course as they rounded the southern edge of Russky Island and began the long way round trip to the Sea of Okhotsk. None of them would feel safe until they had at least made it to the west coast of Sakhalin.

Jack's H.Q

'Jack,' Haruto suddenly appeared on the hologram, 'they have altered course to the north. Their new track was shown in detail of the hologram chart.

Course, speed, waiting points, order of ships through the relatively narrow channel. Convoy reassembly position, refuelling points, tanker rendezvous; every detail that had been painstakingly transcribed to the charts and transmitted to the Russian fleet now appeared in front of Jack and at the same time Tyrell and every ship's Captain and Navigator in the Allied Fleet.

'Fantastic work, Haruto. How did you manage to do this?'

'I encoded a reporting line in the modified chart. Any usage of the charts is sent directly to Northern Planning for assessment as well as to us.'

'Hasegawa, commendation for Haruto and his team for this work.'

'Hai.'

'Well done all. Keep it up.'

The hologram kept the enemy route displayed, as the conference closed off.

'General, is that as important as I think it is?' The Colonel asked.

'More important than anyone will ever know. We are now on the distribution list for their fleet movements. We no longer have to out think them, they are telling us what they are doing.'

'Drones!' Jack pressed the communicator. 'Get this data to your attack team, I want to know the best position to stop their transit.'

'Hai.'

It was only minutes before the optimum position for the coming confrontation had been established. The date and time had been set and all they needed to do now was to wait to see if the enemy fleet changed their plans.

There was nothing to do now except wait.

'Hasegawa, all unit commanders on line please.'

'Hai.'

In less than two minutes all of Jack's commanders were again waiting for instructions.

'OK, here is the current positioning of the enemy assets.' Jack put the positioning data up for all to see. 'As you can see, they are pushing up the west coast of Sakhalin right now. It will be a couple of days before they are in the open and away from support. The next move will be to disable them and then give them the option to surrender.'

A heavy murmur rolled through the collected officers; this was a very big gamble.

'What if they don't surrender? That is a big call getting a fleet to give in.'

'Very true; however, if they do not surrender, I will sink one or two and then give them a second chance.'

It was silent for a moment, then a voice quietly asked 'Who is going to push the button to sink entire ships?'

'Yes, good question. That will be my responsibility. Drones, you and Haruto get the chart hologram organised so I have an indicator and trigger. I want to be able to select and then destroy any one of the ships.'

'Consider it done, Jack.'

'Also, can we get a list of the ships and their manifests, please. I don't want to sink a ship full of fuel if I can get away with one full of potatoes.' A slight laugh emerged at the witticism, but no one was in doubt, many lives were in the balance.

'Tyrell, put your fleet around the bay on the northern most tip of Kunashir Island, you should be far enough away from their detection systems and only a day or so from the expected interception point.'

'Agreed, I have asked for tankers and supply ships to ensure we are fully prepared for battle. And I have asked for a hospital ship to be on standby, and for extra medical supplies just in case they have casualties.'

'Good, arigatō for that. Another box ticked.'

'Roman, Drones; continue your bombardment only as a measure to ensure they have not forgotten we are here, rotate your teams as much as possible.'

'Concur, and thanks to everyone for the extra gun crews; they are making us much more effective.'

'Any questions? No, good. Call me if something arises. Get as much rest as you can. When this goes up, we may get a little busy.'

The hologram closed and the teams all went about their business. Around half an hour later Hasegawa called out. 'Jack, His Majesty for you.'

Jack jumped and was at the hologram before it had displayed the Emperor's image.

'Your Majesty, an unexpected pleasure?' he enquired.

'Just a moment of your time before your world gets turned upside down. We all wanted to give you our best wishes and prayers for the successful completion of your mission. Even the Prime Minister sends his best.'

'Domo arigatō, Majesty. That is most thoughtful; we will do our very best.'

'Is there anything we can provide? Any way we can assist?'

'Actually, there may be one thing, but it is very difficult to ask.'

'Ask as you wish.'

'I feel the political will for this war may diminish markedly when the politicians become aware of the possible casualties; the Prime Minister was aghast when we told him of the Russian losses earlier. I do not want him to get over nervous and sue for peace, giving the Islands back, before we have exhausted our capabilities.'

'What do you want us to do? We can imprison him if that helps?' The Emperor was smiling widely as he spoke.

'As attractive as that appears to be, I am not certain that it is a practical answer to the problem.' They both laughed. 'I was actually thinking of having him stay at the Imperial Palace, as your "guest", to give "political insight" to the outcomes we engineer.'

It was simple to see that the Emperor was giving a great deal of thought to Jack's request.

'Are you absolutely certain you are not a politician? What you are asking is for us to imprison him with his oaths of office, to serve the country and The Imperial Family.'

'I prefer to call it a political point of view, to be given at any instant that you require it.'

'We can do that; it will be simpler if you can get a tactical overview for us to discuss.'

'Consider it done, I will get the SatCon Commander to come to the Palace to setup a Tactical Hologram with the latest data; you will see it as and when we do.'

'Arigatō, Jack. And please do not run for public office; you are so good at persuading people to do your bidding; you would end up with the opposition leader voting for you.'

'You have my word, Majesty, I will never be a politician. Two reasons, the first is I could not lie to everyone on a scale so large, and secondly Fumiko has told me that there is much more to be done in the future.'

'Really? Fumiko Maki has warned you of such a thing?'

'Fear not, Majesty, it is not a threat to our nation. But she cannot tell more at this time.'

'Very well. Good luck to you all. Sayonara.'

'Sayonara, Your Majesty.'

The hologram closed and Jack sat back, closed his eyes for just a moment and then ordered Haruto to Tokyo to setup the requested TacHolo for the Imperial Family.

It was a nervous wait for all. Jack and his team watching the clock to see where the enemy was positioned; The Imperial Family watching the slow pace of the enemy fleet as it crept down the east coast of Sakhalin; and the Russian High Command nervously expecting an attack at any moment and the Command Team of Admiral Litvak and his Russian Fleet wondering if the next hour was going to be their last.

As veterans everywhere would attest, the worst part is the waiting.

Admiral Litvak's Command Bridge

'Make a signal to the fleet. "We are now in a position of no return; we are about to turn to cross the Sea of Okhotsk on our final run to Urup." Now let us be ready, the next forty-eight hours will tell.'

Northern Planning

'Get Jack on the line!' The shout came from the team watching the enemy progress.

'Yes, what is it?'

'Sorry for the early start, Sir. The enemy fleet has just changed course for Urup. ETA at point "Alpha" (ambush site) 27 hours, give or take.'

'Very good. Arigatō, keep watch; and get Eiji on a chopper, please, I will need my interpreter.'

"And now it gets real." Jack said to no one.

'What gets real?' asked a sleepy Colonel as she entered the room.

'The enemy have turned for Urup; in just over a day it gets real. I hope you have had enough sleep.'

She didn't reply; firstly, because she was still so very tired, how did he keep going? And secondly it had suddenly dawned on her that it was almost time for people to die. This was a realisation and a feeling that, as she had suddenly discovered, she was decidedly uncomfortable with; and she was unsure as to how Jack could appear to be so blasé.

'How do you do it Sir?' she asked. 'Be so calm as you plan for men to die?'

'It is all in the planning. I do not plot for wholesale death, although that is a possibility if it all goes wrong; I will keep their people as safe as possible the same as I do mine. In the end it is their commanders that make the decision as to how many will die; none, a few, or almost all of them. In the end it will be their choice.'

As she turned away to get a cup of tea, she said. "This will make for an excellent study case for my Masters. I will be guaranteed a High Distinction pass."

Hearing her words, Jack stiffened.

'NO!' he shouted, as he turned to her. 'I will not permit you, or anyone else, to profit from the fighting and inevitable death that is yet to come. If you think that I am a candidate for your thesis then you have not learned anything about me. If you insist in continuing to push this forward as a tool for your recognition, I will have you jailed.'

'Jailed?' Her complexion began to pale. 'Under what charges?'

'Let's see; You come here to analyse my mental capacities and thought processes, that makes it a medical issue. Does it not?'

'I suppose I does.' She was instantly very unsure where he was going with his argument.

'As a medical assessment of a soldier in the Japanese Defence Forces my medical documents, including all assessments, belong to the Defence Forces and under Military law they may not be released to any entity outside the Defence Forces for any purpose; notwithstanding the possibility of disguising the subject.'

'Hasegawa? The proscribed penalty?'

Hasegawa, as always within earshot of Jack instantly replied from the next room, 'Three years imprisonment and disbarment from all medical authorisations. That includes a reciprocal deal with the Pentagon and by default the American Medical Authorities.'

'I assumed that I would be permitted to use my notes as I see fit, after all, it is my research.'

'It may be your research, but it is my mind and my thoughts and my emotions and I get to keep them, NOT YOU.'

She didn't speak for a few moments, the silence in the room was very uncomfortable. Eventually, she managed a few words. 'I apologise, General, I made assumptions I should not have made. I will pack my bags and leave immediately.'

'Oh no, you don't get off that easily. You will go and get breakfast and then you will come back here. You want to know what it takes to win a war? A war against a numerically vastly superior enemy? I will show you.'

She left the room and almost collided with Hasegawa as he entered. Neither man spoke until they heard the door slam behind her.

'That was good,' Jack said as he looked at his aide. 'How did you come up with the legal details so quickly?'

He looked Jack in the eye. 'I didn't, I made it up. But it is close to the truth, I think it is closer to "dismissal from the service" and "surrender of all clinical works". Either way she does not get her Masters, not out of your mind at least.'

'Arigatō.' Jack bowed to his friend. 'I can always rely on you to support me.'

'You are most welcome. Just make certain I am on your staff for whatever it is that Fumiko says we are going to get up to next, apparently it is going to be a lot of fun.'

'You have been speaking with her?'

'We have spent time together, yes.'

'Serious?'

'Not yet, but you never know what the future holds.'

'I think I need to keep an eye on you two.' Jack was almost laughing out loud.

'Not really, Chie, Tomoko and Reina are doing that.'

'Oh boy, we may be in more trouble than we think.' Both smiled as they thought of the implications of four of the most powerful senkensha ever, keeping watch on the two of them.

'OK, time to check we are ready in all respects.' The two began to travel methodically through every aspect of the campaign that had been put together. One by one, as each item was passed as "ready" and mentally "ticked off", on the checklist they began to relax.

Just as the Colonel returned Jack asked 'Can we get Drones up here. I need to be more comfortable with the Kraken controls before they get to Point Alpha.'

'He will be here in the same chopper as Eiji, said he wouldn't be anywhere else when it goes up.'

'Really?'

'Yes, he wants to see how you will use it.'

'Good, I like enthusiasm. Now, satellites?'

'Haruto reports information is flooding in. Apparently, the Kremlin has not yet worked out that we are using their data, and the reports are that they are still debugging the charts to see who uploaded the modified items.'

'Hmmm, that may be a problem. Get Haruto on the line.'

'Jack, Hai.' Haruto was on line before Jack had a chance to sit down.

'Konichiwa, dare I assume that the Russians will not be able to discover the origin of the modified charts?'

'Assume away, the web trail goes around in circles and crosses itself many times, but it always ends up at a web site called "The Deep" and any good hacker will end up discovering the moderator is one "Neptune, King of the Seven Seas" The only exception is one leg we put in which goes to "Poseidon", so they are just going to be chasing their tails. The server farm which runs the web site is on a small coral atoll in the southern Indian Ocean, or so the address will say.'

'I don't want to know the real details. Again, good work.'

The checking and approval continued for another two hours and they broke for lunch. Following on from a quick meal they returned to the rooms and as they were about to restart a voice came from behind.

'So, this is where you have been hiding? Your absence from the dojo has again been noted. You may give your excuses later.'

'Akio?' Jack spun around to see his friend looking at him. 'It is so good to see you. What are you doing here?'

'Me? I have come to see what you have been doing that is so important that you ignore your obligations to your dojo.'

Jack bowed deeply in a mock apology to his friend. 'I must apologise, Sensei, I have been assigned to this work by none other than the Emperor himself. It is not possible to attend to the Emperors wishes and be at the dojo at the same time.' His words, spoken in jest, sounded more of an abject apology than a joke between friends.

'For the Emperor? Then I think you may be forgiven…'

'Arigatō, Sensei. May I offer refreshments?'

'Hai, if you have real coffee, and not that dish water the air force serves either.'

Jack moved to the table at the opposite wall and made coffee for the Colonel and Hasegawa as well as his friend.

'About time, I see you still have the good coffee.' Akio commented as he took his first sip.

'Life is too short for bad coffee, Sensei.'

'Too true.'

Standing behind them a completely confused Colonel pulled Hasegawa aside, 'What is going on? I though the General was in command yet this man tuns up and it is almost as if the General is a new private?'

Before he could reply Jack turned, 'Sensei, may I introduce Colonel Jonson from the Pentagon, and you already know Hasegawa.' 'Colonel, nice to meet you; Hasegawa, good to see you again.'

'Konichiwa, Sensei.' Hasegawa replied with a bow.

'Colonel, what brings you so far from Washington?'

'I have been sent to assess the effects of battlefield stress and strain on the mental capacities of the Command team.'

'So, you are digging into Jack's brain? Good luck with that.'

'I am sorry? What do you mean?'

'I have been Jack's Sensei for a very long time. We were at the same school together, although we had different classes. As sensei part of my duties is to ensure that my students are mentally well prepared, as well as physically, and that they are focussed and ready. Very important aspects of the life of a practitioner of Martial Arts. Jack's mind has always been clear and focussed, he is probably the most well balanced, mentally, I have ever seen.'

'Interesting.' She replied.

'If I may add a little advice?'

'Please do.'

'Digging into Jack's mind will bring you no benefit, he will only discuss those issues he wishes to. Do not try to get information out of him before he is ready, he will only give voice to thoughts when they are fully formed and no amount of pressure will change that.'

'So, no one can get him to express his feelings? Or innermost issues?' Jonson kept pushing for answers.

'The only one, so far, is Fumiko. But then she already knows the answers before she asks the questions.'

'So, why does he need his Sensei, here? Now?'

Akio smiled as he replied, 'HE doesn't. I am here to assist the unit commanders.'

Colonel Jonson tried not to look perplexed, but her understanding of the human thought processes was being undermined every time she learned something more; she finally came to the conclusion that a lifetime with these men could not unravel the innermost workings of their thoughts.

'I must ask, why is a civilian permitted here? Even with the work you have been given.' Hasegawa asked the question that all were thinking.

'You are looking at "Honorary Major Akio Takamatsu" Sensei to the Northern Army.' Bowing as he spoke.

'YOU? A MAJOR, that is one for the books. How?'

'Following on from the losses early in the campaign, the Emperor asked General Onishi to get a sensei to assist in the preparations. Motoyuki asked me if I was available. It took a while for them to train me, marching, weapons and such; but here I am.'

Just a few moments later Drones and Eiji entered.

'Konichiwa, Jack, everyone.'

'Konichiwa Drones, Eiji.' Introductions were made all round, 'Good flight?'

'Even with the advances of flight and propulsion, it always seems too long; but it was comfortable and smooth enough.'

'Good. Drones, set up the control on the desk. Eiji, I have brought you here as I may need translation at short notice, so make yourself comfortable; do you need a desk?'

'Only a small one, Jack.'

'OK, we will get one from somewhere. Under the windows good enough?'

'Hai.' Moments later two supply privates arrived with a desk, chair, lamp and the usual office supplies as well as a computer terminal.

Just ten minutes after arrival Eiji had his workstation running.

'Hmm, interesting,' he mused.

'Spill it, what is interesting?'

'The Kremlin has just sacked ten IT Colonels for not being able to track the origin of the charts. By the language they are using, and their conversation, they are getting frustrated and some of the more senior Generals are beginning to make arrangements for life after the war.'

'That is excellent, keep it up. Now I think we can bring a little more pressure to bear.'

Colonel Jonson was about to ask when Drones announced, 'Command Terminal is ready. We can ramp it up at your convenience.'

'Are the Kraken in place between Iturup and Urup?'

'In position, secured and primed. Push the button to send them back to the stone age, again.'

'OK, gather round people. Drones show me how this works.'

The group gathered near Jack's desk, almost jockeying for the best view.

Jack took his seat and waited for Drones to begin.

Arranging the control panel directly in front of Jack, Drones began to show the effects of each button. Just three minutes later Jack was ready.

Using the control unit, which looked remarkable like an old-fashioned computer trackball, he hovered over a "KIL" (Kraken Indicator Locator). Just before he pressed the detonator he asked 'Drones, do you think we should have a diversion of some sort? Just to take the emphasis off the Kraken.'

'Given this is the first use, that may be a good idea. It will keep the enemy guessing. As far as Eiji can tell they us they have no information on the existence of Kraken units.'

'Good let's keep it that way.' Pressing his communicator, he called out, 'Roman? Tyrell?'

A moment later the two replied 'Hello, Jack. What do you need?'

'I am about to begin the first phase of the assault forward. Can we get a light bombardment of the enemy base in thirty minutes?'

'Sure, call when you are ready, I will get the gunners ready.'

'What do you need from the Fleet?'

'Nothing yet, be aware they will most likely increase speed when they finally get the word the base is in trouble again; so, we may need to advance timings to accommodate them.'

'OK, thanks for the heads-up.'

'Drones, can we get ten Amazons to shake their generators and comms towers again?'

Looking up from his workstation, hastily set up beside Eiji's desk, Drones replied, 'Already on their way, strike in twenty-three minutes.'

'Good, we shall co-ordinate from here. Drones you have the timings.'

'Hai.'

Colonel Jonson watched from the far side of the room, Akio standing next to her. 'Is this how he does it? This is how he begins a campaign?'

'It is; he has contacted all the Group Commanders involved, they have their orders and he has given the timing to the one man that is positioned to coordinate the strike.'

'Listen carefully,' Hasegawa added, 'Drones will ask for data if he needs it, and he will give the firing orders.'

'Not the General?'

'No, Drones is controlling the timing, watch.'

As the timing clock slowly wound down, every-one was silent.

When the clock showed ten minutes to go, 'Roman, time of flight please?' Drones voice almost frightened Jonson, so unexpected was it.

'Forty-seven seconds.' Came the reply.

'Arigatō.'

Still the clock wound down.

Again, suddenly. 'One minute. All units report.'

'Battery ready. Amazons ready. Kraken ready.' Even Jack had to report to the controller.

'Battery, ENGAGE.' Drones gave the order exactly forty-seven seconds before the strike time.

'SHOOT.' Came the instant reply from Roman, and in the distance, they could hear the thump of the 127s as the engagement began.

They almost held their breath as Drones studied his stopwatch. Ten seconds, five, four, three, two, Amazons, go; Kraken GO.

Off in the distance they heard the, almost single blast as the co-ordinated strike fell on the Russian positions.

General Plishkin's Command Post

'Dammit, do they never give up?' The rhetorical question was fired at anyone that was close enough to hear it.

'Damage reports!'

'Power is out, switching to emergency generator, General.'

'Gun battery received extra damage.'

'Comms tower is down, again.'

'And without guns we cannot strike back. I will personally kill every Airforce General and Navy Admiral if I ever get out of this unholy mess that they have left us in.' Plishkin's staff could sense a tirade coming up and they instantly found other "more pressing" duties that needed their presence elsewhere, anywhere away from the General. 'Just wait until the supply convoy arrives, then we will give it back to them.'

Jack's HQ

'Reports as they come in, if you please.' Jack requested.

Eiji was first to answer. 'Intercepted communications appear to show that Plishkin has just blown up at the Kremlin. He is now demanding the convoy arrive at the first opportunity.'

Jack sat stony faced; 'Thought so,' he whispered to no one in particular.

'Convoy has increased speed, new ETA at point Alpha of sixteen hours plus or minus a few minutes.'

'Arigatō, Haruto.'

'Enemy comms tower destroyed, generator building in rubble, again; they may have power in three to five hours, depends on the level of damage under the broken building. No indication of knowledge of underwater explosions.'

'Arigatō, Drones.'

'Well done to all. Stand down for fourteen hours.'

Everyone left to relax for a while; if it all went as Jack planned, and whatever didn't go as he planned, the Russians would be wondering how to move ahead, if they could move at all.

'Where are you going Colonel?' He asked as she made her way to the door.

'You did say stand down. Didn't you?'

'Yes, but do you see any of the Command Group leaving?'

It was then that she realised that they were all still in the room; Drones, Eiji, Hasegawa were all still concentrating on the displays and information coming from them. Jack and Akio were deep in conversation in one corner. Every so often a report was made and Jack would either give a quick order or he would simply acknowledge the report with "arigatō".

She was frantically making mental notes and formulating questions for them when, suddenly, Jack said 'Agreed. Prepare yourself.'

With those simple three words Jack and Akio left the room and ten minutes later they reappeared; this time in full samurai armour. 'You challenged me,' Jack said, 'I choose katana and wakizashi.'

'Done.' Akio responded to the weapons preference.

The two walked out, in front of the building and as they did so Jack heard Drones.

'Haruto, get some vision of the front of Jack's office, send it to every screen we have. The troops need to see what he is doing, while they are resting.'

'Hai.' Was the muffled reply. And almost instantly every screen from Iturup, to the fleet, to Northern Planning, Central Command and even the Imperial Palace showed the two combatants facing off.

It was a sight that could have come from a Kurosawa film, two samurai facing off. Warily circling each-other waiting for the right moment. A feint here, a foot skip there; each testing the preparation of the other.

Without warning Jack jumped forward and scored two hits closely followed by three return blows from Akio. Now the preliminaries were over, it was time for a real fight and the two each rained blows on the other seemingly non-stop. For over thirty minutes they pummelled and cut away at their opponent trying to gain the ascendency.

Eventually, one had to make a mistake, this time it was Jack. His back foot slipped as he began a forward lunge and the resulting blows on the arms and head saw him fall to the ground.

For the next three minutes he defended himself, but he could not regain his feet and he resigned his mind to defeat. Holding his arms wide out to the sides he released his weapons in surrender.

Just as suddenly as they had begun, Akio stopped. Bowing to his friend he offered a hand to assist him rise. Jack took the offered hand and then bowed in return.

'You have had more practice than I have, and it shows.'

'Arigatō, but you did not see the enormous effort it took for me to overpower you. Even without practice you are a difficult opponent.'

Hasegawa and Eiji emerged from the office with drinks and some assistance to remove the armour. Seemingly from nowhere chairs appeared and the surrounding spectators eventually melted away back to their barracks.

Suddenly Jack shouted 'MEDIC!' and within a minute his personal medic Sergeant Furukawa appeared at his side. As he began to ask what was the problem Jack raised his left hand and the distorted position of the little finger was the only information that was needed to be conveyed.

'Not again! How many times do I have to tell you, get it strapped before a workout!'

'Just fix it, if you please.' Jack's reply was given with the smile that told his medic that he was not angry at being mocked by his medic; it had almost become a game between the two.

'Sensei, if you please?' Furukawa indicated Jack's arm and Akio held it tight for the medic to relocate the errant finger. A little strapping was all that was then required to complete the job.

'Arigatō. One day I will get it fixed.'

As he took his drink he mused 'I wonder,' Jack asked. 'If this outfit is bullet proof?'

'That is easy to test,' replied Akio interested in the concept. 'I have a spare set, let us test it.' A wave of Jack's hand and a soldier appeared to assist Akio to set up the spare armour.

Once mounted on the back of a chair a pistol was aimed at the centre of the Do (chest plate). The first shot gave the answer. A 9mm pistol round would not go through. Then an assault rifle with its high-power round could not get a 5.57mm round through. A 7.62mm (mini-gatling gun) was tried next and it managed to breach the inner most layer but still it did not get through.

'Impressive, I don't think it is worth trying a 50 calibre, they make a mess of just about anything.' Jack was impressed but a 50 was a serious bullet to try to stop.

'Akio was of a slightly different opinion. Let's try anyway. This gusoku (armour) is done for anyway.'

One final test was setup. To everyone's shock, the 50-calibre round did make it through but its inertia was spent as it exited the inner layer of the Do. Any injury would be eminently survivable.

Jack looked at Akio and he looked back. 'One more layer of Kevlar could make this useful.' Akio commented.

'Come inside.' Was all Jack said, and they went into the H.Q. building. The others followed and as they entered Jack and Akio were not to be seen.

Uncharacteristically they had entered Jack's private room and closed the door.

Jack's private room

The room was sparsely furnished, a bed, a trunk for his uniforms, a small wardrobe, desk and chair for personal work and an ensuite for his private use.

Jack sat on the bed and Akio sat on the chair.

'What is with the Colonel? She seems fairly put out over something.'

'The Pentagon sent her, some bullshit about assessing the mental capacities of the command team in a combat scenario.'

'Sounds like your assessment is close to the truth.'

'She eventually admitted that she was using the time to get the information to complete her thesis for her Master's Degree.'

'That sounds rude to me, why is she still here? I thought you would have sent her packing by now.'

'I was going to, but she had already been appraised of many items that are still secret.'

'And so, you decided to keep her here.'

'Yes, and I have expressly forbidden her to use any information about me or my methods that she gains from her inclusion.'

'It actually sounds typical of the Pentagon; do as they wish and bad luck to everyone else involved.'

'Hai, she was unimpressed when I threatened her with jail time.'

Akio spluttered, resulting in a coughing fit as he tried to recover from inhaling his drink instead of swallowing it. Eventually, he was able to ask 'How?'

Jack recounted the conversation and when he was finished Akio simply stated, 'You have not changed since we were in school. A well framed statement would always confuse the ones not ready for it.'

'I try,' Jack replied. 'Now some food,' he called out and, in a few minutes, meals were on the desk.

'You tested the armour, Jack. Are you thinking what I think you are?'

'You know, you are the one person that I could never hide my intentions from. I was thinking maybe I could make some sort of statement, when I force the Russians to surrender.'

'If you do it, then so will I.' Akio laid down the challenge.

'Then I shall get in touch with the manufacturers, see if it is possible to get an extra layer of Kevlar; if not, well it is still as good as the issued body armour we already have.'

The call to the makers did not yield any improved armour, the extra layers would be very difficult to include. There were some new materials that were being tested, but their efficiency would still take a couple of years to prove.

'If you can get a set of your armour sent to my home; I will arrange for it and a couple of weapon sets and my armour to be sent here.'

'Agreed, but let's not tell anyone. We should just turn up one morning. We can't get it here for today but next time; and it will send the Colonel into a tailspin when we do.'

The two grinned at each other.

'She will be so confused, the two of us turning up in armour.' Akio could already see the amusement that they could have at her expense. 'Let her write about that!'

'Yes, maybe I will let her write it, just to see how she handles it. But for now, let's see how the enemy likes my next surprise.

With that the two left the private office and checked up on the progress.

'Enemy has slowed a little, one freighter has a propeller shaft bearing problem, they are trying to fix it without stopping.' Was the first report that came through.

'Good, keep our timing as it is. We can take them when we are ready. Drones!'

'Hai.'

'Are your Kraken pilots rested?'

'Hai, you have control over the deployed units and the pilots are ready for the next assignment.'

'Very good. Commence Operation "Harbour Master", if you will.'

'Hai.'

Drones began to issue the commands to the pilots and within an hour he reported back.

'Harbour Master is initiated. The deployment will be ready to commence in five hours, completion one hour after.'

'Very good, let me know when they are ready.'

'General Onishi, please.'

Hasegawa put through a call to General Onishi's office.

'Jack, how are you? All going well in the North?'

'Motoyuki, yes, all is well. I have instigated Operation Harbour Master. Ready in six hours. I would like to begin preparations for Operation Postal Service.'

'Postal Service? Are you certain?'

'Hai, preparations only; packaging, route planning, delivery systems etc.'

'I will need the Emperor's Authority for this.'

'I can contact him, if that is what you wish?'

'No, no, you have enough to do.'

'Arigatō. Keep me informed.'

'I will, and good luck Jack.'

'Arigatō.' The call ended and everyone in the command room was looking at Jack.

Jack looked around and finally said, 'What? Why are you all staring at me?'

'Are you really going to go ahead with "Postal Service"?' Hasegawa was the one that asked the question that all the others wanted to, none of them wanting to know the answer.

'Not the full plan,' was Jack's reply, 'just inert. We will need to get them to the table and I feel that is the most effective way.'

'If I can speak freely?' Drones asked tentatively.

'Go ahead, you don't need permission.'

'Jack, we are all very concerned about "Postal Service". What if something goes wrong?'

'The units will be completely inert, no one will be able to use them as they were designed. Their purpose is to get the enemy to the negotiation table. Pleading, begging and international pressure have not been successful and I for one am weary of the politician's inability to resolve the problem. If we use this method there will be a resolution and a lasting peace.'

'Then we shall follow your example. Yes?' Drones looked around the room and was rewarded by nods of approval; not only for his raising the issue but for the way Jack was pushing for the completion of the war.

Off to one side Colonel Jonson asked "What is Operation Harbour Master and what is Operation Postal Service?"

'You will be told when the time is right.' Jack replied, even though he had not been addressed in the initial question.

'I am sorry, sir. I should have asked directly.'

'Yes, you should have. But the answer would still be the same. There are only six or seven people in the world that know the details and the Emperor is required to permit any more being included. I am not going to bother the Emperor with that at this time.'

The Colonel did not reply, Jack's tone had been stern enough for her to realise that a discussion was not going to change his decision.

'General, even without knowing the details can I ask who it was that created the operations?'

Jack was concentrating on the hologram before him. 'Move the 59th a little further west, there is a chance of enemy action moving up that rise, towards Mike Rodrigues. Colonel, you have already been told I created the entire battle sequence, just what part of that statement is confusing you?'

'My apologies.'

'Accepted. Drones, ready for some fun?'

'Certainly.'

'Hasegawa contact all divisional commanders. I am about to rattle Plishkin's chains, he may get a little upset.'

'Hai.' Hasegawa replied.

'Drones, let's have some fun.'

Jack began to select the ships in the convoy, as they were displayed before him. Once all the required Kraken units were selected, he called for a connection to the Imperial Palace.

'Jack, you have some information?'

'Hai Majesty, I wanted to inform you that I am about to take the next step.'

'Approved, we will not watch from here, it may be somewhat distressing.'

'Agreed, I will keep you informed.' The connection with the palace was terminated and Jack rose from his chair and went outside, facing east he knelt and bowed his head.

'What is he doing now?' Colonel Jonson asked Hasegawa in a quiet whisper.

'You are a slow learner, aren't you? He is praying that he does not have to kill thirty thousand men this afternoon.'

'Thirty thousand?'

'YES, the enemy convoy has infantry reinforcements embarked, if he sinks the wrong ship twenty-thousand will likely die in the first half hour.'

Jack remained kneeling for a full five minutes. Eventually, he raised his head, made the sign of the cross on his left breast and then stood up. Everyone in the command room was watching him silently.

'It is time.' Jack said as he pushed the "Detonate" button on the console.

Chapter 36
Loss of a Convoy

Admirals Bridge, Russian Flagship

Admiral Anatoli Litvak was sitting in the Command Bridge of the flagship. he had even slept there one night as he was so worried that some misfortune may befall them.

'Admiral, Sir. Acoustic Systems Report multiple underwater explosions.' The Admirals signalman offered the report tablet for Litvak to read.

'What do you mean? Are they earthquakes or volcanic…' at that moment the entire ship seemed to heave underneath them and then suddenly slow to a complete stop.

'What the hell was that?' Grabbing the microphone, he called the captain. 'Captain, what has happened? Have we run aground?' The last question was asked without thinking about the fact that the sea bed was hundreds, if not thousands, of metres below them.

'Unsure at the moment, Sir. Waiting for damage reports. Engineering reports the shaft has stopped rotating; command reports the ship does not respond to steering orders.'

'What is this about underwater explosions?'

'Just getting a reply from the fleet, sir.'

A few anxious minutes went by without explanation of the sudden change in fortunes. Eventually, the Admirals phone rang, the ring tone shattering the tense silence.

'What is the problem, Captain?'

'The entire fleet are reporting the same sir, no propulsion and no steering?'

'Find out why!' Litvak was nothing if not abrupt.

Jack's Command H.Q

'System shows all appropriate Kraken units have detonated, Jack,' Drones reported.

'SatCon?' Jack asked.

'System shows convoy is not moving forward. All ships are floating without engines or steering.' Haruto added.

'Submarines?'

'Unable to tell at this time. We expect them to surface in the next ten minutes.' 'Very good, we wait.'

Russian Flagship

Unable to hold his patience any longer, Admiral Litvak picked up the phone, 'Well Captain, what is going on?'

'Sir we have tried to contact the submarines, one is not responding and the other is reporting the same symptoms with the added problem of flooding in the after compartments.'

'Order them to surface and get those damage reports!'

It was to be a few more tense minutes before any information was to become available. The damage reports showed the rudders and propulsion systems had been damaged by the mysterious explosions, on every ship.

'What can do that?' was the question asked almost simultaneously by the Admiral and the Captain. At that very moment the hologram beeped frantically with a priority message incoming on the international emergency channel.

'Good day Admiral Litvak, I see your convoy has stopped at sea.'

'Who the hell are you?' The captain asked as he looked at the image of a Japanese man, dressed in the casual kimono of a samurai from centuries before.

'I am both surprised and hurt that you don't recognise me. I am General Jackson Nakagawa, Commander of the Northern Army; or as you are probably calling me "That damned Japanese Pest" I know that your General Plishkin has called me that.'

'Nakagawa! What have you done?'

'I have stopped your fleet and here is what you are going to do. First you will shut-down all electronic communication and surveillance systems; second, you will shut-down all weapons targeting systems; third, you will order all your crews to move to their leaving ship positions, civilian crews will board their lifeboats and military will stand-by their rafts.'

'I will do no such thing!'

'You will, and you have five minutes to comply.' Jack was calm and in control.

'I will blow you out of the water!' Anatoli was about to burst a blood vessel.

'Four minutes and thirty seconds.'

'He is bluffing.'

'You think so?'

'Certainly.' The captain was so certain he was right, but even so, deep in his gut, something did not feel right.

The clock seemed to slow even further as they watched the second hand rotate; it felt as though they were watching their lives expire.

'Time is up, will you comply? I will give you five more minutes.'

No one replied this time and the audio on the hologram went silent as the mute button was selected at both ends.

'What are you going to do, Jack? If they don't comply?'

'Let's wait and see what they do first.'

Again, the clock slowly wound down.

'Time is up Admiral, what is your decision?'

This time there was no reply, the images could be seen conferring on the Admirals Bridge, but there was still no sound.

Jack waited patiently, but it was as though he was not even there.

Suddenly the sound boomed through on the Russian ship.

'Freighter, 17907. "Boris Pushkin". Your crew has two minutes to enter and launch the lifeboat!'

'Jack,' called Haruto, 'they have launched their life boat, and are now two hundred metres away.'

'Arigatō.' Jack moved his cursor to the "Boris Pushkin" and pressed the detonate button. It only took the "Pushkin" two minutes before it rolled over and sank. Every eye in the Russian fleet watched, disbelieving the sight before them.

'Now Admiral, will you comply with my demands?'

There was a distinct silence on the hologram, everyone was waiting for the Admiral to reply; and yet he said nothing.

'Come now Admiral, you have just lost thirty thousand tonnes of food and water. Do you want to lose more?' Haruto sent a message which Jack read while still on the hologram, 'My staff tell me that the crews of your freighters are now leaving their ships. What are you going to do?'

Still no reply. The minutes ticked by as they waited for the Russians to formulate their response.

'I will give you the choice, either the "Oceanic God", or the "Oceanic Goddess". Which is it to be?' Jack had deliberately named both the former cruise ships that carried the bulk of the thirty thousand or more troops being sent as reinforcements.

'NO, DON'T!'

'Ah, so you are still listening, good. Do you agree to my demands?'

'Yes; Captain signal the fleet, shut-down all communications, weapons control and surveillance systems.'

'Arigatō, now let's see if they do.'

There was always going to be one Commander that would try to get away with non-compliance. Jack's teams, Drones with the "Big Eyes", Haruto with the satellites and Tyrell with the fleet electronic warfare systems were all waiting for the "one".

'Jack, missile control radar still active on the small frigate.' Reported Tyrell from far over the horizon.

'"Illya Kozlov" has not shut-down, Jack,' confirmed Haruto.

'Drones, indicate the Kozlov.'

As Jack watched his Battlefield Integrated Control Hologram, or "BItCH" as they called it, the indicator for one of the ships turned from blue to red.

'Got it, arigatō.' Jack pressed the button again.

Colonel Jonson almost cried when he did. The others were equally dismayed but did not show any emotion. Just three minutes later the red dot disappeared.

'How could you do that?' Jonson demanded. 'You just killed hundreds of men!'

Jack, disappointed at her outburst, turned his head suddenly and glared at her. She got the message and just as suddenly became quiet.

'Now, Admiral, Have I got your attention?'

'You have.' Litvak replied begrudgingly.

'Good. Now if one of your subordinate commanders decides that he will use his communications systems, be that radio, internet, satellite or even telephone, I will sink two more of your ships; and one will be your flagship. Do you understand me?'

'I do.'

'One of your submarines has failed to report in. I suspect that they had left some watertight doors open, in contravention to your fleet orders. When their hull was breached, they have most likely failed to contain the flooding. We will attempt to locate this unit and determine if any crew survived.

'The remaining ships will shut down and send their crews to their "leaving ship positions" I will send a single warship to each, one at a time. That ship will take the crew off and take the ship in tow. This will take some time to complete and I will permit the preparation of some foods for those ships that will be waiting the longest.'

'The cruise ships which have the army units embarked will be towed without having the occupants removed. DO YOU UNDERSTAND?'

'We do.'

Aside Jack spoke with Drones. 'Activate Operation Harbour Master.'

'Hai.'

'Admiral, you will no doubt receive a call from the Kremlin demanding your activities. I will respond on your behalf, in the spirit of "Brothers in Arms" I will keep you informed of such discussions.'

'Thank you, General. Do I have your word that my sailors will be treated well?'

'They are still alive, aren't they? Of course, we will treat them well. However; any that decide they will try to take matters into their own hands will result in action being taken against another fleet unit as well as their own.'

'Where will we be taken?'

'A small island has been prepared as a prison for you until the war is over. Tyrell, send a ship to tow the flagship to their destination.'

'On its way, Jack.'

'Arigatō. Admiral Litvak, if you wish to discuss anything please raise a white flag and we will contact you; I remind you, do not try to use communications equipment.'

The call was terminated and Jack visibly relaxed. 'That was tense. I need a coffee.'

A cup appeared before him and as he took a sip he asked 'A good outcome, I think?'

All agreed with the notable exception of Colonel Jonson.

'What is the problem Colonel?' You don't like my methods, I bet?'

'You killed hundreds of men without thought. What kind of monster are you?'

'You flatter me. You think I am a monster?' Jack rose from his seat and moved so close to her their noses were almost touching. 'Let me tell you this, I saved the lives of around forty thousand soldiers and sailors today. Yes, a hundred or so died, but their compatriots are still alive. If they do as I say they will be returned to their families.'

'You wanted to see how a combat commander operated, you wanted to see inside my brain, you wanted to get personal benefit from this? Not quite what you thought, was it? You call me a monster? I have not yet released my monster; but I have woken him, and he is hungry for victory! Put THAT in your thesis.'

Jack turned around and sat at his desk, sipping his coffee as he watched Tyrells fleet begin the task of towing the Russian fleet to Japan.

As he watched, his friends could sense that he was about to begin the next phase, and they waited for the inevitable orders.

'Haruto, show me the Fleet Base at Vladivostok.'

The BItCH showed the complex system of active, repair and building berths, the massive buildings and barracks of the huge base.

'Zoom in on the active berths.' While he watched, Colonel Jonson decided that she would try to leave the room; try to get her thoughts together. 'Where are you going Colonel? We are not yet done.'

Reluctantly she returned and, along with the others she watched as Jack prepared to launch another assault.

'Drones, are we ready?'

Drones conferred with his pilots and replied 'Hai.'

'Put them up.' The hologram began to populate with blue indicators all over the Russian base. 'Link all.' The blue dots turned red, and when he was ready Jack pressed the button.

Russian Fleet Base, Vladivostok

'What is going on?' The base commander demanded. As he looked out of the windows, he could see every vessel had begun to settle by the stern at their moorings. 'Reports?'

Assistants were running in every direction; emergency services were unsure which stricken ship to attend to first. It was complete chaos for over an hour. Eventually, some reports began to emerge, and following on from those reports the picture was coming together. Some type of unexpected attack had been carried out. Casualties were very light, it appeared that only ten or so had died and a couple of hundred injured, mostly not seriously.

The Base Commanders hologram came to life again on the emergency channel.

'Commander, I would wish you good morning but I do not think you would share my sentiments.' Jack was being as cordial as he could be bothered. 'You will, by now, be aware that the Fleet heading for Urup is disabled and under my control. To prevent you from attempting to provide assistance I have crippled every ship in the Vladivostok base. Do not try to send ships from elsewhere, do not try to call for assistance from other bases. I will sink them if you force me to.'

Baltic Fleet Base

'What do you mean the submarines have been disabled?' The Base Commander was incredulous. 'How has this happened?'

'We are unsure as to how, but the enemy has apparently blown the propulsion and steering mechanisms off every submarine in the base.'

'Get me reports, I will contact the Kremlin.'

Northern Fleet Base, Murmansk

'How did the enemy get into the base? Have we got any boats ready to go to sea?'

'None, Sir. They have all been disabled.'

'Signal the boats at sea, "Proceed to friendly ports, do NOT, repeat NOT return to Fleet bases." Give them a rundown on the activities at Vladivostok and the Baltic.'

The Kremlin

'Explain yourself?' the President demanded. The Navy Chief of Staff began to outline the problems that had befallen them.

'How is this even possible?'

'I do not know, Mr President.'

'Send the Air Force. They can deal with it.'

'We have tried, they have already destroyed every aircraft we have on the east coast.'

'We may be able to get through this; the public must not know.'

Jack's Headquarters

'Haruto, can we put the recorded interview on the Russian Television system?'

'Soon as you wish. I will patch it through their satellites.'

'Let's do it now, we need to get them on the back foot.'

The State-run television broadcasters had no control over their system, it had been hijacked and they could not stop it from transmitting. Everything they tried, shutting-down the transmitters, closing the stations. Turning the satellites off; it was all to no avail. They simply had to sit down and wait for the control to be returned to them.

The private television stations were under no such constraints. The political masters tried to restrict them but that genie had long since left. They broadcast anything they wanted; and in the interests of ratings they broadcast Jack's message, fearful that if they did not, they would be left behind.

Jack's message was not one of doom and gloom. He simply told the Russian people about the numbers of ships and aircraft that had been lost, along with the crews, and that those losses were the responsibility of the politicians and if they had kept their word, war would not have been an issue.

The riots began in Vladivostok, the police may have tried to stop them if it were not for the fact that so many members of the police force had family serving in the defence forces. They already knew of the losses and the heartbreak that they brought, and they were not in the mood for more lies from Moscow.

It didn't take long. The rioting began to spread; Novosibirsk was the next, closely followed by Yekaterinburg and St Petersburg and soon the people were in the streets in Moscow. All across the country the people were demanding the politicians give those paltry islands back and stop the fighting.

Chapter 37
Loss of a Control

The Office of the President, The Kremlin

'We need a distraction; we need to get a victory over the Japanese so that we can resume some sort of normality. A win on Iturup will at least keep the crowds quiet for a while,' the Home Affairs Minister demanded.

'How? Is it even possible to defeat them? Will we be able to remain in office?' were just some of the often-repeated responses from those present.

Eventually, the President demanded quiet; it was obvious that the debate was going nowhere and he needed to take control of what was left of their political careers.

'Get General Plishkin on the hologram.' Moments later the Image of General Illya Plishkin appeared on the very poor-quality hologram transmission.

'How may I help?' he asked wearily, in between the explosions heard nearby. His unshaven chin and drooping eyes and dirty uniform giving him the appearance of a man that desperately needed sleep, food, reinforcements, information and more sleep.

'Why are you not able to defeat the Japanese? You have the men and the resources, don't you?'

'NO. We have been under constant attack for months. Ever since we managed to dislodge their General his replacement has been attacking us.'

'Why have you not stopped him? You do command an army?' The president was a very unsympathetic man at the best of times, right now he was not being overrun by feelings of enthusiasm and confidence.

'We have tried everything. We desperately tried to get sufficient information to at least find his strongholds but every-time we get access to a satellite it blows up or falls from the sky or goes to Saturn or something, anything except becoming helpful.'

'We have no aircover what so ever; every aircraft that was deployed has either fallen from the sky, blown up on landing or been destroyed on the ground. Same with guns, every time we get them in a position to shoot at the enemy they hit us with so much fire power we can only hope to get our guns back in working order.'

'Surely General, you have tried something different?' The Foreign Minister was almost as effective as a cigarette in a blizzard. He knew nothing of armies, war or even the logistics required to fight.

'Yes, Minister, we have tried. I ordered a cruise missile strike on their general's home in an effort to distract him.'

'Good, good. That helped, yes?' the minister asked hopefully.

'Helped? Yes, it helped; THEM. Their attacks have been more deadly accurate, more vicious, and more sustained. So yes, attacking his home has helped, someone.'

'We dispatched a convoy of supplies and reinforcements, why did they not arrive?'

'Ask the damn Navy, the few reports we got was some ships sunk and the rest interned, towed to Honshu I believe. At least the survivors are being cared for.'

'Can you form any method of attack? Can you take the fight to them?'

'We can try, it may be a suicide mission but we can try.'

'Very well, give it all you have.'

'Yes, Mr President, we will.' Plishkin shut down the hologram and slumped in his chair, which promptly splintered beneath him. 'Burn this piece of shit, it may perform at least one function properly,' he shouted at his aide as he kicked the pieces before storming out.

'Attack, he demands. As if we are just drinking vodka and eating caviar. What does he think we are doing?' As far as Commanding an Army in the field goes, Illya Plishkin had done remarkably well, for a short while. His successes following on from attacking Hokkaido and Jack's home, however, could be measured on the fingers of a man with no arms.

'Get the Commanders of all the divisions here,' he shouted at his aides, he needed to find a way to do something.

Jack's HQ

Drones almost ran into Jack's rooms, so fast he tripped on the outstretched legs of Colonel Jonson.

'Jack, good news.'

Jack didn't move for a few moments then he raised his head from the hologram image he was studying. Turning to his friend, he smiled. 'Then tell me over coffee.'

The newly stirring Jonson commented, almost in her sleep, 'Mmm coffee.'

'Yes, Colonel, COFFEE.' Jack shouted back, 'and it is your turn to do the honours.'

'But, I'm a Colonel.'

'By god, so you are.' Jack had unleashed the beast of sarcasm; never far from the surface he decided to let it out to play. 'And this is Khemkhaeng Thamrongnawasawat; he is a Major, and Hasegawa is a Lieutenant. And it is your turn for the coffee.'

As she finally realised that they were all watching her she finally recognised the fact that she had been told to get the drinks, she was about to speak out then her brain finally clicked into gear; she had never made a coffee or tea or anything since she arrived, Jack had done it most of the time, and now she had to reciprocate.

Ten minutes later the steaming cups were presented to a chorus of "Arigatō" and all sat down.

'Now, Drones, tell us why you hurtled in here like your brakes had failed?'

'I have been analysing the news feeds out of Russia with Haruto. You were right, we have the support of the political opposition. Your television address has resulted in great numbers of ordinary people taking to the streets. Their Navy is holding in port until they can find out what stopped so many ships, submarines already at sea are being diverted to secure friendly ports, they are running scared. We just need to stamp on the politicians and their army now.'

'Good, well done, again, to Haruto; and to you Drones, without both your skills and the dedicated work of your pilots and technicians we would not be in this somewhat dominant position.'

'Now that Operation Harbour Master has been a massive success; we need to initiate Operation Post Master Phase 2.'

'Ready when you say, Jack.'

'Good, arrange for delivery in ten days. Until then we will keep making their lives a misery.'

'Consider it done.' Drones moved to the BItCH and issued the second phase of the operation. Seconds later he announced 'Deliveries arranged for ten days' time at 0300 Moscow time.'

'Perfect,' replied Jack, 'send a confirmation message to General Onishi and the Imperial Palace. Sign it "Taipan 1" for confirmation.'

'Now, Drones, how is Mai getting on without you?'

'She is fine, wishes I was home but she has been keeping company with Fumiko so she is happy with events.'

'Good. Now let's get some idea of how much equipment we can put against the Russians. Get the heads in here, please.

The Heads of Departments and divisional commanders arrived and each was greeted by Jack and handed a drink as they walked through the door.

'I don't know you?' Jack queried one.

'Major Honsho, Sir. I am the temporary replacement for your store's commander. He has gone to get his gall bladder out, expect him back in five days.'

'Welcome, first name?'

'Hiroshi.'

'Find a seat and we can get started.'

'Hiroshi found a chair beside Drones and they introduced themselves.'

'I have called you here because we will soon have to launch a ground assault on the enemy. Roman, your gunners ready?'

'Almost jumping out of their skins, they are impressed with the ability of your infantry in becoming members of the gun teams, no one has ever seen twenty rounds per gun out of a 155 and they are wanting to prove they can do it and keep it up.'

'Arigatō, Catering?'

'Heaps of food, soups are prepared and ready to be cooked for the enemy, if they are needed.

'Drones?

'Amazons and Big Eyes are ready, Kamikaze are prepped if needed; all pilots are rested, all control systems tested.'

'Haruto?'

'The Russians are in a mess. No one; and by that, I mean from the Kremlin down has any concept of the mess.'

'I assume that is because you are feeding them bulls**t?'

'Let's just call them mushrooms, because you keep them in the dark and I feed them.'

They all laughed at the metaphor, the mood eased considerably.

'Hiroshi?'

'Sir, I have checked '

'Jack, call me Jack.'

'Sorry, Jack. I have assessed the supply storage, there are over ten million rounds each, in reserve, for the 50cal's, the miniguns and assault rifles. Two million for the pistols and side arms. A hundred thousand 30mm for the ARV's and a further five-hundred thousand for the 50cals on the IFV's. Grenades by the tonne as well as a stack of strange devices that are marked "Amazon Drop" Don't know what they are. There are also two ARV's, damaged and barely moveable but still working.'

'Excellent. That is what I wanted to hear.

'Cavalry?'

'All units fuelled, armed and ready to go. No defects reported.'

'Are there any defects not reported?'

'Only one of the tank commanders, but we all accepted that he was little nuts before he arrived.' The entire room erupted into laughter, they all knew the one tank commander he was referring to, widely recognised as the one man that could get a tank into and out of an otherwise impossible position.

'And, might I just add, Jack. We are ready to avenge the loss of Hiro and the others; as the Australians say "We have unfinished business" here.'

'Good, when we go your tanks will be leading the push in the centre so be ready.'

'Mike, recon?'

'Well rested and fed, actually getting a little fat is closer to the truth. We have setup a defensive position on your left flank. Weapons are clean and ready; ammo packs are all full.'

'Great, we hope you don't have to go into action but you never know.'

Jack got each of the infantry commanders to give their status and following on he began to give the sequence he was planning for the final push.

'We are planning a surprise for Moscow; it will be delivered in ten days. I want to rest until then and when we go it will be fast. Be ready and remember, no battle plan survives first contact, we may have to react rather than act. Good luck. We will have another meeting closer to chaos time.'

All rose and returned to their units, bowing in respect to Jack as they left the room. Once they were all gone Jack sat back and smiled.

'For someone going into battle soon you are remarkably relaxed.' Commented Colonel Jonson.

'I have done all I can, up to this time. There is room to change plans, if needed. The commanders are fully appraised and ready. The army is fed and rested, more than we can say about the opposition. We have sufficient ammunition to complete our mission and we can annoy the enemy almost at will. Why would I not smile and relax?' Jack replied, almost enjoying her discomfort, 'And you can put that in your papers. Yes, I know you are still planning to write about me, whether I permit it or not.'

The Colonel blushed deeply, she had always been able to keep her emotions under wraps, but Jack seemed to see through her defences, he was a most disconcerting man to deal with, and still she could not get any real assessment of his abilities or his mental capacities.

General Plishkin's H.Q

'How can we move against them, General?' Asked Bokova, the General's aide.

'I am trying to think, there must be a weak link, somewhere we can breakthrough and attack from behind.' Plishkin was getting desperate, the few options were, seemingly covered, by the massive numbers of enemy ground forces.

'There does not appear to be any way around them.' Bokova commented.

'No, there is no way around them,' he thought for a moment and then it was as though he had been given a divine intervention. 'No, we can't go around them but we may be able to get **through** them.'

'What? What do you mean?'

Quickly spreading the last of his topographic maps on the table, he checked the ground for steepness and tracks. How could he get a division or two up the hills and into the rear?

'If we go straight at their left flank, firstly they won't be expecting us, the element of surprise will give us enough inertia to crash through their 59th division and then into the rear, from there we can attack their support infrastructure. We may be able to create enough damage to allow us to attack with the other divisions.'

'A little risky, General?'

'Yes, but this is war; everything is risky. Get the divisional commanders; I need to prepare.'

'Yes, General.' Bokova left and began rounding up the divisional commanders, leaving the engineers to try to restore power and the plumbing.

The tank commanders were the worst of all those remaining, their companies had borne the brunt of the attacks of Drones and his Amazons. With few other targets and his pilots getting innovative rather than bored with inaction, they had sat down and plotted and planned. The result was they managed to adjust both the drop time and the adhesives to allow them to drop high explosive packs on the barrels of the Main Battle Tanks. No gun, no tank. When the Russians began to protect the guns with camouflage netting the pilots managed to get the drones to fly with the explosive pack aimed at the rear of the tank. With no power unit the tank became an immobile gun, and a prime target for Roman and the 86th.

'OK, silence.' General Plishkin demanded. 'We are going to attack the enemy on the right side. I need the fittest and strongest men from each division for this assault.' As he explained the proposal the commanders were almost becoming enthusiastic at the prospect.

'Do we have sufficient ammunition?' was the first question that would be asked.

'The assault division will have as much as they can carry, it is imperative that they have the chance to break through and they will need to carry sufficient ammunition to achieve this aim.'

The commanders were suddenly silent, they all knew more than well that if the "assault" company were to have as much as they could carry then the rest of them would almost be reduced to sticks and rocks, so short of supplies were the Russians. One of the more senior of the divisional commanders began to question the draining of the pitiful ammunition supply when he was told with no question that he would be charged with "Lacking fighting spirit" if he continued to be disruptive.

From that moment the Russian defence of Iturup was doomed. If the assault division as much as faltered in their work, the remaining divisions would not be able to withstand the resultant tide of Infantry and Cavalry that would swarm over their positions; and the Divisional Commanders were not game to bring the faults of the plan into the light.

In complete contrast over in Jack's camp a corporal knocked on the door to Jack's planning room. 'Daizen come in.' Daizen Akimari was surprised to be addressed with such familiarity. 'Is there something you need?'

'No Sir, but I have thought of something.'

'Speak up.'

'The word is that you expect the Russians may attack on our left flank.'

'Hai, that is one possib.'

'As the 59th have moved more to the left would it not be better to do a similar thing with the 61st?'

'Possibly, why do you ask?'

'If the 61st do not move it leaves the 59th alone, move the 61st and the 91st a little to the left, the Cavalry can fill the gap and they will be ready to run down the track into the enemy camp.'

'Hmm. Let's see.' Jack pushed the controls and the hologram showed the disposition. Further pushes of the buttons showed the deployments. As the two discussed the movements, Colonel Jonson watched and listened.

'You are absolutely correct. Hasegawa!'

'Hai, Jack?'

'Get these movements to the commanders of the 61st and the 91st. Inform the Cavalry as well. And get a commendation for this man, Daizen Akimari. Excellent work Sergeant Akimari.'

'That is Corporal, Sir.'

'Not any more, it isn't. Keep it up, I need information and ideas like this.'

Akimari left and Colonel Jonson edged closer.

'General, you take advice from a corporal?'

'Of course, his view could save a thousand men or more, why would I not listen?'

'I must say, I find that now I am in constant awe of your style of command. I don't think the Pentagon will be best pleased with any report I write; you do not comply with any of the models they teach and yet you still manage to get better results than they can predict.'

'How do you think the U.S. Navy would have handled the Russian Fleet?'

'Not certain, I would like to find out, is it possible for me to push the scenario to a friend of mine that works at the "War College", would that be acceptable?'

'Only if you do not mention any of the tactics we have used. Give them three months preparation and let's say they have three weeks' notice; casualties must be kept to a minimum and statistics reported. Give them the same fleet concentration we have. Be interesting to see how they go?'

'I will do that; I will have the signal ready for your approval in an hour or so.'

"Finally," Jack thought, "She is coming around to a different way of thinking."

The next morning Colonel Jonson was having breakfast with Jack when Hasegawa entered the room. 'Jack, Colonel, Annapolis (U.S. Navy College) has agreed to test your scenario. The Graduating class of C.O. (Commanding Officer) X.O. (Executive Officer) designates has been given until the weekend to formulate one battle plan between them.'

'Good, keep us informed. Hardly seems fair, one against thirty.'

'Never mind, Jack. The thirty will get over it, eventually, defeat is difficult to handle but in large numbers they should be able to deflect sufficient blame away from themselves.'

The three shared in the joke, it would have been amusing if the outcome had not been so one sided. Jack's plan completely outshone the entire class. And to add to their embarrassment it was an Infantry Officer that had done it. Just two years into the future, Tyrell would use it as a basis for the rewriting of the Fleet Operations Manual.

Chapter 38
The Last Russian Effort

'Get the commander of the Assault Division in here!' Plishkin was getting more abrupt every day. His mood hovering between depression and outright rage, no one knew which it would be at any given moment.

Eventually, the Colonel selected to lead the attack arrived at the H.Q.

'Why has it taken you so long to get here? When I want to see you, you make sure you are here!' Plishkin's voice was rising in tone as he spoke, a certain sign it was going to be a bad day for all within sight.

'I apologise, General. I was inspecting the division to ensure they had all the ammunition and equipment they need.'

'And? Do they?'

'The cold weather clothing will not last another winter, if we are still here. Same for the body armour, it is all worn and in need of replacement.'

'What about their weapons?'

'They all seem to be clean and working.'

'Is there anything else they need?'

'New boots, the constant wet weather has taken its toll on the ones they have.'

'Very well.' Plishkin sounded a little sarcastic, but the effect was lost on the Colonel; a dour Muscovite he was as unfeeling as Plishkin was angry and he had better things to do than engage in verbal banter with a man he did not particularly like in the first place.

'Plan of attack. You will lead the division through the Japanese lines, here,' he pointed to a portion of the map, indicating a position on the far right of the Russian lines. 'You will make your way up this incline and around the end of this escarpment. Half way round is the place the Japanese have moved their defensive division to. They are isolated, you need to break through and make your way into their rear areas. Their armoury and stores are just here,' he indicated an area towards the top of a small hill. 'There are no other forces within the area.'

'That is a very steep rise, it will be slow work to get to the top, 35 to 45 minutes at a minimum.'

'And that, Colonel, is why you have been assigned a composite division. You have the fittest men from every unit, and you have a two to one numerical advantage. Make good use of them, you must not fail!' Plishkin thumped the table for emphasis, a move that ensured everyone in the room knew he was in charge.

'Yes Sir. We will depart at midnight and attack just before dawn.'

As he left the building, the Colonel had mixed feelings. On one hand he was happy to be out of the way but to oppose that thought he had the uncanny feeling that he would most likely not survive the next forty-eight hours. For one brief moment he contemplated surrendering to the enemy; but that would never sit well with his beliefs and it was dismissed almost as soon as it had risen.

Jack's H.Q

'Haruto, is there something happening in the Russian camp?'

'Nothing I can give a name to, Jack. Why do you ask?'

'I just have a feeling, like that feeling you get just before a thunderstorm? You know something is going to happen, but you don't know exactly what.'

'I am with you on that. They have not made any significant movements in the last few days, may be a week. Unlike Plishkin.'

'I agree, keep up the surveillance on the Russian forces as they take the captured ships to Yokosuka. I will have Drones keep watch on the fleet movements.'

'Hai.'

'You think there may be a problem, General?' Colonel Jonson was unusually concerned with the possibility of the Russians doing something unexpected.

'Something is happening in the Russian camp. They have not tried to manoeuvre into a position to counter us for some time. Their big guns have been silent for a while and there is no attempt at signal traffic. They have not even tried to complete repairs to their power systems. Something is up, and we will need to be ready.'

For the rest of the day there was no further news; but the strange feeling would not let Jack alone, it was almost as though he was being told what was happening. "I wonder if this is what Fumiko feels when she gets her warnings?" he mused, then dismissing the issue he was pleased to see no one had heard him.

But, no matter how many times he dismissed the feeling, eventually it returned.

0500, Jack's Western Flank

'IN COMING!' The shout was cut short as the Rocket Propelled Grenade (RPG slammed into the middle of the 59th division's new front line. Closely followed by more and more rounds it quickly became obvious that this was a full-scale assault.

'Stand TO!' The shout came from the command team of the 59th. The order was completely redundant, they were already fighting the Russians and it seemed that there was an inexhaustible number of enemies attacking.

Jack's H.Q

'Jack! It's on, the Russians have attacked the 59th.'

'Damn. All divisions stand to, safety's off. Get the command of the 59th on line.'

'No connection.'

'What's going on?' Colonel Jonson appeared in the doorway, dishevelled and clearly confused.

'59th is under attack.' Hasegawa shouted across the room. 'Get over here and keep out of the way.'

Jonson moved to the corner position beside Jack's desk and watched as he marshalled his army. A stream of orders was going out, no one acknowledged them, they were just obeyed.

'61st, try to get to the 59th, reinforce their position. 91st and 93rd move west to 61st position, cavalry fill the gap all units to jump point "Bravo".'

'Haruto, Drones give me EYES!'

The hologram suddenly burst into life showing the satellite view of Jack's left flank.

'Damn. They have almost made it through. Drones, do NOT launch Amazons, we do not have clearance between them and us. ANALYSIS!'

'Looks like the 59th have taken a pasting, the Russians must have 15,000 or more.' Hasegawa gave his report almost as calmly as if he was ordering sushi at a restaurant.

It wasn't that the 59th were not fighting, they were completely outnumbered and the casualty lists would reflect that.

'JACK! they are moving through the lines, looks like they are heading for the armoury and supply area.'

'And all we have between them and us is the Recon units.' Jack spoke almost silently. The room fell quiet as they all waited.

For almost a minute no one spoke, the silence was deafening.

'Mike! You have 10,000 or more Russians coming up the rise at you. Get as many of your guys to the armoury as you can, take anything you want, 50cals, miniguns, RPGs, ammunition. Take the two damaged ARV's and 30mm ammunition as well. Get yourselves into a defensive position. They will be on you in around thirty minutes, give or take. If you can hold them up, I can get to their flank and take them out, but I need time.'

'Got it.'

The entire time that Jack was briefing Mike, Akio was speaking with the Armourers.

Mike Rodrigues sent almost three-quarters of his men to the armoury and when they arrived, they found cooks, medics and drivers all filling the ARV's and trucks with weapons. The Marines had barely arrived before the Staff Sergeant Storeman sent them back with a dozen heavily laden trucks.

By his estimates the Russians were still twenty minutes away when Mikes team had rearmed themselves. A rumble behind them saw the two ARV's almost stumble into position; barely able to move under their own power they gave the appearance of two wounded bulls preparing for a fight to the finish.

'Jack! We are as ready as we will ever be. I know this isn't the right time to remind you, but if you remember, we are not permitted to attack the enemy, we are only allowed to defend ourselves.'

A voice behind him made Mike turn. He saw a bespectacled storeman Private standing there, beside the ARV.

'What is it?' Mike asked.

'I can make it so you are only defending yourselves, and us.'

'Let him do it Mike. Good luck.'

The Private began to outline his idea and Mike readily agreed. This was going to be dangerous but it was the best plan they had.

'Jack, we should get ready.' Akio whispered into Jack's ear.

'Hai.'

'Eiji, I want you beside me, you too Colonel. In body armour with an assault rifle. Be prepared to run we will need to move quickly.' Jack turned and, along with Akio, entered his private room.

Just five minutes later the two emerged. Both wearing glistening black Samurai Armour with a daisho (matched pair of katana and wakizashi) at their left sides; a 9mm pistol with twenty round magazines and an assault rifle.

With the rifle in one hand and kabuto in the other they were completely out of place and everyone looked on in amazement.

'Really!' Hasegawa almost shouted. 'You are going to war in gusoku (armour)?'

'Why not, just as effective as body armour and it covers more of me as well. Should upset the Russians too.' Jack replied, 'Let's go people. Time to earn your pay.'

At that order; Jack, closely followed by Akio, ran from the room calling for the 61st and 91st to follow him. Instantly ten thousand soldiers began running to the flank of the advancing Russian Assault team with another ten thousand following.

'Drones, get some Big Eyes up for Mike, he needs information.'

'Already done. Looks like the Russians are having some difficulty with the steepness of the terrain.'

'Big advantage, Jack. The Russians are slipping on the icy ground and their white uniforms show up clearly against the dirt and trees.' Mike Rodrigues sounded pleased.

'Great. Haruto give them as much assistance as you can. Good luck, guys. We will be there around forty-five minutes maybe a little more. Hold them off as long as possible.'

'Will do.'

The Russian assault division was making very hard work of the steep terrain; muddy and icy underfoot it was difficult to get a grip on the ground, add the fact that the Russians boots were now very worn and the smooth soles were all but useless in the attempt to scale the hill. Their mood was good, despite the setbacks, they had smashed through the thinly placed 59th division and were now moving towards their objective.

Meanwhile; Mike Rodrigues and his marines were preparing a welcome that the Russians would never forget. Well positioned and, even with the enemy making ground towards them, the cooks were supplying a meal to keep them ready.

'Range?' Mike called into his communicator.

'350 metres.'

'We may well be waiting for them until after sundown at this rate.'

'Well, let's settle in and enjoy the wait. The longer they take the more tired they will be.'

Almost ten minutes later the call came in '240 metres!'

'OK, Stand to.' Mike responded; his plan was to wait until the Russians had entered a "killing field" before he moved. A natural break in the vegetation marked the 220-metre mark and at that point it would be difficult for them to find a safe point.

The stores clerk looked at Mike and nodded; Mike nodded back. Standing up the young soldier looked at the advancing troops and miraculously no one shot at him, the track before him seemed to be seething with moving figures, he raised his assault rifle and began taking shots at the advancing Russians.

Absolutely nothing happened for almost ten seconds then all hell broke loose. Thousands of Russians began to shoot, not so much at him, or for the most part near him, just shooting. He ducked down behind the fallen tree that they were using for cover and said 'Sergeant! I think they are shooting at you.'

'I think you are right.' Mike replied with a grin. 'RECON, RETURN FIRE!' Mike shouted to his team and instantly the ARV's opened fire.

They could never be accused of hiding from a fire fight, but the steady whump, whump, whump of the 30mm cannon coupled with the rattle and crash of the associated 50 calibre machine guns mounted on the ARV's made the Marines even more bold. Almost as one they stood up and the noise increased as fifty marines opened fire with their machine guns. Thirty more added the screeching whine of the mini-guns to the cacophony and the remainder began to dump rocket propelled grenades into the approaching Russians.

Hiding behind a tree the Colonel demanded 'Where the hell did they come from? Plishkin told us there was no one here.'

'Must be at least four companies (400 men) up ahead, or maybe an entire division,' his second in command guessed, as they tried to find a way around the ambush. Unfortunately, their conversation was the last either would have. Seconds later six 30mm rounds brought the tree down on top of them. Now leaderless the Russians tried to keep under cover as they made an attempt to leave the site and return to their own lines.

'Jack! We are running low on ammo! How much longer?'

'Can you do ten minutes?'

'Possibly. Tell us when to stop.'

The horrendous rate of fire was maintained; the barrels of the 50 calibres were beginning to glow in the gloomy light; the 30mm were silent, nothing left to shoot with. The miniguns were also about to go silent and the last of the RPG's had long since left their launchers.

'HURRY UP JACK!' Mike shouted above the noise.

'Standby!' came the reply.

'STANDBY! CEASE FIRING!' Jack screamed and suddenly the noise stopped. In the brief silence the Russians were completely at a loss as to why their enemy would stop shooting; that was until their worst fears were realised.

Down the hill, at full speed ten thousand Japanese Infantry charged directly at the Russian flank. The few that were brave enough to look would claim they saw two Samurai, in glistening black armour, leading them.

The shock was sufficient to prevent the Russians opening fire; that and the fact they were almost out of ammunition.

The 61st Division had no such problems, assault rifles blasted everything that even tried to move. Just as the Russians began to return fire their slim hopes of being able to return to their camp were completely crushed. The 91st Division charged at their rear cutting them off from all hope.

The fight itself was not a long one; Mike and his Marines had stopped the Russian attack and had held them up long enough for the advancing infantry to destroy them completely. The few that wanted to fight were quickly dealt with and the rest surrendered just as quickly.

Once the fighting stopped Jack began to marshal his forces.

'Tyrell, bring the fleet towards the bay. Haruto, give Tyrell the coordinates for medevac for the 59th. We will need medics as well.

'Roman, Drones; give their camp a pasting. All teams prepare to advance. 61st and 91st reload.'

'Jack we are low on ammunition.' One of his company commanders advised. No sooner had he spoken than a pair of large trucks slid, almost sideways, down the hill to Jack's position, stopping only when they had run into a fallen tree, brakes were useless on that terrain.

As soon as they stopped the teams in the rear began to heave ammunition crates out of the trucks for the waiting infantry to reload their weapons and refill their bandoliers.

'TEN MINUTES!' Jack ordered, and right on schedule they began their move on the Russian camp.

Once again running they made good time and as they began their approach, they could hear the shells and grenades exploding in the distance.

'ALL DIVISIONS ATTACK!'

Three simple words that saw the best part of eighty thousand soldiers, with armour in support, charge towards the Russian camp.

'Colonel Jonson, are you ok?' Eiji asked.

'Not really, I don't think I can run much further.'

'You have to, Jack wants you alongside him when he enters the Russian camp.'

'Why?' she puffed as she tried to keep up.

'So that you can see how he ends this war. You want that in your thesis, don't you?'

Those words seemed to spur her on and she was reasonably close when they entered the outer edges of the camp.

'CEASE FIRE!' Jack ordered Roman and Drones. Seconds later the last of the shells exploded and the camp was eerily quiet. As the Russians began to emerge from their protective dugouts, they were confronted by a massive army waiting for them. Only a few were brave enough to shoot and those were quickly dealt with.

First a couple threw their weapons down and when the Japanese took them aside a few more surrendered. As they realised, they would not be shot, armed or not, more surrendered. Soon the capitulation was almost complete.

Chapter 39
Surrender

The Russians, poorly clothed, hungry, out of ammunition and dispirited had been defeated; not just a defeat, in the end this was a capitulation.

As Jack and his team moved through the camp, the completely out of breath Colonel Jonson trying to follow, he began to issue orders.

'150th, establish a weapons dump at the eastern end, near the caves entrance. Catering, bring the kitchens and foods in to the east as well. A meal for everyone once they have surrendered their weapons.'

Grabbing a soldier by the jacket he demanded 'Where is your Commander!' The soldier was probably not fluent in English, if he could speak any at all, and Eiji repeated Jack's words in fluent Russian as they were being spoken.

Quickly the terrified soldier pointed at a large building with double doors at the entrance. Jack pointed at a number of his senior sergeants and they began to move towards the doors.

Russian HQ

'Thank God the bombardment has stopped. Is there any news from the Assault Division?'

'Nothing General, last report was they had broken through the Japanese 59th division and were proceeding along the planned route into the enemy rear.'

'Very good. Maybe we can give some good news to Moscow. Keep trying to contact them.'

At that very moment, with Plishkin smiling at his command team, the doors crashed open and a dozen very big Japanese men entered; assault rifles ready they pushed their way inside until each had his own targets in their sights.

'DO NOT MOVE! WEAPONS ON THE FLOOR!' Eiji ordered the startled officers in his clipped east coast Russian accent. 'HANDS UP!'

The officers all complied; Jack could see the surprise in their eyes as he entered the room, mud spattered armour notwithstanding, it was simple for all to see, THIS was the man in command.

Jack withdrew his pistol and handed it to Eiji on his right; unclipped his kabuto and sword and handed them to Akio who was standing to his left with Colonel Jonson, leaving his assault rifle hanging from its sling.

'Which is Plishkin?' Jack demanded.

The Russian General moved forward and announced 'I am.'

Jack moved towards him until he was less than an arm's length away. Without forewarning Jack lashed out with a left hook that could have felled a bull, instantly fracturing Plishkin's right eye socket.

The Russian screamed in pain as he grabbed his face, Jack shouted 'THAT IS FOR MY MOTHER.' The look from the general was disbelief, then Jack hit him with a straight right, breaking his jaw. The Russian was now barely standing as Jack shouted 'THAT WAS FOR MY FATHER!'

The disbelief was slowly fading as Plishkin came to the realisation of who he was facing.

Jack grabbed Plishkin's body armour by the shoulder tabs and twisted him around exposing the unarmoured gap of around 100mm at the side. Three quick, massive hits to the ribcage saw three fractured ribs.

'THEY ARE FOR MY THREE GROOMS!'

None of Jack's team had moved, all still kept their weapons aimed at the now disbelieving Russians, but Jack was not done. A kick to the knee saw General Plishkin crash to the floor in agony, his knee broken beyond repair.

'AND THAT IS FOR THE MARE YOU KILLED WHILE SHE WAS FOALING!'

It was at that point that a Major, standing in the far-right corner made the fatal mistake of reaching out for a pistol left on the table.

'NYET' (NO) shouted Eiji as he raised Jack's gun and put a bullet in the Majors head beside his eye. He was dead before he hit the floor.

'Good shooting, Eiji.' Jack complimented his translator.

'Not really, it should have been between his eyes, your sights are out of line.'

'Really? Still a remarkable shot, well done. Where did you learn to shoot like that?'

'I qualified for the Asian Games last year.'

'Well done.'

As Jack and Eiji spoke; off to the left, a Colonel began to move away, Akio drew his sword and had it at the Colonels throat before he had moved half a step.

'If I were you, I would stay right where you are.' Akio warned him and the Colonel instantly stopped moving fearful of the consequences.

Jack turned and asked 'Who is the ranking officer now that your General is incapacitated?'

'Th, th, that would be me. Colonel Karan Hartchev.' His voice faltering as he felt the threat of Akio's blade against his throat.

Jack looked him in the eye, instantly confirming that the control now rested firmly on the shoulders of the Commander of the Northern Army. 'You have a choice, Colonel. Either you can surrender, unconditionally; or you can continue fighting, if you prefer. Which is it?'

The Colonel looked carefully around the room; trying to confirm the choices he was presented with. The eyes of his officers were desperately seeking guidance and at the same time they wanted to be done with the business of war. A collective sigh of relief could be heard when the Colonel said "We surrender."

'A wise decision; you have saved many lives today. 'Turning to the men he had brought into the Russian H.Q. Jack ordered 'Lower your weapons and search them.'

Half of the soldiers did just that, the others still held a firing position until all threat of retaliation had been negated, and then they lowered their weapons. 'General?' Began Colonel Jonson, but that was all she managed to get out.

'Tyrell? Get some engineers to clear the airstrip as a transit point. Bring the hospital ships in, send every combat medic you have.'

'Drones, Complete Operation Post master.'

'Mai, a signal to my family, Cc the Imperial Palace, General Onishi, the Combined Chiefs of Staff and the Northern Planning Cell. Message reads "Deuteronomy 32 V 41-42" Authentication Taipan 1. Arigatō.'

'Mike, bring your guys down the hill and into the centre of the camp.'

Turning to the Russian, 'Colonel, you will get your engineers to clear the entrance to the cave system at the eastern end of the camp.'

'No, you can't. It is too dangerous to do this,' he protested. Jack spun and stared directly at the Russian.

'Once again you are faced with a choice; either your engineers clear the caves entrance or I will order a strike to blast it clear, CHOOSE NOW!'

Faced with an impossible selection he finally ordered his engineers to clear the entrance to the cave system.

'There, it is so much easier if you do as I wish. Hasegawa, can we get some coffee in here, please?'

Ten minutes later a catering truck appeared with coffee and food. Jack served everyone present and then, again, turned to the Colonel. 'Once your men have cleared the entrance to the caves you will have your entire army take their weapons to the entrance. Once they have deposited their weapons and ammunition, they will be given a meal and then they will assist with the triage of your injured.'

Again, Jack spoke into his transmitter, 'Roman? Stand down your gunners. Give them my eternal thanks.'

Jack held out his hand to Akio who returned his katana and Kabuto to their owner. As he clipped the sword on his armour Akio commented, 'This is a really good weapon, Jack. Balance is perfect, as is the edge. Where did you get it?'

'That, Sensei, is "Revenge" belonged to none other than Tokugawa Musashi himself.'

'This is the Shoguns katana?'

'It is.'

'And yours?'

'This is "Vengeance" another of his weapons.'

Akio bowed. 'It is a privilege to have been permitted to use it. Arigatō.'

'You are welcome, Sensei. Now to other business. Colonel Hartchev, you will signal your Command in Moscow that the war has been lost. They will be somewhat aggrieved at first but I have arranged a delivery that will confirm the end of hostilities. Hasegawa will assist you. Send your officers out to assist with the surrender of your weapons, remember your troops must only carry their weapons by the muzzle and the magazines must be removed. Noncompliance may result in them being shot as they will be suspected of preparing to return fire. Colonel Jonson, Sensei, Eiji come with me.'

At that Jack left everyone with their responsibilities. As word spread through the Russian ranks, they were more than eager to comply. As the explanation of the soup was given the Russians were all pleased to finally get a meal, and the next day would see them getting a full diet.

As Jack walked through the camp, his small entourage following, the full effects of the devastation could be seen. Not a single building was unscathed and everywhere they looked they saw the bedraggled faces of the defeated army.

Turning the corner near one building, Jack saw a medic trying to stitch a gash in the arm of a very young Russian. Handing his assault rifle to Akio, Jack held the man's arm still and closed the wound, freeing the medic to use two hands to finish the job. 'Tell him he will be fine, Eiji. Just keep still and he will get pain relief as soon as it is available.' As Jack spoke, Eiji translated and the man visibly relaxed. Once the job was done, Jack thanked the medic and then moved on through the camp.

'Why is he doing this?' Jonson asked Akio in a quiet whisper.

'It is one thing to command an army, it is quite another to gain its respect; and it is a miracle to get respect from your enemies. He is giving assistance and reassurance to all he sees; they will quickly spread the word that he is not here for revenge and that now the war is done they will be cared for.'

Just then Jack spotted a man lying almost completely under a wall from a collapsed building. Pulling at the debris it took just a few minutes to release the man. Anyone could see that the extensive injuries were not survivable, Jack called Eiji to his side to translate.

'Sensei, get a medic with some opiates for this man.' Looking at the gasping soldier, Jack asked 'Are you Christian?' and through the bouts of pain from his shredded intestines he nodded to the translation. Jack held his hand and began to pray, not loud but clearly. With Eiji converting each word instantly the soldier began to breathe a little slower as his life ebbed away.

Moments later a medic arrived and gave a him quick injection. Less than two minutes later the man passed away. Jack stood up and moved away, no more than two metres, knelt down and placed his rifle and katana before him and bowed his head.

For a full five minutes no one that witnessed the scene moved. Japanese and Russians alike all stood silently, waiting. Eventually, Jack retrieved his weapons, turned to the dead soldier and saluted. Turning to Colonel Jonson, with tears flowing down his cheeks, he said, 'Put THAT in your thesis.' And moved away as the stretcher bearers took the remains away to the identification station.

'Jack, you are bleeding.' Eiji had noticed the blood dripping from his arm and the trail of blood he left while walking. Find a medic when we have done what needs doing.'

For the next three hours they moved through the camp giving help where they could. Finally, they had moved through the former Russian camp and were within sight of the field kitchens. Jack suddenly stopped and turned around, listening intently. Slowly he retraced his steps and turned down a narrow alley. Akio and the others followed wondering why he had made his way into the narrow area full of the wreckage of a collapsed building.

It was almost at the same time that they saw the source of Jack's attention. Lying, almost completely buried was a Russian soldier. Visibly shaking from the intense cold and feebly crying out for help in a last desperate attempt to live. Jack and Akio began tearing at the debris and Eiji ran to find some healthy Russians to do some heavy lifting. For almost twenty minutes they struggled with the wreckage and eventually there was just one large, heavy piece of steel framework laying across the legs. Gathering all those working and lifting together they held the steel up long enough for Colonel Jonson to drag the man out into the open.

For her part, Colonel Jonson was surprised as to how heavy he was and how difficult it was to pull the man clear as she struggled to haul him out of the way. Eventually, they had him clear and the heaving men dropped the steel frame back onto the ground, lungs heaving and muscles screaming at the extreme effort it had taken to hold the frame up long enough to save the man.

Two medics, waiting patiently to one side had given him pain relief and began to assess his injuries. After a few minutes one looked up at Jack.

'He appears to be relatively uninjured, if we leave his legs out of the equation. He is suffering from hypothermia and that is the most important thing right now.'

Jack looked at the man's pleading face and handed his assault rifle to Eiji. Crouching down he spoke quietly.

'This is going to be both painful and difficult to do.' Eiji translated and as everyone watched, wondering what was going to happen, Jack pushed his hands under the Russian and picked him up. Moving both quickly and gently Jack carried the man out of the alley and turned, not towards the medical facility at the western end of the camp but towards the field kitchen set up in the east. With Akio and Eiji leading the way and clearing a path through the throng of interested people Jack shouted for the cooks to get a seat for him.

Gently letting the man down on the chair, he directed the cooks to place him as close as possible to the steaming kettles full of soup for the defeated army. As soon as he had ensured the man was not going to fall from the chair, Jack let the medical staff begin their difficult tasks. First trying to save his life and then his legs.

The heat from the kettles soon had his core temperature beginning to rise, a lot of soup helped lift his temperature from the inside and also gave him some much-needed fluid replacement to help ward off dehydration.

The legs, however, would soon prove to be a significant problem.

'Sir we cannot fix his legs here, they need surgery.'

'What is the diagnosis? Best estimate.' Jack replied.

'Both femurs are fractured, straight across the bone. Should be simple enough to correct with plates and screws. The lower legs are a very different prospect, compound fractures, through the skin, as well as many small pieces of floating bone, he may lose both below the knee.'

'Arigatō.' Jack answered, keying his transmitter he called for assistance. 'Tyrell, we need a medivac chopper at the east end of the Russian camp and put a surgical team on standby; one patient, hypothermia and multiple upper and lower leg fractures and there is a possibility of compartment syndrome, but the legs were not crushed to the point of preventing blood flow so that may or may not be a pressing issue.'

'Roger that, on its way.'

Watching the event from a professional point of view, Colonel Jonson was finally becoming comfortable with the way Jack held his command together. Not with orders or demands of obedience; but with care and concern for his army and his former enemy. "This will make for compelling reading when I finally get to put it down." She thought as the medevac chopper landed a short distance away.

Imperial Palace

'Your Majesty, Signal from General Nakagawa.'

'What does it say?'

'It appears to be cryptic it says "Deuteronomy 32 V 41-42" I do not understand.'

'Call his family, they will know.

Central Command

'General Onishi sir, Signal from Northern Army Command.' The communications Sergeant reported.

'Yes?'

'Signal reads; "Deuteronomy 32 V 41-42".'

'Who sent it?'

'Authentication is Taipan 1.'

'What the hell does it mean?

Jack's home

'Asa, there is a message from Jack, they have brought it down from the communications people, but it is some sort of code.'

'Show me, Emika.' Asa took one look at the piece of paper and reached for the family bible. 'Let me see, Deuteronomy, chapter 32,' she thumbed through the huge family bible, 'Verse 41.' Asa read through the quote and as she did so a call came from the Imperial Palace.

'Your Majesty, how can I help?'

'Do you understand the message from Jack?'

'I do, it is a quote from the bible.'

Asa read the text from the latest revision.

"I will whet my glittering sword, and with my hand take hold of judgement; I will render vengeance to my enemies, and this is how I will reward those that hate me. I will make my arrows drunk with blood, and my sword shall devour flesh; and with the blood of the slain and the captives I will bring revenge upon the enemy."

'I believe he has done it. He has won.'

'Praise the gods. Arigatō Asa. I will get your brothers home for you, celebrate as a family.'

As he spoke Hana entered the room and quickly became ecstatic at the news. There could be no other explanation for the quote.

The Kremlin

'Mr President, there has been a delivery.'

'Explain yourself.'

'A large crate was left at the loading dock last night. The packing documentation states that only you are to open it.'

'Very well.' The president was less than impressed, however his curiosity demanded he open the crate.

Russian Navy, Baltic Fleet Base

'What do you mean a delivery?'

'A crate was delivered last night; it is being held at the main gate. There is a note on the top saying "TOP SECRET. For Base Commander - Only."

'Very well. I will be there shortly.'

Russian Nuclear Submarine Base, Murmansk

The phone rang incessantly, the Base Commander did not like to answer it while he was busy, this time it was with one of the secretaries.

'Wait here, my dear. I won't be long,' he told her. He did not know how wrong he could possibly be.

'What is it? I said no interruptions!'

'I apologise Admiral. There is a matter of great urgency. The President is calling.'

'Very well, put him on.' The phone clicked and the hologram presented the image of the president. 'Sir, what can I do for you?'

'You can get dressed and go to your main gate and open the crate that awaits you.'

'How do you know about the crate?'

'Because I got one as well and so did the Commander of the Baltic Fleet.'

'I will call back once I have opened it.' Rushing back to his private quarters he told the secretary, 'Get dressed and get back to work, I have been ordered by the President to attend to some business.'

'Are you sure?' she asked, clearly disappointed.

'YES dammit, get out.' She left quickly and the Admiral dressed and called for his car.

Arriving at the gate he flung open the door and demanded, 'Where is this goddam crate that everyone is so fired up about?'

'Under the roof at the rear of the loading area, Sir.'

The young sailor was now both frightened of his Commanding Officer and overly curious about the crate.

'Come with me,' the Admiral ordered. 'And get some tools.'

Rushing through the building the sailor emerged with a tool bag just as the Admiral was reading the note attached to the top.

'Carefully remove the screws out of the top and then leave.' The young man did exactly as he was told, and, once he was out of sight, the Admiral removed the cover.

Sitting on top was another instruction sheet.

You have completed the first task. Connect a hologram call to your President and wait until all are on line. Do NOT proceed further until instructed.

The same process was being completed at the Baltic base and the Kremlin. It took around half an hour before all three sites were at the same point. The President was now given the next instruction.

"Connect your hologram call to Net-site 8810-8100-9090-001-8734 and connect all sites to the call." The President did so and he was rewarded with the image of Jack sitting sipping coffee; the apparent background view of the mountains from his home was a peaceful setting.

'Konichiwa. Would you like me to have my translator present or can we agree on the use of English as a workable language?'

The three Russians agreed on English.

'Good. Now I trust you have not yet proceeded further than your instructions.' Agreement was given and Jack continued.

'If you now remove the green foam cover you will see a familiar device within your crates, Mr President you will see two. Remove the cover now please.' Carefully the Russians removed the foam cover and there before them sat warheads from the Russian missiles that had been used to begin the entire fiasco.

'Gentlemen, these are from your submarine the "Boris Yeltsin". You may check the serial numbers if you wish, I will wait.'

'Are they live?'

Jack gave a small laugh. 'No, it would be entirely counterproductive for them to be live warheads. We had them rendered inert just after we took them.'

The Russians began abusing any and all within earshot, angry at the possibility that the Japanese had the weapons and even angrier that they had been able to deliver them to such important facilities.

'ENOUGH!' Jack shouted 'Enough of the histrionics. You knew the weapons were on Iturup, it was always going to be a possibility that they would fall into my hands; and now, here they are.'

'What do you want?' The president was fearful of the demands that would now be placed on his country.

'Surprisingly little. You will contact our Diplomatic Mission in Switzerland and make arrangements for peace. The Islands seized will be returned to Japanese control. Once you have done this you will return everything that has been stolen from the Ainu. You will rebuild their homes and infrastructure. The border will be re-established at the same point that it was when you created the invasion. You will remove all military from the Kuril Islands.'

'You ask too much. We will not accede to your demands.'

'And you forget that I still hold over 1300 of your warheads and the next ones that are returned to you will be live and falling from a high-altitude aircraft. Is that clear enough for you?'

'You hold all the aces, or so it seems.'

'And you have the power to either continue or prevent a continuance of the war; you choose.'

'You would not dare!'

'Your General thought he could push me out of the war and he is now undergoing surgery to rebuild his face and replace his knee. You cannot bluff me; I will win this war and the next move is yours.'

'If we do as you wish, what then?'

'Your elections are due in six months; I expect them to be an honest and fair election. And I expect you to abide by the decision of the people. If they want you to continue, they will vote for you; if they do not want you, they will not vote for you. It is a simple proposal.'

'And what will you do with the weapons?'

'They are in a secure storage; we will keep them. Call it a "security deposit", a surety to ensure your future co-operation.'

'Your nation is strictly opposed to the use of nuclear weapons; how will you justify having them?' Asked the Baltic commander.

'DO NOT LECTURE ME, ADMIRAL. I know only too well the restrictions and the political demands of my country. I also know and understand the fact that the weapons are a very effective bargaining chip should you choose to ignore whatever peace agreement the politicians create. You will not be able to get them back either by bargaining or demanding. AM I CLEAR?'

'General, we will abide with your requests. They appear to be reasonable. What guarantees do we have that you will not use the weapons against us?'

'None, they are weapons of war and may be used as such. Rest assured we will not make excessive demands of you now or into the future. Also, we will not begin a war with you, we wish to live in peace and this is one way to cement the fact that you will abide by such a peace.'

'You win and you have my word, we will make the requisite approaches with your Diplomatic Mission.'

'Arigatō, Mr President. I am certain we will speak again. I will have my medical teams begin to prepare your casualties for repatriation. The uninjured will be put to work retrieving the bodies of your soldiers from the battle grounds, also for repatriation. As soon as we can, I will arrange for you to send a hospital ship to collect them.'

'Now I must leave you to your business, I need to speak with my leaders.' Jack closed off the hologram and breathed a huge sigh of relief.

'Masterful negotiations, Jack. I will inform the Prime Minister he will be receiving some diplomatic overtures in the near future.' The Emperor had been listening on a connected line.

'Arigatō, Your Majesty. I have gone as far as I can with this, it is now in the realm of the politicians. Let us pray we have done enough and they don't stuff it up, again.'

'Arigatō, Jack. When you feel you can leave the area, come to the Palace. There is much to discuss.'

'Hai, Majesty.' Jack bowed and closed the hologram. For the first time in years he felt at peace.

The doctor would come every day to check Jack's wounds, the dressings were changed and the medication for the infections was prescribed. Jack was still working hard; the administering of the Islands could be done from his home but he was still the one in command.

Eventually, there had been sufficient progress made and it was time for the locals to take their islands back. Harucor and Chikap Anchicar were the first to return to their ancestral home. Theirs was one of the first homes to be completed and soon many others were flooding back

Curiously there was a group of around a hundred and fifty Russians, part of the clean-up and rehabilitation teams, that asked for permission to remain.

'You will need permission from the ruling council. I cannot make that decision. I notice you are a mixture of men and women in your group, you do understand that you will not be permitted to create a Russian community?' Jack was trying to be diplomatic about the possibility of their remaining.

'We understand that, General. We do not wish to recreate a piece of Russia; we wish to become part of their community. To be completely honest, some of us have struck up friendships with the locals, men with local women and women with local men. Most of us are from the rural areas and this is almost ideal for us, no big cities, no rushing traffic; a slower pace of life. We spent far too long as a part of the army, we wish to give something back.'

'I will speak with the Ruling Council. They will make the decision. I will ask for Alex Gripkin, the former Ambassador to be appointed as a special envoy, his wife Sakura has family ties with the Ainu and the two may well be able to assist in the assimilation process.'

The following week Jack made the call and put the proposal to Harucor and the council. They were very happy to get a group of people to migrate into their community. Most of whom were already committed to relationships and all wanted to make a new start. They would make good replacements for the younger ones that had decided to remain in the cities. The lure of bright lights and a city lifestyle had been a little too much for some to resist.

'Jack?'

'Hai, Fumiko.'

'You are to visit the Palace soon. It will be a mixed visit, some good and some not so good news. You may need to be a little careful.'

'I will be. Would you accompany me to the Palace?'

'I would like to.'

'Then we shall go tomorrow.'

As soon as breakfast had been completed Jack and Fumiko took his helicopter to the Imperial Palace in Tokyo.

Chapter 40
A Visit to the Palace

'General Nakagawa, and Fumiko Maki, your Majesty.' The palace aide bowed as he held the door open, gesturing for Jack and Fumiko to enter.

Jack moved to the Emperor and released his katana from the mounting on the side of his dress uniform. Kneeling down he presented the weapon to the Emperor. Tsuka to the left and edge away from the Emperor; the most benign method of presenting to the Emperor.

Reaching out the Emperor placed his hand on the weapon and said 'Keep your weapon, General. You have earned the right to bear it in our presence.'

'Arigatō, Majesty.' Jack rose to his feet, slightly unsteady as the wound to his leg was not healing as quick as he wanted, still holding the weapon, the Emperor gestured to a seat for them and both Jack and Fumiko sat down.

'I must congratulate you, Jack. Your victory was the most brilliant ever witnessed. And keeping casualties to a minimum was a most welcome result.'

'Arigatō, Majesty, it should have been better but we have won and that is the most important part of the result.' Jack was not feeling the Emperor's enthusiasm for the statistics. Far too many lost as far as he was concerned.

'There will be a presentation tomorrow for you and your senior officers, the remainder of the army will be awarded as they are available.'

'Arigatō, Majesty. You are most kind.'

'The least you deserve. However; there is a small problem, next week you will need to be available for the beginning of the trial of General Plishkin, you had him charged with war crimes and his case is before the International Court of Justice beginning Tuesday.'

'I will be there; dare I assume General Ito will be able to let me have a flight?'

'Assume as you wish. If he does not you can have my private jet.'

'Arigatō, Majesty. You are still most kind.'

'Stop with the grovelling, Jack. Have coffee and tell us how you did it.'

Jack smiled as the coffee was served and the Crown Prince joined them as he spent the next two hours describing the final days of the war.

'This Colonel Jonson, she will be giving her report to the Pentagon soon?'

'I believe so, I did not want her to do so, I feel it is a private thing the inside of my mind. But she was a helpful focal point of distraction for me and I think she was very surprised at the complex world I live in.'

'Don't worry, Jack. All will be well with her report.'

That was the first thing Fumiko had to contribute to the conversation.

'Are you certain?' the Emperor asked.

'I am.'

'Then there is nothing to worry about, Majesty. If Fumiko says it is good, it is good, and I will not argue with her.'

The Pentagon

'Colonel, you were sent to probe the capacities of his mind and you come back here saying that you have no important findings. THAT is difficult to believe.'

'I am sorry if you do not like what I have, but he is a complete contradiction to everything we think we know.'

'Explain yourself.'

'Well, we can teach what he does, that is easy enough. We can teach how he does it, not quite so easy but still achievable. What we cannot teach is how he organises the requirements in his brain. How does he keep the demands of every soldier under his command in the front of his mind and still have room for creating new weapons, devising methods of using those weapons, finding people that can make the most effective use of what he has and, more importantly, when he needs it.'

'He knows everyone that is in his army, by name; they are encouraged to speak out, loudly if necessary. Bring errors to his notice, create changes if they are needed.'

'You have some examples?'

'A Corporal knocked on the door of his office, just before he sent the army at the Russians. Jack acknowledged him by first name. The Corporal gave him a planning error he believed had been missed.'

'Like what?' The General investigating the war was becoming more incredulous with every minute

'The Corporal had noticed that the division on the left flank had been placed in a position that left them exposed and without sufficient support. He advised…'

'This Nakagawa permitted a Corporal to question the placement of an entire division?' The General interrupted Colonel Jonson.

'Not only did he permit it, he took the advice of the Corporal and moved other divisions to cover them.'

'I would have busted him to buck private.' The General was astounded at the way Jack operated.

'I understand, Sir. Most would. But Jack not only heard the concerns but he promoted him as well for the foresight.'

'Unbelievable. How does he keep discipline?'

'That is the amazing part, his discipline is kept by the army itself. He demands a great deal of work and he gets it, keeps the soldiers happy and they give him total support. It is really amazing to watch as it happens.'

'I suppose the Corporal is an unusual event.'

'No General, not at all. The Major commanding the remote Drone systems was a private and he will be promoted to Colonel in the near future. Brilliant man, devised several weapons and over saw the construction and testing of them as well. His SatCon was responsible for putting the Russians off line for the entire war.'

'We will need to speak with that man, the SatCon Commander, find out how he did it.' The General was finally getting enthusiastic about the way Jack worked.

'I don't think that will be possible, the methods used as well as the proprietary software is highly Top Secret, they will not likely let that go.'

Imperial Palace

'Is everyone here?'

'They are, Majesty.'

'Good, let us begin.'

'I call forward General Roman Garcia.' Roman stepped forward and saluted.

'General Garcia, for your commanding of the Artillery Battery and exemplary field support for the Northern Army; you are hereby awarded the order of the Rising Sun, Grand Cordon. Congratulations.' The Emperor placed the sash of silver, edged with red around Roman's chest and the medal was fixed to his left breast.

'Arigatō, Majesty.' Roman thanked the Emperor, saluted and moved away.

'I call forward Fleet Admiral Tyrell Backhouse.'

Tyrell moved forward and the ceremony was repeated.

The awards were made for every unit commander, in descending rank. The Divisional Commanders received the second-class medal, known as the "Gold and Silver Star"; the administrative officers received the third class or "Gold Rays with Neck Ribbon" and so on. Each award made according to the level of work completed.

'I call forward, Major Kheaeng Thamrongnawasawat.' The Aide made several attempts at pronunciation, none of which were close. Eventually, he gave up 'Major Drones.'

Drones was awarded the Rising Sun Grand Cordon as was Haruto Saito.

'In recognition of the incredible work completed by these two Majors and their contribution to the success of the campaign; both are promoted to Colonel.' The Emperors Aide moved forward to hand the Emperor the rank badges for their promotion. This was probably the quickest a private had ever moved up in rank and Drones was very proud to have been able to assist.

Mai was the next to be called and she was awarded the Second-Class Rising Sun as was a, somewhat embarrassed, Colonel Jonson.

Mike Rodrigues followed and his Grand Cordon was very well received for his part in holding up the Russian attempt at a breakthrough.

The second last to be called was Akio. Awarded the Rising Sun Grand Cordon he was slightly embarrassed as he felt he had not done anywhere near what the others had achieved. He bowed and thanked the Emperor; this was far more than he had expected.

There was one left to be awarded.

'I call forward General Jackson Nakagawa.' The name was almost lost in the cacophony of cheers that erupted as his name was spoken. Every member of the command teams as well as those of the ground troops present and the commanders that had already been awarded were cheering.

Finally, the crowd became a little quieter and the Emperor began his speech.

'General Nakagawa was running the Planning Group when war broke out, that much you all know. When General Tanaka was relieved due to wounds it was General Nakagawa that was pushed into the unenviable task of commanding an army that was hard pressed by a powerful enemy. That he regrouped and forged a way ahead is now fact. To be able to continue to push the enemy back he found new weapons, new tactics and a determination not seen for many decades.'

'To bring the enemy to the negotiation table and be able to bring peace to us all is a feat that was not expected. He has re-established the presence of the Ainu in their homelands, he has been able to get the enemy politicians to agree to a return of the islands and the property as well. I do not think it will be possible for us to list all his achievements, those we have already addressed will be sufficient.'

'It gives me the greatest pleasure to award General Nakagawa the highest honour we can. The Supreme Order of the Chrysanthemum, Grand Cordon.'

At that point Jack saluted the Emperor and removed his uniform cap. Kneeling he unclipped his katana; this time he wore "Emperor", the dress sword of his ancestor, and presented it with both hands. The usual, official greeting he gave his Supreme Commander, who after placing his hand on the weapon, refused to take it.

The Emperor placed the sash across Jack's chest and the medal around his neck.

'Congratulations and domo arigatō, General. We could not have done it without you.'

Off at the rear of the huge crowd a cheer arose. "BANZAI, BANZAI, BANZAI." Giving the requisite thirty thousand years of good life to both Jack and the Emperor

Chapter 41
War Crimes

"All Rise" The clerk of the International Court of Justice ordered and all present stood in respect for the three Justices as they took their seats.

'Docket 22301212001, The case of War Crimes. Defendant General Ilya Plishkin of the Russian Army.'

The two groups of lawyers sat at their opposing desks looking directly at each other. This placement of desks deliberately used to avoid the accuser or defendant from using body language to influence the Justices.

'Who is the first witness?'

'Asa Nakagawa.'

Asa was called and she gave her testimony; that the night had been quiet until it was split by three massive explosions. The resultant fire had eventually been contained and the dawn had shown the cottage and the chapel had been destroyed. And the stables had been similarly blown to pieces.

'You claim that you knew the Russian army was to blame, how?'

'Who else would do such a thing? The only reason anyone had to destroy the buildings was because Jack was making their lives miserable, and who would that be? THE RUSSIANS.'

'It could have been a gas explosion?' the lawyer put forward a possibility in an attempt to deflect the probability.

'It could,' Asa agreed. 'Except for a couple of problems with your supposition; first there was no requirement to have gas connected to either the cottage or the chapel; second, who would have a gas connection to a stable?'

The lawyer was frustrated and began to delve into the documentation before him.

'If that is so, how do you explain this gas bill from the utility company?'

Asa gave him the sort of look a mother saves for a stupid question from a child. 'May I see the paper?'

The document was handed to her and she made a great pretence of looking carefully at every word. 'You are an idiot.' She said as she handed the bill back.

'I beg your pardon?'

'I said "YOU ARE AN IDIOT",' she repeated, slowly so even the lawyer became uncomfortable, 'and deaf as well, it seems.'

'And why do you say that?' He replied smugly.

'Because that bill is for the castle, not the cottage. Do you really think two elderly people could use that much gas in a three-month period?'

The lawyer looked carefully at the bill and then spoke briefly with his companions. 'No more questions.'

The defence team then called an expert on military law.

'You have read the articles of war. The claim is that the action attributed to General Plishkin is a war crime, is that so?'

'Given the missile strike destroyed the small buildings It should be viewed as a mistake, an error in targeting.'

'Is that true, is it possible, an error in targeting?'

'Certainly.'

'Your witness.'

Jack's lawyer stood and announced 'No Questions at this time.'

The defence lawyer was now supremely confident in winning the case. All the testimony had supported their argument.

'Prosecution? Your first witness?'

'We call Colonel Karan Hartchev.'

'You can't use him as a witness!'

'Why not, he was there.' The lawyers argued for a few minutes before the Justices gave their consent to the prosecution's request.

'Colonel, you were present when the missile strike was ordered?' 'I was.'

'Why was it ordered?'

'General Nakagawa had been systematically destroying everything we had, General Plishkin needed a method of distracting him so he ordered a strike on Nakagawa's home.'

'He knew it was General Nakagawa's home and he still ordered a strike? Is it possible that there was a targeting error?'

'No, the stated accuracy of the weapon is good enough to ensure that, once launched, the target is hit.'

'Was the possibility of an attack on the castle ever discussed?'

'It was, but General Plishkin said he did not want to damage the heritage site; he believed it was a museum.'

'So, he deliberately targeted the cottage?'

'And the chapel and the stables.'

'You watched as General Nakagawa attacked General Plishkin, did you not?'

'I did.'

'And what were your thoughts?'

'That Plishkin got what he deserved. He was advised not to attack the small buildings, but he did anyway.'

'What did General Nakagawa say, as he struck General Plishkin?'

'The first hit was for his mother, the second was for his father. It was then I knew that civilians had been killed in the strike. I believe he got what he deserved.'

'No more questions.'

There was really no point in the legal argument going much further, but somehow, they managed to keep the legal fight going for a few days. The fact was, no-one could make any indentation in the prosecution argument.

The Justices were not out for long, in their deliberations, they returned with a unanimous decision of guilty and the former General Plishkin was taken away to begin to serve his twenty years imprisonment.

Chapter 42
Back in Hokkaido

'Come it is time for lunch.' Emika ordered Jack and his family to the table. Curiously the one extra was always there; ever since the end of the Border War, Akio had become a fixture in the house, and no one even wondered why.

'Emika there are two extra places set, why?'

'You are getting visitors today. They are coming for lunch.'

'Why did I not know? And who is it?'

'They are here.' Chie answered and shortly the sound of a helicopter could be heard.

'No matter how often I see it, I still enjoy the view of the castle from so high up.' The words were almost shouted to be heard above the noise of the rotors.

'As do I, Shogun. It is a beautiful building.'

'Then I suppose I should greet my guests.'

'Stay there, Jack. I will bring them through.' Chie announced in the "Don't argue with me" voice she used.

'As you wish.' Jack relaxed in his chair and waited. The conversation turning to the condition of the colt that had survived the Russian attack.

'How is he, Jack?'

'Uncle has had him weaned and he is now showing his true nature. He appears to be quite a handful, doesn't like loud sudden noises, probably won't have the temperament for life with the Guard. I am the only one he allows near him at the moment.'

'Then you will have to train him and ride him yourself!'

Jack jumped up and was already bowing before he had "hit the ground"

'Your Majesty, I was not expecting you.'

'And yet here I am. Mark this date on the calendar, please, Jack was surprised by a visit.'

Everyone laughed at Jack's obvious discomfort, it was a rare day indeed that Jack did not know exactly what was going on.

'And why did my personal senkensha not keep me informed?' he demanded, only just keeping a straight face.

'Because I wanted to see what happens to mere mortals that do not have the advantages you normally have.'

'And was it worth it?'

'Oh, most certainly. Quite amusing.'

'Well at least you enjoyed yourself. Come Majesty, Shogun, join us.'

They all sat for a meal, not lavish, quite austere actually, but full of flavour and well punctuated with conversation.

The meal ended and the family and guests left for the rear deck to sit and have coffee. A relaxing time for all.

'Am I allowed to ask why you came so far for lunch? And please do not say it was the meal.'

'OK, Jack. This is the why. Following on from the war there is almost nowhere for you to go. Your victory over the Russians has placed you at the very top of all military positioning and you always say you do not want to be promoted. And yet we find that staying where you are is almost impossible,' replied Hiroshi Kobaya, the Shogun, Commander of the Imperial Guard.

'Thank you, Hiroshi. But your words present more questions than they convey answers?'

'As you say. I have spent considerable time discussing the possibilities and there may be a solution to the enigma that you present. We cannot leave you in your current position, the populace will be outraged that we cannot promote you following your work. We cannot promote you, you don't want it and there is nowhere to put you anyway, and there are many more senior officers that would resent you for it. So, we need to create a position that is unique, for you.'

Jack looked back and forth between the Shogun and the Emperor. If it had been possible to see his brain working, the sparks from the overloaded neurons would be blinding.

'You mean?'

'Yes, Jack. I want to appoint you to the position of "Captain of the Imperial Guard" Your primary position will be "Deputy Commander of the Emperors Personal Guard" but you will also be an official escort to Princess Teimei. Of course you will retain the equivalent rank comparison to your current position of Four-Star General.'

'So that is how you wish to circumvent the gossip. Give the Princess an older escort, one that could not possibly be anything other than an official escort; and then no-one can complain or draw inference that there is a relationship in the air. A very good plan.'

'Well, Majesty. If Jack says it is a good plan, then so it is.'

'You accept, then?' The Emperor asked.

'You know full well that I cannot refuse. If my Emperor wants me to be a Captain of the Guard then so it will be.'

'Arigatō, Jack. I am most grateful you agree. Do you not have any demands? Any requirements?'

'I would like to bring Fumiko as my personal assistant and also Akio Takamatsu as my personal Sensei, if possible?'

'A Sensei of his standing, specialising in the skills of swords, will only benefit the Guard, Your Majesty.' The Shogun was pleased to be offered the services of such a skilled master.

The Emperor looked at the Shogun and commented, 'We have several suites vacant in the lower levels. Jack and Akio can be comfortable there and they will be close to the personal suite of the Princess.'

'I will make the arrangements.'

The deal was done; Jack, along with Fumiko and Akio were now firmly attached to The Imperial Guard.

'Report to the Imperial Palace on the first of next month, once you have completed your induction you will visit the Armourers and the Tailors for your new equipment.'

A chorus of "Hai, Shogun." Accompanied by huge smiles was all the reply they needed; Jack was now a Captain of the Guard.

'Now, Captain, I think we should toast this day with sake.'

Jack called for Emika and she had a barrel of vintage sake brought up from the cellar. No sooner had they tasted it than it was taken away and a new barrel was brought up.

Jack was mortified at the taste, 'I most humbly apologise; something must have gone wrong, we have never had a barrel go off before.'

'Akio, I assume you have your own weapons? I know Jack has the pick of many of the finest examples available.'

'I have many fine training weapons, Majesty, and several top-quality display items; but for a fighting weapon I will borrow one from Jack.'

'Not at all, my friend, we will visit with Watanabe Korehira tomorrow, I feel a new daisho each will be the best way forward.'

'You deal directly with Watanabe Korehira? I have been trying to get a daisho from his workshops for several years.' The Shogun was clearly surprised at the revelation.

'Then try no more, come with us. Tomorrow will be a very good day for us all.'

'For you maybe, but the new Ambassador from Russia will be making his initial visit tomorrow and I must attend.' The Emperor replied, 'Shogun, go with them, the Russian can have an unescorted visit without the trappings of a full diplomatic audience, that is more than they deserve.'

'Arigatō, Majesty. You are most kind.'

They all drank a little too much sake, but not so much they could not perform their duties. The following morning Jack called General Ito and asked for a helicopter for the day for the Shogun to attend to official business for the Emperor.

'Never seen him so eager to assist, what have you done to him Jack?'

'Not really certain, but I did manage to correct some errors in his judgements a while back. Been nice to me ever since.'

'Well, whatever it was, well done.' The Shogun was impressed with the support Jack could garner at a moment's notice.

The helicopter landed in a small clearing a short walk from the family home of Watanabe Korehira. As they neared the house, Korehira waved them inside.

Once close enough for protocol, Jack bowed to his friend and received a bow in return. Introductions were made and, given the rank of the guests, refreshments were served immediately.

'I will have one of my minerai kenshi (apprentice swordsmith) assist the flight crew.'

'Arigatō. I feel we may be here a while.'

The morning gave way to lunch and the coffee gave way to sake. The four men enjoying each other's company as if they were all lifelong friends.

Later in the afternoon the sake gave way to whiskey and eventually Jack suggested that they all go to a local restaurant for dinner. Returning from the restaurant the whiskey gave way to even more whiskey and eventually they all found their way, or more correctly were taken, to a bed somewhere in the house.

The following morning saw four hangovers decide not to have breakfast but to partake in several cold showers and some decidedly necessary coffee to help alleviate the agony of "not seeing friends more often".

Just before lunch, Korehira asked 'So now we have, again, cemented our friendship; what brings you here?'

'Akio and I have been appointed to the Imperial Guard.'

'Well, that is wonderful news, we should celebrate.'

A chorus of "I don't think so" erupted and all laughed.

'Maybe another coffee, will do this time.' Korehira suggested.

'Yes, coffee. As I was saying, we have been appointed to the guard and we will need new ceremonial fighting weapons.'

'So, three daisho, then.'

'No, actually three daisho for us and a new ceremonial daisho for the Emperor.'

'That is going to be expensive, Jack.'

'I know.'

'Jack, I can't let you spend so much on me.' Began the Shoguns protest. 'It is too much.'

'Let me worry about that.'

'You do realise that it is strictly forbidden for a member of the Guard to accept gifts and gratuities?' The shogun announced the official caution; gifts and gratuities were always assumed to come with the need for a reciprocal and any member of the guard that was beholding to any other person was regarded as a liability, their loyalties would be assumed to be divided between their Emperor and the one they owed a debt.

'Which is why I am selling them to you, for a hundred yen each.'

'That will still cost you a fortune?'

'So be it, I am a bad businessman.' Jack grinned. 'But that is as close as I can go to a gift.'

'Arigatō, Jack. This is too much.'

'Not for a friend. Now, Korehira, what do you have on hand?'

The remainder of the afternoon was spent selecting and adjudicating the relative merits of many of the finest weapons to emerge from the forges of

Watanabe Korehira. Eventually, as the sun began to set the selections had been made and the price had been settled.

'Jack,' began Akio, 'You do realise that you have just spent over two million U.S. dollars?'

Jack looked at his friend and simply replied, 'And worth every cent.'

The following morning, this time after a proper breakfast, with the Emperors gift securely held in its katana-zutsu (katana carry case) the helicopter departed with a promise from its occupants to revisit sooner rather than later. 'Stop at the Imperial Palace and wait for us.' Jack ordered the pilot.

'We will visit the Emperor and present his gift. Hiroshi you can continue your business while Akio and I go home and begin to get ourselves together for the move.'

'So, already taking over; giving orders to all and sundry.' Hiroshi could no more contain his laughter than he could keep the smile from his face. 'Arigatō, Jack. I will be looking forward to working with you; and you too Akio, I will need to improve my skills if you and Jack are going to be a permanent presence at the Palace.'

'Don't be surprised if you get some complaints, Akio does not accept second best in his work.'

'Good, we will all benefit then.'

The helicopter landed and the three men made their way through to the Emperors receiving rooms. As they marched even the palace cats decided to watch from the doors rather than the middle of the walkways as they usually did. All except Isamu, the "leader" of the cats. He forced them to walk around him using the simplest method; he simply refused to move.

The aide knocked on the door and announced the visitors. The three moved inside and bowed to the Emperor.

'I trust you had a productive visit with Watanabe Korehira?' the Emperor asked.

'Most productive, Majesty. So much so that we ended up with a spare daisho. I thought you may like it?'

Jack opened the case and the gleaming gold and black lacquered saya gave a hint to what was inside. The saya (scabbard) was gleaming black with gold silk sageo (tie cord for securing the weapon) The design on the saya was inlaid mother of pearl sakura (cherry blossom), the kojiri (tip of the saya) was a solid gold cap.

The ito (tsuka handle) was decorated with the same gold silk as the sageo. Underlaid with a black same (dyed ray skin under the ito) and the menuki (decoration) and kashira (butt cap) were both also solid gold as were the tsuba (guard), the fuchi (tsuka collar), the habaki (blade collar) and the koiguchi (saya opening collar).

The highly polished and finished blade was as sharp as could be ever made. The matching wakizashi was the same, just a little shorter and the katana-zutsu was lacquered and inlaid to match the contents.

'A truly magnificent example of the work of a Master Kenshi (swordsmith),' the Emperor almost whispered as he examined the gift. 'But surely it is too expensive to simply give away?'

'Not at all, Majesty; over the centuries my family have had many weapons made at the Watanabe workshops. This is simply one of his very best pieces of work. He, and I, are more than happy that it will be used and not left to gather dust on a wall somewhere; owned by someone that simply wants to be able to say he has a "Watanabe daisho" in his collection, and impress his friends with the simple statement not with his ability or any real requirement.'

Chapter 43
Induction

The family gathered for the evening meal; Asa, Hana, Reo and Sora were all chatting away with Akio and Chie. Just spending quality time together before the meal was served. Emika was busy cooking and the grooms were closing the stables for the night. A normal closing to the daily routine at Jack's house. With one small exception. Jack was nowhere to be seen.

'Where has he gone this time?' Hana asked. It was a rhetorical question, spoken with a little sarcasm and a smile.

'Fumiko is taking care of him.' Chie answered.

"Taking care" would normally indicate that she was giving some type of assistance; in this case she was simply kneeling behind him while he finished his prayers at his parent's graves.

As he regained his feet, he turned and thanked Fumiko for her support. He always found it difficult to be near the remains of the chapel and his parents graves. He felt he should have been able to prevent their deaths, and in some measure, he blamed himself.

Looking around at the area there was almost no indication that a chapel had once stood nearby. The only piece remaining was the "corner stone" which had been retrieved from the rubble and placed back in its original position.

The builders had already begun to lay the foundations and prepare for the rebuilding of the family chapel close to the original position.

'Come, Jack,' she said, 'they will be wondering where we are.'

'You think so?' he asked.

'No, but it sounded right to say so. You know full well that they know exactly where we are, and why.'

'Yes; but in my defence, I still find it a little difficult to not be here.'

'That is why they have left us alone, here. They all come when they feel the need to do so.'

'Why is it that I feel as though I will not be able to do this much longer, come here?'

'Because you have many very important events in the future. None of which will be here. You will be away for some years and you will not have the benefit of a chapel. Use this while you can, keep it in your mind for when you cannot.'

'Arigatō, Fumiko. As always your words are a great comfort to me.'

The final family dinner was a lavish affair, foods came and went as did drink and confections. They all ended the night on the rear deck looking at the lights, dotted across the mountains and twinkling in the distance.

The next morning the helicopter lifted off at ten and made the quick trip to the Imperial Palace.

'They have just landed, Your Majesty.' The Emperor's assistant announced as he waited at the door for further instructions.

'Very good. Show them to the official receiving room.'

'Hai.' The assistant hustled away to ensure the guests were taken to the proper rooms.

His family were all led to the official room and shown to their seats. Jack and Akio were taken to a separate room to dress in their new uniforms. Fumiko helping Jack to get all the medals and other accoutrements correctly positioned on the different design uniform. The only item missing was the unique rank insignia of The Guard.

Eventually, the clock turned to two pm.

'All rise.' The order was given and marked the beginning of the ceremony. All those present to witness the induction stood and waited.

'Their Imperial Highnesses, The Crown Prince and Princess.' Everyone bowed as the Prince and Princess moved to their seats and bowed in return.

'Her Imperial Majesty, The Empress Akahana.' Everyone bowed deeply, honouring the Empress.

A minute later; 'His Imperial Majesty, The Emperor Daiki.' Again, all bowed, this time waiting for the Emperor to move to his seat and bow in return. Once everyone had become comfortable the announcer began.

'Today we are here to induct two new members in the Imperial Guard. I call forward Major Akio Takamatsu.'

'Akio moved forward and saluted the Emperor, removed his cap and handed it to an assistant waiting with him. Kneeling, he unclipped his daisho and placed them on the floor, tsuka to the left and edge towards himself.

'Akio Takamatsu, you have been appointed to a position in the Imperial Guard. Do you undertake this position voluntarily?'

'Hai.'

'Your position will require you to defend all members of the Imperial Family at all times, even unto death. Do you still agree to the position?'

'Hai,' he replied without hesitation.

The Emperor moved forward and an aide opened a carved cherrywood case and offered the Emperor the rank braid within. A group of three gold coloured silk braids; layered to place them in loops within each other, the Emperor attached the rank braid for a Chief Samurai to the right shoulder, outside the sleeve and surrounding the badge of the Imperial Guard.

'Congratulations; regain your weapons and rise, Chief Samurai Takamatsu.' The Emperor addressed Akio directly.

'Domo arigatō, Majesty.' Akio stood and was handed his cap. Placing it on his head he saluted and then turned and made his way to the side, making room for Jack.

The audience applauded loudly and Akio had a massive smile on his face as he moved away from the Emperor.

'I call forward General Jackson Nakagawa.'

Jack marched in and stopped before the Emperor. Removing his cap, he handed it to the aide behind him. As usual, for Jack, he knelt and unclipped his daisho at the same time. Holding it with both hands, tsuka to the left and edge towards himself he raised it as though it were a gift, his normal greeting to the Emperor.

'You may keep your weapon.' The Emperor announced and Jack replied "Arigatō." As he placed his weapons on the floor.

'Jackson Nakagawa, you have been appointed to a position in the Imperial Guard. Do you undertake this position voluntarily?'

'Hai.'

'Your position will require you to defend all members of the Imperial Family at all times, even unto death. Do you still agree to the position?'

'Hai,' he replied without hesitation.

The Emperor moved forward and an aide opened a second carved cherrywood case and offered the Emperor the rank braid within. A group of four gold coloured silk braids; layered to place them in loops within each other, the Emperor attached the rank braid for a Captain Samurai to the right shoulder, outside the sleeve and surrounding the badge of the Imperial Guard.

'Congratulations; retrieve your weapons and rise, Captain Samurai Jackson Nakagawa.' The Emperor addressed Jack directly.

'Domo arigatō, your Majesty,' he replied.

With that simple statement the official portion of the induction ceremony was complete. As they all dispersed, they were led outside to enjoy the "Garden Party" that always followed an induction ceremony; family and guests first and the Imperial Family following them. The new inductees would be "presented" to them all, a few minutes later.

As Akio and Jack emerged into the palace grounds, they were astounded to see the vast majority of the guard waiting for them, cheers and applause quickly gave way to shouts of "Banzai" for them and the Imperial Family. Jack and Akio were very popular new members of the Imperial Guard.

Chapter 44
A Legal Problem

The Pentagon

'Colonel Jonson, come in here please.' The hologram on her desk shutdown as quickly as it had started up.

'You want to see me Sir?' The Colonel was confused, the request was stated as just that, but the underlying inference was that it was an order.

'Just got this, Colonel,' he pushed a signal across the desk. 'Care to elaborate?'

Jonson read the signal and then re-read it. 'It appears that General Nakagawa has listed me as a witness in a legal trial, I have no idea why.'

'He says he is going to collect you on his way through to The Hague. Let him know you will be ready, but he will have to speak with me and our legal team from JAG (Judge Advocate General).'

'I will call him and make certain he knows your requirements.' Jonson left and placed a call on Jack's private line.

'Konichiwa, Colonel. I gather you have received the signal?'

'Good morning to you too Sir, yes and I have been ordered to ask you to speak with General Moreton and the team from JAG before we depart D.C.'

'Not a problem, Akio and I will be travelling with a lawyer as well, I will be there in one week, so Wednesday next week. Wheels down at Andrews (Airforce Base) at approximately 1100 local, we can meet after lunch, does that suit your requirements?'

'Fine with me, I will get General Moreton to clear a couple of hours from his schedule.'

'Arigatō, see you then.'

The hologram closed off and Jonson was left wondering exactly what was going on. She then returned to the Generals office and explained the call.

'Did he give any ideas about what was happening?'

'No, Sir. But he did not appear to be concerned at all.'

'Hmmm. Your professional opinion?'

'You mean as his psychologist?'

'Yes.'

'He always gives the appearance of being in control, in this instance he does not exhibit any distractions, I do not think it is as serious as the signal hints.'

'Very well, next Wednesday it is.'

The Wednesday morning arrived, and Colonel Jonson simply waited for the morning to pass away. A call from the Traffic Controllers at Andrews alerted her to the fact that Jack's flight had arrived and had been cleared by Border Control. Jack and Akio had lunch on the plane and at 1230 a car took them to the Pentagon for the meeting.

The office intercom gave a quiet "ping" as it indicated that General Moreton's secretary wished to speak.

'Yes?' He answered, as always, sounding a little gruff. 'Colonel Jonson is here with your 1300.'

'Send them in; and call JAG, find out why they are late.'

The door opened and Jonson waited for Jack and Akio to enter. Wearing their "day" uniforms, black with medal ribbons and a katana at the side, they did not appear to be a member of any military group that General Moreton could think of.

Jack held out his hand. 'Jack Nakagawa,' he introduced himself and the two shook hands. 'This is Akio Takamatsu, my sensei.'

Greetings all round and they sat, waiting for the lawyers to arrive.

'General Nakagawa, I must say I was quite confused when I got your signal?' The statement was more question than anything else.

'That is Captain Nakagawa.'

'Captain? That is a huge drop from General?'

'No, I apologise, I am not making myself clear; I am a Captain Samurai of the Imperial Guard; I still retain the equivalency of my previous four-star status. Akio is a Chief Samurai, equal to a senior Colonel.'

'OK, that is going to confuse a lot of people.' Colonel Jonson commented.

'It does,' replied Akio, 'but it is always fun watching their faces when they get it completely wrong.' His grin was as wide as ever.

'So, tell me; if you are still a four-star, who is your Commanding Officer?'

'I report directly to the Shogun, and he to the Emperor.'

'That is a very shallow reporting line,' he commented on the apparent lack of political levels for the guard. 'We have under ministers, secretaries, Secretary of Defence, and a few hanging on before we get to the President.'

'We were appointed by the Emperor, and we do not form a part of the Defence Forces, so we by-pass all the usual governmental levels.'

'Interesting concept, I wish we could get by without the political interference.'

'Ours is a system that does not work for the regular military, we are the Emperor's Guard and as such we do not perform any other function than the protection of the Imperial Family and their residences. A military group, however, is the enforcement arm of their government and they must be viewed as a part of the government; hence political oversight. It helps us that we are a relatively small group and are not a part of the armed forces.'

The small talk continued for some time and General Moreton was getting more than a little angry at the tardy appearance of the lawyers. Finally, the intercom beeped, as the general's secretary announced their arrival.

The door opened and a posse of lawyers and assistants flooded the room.

'About dammed time; where the hell have you been? Captain Nakagawa was getting ready to leave.' It was a small lie and Jack acknowledged it with an imperceptible nod, Akio and Jonson were both watching Jack and picked up on the small gesture.

'My apologies, General Moreton. We were held up in the traffic.'

'No telephones?' Jack asked innocently, deliberately baiting the lawyer just to see how much it took to get him angry.

The lawyer, a full Colonel, completely ignored Jack's question and began to prepare for the briefing.

After waiting for a minute General Moreton spoke up, 'Captain Nakagawa asked you a question? You just going to ignore him?'

'General, I am not in the habit of being questioned by a captain.' The terse reply was met by a stony silence from Moreton and a burst of Japanese from Jack and Akio. In the brief moments after, Akio stood up and moved the hologram controls to allow easier access.

'If I may General?' he asked.

'Fire away.' Moreton did not know exactly what was going to happen but his discussions with Colonel Jonson had prepared him enough to know that there would be a slap-down coming soon.

The hologram came to life with a view of the inside of the Russian H.Q. just at the end of the Border War, as it was now being called. Taken from Jonson's combat body cam, the image was just behind and to one side and showed Jack and Akio standing side by side.

'What the hell is this?' the lawyer demanded; the only reply was Jack's voice demanding to know which was General Plishkin.

The lawyers sat, unbelieving, as they witnessed the beating that Jack handed the Russian. Once it was over; Akio closed-down the hologram and sat back in his seat relaxing and sipping his coffee.

Finally, one of the junior lawyers had the courage to ask, 'Who was that?'

'That was me,' Jack replied. 'The victim was General Plishkin, Commanding General of all Russian Forces in the Kurils.'

'And that is why we are here. So, don't anger Captain, formerly "General, Commanding Japanese Forces Northern Pacific", Jackson Nakagawa.' Smiling, General Moreton added, 'I understand he doesn't like lawyers.'

One of the assistants pushed a tablet in-front of the senior lawyer and all waited as he read the short history of Jackson Nakagawa as shown on his Wikipedia entry.

Finally, the lawyer looked up. 'You did that? All that?' he indicated the page before him.

'And a lot more,' Jonson added. 'And, as his therapist, I must say I am surprised you still have all your teeth.'

It took a while for the words to penetrate but eventually he began to stammer an apology.

'Don't apologise for not knowing.' Jack snapped back. 'Your office was told what was happening here today and you did not do your due diligence. If you had, you would know who I am and what I have achieved. General Moreton I think a Colonel is far overpowered for the job at hand, a junior lawyer and one assistant will be sufficient to cover the U.S. Army's involvement in this issue.' Moreton gave Jack a quizzical look and it was replied with a nod.

'Colonel, leave the assistant and his tablet and the lieutenant; the rest of you can leave.'

'General, may I remind you that this case is to be heard at the International Court of Justice. Its high status demands a very senior legal team.' The Colonel replied.

'Do I detect a serious level of personal aggrandisement?' Jonson asked. 'You don't want this for the important legal battle it is, you want the glory that comes with winning a case in the highest court in the world. General Moreton, I have a couple of Masters students that would benefit greatly from analysing the Colonel and his desire for acknowledgement?' The question was a slap in the face, and the lawyer could not dispute it.

'Thank you, Colonel, that will be all.' General Moreton dismissed the lawyer and his entourage and once the door had closed behind them everyone visibly relaxed.

'Lieutenant, you seem pleased to be the one left behind?'

'Sir, I feel privileged to be assigned this case. Even if it just as a buffer for Colonel Jonson.'

'Why do you put it that way?' Moreton was interested in the thinking of the young officer.

'The U.S. involvement in the Border Wars was minimal, to say the least. Less than a hundred Marines, a few ships and around a thousand sailors, and of course Colonel Jonson. I will be there simply to defend U.S. interests. Given the charges laid, my input will be minimal.'

'And that,' interrupted Akio, 'is the difference between him and the Colonel; no personal agenda.'

'Quite right. Arigatō Sensei.' Jack addressed his friend using his most formal title. As he spoke, he pushed some buttons on the hologram control. 'Haruto, can you get control of this?'

'Already have it.'

'Who is he?' General Moreton was extremely concerned, the implication stated that a stranger, a foreign stranger, now had access and control of the Pentagon's Hologram Communications System.

'General, may I present Colonel Haruto Saito, Officer Commanding SatCon Central Command.'

'General, nice to meet you.'

'And you too, Colonel. This is supposed to be the most secure comms system in the world.'

'Funny about that, the Russians thought that about their Combat Communications and Command Protocol; and they still don't have any idea why they can't contact some of their satellites.'

'Captain, your man here seems to be having a great deal of fun? This is very serious.'

'I agree General, Haruto what have you been getting up to?'

'Nothing much; just having a little fun now that the fighting is over.'

'Ok, what have you done?' it was almost an accusation, but not quite.

'Well, truth be known, I have been sending pictures of the, let's call them "wayward" members of the former Russian Government as they try to cover their naughty ways.'

'Sending them where?' Moreton was intrigued.

'To their current political masters.'

'Can I ask why?'

'They caused the deaths of a lot of innocent people, ours and theirs. As the Australians say, "Paybacks are a bitch".'

'How do we know you are not doing the same to us?'

'Because we do not care how other countries are run, as long as they don't attack us.'

'As I told you, General,' Jonson began, 'they do not follow much in the way of convention. All is fair in war; maybe not right but all is fair.'

'Remind me not to make you angry Captain.'

'Then call me Jack; there are many times when rank just gets in the way of a good conversation. By the way, Caroline, congratulations on achieving your PHD.'

Jonson looked shocked; this was the first time Jack had used her given name.

'But I haven't even applied for my Doctorate?'

Jack smiled. 'Haruto?'

'Hai, one moment.' Seconds later a document appeared on the hologram. They all read it at least twice. Colonel Caroline Jonson was now Doctor Caroline Jonson, PHD.

'How did this happen?'

'You ticked the wrong box on your application form. This has all gone through and the Board of Medical Services at Harvard approved your doctorate this morning.'

'But how did you get the copy?' she asked, clearly astounded at the events unfolding before her.

'Would you like to take a moment to think about who you asked that?' Jack replied.

Caroline looked around the table, smiling faces all around her, then as she looked at the hologram image of Haruto it finally clicked.

'You hacked Harvard?'

'You sound surprised; and we prefer to call it "accessed data"; "hacked" has so many centuries of poor connotations.'

OK, down to business.' Jack suddenly began to address the situation. 'Drones, do we have the legal team online?'

'They have just lifted off from Singapore. Give them a minute.'

'Who the hell is "Drones"?' General Moreton was getting the feeling he had been overrun.

'Drones; meet General Leroy Moreton, he is the Head of Medical Services. Leroy, this is Colonel Drones Commander Remote Surveillance and Ranging Services.'

'Nice to meet you Leroy. Congratulations, Caroline. Well done, was it worth the terrifying dive into Jack's brain to get there?'

'Now it is done I feel that it was very much worth the journey, if you had asked me a month after we had met, the answer may have been very different.'

'Can I ask a question or two please? This being my office and all.' Leroy Moreton was not expecting everyone to laugh, after all he was the General Commanding Medical Services and such a request would usually be met with a polite "yes, Sir" or a similar response.

'If you wish.' A small voice from the depths replied.

'And who was THAT?' Leroy was now getting frustrated; so many voices and images on HIS hologram that no one had authorised.

'My name is Fumiko; I am Jack's Personal Assistant. Jack, the Shogun sends his apologies, a planning meeting with the Crown Prince is lasting a little longer than he thought.'

'Arigatō, ask him to join us when he can.'

'Hai.' Fumiko left the call and they began to get the meeting underway.

'Leroy, you had a question?' Jack asked.

'I was wondering if this is what it is like all the time around you? People jumping in, dropping a snippet of information and then dropping out just as quick?'

'Actually; Sir, it is. What you have just seen is a small part of Jack's life. It was much busier during the Border Wars.' Caroline interjected.

'I am beginning to see why your reports appeared to be a jumble of information.'

'I must apologise, again, for that. But it was actually a lot busier during the war.'

'Your thesis is beginning to make a lot more sense.'

'Thank you, Sir.'

'Legal Team on line, Jack.'

'OK, down to business. You have all read copies of the charge sheets, any questions? Comments?'

The real business of the meeting went for over two hours, no point was left unsaid or unquestioned. The more they discussed it, the more headway they made. As the meeting was drawing to a close there was one question that had been left unasked.

Eventually, it was Akio that spoke up.

'Are you certain you want to yank their chain that hard?'

Jack thought for a moment. 'Hai. This is a very trivial matter and yet they have decided to take it to the highest court possible. I need them to be on the back foot, this will do it.'

'So why do you need Colonel Jonson?' Leroy was still a little confused.

'She is, essentially an independent witness, her combat camera files will give a clear and unequivocal answer to the charges.'

The hologram beeped. 'Many apologies, Jack. The Ministers would not stop talking.'

'No apology needed; Hiroshi Kobaya this is Leroy Morton; Leroy, Hiroshi. I will get Mai to send you a copy of the entire meeting to bring you up to date. What I need is a confirmation that, firstly Full-Dress Uniform is appropriate and that a daisho is a required part of that uniform.'

'You need this in writing?'

'Written up as a part of the Manual of Uniforms will be sufficient.'

'The Emperor has asked if you need some regal assistance?'

Jack thought for a moment. 'Can you ask him to make it an order from the palace? That will stir them up.'

'Consider it done. And it is your turn to buy dinner.'

'Done, meet us in London this time next week, there is a little place near Sandhurst that I like. Leroy, come with us.'

'I think I will. I just need to convince the wife that it is essential I go.'

'Bring her with you, in fact we have enough time, we will stopover for an extra night or two and you can fly with us.'

'Caroline, do you have a dress sword? Or as a medical officer are you not permitted to wear one?'

'Despite going into battle with an assault rifle, we are generally not permitted weapons.'

'Wait, you went into battle, armed?' Leroy was both amazed and angry at the break in protocol.

Jack leaped to her defence. 'I ordered her to be armed, we were going into a fight against several divisions of infantry and armour, she needed to be able to protect herself. As it turned out, hers was the only weapon not fired that day.'

'OK. I can't pretend to be happy, but she was under your command. No harm, no foul, as they say.'

'Are there any Cavalry units near us?' Jack, as usual, had changed the direction of the conversation without notice.

'Fifth Cavalry Regiment is at Fort McNair awaiting deployment.' Haruto was quick to reply.

'Leroy, can we get Caroline attached to the Fifth for a day?'

'Yes, but why?'

'If she is attached, she can wear the uniform and insignia of the Regiment; that means we can get her uniform patches, in addition to her medical insignia, and a sabre to wear. It looks better than an officer's dress sword, it has an air of purpose not unlike a katana.'

'You are doing this, all of this, just to create an impression?'

'Certainly, if we walk in wearing daily work uniforms we will be seen as lower in status. Put us all in dress uniforms, and with real weapons and we stand out as being at the top of the tree. By the way Caroline, do you have all your medals yet?'

'No, not yet.'

'We need to get onto that. Hasegawa, can we get the Active Service, Foreign Service, War Combat and Special Merit medals for Colonel Caroline Jonson?'

'They will be mounted and dispatched today.'

'Arigatō.'

'Wait a moment, you had wound, a rifle round went across your arm. Leroy, we need to get a Purple Heart for her as well as the Foreign War Service medal.'

'Jack, it was just a stray shot.'

'None the less, you were wounded in combat.'

'Colonel, you did not report this?' Leroy was finally getting the message that things simply happened around Jack without any heavy demands.

'I was not concerned, a couple of stiches and a dressing was all it took, there were so many others wounded that I did not feel right making a fuss of it. Even Jack had three or four bullet wounds and he waited for the others to be treated.'

'I will have it ready this evening, ceremony tomorrow 9am.'

'Thank you, Sir, that is so very kind of you.'

'You are welcome and call me Leroy, that seems to work around these men.'

The Commander of the Fifth Cavalry presented Caroline with her Regimental Patches and Sabre; the other awards were made, the Purple Heart, Foreign War Service and the Japanese medals were presented and proudly worn. Two days later they left for London and then The Hague.

The ground transport arrived at the court building, an impressive almost cathedral like building completed in the early 20th century, the heritage building and its surrounds were incredibly beautiful. The grounds were manicured lawns and sculpted trees and bushes.

Jack's motorcade drove up the driveway and stopped at the main entrance. Each member of his team attaching their daisho as they emerged.

Once they were all ready, it was Jack that was leading them as they entered the building. As they approached the Concierge desk, needing to be directed to the appropriate court room, a group of armed security guards rushed out and levelled their weapons at them.

'Don't move!' their supervisor shouted, and everyone stopped, except Jack, he took several steps forward and fixed the supervisor with a stare that would take the initiative from the guards.

'Put your weapons down!' Jack ordered and half of the guards complied.

'I am—'

'I don't care who you are, remove your weapons!' the guard shouted.

Again, Jack stared at him. 'Does it make you feel powerful to shout at people? Because it does not work with me. Either speak quietly with respect or don't speak at all.'

The supervising guard was now a little unsure, no one had ever challenged them before and he was just a little unsure as to how to progress. Eventually, he found the words he was looking for.

'Weapons are not permitted.' Was what he said and yet, somehow, the words did not feel right to him immediately he had spoken.

'Then why are you carrying them?' Jack asked in a simple, quiet voice.

'We are the guards here and you are not allowed to have weapons.'

'Ah, so it is a power stance. You have the weapons so you are in charge. You know, the Russian Army once thought that too.'

The reference took them by surprise, no one had ever argued with them before and now they were becoming unsure how to proceed.

'Either place your weapons on the table and back away, or leave!' The Supervising Guard had finally managed to make a definitive statement.

'I thank you for the choice, we will leave. Return to the cars.' Jack ordered and they all turned around and left the building. Jack waited for the word that they were all in the cars and then he turned and left, as he passed through the main entrance into the warm sunshine he turned and addressed the supervisor,

'Kindly inform the Judges of your decision to eject us, they will be expecting us in court in around twenty minutes.'

Before he could be stopped, Jack was in the car and they made their way to the landing area and were back in their helicopter and on their way to The Royal Military College at Sandhurst.

Back at the Court, all hell was breaking loose.

'Where are they? They have been summoned to court,' the Russian lawyers were shouting, demanding Jack and his team be arrested and tried for Contempt of Court.

After a lot of argument, it was finally decided to call the Imperial Palace to find out what had happened, the call was rerouted to the Shogun.

'Imperial Guard, Shogun speaking.' Hiroshi answered the phone in as gruff a voice as he could, he knew exactly what was going on and he was always going to help his friend.

'Good day, sir. I am calling from the International Court of Justice; your Captain Nakagawa was to appear here this morning and he has not arrived. Do you have a reason for this?'

'He did arrive. Your security detail ordered him to leave, so he did, along with his legal team and witnesses.'

'Oh. Thank you. I will investigate, may I call you back?'

'Of course.'

'Get me the Senior Guard on duty this morning!' The Clerk of Court was furious, it was far beyond the duty of the Guard to prevent the appearance of the accused.

A few minutes later, 'You wish to speak with me?'

'Yes, come in, sit.'

The Supervising Guard entered the room and closed the door behind him.

'You turned a group away this morning, why?'

'Everyone of them was wearing a weapon.'

The Clerk of Court was instantly intrigued. 'What sort of weapons?'

'They all had swords.'

'Swords?' The Clerk thought for a moment and then asked 'Were they in a dress uniform?'

'I suppose it was, yes. They all had medals, not ribbons, and some had stars on their jackets as well.'

'And you are still alive to bear witness to this.'

'I don't understand?'

'The man you sent away, with his legal team and witnesses was none other than Jackson Nakagawa, the man that defeated the Russian Army, and Airforce, and Navy; he was supposed to appear before the court this morning and now no one knows where he is. Thank you for this mess I now have to fix.'

'But he should still not have been wearing a weapon!' The Guard protested loudly, but the Clerk of Court was no longer listening.

Chapter 45
Dinner with Friends

Signals Communication Room
Royal Military College, Sandhurst

The young signalman was on his first watch, ever. Just graduated from the School of Signals a week before, he had been posted to the Signals Office at the College and this was his first job, delivering a simple signal.

'Where is the Deputy's office?' he asked the duty sergeant.

'Third floor, turn right out of the lift. It is down the hall on the left.

He approached the door and checked the nameplate "Deputy Commandant, Colonel Mark Gibbs R.M. (Royal Marines). Taking a breath, he knocked firmly but not too loudly.

'Enter!' came the reply from within.

The young signalman opened the door and saw the Colonel sitting behind his desk reading from what appeared to be a very small, very old book titled "Go Rin No Sho".

'Signal Sir, Duty Sergeant said to hand it directly to you.'

'Read it please,'

'Message reads, "Arriving H 10M 10P".' (Helicopter, ten minutes, ten passengers)

'Odd, is there a signature or authorisation?'

'It says signed "Taipan 1" nothing else. We could not find a reference in the manuals.'

Mark put the book down instantly. 'When was it received?'

'Less than five minutes ago.'

'Go to the Commandant and inform him we have visitors arriving.' A wave of the hand sent the private scurrying off in confusion; everyone he knew said he was going to what was probably the quietest billet in the army, yet here he was with his very first signal and everyone was instantly rushing about.

He arrived at the Commandants office and then read the signal to the Commandant; who promptly responded with "Shit, we have a parade ground full.

Colonel Mark Gibbs knew exactly what was happening and he knew that sufficient room to land would be required. He opened the window and shouted "Sergeant Major, clear the parade ground, inbound helo."

Every window with a view to the parade ground was crammed with faces. Word had spread like wildfire that someone was arriving in a hurry, and everyone wanted to know who.

Just five minutes later a large passenger helicopter could be seen approaching the open area. Even though the signal had given the impression that everything was in a hurry, the pilot was not. Hovering for a few moments, he then placed it down gently in the centre of the parade ground.

The passenger door opened just as the Commandant and his Deputy arrived.

'What the hell are you doing here?' Mark quickly moved towards his friend and they embraced. 'Last I heard you were kicking Russians all over the place.'

'Yeah, that was fun.' The two smiled and chatted as the remainder of the passengers emerged.

Introductions were made all round and cadets were assigned to retrieve the luggage. Suites were made ready for the senior officers and rooms for the juniors. Once clear, the helicopter was taken to a nearby RAF Base until it was required for the return journey, while the former occupants were taken to the officer's mess for refreshments

'So, what actually brings you here, Jack?' Mark asked the question that everyone wanted answered.

Jack gave a quick explanation of the events at the International Court.

'You mean to tell us that you have deliberately NOT appeared at the highest court on the planet?' The college commandant was stunned.

'You make it sound like it's a bad thing when you put it that way. I prefer to think of it as "complying with an order from an officer of the court".' Jack was smiling widely as he recounted the morning, 'I didn't have anywhere else to go so I thought "Mark is a good friend, maybe I can stay with him for a couple of days" so here we are.'

'You make yourself an international fugitive and the first place you go is a military base. That takes guts.' Mark was still astounded.

'Maybe, but I thought we can all go to Katsuo's for dinner.'

'He will be very pleased to see you; I will call for reservations.'

At that point a steward approached the table. 'Excuse me, Sir,' he addressed the Commandant, 'there is another unexpected visitor, he appears to be wearing a similar uniform to Captain Nakagawa.'

The commandant looked at Mark, and Mark looked at Jack; Jack nodded and the steward was told to bring the visitor in.

As they approached the table, Jack stood up and bowed. 'About time you arrived Hiroshi.'

'Yes, yes, I had to come through the gate not fly over it.' The shogun replied with a grin and took a seat. More introductions and explanations all round. 'Arigatō, now Let's get out of these uniforms and into some more comfortable clothes.'

All the guests were taken to their rooms and were back in the mess within an hour. The questions did not stop until they were ready to leave for the restaurant.

'Colonel Gibbs, when you told me you knew Jackson Nakagawa, I thought you meant you had met him, I was unaware you were drinking friends?' The commandant asked.

'Well, Jack and I trained at a dojo nearby, and from that we became very close friends.'

'And he is one of only two that have beaten me in the dojo.' Jack added.

'And who is the other?'

'That would be me.' Akio raised his hand and acknowledged the accolade.

'Tell us more of the Border Wars?' Mark asked.

'Over dinner. Jack replied.

As they approached the restaurant Mark confessed 'I didn't tell Katsuo you were coming, I just asked for a table big enough for us all. Luckily a birthday party cancelled at the last moment and he can accommodate us all.'

'Good. Let's see how he reacts. Get everyone else inside first, I will make the grand entrance and ask if he has a table for the evening.'

Katsuo Kobayashi was looking forward to having one of his good friends in the rooms for dinner, it had been a long time since they had time together and he was anticipating a good evening with lots of sake between them.

Waiting at the door and looking for his friend, Katsuo was eager for him to arrive, it had only just registered that Mark was bringing a large group of fellow diners when he spotted the bus arriving.

Mark was first out of the small bus they had taken for the evening and he was greeted as the old and close friend he was. One by one they all entered the restaurant and each was introduced to their host. When he introduced Akio, Katsuo was overtaken with emotion, a member of the Imperial Guard in his rooms. The next was The Shogun and Katsuo bowed so deeply they thought he must fall on the ground.

'Arigatō, please not so low, such a bow should be reserved for the Emperor.'

Katsuo was instantly apologetic.

'Please do not apologise, I really appreciate the honour you do me.'

Showing his distinguished guests to their table, he didn't even notice the spare seat at the table as he took the orders for drinks. As he ordered the waitress to bring water for the table, he heard the bell over the door ring, heralding yet another customer. Inwardly smiling he began to think that the cancelled party would not be a loss after all.

He overheard the new customer ask the waiter at the door for a table.

'I apologise we have no spare seats tonight,' he was told politely.

'Perhaps I could speak with the manager?' Jack asked with a disappointed tone to his voice.

'I am the owner; how can I help?' Katsuo was approaching from behind.

'Perhaps a chair for an old friend?' Jack asked as he turned around. 'And maybe a guinomi (traditional cup) of your very best sake served at 42 degrees.'

Instantly a tear rolled down his cheek. 'My friend, for you the world. For Mister Mark,' he turned and wagged a finger at Mark, 'A seat out the back in the car park.'

Mark grinned and said 'I apologise, but it was too good a chance to miss.'

'And that is fair, you are forgiven.' Katsuo led Jack to his seat; and Jack promptly gave him the billing details for the evening.

'No, not again. You must not keep paying here.'

'Sorry, Katsuo, but I have been appointed to the Imperial Guard, and...'

'And you are not permitted to receive gifts, I know. But how do I repay you, for everything?'

'You already have; your friendship is all I need.'

Off to one side the Commandant whispered in Mark's ear, 'How can he afford to pay for us all?'

'I will give you a hint,' Mark whispered. 'His passions are his fleet of Bentleys, his Vintage Aston Martin and Friesians, He lives in a castle that he owns. And his family are one of the wealthiest in Japan, that makes him mega-rich and don't even bother trying to pay your share, it won't happen. Enjoy the evening and the company, that is all he asks.'

'My god, you hang out with powerful people, don't you?'

'Yeah, took me taking a couple of whippings in the dojo to get this far.'

'You mean you let him win?'

'No, I had to beat him, and beat him fair and square, he does not like it when an opponent does not try everything.'

'Now, Katsuo, is Simon working tonight?' Jack's question turned the conversation around.

'He is, in the kitchen preparing your meals.' Jack got up and excusing himself from the group he went to the kitchen.

'Who is Simon?' Caroline asked.

Akio grinned broadly. 'You mean you have mined deep into his brain for months and you never discovered Simon? Mark, would you do the honours?'

Mark nodded and gave the gathered diners the story of the evening that Jack and he had prevented the assault and robbery of the entire restaurant.

'I can't believe it!' Caroline eventually spluttered. 'All those months and he never mentioned it.'

'That is Jack.' Akio simply stated the fact that his friend does not seek justification in his every move. 'I am willing to bet he did not tell you that he bought Simons Grandmothers house after Tom and Johnny were put away by the Judge, either.'

'No!' At this point everyone was wondering what would be the next revelation. 'And he also pays for Simons wages and college tuition.'

By now all were intensely interested in what would be next.

'Why did he buy the house?' This time it was the shogun that asked.

'Simon and his grandmother were doing it tough,' Mark replied. 'So, Jack bought the house as an investment and they live there for one pound per year, rent.'

'That is ludicrous!'

'You may think so, but; Jack has a property, Simon and his grandmother keep the maintenance up to it, the two have a place to live and another cycle of poverty and want are removed from society. The only stipulation is that Simon keeps working. Katsuo agreed to put him on as "minerai shefu", apprentice chef.'

'Why?' Caroline asked, her original presumption of Jack had been turned over several times since she first met him. This was not a hard-nosed authoritarian military commander; this was a caring human being that looked after those close to him and those in need as well.

'Jack does a lot of this work. None of you would be aware that his family trust, controlled by his sisters, runs three shelters in Sapporo. One each for homeless men and women and one for victims of family violence. His military salary and that of his two brothers go directly into the trust, they serve for no pay. The money as well as a grant each year from the estate income and some philanthropical donations from across Japan sees the shelters well supported.' Akio was the only person in the world, outside the family, that knew the details.

'And he can still afford to buy us dinner? I had no idea he was so deeply involved in charity work.' The Shogun was almost overwhelmed with the revelation.

'He prefers to keep it secret, simply to stop the tricksters from making demands of him and his family.'

At that point, Jack emerged from the kitchen and everyone turned and looked at him.

'So, Sensei, you have been disclosing my private life!'

'Of course, these are friends and they deserve to see, and know, a little extra of you.'

Jack looked suspiciously at his oldest friend. 'I suppose you are right. But, Caroline, you do not get to update your thesis from these revelations.'

Caroline looked at him as he cast his gaze around the table, gauging the reactions of his friends. 'Thesis, nothing, I want to write your biography and then donate the profits to your Family Trust.'

Jack's head snapped as he turned to face her, his eyes giving nothing away but the action had everyone on edge, he had been caught out; he could hardly ignore the possibility of big profits being donated and yet he still would prefer to keep his private life private.

Eventually, he spoke, 'Very well, you have my permission. Leroy, we will need to get Colonel Jonson attached on a semi-permanent basis to the Imperial Guard; Hiroshi, dare I assume we have your permission?'

'I will ask the Emperor.' Hiroshi stood up and moved outside to make the call, just two minutes later he returned and nodded to Jack and Leroy Moreton.

'I guess we will have to keep the temporary shrink for a few months more.' Leroy laughed at his own joke and the others joined in.

'Caroline, you will remember Fumiko?'

'Yes, young woman, incredible insight.'

'Interesting way to put it, but yes, that's her. She has forewarned me of several momentous events that are upcoming, you will need to be close by when they begin.'

'Don't worry, I will be right there.'

As the conversation twisted around Fumiko and her abilities to the skill level of the people Jack had gathered around him for the border wars, the meal began to appear before them, and the empty plates disappeared just as quickly.

The door opened with its usual accompaniment of tinkling bells and Mark, who was directly in line with it visibly stiffened.

'Tommy Penny, and brother Johnny; what brings you two back here?' Jack and Akio both saw Mark's muscles begin to tighten as he anticipated a fight.

'Please, Mr Gibbs, sir. We wanted to apologise, that's all. And to give a warning.'

'YOU WHAT?' Mark was now ready to jump the table and "get stuck in" as he liked to say.

'No, no, no, not that way. Mr Kobayashi, we were wrong to try to stand over you. I have seen what Mr Jackson has done for Simon and I want to thank you both, it is more than I could do. And thank you for looking after my mum too. I am sorry for my previous ways. So is Johnny.'

'I forgive you; I hope you have made better choices now?'

'We have, Mr Kobayashi, we now work at a distribution centre and we are out of the "bad boys" game.'

'Good.'

'You said you have a warning?' Jack did not even turn his head as he spoke.

'I have heard, on the grapevine so to speak, that a couple of my former companions are going to try to pick up where we left off. They may be here later tonight. Now I don't want you to worry, me an' Johnny can deal with 'em. It's just that you paid me for "protection" and even though I could never give your money back, we would like to give you the protection you have already paid for.'

'How do you mean?' Kobayashi was concerned now, another fight inside the restaurant could be a problem.

'We will wait for them outside and when they get here, we will deal with them.'

'Sensei, a few tips for them, I think. They may be a little rusty after their time away.'

'Hai.' Akio rose from his seat and moved outside. 'Don't eat all the Unagi, I won't be long.'

Leaving the others Jack and Mark, closely followed by Hiroshi, went with them.

'Remember, keep the fingers straight, in line with the arm and strike for the rear of the throat from the front.'

'Can't we just punch them?' Johnny asked, slightly confused.

'Think of it this way, a punch is effective, but the blow is spread across the knuckle. If the blow is not timed correctly, striking across the bones of the fingers is the quickest way to break them; with the fingers, hand, wrist, forearm and elbow all in line the power is increased and the likelihood of injury, to you, is decreased.'

He then showed the best way to perform the hit. 'Remember, aim for the front of the throat if you wish to hurt them, aim for the back if you wish to kill.' The last words resonated deep within Tom's brain. "This man has just shown me how to kill a man." That gave Tom a lot to consider, the people he had previously tried to fight were trained, and at ease with killing if they had no other course of action. He decided they were dangerous men to keep as an enemy.

'I get it. That sounds right.' The three practiced for a few minutes and then Akio returned to the meal. It was not too long before the expected arrival.

'Oy, Tommy. I thought you were still inside.'

'You wish, Nick.'

'Well, no point in your being here, is there? You being on parole and all.' Nick smiled. 'Me and Frank are taking over your patch, so you can "retire".' The two thugs laughed at the former hard man of the town.

'Don't think so Nick, my BOY.' Tom placed a little extra emphasis on the word boy. 'You see, Mr Kobayashi and the others have paid me for their "protection" and Johnny and me are going to do what we were paid for.'

'You need to think again!' Nick made the mistake of trying to intimidate his opponent by getting too close. For his trouble he got Tom's left palm on the forehead tilting his head back, and that was quickly followed by a straight fingered hand to the throat. Nick gasped and fell to the ground struggling to breathe. Frank, was trying to get away but he slipped and fell, lying on the ground he was genuinely frightened for his immediate future.

Jack and the others all came out of the restaurant and surveyed the scene.

'Thank you, Mr Akio. Your teachings are very effective. And thank you too, Mr Nakagawa, for everything.'

Nick had just begun to breathe again.

'Tommy, did you say Nakagawa?' Frank asked in shock.

'What if I did?' He replied, his tone indicating his displeasure at the two trying to take over.

'You mean Jackson Nakagawa?' Franks voice was now tinged with a little fear. 'That's right.'

'THE Jackson Nakagawa?'

'You are repeating yourself, Franky, my boy.'

As he regained his feet, Frank looked at the prostrate Nick. 'You f*****g idiot,' he spat at his supposed friend. 'You just f*****g declared war on the man that thrashed the entire f******g Russian Army. WE ARE DONE!' Frank shouted at Nick. 'You and me are DONE!' and he ran off. Well, as far as "ran" could refer to a 135kg 1.6m tall man could. Frank was almost having a heart attack when he left, not wanting to be anywhere near the fallout from the evening's debacle.

Scrambling to his feet, Nick stammered hoarsely, 'S, s, sorry Tom, sorry.' And ran away.

'Come inside, you two.' Jack asked Tom and Johnny inside the restaurant. 'Sake, arigatō, Katsuo.' Cups appeared and sake was poured. The two, former antagonists looked at each other in silence.

'You have taken a great stride today, how do you feel?'

Tom Penny looked back at Jack for a few moments. 'It feels good, I have done something that will benefit someone else.'

'If you need help, contact Kobayashi san, he can contact me.'

'I will do that, and thanks again.'

Tommy and Johnny left them to finish their meal.

'You sure know how to make friends.' Leroy Moreton was astounded at the turn of events. Once Mark and the others regained their seats, they were told of the short sequence of events outside.

'You fight a man and have him jailed, you save his son and mother from the streets and then you make friends with him? You are almost impossible to predict, in fact the only thing certain around you is that nothing is certain.'

'Thank you, Leroy, perhaps Caroline can use that as a foreword in her book?'

'If she want's, I will write the foreword for her.'

'Thank you, Leroy, I will keep you to your word.'

With all the "entertainment" for the evening complete the friends spent the rest of the evening swapping stories and simply enjoying each other's company.

Chapter 46
Return to Court

The evening ended with everyone having consumed far too much food and a similar excess of sake. The driver returned them to the academy and all fell into a deep, alcohol induced, sleep.

They all met at 8.30 for breakfast the next morning, most were much the worse for the evening but a filling meal and a surplus of coffee at least had them functional.

A steward approached and, after handing the Commandant a piece of paper, took two steps back and waited for a reply.

'Well, Jack. It appears the International Court has finally tracked you down. Your appearance has been rescheduled for the day after tomorrow at 11am.'

'Good. Is there a return address on that signal?'

'Yes.'

'Could you please ask if there are still restrictions on the wearing of our dress uniforms?'

The commandant sent the steward for a signal man who was waiting just outside the entrance. The signal was sent via the tablet the man was carrying and the reply was almost frightening in its return speed.

'I do not know how you do it, Jack. Your team are permitted to wear your weapons.'

Jack smiled as he looked at the signaller. 'Send a reply, please. We will attend at 11am, as requested. Sign that Captain Nakagawa.'

The signaller sent the message and left them to their morning.

'Hiroshi, arigatō to you and the Emperor. Must have hurt them pretty bad getting a demand they could not refuse.'

'You are welcome, I suppose they will be a little upset, but you win this round.'

'And I will win the fight.'

The discussion went back and forth until the "breakfast meeting" morphed into lunch.

'Lieutenant, we will have a war conference at two this afternoon.' Jack informed the young lawyer. 'We will complete preparations and leave for The Hague first thing tomorrow.' Jack activated the hologram and called out 'Hasegawa, we will be arriving at The Hague around 11am tomorrow, can we get a fleet of cars to transport us to our hotel? And again, from the hotel at 10am the next day? Have them wait at the Court for us, I am not planning to be there long.'

'Hai, consider it done. The Ambassador has invited you all for an official dinner that evening, 7.30 for an 8pm sit down.'

'Very well, 7pm pick-up.'

'Hai.'

The hologram closed off and they all simply looked at each other.

'You seem very confident?' Caroline asked, more to relieve the suddenly uncomfortable silence than for any real need for information.

'I have mentally thrashed the charge sheets several times, as well as the legal precedents; the charges are trivial at most, if I have to, I can close this without the use of lawyers, no offence lieutenant,'

'None taken, sir.'

'Arigatō. The trial will consist mostly of their legal team making outrageous claims and lengthy addresses to the Court. My response will be short, almost brutally so, and factual. The Combat cam files will back me up and then we can go for a late lunch.'

'You don't think you are being a little overconfident?' It was Mark that was being the "Devil's Advocate"

'Perhaps I am, but the wording they have used in the framing of the charges puts them on the back foot. I am betting they do not believe that I have had the documents translated several times, including having Eiji convert them from the original Russian into Japanese. They have also been translated from Russian into French and then English as well as Russian directly into English. Every translation has simply highlighted the same grammatical sequences and the factual errors contained therein, that is their mistake. It will be short.'

'Now that is what I would call a "well prepared client".' The American Lieutenant smiled as he spoke, this was a huge lesson in how he would conduct his future. In the future he would often recall the case; and how he learned more about preparation in the few days he was with the "Captain", as he referred to Jack, than he learned in years in Law school.

The International Court

The fleet of limousines, all matching Bentleys, slowly made their way up the entrance driveway to the front of the court. As each arrived at the main entrance the occupants would alight and wait patiently for the next car.

Finally, Jack arrived with Hiroshi, in the last car, and observing the tradition of the guard the most senior officer present, the Shogun, was the last out. As Jack was the reason that they were all there in the first place, he had the honour of leading them into the building. Every member of his entourage was covered with military decorations. Those that had been with Jack in the Border Wars had the most; medals, breast stars, sashes, neck ribbons and the ever-impressive daisho at the side.

'I thought you were going to wear "Emperor and Queen"?' Akio queried Jack's choices as they passed inside.

'Changed my mind at the last minute, I think "Repulse and Vengeance" are a better choice, make a statement by wearing combat weapons.'

'Hai.' Was the simple reply.

As they made their way inside, a guard led them to the appropriate court door. As they entered, one of the Court Guards muttered under his breath 'He still shouldn't be wearing weapons. He can do a lot of damage.'

Akio heard the man and moved to confront him. 'If the Captain wanted to cause damage, he could either bring a division of infantry, or just drop one of the 1300 nuclear weapons he has at his disposal. The fact you are all still breathing is testament to his kind nature.'

It was difficult to say whether the guard was more taken by surprise by Akio addressing him or by the fact that Jack could actually destroy them all. Either way he was silent from that moment on.

'All Rise.' The Clerk of the Court ordered, and everyone stood as the three Justices made their way to their seats. 'Be seated.'

There was a considerable shuffling of documents and hologram controls, eventually those present became settled and the Clerk got to his feet a second time.

'The International Court of Justice is now in session. Special Authorisation has been granted for Ilya Plishkin, former General of the Russian Army, to bring this action. Council for the Plaintiff, please present your case.'

Plishkin's lawyer regained his feet and began. 'We have brought this case to highlight the criminal actions of General Nakagawa during the closing stages of the so-called Border Wars. The charges are serious enough for the case to be heard here, in the highest court in the world. We will present evidence of illegal assault of a prisoner of war and subsequent cruel treatment of both the plaintiff and those under his command.'

Akio and Caroline both looked at each other and then at Jack. Jack simply shrugged his shoulders in a gesture of indifference. Hiroshi whispered to Leroy Moreton "Are they serious?"

"Apparently so." Leroy replied, he was as astounded as everyone else on Jack's team.

'Does the Defence have a response?'

Jack's lawyer stood and replied 'We will defend these preposterous allegations.' And then sat down.

'Is that your opening argument?'

'It is.' The legal team were under strict orders to speak in as forceful manner as possible but not to say any more than was absolutely essential. When asked later why he had ordered his legal team to act that way, Jack simply answered that "the opposition would have to do all the work if his team did not provide any answers or provocative statements."

'The plaintiff will call their first witness.'

'We call Ilya Plishkin.' The former General was taken to the witness stand and sworn in.

Plishkin made his way to the stand, flanked by two prisons officers; he was, after all, still a prisoner.

'Will you take an oath or an affirmation?'

'I will take an oath.'

The oath was given by the clerk of court and repeated by Plishkin.

'Mr Plishkin, in your own words what occurred on the day in question?'

Plishkin began to outline the events of the day and eventually he got around to the moment that Jack and his team crashed into the headquarters room.

'I heard them smash the doors in, I was consulting the deployment maps at the time. When I realised who it was, I decided to surrender. Our position had become untenable, insufficient food and ammunition would be the eventual downfall of my army. We simply could not continue. As I surrendered, HE!' Plishkin pointed at Jack, 'began to beat me, not just one punch or two but a continual unceasing assault. Eventually, I blacked out and by the time I came to I was a prisoner and being assessed by a triage medic.'

'How would you say this beating, a beating of an effective prisoner of war, affected you?'

'I became depressed, this is not how civilised people act. We were denied the chance to surrender properly and we were poorly treated even the next day.'

'Explain that please?'

'It was not until the evening meal on the following day that my soldiers were given a real meal. Many were still awaiting medical treatment. Many had lost limbs and were suffering as a result. They were savages, not caring for anyone.'

'Thank you, Mr Plishkin.' The lawyer had a smug grin, he thought he had presented a valid and strong case against Jack, the only real target they could attack. 'You may question him now.' The lawyer sat down and smiled as he spoke with his support team.

Jack and his team simply sat and spoke in hushed voices, slowly they became more animated and Jack eventually said, reasonably loudly, 'Either do it as I say or go, YOUR CHOICE!'

The rest of the court was silent, Plishkin and his side grinning as they thought that they had the upper hand; Jack's team were, apparently, divided and fighting amongst themselves.

Jack's lawyer eventually stood up and said, 'We assume that the defendant has evidence of these so called "accusations"? or are they just that, accusations without evidence? Do they have an actual victim of this supposed indifference?'

'We have an engineering corporal, Vladimir Aslanov, that lost both his legs, his medical treatment was insufficient at the time of triage and following on from that time.'

'Your Honour's, we would like time to examine this evidence; it has not yet been delivered to us and it is not referenced in the trial documentation. Also, we would like the opportunity to cross-examine this witness.' Jack's lawyer sat down and a brief aside was rewarded with a slight nod of approval by Jack.

'Agreed, the plaintiff will provide the documentation and the witness is to be made available tomorrow morning. We will reconvene in thirty minutes.'

Every one stood and bowed to the judges as they left. Plishkin and his team followed their departure. Jack, however, did not make any move to leave. His legal team were almost out the door when Jack called out.

'Where do you think you are going?'

'Outside, we are in recess.'

'And we have work to do,' Jack replied as his team slowly returned to their desks. Jack began to work the controls on the hologram.

'Mai, are you available?'

Here Jack. What can I do to help?'

'First I will need to speak with Motoyuki.'

'Here he is.'

'Jack? I trust the court case is going well?'

'Possibly, they have just introduced a surprise witness. I need to borrow Haruto for a while, is that ok?'

'Sure, use any resource we have, if it will help.'

'Thanks, stay around, I may need you again.'

The next voice was Haruto, 'Mai said you need some help, Jack. What can I do?'

The Russians have called Corporal Vladimir Aslanov as a material witness; we are getting a copy of his medical documents but they may have been altered.'

'Say no more, their Medical Services database leaks like a sieve. The advantage is that the system keeps copies of every document as it is saved; so, if they have altered the documents, we can get both copies. Give me ten minutes and I will send it to you.'

'Arigatō, Haruto; get it to Mai. Mai can you run it through the comparison software and find the alterations I believe will be there?'

'Certainly, I will also get Tyrell to get the original treatment notes from the U.S. Navy.'

'Arigatō.' Jack stopped for a moment and was deep in thought. Just a few minutes before the Judges were due to return, he addressed his team.

'Now, this is how I expect it to play out.' For the first time ever, his briefing was exactly that, brief. As Plishkin and his team arrived the hologram again came to life. Mai spoke briefly, almost in a whisper.

'Your requested documentation and the comparison report are on your tablet. There are many changes that have been omitted in the most recent version. The triage report and treatment regime are also there, as is a copy of the letter of thanks from Corporal Aslanov.'

'Good. Thanks Mai, this will make things a lot better, they are going to regret this for a long time. Stay on line please, I may need some extra assistance.'

The judges finally returned and the court was ready to continue.

'Do you have the documents?'

'We do.' Plishkin's junior lawyer handed them to the Clerk of Court and he in turn gave them to Jack's team. Jack and his lawyer compared the reports and after around ten minutes the silence was becoming oppressive. Jack and his team exchanging opinions and revelations in Japanese and becoming more animated as they did so. As Plishkin and his team witnessed their opponent's arguments they smiled at each other and were expecting a significant shift in the proceedings, and just a few minutes later, a shift was what they got.

Jack's senior lawyer rose to his feet and addressed the court.

'We would like to call Illya Plishkin,' he announced and Plishkin was returned to the witness box.

'Mister Plishkin, there are a significant number of changes that have been made to the medical reports for the Corporal; how do you explain this?'

Plishkin blushed and stammered, 'I, I, I do not know what you mean.'

'Really? Let me walk you through one example, just one for now. The report you provided, dated just two months ago, states "his legs were so poorly treated that amputation was inevitable". Yet the original report from the Russian Eastern Command Medical Centre shows that, and I quote, "With proper medical and physio-therapy care this man should regain full use of his lower limbs". Explain that please?'

'Where did you get that report?'

'We have our own sources; now explain it please?'

'I assume the treatment regime was corrected following a further analysis.'

'Hmmm. That may be so, but why does the report you gave us have no reference to the reason for the change of treatment or even the original diagnosis; yet the original report has every step of his treatment laid down as it happened. And the original report has the treating doctors name clearly noted on every document as well as the treating nursing staff; yet your document has no such detail.'

Plishkin and his team descended into chaos and Jack team waited patiently until the noise subsided. At that time Jack's junior lawyer beckoned the Clerk of Court and handed him the supplied report and the original as well as the comparison.

'These are for you to make your own checks of the documents, please keep them as we have our own copies.'

'It appears that a number of important issues have been uncovered; as such we will have to fully investigate them. We will adjourn until next Monday morning. The plaintiff will ensure that the witness is available for cross examination at that time.'

The senior of the three judges banged his gavel three times and the court was dismissed, leaving everyone to depart for their respective accommodations. As they drove away Jack called Mai.

'Mai, find this Corporal Aslanov and connect me to him, I want to know why this has suddenly become a problem big enough to be included in this ridiculous farce.'

'Already done it Jack; he says he has been promised prosthetics if he testifies for Plishkin. He does not want to testify, but the lure of being able to walk again is too much for him.'

'So that is their ploy; let him know he will be taken care of. Don't say any more than that, his testimony needs to be as accurate as possible, not tainted with possibilities.'

'Hai.' Mai closed off the call and all remained quiet for the rest of the journey back to their hotel.

The only ones to actually speak with Jack for the next three days were Akio and Caroline Jonson; the rest were left to their own devices for the three days they were waiting.

Jack, for his part, simply sat and drove thoughts around his brain. While the two had seen this often enough it was still disconcerting to see his level of concentration as he planned his replies to the inevitable questions.

Eventually, they all met for breakfast on the Monday morning.

'How was your weekend Jack?' It was Leroy that had asked out loud what everyone was wondering.

Jack suddenly looked up as though he had been stung. 'Weekend? What day is it?' he asked innocently.

'Monday.' They all chorused.

'Really. Must have been uneventful, I don't remember any of it.'

Monday Morning

'The court will come to order!' The clerk of court announced, and all became silent.

'Defence, do you have any questions for the plaintiff?'

No questions at this time; we reserve the right to recall Mr Plishkin later should we decide that we need to hear further from him.'

'Very well. Does the plaintiff have more witnesses?' The senior of the Justices was clearly unimpressed with the flimsy evidence so far provided and the evident lack of enthusiasm for a cross examination.

'Just one, we call Vladimir Aslanov.'

Room to move was made between the doors and the witness stand and Aslanov slowly pushed his wheel chair to the front of the court.

'Will you take an oath or an affirmation?' The clerk asked. The oath was taken and he was placed in front of the witness stand.

'Mister Aslanov will you tell the court what caused the loss of your legs?'

'It was the morning of what was to be the last day of the border wars. During a particularly violent bombardment I took shelter beside one of the communications sheds. As I tried to make sure I was as safe as possible the aerial tower collapsed on me.' As he gave evidence, he made eye contact with Jack, far from being overawed by the contact he appeared to Jack to be seeking, pleading, for help.

'Go on.' Prompted the lawyer.

'I was knocked unconscious for a short while and, when I came around, I was trapped under the steel frame. I tried to call out but no one came to help. I assumed it was because I had taken shelter in a small area and no one could see or hear me.

'I remember I tried to crawl out but the pain was too intense, I could feel and move my feet and toes but I could not get out. I must have been trapped for a long time and I do remember the shooting stopped. That was when I tried to call

429

out again but still no one heard.' A small tear made its way down his face as he recalled the traumatic experience. 'Eventually, I heard some voices and I hoped and prayed that I would be rescued; soon a team of people arrived and managed to lift the wreckage far enough for one of them to pull me clear.'

'Take a moment.' The lawyer said as he handed the now distraught man a tissue to dry his eyes. After a few minutes he continued. 'What happened next?'

'The man that organised the team to get me out had the medics give me pain relief and then he picked me up and took me to the field kitchens.'

'He didn't take you to the medical facility? Despite your crushed legs he took you to the kitchen?'

'Yes, he had a chair placed between the kettles and blankets wrapped around me and then he gave me hot soup while the medics began the treatment. Eventually, I was taken to a helicopter and then to a hospital ship for surgery.'

'Do you know who it was that did this to you?' The lawyer's language deliberately pushing a tone of blame.

'Yes, it was none other than the Commander of the enemy forces, General Nakagawa and his command team.'

'So just to be clear, he took you for food before he provided medical aid.' Before he Aslanov could answer the lawyer continued. 'What treatment did you eventually get, your injuries were significant, what was done to help?'

Confused at not being able to fully explain he eventually he managed to continue, 'It took a long time for the medics to clear me to travel to the ship. Once I had been taken to the x-ray and MRI screening as well as the toxicology assessment, they finally took me into theatre. My upper leg fractures were corrected and they did what they could for my lower legs.'

'Your description does not sound positive?'

'As it was explained to me, the multiple fractures and bone fragments made the reconstruction of the lower legs a very difficult goal to achieve.'

'How were you after the operation?'

'I don't know, is the short answer. I was kept sedated for the most part and when I was brought back to an awake condition, I was told that it would be some time before it would be guaranteed if my legs would heal.'

'When were you repatriated to Mother Russia?' The lawyer was deliberately using as much evocative language as possible, to try to gain the sympathies of the court.

'It was just two months. I was told early one morning I would be going home that afternoon, almost before I could process the information, I was on a flight home.'

'You were reassessed when you returned to Vladivostok, what was the doctors report?'

'I do not know; it was not explained to me. I was in a room with other survivors and none of us had our wounds or treatment explained.'

'I will read it for you.' The lawyer was beginning to get a little too close to perjury and his demeanour was starting to show it. "The injuries for this man are far too significant for the expected outcome of full use to be a realistic goal. A full examination and reassessment in two weeks, this examination is required with a view to amputation." It is obvious that the further testing resulted in the amputation of both your legs. How did that make you feel?'

'Feel? I became depressed, I had a new born baby to take care of and I could not even aspire to leaving the wheel chair, it was so abrupt and unexpected; here I was with little or no prospects; how was I supposed to move forward?'

'No more questions. Your witness.'

'We have no questions at this time, we reserve the right to recall the witness if we need to do so.' Jack's lawyer was still under orders to keep the replies as short as possible.

'No more witnesses. Your Honour.'

'The defence may call its first witness.'

'We call General Karan Hartchev.' At the mention of the name. Plishkin and his legal team began to furiously debate their options and eventually to voice their objections.

'I am sorry, is there a problem with us calling the General?' Jack's lawyer had asked the question perfectly, a disguised cross between surprise and sarcasm it had the perfect effect.

'You cannot call him!' The Russians shouted as they began to stand.

'Why not? He **was there**, you know.'

'He was the second-in-command his loyalty is to Russia and his superior officer.'

'As it should be,' replied Jack, bypassing his lawyer. 'But he is now a General, commanding his own forces. His former Commanding Officer is just that, FORMER, there is no reason we should not call an eye witness to the event, or do you have something to hide?'

The Russian team began to descend into chaos as they tried to find a way to prevent Hartchev from testifying.

'While you are having a discussion, we will continue with proceedings, shall we? We call General Hartchev.'

The Russians were still arguing as the witness took the stand and was sworn in.

Jack had, meanwhile, taken control of the entre situation.

'General Hartchev, Firstly, congratulations on your promotion, it is well deserved.'

'Thank you, sir, such praise from someone as respected as yourself is gratifying to receive.'

'If we can get down to business. You testified against the then General Plishkin at his war crimes trial. Why was that?'

'Because he had ordered a strike against a group of civilian buildings that was not a part of the combat area. The people inhabiting those buildings were non-combatants and were not involved in the war. To attack them was wrong and against the Rules of Combat.'

'Thank you. You have heard the evidence of Mr Plishkin, what are your thoughts?'

'He is lying. He was no more willing to surrender than he was going to fly to the moon.'

'Thank you. Your witness.'

Jack sat down and had a somewhat animated conversation with his legal experts. They didn't want him to speak unless necessary and he was determined to conduct his own defence.

'General Hartchev, you don't like our client, do you?'

'He brought shame upon us; the Eastern Army was a proud fighting force and he shamed all of them by attacking civilians.'

'I will take that as a "No", then.'

'Take it any way you wish.'

'You believe he was not conducting the war as effectively as he should?'

'He was wasting the lives of many brave young Russians; his tactics were not suitable for the conflict. His early successes were due almost completely to the methods of the first General he was opposed to. When the direction of the war changed, with the advent of General Nakagawa on the other side, he was not capable of commanding the army he was given.'

'Damming words, General. You sound like you are a fan of General Nakagawa?'

'During the war, I was constantly amazed at the variety of weapons he had at his disposal and the methods he had of using them, innovative weapons and tactics. I have since that time read many papers on his methods and his capabilities. He is a true military genius, if we had not been on opposing sides, I would have enjoyed working with him.'

The Russian lawyer spoke briefly with his team, he was not getting anywhere with trying to mitigate his testimony and its damage; they decided that it was probably best to get him off the stand as quickly as possible.

'No more questions.'

'Next witness for the defence?' The senior of the three Justices was keen to move along the proceedings.

'We call Chief Samurai Akio Takamatsu.' Jack had relinquished the control back to his legal team.

Akio moved to the stand and took an affirmation, a position in full concurrence with his slight ambivalence about religious matters.

'Chief Samurai, you were present that day, can you tell us of your perspective?'

'Please call me Akio, titles can be obstructive at times. I was standing at Jack's left side as he entered the enemy headquarters. We had a number of senior non-commissioned officers enter first and they had all the occupants in their sights. No one spoke, I am still unsure if I found that confusing or amusing, you would normally expect something to be said.'

'Jack handed Eiji his pistol and he then handed me his kabuto and katana.'

'Who is Eiji?'

'Eiji was Jack's interpreter, fluent in Russian, English and a couple of other languages as well, his job was to convey to the enemy any orders, in their own language, to ensure there was no possibility of confusion.'

'Why would he divest himself of all weapons?'

Akio could easily see where the questioning was going and he was only too happy to go along with it.

'Jack did not give up all his weapons.'

'What did he have left? You say he gave up his pistol and sword.'

'Yes, but Jack's other weapons are not so easily removed. His hands, feet and even his head are very effective weapons, include knees, elbows and fingers. You get the idea.' Akio looked at the bench.

'We do,' replied the Justice.

'What happened next?'

'Jack shouted "Which is Plishkin?" to which the plaintiff replied.'

'And then?' The lawyer gave the impression that it was difficult to get sufficient response from Akio.

'Jack hit him five times and kicked him once.'

'Is that all? A total of six hits?'

'That was it.'

'He did that much damage with only six hits?'

'Hai, sorry, yes.'

'After that?'

'Jack called for medics to treat him and placed him under arrest for War Crimes. Following on, Jack asked who was the senior officer and the then Colonel Hartchev replied. Jack gave him the ultimatum, surrender or suffer the consequences. Fortunately, General Hartchev was a good commander and he could see that further fighting was not going to end well, he surrendered immediately.'

'On a side note, there was a Major in the headquarters room that was shot dead. Why was that?'

'Those present were ordered to place their weapons on the floor, the Major tried to be a hero and reached for a gun on the table, Eiji shot him before he could raise the weapon.'

'A remarkable shot, in a crowded room?'

Akio smiled widely. 'Not at all. As we found out that day, Eiji is a crack pistol shot; good enough to win international competitions. His placement was almost perfect, one shot one dead and no one injured, if you ignore the ringing in the ears from such a close range.'

'Thank you. Your witness.' The lawyer sat down and Jack thanked him as he did so.

'You say he gave you his weapons, why would he not just shoot my client and be done with it?'

'I cannot say, I am not qualified to give evidence as to his state of mind.'

'I think you are more than qualified. You are his sensei, are you not? You do teach him how to focus and fight?'

'Is that what you think I do? I teach him to quiet his mind and to focus on the task at hand and I analyse and correct his movements and use of the traditional weapons; that does not mean I can read his mind. Ask Colonel Jonson if you want to find out what goes on in his head, she has a better understanding than anyone in the world. But I can tell you this; if it were me, I would have used a katana and an "O-kesa" cut.

'Can you explain that? For those of us unfamiliar with the ancient Japanese term.' The lawyer was condescending in tone and about to get a lesson.

'O-kesa is not an "ancient term", as you call it. It is a statement of fact; the cut is from the shoulder to the opposite hip. It severs all bone and flesh between the origin and finish points death is instantaneous, IF it is done right; an inexperienced swordsman with inferior weapons will leave the subject in considerable agony for a long time as he tries to remove the weapon from a partially severed bone.'

The lawyer was completely unprepared for the description, and he continued shakily. 'You are able to do this?'

'Certainly.'

'And General Nakagawa?'

'Again, certainly. He has the skills and the weapons to do it.'

'Could you elaborate please, some more information about the weapons? What makes one inferior and another superior?' The lawyer had completely lost track of the cross-examination, he was now more interested in the concept.

'The superior weapon will have been forged by a superior Kenshi, swordsmith. The materials will have been selected from the finest raw materials. Inferior weapons are not. The sharpening and polishing are critical to the performance of the weapon.'

'And you have these weapons? At your home or dojo?'

Akio, again, smiled as he unclipped his katana. Holding it at the centre of the saya he almost presented it to the lawyer. 'No, I have it here.'

The lawyer simply stood in awe at the sight of the weapon being held out for all to see. 'And him?' he pointed at Jack who held up his daisho and Hiroshi also held up his swords.

'As members of the guard we do not have dress weapons, all are combat ready. Jack's weapons were used by none other than Tokugawa Musashi during a riot in London almost three centuries ago. Look it up on the internet and you will see how effective they are.'

'No more questions.' The lawyer had strayed far enough and now even he could see the need to get back on track.

'I feel that we should now break for lunch. We will reconvene at 1.30.' The Justices were beginning to stand as the Clerk of Court said "All rise"

'How do you think it is going so far?' Hiroshi asked as they waited for lunch to be served.

'We have them done; I want to put Caroline up next then me.'

'Why do you want to testify?'

'Put it this way, Hiroshi. What I want is a finding of "Not Guilty" that way it is done for ever. I will not do this again when someone decides they have a possibility of making more money.'

'Fair enough.'

Lunch came and went and when they all filed into the court for the afternoon session no one made side comments on the weapons they wore.

'Is the defence ready to continue?'

'We are. We call Colonel Doctor Caroline Jonson.'

Caroline made her way to the stand and took the affirmation.

'Doctor Jonson. Please tell us in your own words what happened that day.'

'It was exactly as Chief Takamatsu said. Jack divested himself of weapons and his helmet and then called out Mr Plishkin. The fight was short and one sided.'

'Why do you say that, "one sided"?'

'It was over almost before it had started, Mr Plishkin had no ability to attack and by the time Jack was done Mr Plishkin could not even stand, let alone fight.'

'Thank you, Doctor. Your witness.'

'You say you are a doctor, doctor of what?'

'Psychology and clinical psychiatry.'

'So, you understand the mind of General Nakagawa, and can give us a reason why he beat Mr Plishkin unmercifully and unceasingly?'

'Firstly, while I understand the reasoning of the mind, every person is different, their motivation, their personal preferences are governed by their upbringing and the circumstances they find themselves in at any particular time. It is not possible to say that because something happened then the resultant action will be this.'

'Secondly, having been given the privilege of watching his work and seeing his methods, I can guarantee that Jackson Nakagawa does not fit a profile that can be laid down in a text. His mind does not function like most.'

'That is difficult to believe, can you give an example?'

'Certainly. Your Mr Plishkin, tried several times to attack the Japanese positions, several times he was defeated. His training forced him to attempt even more difficult and risky ventures in order to try to defeat the opposing army, all of which failed. When Jack was presented with the problem of how to eject the Russian Army from Iturup, he found several methods of, not attacking directly, but forcing his enemy to react to his attacks. As General Onishi said, the commander that can force a reaction has control of the battle field.'

'Professionally, why did he give Mr Plishkin a prolonged beating? Surely a few hits would have been sufficient?'

Caroline looked at the lawyer with deep suspicion; staring directly into his eyes she could see he was nervous about something. 'You are worried, aren't you? You think this is going badly and your payday is not going to be as big as you want. What is your driver here? Debts?'

The Russian lawyer suddenly began to sweat, just a few beads on his brow, but enough to give her comments impetus.

'That's it, isn't it. You have bad debts and you need to win this to escape your fate.' She turned to the Judges. 'We can stop this now, please show the hologram vision from my Combat Camera.'

The Clerk of Court started the recording and the result was exactly as Akio and Caroline had stated.

'No further questions.' The Russian case had all but collapsed, but Jack and his team were not yet finished.

'I call Jackson Nakagawa.'

'Do you wish to take an oath or affirmation?'

'I will take an oath.'

'Which religious texts do you wish to use?'

Jack crooked a finger at Akio who left the desk and presented Jack with his family bible. Jack took the oath and Akio returned the bible to its travelling case.

'You ask for a bible, why is that?'

Jack looked at his lawyer as though he was an idiot. 'Because I am a Christian, why else would I ask for a bible?'

'Yes, good.' His lawyer was playing the part to perfection.

'Why did you beat Mr Plishkin so badly?'

'I didn't. I gave him one blow for each unnecessary death he caused by attacking my parent's home.'

'Just one blow each?'

'Yes. Replay the hologram, with audio.' The hologram was replayed and Jack could clearly be heard shouting the reason for each blow as he made them. This time the hologram was allowed to continue playing and it showed Jack clearly giving the option to surrender to Colonel Hartchev.

'Arigatō, Your witness.' Jack gave a small nod and turned to the Russians as they tried to formulate a reply of some kind.

'You deliberately withheld food from the defeated forces for over twenty-four hours. Why?'

'I didn't. We fed them a soup with a little bread straight away. They had been without substantial food for some time and my medical experts said it would be best to give them a soup first until they could withstand a more substantial meal. As each man surrendered his weapons, he was fed.'

'That is not how it happened; you know that.'

Jack was incensed, the deliberate lie was a personal affront.

'Show the hologram.' Jack hissed between clenched teeth.

Sure, enough the hologram showed the Russian soldiers being given food in exchange for their weapons.

'What is your next baseless allegation?' Jack snarled.

'You withheld medical treatment.'

Jack simply pointed at the junior legal aide that was controlling the hologram. The vision that appeared showed Jack holding the arm of the Russian soldier as the medic stitched it together and then it showed Jack as he prayed with the dying young man he had pulled from under a collapsed building.

'Is that enough evidence or do you want more?' Jack snarled as he spoke; looking around the room at each and every person in it. He could see the Russians were in shock, they had not been given that much detail. The court officials were trying to watch but it was very confronting. More than one of the gathered press could be seen trying to prevent themselves from vomiting on the spot. 'You think that was bad? Watch!'

The hologram continued, showing the walk through the Russian camp and Jack suddenly turning and retracing his steps. The video continued to show the rescue of the young Russian from under the debris and all were astounded when Jack ordered the medics to supply pain relief before picking him up. The court nearly erupted when it showed Jack gently placing the man where he could get the most warmth and food. The audio clearly repeating the request for a medevac and operating theatre. Once the soldier had been dispatched, the hologram showed Jack serving food to his former enemies

'Not pleasant, is it.' Jack pointed again and the hologram turned off. 'I apologise for the vision, but that is war, that is what we dealt with every day.'

The three Justices spoke for a minute and then looked up. The senior Justice spoke.

'It is patently obvious, even to the most casual observer, that there is no evidence to support the plaintiff's case. General Nakagawa, please rise.'

Jack did not move, he continued to wait.

'General?'

The Clerk of Court passed a note and the Justice nodded.

'Captain Nakagawa, please rise.' Jack stood up and bowed to the Judges.

'It is the judgement of this court that the charges are not proven. Jackson Nakagawa you are NOT GUILTY. This court is adjourned.

'If I may?' Jack spoke, no one knew what he was going to say but no one was willing to stop him at that time.

Pointing at the legal assistant he ordered, 'Get Mai Thamrongnawasawat on line.'

A few moments later her smiling face appeared. 'Hai, Jack; how can I help?'

'I need to speak with General Onishi.' Seconds later Jack's friend appeared.

'Yes Jack? What can I do for you?'

'You will remember Vladimir Aslanov. The Russian Medical Command has seen fit to either ignore or change the recommended medical treatments advised for him, this has resulted in both his legs being amputated. Can we get him added to the Veterans Prosthetic Program?'

The senior Judge began to loudly bang his gavel shouting for Jack to stop. An order Jack would obviously ignore.

'Sorry Jack. If he was still held as a P.O.W. we could do it; but as he has already been repatriated, he is now the sole responsibility of the Russian High Command.'

'Hmm. Arigatō, please stay on line.' The Judge kept banging his gavel.

'Mai, I need to speak with the Board of Directors for the Trust.'

'Certainly, one moment.' The banging continued, trying to get Jack's attention.

'Board of Directors.' Mai announced.

The banging still continued.

Jack turned to the images on the hologram. 'Konichiwa. I apologise for the unannounced demand.' Before his sisters and brothers could acknowledge him, Jack began to give them the story behind Vladimir Aslanov's predicament. 'I ask if it is possible for the trust to approve the required treatment for this man. I will need to recuse myself from this decision due to a conflict of interests.'

'Understood, please wait.' Reo had picked up on the problem presented and muted the hologram. The four could be seen animatedly discussing the issue and after a tense few minutes they turned back towards the court.' The banging by the Senior Judge continued as he called for order.

'We have assessed your request and while we are sympathetic to the plight of this man, his rehabilitation falls beyond the scope of the trust.'

'Arigatō, may I ask if the trust will be willing to underwrite the costs and when the treatment is complete, I will repay the trust?'

'That is permitted.' Asa replied with a smile.

'Arigatō, please stay on line.' The audio went dead and Jack's family sat quietly watching the proceedings. The Judge continued banging his gavel in a vain attempt to regain control.

Finally. Jack spun around and looked at the senior Judge.

'Bang that thing again and I will turn it into tooth picks.'

No one could say exactly what it was that made the judge stop. It may have been the order; it may have been the threat or it may have been the command presence of the man that now very clearly held the floor. Whatever the cause was, silence now fell on the court room.

'General Onishi,' Jack began again. 'Can we get him added to the prosthetics program being run from the Northern Army Command Hospital? Send a full itemised invoice to the Trust and I will cover the costs myself.'

'If that is what you want, we can do that.'

'Arigatō.' Jack bowed. 'General Hartchev, can we get Vladimir's family yourself and your wife on a flight to Singapore?'

Karan Hartchev was surprised to hear his name and it took a few seconds before he answered.

'Certainly. How soon?'

'Hmm, just a moment. Mai, get General Ito please.'

Everyone in the courtroom was silent, none had ever seen Jack at work and the number of people he could call and get support from astounded them all.

'Yes Jack, what can I do for you?'

'Kei this is Karan Hartchev; Karan-Kei. I need a VIP navigational exercise from Tokyo to Singapore returning with some extra passengers. On arrival in Tokyo, transport to the Northern Planning Cell, please. I will leave you two to resolve the timings.'

Jack turned towards Plishkin and his legal team. 'You have me brought here to face charges that are evidently false; you want me to suffer the same fate as yourself. Have I done enough for Vladimir? Do you want more from me?'

At that point Jack's personal communicator rang. As he answered it he held up one finger to the court indicating he wanted silence. Speaking rapidly in Japanese he eventually finished with "arigatō, Majesty" and shut down the call.

Looking at the Judging Tribunal he bowed. 'I thank you for your forbearance, there is one final item I need to address,' he did not wait for a reply. 'Mai, get The President of Russia on line please.'

'And if he does not wish to speak?'

'Remind him I still hold his warheads and the proposal I have will be beneficial to him, personally, and Russia as a nation.'

'Hai.' Mai replied and just two minutes later the president appeared.

'How may I be of assistance?' The president was nothing if not straightforward.

'Before I give my plan for your approval, I have a question or two.'

'Continue.'

'Mr President, how much would it cost for all the veterans of the Border Wars to receive the medical and psychiatric treatment they need?'

'Difficult to say, exactly. The last figure from Defence Medical command was in the region of three million New Roubles.'

'And what does it cost to build a nuclear warhead?'

'That is highly classified.' The president was now very wary of the direction of the conversation.

'A round figure will be fine; I do not need the exact cost.'

The court was completely silent; those that knew Jack were slightly perplexed at his speaking in riddles, but all waited to see what would happen. After all, the man that could call one of the most powerful men in the world, and have him comply with his demands, was one that needed to be listened to.

'Roughly a million and a half New Roubles.'

'OK.' Jack thought for a moment and then continued. 'I want you to reduce your latest construction order for warheads program by five. You will then place the saved monies in an independently administered trust for the needs of the Veterans of the Border Wars. In return for this, I will return five warheads to cover the shortfall in your inventory. Is this acceptable?'

'You drive a hard bargain. You said I would benefit personally, how does this deal benefit me?'

'You will get the approval from the public, both internationally and at home, for being able to reduce the cost of your weapons inventory and being able to provide for your military veterans without extra costs or taxes. That alone should ensure your re-election.'

'How will you return the weapons?'

'I will arrange for Admiral Litvak to collect and transport them.'

The president thought for a few moments. 'Agreed I will have the Minister contact the Admiral.'

'There is no need for that, I will do it all from this end.'

'Very well, I will send proof of the changes to the financials and production. Thank you for your willingness to help.'

'Not at all, Mr President, I am just trying to help some war veterans that need as much assistance as possible.' Jack bowed and the image of the Russian President faded.

'Mai, Admiral Litvak, please.'

'Already on line.' Mai replied with a smile; a smile that was warmly returned by Jack.

'Anatoli, how are you?' Jack greeted the Russian Eastern Seaboard Commander with a friendliness that belied their almost non-existent relationship. 'Dare I assume that you heard my conversation with your President?'

'I am fine, sir; yes, I heard.'

'I will get Karan Hartchev to arrange for you and your wife to arrive on the same flight to Singapore as he will. I would like you to both come to the Northern Planning Cell for a full debrief and to arrange the handover. General Ito will assist with the travel north. Shall we say Friday next week?' The last was a rhetorical question and everyone simply accepted the demand.

Finally, Jack paused for a drink. Before anyone could speak, he continued.

'Mai, a message to all commanders Allied Forces, From Commander Northern Army Conflict Command. A full war debrief will be undertaken from next Friday. All Commanders and their domestic support staff are required to attend. Sign that Taipan 1.'

'Hai.'

'General Onishi and General Ito, I will require you there as well. I assume Himari and Yumi will be available?'

'Hai. Silly question Jack, Yumi will not let me go alone anyway.'

'Hai. Same for Himari.'

'Thank you all for your time and forbearance.'

Strangely no one left the hologram call.

Jack bowed to the court bench and then turned to Plishkin and his team.

Slowly he walked to the edge of their tables eventually standing over them with both hands planted firmly on the table top. Caroline would eventually describe it as "an intimidatory stance, deliberately invading their space and placing them on the defensive."

'HAVE I DONE ENOUGH!' he demanded forcefully. 'I have helped every single one of your wounded military, far more than any of you have even tried to do; I even returned the prisoners-of-war in the best possible physical condition as well as repatriating the bodies of the fallen. IS THAT ENOUGH!'

No one spoke, Jack's presence alone was enough to ensure he still had command of the room.

Jack turned to the bench and bowed deeply, far deeper than protocol demanded. 'My Lords Justice. I apologise for my outburst, however there were many items that needed to be addressed. I now need to make good my promises and ensure that others keep theirs.'

'Your apology is accepted. How will you ensure that your former opponents will do so?'

'They will be reminded that I still hold a great number of their weapons and I am quite willing to deliver them as they were originally intended.'

The chief Justice spoke briefly with his associates, 'I think we will make a representation to the Russian Government to ensure that the agreements are kept; after all the decisions were made in the highest court in the world as such, we can keep track of the results.'

'Arigatō, I thank the court and its Justices for their rulings. I would also like to thank my legal team and my friends for their support. I would also like to congratulate the Clerk of the Court Mr Kruyff, congratulations on your twenty-year wedding anniversary today, I have taken the liberty of sending a bottle of champagne and some flowers to your home.'

'Thank you, but I am unable to accept, it is a breach of the guidelines, bribes are not acceptable.'

'A bribe? is that how you see it? It would be a bribe if I asked for something in return, I do not. It would be a bribe if you had performed a task for me outside of your duties, you did not. It is simply a gift for someone that should have been at home enjoying a special day with his wife.'

Jack led his team in applauding the man and the rest of the court followed suit, all except the Russians who were still arguing amongst themselves about everything.

Chapter 47
Back to Japan

The flight home was completely uneventful, just good friends enjoying each other's company.

Around half way home the co-pilot made his way into the cabin and presented a message tablet to Hiroshi, who read the note and nodded as he returned the tablet.

'Jack, the Crown Prince wants you to take a week off after your "debriefing", then he has a rather difficult assignment for you.'

'Any ideas what?'

'I will let him tell you. What will you do with your week?'

'I will visit with Watanabe Korehira during that time, there is some work I want done and then I am going home for a few days sleep.'

'Understood. Can I get you to take my dress katana, the mekugi (securing peg) needs replacing as does the same.' (Ray skin under the ito)

'Consider it done. Caroline, will you come with me?'

'Of course, I will. The more I find out about you the better.' Spoken with a broad smile, she was feeling privileged to finally be included in his private world.

The hyper jet touched down at Haneda Airport late in the afternoon and once cleared by Border Control they were joined by Motoyuki and the others based in Tokyo. A short wait in the private lounge and they were soon joined by Tyrell, Daisy, Roman and Grace. Soon the guests were all onboard and on their way to the final destination. Jack and Caroline, along with Vladimir Aslanov, had already returned to his home that morning and received a welcome home fit for the Emperor himself.

The huge passenger helicopter finally approached Jack's home. Those that were regular guests were giving a running commentary about the magnificent castle that none of the others expected to see.

Landing in front of the castle the guests were guided into Jack's home and all were more than impressed with the displays of artefacts that abounded within. Finally making their way to the rear deck they found Jack waiting for them.

Jack welcomed them all and had his staff show each where their rooms were for the duration of their stay.

'Tyrell, Roman; you are in your usual suites. Same for you Motoyuki and Kei. I have made a suite ready on the ground floor for Vladimir and Svetlana, better wheelchair access. If anyone has any extra or special needs that arise, please ask. I know it has been a long journey for some so we will have a meal in two hours and get to know each other. All other business can wait until tomorrow.'

When the conversations began, just after lunch, it, at first, quite stilted. No one quite willing to ask any questions that may be awkward or embarrassing in some way.

'So, Anatoli,' Jack began to break the moment, 'how are your plans for retirement coming along?'

Anatoli Litvak was shocked, he had never expressed his plan to anyone except his wife, Tatiana. 'How do you know that? I have never spoken about it.'

Fumiko tried to cover her grin, Grace and Daisy both saw her and Daisy giggled. That caused Grace to erupt in laughter.

'What is going on?' Anatoli demanded.

'We are so sorry for laughing, it's just that we have become so used to not being able to keep secrets around here it came as a surprise to us.' Daisy began the explanation, 'Fumiko here told us what was going on just before dinner.'

The demand for an explanation resulted in the now usual shock and initial disbelief followed by many questions.

'You mean she can tell us what will happen?' Tatiana finally asked.

'Under some circumstances, yes. Don't worry, your retirement will be received as a well-deserved reward for your life's dedication.' Fumiko's voice changed pitch, 'When the time is right you will be summoned by Jack, his need for your expertise will be overriding and you will fight with him in the war yet to come.'

'Another war?'

'Do not concern yourself, Jack will keep you safe. You will be a part of the most incredible army ever seen.' Fumiko slumped slightly, her head resting on Jack's shoulder.

'Hot sweet tea.' Chie demanded and a pot almost instantly arrived at the table.

'What does she mean, another war?' Anatoli was now more interested than concerned with the prediction.

'Fumiko has been giving these predictions since before the Border Wars began. Apparently when it happens, we will have a real fight on our hands; but do not worry. She also says we will win; we just need to be ready when it happens.

The following dawn, Jack was to be found in his usual place. Kneeling and facing east as he prayed. As the sun began to rise Fumiko knelt slightly behind him, waiting patiently for him to finish his morning ritual.

'Come breakfast is almost ready and your guests will rise soon enough.'

The two sat and, before they could begin, Chie arrived to eat with them.

'This is the best way to begin the day, breakfast with my closest friends.' Jack commented, not expecting a reply.

As they finished the meal Jack took a coffee out to the rear deck and sat as the warmth of the early morning slowly invaded the house.

'There he is.' Jack heard a clearly Russian accent behind him. Without turning he called out, 'Come, sit with me.'

Anatoli and Karan both found a seat and the three looked at each other slightly awkwardly. Eventually, Jack asked, 'You must have questions for me?'

Another slightly less awkward silence and eventually, Karan asked, 'Why have we been invited to your debriefing? Surely it would be for your staff, not your enemy?'

Jack gave a small laugh just as Fumiko arrived with coffee for them all.

'That is an interesting way to begin, most want to know about the house first. I asked you here as I wanted you to know why I prosecuted the war so severely, and to ensure you understand it is not a personal vendetta for me, even though I could have justified it as such. The war was an issue that was presented to us all, by our politicians, and had to be resolved.'

'How did you stop the resupply fleet? Would you really have sunk the troop transports?' Anatoli needed to understand how close he was to dying.

'Actually, that was a bluff. My psychologist once accused me of being a monster, I could not kill so many in one attack, even though we were at war. The bluff worked, I felt that no decent commander would ever put so many at such a risk, it appears that you are, by my standards, a decent commander. As to how I stopped the fleet, I am not at liberty to say, it is secret.'

'We both know that Plishkin attacked your home, yet we do not see any damage? How is it that the strike was a success yet nothing is damaged?' Karan was a little perplexed.

Jack smiled. 'Come with me,' he stood up and began to walk away from the house, just a short walk along the tree line they came across a narrow dirt path and walking down they emerged in a grassy glade where there were three steps sitting alone at the end of the track.

'This was my parents' home; my family have decided not to rebuild it just to keep the access steps as a reminder.'

Jack began to walk off, beckoning his guests to follow. They moved along a second pathway and around three hundred metres along they came to a small chapel. Instantly recognisable with a cross over the door as well as one on each side. Jack moved inside and without waiting for his guests he knelt and gave a quick prayer; Anatoli and Karan remained silent as he did so. Standing up he crossed his left breast and returned outside, rounding the right side of the building they were confronted with a pair of graves and Jack again kneeling.

The two Russians remined silent.

'My parents.' Jack announced and moved away, clearly distressed.

Jack emerged from the tree line and walked across the grassy area towards the newly reconstructed stables. The three stood at the open doors and looked inside. Three horses were stabled and as the black stallion at the far end caught scent of his master he began to stamp and whinny loudly.

'That,' he announced, 'is Kyoto. He was foaled when Plishkin's strike destroyed these stables. He was originally destined to be a mount for the Emperor, however after he was checked he is too nervous and unpredictable for such an important duty. His dam was worth around three hundred million U.S. dollars in breeding fees. If he was quiet enough, we could charge anything up to 3 million per service. Watch this.'

Jack walked away to a place he was out of the direct line of sight and the horse became quiet again. Holding his finger to his lips to ensure they remained silent, Jack dropped a steel bowl on the concrete floor. The chaos that ensued saw Kyoto almost destroy his stall; the animal was so frightened that the only way Jack could calm him was to turn up some classical music and hold the lead rope, all the time speaking to him.

'This is the only way we can calm him. His preference at this time is Beethoven's Moonlight Sonata.'

The three returned to the deck and fresh coffee waiting for them.

'The monetary cost of the horses is probably enough for most men to kill. As you can see there were literally hundreds of millions of dollars on the line; but I can tell you he got the beating for the unwarranted assault on civilians. Yes, I had to cover the entire cost of the losses and that is on me, but that strike gave me the impetus and determination to win.'

'What would have happened if we had managed to get the fleet off loaded on Iturup? What would you have done?'

Jack thought for a few moments. 'At that time, we had the upper hand. We would have launched air strikes on the ships while they were at their most vulnerable, as they off loaded. The first strikes would have been against the troop carriers, the death and destruction we could have created would have destroyed any improvement in morale the fresh troops would have brought. We could have sunk the fuel tankers as well and that would have created fireballs in the dock area. Your fleet would have been far too busy fighting off the coalition attacks as well as the air assaults. Our gunners already had the range of the dock areas and could shell them all day and night if necessary.'

'It is probably as well that you are not as irrational as Plishkin. Your plans appear to be well thought out. For what it is worth, the other commanders are very much impressed with your approach to fighting. I would like to have known you in better times.' Karan was glowing in his praise of his former enemy.

'Arigatō, it is kind of you to say so, perhaps in the future. Anatoli, to return the weapons we will need you to bring a single warship, a destroyer size should be sufficient.' Jack was suddenly working again resolving the last of the "real" issues. 'There are two bays on the far south west coast of Iturup, the southern one is almost fully enclosed and not suitable, the one immediately to the north is open but sheltered. Once your ship is anchored, suitably far off shore I will get the weapons delivered by helicopter. No one will be permitted to land on shore and the ship will be required to leave as soon as the transfer is complete. You have my word that we will not have ships or aircraft deployed in the area but it will be under satellite surveillance. Is this acceptable?'

'Certainly, when?'

'Contact your base and have a ship assigned, when it is ready the delivery will commence; have the captain time his arrival for 0800 at the anchorage and we will have the helicopter deliver at 1000. I estimate that it should be completed by 1200 and your ship can depart before 1300.'

'You seem to have thought of everything. Agreed, two days' time?'

'That is acceptable.' Jack called out 'Haruto can we get in touch with The Russian Eastern Naval Base for Admiral Litvak?'

'Ready and waiting.' Haruto replied.

Anatoli made his arrangements and then signed off.

'Good, now let's see who else is moving.'

The three went back inside and joined the conversation with the others. Around an hour later Anatoli asked 'Perhaps we should excuse ourselves, to let you all continue your debriefing.'

Almost as one the others laughed.

'Have I said something wrong?' Anatoli was clearly confused.

'No, nothing wrong.' Tyrell replied.

'A "debrief" is Jack's way of saying "come to his place for drinks and companionship".' Roman added.

'And your commanders all agreed to this?'

'Not at all, they think we are actually discussing what happened.'

'Now I am really confused.' Anatoli was unsure of the command structure of his former enemy.

'It is very simple; our Chiefs of Staff would never let us attend if they knew. It is far too expensive to transport us all just for fun.'

'Actually, there are a couple of the Chiefs that know. Firstly, General Ito and secondly me,' Motoyuki had picked the right place to join the conversation, 'but to be fair we enjoy coming here as much as any. By the way, if your wives are joining with ours then we will all be spending a lot more time together.'

It was at this time the mood lightened considerably and the "meeting" became considerably more relaxed.

It was just after lunch that the hologram beeped with an incoming message.

'Haruto, what can we do for you?' Jack asked.

'Actually, I have a message for Karan and Anatoli.'

The two Russians were automatically concerned, how did one of Jack's officers get a message for them?'

'Go ahead.'

'The latest intelligence shows that the High Command is purging the officers that "lost" the war. You may be better off resigning and going into early retirement.'

Concern turned instantly to worry; it had not taken long for the Kremlin to get to them.

'How do you know this?' Karan asked directly.

'There is much signal traffic coming out of the Kremlin and your countrymen are jostling for position.'

'Again, I ask. How do you know this?'

'Haruto is our Commander of Satellite Services. Haruto I assume you can back this up?'

'Yes Jack. Confidential emails for you to check.' The documents emerged on the hologram before them and a quick read through was all that was needed to confirm the assessment.

'Arigatō Haruto. Gentlemen? Your response?'

'It appears that retirement is on the near horizon for both of us.'

'Get it done quickly and your resignation will be accepted without question or repercussions.' Fumiko turned and left the room.

'You can do it from the reading room if you wish.' Jack added to the quickly spiralling conversation.

'Yes, we will.' Emerging just a few minutes later the two looked at all in the room. 'It is odd, but I think a weight has been lifted from me.' Anatoli agreed with Karan and the two relaxed visibly.

The next five days were spent cementing relationships and getting Vladimir Aslanov settled into the treatment plan and his family settled into accommodation nearby.

The next morning Jack could be found at dawn, meditating on the deck.

Eventually, without turning his head, he spoke, 'You are early this morning, is there something specific you need?'

Fumiko kept her head bowed and replied, 'We need to talk.'

To a normal male, those words could either be filled with foreboding or they could instil terror; for Jack it meant he would need to resolve some type of issue and that would be best discussed over coffee.

Jack turned and smiled at her. 'You had better come with coffee if you wish a deep discussion at this hour.'

'Of course, there is coffee. But we need to speak now while we are alone and we can be candid with each other.'

'Sounds serious.'

Fumiko said no more until they were seated.

'Now, my young lady, what is it?'

Fumiko took a very deep breath before she began; despite her close ties with Jack she felt she was about to cross a line. 'Caroline is becoming very deeply embedded in your life.'

'She is doing a great deal of work; it is natural she would be close.'

"Why are men always so blind to the obvious" she thought to herself. 'No, I mean she is VERY close.' Fumiko was now visibly trembling; she was clearly very worried.

'You are really concerned, aren't you?' Jack noted as he took a swig of his coffee.

Fumiko decided that she would have to be blunt. 'She is NOT the one!'

Jack spluttered and choked as the coffee went everywhere except down his throat; eventually the coughing fit subsided and he was able to talk.

'Is that what this is about?'

'It is a fair comment, given what I know.'

'I understand, but let me say this. Firstly, domo arigatō, you always have my best interests at heart. Second, Caroline is covering a great deal of territory as she prepares to begin my biography, it is accepted she will be close to us all. And lastly, I know she is not the one, I do not feel any personal connection with her. I will know when the time is right.'

'You mean you are not romantically interested?'

'No, we both know that, don't we?'

'We do.' The two began to laugh as the gravity of the chat dissipated and the dawn gave way to a clear warm morning.

Eventually, Caroline joined them on the deck and a breakfast appeared, seemingly out of nowhere.

'So, what are we up to today?' Caroline asked between a mouthful of eggs and a sip of coffee.

'Today we will go to Shimane Prefecture to visit a family friend, I have a favour to ask. Then we will come back here and maybe relax for a day or two. I also need to go to Sapporo for a day to help Asa and Hana.'

'What are they doing?' Caroline asked.

'You will see when we get there.'

Just an hour later the helicopter lifted off for a fast trip to Shimane Prefecture and the forges of Watanabe Korehira.

'Jack, another visit? And so soon.'

'Yes, my friend. I have a job, a minor one but a job none the less.'

'Come, it must be time for sake.'

'Not after the last time, you have very strong sake here.'

The two grinned at each other and made their way into the house, followed by Fumiko and Caroline. Once settled inside Jack made the introductions.

'So, Caroline, how difficult is it to get into his head?'

'Probably as difficult as flying to Mars without a spaceship.'

'Yes, I have heard that. The news feeds are all saying that the Russian High Command have still got no idea what went wrong on Iturup. Tell me, have you ever seen a forge in action?'

'No.'

'I will have my son give you the guided tour.'

Caroline expected a boy around twelve or thirteen to appear, but was surprised by a very handsome man in his late thirties. The two made their way across the compound towards the Tatara (the name given to either the forge house or the forge itself).

'That may have been a mistake,' Fumiko announced.

'Why so?' Korehira was instantly intrigued.

'They may well forge something else as well as metal.' Jack noticed Fumiko's voice was slightly deeper.

Korehira looked at Jack and Jack smiled. He began to tell the story of Fumiko and her abilities.

'So, you know these things?'

'I do.' She replied.

'It is going to happen? No question?'

'It will be as I say.' Fumiko was slowly returning to "normal".

'Then this is truly a day for celebration, my son has been too busy to find a partner and now, it seems, one has found him.'

Korehira's words were as prophetic as Fumiko's, the two appeared an hour later hand in hand, both smiling and blushing at the same time.

'So, Fumiko was right.'

'What?' began Caroline. 'But we only just met, how do—Oh never mind. She is never wrong, is she?'

'No, and it is wonderful to see you smile.' Korehira said to his son and Jack simply grinned with Fumiko. 'Now, son, go fetch the special item Jack ordered.' Moments later he returned with a katana-zutsu and handed it to Jack.

As his hands caressed the exquisitely finished hand carved case Jack looked up at Caroline. 'When we first met, I didn't want to speak with you. I was rude and there can be no excuse for that. Over the subsequent months you persevered, observing and understanding my personal dislike of being analysed, you still kept going. I like that you did not simply give up. This is a gift for you. Wear it with pride.'

He handed the box to Caroline and she took it with care, ensuring she did not damage it. As she looked at it, she could see the inlaid crest of the 5th Cavalry on the lid. Gently opening it she could see the work of art that lay within.

'Everyone thought I was slightly insane when I asked for you to be attached to the Fifth Cavalry, this was why.'

Caroline slowly lifted the contents out of the deep velvet cushioning and she gasped when she realised that she was holding a duplicate of the sabre she had been given as being a part of the cavalry; but this was so much better in every way. Solid Gold fittings all over, beautifully handcrafted scabbard, engraved hilt; every part of it was stunning.

'Take care,' warned Korehira. 'The blade is every bit as sharp as one of Jack's weapons.'

Eventually, Caroline spoke 'How?' was all she managed to get out.

'I had a sabre scanned and the details sent here, Korehira and his son, Itsuki, created the only one in existence; a sabre, forged, sharpened and polished the same way as a katana. When word gets out, you may have a lot of requests for work for the same style.'

'And they will all be politely refused. That was a difficult item to create, the curve of the blade, coupled with the thickness made it difficult to balance. I do not wish to do too many more of them.' Itsuki was adamant. 'That and the fact I want Caroline to have the only one in existence.'

'And so, she has.' Korehira commented.

'Jack, this must have cost a fortune?' Caroline asked.

'Do not count the money, it comes and goes; count the friends, they stay for a while; and looking at Itsuki, you will be here for a long time.' For the second time the two blushed. 'Wear it for a formal parade one day and embarrass everyone else, that is what I do.' Jack had the last word on the subject.

Suddenly Fumiko sat bolt upright, Jack watched as her eyes glazed slightly; everyone was silent. 'Many more of your masterpieces will be needed, thousands. A war beyond all comprehension is coming, your weapons will win this.' As she finished speaking, she fell back in her seat. Jack jumped up and checked her announcing all was well.

'That is dangerous, Jack.' Korehira was the one that spoke out first. 'If she is as powerful as you say then we are in for a rough ride.'

'Fumiko has been giving these foretelling's for some time, she is always right and we will need to be ready when the time comes.'

Fumiko's words did not stop them from enjoying the remains of the day; eventually they boarded the helicopter and made their way back to Jack's home, exhausted they fell into their beds and slept until mid-morning, except Caroline, she stayed with Itsuki to "do some more research" into Jack's life and friends.

Chapter 48
Orders from the Crown Prince

'You sent for me, Your Highness?' Jack bowed deeply to the Crown Prince as he entered the private office.

'Yes, thank you for coming; did you bring your psychologist friend with you?'

'She will be here soon; she is currently in transit from Shimane Prefecture.'

The two had refreshments served as they waited. Despite their long-standing friendship, the conversation was hesitant and punctuated by periods of silence. By the time Caroline was announced Jack was concerned that there was something very serious going on.

As Caroline entered and bowed, the Crown Princess also entered but via the private door. An aide appeared from almost nowhere and presented the Princess and Caroline with tea and coffee, and disappeared almost as quickly.

'I know you will both be wondering why I have asked you here,' the Crown Prince began, 'It is very embarrassing to ask this of you and I hope you can come up with a plan to help. Our daughter, Princess Teimei, has fallen in with a group of undesirable girls at her school. The girls have altered her thinking and her attitude from a caring and considerate young lady to an entitled and argumentative teenager. We have tried reason and punishment to no avail. She will not be guided by any of the methods we have tried. In short, we desperately need help; if she is to become Empress, in the future, she must change her attitude.'

'Your Highness, if we are to try, what are the boundaries?' Jack asked after a short period of thought.

'Physical punishment is, naturally enough, not permitted. You may take her away from the palace, anywhere you wish to go. If needs be, disconnect her from her social media and definitely disassociate her from these so called "friends".'

Jack was already beginning to form a plan in his mind.

'When was it that she began to change?' Caroline asked.

'When she started at the boarding school, to complete her last two years of secondary schooling and prepare for university.'

'Good, that is a point we can begin with.'

'Please, share with us, what are you thinking?' The Crown Princess was clearly desperate for some way forward.

'We will visit the Head of the school, words will be said that will not be pleasant, but they will be said,' replied Caroline. 'I will do this, as a doctor my demands may carry more weight.'

'Jack, you are quiet?'

'I was thinking that we must first, and foremost, before anything else; remove her from the influence. I feel she may benefit from what the Australians call a "reality check" she needs to see what real life is about. Following that she needs to see what real people do, how they live and how they cope with the daily stresses of life.'

'Do I detect a plan, already?' The prince was clearly already buoyed by the positive direction the discussion was taking.

'I feel that Princess Teimei would be greatly appreciated by the local people if the Emperor were to send her to Iturup, a good-will visit with the newly restored population will be beneficial to both her and the Crown. It will also serve to show that the Imperial Family are still thinking of them and with that comes the assumption that the remainder of the country are also of a like mind. We can stop at a couple of places on Hokkaido on the return journey that will show her just how privileged she really is and how much she really owes to the country.'

'Tell me more?' Asked the Princess.

'I would, but if she is going to react the way I hope, then it will be best if you are unaware of the situations she may encounter. If she is to be rehabilitated, then she will eagerly want to share with you; and I do not want you to be concerned with our methods.'

'Caroline, your thoughts?'

Caroline smiled. 'I have been a witness to Jack creating miracles from nothing. If he has a plan, then I think you should trust the plan.'

'Without question?'

'Certainly.'

'Then we will begin. I will speak with His Majesty and you shall begin a low-key visit to Iturup.'

'Arigatō, your Highness. We will take a small security contingent, no more than three samurai, including Chief Takamatsu.'

'Always the sensei goes with you?'

'He is the one I trust most with my life; we have known each other for a long time and we work well together.'

'When will you be ready to go?'

'I feel it is best if we leave tomorrow, no fanfare, no press releases and the Princess is not to be told until just before we are ready to leave. Her personal assistants can pack some suitable clothes while she is at school today. Tomorrow morning, we can ask the Emperor to speak with her. Get the I.T. department to shut down the palace network for "maintenance", from now until we have gone, so she cannot warn her friends. And I will speak with Harucor and Chikap as well as Sakura and Alex to arrange a small greeting. We will need to keep her mentally grounded for the time we are away; so, we will not be making a great deal about the visit being official or regal in any way.'

'How do you do it, Jack? You already have a plan working and I have not finished my tea?' The Crown Princess was astounded at the speed the plan erupted.

'He always does this,' Caroline interrupted. 'He does not have a brain as we understand it, he has a "Devious Plan Creation Centre".' They all shared in the joke, all except Jack.

'That's a bit harsh, a fair assessment, but harsh.' Then he began to laugh at the joke as well.

'Then it is decided. Tomorrow we begin.'

'If I may make one more suggestion?' Jack asked before he left the room.

'Go ahead.'

'Do not tell the princess yourselves, let the news come from the Emperor and ask him to frame it as a personal favour; no girl can refuse her grandfather's personal favour.'

'That is cruel. But I can see your thinking. Shall we aim for a nine o'clock departure?' The prince was now beginning to feel optimistic.

'Nine it is.'

Farewells were spoken and Jack and Caroline left to begin planning in earnest. By the time they had made it to his rooms the plan was all but complete.

'Akio,' Jack called to his friend, 'get some gear together, tomorrow we will be going home and then to Iturup.'

'Any special reason?'

Jack and Caroline spent the next half-hour explaining the problem and the proposed solution.

'Well, do you think it will work?' Jack asked, always wanting, and valuing, his friend's opinion.

'Of course, it will work.' Fumiko spoke from the side of the conversation. 'BUT. You will not survive unscathed; you will survive but it will have a down side.'

'Will you be with us?' Akio asked.

'Only as far as home, then I will spend the time with Mama. When you return, I will accompany you on the remainder of your journey.'

'It is settled. Akio, select two Senior Samurai to accompany us.'

'Hiroya Furukawa, the combat medic will be one and I will find a suitable "twin" for him, same size, make a pair as official guards.'

'Very well. Now we must discuss the desired outcomes and the possible problems we will encounter on the way.' The next two hours were spent honing the plan and discussing it all with the Chiefs on Iturup.

A call to General Ito saw a helicopter arrive at the palace at 8 am and leave just an hour later with a very sullen princess pouting, arms folded, in a corner seat.

A two-hour stopover at Jack's home saw the departure of Fumiko and the helicopter then left for Iturup.

On Iturup

They landed at the now refurbished airstrip and a rough trip down some rutted dirt tracks was all it took for the complaints to begin.

'Why is the road so bad? Don't they have any decent cars? Why is everything so dirty?' The list of complaints did not stop for the entire trip.

'STOP!' Jack suddenly shouted. The cars slid to a halt and Jack jumped out, closely followed by Akio and Caroline.

'I'm not getting out, Teimei continued to pout and grumble in the rear as she watched as the three walked off to the edge of the forest. 'Why do we have to stop here?' she demanded; no one replied.

A few moments later they emerged, finding a couple of sticks they fashioned a marker and hammered it into the ground using a rock as a hammer. Akio made some notes on his tablet and they climbed back into the car.

'Why did you need to stop?' Teimei demanded, and still no one answered. Jack and Akio looked out of the window and Caroline sat with a small tear sliding down her cheek.

'What is wrong with you people?'

At that remark Jack all but exploded. 'GET OUT!' he shouted. Teimei was firstly affronted; then, as the tone of his voice registered, she became a little frightened. Before she could actually move, Jack had rounded the rear of the car and pulled the door open. Grasping Teimei he literally pulled her from her seat. Almost dragging her behind him they all but disappeared into the edge of the forest.

'LET GO OF ME!' she demanded but Jack did not let her go until he had arrived back at the point Akio had noted for reference.

Pointing down he indicated the helmet, complete with the insignia of the 91st Infantry Division and the bullet hole that had ended his life. He had spotted the rounded top of the helmet through a clearing between the trees as they drove down the road. The recent rains had washed the helmet clean and it was easily identifiable in the mud.

Pushing her head so she could not help but see the object he snarled at her. 'That is the remains of a soldier I led here during the Border Wars, his family have been waiting for him to be returned to them, SHOW SOME RESPECT!' Jack released the Princess and she didn't move, she simply stared at the helmet, eventually she made out the outline of some bones and one end of his assault rifle.

Suddenly overcome with some guilt she mumbled an apology. Jack never heard her; if he did, he did not show it. Eventually, she looked at Jack and saw him praying over the dead soldier. Her mind filled with questions and emotions, she had never had to deal with death and to see the results of a violent death right before her eyes made her realise, she was not the centre of the universe. This man had died trying to help others.

Her rehabilitation had begun.

They returned to the car and the journey to the settlement was completed in silence.

As the car arrived, at the most impressive building in the settlement, they were met by the ruling council and Alex and Sakura Gripkin. To say she was stunned would be an understatement. She was not greeted as she expected; it was Jack and Akio that were the centre of attention, only after Caroline had been introduced was she then presented to the senior councillors of the settlement; deliberately left to last it was done to reinforce the fact that she was not the most important person on the island.

The first day was spent looking at the progress the settlers had made, crops were beginning to grow, and buildings were being repaired.

'Why are they making such a fuss over some corn and rice growing?' Teimei asked in confusion, she simply could not see the importance of it.

'Because they have nothing else, that is going to be their main food source for the coming winter.' Akio answered curtly.

'Why don't they buy something?'

'Do you see shops? No, this is all they have and yet they are happy. Their fishing boats will come back tonight and, God willing, they will have some fish for them to eat; but there is no guarantee they will.'

'What if they don't?'

'Then they go hungry and try again tomorrow.'

'Someone should help.' Yet another small slip of reality got through to her young conscience.

'Who?' asked Caroline, innocently.

'I don't know, someone.'

'What about you? Could you help?'

'I don't know how, I can't fish.'

'No, but you could tell people that they need help, someone may hear **you**.' Caroline was pushing her to think outside her experiences.

'Who is going to listen to me?'

'Entitled Teimei, the Tokyo schoolgirl? Not many, but Princess Teimei? Now she could have the best interests of the people of The Kuril Islands at heart.'

'How can I do that?'

Caroline had pierced her barriers. 'You could try to show the world the problems these people face instead of complaining about the shade of eyeshadow that you have. Social media may be helpful?'

'My friends would make fun of me!' Teimei snapped back.

'Then they don't sound like real friends to me.' Caroline had managed to push her thinking to a new, more realistic level. The discussion did not go much further that day, or for the remainder of the visit, but the Princesses attitude had visibly softened.

For the next three days they toured the settlement, helping where they could and encouraging where it was needed.

As they entered the helicopter Jack spoke with both Harucor and Alex, 'I will give your request to the Emperor, he should be able to bring some imperial pressure to alleviate your food shortage; failing that I will simply embarrass the Prime Minister for not supporting you at your most pressing time.'

'Arigatō, Jack. Come back soon.'

The helicopter lifted from the ground and was soon on its way back to Jack's home.

Jack's Home

The flight was remarkable, simply because it was quiet, very little conversation and, notably, no complaints from Teimei. They landed on the estate a short walk from the castle and Jack's grooms took the baggage to the appropriate rooms.

'I am going to sleep for a while.' Teimei announced. And she was a little shocked when no one replied. Significantly she did not ask for her tablet or communicator before she went to her room.

'Perhaps, we have made some ground?' Caroline whispered to Jack.

'Let's hope so.' Jack replied. 'Let's hope so.' Two hours later Teimei reappeared in the sun room.

'Where is Jack?' she asked.

'He is at the old chapel, down that path and follow it to the left.' Akio answered curtly.

Teimei walked down the path and stopped suddenly when she saw him kneeling before two headstones. She looked at him, unsure if she should speak when Caroline softly whispered behind her, 'Wait until he is done, he is praying.'

Teimei turned her head and looked at Caroline; she was about to berate her for daring to give orders to a princess, when Jack said 'I am done, come join me.'

Teimei knelt beside Jack and asked, almost timidly, 'Who were they?'

'They were my parents, killed by Plishkin during the border wars.'

'I am sorry, I didn't know.'

'You are not expected to know, Caroline understands my need to be here at times and she knows not to disturb me when I am.'

'Tell me more, please?' Jack noted it was a request, not an order and once they had returned to the house, they sat on the rear deck as he related the particular part of the border wars to the young Princess. Another breakdown in her series of walls, they were moving in the right direction.

That evening Teimei and Caroline spent more than two hours talking about the "friends" she had made and what was and was not appropriate in the world. It was a point of breakthrough for her. They could all see her attitude changing.

For two days they relaxed then Jack announced that it was time for Teimei to discover what his family actually did. The cars took them to Sapporo and into an area not often frequented by the "well to do".'

'Why are we here?' She asked; gone was the demand, now it was a real question.

'You will see.'

They drove past an army barracks; the sign at the gate proudly announcing that it was the "Home of the 59th and 61st Infantry Divisions".

'Isn't the 61st your division, Jack?' Caroline asked, more to begin the conversation than an enquiry for knowledge.

'It was; and they still like to call themselves "Jack's Pack",' Akio replied.

'We are almost there, now you are about to see something that is not often shown to the world at large.'

The car stopped at a nondescript building; large, red brick and ugly. The banner over the door announcing "Asa's, home for families". They all walked in, the doors opening onto a large entrance area, furnished with nondescript, second hand couches and chairs, a few tables with writing implements and official looking forms waiting to be filled out. Some boxes of toys in the corner to keep little children busy.

'What is this place?' Teimei asked. Before she got an answer a shout from behind the official looking desk drew their attention.

'Jack! About time you lazy thing, get in here and give me a hug.'

Jack moved quickly to his sister and hugged her as ordered, as he did so he whispered the reason for his visit and she whispered back her assent.

'This,' he announced, 'is…' before he could finish, she said, 'Teimei, Jack is showing me his world.' Jack and Caroline both made a mental note of the lack of title.

Asa nodded. 'Welcome Teimei.'

They all sat down and Jack went with Asa to get the refreshments. When they returned, Jack served them all and there was a short wait before the conversation took off.

'What do you do here, Asa?' Teimei asked.

'This is a shelter for women and children that have been abused and have nowhere else to go.'

'Who pays for this?' It was a blunt question, asked in the right spirit but as blunt as only a teenager could be.

Asa looked at Jack, allowing him to pick up the conversation.

'We do, and by we, I mean the family trust. We get some donations from philanthropic groups but it is all run by us. This facility and one for homeless women, on the other side of the camp, is run by Asa and Hana, my sisters. We also have one under a hired manager for homeless men, but that is on the other side of the city.'

'You pay for everything?'

'For most of it. We get a lot of the women and older children that live here doing much of the work, cooking, cleaning, and the outside areas.'

'Fortunately, thanks to Jack's connections.' Asa butted in. 'The 61st division provide emergency security for us; if there is a problem, we activate the duress alarms and a lot of soldiers come to help.'

'Does that happen a lot?'

'No, but it is comforting to know we can count on them. They share the duty with the 59th division, also in the barracks.'

For two days they helped around the facility, cleaning, cooking, talking with the people that had made it their temporary home and those that had decided to trade their labour for a permanent home. Living in the small rooms on the very top floor of the building, they were enjoying their time helping the less fortunate ones there.

As so often happens with such events, the good times were bound to end, sometimes they just fizzle out and sometimes they are ended by force. This time it was ended by violence.

It began on the morning of the third day. They had extended their stay by an extra day to help with some new "clients" as Asa called them.

The day started out quietly enough, several families were given clothes and rooms, and shown around the facility. Lunch came and went and around mid-afternoon they were all having tea as the last family arriving for the day were made welcome.

Suddenly the doors crashed open and a man burst into the room brandishing what looked like a sugar cane knife. Around half a metre long with a wide blade, they had been designed for the manual cutting and clearing of the huge sugar cane plantations of Australia and central America; it had a sharp spike on the rear of the blade which allowed the worker to pull the cut cane stalks towards them for removal of leaves and cutting to length for transport.

The man was obviously drunk and his constant screaming was frightening for the women there. Unfortunately, there was no one close to the duress alarms and that meant that Jack, Akio and the two Samurai were the only ones that could do anything.

Jack jumped up and began shouting orders, 'Akio, you two,' he indicated the two samurai. 'Protect them,' he pointed to Teimei and Caroline. The guards herded them into a corner that would provide some defence from the assault.

Jack turned and addressed the man, trying everything he could to get him to give up his weapon. For almost fifteen minutes it appeared that Jack was going to be successful, right up until the man's former partner appeared in the room; she had come to ask for an extra towel.

It was so innocent, her request, but the sound of her voice seemed to spur him into some sort of fury. Screaming at everyone in general and no one in particular he suddenly lunged at Jack, who was the closest.

Despite his training and discipline, Jack had been distracted by the woman and the first blow slammed into Jack's upper left arm. Blood instantly soaked his shirt, an indication of how deep and severe the cut was. Jack did not have time to react before the second blow sliced across his chest from the left shoulder to the right side. This was now the time that either Jack or the man were going to win.

At this time Asa made it to the duress alarms and began banging desperately on it to get the required response.

Finally, with his survival instinct kicking in, Jack managed to kick the man in the knee, putting him off balance for just a moment; just long enough for Jack to land the first blow to his head. The combined hits, both on the left side knocked him to the floor and Jack took his opportunity.

Quickly stamping down hard, everyone heard the bones in the man's hand crack, fingers were so badly broken they would never work properly again. Jack then landed, knees first, on the man's chest. Despite his left arm being all but useless, Jack managed to grasp his shirt with the left hand and, using his right fist only, beat the man almost to death. His face bloodied and unrecognisable, the man could not get to his feet.

As Jack finally stood up, he staggered a little and then turned, seeing the Princess and the others safe he turned back to the assailant and swiftly kicked him in the groin followed by a kick to side of the leg, just above the knee. The damage to the nerve would stop the man from ever walking without a limp for the rest of his life.

'Will someone get a medic?' Jack asked and then he fell to the ground, almost unconscious.

As if in response to his request the door opened, and two dozen soldiers rushed into the room.

'Get that piece of shit outside!' Akio took control of the situation.

'Drag that table into the middle of the room.' Hiroya Furukawa, Jack's "personal" medic had taken charge. Two soldiers dragged a long dining table to a place where it could be useful. 'And cover it in towels.' The woman that wanted a towel found the pile behind the desk and brought a dozen to the table, spreading them out as she did so.

'Pick him up and put him up here.' Hiroya was now fully in charge.

'Get some pressure on his wounds.' Some of the soldiers wadded the towels and began to considerable task of staunching Jack's wounds.

Over the commotion another voice was finally heard. 'Stop! Do nothing more until an ambulance gets here, you may be doing more damage than you know.'

Everyone stopped for a moment and the owner of the voice was finally identified.

'If we don't do something now, he will die!' Akio was incensed that some officer thought he could take over.

'I order you to do nothing more!'

'And I order you to go away!' The relatively small female voice was clearly heard over all the noise.

The Colonel was almost going to shout but something in his brain stopped him, instead he asked 'And who are you?' he asked.

'I am Princess Teimei, and I order you to leave this room, Chief Samurai Takamatsu, Senior Samurai Furukawa, continue please.'

'Arigatō.' Akio gave a brief bow and Hiroya returned to his work. 'Get word to the barracks, as many combat medics as you have, here, now!'

Just minutes later around twenty medics arrived, each carrying bags of medical supplies.

Pointing at the first, Hiroya said 'Get a blood donation site set up,' pointing at the next, 'As many O-Neg donors as you can find. Cut his shirt off, check his wounds.' The medics began to function as a team and they quickly confirmed that there were just the two wounds, left arm and chest. By that time, they had four trying to stop the bleeding gash across his chest and two more on his arm.

Jack was still conscious, but struggling to stay that way. It was not a long time since the attack but it was now getting to be desperate, Jack needed the transfusions and the wounds closed and he needed that done quickly.

As the first donations were being taken a medic inserted an IV line and the life-giving fluid was squeezed into his right arm. As the first bag emptied Jack began to rally.

'First step to recovery.' Caroline whispered to Teimei as they watched from the side-lines.

'We need to begin but we cannot give him enough local anaesthetic to relieve the pain.' The senior medic commented to Akio.

As Akio began to formulate a plan, he heard Jack speak.

'Get the teams together, and get them ready to begin stitching. Get a single dose of the new anaesthetic prepared. When everyone is ready to go, give me the dose and everyone works at the same time. You will have twenty minutes before I come around; I don't expect to see any needles except the IV when I do. Now hurry.'

And hurry they did, just three minutes later they were ready to begin.

'Do it!' Jack commanded and promptly was put under by Furukawa. Eighteen minutes later the last stitch was in place and the medic teams were clearing their trash away as he came to.

'Turn him slightly on to his right side.' Furukawa ordered. And as they did Jack vomited all over the floor. 'Sorry, people, that is a side effect. When they wake up, they vomit.'

The soldiers began the clean up just as the police arrived to take the offender away to, firstly the hospital, then to the watchhouse.

As they rolled Jack back over, he visibly relaxed. Asa got a bucket of warm water and some wash cloths and was about to start cleaning the drying blood from her brother's body when Teimei asked, 'Please, may I?'

Asa was unsure what she meant, but as the washcloth was taken away from her she understood, Teimei was going to wash him; in a remarkable turnaround she had finally realised that her role was not as a privileged member of the world, but she was a servant of the Japanese people and she felt it was important that she perform the honour for him.

Asa let the young girl take the cloth and watched as she gently wiped the blood from his wounds as the tears flowed down her cheeks.

When she was almost done Jack whispered to her, 'My Princess, do not weep, I am alive and you are unharmed. That is all that matters. And your tears are making my chest wet.'

'Teimei looked at Jack and saw his familiar smile, she could not help herself as she began to laugh with him.

Once she was done, she called the senior medic who gave Jack a huge dose of antibiotics. The ambulance arrived and the doctors at the hospital sent him home the next morning, with orders not to do too much to stress the wound sites. A rule he gladly complied with.

As she turned around, she could see the strained and exhausted faces of the medics. They were all relieved Jack had pulled through and they continued to clean up.

'Where is that Colonel?' Teimei asked in a soft voice.

'Still in the corner, where he belongs.' Akio replied.

The Princess turned and looked at the second of her guards. 'You are a communicator?'

'Hai, Your Highness.'

'Can you setup a hologram call to the Palace, please?'

'Hai.'

Moments later the Emperor appeared on the hologram. Teimei bowed deeply.

'Sofu (grandfather), we have had a problem here at one of Jack's family charities.'

'Go on, Teimei.'

The young Princess spoke clearly and evenly and gave every detail of the incident.

'What do you want done?' The Emperor asked once she had finished.

'Firstly, I think the Colonel should be removed from this position, he may have lost the support of the division by his attitude to Jack's medical needs. The 61st was Jack's division and they still associate closely with him; they will not react kindly.'

'That is a big call, contact General Onishi, he can advise and take any necessary action.'

'The second request is for the Major to be promoted to take his place. The Major had control, and the security detail all complied with his demands.'

'Again, I will support your request with General Onishi. Anything else?'

'I feel that the security detail for the Family Centre should be a permanent thing, the division can assign soldiers on a rotational basis, one female and one male to assist in the registration and settlement of new clients, they will also be available if there is another incident.'

The Emperor agreed, 'Bring all these items to the attention of General Onishi, have him call me if he has any misgivings. And, arigatō, Teimei, your work has been most beneficial to those that desperately need assistance.'

Teimei and the others sat and relaxed for a short while, then she called General Onishi in Central Command. After outlining the requests and the reasoning behind them Motoyuki Onishi agreed and their conversation was terminated. He didn't tell her that the Emperor had already called and given him the authority for the changes; the two had decided that it was time for Teimei to make some important decisions on her own.

Chapter 49
Return to the Palace

Central Command

'Get me the Colonel in command of the 61st division.' General Onishi was not in a mood to be kind, his close friend had almost died as a result of the order of the Divisional Commander.

The hologram came back to life and the image of Colonel Sugimoto appeared before him.

'General, what can I do for you?' The Colonel was hoping the call was just to understand the events of the day.

'Get to Central Command, I will see you at 0800 tomorrow.' The hologram shutdown and the Colonel was left with the uncanny feeling that it was not going to end well.

The knock at the door was firm and its owner was hoping to convey the thought that he was in the right.

'Enter!' Onishi replied to the knock.

Colonel Sugimoto entered and saluted; Motoyuki did not reply, he did not even acknowledge the presence of the Colonel.

After a few tense moments, Motoyuki looked up and said 'Sit.' No more, no less. He had taken a leaf out of Jack's book of "Military Philosophy" and placed the colonel at a distinct disadvantage.

Eventually, he put down the documents and turned to the Colonel.

'What the hell were you thinking? Do you know who it was you refused treatment to?'

'I don't know what you mean?'

'In the shelter, what is the name of the man you refused to arrange medical treatment for?'

'I do not understand, he was just a visitor to the centre.'

'Just a visitor, JUST A VISITOR!' Motoyuki was incensed at the indifference of the man. 'THAT man was not only the man that owns the centre for families, he pays for it from his own pocket, and his sisters run it. AND he is a friend of mine, a long standing, personal friend of mine. Add to that the fact that he is a Captain of the Imperial Guard and the Personal Escort of none other than Princess Teimei, who was also present there. You want me to keep going?'

Colonel Sugimoto simply sat there with his mouth open, no words would emerge no matter how he tried.

'Oh, and one other thing. His name is "Jackson Nakagawa"; does **that** name mean anything to you?' The question was rhetorical, and yet the Colonel still tried to justify his orders.

Eventually, Sugimoto found his voice. 'I didn't know. Why did no one tell me they were there?'

'What, you think a man such as Captain Nakagawa needs to keep you informed of his life? I now have the Princess and through her the Crown Prince and the Emperor climbing all over me on this.'

'I apologise, General, I was unaware…'

Motoyuki held up his hand. 'STOP, no excuses. You realise that the 61st still hold their connection to Captain Nakagawa close. Do you think they will be happy to be commanded by the man that almost caused his demise? You are so lucky that his senior Combat Medic was also a former member of the 61st. He at least managed to get them working as a team; and saved Jack's life as well.'

'I will have to work hard to regain their confidence.'

Motoyuki looked hard into the face of the Colonel. 'You were promoted into that position; I can tell you I had a dozen very senior men wanting to be associated with the 61st and the 59th as well, YOU, got that chance and you butchered it.'

Motoyuki waved his hand when Sugimoto began to make his excuses. 'SILENCE. You will be posted to Central Command as Barracks Officer, work hard and you may be given a Combat Command in the future. Dismissed!'

Colonel Sugimoto got to his feet and saluted; as he turned to leave his mind was working furiously on how to save his career. He was still thinking about it when he arrived at Central Command to take control of "parks and gardens" as his new position was known.

'I need a coffee.' Motoyuki asked his secretary and one duly appeared on his desk. 'God, I hope Jack is OK,' he said to himself. 'Get Chief Samurai Takamatsu on the line!'

'Motoyuki, you are well I trust?' Akio knew exactly why the call had come through and he was waiting for his friend to continue.

'I am, thank you for asking. The real question is how is Jack?'

'He is fine, last report has him harassing everyone to get away from the hospital and doctors.'

'I will speak with the Shogun and get Furukawa assigned permanently to him, that will get him home for his recuperation.'

'Arigatō, just so you know, the princess will not leave here until Jack can travel with her.'

'So, he made a breakthrough, good. I knew he would. Dare I assume the Emperor and crown prince know and agree?'

'Princess Teimei told them she would not return until Jack was fit enough to escort her.'

'Very well. We must have dinner when you all return to Tokyo.'

'Deal.' The call was ended and Onishi began to make the necessary orders for the promotion of Major Matsuda to Colonel and assign him Command of the

61st Division. "I think the Princess has been imprinted with some of Jack's determination, now she has me promoting a man on her instructions. Still I suppose it could be worse, at least the 61st like him."

Jack's Home

'At last, you return.' Fumiko was mocking Jack, but deep inside she was pleased to see him in good health.

'Yes, I have returned. I know you said it would be dangerous, but I did not think it would be this bad.'

'You will be fine, and next time you will be better than this.' Fumiko turned and walked off only to return with coffee and biscuits.

Quickly joined by Caroline, Akio and Teimei they all began to catchup with events.

'You mean Onishi sacked the Colonel?' Jack was astounded at the revelation.

'He did, but only because Teimei demanded it.' Caroline replied.

'And how did it feel, Teimei, to change a man's career with a word?'

'I think he was out of his depth; he could not solve the problem at hand and he resorted to basic concepts, not resolving the real needs of the situation.'

'And was it easy for you? To make the demand?'

'Once I saw how well Akio and Hiroya worked, how quickly they took control and got the result they needed, it became a lot better for me. The support I received from the 61st and the 59th for overriding the original command proved to me that the order was right.'

'She made a real impact, Jack. The 61st may be "Jack's Pack" but the 59th have now taken the nickname "Teimei's Tribe".' Caroline was proud of the young princess and her progression into the complex life of the Imperial Family.

'Good to hear. Now, my Princess, tell me, have you prepared your homecoming speech for your parents?'

Teimei looked at Jack, then Caroline and Akio and then back to Jack.

'I knew, at the time, you had been ordered to take me away from my so called "friends". I know I was not a nice person; the fact is that you all helped me to find my way. The world is not as simple as the entitled believe; there are a lot of people that need help, just to survive and I know you all do more than your share to help. I will return to school but I think it will need to be a different one to the one I was at. They were not good friends, and I have no desire to spend time with them.'

'And who do you think are good friends?' Caroline was asking more to keep the conversation moving, to keep the Princess explaining her thoughts.

'I would like to think that you are all my friends, you have worked hard to change my thinking and to show me a different way, how to help. That is more important than the shade of lip gloss I want to wear.'

'Arigatō, my Princess. All we need to do now is get you back to the palace to speak with your family.' Jack was smiling widely at the change they had engineered in the life of the young lady before them.

The Imperial Palace

'Her Imperial Highness, Princess Teimei.' The aide announced to the Emperor and the rest of her family as she entered the receiving rooms.

Stopping a respectful distance from them she bowed deeply to each in turn, Emperor, Empress, Crown Prince and Crown Princess. For the first time in almost two months, she did not have a personal escort with her, this she must do for herself.

'Welcome home. How was your journey?' The Emperor's question was simple enough but it triggered a wave of emotion as the princess explained everything that Jack and his friends had done and how it had affected her. Once she was finished; she rushed over and hugged her father and mother.

'I am so sorry; I have been a very nasty person. Arigatō, for sending me away with Jack and the others. They taught me so much, and sometimes it was not pleasant. Watching Jack get so very badly hurt while he protected me and seeing Akio and the others not going to his assistance simply because he had ordered them to stand in front of me, was a real moment in my life, a moment I will never forget. I realised that if Jack was to die that day, there were three more Samurai waiting to protect me. That so many are prepared to possibly die for me and also for all of you, showed me that I need to be able to do more for others. My former friends were so very selfish, I will not need them to continue my life, I have real friends now, here in the guard, at Jack's home and also on Iturup, friends that care.'

She stood upright and formally bowed to all. 'Domo arigatō.'

'I knew you could do it, we just needed to find a method to make it happen. Saying that; where is Jack?' The Crown Prince needed to speak with the architect of his daughter's change.

Jack entered the room and bowed; 'Forgive me, Your Majesty, it is difficult for me to kneel at this time.'

'You are forgiven, even though I have told you that kneeling is not required.'

'Not for formal acknowledgement perhaps, but I feel it is a necessary honour I do for you.'

'Always the answer. I feel it is time for me to forego my constant reminders and for you to continue to do things your way.'

'Arigatō, Majesty. It is so kind of you.'

'Now, how did you do it, you must have some impressive magic to achieve such a broad change?'

Princess Teimei blushed deeply and Jack smiled at her discomfort.

'I did very little, I showed her some of the results of the Border Wars; I showed her the efforts some have to make just to survive; and we showed her some of the less fortunate of society. She made the connections and changed her thinking, I actually did very little. Caroline Jonson did much of the mental work and Akio and Furukawa the rest. I believe she will do you great honour in the future.'

'Arigatō, Jack. What do you mean "great honour"?'

'I am unsure of the exact nature, Fumiko Maki told me and I am simply repeating her words.'

'Well, if Fumiko said it…'

'It must be true!' they all finished the Emperor's sentence together and finished with smiles and laughter.

'Now Jack, coffee and stories.'

Chairs and refreshments were brought in, as were Akio and Caroline and for the next hour and a half the friends regaled the time they spent together.

'Sofu, can we get the Prime Minister to help the Ainu on Iturup and the other islands? They are desperately short of foods and other requirements?'

'Certainly, better still, I will have him come here tomorrow and you can tell him yourself, make certain you know what basics they need and you can be the driving force behind the request.'

'Oh!' She replied. 'I don't know if I am ready for that yet.'

'Believe me, you are ready. And I will be behind you, just to add a little realism while the politician tries to find a way to deny your request.' Jack encouraged her to believe her abilities.

'I will do that then. I already know most of what they need, I will speak with Harucor and the council this evening and get a full list.'

'That's better, you will succeed.' The crown princess was impressed. She was even more impressed when the Prime Minister immediately conceded the point and supplied the support so desperately needed in the far north.

Jack's mission was complete, the princess was now an important asset as a member of the Imperial Family.

Chapter 50
Life Gets Quiet (for a While)

Jack returned home to continue his rehabilitation; his left arm was very weak, as the muscles had been almost severed to the bone, he knew it would be some time before he would be able to move freely, let alone have sufficient strength to perform his duties.

It was to be almost three weeks before he returned as the personal escort for Teimei and another nine weeks before he could begin conditioning training to regain the strength he needed, he was sadly out of condition and it was Akio's job to rectify that.

Every day at dawn the two would go for a five-kilometre run, followed by a workout in the weights room and then breakfast. The rest of the morning was dedicated to completing any professional correspondence and answering calls from all who thought he could be of assistance.

Frequent callers were the Council of The Kuril Islands, when they needed help; the planning centre in Tokyo when they wanted to give a new officer or, sometimes an entire class from the academy, something to keep them up at night.

The Imperial Palace would often ask for planning assistance for processions and parades; and people like Watanabe Korehira would ask for a "professional assessment" of a newly forged weapon. This would entail Jack, Akio and Caroline travelling to Shimane Prefecture for a "week's testing of weapons"; the correct translation was "look at what I have made, now let's have a drink".

Strangely enough, on the weeks that Caroline was with them she also had "professional appointments", translation "I want to spend time with Itsuki" and no one objected to that either.

Eventually, Caroline submitted her application for discharge from the U.S. Army. The hologram call from General Moreton was always going to come and as he looked at her, he asked 'Are you certain you want to be discharged?'

When she replied in the affirmative, he simply agreed, 'To be honest, we thought you had already left us. Good luck with the future.' And that was the end of her involvement, with the American Army at least. Her attachment to the Imperial Palace was to become, eventually far more demanding; but that was far into the future.

In the mean time she would be able to spend time with the three men she admired most in the world. Itsuki, for their romantic connection as well as his skill and dedication to his craft; Akio for his ability to instil discipline and weapons skills; and of course, Jack, the one man she wanted to understand more than anything else in the world, but she knew she would only ever scratch the surface.

For all of them, life was good and they all enjoyed their shared time together.

Eventually, Jack and Akio were able to begin sparring with weapons, bokken (wooden swords) at first, then a single steel blade training katana. It was obvious that Jack's left arm was going to be a problem, but then again that was why they were training, to bring him back to full fitness and that would only be accomplished by time.

The single katana gave way to a wakizashi and katana pair, and Jack's power improved quickly. Once a week the two would attempt "tamashigiri" or test cutting. The tatami mats, rolled and bound were as close as they could get to the original test of a human torso; a practice that had been abandoned centuries before, and a skilled swordsman with a good weapon could slice through without any trouble. Right-handed, Jack was fine, left-handed took a lot more time and effort to get it right. Eventually, he managed it and the next morning he and Akio decided it was time for full contact combat training.

By the time they had finished there was a gallery of spectators viewing from the rear deck. Every successful blow applauded and at the close, two very tired and weary samurai finally called for a close to the proceedings.

'Well done, Jack,' Akio bowed to his friend. 'I can tell the Emperor you are ready for full duties.'

'Arigatō, but why don't we surprise him with a visit at the palace? I have some planning for the Bunkyo Ume Matsuri (plum blossom festival) to be completed anyway.'

'Deal.'

The two showered and had breakfast before arranging to go to Tokyo the next morning. The day went quietly and before they knew it sunset was upon them. Sake and tall stories were the order of the evening and eventually they made their way to their rooms.

As was now usual, Jack could be found at dawn facing east as the sun rose above the horizon. Once he was finished, he got to his feet and returned inside, the warmth of his home a sharp contrast to the biting cold of a late winters' early morning.

Breakfast came and went without a great deal of deep conversation and by mid-morning they were dressed in their day uniforms and ready to return to the palace. The helicopter flight was quick, the improvements in engine and rotor technology had increased flight speed as well as decreased fuel usage and noise.

'Helicopters are a great way to fly.' Akio announced to no one in particular.

'They are, and dammed expensive to run,' Jack replied. 'That is why I get General Ito to supply it.'

They laughed at the mildly amusing statement as the Imperial estates came into view. Moments later they were on the ground with a dozen members of the guard retrieving their luggage. First stop was the Emperor's receiving rooms.

As the two moved through the palace, the staff working in the various rooms would stop and bow in respect; and as they slowly got closer to the Emperor's rooms, the one member of the palace staff that everyone else made room for, stopped in the middle of the passageway that he had made his own domain. Jack stopped and addressed him. 'Konichiwa, Isamu. I trust you are well?'

The huge Savannah cat, known as the "ruler of the palace", gave a guttural howl and then purred loudly, which was as close to a command as he could give, and Jack dutifully bent down and gave him the demanded scratch behind the ears. Satisfied, Isamu left the two to continue on their way.

'That animal rules this place.' Akio commented.

'He does, and don't let him hear you say it out loud, his claws are quick and sharp.'

The two smiled and continued to their meeting with their Commander-in-Chief.

The Emperor's aide knocked on the door and received a muffled "Enter" from within. As he opened the door he moved inside and announced 'Captain Nakagawa and Chief Samurai Takamatsu, Your Majesty.' A brief bow and the aide departed, closing the door behind him.

Jack, as usual knelt and offered the Emperor his weapons and Akio followed suit. Formal refusal completed the official greeting.

Once alone the Emperor moved quickly to the two and greeted them a little less formally.

'Jack, so good to see you have recovered and we must thank you, both of you, for your working with Teimei. I understand your efforts were not only successful but continue to reap results.'

The rear door opened and the Crown Prince and Princess entered with the Empress. Closely following behind them was a steward with the refreshments which were served; before they could continue their conversation, the Emperor indicated that they should all sit.

'Arigatō Majesty, we believe that the visits were more than successful. Princess Teimei has improved the relationship with the Ainu as well as her standing with the political leaders; she has shown that she has the ability to get them to work together.'

'And the problem in Sapporo?'

'The entire process was difficult; she had not previously had need nor opportunity to see how difficult some people's lives are. She had great empathy for them all and helped my sister, Asa, in her daily work for the short time we were there. I must say that Doctor Jonson was a great help for us, we could show Princess Teimei as much as we wanted, and the fact is, she had not been aware of the issues of life outside the palace and of the work you all perform. Once she understood some of the daily lives of others, she adapted her thinking and her understanding and changed her perspective. That made our job so much easier, her thinking was augmented by Caroline's reinforcement of the improvements her life would receive and the result is the confident, caring young woman we now have with us.'

'And her so called friends?'

'It was The Princess that decided to relinquish that part of her life, I think she felt more fulfilled by helping others than by concentrating on the frivolous parts of life. She will be a great asset to the Imperial Family and a great joy to you all, I am certain.'

'We can only thank you. It was a difficult task you were set, and you both completed your duties with what has become the normal way for the guard; a minimum of fuss and with spectacular results. Tell us more about the intruder you encountered?'

Jack related the incident and the aftermath, exactly as it had occurred, no detail was omitted and a little extra emphasis was placed on the part played by the Princess.

'I must say,' the crown prince began, 'before your tour of the north, I do not think Teimei would have been capable or confident enough to have made such a command. To take on a Colonel that commands a combat division is a big step.'

'Not only did she take him on, she won the argument. A great leap forward, under the circumstances. Personally, she probably saved my life by getting him away from the incident; I know Akio and Hiroya would have ignored him, but to have her take control cemented all we had done. I am in her debt.'

'As she is in yours, arigatō, Jack. We trust you are fully recovered?'

'I am, Majesty, and ready for my next assignment.'

The Shogun was called and the planning for the Bunkyo Ume Matsuri (Plum Blossom Festival) began in earnest.

Osaka Festival Planning Office

'This year the official festival review will be held at Osaka Castle...' The government official and then the Mayor of Osaka droned on for what seemed to be forever before they finished their briefing. Questions were asked and answered, and everyone seemed to be satisfied. Finally, the meeting broke up and everyone went their way.

'Thank the gods I am out of there.' Teimei whispered to Jack as they left the building, 'I was almost asleep for half of that. How can they make a semi-interesting subject so boring?'

Jack grinned widely. 'I am glad it was you I was seated with, I actually did drop off once or twice; they must have been either too polite or they were watching you, they did not notice me.'

'Unfair,' she replied. 'If I have to sit through it, so do you. Stay awake next time.' It was an order, but her grin belied the humour behind it.

'As you wish, my Princess.' Jack gave a small bow in deference. 'But I fear I will need more coffee next time.' The two were seen smiling as they made their way to the waiting car to take them back to their rooms at the Kyoto Imperial Palace.

The festival went exactly to plan, no delays, no inconveniences, no troubles.

'That is done, thankfully without interruption.' Teimei commented.

'Yes, it was all good. Now, our next appointment will be Hanami in Sendai; The Floating Lantern Festival in July and then Shichi-Go-San (children's festival, literally seven-five-three years of age) in Nagoya, in November.' Jack listed the currently booked festivals for the remainder of the year.

'Sofu (grandfather) has given us a good calendar; enough to keep us busy and still have time to squeeze other events in should we be requested.'

'Hai, it is good. We will also have the Official visit of the British Royal Family later in the year, that will be a very busy time for all of The Guard.' Jack agreed with Teimei and they continued to analyse the schedule.

'Let us concentrate on the next one, to begin with.' Teimei and Jack worked their way through the requirements of each festival and event as they arose. All were completed without any problems and when the year finally closed, they were all at their own homes with family for the New Year Celebrations.

The New Year was to prove to be a little problematic. Some of the festivals were moved in both date and location and inevitably clashes were happening. Some were cancelled due to unrest with some protest groups demanding the Government change the political stance on several key issues; the always contentious problem of how to help the homeless and the less fortunate would always sway between providing massive assistance packages and support, to give them enough to survive and make them work for their existence. Literally from one political extreme to the other and back again.

It just happened that at this time the pendulum had swung rather quickly towards the "give them nothing" side; and the "greater assistance" groups were becoming more agitated every day; most were politically active but some were getting physically aggressive as well.

The die had been cast and no-one could have foreseen the outcomes of the decisions made as the two opposing factions made their positions known more widely every day.

Planning Rooms of The Imperial Palace

'Your Majesty; there is some evidence that a protest will be held at the Tokyo Hanami Matsuri (Festival of the Cherry Blossom).' The senior planning officer was trying to be diplomatic as he brought what he thought was an important issue to light for the Emperor.

'And what do you think we should do?' The crown prince was renowned for asking questions in a relatively blunt way; he had long ago found that the best way to get answers from some individuals was to ask a blunt question and let them try to work out what was the best reply.

'I beg your pardon, Your Highness, what do you mean?'

The crown prince smiled inwardly, spending time with Jack had the benefit of learning how to get people on the "back foot" as Jack called it, make them answer without giving them a preferred position.

'You have raised a problem, what is, by all reports, a very real problem; What are your recommendations?'

'I...I...I...' The man was clearly having a problem pronouncing his possible resolutions for the issue.

'What he is trying to say,' began Jack from the back of the room, 'is that there may be a safety issue we need to plan for. Do we attend? Do we all abstain from the festival? Do we call the Police Chief and demand all Tokyo Police to be at the grounds? Do we activate the Army to provide a defensive perimeter? Do we place the entire Imperial Guard around the Imperial Viewing Dais? Do we send only one or two members of the Imperial Family or do we all attend as originally planned? Speak up man, surely you have some idea of what you want us to do?'

The planning attaché was now almost unable to speak; his mind was caught between "How do I tell the Emperor what to do" and "What if Captain Nakagawa has a better plan and I appear to be unable to do my job?".

'Captain, perhaps you can assist?' Princess Teimei proposed a possible method to resolve the impasse.

'If I may?' Jack asked, more from being polite than any real desire to do someone else's planning for them.

'If you would?'

Jack sat and stared at the planning hologram for almost two minutes.

'We can set the viewing platform here,' Jack indicated the position on the hologram. 'The transportation containers can be stored here, behind the stands, we can leave a gap of three metres between them and stack them two high. That gives a barrier to prevent access from the festival area, small areas are easily defended by a few against much higher numbers of opponents.'

'How do you know that? Surely a few defenders would be easily overrun?' The Planner was sceptical at least.

'Ask the Persians that tried to take the Thermopylae Pass, they were held up by a relatively small Greek army, despite a numerical superiority of at least fifteen to one. The Greeks may have lost the battle in the end, but they stood firm and held up a superior force for many days. I propose that a company of the 59th be available to assist if we need to evacuate, they can wait near the Akasaka Palace. The area behind the containers, on the roadway can be closed off and the imperial carriage can wait there along with the Emperors Personal Guard. If we need to leave quickly it is a short distance from the viewing stand to the waiting carriage and escort. The police can pick up the carriage escort duties when it makes it to the grounds of the Akasaka Palace, where the 59th can take over as a protective force; IF we need to evacuate! If we don't then all is well.'

'Can I ask why you specify the 59th? Are you not more closely aligned with the 61st?' Asked the empress.

'Majesty, the 59th are more closely tied with Princess Teimei, they will be more invested with the safety of your selves and the princess, a little more enthusiasm for their patron.'

'Good, it is pleasing that she has made such a strong bond.'

'When did you come up with that plan? You must have worked on it for a long time?' asked the planning official, convinced that Jack had been covertly planning for some time.

'I started when you said "there is some evidence that a protest will be held at the Tokyo Hanami Matsuri" and I finished just then.'

'That is unbelievable; we have been wrestling with this problem for almost a month and you complete it in five minutes.'

Jack grinned. 'What can I say? It is a talent.'

'If you have time; I have several more events that would benefit from your skills?'

'My apologies, I have more than enough to keep me busy with my current workload. I simply do not have time for such endeavours.'

The planning attaché was unsure if he had been fobbed-off or just denied a chance to resolve some issues; either way he would not be getting the help he so desperately wanted.

Jack's plan was analysed and implemented; the only change was to the creation of the fencing for the official viewing areas, there were no post supports available and as such a fence could not stand alone. The problem was resolved by erecting transportation containers along the sides and getting the Tokyo Arts College to decorate them with suitable murals; a simple solution that could be completed with a minimum of fuss.

The very next meeting of the security group was almost in uproar when Jack arrived with Fumiko alongside him.

'Why have you brought your assistant?' closely followed by 'She is not permitted to attend!' Were just the first questions asked; or perhaps, demanded, would be a better description.

'If you wish me to assist, then Fumiko will stay, make your choice.'

Amid much complaining, Fumiko was eventually permitted to remain.

The discussions began and were, mostly, attempts at changing Jack's initial plan. As each change was put forward the relative merits were discussed; Jack would remain silent and every so often Fumiko would whisper in his ear and Jack would nod sagely; but he did not reply.

Eventually, after almost half-an-hour, one of the delegates asked, 'Why are you silent Captain? Do you not have any input?'

Jack looked at the man his eyes "piercing" the man's brain; so intense was the stare that he instantly felt uneasy. Trying to dissipate the uncomfortable feeling he asked, 'What is your assistant advising? We would all like to know?'

'She is giving me her insight into the changes.'

'Well? Tell us all.'

'She advises me to distance myself from the changes you propose, they are dangerous; to the Emperor, the Empress and the rest of the Imperial Family. You want to close off the rear of the official stands, that imprisons the Imperial Family within the compound, UNACCEPTABLE! You wish to save some money by moving the stands to an area that does not permit a simple departure if there is a problem, also UNACCEPTABLE. You were given a plan that enabled the safety of the Imperial Family and you want to ignore that. Your choice, I will not be available for any further planning meetings.' At that Jack and Fumiko left the meeting.

The remaining delegates were left arguing, the noise slowly rising as they became more animated. In the end, there were no decisions made and the meeting ended in chaos.

Imperial Palace

'Jack, explain yourself? Why did you leave the meeting?'

'I must apologise, Majesty. The changes they proposed would place you and the family in a precarious position. They wanted you to be fenced in with the entire parade and the spectators, with only one way out. The proposal was simply to save some money on the festival costs. Again, I apologise, I will not permit your safety to be compromised for commercial reasons.'

'You feel that strongly about it?'

'I do.'

'And you Fumiko, what do you say?'

'The initial advice was that there would be a protest,' her voice lowered, 'There will be a protest, and you will be in some danger if the plans are altered, accept Jacks plan and you will all be safe.' She drew a deep breath and visibly relaxed.

'Arigatō, Fumiko; and you Jack.' The Emperor rang a bell and an aide arrived soon after. 'Call the head of the planning committee and have him come here immediately.

The aide left and just a couple of minutes later he knocked on the door.

Bowing deeply, he reported, 'Majesty, the head of the committee will be here in just a few minutes.'

'Good, bring him in when he arrives.'

The head of planning was shown into the Emperors receiving rooms as soon as he arrived. The sight that met him almost shocked him. Jack and Fumiko were both sitting and sharing, not only refreshments but also some joke he was not privy to, laughter emanating outside the rooms as he arrived.

'Head of Planning for Hanami.' The aide announced as he held the door open to show the man in.

The Emperor did not offer refreshments, nor did he offer a seat. Leaving the man standing, the Emperor waited for a moment while the traditional bow was completed.

'I have been appraised of the situation by Captain Nakagawa, what do you have to say?'

For almost five minutes the man spoke with ever increasing rapidity. Eventually, the Emperor held up his hand, to silence the excuses.

'Enough. If you wish to save some money on the security arrangements then we shall do so.'

'The Head of Planning smiled widely within his own mind, it was a rare day that anyone could say they had been given what they wanted at the first attempt.'

'Arigatō, Majesty.'

'Do not thank me so quickly, if money is what you want to save then you will do so, BUT! We will not be attending, that way you can save much more by not needing any of the security arrangements or the official viewing platforms or the fencing. Arigatō. You may leave.' The man was summarily dismissed and escorted from the Emperor's rooms.

Once the door was closed Jack looked at the Emperor. 'I must say, I did not expect that.'

'Don't worry, Jack. In a couple of days, I will summon him again. That will give him some time to squeeze some more money out of his sponsors. The festival will go ahead as you planned. I have simply given him a gentle nudge in the right direction.'

'I hope you are right, or else I get an early vacation.'

'Sorry, Jack.' Began Fumiko, 'No early vacation for you.'

Silence suddenly descended over the three; quickly followed by laughter.

'So be it.' Jack finally replied, 'I will prepare the Guard and get the 59th down from Sapporo.'

'Excellent idea, Jack. Arigatō Fumiko, as usual your abilities will prove to be the most decisive tool we have.'

'You are most welcome, Majesty. Anything I can do to assist.'

Chapter 51
Festival Time

The week of festivities finally drew close. In the week leading up to the day, Jack, Akio and the Shogun could be found touring the viewing site and checking security arrangements, with the Assistant Planning Clerk closely following taking notes for corrections.

'Get the containers turned around, I want the openings pointing out, away from the arena.'

'May I ask why? Nakagawa San (Nakagawa Sir).'

'The openings have hand and foot holds; if we turn them around, they are the same as a brick wall.'

'Again Sir, may I ask why this is important?'

'If we have the rear facing the arena; then anyone trying to exit the arena, for any reason, will be restricted to the gap between the containers. By doing this we restrict the numbers that can use the area. Prevent them from climbing and we control the passage.'

'Ah, I understand, I think.' The man was clearly still confused.

'Why do you think we want this gap? Here between the containers?' Jack asked but he received no real response.

'We are placing the imperial carriages here after the Emperor and empress have arrived. Should they and the Imperial Family need to leave in a hurry they only need to come through here,' Jack pointed to the gap between the containers, 'which is less than twenty metres from the rear of the viewing platform and they are away. This is the emergency exit for them. The Emperor's Personal Guard will also be waiting here to escort them.'

'Now I do understand, I will have the containers turned around before lunch. Arigatō, Nakagawa San.'

'You are welcome.' Jack and the others continued their inspection tour and when they were done, they were satisfied with the arrangements.

'Time to relax for a while.' The Shogun announced, 'We shall "inspect" the catering arrangements for the escort, next.' Akio and Jack both knew what he meant and they were soon seated and enjoying tea, in the catering tent far behind the viewing platforms, while they discussed the scheduling for the actual day of the Festival Parade, which was now very close.

Next stop was a ride from the official viewing area to Akasaka Palace; their huge Friesian's loping along gently completely unfazed by the traffic as they rode the one kilometre or so to the palace; as they rode, they were constantly checking the route to ensure there could be no interruptions to the journey.

Once the festival appointments were completed, this was where the Imperial Family would be stopping for the official reception and the evening banquet. The plan then called for them to be driven back to the Imperial Palace and that would complete the days engagements.

Fate, however, would require a slight change of plan; Hiroshi and Akio always knew it was a possible outcome, but Jack was almost certain and he was already making mental notes on possible changes to the route planed from the reviewing area all the way through to the Imperial Palace.

Once inside the palace grounds they allowed their horses to pick up speed and canter to the palace proper where they were handed over to the grooms.

'Are you happy with the route and transport?' Hiroshi asked, he had already noticed Jack's change of demeanour and that could only mean one thing, he was concerned.

'The route and transport arrangements are good.' Jack announced, the others were waiting for the "but" that was implied by Jack's tone. 'But; I feel we should have an extra company of the 59th waiting at the Meiji Memorial Picture Gallery as well as the company we are putting in the grounds of the Akasaka Palace.'

'Two Companies? That's a lot of soldiers, do you really think it necessary?'

'I don't know, I feel that if we have to evacuate the Imperial Family we will need the ones at the Palace for direct protection, that is the direction we will be travelling; the other company will be able to restrict the movement of any protestors and can effectively contain them, once they are prevented from escaping then the police can have them. Of course; if all goes well, then they will be bored with the waiting. Let's hope for bored.' Jack's preference was well stated, but both Hiroshi and Akio knew that if he was concerned then that would be a good reason to be extra vigilant.

Jack pulled his communicator from his pocket and made a call.

'Chief of Staff's Office, who is calling please?'

'Captain Nakagawa for General Onishi.'

'Certainly, Captain. One moment.' Such was Jack's reputation and his friendship with Motoyuki the call was put through immediately.

'Jack, how are things at the palace?'

'As good as they can get. How about in Central Command?'

'Same, same. What can I do for you?'

'Is it possible to get Drones and Haruto to do some work for me?'

'Sure, what do you need?'

'I would like satellite surveillance of the Hanami festival site from tomorrow until after the festival ends, and I would like Drones to give me visual coverage for the day of the festival parade.'

'Certainly, are they looking for anything specific?'

'Not that has been identified by the usual intelligence networks.'

'So why the need for extra eyes?'

'That is easy, just one word…'

'Let me guess, Fumiko?'

'Absolutely right.' Jack smiled as he thought of how far they had come and how much they could depend on each other.

'Consider it done, Haruto will let you know when the bird is on task, I will have Drones and Mai at the Palace tomorrow along with the pilots and portable equipment.'

'Much appreciated, Arigatō. When the festival is over, I will come and pay my respects, time we all had dinner together again.'

'Agreed. Let me know if there is anything else that I can help with.'

'Sayonara.' The two closed the conversation.

'Feel better now?' Hiroshi asked.

'To a small extent, at least we can get aerial surveillance now.'

Chapter 52
A Day Not Easily Forgotten

The day of the festival parade dawned the same as any other day; the sun gave the promise of a warm but not too hot day and a gentle breeze was already making its way across the city. Members of the Guard were brushing their horses in preparation of an expected busy day. All the kura (saddles), omogai (bridle), tazune (reins), the traditional abumi (stirrups) and the other pieces that make up the "tack" as it is more commonly known, had been the subject of a week's worth of heavy polishing.

Once the leather equipment had been polished, the silver adornments were also polished and the tack would be assembled and the horse "dressed". The members of the Guard were also polished and dressed, the gusoku (armour), polished with a special treatment, made them glisten like they were wet. No medals or stars are worn, the only indicators of rank were the coloured laminar plates of the sode (shoulder pieces). The centre plate was silver for the lowest rank of Samurai; top and bottom plates for the Senior Samurai; top, middle and bottom for the Chief Samurai; Captains had two top and two bottom plates painted and the Shogun had all five armour plates gold plated.

For all ranks the agemaki or "clover knot" is fastened to the Do (chest plate) of the armour, green with silver traces of the Order of the Golden Kite (second class) for the lower ranks and equal parts silver and green of the Order (first class) for captains and above.

Jack's uniform was completely different. As the personal escort for the princess, he was permitted to wear "Dress Uniform - Soft", the standard dress uniform of the Guard, but not including medals, stars or sashes. Medal ribbons were the only indicators of his extensive service and the "Captains Braid", the four strands of gold silk worn over the right shoulder, were the only indicator of rank.

As 10am approached the cars carrying the Imperial Family approached the Akasaka Palace and the company from the 59th division formed a guard of honour for them as they left the vehicles. Once the Emperor and his family were ready the two Imperial State Coaches were brought to the forecourt of the palace.

Twin Landau carriages; a four-wheel convertible carriage with low side for better viewing of the occupants, drawn by four "Imperial Blacks" with two drivers at the front and two footmen at the rear, were the order of the day. The Emperor's carriage was distinguishable as it was carrying the Imperial

Chrysanthemum on the doors, the second carriage was for the Crown Prince and Princess seated at the rear and Princess Teimei and Jack seated at the front.

The Crown Prince's carriage was to leave first with Akio following the carriage and an escort of four samurai behind him. The Emperor's carriage departed around ten minutes later with the shogun immediately behind the carriage and a further ten samurai as escorts.

The cortege made its way around the outside of the viewing area and then completed a lap inside giving the huge crowd a chance to see all the occupants. Finally stopping before the Imperial Viewing Platform, the steps were lowered and the door opened to let them all alight. Crown Prince first, then the Crown Princess and Teimei, last was Jack who followed them all up the stairs to their seating positions. Off to the far side of the platform sat the Prime Minister and the senior ministers of state. Before they took their seats, the royal party bowed to the crowd and waved as they waited for the Emperor's carriage to arrive.

The timing of the arrival was almost perfect, the Crown Prince's party had made their way to their seats and the carriage had been relocated behind the barriers and the crowd had become a little quieter. Just as everyone was becoming involved in their own conversations a roar could be heard, getting louder every second it was accompanied by almost everyone waving the national flag. The Emperor's carriage had entered the arena.

Jack pressed the button on his communicator, 'Haruto? Anything to worry about?'

'Nothing overtly obvious, Jack, but cloud is making it difficult for us to see anything definite. There was some phone traffic but that was inconclusive.'

'Arigatō, Drones?'

'I am concerned about the number of supporters we can see, there are a lot wearing a bright blue shirt but no float matching them. They may just be a marching group.'

'Hai, keep a close watch on them, call if something obvious shows up. Arigatō.'

Everyone present got to their feet and shouts of banzai could be heard all around the area. Eventually, the carriage came to a stop at the steps for the viewing platform, as they made their way down the few steps of the carriage, all the Samurai present saluted as did all the military and ex-military present. The civilians all bowed in honour of their Emperor. The Emperor and Empress made their way to their seats and waved to the crowd before the National Anthem was played; once it was finished, they sat. Sitting was the signal for everyone else to relax and sit down as well.

The first display was from a marching band and they made their way up and down and around the arena to the delight of all present. The displays arrived and left as each had their turn and then the parade itself began. Entering from one end of the arena they moved down the side and across in front of the official viewing stage then they returned along the other side and back to the starting area along a series of roads that enabled the tens of thousands of spectators to also view them.

It was spectacular. A total of one hundred and twenty floats, all accompanied by dozens of supporters, some walking and some riding on the float, who sang and danced to various tunes and songs as they made their way through the arena and out into the street.

'Jack? What is it?'

'Hmmm…' Jack's mind was elsewhere at that moment.

'JACK!' Teimei nudged him with an elbow.

'Huh, what?' He finally came back to the moment and looked at the princess with confusion on his face.

'What is wrong? What did Haruto and Drones say?'

Jack leaned over and spoke very quietly, 'There appears to be a large number of people waiting for their moment to enter the arena, the problem is that they do not appear to be supporting any floats or bands, I have checked the programme and there is no mention of a group in blue. Be aware and ready, this may not go as we wish.'

'Will you alert the Emperor?'

'Your parents first then the Emperor.'

Jack leaned forward and spoke directly to the Crown Prince and Princess. He finished the conversation with "I will move forward and inform the Emperor." And he received a slight nod of assent before moving.

Standing up he moved from his seat at the end of the row and moved down the few steps and along in front of the Emperor. He squatted down and began to explain what was happening and his thoughts and his preferred emergency plan; should it become necessary.

Both the Emperor and empress nodded their assent and, once he was finished, Jack moved back to his seat. The concern was clearly written on his face and Teimei was becoming worried.

'Jack? Will we be safe?' Her question was almost spoken with hope, but it conveyed the deep worry she was feeling at that moment.

'I am unsure, at the moment. There are signs that it may not be as we would hope.' His reply, while not exactly cryptic, was not as reassuring as she had wanted.

The minutes slowly ticked by, as the festival continued her fears slowly subsided, and she began to relax, just a little.

Jack appeared to tilt his head and he placed his hand over his ear as he received a message.

'Jack, they have brought posters and placards out into the open. They have managed to secrete the support poles that hold them up, these poles have been fashioned into makeshift weapons. Get ready!'

'Arigatō, Drones. Get video for the police, they may want to prosecute.' Then he nodded to the princess and leaned forward to tell the crown prince and princess the developments.

'Make your preparations, I will inform Otosan. (father)' He leaned forward and spoke quietly.

'Captain Nakagawa is most concerned; he is making preparations.' His message was acknowledged with a small nod.

'Shogun, Akio. Ready the carriages and mount the Guard. Be ready.

Without an audible response the guard prepared to depart the festival grounds.

'GO NOW!' Drones voice burst into Jack's earpiece. 'They have entered the arena and are beginning a protest; total numbers calculated to be in excess of a thousand. Must have been hiding under the tree canopy to keep out of sight.

They are in the middle of the parade, keeping themselves surrounded by the participants.'

Jack stood up and immediately moved to the front of the viewing platform and informed the Emperor.

The entire Imperial Family stood up and made their way down the rear evacuation stairs and between the containers towards the carriages. First onboard was the empress, closely followed by the Emperor and as soon as they were seated their carriage lurched forward to begin its journey back to the Akasaka Palace. Holding on tight to the grab handles on the side of the carriage the two held hands as they picked up speed, the hooves of the Imperial Blacks thundering on the ground as they galloped away.

The Crown Princess and Princess Teimei were next to mount their carriage closely followed by the prince; Jack waiting patiently, if nervously, by the door for everyone to be seated.

It was at that point that it began to go wrong. One of the horses, spooked by the noise and frantic movement around it, managed to step over the traces and its leg was now unable to move. Jack threw his uniform cap into the carriage and moved to soothe the frightened animal as the footmen tried to correct the problem. Precious seconds slipped by and the protestors could be heard getting louder.

'JACK! Get out of there!' Drones was now sounding frantic. 'They are approaching the viewing area and getting more agitated by the minute.'

Jack did not respond; he was now becoming worried that they would not get away in time. Just as quickly as it had become entangled, the horse and several attendants managed to get it untangled.

Jack moved back to the door, unclipping his daisho as he moved. Looking around he noted that everyone was ready to leave. He turned and saw the first of the protestors approaching the "tunnel" he had created with the transport containers. He turned back and looked at Teimei, extending his daisho he told her to 'Hold these.' She reached out and grasped the mounted sayas and as she did, Jack withdrew the two weapons.

'GO!' he commanded. 'Get out of here. Akio, once every one is safe come back for me, not before.' As he turned towards the oncoming mob, he heard the driver shouting and whipping the horses as the carriage began to pick up speed. He also heard Teimei.

'JACK! NO!' even though he had heard the shout he did not turn his head. He was now concentrating on the huge mass of people trying to squeeze into the relatively narrow gap he had left them.

Stretching and flexing his arms as he ran, he prepared to hold them up as long as possible.

Akasaka Palace

The Shogun had raced ahead of the imperial carriage, once he had determined that it was safe to leave them and arrived at the palace well before hand. The commander of the 59th division raced out to see what was happening and he was greeted with "Send a Company to the Imperial viewing area, rifles and ammunition, fix bayonets and be prepared for hand to hand if necessary."

The commander ordered the third company to rush and they instantly began running the kilometre or so to the viewing stands. None of them even stopped to acknowledge the Emperor as he passed them as his carriage rushed towards the palace. Nor did they slow their pace as the Crown Prince's carriage raced by.

At the Viewing Platform

Parts of the mob had stopped and were haranguing and threatening the few remaining politicians that had not yet managed to engineer their escape. The rest were all trying to enter Jack's "choke point" together.

Jack meanwhile was slashing his way through the first of the protestors and he had managed to slow their progress around half way between the containers. As a great Sensei once told his gakusei (students), "Do not spend your energy trying to kill every enemy, slash at the arms, legs and body. If you can disable them, they are not a threat and you can concentrate on those that still oppose you. Remember, in battle there are two things you should not waste, time and energy. To ensure an enemy is truly dead takes both of those things away from you." Words that Jack found, at that very moment, to be very useful to him.

The wounded were beginning to create a barrier of human bodies between him and the mass of people that were still trying to get through. Many wounded were being trampled as the fight wore on.

Jack, however, was not getting it all his own way. Many had managed to stab him with their makeshift weapons and even though he had not personally heard the crack of a gun or felt the impact of a bullet, he had been wounded several times himself.

The fight continued for several frantic minutes; first the mob surging towards him and then his onslaught pushing them back, increasing the pile of wounded between him and his opponents.

Unbeknownst to him, the other company of the 59th were cutting off the possibility of the protestors being able to run away from what was quickly becoming a debacle and with Jack almost preventing the forward momentum their options were becoming fewer by the minute.

Unfortunately, Jack's body was now beginning to suffer from the beating he was taking and, as he became progressively weaker, he began to retreat slowly away from the safety the narrow alley had afforded him.

Deep in his mind he became aware of a familiar sound, the rhythmic thump of heavy horses was becoming louder and eventually he heard the shouts of his friends.

'Stay there, Jack!' the first voice commanded him and he stopped where he stood, both weapons pointed down at the full extent of his arms. The protestors had also stopped and Jack was not willing to take his eyes off them. Off to one side he made out the armour of Akio, also holding two weapons. Turning his head slightly he saw the Shogun on the other side.

'Couldn't bear to let me have all the glory I suppose?' He asked, his voice trying to sound unconcerned.

'Quite happy to let you continue, but you will have to share, just this once.' Hiroshi grinned as he spoke. 'Besides there are a hundred of the 59th behind you as well as a dozen samurai.'

'Sounds like overkill to me. But I bet they,' Jack pointed his wakizashi at the now hesitant protestors, 'still think they out number us.'

'Probably. Sensei, your tactics?'

'March towards them, swords ready. 3 Company fix bayonets and prepare to fire!'

The hundred men of 3 company all complied with their orders. Bayonets were fixed and assault rifles cocked, ready to fire.

'Right, let's go.' As Jack gave the order the Guard began to move towards their opponents. The closer they got the more menacing they appeared to be. With Jack leading them in his day uniform and the others all in armour they gave the appearance of exactly what they were, men ready to die for their cause. The real question was, were the rioters prepared to do the same?

The answer came just as Jack, in the lead, was around three metres away from the pack. First one threw down his placard then another and another, slowly they all surrendered. One by one they were taken aside and, eventually, the police would handcuff them and lead them away.

Jack turned to the others and announced, 'I need a horse, I need to get to the Emperor.'

'We brought "Shotgun" with us,' Akio announced and Jack thanked him.

All the Samurai mounted for the return to the palace. Before most were ready, Jack had left. His parade horse, Shotgun, thundering along the roadway so quickly that the rest had trouble catching up. It was only a relatively short ride and the guard were quickly reining in their mounts as Jack made his way to the rooms where the Imperial Family would be waiting.

As he cast his eyes around the room it was Teimei that first spoke.

'Thank the gods, you are safe.' She rushed to him and threw her arms around him, but she felt something was wrong. He had simply stood there, weapons in hand, swaying slightly, eyes a little glazed.

Eventually, he spoke, 'I think I need a chair.' And with that he slowly began to drop to the floor, the only reason he didn't fall down completely was that Akio and Hiroshi held him, one each side. A footman pushed a chair behind him and they lowered him down gently.

As Teimei backed away from him she could feel her hands were suddenly sticky and when she looked down, she almost screamed at the sight of bright red blood on her palms. For several seconds she looked and eventually the Emperor spoke.

'What is it Teimei? What is wrong?' The princess turned slowly, palms upwards and hands out stretched. Tears began to roll down her cheeks, but no words would form.

For an agonisingly silent few seconds, no one moved; Akio was the first to react. 'FURUKAWA!' he shouted at the top of his voice, again and again he shouted and suddenly a breathless Furukawa entered the room.

'What is wrong?' he demanded as he gave a close inspection to each of the Imperial Family, fully expecting one or more to be injured. His eyes visibly widened when he saw the hands of the Princess but he quickly dismissed her as a patient; despite the blood on her hands and her dress she appeared unharmed.

When he looked in the direction of the Guard Commanders, he was stunned to see Jack's face was almost white and he appeared to be unconscious.

His training finally kicked in. 'Bring that table here!' he ordered and Hiroshi dragged it closer, 'Get him up on it.' The three managed to wrestle Jack onto the table, flat on his back. The medic looked at Akio and ordered him 'Get some more medics and combat kits.' Not a request, a simple order that was obeyed immediately. No one questioned him, Senior Samurai Furukawa was now the one in command.

His medical kit, arrived along with an extra pair of samurai to fetch whatever was needed, and Furukawa began to cut away the uniform. As Akio removed the shoes, Furukawa cut through the jacket and then the shirt. As he worked, he announced 'Your majesty, this is not going to be pretty, you may wish to wait in another room,' he did not even lift his head as he worked, it was a simple suggestion that was made as he began the triage of the patient before him.

'Hai, we will be in here.' The Emperor shepherded his family into a side room and Teimei insisted that the door remain open. The palace staff provided refreshments which were accepted but they had no taste, there was a far more important event that still held their minds.

Two more medics from the 59th arrived and began, under instruction, to bandage the minor wounds. 'Can I get someone to remove my armour, this is difficult enough without the restrictions.' Hiroshi and Akio unbuckled and removed the many pieces one by one as Furukawa worked.

For Teimei the world seemed to have stopped. She stood quietly praying, to whatever god would listen, that Jack would survive. As she watched the medic try to repair the damage again. She took a sharp breath as the huge scar across Jack's chest emerged from the cut shirt; the memory of the last time she had witnessed him protecting someone was too fresh not to elicit a reaction.

Her eyes never wavered as she watched the medic spray the combination anaesthetic/pain suppressor into each wound before he probed and pushed looking for debris and deep damage before he ordered the wound closed.

As he methodically worked each wound a door opened and a man entered.

'Stop!' he demanded. 'I am a doctor and this man must be treated in a hospital, there is no sterilisation of your equipment or yourselves.' Teimei looked at Furukawa and it was then she realised that he was almost wrist deep in Jack's abdomen without even gloves as protection; never the less she was incensed, yet still unable to move.

'Stop! I said.' The doctor ordered a second time and his demand was answered by a powerful female voice from one side.

'GET HIM OUT OF HERE!' Everyone, with the noticeable exception of Furukawa stopped and looked for the owner of the voice.

'I SAID "GET HIM OUT OF HERE!" NOW!' Jack, in a fog of anaesthesia slurred as he spoke, 'Do as the Princess orders.' And two samurai all but dragged the doctor out of the room, closely followed by Teimei.

'Do not return.' Were her only words as she closed the door, shutting him out.

The medics, meanwhile had managed to get Jack stable, and the superficial wounds were dressed. There were still a few major problems to be resolved, the results of gunshots, but he was going to survive.

Just before the ambulance arrived a hologram call was received by the Emperor.

'General Onishi? To what do we owe the pleasure?' He was trying to be the politest he could be under the circumstances.

'Good news, Your Majesty. When Jack moved to oppose the rioters, Colonel Drones took it upon himself to get as much surveillance as possible. He has not only identified the ringleaders of that gang but he has also had them followed to their base of operations. The Police are already on-site making arrests.'

'Arigatō, General. Our thanks to the Colonel and his team.'

'You are most welcome. There is more; Drones also identified the shooters and had them followed as well, three have been arrested and the fourth will be taken into custody soon.'

'How did he mange to do this? Find them so quickly?'

'Drones and Jack are very close friends; they work well together and Drones decided to keep a close watch on proceedings. We owe it all to Jack's methods of encouraging people to perform as best as they can. This is the result.'

'Excellent work, again arigatō General. And thank the Colonel and his team as well.'

Once he was loaded into the ambulance Furukawa got in beside him, despite the protests of the driver and the paramedic. When they arrived at the hospital a fully briefed theatre team was ready for him. Once the emergency was over the chief surgeon found Jack's medics and thanked them for the quality and precision of the work they had completed; the triage and treatment had improved

Jack's chances of survival from low to very high. He had once again managed to survive against the odds.

As he was wheeled into a private room the entire Imperial Family arrived for the medical reports and to check on him for themselves. Princess Teimei was not going to take anyone's opinion, she wanted to see for herself.

'Where did the scar on his chest come from?' The surgeon asked.

'That was from a fight he had protecting a number of people in Sapporo.' Teimei replied.

'We can repair the scar and make it all but invisible, just say the word.'

'NO.' Teimei replied, almost too forcefully. 'He is not concerned with the superficiality of cosmetic procedures; he is happy to keep his scars.'

'Are you certain?' The crown prince asked. 'Did you discuss this with him?'

'I did, papa. He told me that without the scar he could not back up his stories in the pub.' She could not prevent the grin crossing her face as the crown prince answered, 'Only Jack would think like that.'

Chapter 53
Recuperation

Jack only spent a week in hospital, the surgical team were so impressed with his progress that they were happy for him to recover at his home, as long as he had a medical team available.

It was the Saturday morning, eight days after the festival that the helicopter landed gently on the front lawn and Furukawa and Akio were first to emerge. Jack slowly climbed down from the cabin and walked stiffly across the grass into the waiting cordon of Chie, Fumiko, and Emika.

'Mother sends her best, Jack,' Chie spoke as she gently hugged him. 'She says you will recover without too much problem. Fumiko thinks it will take some time.'

'Arigatō, Chie. What do you say? Who do you agree with?'

'As is normal, around you, Fumiko is right. It will take some time. But she is confident you will be fully fit when you have to attend your next big event.'

'Cryptic, as usual.' Jack eyed he with a mixture of suspicion and amusement.

'You need no more than that, for now. Just get better.'

They all entered the house and a meal appeared before them. The conversation was flowing amongst the friends when Caroline and Itsuki appeared at the door. More welcomes and more explanations. At one-point Jack and Caroline found themselves alone on the deck.

'How is life for you, Caroline? Are you and Itsuki getting on well?'

Caroline looked at him with a hint of suspicion. 'Who has been telling you things?' She demanded.

'No one. I am simply interested in the lives of my friends.'

'Oh god. I am sorry for being suspicious. I asked to be able to tell you myself and I thought someone had beaten me to it. You know what it is like living with Fumiko, there are no secrets.'

'Not normally; but this time she has kept one. Out with it.'

Caroline took a deep breath. 'Itsuki and I are to be married; I would like you to give me away, if you can.'

Jack struggled to get to his feet, eventually Caroline helped him up and as she did, he embraced her. 'Congratulations. Of course, I would be delighted to escort you down the aisle.'

Caroline almost began to cry; she was so relieved. With the loss of her parents a few years before she did not have anyone to stand with her, now her closest friend had agreed.

'It's ok, he said yes.' Fumiko's distinctive voice emerged from the hallway, and the entire group of friends and family followed it onto the deck.

'There is more.' Itsuki spoke in his quiet, respectful voice. 'We were hoping you would agree to let us have the ceremony here.'

Jack looked around the surrounding smiling faces. 'So you are all ganging up on me. Making it so I cannot refuse.' The smile belied the accusation. 'Of course, the wedding ceremony will be my present to you both.'

With that the friends all sat and began to make plans for the celebratory event.

As afternoon gave way to evening, they all ate and chatted until eventually it was so late that even Jack had to admit defeat and retire for the night; sleep, however, was an elusive goal. The combination of his injuries and his mind working at a frantic pace as he turned over ideas for the planned wedding.

Dawn eventually began to break as he made his way down to the now, completed, chapel. Despite the outer shell being ready, there was still some fitting out to be completed. Finding a discarded bucket, he turned it over and settled down gingerly. Eventually, he managed to get comfortable and began his prayers. For almost half an hour he sat immobile, and when he finally looked up, he saw his closest friends sitting with him.

'Suddenly you are all Christian?' he asked the rhetorical question and did not expect to get any reply. Furukawa was probably the last of his associates that he thought would be religious, to have him speak out was a true revelation.

'I think it is safe to say that while we do not exactly follow your religious inclinations, we have seen the benefit you get from it, so we thought it may help us all if we join you. That and the fact that you may not get up if we aren't here to help you.'

'Good point, help me up and we can get coffee.'

With Akio and Caroline beside him, and his entourage following, they made their way back to the house where coffee was ready and waiting. A couple of hours later they were beginning to get hungry.

'Emika,' Jack called out and a few moments later she appeared.

'Hai?'

'Is breakfast almost ready?'

'Not yet, we are waiting for some more guests to arrive.' She then turned and left them without any more explanation.

It was just over an hour before she called them for breakfast and as Jack hobbled into the dining room he was almost knocked down as he was "mugged" by a horde of nieces and nephews, along with their parents, his brothers and sisters.

'How many times do you need to get injured? Why don't you get out of the way?' Asa asked, never the one to hold back, she feared for her brother's safety.

'It is very simple, I would be perfectly safe, if only people would stop trying to hurt those I protect.'

'Why don't you let someone else do it?' Hana would not let the question go unanswered.

Before Jack could reply, Caroline jumped into the conversation. 'The reasons he does this work are many and varied. His protective instinct and his commitment to those he is assigned to are the subject of much debate and I can tell you that, even though I have had more time with him both personally and professionally, I have the best insight into his actions. Yet he still confounds us all. I am now at the point where I want to simply follow him to see what happens next.'

'But he is always in the thick of the fighting, how can we be certain he is safe?'

'My lady,' Fumiko spoke out, 'he will be safe, now and forever. He will soon find his life's partner; she will be the most unexpected of all time. He will never be in danger of being severely wounded. Believe in his capabilities, he is unique in his field; even the Russians respect him.'

'Arigatō, Fumiko. While your words are comforting, they still do not put us at complete rest. We worry.'

'And you are right to worry, my dear sister,' Jack had joined the conversation. 'But please know, I will always return here. This is our home, we will always be with each other, even far apart, we are together.

The wedding was a huge success, a massive crowd of well-wishers turned up for the ceremony. General and Mrs Moreton, Motoyuki and Yumi Onishi, Tyrell and Daisy and Roman and Grace all arrived and were immediately put to work assisting with the decorations and catering.

The festivities continued for almost a week; well, it would have been a week if the ceremony had been held on the first day. Suffice to say it was three days of meet and greet, one day of a wedding, and three more days of celebrating. In the end Jack found he had done some more damage to his leg and he would need to undergo some corrective surgery. The "wedding week" finally ground to a close. Visitors bade farewell and the house eventually became quiet again.

Reo and Sora, Jack's brothers had made the decision to leave the Navy, the incident at the shelter in Sapporo had made them acutely aware that they needed to be more visible around the area to help prevent the escalation that so easily occurs when emotions get high. They still kept the 59th busy as well. Princess Teimei had, as patron of the division, arranged for a permanent presence in the two shelters on their side of the city and Jack had done the same with the 61st on the other side.

Life was looking good; the busy schedule was becoming quiet. At one stage Jack asked if he was being deliberately left out and the reply was that as soon as he had finished with the corrective surgery and he was back to full fitness then he would be returned to full duties.

He accepted the conditions and the surgery was scheduled. Unfortunately, it was not good news. The tendons attaching the hamstrings to the bone were in a very poor state and it took the surgeons a lot of work to correct the problem.

As so often happens, correct one problem and the resulting shift in stresses produce a corresponding problem elsewhere. This time the repair of the right thigh left him with an over strained left knee and the doctors were again summoned to correct the problem. Repaired meniscus, and tightened tendons saw him limping around the house bemoaning his run of bad luck.

Little did he know, his was only one small piece of "bad joss" as the ancient Chinese called it.

The hologram beeped for the third time that hour. Jack was becoming weary at the constant interruptions.

Despite the fact that his injuries were rapidly healing he was still wary of rushing around. Pressing the answer button, he was pleased to see Motoyuki appear on line.

'Konichiwa, my friend. A pleasure to see you.' The replied pleasantries were strained and Jack was instantly wary.

'What is up? You are clearly concerned.'

'Can I come and see you?' The curt reply only caused Jack to become more worried, this was not the way his friend usually spoke.

'Of course, when?'

'I am on my way; the helicopter will land in just half an hour.'

'When you arrive, come straight to the library, we can talk there.'

The helicopter landed and Emika took the crew into the house for a meal. Motoyuki made his way through the house to the library.

'Come in, my friend. Sit.' Jack indicated a chair and Motoyuki sat down, the old-fashioned leather briefcase resting on his lap. Jack placed a plate of biscuits and a coffee on the table beside him, and took a seat opposite.

'Now what has you so spooked?' Jack tried to ease the obvious tension, to no avail.

Motoyuki unlocked the wrist restraint and opened the case, from the interior he produced a sheaf of papers. Jack noted that the cover sheet was clearly labelled "MOST SECRET. Copy TWO of THREE."

'Tight security, what is going on?'

'Read this.' Was the only reply. Jack sat back and began to work his way through the papers.

Eventually, he gave them back and sat back in the chair, his mind racing as he tried to make sense of the report he had just read.

'This is real?'

'It is.'

'It is happening now? In the North-West of Australia?'

'Hai.'

'Aliens? As in creatures from space?'

'Hai.'

'How did aliens arrive and land and set up an advance base without anyone knowing? Without anyone noticing?'

'We don't know. The UN is currently assembling a multi-national force to try to gain access to their base. I cannot say more than that.'

'Just a moment,' Jack activated hologram and the appearance of Haruto appeared before him. 'Haruto, I have General Onishi with me.'

'Konichiwa. Motoyuki, may I speak freely?'

'Please do, we are all sworn to secrecy in this.'

'Jack, we have tasked several satellites over the site, can't get anything out of there. It is as though there is nothing there.'

'How did we find it? Someone must have some knowledge?' Jack was becoming a little frustrated with the lack of detail. 'Does anyone have satellite scans?'

'Don't think so, we have stolen two Chinese and an extra Russian bird, but there is no real information, no images to see, just some IR outlines.'

'The site was discovered by a couple of kids; they have been moved away and the military have taken over the area.'

'I understand, this is very dangerous. Let me know any information you can.'

Haruto closed the link and Jack returned to his ruminations. Eventually, he spoke again. 'What do you want me to do?' Jack eventually asked, his mind was churning, trying to make sense of the revelations that had been presented to him.

'Speaking as Chief of Staff, we do not have a plan as yet. Speaking as a Military representative of the Human Race, we are planning a series of attacks. The effectiveness is not guaranteed.'

'We may well be in trouble. We will have to wait and see.'

The military gathered in the desert near the newly established alien "base", and following a full artillery barrage a frontal assault was ordered.

The guns blazed away from 4AM but when the spotters looked there was no damage at all; they could see where their shots struck the "shield" but no damage was evident. The troops waited at their starting point and when the order to advance was given they went to their deaths, the defensive shield instantly killing all who came in contact with it. It appeared that nothing on earth was going to stop the invaders.

Getting frustrated the Heads of State, the Emperors, Kings, Queens and Presidents as well as the UN wanted a better plan than just charging at the enemy lines like it was World War One all over again, and the call went out for a different view and a better plan.

The head of the UN Security Council asked for the name of the very best ground forces commander there was. Everyone put up their favourite. The Russians wanted Kosmalov; the Chinese wanted Yuang, the British wanted Armstrong and the Americans wanted Crasten; but the universally acknowledged master was Captain Jackson Nakagawa, formally a General of the Japanese Defence Force.

The Imperial Palace

The Emperor sat in his rooms in the Imperial Palace in Tokyo. As he read the latest briefing report from the UN, he began to get even more worried, despite not showing it. Ringing a small bell his personal aide entered and bowed.

'Yes Majesty, how can I be of assistance?'

'Recall Captain Nakagawa from leave, it seems that we will be in need of all of his impressive skills.'

'Hai Majesty,' and he turned and left.

A short while later the Emperor's aide knocked and waited for permission to enter.

'Come in.'

'Captain Nakagawa is here Majesty.'

'Show him in.'

The captain marched in and stopped around two meters from the Emperor, then, as was his usual approach, he unclipped his weapons from his side. As he knelt on one knee, he offered his katana in acknowledgement of his supreme commander's position. No one else in the world was the recipient of this overt sign of fealty.

Following a small bow in return from the Emperor, he stood and spoke

'You have summoned me your Majesty.'

'Hai, Jack. My apologies for cutting your leave short, I trust your leg has healed?' Without waiting for a reply, the Emperor continued, 'Have you been kept up to date with the latest happenings from Australia and the UN?'

'Only the barest of important information, as I understand it the details are classified, but I have a fair understanding of the implications.'

'The Secretary General of the UN has asked that you be placed in command in the area and given all assistance you require to either subdue or destroy the invaders. All members of the Security Council and every member nation have pledged their support. This is the most dangerous situation that this planet has ever been subject to and they have given you the job of seeing it to its conclusion.'

'I will make preparations to leave immediately. Am I permitted to have my own staff officers?'

'You may take whoever you wish.'

'Arigatō.' Turning to the Emperor's aide he continued.

'Chief Samurai Takamatsu as my Sensei and Deputy. Senior Samurai Hasegawa as my Administration Officer. Fleet Admiral Tyrell Backhouse from the United States is to command fleet operations. General Roman Garcia is to command a land battery consisting of the 123rd, 165th and 187th Medium Battery's, 86th Heavy Bombardment and the 93rd Artillery Support Group. Colonel Drones with his long-range surveillance "Big Eyes" drone units and pilots, and Colonel Haruto Saito and his team for satellite works. And a company of samurai from the guard. Ask the Americans for Lieutenant James Cruz to be attached as my Intelligence Officer.

'Hai.' The aide replied and scurried away to begin issuing the requests to the American and Mexican governments.

The Emperor waited until his aide had left. 'The Air Force has been ordered to place a hyper jet at your disposal. Good luck my friend, you may just need it.'

At that the interview was understood to be over and Jack left to make ready for what was promising to be a long trip overseas.

たくさんのコリン

Takusan no Korin

Continued in "War Chief" by this author.